Markus Heitz studied histo… …age and literature before writing his debut …*chatten über Ulldart* (*Shadows over Ulldart*, the first in a series of epic fantasy novels), which won the Deutscher Phantastik Preis, Germany's premier literary award for fantasy. Since then he has frequently topped the bestseller charts, and his Number One-bestselling *Dwarves* and *Älfar* series have earned him his place among Germany's most successful fantasy authors. Markus has become a byword for intriguing combinations: as well as taking fantasy in different directions, he has mixed mystery, history, action and adventure, and always with at least a pinch of darkness. Millions of readers across the world have been entranced by the endless scope and breadth of his novels. Whether twisting fairy-tale characters or inventing living shadows, mysterious mirror images or terrifying creatures, he has it all – and much more besides.

Praise for Markus Heitz

'Heitz keeps on delivering'
Upcoming4.me

'Heitz is venturing into new territory and proving that he can really write a thrilling tale. Recommended reading for all thriller fans'
Papiergefluster.de on *Oneiros*

'I'm definitely hook line and sinkered . . . The world building is intriguingly gorgeous . . . A fast addictive read that will draw you in and leave you wanting more'
Liz Loves Books on *Aera*

'Tolkien with a dash of Gemmell and a sprinkling of George R.R. Martin'
Malazan Empire

'Very entertaining . . . [These] books are worth reading'
Dat Book Reviews on The Dwarves series

'Driven by unrelenting action, [the book] springs to life through the vivid, vigorous writing'
Kirkus on the *Legends of the Älfar*

'If your bookshelf is already home to Tolkien, Martin, and company, *Righteous Fury* will find a comfortable spot to fit in'
Booklist on *Righteous Fury*

'A real joy to read'
Falcata Times

'*The Dwarves* is a well-constructed classic fantasy story that I greatly enjoyed'
Speculative Book Review

'An exciting new turn for Markus Heitz; an exciting, scary fantasy novel. Those looking for entertainment will certainly find it with *Oneiros*'
Phantastik-news.de on *Oneiros*

Also by Markus Heitz

THE DWARVES

The War of the Dwarves

The Revenge of the Dwarves

The Fate of the Dwarves

The Triumph of the Dwarves

LEGENDS OF THE ÄLFAR

Righteous Fury

Devastating Hate

Dark Paths

Raging Storm

DOORS

Doors X Twilight

Doors ? Colony

Doors ! Field of Blood

Oneiros

AERA: The Return of the Ancient Gods

AERA

THE RETURN OF THE ANCIENT GODS

MARKUS HEITZ

Translated by Emily Gunning
and Charlie Homewood

Jo Fletcher
BOOKS

Aera Prologue first published in the UK in 2015 by Jo Fletcher Books
Aera Book 1 first published in the UK in 2015 by Jo Fletcher Books
Aera Book 2 first published in the UK in 2015 by Jo Fletcher Books
Aera Book 3 first published in the UK in 2016 by Jo Fletcher Books
Aera Book 4 first published in the UK in 2016 by Jo Fletcher Books
Aera Book 5 first published in the UK in 2016 by Jo Fletcher Books
Aera Book 6 first published in the UK in 2016 by Jo Fletcher Books
Aera Book 7 first published in the UK in 2017 by Jo Fletcher Books
Aera Book 8 first published in the UK in 2017 by Jo Fletcher Books
Aera Book 9 first published in the UK in 2017 by Jo Fletcher Books
Aera Book 10 first published in the UK in 2017 by Jo Fletcher Books
This omnibus edition first published in ebook in Great Britain in 2017
This paperback omnibus edition published in 2022 by

Jo Fletcher Books, an imprint of
Quercus Editions Ltd,
Carmelite House
50 Victoria Embankment
London EC4Y 0DZ

An Hachette UK company

Represented by AVA international GmbH, Germany www.ava-international.de
Originally published as Die Rückkehr der Götter in 2015 by Verlagsgruppe Droemer Knaur GmbH & Co. KG, Munich, Germany

A CIP catalogue record for this book is available from the British Library

PB ISBN 978 1 52940 198 1

10 9 8 7 6 5 4 3 2 1

Typeset by CC Book Production
Printed and bound in Great Britain by Clays Ltd, Elcograf S.p.A.

Papers used by Jo Fletcher Books are from well-managed forests and other responsible sources.

Extracts from:

DOS AND DON'TS
An informative and entertaining guide to the world of 2019 and its various gods.
With new case studies and evidence.

342nd digital and enhanced multimedia edition, November 2019.
The publisher accepts no responsibility or liability for the actions of any individual acting on information contained in this publication.
– Download: 99 Cents –

Dear readers,

With this brief multimedia guide, we aim to provide a review of the far-reaching and dramatic events of the past few years . . . Let us go back to the year 2012:

From one day to the next they reappeared: the gods.

The *old* gods. The ones the Bible meant when it said 'You shall have no other gods before me' – whose existence the Christian holy text had never denied or disputed.

Some gods reclaimed their old sites of worship, long repurposed by other religions, predominantly by Christians. Magnificent buildings were razed to the ground and replaced with forgotten icons.

Perhaps some of you will remember the confusion, the chaos that overtook the world; perhaps some of you were even there when the gods first appeared. For you, dear reader, and all our other patrons, we have delved into the archives and collected some records of the events.

PROLOGUE

#1

Transcription of radio program *Antenna Hamburg*, Germany, 21.12.2012, 0014 hours

PRESENTER: 'That was the weather report for this beautiful winter night. And now, as always, it's your chance to ring through to the studio and tell us how you'll be celebrating this festive period. Here's our first caller now, a big hello to Iris from Horn.'

IRIS: 'Yes, hi, I just . . . it's completely insane!'

PRESENTER: 'What are you and your friends up to then?'

IRIS: 'We were just getting in the car, then there was this light and . . . but it wasn't a light. It was some kind of vehicle with a man on it.'

PRESENTER: 'On the street?'

IRIS: 'In the sky! I swear to god! With a . . . I don't know. Looked like . . . he had two birds that were flapping all around us! At night!'

PRESENTER: 'Yo, Iris, am I right in thinking you guys have had a few already tonight?'

IRIS: 'I'm serious! And now . . . shit, there's another one. He's got a hammer and . . . fuck! Fuck, he just knocked down the church! The whole building's just collapsed! And . . .'

The call breaks up at this point.

In the 21st century it hadn't occurred to anybody that the gods might return. Appearing right in the middle of their meagre conception of reality.

Pyramids, temples, shrines and all kinds of holy sites or mythical locations regained their original significance.

The gods came in their hundreds – and they acted. Reports came thick and fast of sightings and miracles.

Here is our next report.

#2

Transcription of TV program *ZDF Daily News,* Germany, 1.1.2013, 0019 hours

PRESENTER: 'Reports of sightings of mythical beings are flooding into the studio as we speak. Experts are viewing this as a deliberately coordinated attack, perhaps carried out by a network of pranksters inspired by the hysteria surrounding the 2012 Mayan apocalypse predictions. Some of the videos uploaded onto social media sites are of extremely high quality and production value, whereas others are clearly amateur recordings in a style more reminiscent of the *Blair Witch Project*. We're going live to David Brauer, who is in Berlin with a camera crew at the Brandenburg Gate and has seen some astonishing events in the past couple of hours. David, what's going on out there?'

BRAUER: 'It's hard to tell exactly what happened, but in the middle of the fireworks display there was a huge flash of light, like a lightning strike, and all the fireworks immediately stopped. Then there were some loud bangs, but no corresponding explosions could be seen. And then a huge figure appeared, which has been described by most people we've spoken to as a "Viking giant". The figure had only one eye, and was shouting in a language similar to Germanian.'

–Montage of pictures sketched by the team and footage from mobile phones–

PRESENTER: 'David, in your opinion, could these events, which are causing worldwide chaos and confusion, simply be a prank on an enormous scale – perhaps carried out by a group of hackers and pranksters?'

BRAUER: 'Yes, in fact that's what everyone is assuming at this point. The police are searching the roofs of the surrounding buildings and the Brandenburg Gate itself for any evidence of projectors or equipment used in the prank. It's likely that very high specification machines were used, probably modified film projectors.'

PRESENTER: 'How are the police explaining the non-explosion of the fireworks?'

BRAUER: 'The police are assuming that the people responsible for the projection also tampered with the pyrotechnics by wetting the powder chambers or the internal ignition mechanisms. That would have been entirely possible.'

PRESENTER: 'And we've heard that after this unplanned interruption, the celebrations carried on, is that right?'

BRAUER: 'Yes, they certainly did!'

–He stands to the side, behind him can be seen a large pile of wooden barrels–

BRAUER: 'It seems the culprits used the distraction to leave about fifty kegs of mead in the square. And I can tell you one thing . . .'

–He raises a cup of mead to the camera–

BRAUER: '. . . it tastes fantastic.'

Things, however, do not always go so smoothly if the gods are unhappy with something in their area of influence.

Read for yourself:

#3

Transcription from private radio channel of the Italian coastguard, patrol cruiser *Brentano*, Italy, 26.12.2012, 2112 hours

COASTGUARD: 'Unidentified vessel, we have received an emergency broadcast from your location. Please identify yourselves.'

VOICE: 'We're taking on water, we had a collision with a . . . a thing!'

COASTGUARD: 'We can see you now, at one o'clock. Your ship *Bravewave* is listing heavily. We won't be able to tow her.'

VOICE: 'You have to come and get me off here before that thing surfaces again!'

COASTGUARD: 'Your ship isn't listed on our system. What is your cargo, sir?'

VOICE: *–silence–*

COASTGUARD: 'What cargo do you have on board, sir?'

VOICE: 'Just come over and get me, god damn it!'

COASTGUARD: 'We're right by you now. How many people need to be evacuated? Are there any injured?'

VOICE: 'I'm the only survivor. That thing killed everyone on board. With a trident.'

COASTGUARD: 'Can you repeat please, sir? It sounded like you said *trident*.'

VOICE: 'Please! I'm sinking!'

–Recording from camera on the stern of the coastguard's boat:

A wave rises spontaneously from the calm sea and pushes the listing vessel completely on its side. The light on the ship goes out, and the vessel sinks while a glowing trident appears to pierce through the bow.

COASTGUARD 1: 'What the hell was that? Where did that wave come from? Was that . . . a torpedo?'

COASTGUARD 2: 'I don't know! Look, what are those packages floating on the water?'

At this point, we would like to issue a warning to travellers:

When travelling abroad, ensure you do some research before leaving, specifically on which gods are responsible for the regions you will be visiting. This can prevent misunderstandings with both the gods and the country's inhabitants. Provocation of the gods – as our next example will illustrate – is to be avoided at all costs.

#4

Online video, Ireland, 29.12.2012, 1823 hours

–Teenagers in casual clothes stand by a river–

TEENAGER: 'The light was coming from there. Seriously! And then there was this voice singing, really lovely, and then over there this guy just rose up straight out of the river.'

–The camera pans over the calm river–

CAMERAMAN: 'There's nothing there, you nutter.'

TEENAGER: 'No, there was something. And it was speaking this weird sort of Gaelic, and I think it said its name was Nechtan. I didn't understand it properly but . . . it was saying something to do with the river. And something about getting permission or something like that . . . And then he went back into the water.'

CAMERAMAN: *–laughs–* 'Yeah, sure.'

TEENAGER: *–holds a hand in the water–* 'See, it's totally clean and it doesn't smell of all that crap they pump in there anymore. The Boyne is clean again, just like that.' *–stands up and pulls his trousers down, urinates into the river–* 'Can't stay that way forever, obviously.'

CAMERAMAN: 'Sean! Put your dick away and get away from there! Sean . . .!

SEAN: 'Oh, shit, what . . .'

–A hand shoots out of the water, grabs his genitals and rips them off. The boy falls to the ground screaming and holding his crotch–
[2.2 million clicks in 21 minutes.]

Some gods went on camera and gave interviews, filling their long-ridiculed followers with vindication.

And in doing so, they showed us their personalities.

#5

Online video, Sweden, Oslo, 29.12.2012, 2111 hours

–A guy in a Loki costume from the film The Avengers*–*

MAN 1: 'I am Loki, mortals! I have come to . . .'

–The door opens, a man in a perfectly tailored suit enters–

MAN 2: 'I'm sorry my good man, but you are a fake' *–smiles into the camera–* 'Hello, dear viewers. I'm Loki and I would like to introduce myself. You should be aware that a new era has begun.'

MAN 1: 'Get out you idiot! This is a live stream!'

MAN 2: *–looks at Man 1 askance–* 'What a strange costume. Nobody's going to follow you wearing that, my boy. But here, play a game with me: if you manage to say my name correctly ten times in a row within three seconds, I'll make you so rich you'll be practically buried in money! And I'll get you a better costume' *–nods to the camera–* 'I give you my word!'

MAN 1: *–looks confused–* '. . . okay? Loki Loki Loki Loki Loki Loki Loki Loki Loki Loki!' *–laughs loudly–* 'Bam! Take that!'

MAN 2: 'I meant my other name: Hveðrungr.' *–shrugs his shoulders–* 'But I am a man of my word.' *–He makes a hand gesture and the ceiling falls down in large chunks, completely burying Man 1 and his chair–* 'Well, partially anyway – you're certainly buried.' *–looks into the camera–* 'Dear viewers: the stories are true – I'm back.

Follow me. Play with me. Make a bet with me, but try to do better than this young man.' *–smiles and makes a bow–*

Our next film, however, demonstrates that things can go quite differently, and that some gods can even contribute to the greater good.

We apologise for the poor quality of the recording.

#7

Online video, West Africa Sierra Leone, 23.12.2012, 1427 hours

–Blurry footage, dirty lens, dust, a small, simple village–

–A group of armed men with no uniforms are marching through the area, terrorising a village. They shove the villagers to the ground, kick and beat them, opening the gate to the cattle pen and releasing the cows–

SUBTITLE: 'Move, move! Where are the stones?'

–People who show any resistance are shot. Shortly there are a dozen people lying on the ground, blood oozing into the earth–

SUBTITLE: 'We've done nothing wrong! Nothing! The diamonds were all given away!'

–The camera pans towards the ground where a very large black scorpion with remarkable brown markings is creeping out of a crack in the dry earth and scuttling towards the soldiers. With exact, targeted jabs, the scorpion stabs through the thick leather of their boots and stings each of the attackers in turn. Attempts to stamp on the scorpion or shoot it have no effect. The men die almost immediately, screaming in agony–

–The scorpion creeps back into the crack in the ground–

–The villagers kneel before the crevice and cry loudly–: 'Asase Yaa!'

SUBTITLE: 'The earth goddess has saved us, she saved us!'

Summary of examples #1 to #7:

Whether the Great Spirit or Mictlantecuhtli, whether Anubis, whether Odin and Thor, whether nameless deities of nature or the legends Mars and Hephaestion, whether Olorun, Mother Earth, Loa, or Shiva or *Kami*, whether manifestations of Buddha or Cai Shen – they existed. Real.

Faith became *knowledge.*

But why did they suddenly appear in the year 2012?

There are many theories surrounding the date of the gods' manifestations, ranging from pure coincidence to calculated and complex intentions. Here at *Dos & Don'ts* we wish to avoid speculation on this matter.

The Mayan calendar, a system that follows an entirely different concept of time, and which ends in 2012, is often cited as an explanation, interpreted by many as the 'end of the world'.

In fact, *D&D* research has so far uncovered no Mayan texts pointing to the downfall of the current world, or indeed the beginning of a new one. Only Tablet 6 (found in El Tortuguero, west of Palenque) mentions anything interpretable as prophecy: the deity Bolon Yokte' K'uh will appear in a great spectacle.

Yet the manifestation of so *many* gods was never described.

Accordingly there were also no mentions of the Christian god or Allah or Jahwe (*more on this later*).

An explanation oft cited by sceptics is a model written by ***Malleus Bourreau***, detective at Interpol and renowned atheist, who investigates criminal cases with suspected godly influences. (*See chapter: People of Note*).

What are the gods doing worldwide?

Regrettably, even this expanded and updated edition of *Dos & Don'ts* cannot give a full account of the activities of the gods across the world. For further information on the locations and dealings of gods in particular regions, please purchase the enhanced *D&D* guide, *Gods:Where They Live and What They Do* in the *D&D* Shop (available in PDF or app format).

The general picture looks like this: Some gods live among mortals in the old temples, in new buildings, in high-rise apartments; some live alone in underground bunkers or towers miles above the ground.

Some of them have founded companies to broaden their influence in the mortal world, becoming involved in securities and engaged in the economy. Naturally, the larger corporations have shown enormous interest in doing business with the gods.

At this point we offer a piece of advice: under no circumstances should you purchase bonds issued by Loki, unless you are particularly well versed in stock price volatility.

To date (Nov. 2019), the record for the greatest rise and fall in stock prices is held by *LOKI Enterprises Personal Security Ltd.* Their manufacturing of a one hundred per cent bulletproof vest was proving to be incredibly successful, until it came out that each product contained a randomly positioned intentional weak spot that could be penetrated by small calibre bullets.

Other shares that have proven difficult in the recent past

are those connected to the goddess Athena. Her enterprises are plagued by various legal disputes concerning copyright law and trademark protection.

Perhaps the most solid businesses in the current market are led by the gods Hephaestus and Vulcan. However, we would encourage any readers interested in investing to seek information and advice on the business dealings of the gods from an independent financial consultant.

An exciting detail for the adventurous among us: rumour has it that some gods have been taking specially selected humans with them to other planets. These lucky few have brought back souvenirs from their travels, and others have even constructed buildings on these planets in order to stay there for longer periods.

Dos & Don'ts has not yet sourced any substantial evidence concerning the authenticity of these extra-terrestrial holidays, and it is equally possible that these reports are deliberately misleading or entirely false.

The Mystery of the Big Three

According to *Dos & Don'ts* research, Christians, Muslims and Jews across the planet are still waiting for information regarding their deities: God, Allah and Jahwe.

Dos & Don'ts do not wish to engage in speculation on the topic, or call the existence of the missing gods into question.

It is entirely possible that the awaited deities have already manifested and are wandering the globe anonymously, or perhaps have been performing miracles falsely attributed to other, more vocal gods. Following extensive research, *D&D* is still unable to provide an answer to this question.

The failure of the so-called Big Three to make themselves known has had far-reaching consequences:

Once the mightiest religions in history, Christianity, Islam and Judaism withered into nothing more than godless cults. Their followers were scorned and ridiculed, forced to worship in secret, or worship under strict regulation from the now dominant deities (*see chapter: Religious Minorities*).

Mass conversions and wars followed swiftly after the events of 2012, until society finally adjusted. (*See chapter: How the World Changed*).

Conclusion to our brief introduction:

The world has undergone a great change.

Things are bleaker – many analysts have drawn comparisons between our current times and the mood evoked in films such as *Blade Runner, Sin City* or the classic twentieth century film noir.

But there is a positive to be found in all this: humanity persists.

Here at *Dos & Don'ts,* we are wholly convinced that even from today, in November 2019, the world will continue to change.

And we are equally hopeful that this change is for the better – after all, even gods cannot find pleasure in driving humanity to destruction.

[. . .]

Extract from *DOS & DON'TS*

342nd digital and enhanced multimedia edition, November 2019

From chapter: People of Note

[. . .] We also wish to mention a man unanimously considered by the *Dos & Don'ts* team to be a critical figure in the debate surrounding the gods: **Malleus Bourreau.**

Due to his notoriety we will not be publishing a photo of him, nor any information concerning his whereabouts.

Though his position as special inspector for Interpol necessitates a low profile, it would be remiss of us not to mention him here – despite his efforts at anonymity, he is undoubtedly an influential figure.

Malleus Bourreau was born in Germany (now Germania), and is currently in his mid-forties. His life story is something of a mystery. Though rumours abound regarding his family, his Culebras, his childhood and his activity in the years following 2012, *Dos & Don'ts* wishes to distance itself from the circulation of such unreliable information.

Bourreau is not particularly remarkable in stature or appearance. He wears his black hair short on the sides, a little longer on top and shaved on the neck. His facial hair varies, but currently (Nov. 2019) he is thought to be sporting a Fu Manchu moustache with a small beard.

Underneath his right eye runs a barely visible horizontal scar. In public he tends to wear a black hat and sunglasses, which render him almost unrecognisable.

In brief, Bourreau fought on varying sides during the Great Change, but eventually joined those battling against the gods. When the gods claimed victory, Bourreau surrendered and made use of the amnesty that came with it. His outstanding instincts were noticed by the authorities and he was pulled back into his old profession as an investigator, this time working for Interpol.

The reasons we at *D&D* saw fit to include Bourreau in this chapter are twofold. Firstly, the sheer number of god-related investigations he has carried out for both private and public clients makes him a key player in our field of interest. But perhaps more intriguingly, he also holds an extraordinary opinion on the return of the gods, one which is gaining popularity in niche circles:

Bourreau is an **atheist**, one of the least common belief systems in today's decidedly religious climate. (see chapter: Religious Minorities – though the term 'religion' does not technically apply to atheism, for brevity and convenience we include it in the chapter alongside Christianity, Islam and Judaism).

As Bourreau's exceptional beliefs are best represented by his own words, let us examine this extract from an audio interview for the online forum *Immortals Today*, conducted during a court hearing in 2018.

REPORTER: 'Inspector Bourreau! One question: how can anyone still be an atheist in this day and age?'

BOURREAU: 'What do you mean by that?'

REPORTER: 'You reject the gods because you don't believe in them. But we've just seen you coming out of the courtroom, having overturned a verdict in a murder trial by *personally* proving that the crime was committed by the god Hodur. How does that make sense?'

BOURREAU: 'I know that there are no such things as gods.'

REPORTER: 'How do you know that?'

BOURREAU: 'Where were they before?'

REPORTER: 'You're answering with a counter question, that's a little evasive.'

BOURREAU: 'I'm aware that you're not willing, or able, to follow my argument, which I understand to a certain extent. These beings who appeared in 2012 are certainly something other-worldly, but they're not the gods we know from sagas and legends or creation stories.'

REPORTER: 'So, what are they?'

BOURREAU: 'Potentially extra-terrestrials who have figured out that people such as yourselves would fall to their feet and become blinded by reverence as soon as they appeared? All rational thought has been abandoned and people simply obey without questioning. That's what they're aiming for. That's why they appeared as gods.'

REPORTER: 'Does it even matter how we understand these beings?'

BOURREAU: 'To me, yes. If I can prove that an alien committed a murder, I can arrest it and reprimand it according to the laws of our international justice system. If I bring a god before the court, the judges and lawyers run a mile. That's the difference. For me they're just another kind of being – there's nothing divine about them.'

REPORTER: 'But you are largely alone in that opinion, correct?'

BOURREAU: 'Because the majority of people are short sighted and only concerned with their own personal interest: they follow a god and are rewarded for it. But one day they will have to pay for the complacency they enjoy today. And it won't come cheap.'

REPORTER: 'Inspector, there are many who believe your actions during the Great Change, when you fought against the gods, were simply insane.'

BOURREAU: 'I only fought those who were guilty. I couldn't care less about the other ones.'

REPORTER: 'How, in your opinion, is it possible to prosecute a god?'

BOURREAU: 'By setting up a court system that applies to them. That's my most pressing concern, and if the gods had any sense of responsibility they would have done it themselves long ago. Let me give you an analogy: people can be sentenced in court for committing cruelty against animals. The animals don't even understand, but we do it anyway.'

REPORTER: 'You're comparing us with animals?'

BOURREAU: 'You're a lapdog. Just like the one sat next to the goddess Hecate on the amulet you're wearing. Not a particularly imaginative choice, I must say, given the variety of gods you have to choose from.'

REPORTER: 'So, what happens if we prove that extra-terrestrials don't exist, and the atheist is forced to acknowledge that he was wrong?'

BOURREAU: 'The whole thing could still be explained as a form of mass deception by world powers, executed through national experiments with drinking water and air pollution. Or maybe I'm lying in a coma somewhere and imagining the entire situation. A nightmare.'

REPORTER: 'Then why would you stay willingly in this nightmare, inspector? Maybe if you try to kill yourself in the dream you might wake up.'

BOURREAU: 'No. Someone has to maintain a semblance of rationality in the face of madness. Apparently that task falls to me. And now if you'll excuse me please. I have another case to settle. One of many.'

To clarify what it is that motivates this extraordinary man, we now present our depiction of an episode brought to light by the *Dos & Don'ts* hidden camera team.

D&D has recreated the scenes with actors, but made every effort to preserve the authenticity of the material. The scene played out exactly as it is portrayed in the following clip.

>>>Free Clip 'Freyr's Eve'

Germania, Free City of Bremo (Bremen), October 2019

Malleus Bourreau climbed out of his BMW i8 and flung on his black hat in one fluid motion. It was late in the afternoon, and the clammy winter darkness had already enveloped the city. The side street smelled of wet asphalt, damp paper and exhaust fumes, and had no lighting. The two solitary streetlamps had both been destroyed, their LEDs and glass panes smashed into fragments.

After a quick glance around, he stepped into the nameless self-service café, part of the *BlackBean* chain.

Just one more hour. He pushed his credit card into the slot on the counter, chose a double espresso with aromatic milk froth, and took a seat by a window that was as good as opaque.

Ten small tables in the café were all unoccupied, and except for Malleus there was only a gooey-eyed young couple sitting almost on top of each other and swiping through photos on a tablet. A *BlackBean* employee in overalls was making a lacklustre attempt at wiping down the machines. Fronted with black and chrome plastic with various spouts, they spat out a variety of speciality coffees for very little money. There were no waiters, and the disposable cutlery ended up either in the bin or on the floor, depending on the customer. Cold neon light made the furniture look even uglier than it already was. Anyone with enough money avoided these cafés. Even in Bremo.

Better so. Malleus sipped at his drink and looked across the street. The window was perfectly positioned to give him a view of the unimposing remodelled factory opposite without being discovered.

Bremo had been largely spared in the destruction of the Great Change. On his drive through the city he hadn't seen any damage to the buildings, and in fact, the cranes were building new houses, plus a new temple whose attribution he couldn't quite place. That was unusual as the Germanic gods generally didn't tolerate any clearly visible competition. In more general terms, too, Bremo's architecture had changed; runes and modern interpretations of Germanic art, murals and ornamentation adorned the buildings. LED billboards attached to growing skyscrapers, zeppelins and hot air balloons crowded the sky. Invitations to various winter solstice events blared across the city, the fragments of marketing spiel and garish music occasionally floating into the *BlackBean*.

The numerous Christian buildings in the city had been transformed into social housing and private apartments – plenty of uses had been found for the city's impressive churches and cathedrals. Smaller Christian buildings had been torn down and replaced with newly created pagan groves and gardens. The Germanic gods lauded their victory over the religion they had driven out of their followers' heads with obvious satisfaction.

I'll go and see the temple later. But first: the case. Malleus took his PDA – personal device – from the right pocket of his worn-out military coat, laid it on the small table in front of him and pulled out his metal cigar case; inside were his treasured Culebras, a lighter and a wooden splint, which he used to light the twisted cigars.

Ignoring the dirty looks thrown his way by the happy couple, he took out a cigar with a green band and sniffed along its edge. The smell of it alone helped him to think more clearly, stimulated his intellect.

Malleus had researched long and hard before finally finding the location he would be heading to in a little less than an hour.

His Swedish colleagues had given him a tip off regarding the individual he was following, who had recently left Uppsala on a ferry.

Once Malleus had identified the route through Germania most commonly used by his target, he immediately headed to Bremo. It was here that the scheme had begun, to which hundreds had fallen victim. A few had even lost their lives in the process – and not as a voluntary sacrifice.

Compared to those lives, the millions he's been swindling out of his followers are almost negligible. Malleus stroked the ends of his Fu Manchu moustache thoughtfully. He activated the PDA, opened the i8's autopilot and sent the car to search for parking spaces in the area. He didn't want to leave it parked outside the café – he was trying to avoid attracting any attention. Then he lit the splint and subsequently his Culebra, while the electric engine of the BMW started up and purred off down the street.

'It's no smoking in here,' commented the male lovebird in annoyance.

The smoke that spilled over Malleus' lips welled into a cloud that formed the unmistakable shape of a penis in the air, dissipating into indistinguishable curls a moment later. The insult had not been intentional on his part. It had something to do with the case that had led him into the café in the first place.

'I do apologise. I always smoke a cigar with my coffee, force of habit,' he answered politely. 'May I invite you and your friend to join me by way of apology?' Malleus' eyes, obscured by blue contact lenses, fixed on the couple, noticing details, anomalies, characteristics.

'No, it's fine.' The man got up and pulled the woman with him. They left without a word, and were followed soon afterwards by the *BlackBean* employee.

As soon as he was alone, Malleus took out his weapons from his coat pocket.

They were modern replicas of the Apache Knuckle Duster Pepperbox – two titanium knuckledusters with fold-out miniature 9mm revolvers, plus an integrated double-edged flick knife. Since the Great Change he preferred not to use heavy weaponry. The weight, the sound – too many memories. *Bad memories.*

Malleus checked the chambers and carefully hid them in his coat again. He was ready for the worst case scenario.

Satisfied, he puffed on the Culebra, the burning tobacco crackling gently as he inhaled. The smoke seemed momentarily to take on the shape of a man's face, then dissolved into thin wisps. *Today it ends.*

Despite the bad weather, there was still an unusual amount of movement on the other side of the street. People strolled with a casual air through the dark, deserted alley and through the entrance to the old factory building, as if by sheer coincidence.

Malleus counted these people. After around thirty minutes he'd counted 200 men and women of varying ages, wearing a range of clothing styles. The side street was clearly exerting a mysterious pulling power, affecting people from all levels of society.

After forty-five minutes, the flood of people ended.

My cue. Malleus stood up and threw the plastic cup into the bin. In the doorway of the café he paused to adjust his hat, ran his fingers over his beard and set off. *Fifteen minutes until a god is overthrown.*

He paced over to the entrance, raising the collar of his military coat, which when combined with his hat, gave him sufficient shelter against the light evening drizzle.

Malleus had organised the support of a SWAT team with the local authorities, which he would call in should it be necessary. But on the whole he preferred to solve his cases alone, if circumstances allowed. He guessed he would be able to handle the Bremo case.

Slightly hidden in the entrance, which led to a torch-lit courtyard, a bulgingly muscular man with a sharp suit and a thick coat was about to close the iron outer door.

He saw Malleus and paused, pulled out a tablet computer and after a momentary glance continued to block the passageway. Apparently there was a guest list. 'Sorry, this is a private event.'

'I'm sure it is. But unfortunately *private* doesn't apply in this case.' Malleus flashed his identification. 'Bourreau, Interpol. I'd like to speak with Mr Freyr before his appearance tonight, if at all possible?'

The doorman looked around as if to ensure that nobody else was following the inspector. 'You've come to the wrong event, inspector. This is a concert.'

'How wonderful, Mr Freyr is clearly a man of many talents. As far as I knew these events were mainly about him demonstrating his power as a god of fertility. I'll leave out the jokes about his big instrument, shall I?' Malleus stuck his hand in his coat pocket and slipped his fingers through the rings of the knuckleduster. 'I take it you're Skirnir?'

'Who?' The doorman appeared baffled.

He sighed. *The same crap every time.* The people never bothered to properly research the gods they so blindly followed. 'Skirnir, according to mythology, is the friend and assistant of Freyr.'

'Oh right. No.' The man was smiling indifferently. 'Whatever you say, inspector. Good luck with the search.'

'Do I need to show you my warrant, or are you going to let me through?'

'Show me whatever you like. You're not getting past this door.' The man moved to push the iron door closed. 'I could whip up an ID badge like that myself with a few minutes and a laminator.'

Malleus stepped forwards and drew his hand from his pocket, the Apache gripped tightly in his fist.

In a split second, the doorman pulled out a thigh-length dagger from his coat and stabbed at Malleus.

So, you are Skirnir. Malleus turned to the side, letting his coat whirl loosely in the air to confuse his attacker.

Taken aback by the flapping material, the doorman took a step to the side, straight into the path of a powerful punch from Malleus' concealed fist.

The titanium rings slammed against the man's lower jaw, breaking the bone and dislocating the joint with a loud crack.

Chunks of tooth and blood sprayed from his lips, his head snapped backwards and the rest of his body followed in an unconscious arc. The man collapsed motionless at Malleus' feet, blood pouring from his mouth onto the rough stone floor; the impact of the fall had added a deep facial cut and a broken nose to his injuries. The dagger crashed to the ground next to him.

Malleus quickly restrained the doorman with cable ties, securing his hands behind his back and darting into the hallway, lit only by the flickering of the torches bracketed to the walls. He left the door open for the SWAT team, just in case.

The doorway opposite him led into the largest building in the factory complex, whose huge windows emitted a warm light into the evening chill. Muffled conversation spilled from the building, the men and women inside clearly full of anticipation for what was to follow.

Malleus was familiar with such fertility rituals, which tended to take place in conjunction with other forms of debauchery, such as at the Bacchanals.

The 200 women and men would almost certainly be standing naked in the beautifully decorated hall, awaiting the appearance of their god Freyr. He would then collect offerings in the form of large amounts of cash, and following this select a few women to pleasure. Finally, everyone would give in to their basest desires and pay homage to Freyr in the hope of becoming pregnant with the children each visitor was so desperate to conceive. Should the long-awaited pregnancies appear, Malleus was certain it had nothing to do with the miracles of Freyr. The man was a crafty, ruthless crook.

And a murderer. Malleus crept into the inner courtyard and headed down the passage that didn't lead to the large hall. He was looking for a dressing room – and found himself blocked by a second doorman.

The startled attendant opened his mouth to utter a warning, but was cut short by a hefty punch to the solar plexus with the knuckleduster, and collapsed into a wheezing pile on the ground.

Malleus tied this one up too, rolled him to the side and entered the door his opponent had been guarding without so much as a knock.

In front of a large illuminated mirror sat the muscular man who had been on Malleus' wanted list for over two months. As the suspect had used many aliases in the course of the investigation,

Malleus decided to just stick with the name Freyr until finger-prints and DNA matching could confirm his true identity.

His white bathrobe was slightly open and Freyr was powdering his face; his forehead was adorned with a rune, and a tattoo sprawled across his chest, showing a wild boar with golden bristles along its back. This was almost certainly a depiction of Gullinbursti, Freyr's legendary steed fashioned by the dwarves Sindri and Brokk. The god could ride faster on this boar than most could ride on a horse, according to the sagas.

'Forgot to knock again, Mads?' Freyr scolded without turning his head; his long blond hair glistened and bounced as he primped.

'I'm sure Mads would have knocked. Not my style though,' replied Malleus, showing his pass for the second time. 'Bourreau, Interpol. You're under arrest.'

Freyr paused and slowly turned his head to face the door. Aside from a narrow window, there were no other routes of escape. 'What for?'

'Several counts of incitement to murder, murder itself, business fraud,' answered Malleus, 'and tax evasion. But my Swedish colleagues will be more interested in that one.'

Freyr threw back his head and laughed. 'You want to arrest a *god*?'

'If you are one: yes. But as you're nothing more than a conman, this should go quite smoothly.' Malleus looked around. There were a good number of cases with luggage tags scattered around the room. Apparently Freyr and his team were planning to move on after tonight's event. 'I'm afraid your European tour is cancelled.'

'I haven't murdered anybody.' The man got slowly to his feet. 'And I *am* a god! I can . . .'

'You're a shit,' Malleus continued in a soft, deliberate tone. 'An asshole who exploits the faith of troubled people desperate to have children. Nothing more than deception and lies, to get your hands on as much of their money as possible.'

Freyr's affected cheeriness vanished, his lips thinned.

'You murdered Lionel Albrecht, amongst others, out of fear that he would persuade his wife to stop receiving your godly services, because she continually failed to become pregnant,' began Malleus.

Freyr's expression became hostile. 'You've come alone, inspector?'

'Subjects such as yourself don't present much of a challenge.' Mallleus was aware that the man was about to attack him. 'Albrecht's wife witnessed the murder and informed the police. In addition, we're also aware of several other murders amongst your followers, in which the women killed their husbands at your command. Apparently you're very sensitive when it comes to questions about your reproductive abilities. And even more sensitive when it threatens your income.'

'How dare you!'

'We conducted DNA tests in all the known cases. You have exceptionally human-looking DNA for someone who is supposedly a god of fertility.' Malleus braced himself for the imminent attack. 'I've got you by the balls. And you're not going to wander off back to Alfheim to live with the fairies – you're going to spend some serious time in a very human prison. But before that' – he gestured towards the door – 'we're both going to go out there and explain to those poor blinded people that they've been had, in both senses of the word, by a mortal, human man.'

Freyr abruptly kicked the chair in front of him so that it slammed right into Malleus' knee.

Malleus winced in pain and buckled slightly.

His attacker jumped past him and through the door.

Malleus grabbed at the bathrobe, but it slipped through his fingers.

'You'll never catch me!' Freyr tore out of the room and through the hallway. 'I am a god!' But in the dim light he failed to notice the tied up body Malleus had left there minutes earlier, and toppled over the lifeless doorman onto the ground.

As he stumbled to his feet, Malleus reached him and seized a handful of his long, blonde hair. 'Yes I will,' he replied, and pulled his head back, attempting to press the man against the wall and cable tie his hands. 'You're under arrest.'

Somehow Freyr untangled himself from Malleus' fingers and escaped, leaving him with a handful of bloody, blonde strands of hair in his fist. Snorting with rage, Freyr ran a few paces, then spread his arms in a grandiose pose reminiscent of a wrestler; his muscles and tattoos twitched.

'Father Freyr, lend me your power!' he called, and his grey-green eyes were suddenly filled with iridescent light; the golden bristles on the tattooed boar began to glow. 'The mortals wish to imprison your son, who is fulfilling your will on earth. Do not allow this, stand by me! I offer you this man as a sacrifice.' He threw himself with a wild grunt at Malleus, hands outstretched.

A demigod! Malleus avoided the vicious attack with a swift pivot. The man's knuckles narrowly missed his throat, instead smashing into the wall behind him in a spray of plaster and brick.

Growling, Freyr turned and flailed with dust-covered fists at Malleus, who jumped backwards, putting a safe distance between himself and his attacker, who seemed to have exchanged his reason for superhuman strength.

The fight was moving backwards; back in the direction of the improvised dressing room. Freyr seemed to have abandoned his intention to flee and was now wholly determined to simply kill his opponent, as promised to his supposedly godly father.

Just like he killed his other victims. Malleus waited for the opportunity to counterattack.

He took one, two steps back into the dressing room, encouraging Freyr to follow him, then grabbed the door handle and swung the heavy metal door against his attacker with all his strength. The steel struck Freyr directly on his forehead and threw him back against the wall, where he crumpled into a dizzy heap.

'Well, that was quite the divine comedy,' commented Malleus, giving Freyr one last punch with the knuckleduster, just to be safe. 'Or half-divine anyway.' The man's eyes lost their fanatic glow and drooped shut, the golden lines on his tattooed chest vanished.

Malleus perched on the makeup table, pulled out his case of Culebras and selected one with a red band. Demigod or not, he had caught his suspect.

He inhaled deeply and blew a thick cloud of smoke towards the unconscious Freyr, which momentarily formed the shape of a laughing face.

Continuing to puff on his cigar, Malleus quickly searched through the cases in the room and found plenty of evidence for the conman's activities, as well as a Swedish passport bearing the name Olle Viklund; the seal and stamps were authentic. A blood analysis would show whether the man had drugs in his blood, which would account for his extraordinary show of strength.

Even if you really are a son of Freyr, thought Malleus as he peered through his dense cigar smoke, *your daddy isn't coming to help you.* Chuckling quietly to himself, he stood up, and packed the passport, several bundles of cash and the makeup brushes into his pockets. *Gods don't use face powder. They just look supernaturally divine.*

Time for the deterrent. Malleus took one more drag on his cigar and enjoyed the faint head rush it gave him.

Then he bent down, grabbed a thick handful of long blond hair and dragged Olle Viklund, aka Freyr, behind him like a sack of potatoes through the passageway to the great hall, where his followers were patiently awaiting his arrival.

The sight of their supposed god combined with the evidence he had just found would open their eyes. They would bashfully clothe themselves and leave the hall without another word.

Shame was usually the overwhelming reaction when he exposed a conman.

But Malleus was ready to bet that those same people in six months or a year, or maybe even just one month, would be swearing allegiance to another god. One that they were totally convinced was real, no doubt about it, not like the last one.

Until I reappear. Malleus smiled grimly and ran his fingers over the ends of his moustache. *The Houdini of the modern, god-filled world. Exposing the charlatans, one by one.*

Emphatically, he swung open the doors to the hall, to a chorus of horrified gasps.

[. . .]

Extract from *DOS & DON'TS*

342nd digital and enhanced multimedia edition, November 2019

From chapter: How the World Changed

[. . .] The historically minded amongst our readers have often expressed the wish for a concise summary of the most significant world events from 2012 until the present day.

Dos & Don'ts are proud to provide exactly that in the following chapter.

For a deeper analysis of individual historical milestones, we recommend that our readers conduct wider personal reading, guided by our own anthology, *D&D: The Continents, The Gods, The Great Change (24th digital and enhanced edition, May 2019)*

As our readers have come to expect, this chapter includes >>>*exclusive historical content*, available only in this *D&D* edition.

To begin with, we'll discuss **December 2012**, now referred to as 'the phase of wonder, awe and disbelief'.

The world initially believed that the events around 21.12.2012 were some form of prank executed by a network of hackers, actors and enthusiastic nerds, an attempt to give the world a little fright – until the first undeniable miracles and attacks by gods and legendary beings began to occur (see Introduction, cases #1-#7).

The first large wave of conversions began in **early 2013** in Europe (incl. Russia), as Christians began to worship Germanic, Slavic and Celtic/Pagan deities. Those few who had always followed the old rites were shown particular favour by the gods. Nature faiths such as Wicca also experienced a sharp rise in followers.

The Christian churches endured, but were powerless to prevent the dwindling of their congregations.

>>>*Exclusive historical content*

One particularly interesting case is that of the priest Adrian Tuschmann, who presided over a small parish near Cologne, who during a sermon suddenly pulled out a copy of the Malleus Maleficarum, a treatise on the prosecution of witches, and began quoting it at length.

This led to the events of the evening of 30th April 2013, historically recognised as Walpurgis Night, when the priest and a small group of his followers appeared at a gathering of the village youth. The gathering was a celebration, where the villagers intended to dance through the night into May morning – but this was interrupted by Tuschmann. The priest insisted that by indulging heathen customs the people would secure their own damnation, and instead of dancing around the fire, they would be burning in it.

When a number of the youths at the gathering mocked the priest, he attacked them, pushing them into the fire while his small group of followers prayed for their souls.

The teenagers were rescued from the fire in time, but were taken to hospital with severe burns.

Following the incident, Tuschmann disappeared. The next day

he was found hanged on his own bell rope, with a pagan rune scratched into his forehead.

The first waves of conversion in the Middle East and other Muslim states were reasonably moderate, as both Sunnis and Shias were largely very strongly committed to Allah. In addition to this, very little was known by the general population about the old gods, such as Marduk.

The exception was Egypt.

Here the gods found it extremely easy to reclaim their followers. Egyptians flocked to the ancient gods in their thousands, which was observed with suspicion by Israel and the neighbouring Muslim states. The Egyptian president declared himself to be the new Pharaoh.

>>>*Exclusive historical content*

At this point we must mention the case of Amunet Syrah Abdelghani.

This young woman was working at the pyramids as a tour guide, when one day she went missing whilst on a tour and could not be found for days. A search party was sent out but failed to find any trace of her.

When, four days later, she suddenly reappeared in her apartment, she had no memory of what had happened to her. There were no signs of mistreatment or violence on her body, in fact the opposite was true: she had been bathed, oiled, and her clothing smelled of fresh perfume.

During her evening shower, Abdelghani noticed a mark on her stomach that resembled an ancient hieroglyph. Though it didn't seem to be a tattoo of any kind, the symbol was permanent and could not be removed.

Nine months later the young woman gave birth to a healthy baby girl, bearing exactly the same mark on her own stomach.

The events of 2013 can be summarised thus: the world underwent an extreme change, which was feared by many, welcomed by others, and sometimes even celebrated.

The countries that suffered the most were those that had previously been governed by the larger monotheistic religions.

The polytheistic countries of Asia had a clear advantage: they hailed the gods, beings and creatures who appeared as confirmations of their ancient beliefs.

There were even reports of miracles in Australia and the Arctic regions.

We now reach the year **2014**.

The new year brought little peace or rational solution for the mysterious manifestations of the previous twelve months. On the contrary, this year only widened the gulfs between religions, fuelling jealousy and resentment.

In Europe the newly converted and the old faithful were showered with gifts by their gods. These gifts ranged from houses that appeared out of nowhere, to gold and riches – they even had their diseases and injuries healed.

The endless footage and photographs on the internet left their mark. It was the most effective and cheapest propaganda the gods could have wished for.

It should not be forgotten, however, that tensions between the converted and the original believers were widespread, and to this day there continues to be unrest amongst the subgroups of followers, ranging from minor squabbles to significant conflicts.

To avoid misunderstandings, the original believers are often conceptually split into *Traditionalists* and *Neo-Pagans*. (Though the latter generally denotes followers of neo-paganism, this is itself a broad category – ranging from pedantic offshoots even stricter than the traditionalists, to the looser understanding of paganism born out of the Woodstock era, which has nothing to do with the traditional rites and rituals of the gods.)

There were countless reports of robbery, extortion and manslaughter in which the original believers demanded compensation from the newer converts, seeing themselves as deserving of more rewards due to their longstanding loyalty to the gods.

If an individual was thought to have converted not out of religious conviction, but through pure financial calculation, it was not uncommon for them to be murdered by their fellow believers.

This happened on several occasions to prominent politicians who pulled out of the established parties in order to align themselves with the new political trends dictated by the gods. There was much talk of *tribunals* in these cases, which some have compared to the Spanish Inquisition of the fifteenth century.

>>>*Exclusive historical content*

I.

Sean O'Connor and his Banshees became famous for putting converts on trial in Ireland. Anyone who didn't pass the trial was said to have 'heard the cry of the banshee', as the murders were euphemistically described. O'Connor was apprehended only years later and died under mysterious circumstances.

II.

Another example was the Trial of the Stones in Carnac, which continues today (Nov. 2019).

People whose motives in converting are brought into question, or who are thought to be deliberately disrespecting the gods or blaspheming, are forced to walk through the standing stone fields of Carnac on the night of a new moon. The region in Brittany is renowned for its thousands of standing stones, grouped into rows.

Whoever comes out of the stone fields alive is permitted to stay in the congregation. The dead are collected on the next morning and burned.

Many people emerge with deep wounds; some never recover mentally from the experience, though none of the victims can remember exactly what happened to them during the night in the fields.

An unusual and noteworthy fact: the Indian deities have an unexpectedly significant presence in London.

Though the gods tended to stay largely in the geographical areas where they had manifested and had most influence, Shiva and Co. made the move to the English capital in 2014.

The Hindu population rose continuously over the coming months, and London became the toehold for Hindu deities across Europe.

Missionary work was strictly avoided by the Hindu gods, presumably out of respect for the predominant Celtic gods in the region. However, to this date (Nov. 2019), the strong Indian and Hindu influence on London should not be overlooked.

Let us throw a glance across the pond.

In 2014, tension rose in the United States: while anxiety amongst the white population reached a crescendo, the First Nations, formerly known as Native Americans, were growing stronger.

Spurred by the return of the Great Spirit, they demanded a proportionate representation for their people in the US government, alongside remunerations and a substantial transformation of the American economy, with an emphasis on ecological policies and green energy.

The unease amongst the white population had remarkable results – increasing numbers of Americans sought to claim indigenous roots, presumably in an attempt to escape the wrath of the Great Spirit, or Manitu, or whatever other name this god was known by, and where possible to be rewarded for their newly discovered Native American heritage.

Genealogists were suddenly inundated with work, and due to widespread falsification of archive material, DNA-testing was carried out on a national level.

>>>*Exclusive historical content*

It was in this context that US senator William T. Olderman made himself a figure of ridicule, as he proudly presented a stack of documents and birth certificates proclaiming him to be the descendant of the Comanche chief Po-bish-e-quasho (also known as Iron Jacket). Iron Jacket was known for wearing a Spanish chainmail shirt that protected him from light munitions, giving him a reputation of invincibility.

Olderman began regularly wearing shirts made of chainmail, and painted half of his face in the Comanche style to display his heritage.

He went on to marry a First Nation woman descended from the Wyandot.

Until his death Olderman insisted that he could feel his First Nation roots in his Comanche blood.

Thus the unsettling year of 2014 continued: the world

continued to change, but the remaining political leaders of Christian, Islamic or Jewish faith were secretly preparing to retaliate.

They refused to see their religions defeated by the mere failure of their gods to appear on cue. Preparations were made for quick, devastating actions against the centres set up to worship the new gods, though not everyone at the table was in favour of such drastic measures: there were many votes against and abstentions.

This dissidence was quickly resolved: politicians who had converted to the ancient gods were simply excluded from the discussions.

The vote then quickly showed a clear majority in favour of *Operation Theoclast: direct attacks on the gods and their domains.*

Who could have predicted how dramatic the year **2015** would be: *Operation Theoclast* began almost immediately, though without any clear idea of whether this would be a truly coordinated international effort.

As planned, the militaries of certain states carried out strong attacks on the newly erected centres of worship for the gods. This occurred predominantly in Europe and North America. In Asia, Middle and South America, and Middle and South Africa, next to nothing happened. (Details on the Great Change can be found in the *D&D Self Study Series: The Great Change – Winners and Losers.*)

But in Europe there was widespread dissent – the Scandinavian states decided on neutrality, and Greece and Italy unexpectedly dropped out of the operation.

In Germany the picture was mixed.

The followers of the new Germanic gods put up substantial resistance. Artillery and explosives were used extensively, and only with considerable force and heavy weaponry were the troops of *Operation Theoclast* able to advance in the face of the state police.

>>>*Exclusive historical content*

In 2015 the damp, wooded countryside of Bramsche saw a small-scale recreation of the legendary Roman Battle of Varus in AD 9.

Advancing special troops were baited into an ambush by the leader of the Germanic forces, Irmin Menius, and torn to shreds by state soldiers. The thick treetops prevented Theoclast-deployed helicopters from engaging in the firefight, and the trapped forces were slowly and painfully eradicated.

Video clips from the battle drew attention for their remarkable footage of the statue of Arminius, leader of the Germanic forces who defeated the Romans in the original Battle of Varus. The statue, over twenty-eight metres high and brandishing a seven-metre-long sword, appears to have engaged in the battle and taken down at least two helicopters by throwing tree branches.

Though one may initially disregard these clips as clever video editing or CGI trickery, on examining the statue in its rightful place on the Grotenburg, one can observe bullet holes and even blood on its sword, which has been independently verified by *D&D* researchers as human blood.

Things were less drastically violent in China. Even before 2012, the country had been a colourful melting pot of different religious orientations.

But the Communist authorities had no interest in sharing their power. They carried out a so-called 'Enlightenment Campaign', which was at least minimally inspired by *Operation Theoclast.*

Temples were torn down or repurposed as sport stadiums and events arenas in an attempt to expose the illusory nature of the gods. Followers of the Chinese folk religions were subjected to severe reprisals.

News of these measures slowly trickled through to Europe. *D&D* have exclusive access to many of the verified recordings from China. It was reported that the Eight Immortals of Chinese mythology were appearing on various occasions, when the state reprisals against their followers were too violent or unjust. Several secret recordings support these accounts.

In one photograph a man in traditional Chinese clothing is clearly visible riding on a black tiger and holding a golden rod in one hand. In the other hand he is gripping a long spear, which is piercing the chest of an Enlightenment official.

Lei Gong, the Chinese god of thunder, also appeared in many locations, and with his bird's feet and feathers he makes quite an unmistakable impression. With his hammer and chisel, which traditionally represent the thunder he controls, he appeared at various ruined temples and rebuilt them. He also used his beak, lined with sharp fangs, to eviscerate a number of state officials.

Of course, the Chinese government denounced these images, videos and witness statements as simple falsifications and propaganda. However, here at *D&D* we have conducted extensive analysis of the materials in question and come to the conclusion that there has been no editing or manipulation of the footage at any stage.

The summary of **2015**, then: by the end of the year the remaining Christian, Islamic and Jewish powers who took part in *Operation Theoclast* stood with their backs against the wall, reduced to fighting for their very existence.

The governments and instigators, politicians and spiritual leaders knew that their fate was about to be decided. And they were quite aware that the ancient gods were seldom inclined to leniency or mercy.

In **2016** the gods launched their retaliation against the nations involved in *Operation Theoclast*, igniting the second wave of the Great Change.

Entire villages, towns and regions were laid to waste by the gods, and their followers enacted devastating acts of violence and destruction with conventional weaponry.

It was not long until ceasefires were reached and new governments founded.

The gods were generous, and refrained from carrying out much of the retribution they had planned against the politicians, who they essentially wished to exterminate. Instead, they healed the injured and helped to rebuild the states they had destroyed, with miracles on large and small scales. They founded charities, and their blessings were in high demand.

However, the countries where *Operation Theoclast* had taken place still bear the marks of that devastating conflict: Spain, Portugal, France, England, Northern Ireland, Austria, Germany, the Benelux countries and of course the Christian and Russian Orthodox countries in Eastern Europe.

>>>*Exclusive historical content*

One peculiarity that has never been fully explained, even by the experts at *D&D*, are the reports of appearances made during the conflict by divine and mystical beings who have *nothing* to do with European culture.

The majority of atrocities committed during the wars have been traced back to these beings: entire populations disappearing from villages and towns, areas that had never been under fire. Many bodies remain unaccounted for.

The few witness reports regarding the appearances of these entities are inconsistent and contradictory, and so far no video footage has emerged. They disappeared as quickly as they attacked.

To this date (Nov. 2019) no Celtic or Germanic gods have claimed any association with these beings. *D&D* has assigned a research team to the case.

The year **2016** in summary: governments were swept away or conformed to the wishes of the gods. Many conflicts in the countries most affected by the Great Change carried on through the end of the year, but all in all, the people of Europe had understood and accepted that the gods were here to stay. And they were real. (Details on events in the rest of the world can be found in the *D&D Self Study Series: How the World Changed.*)

2017: the power relations in Europe changed considerably. Italy, Greece, the Republic of Ireland, the Scandinavian countries of Iceland, Sweden, Norway, Denmark, Finland, and additionally Scotland, Italy and Greece all continued to stabilise and in doing so achieved economic advantage in Europe. They had all remained neutral or accepted the gods during the Great Change.

The invaded and conquered *Theoclast* countries of Spain, Portugal, France, England, Northern Ireland, Austria, Germany, the Benelux countries and the Christian and Russian Orthodox countries in Eastern Europe were gradually beginning to recover. (Details in *D&D: How the World Changed.*)

The rebuilding of Europe was in full swing, the economy was boosted, the gods acted benevolently and used their powers for the health and social benefit of their people, attending to culture and public affairs. Many gods joined or founded companies, and constructed their own temples, or renovated entire quarters for their followers.

>>>*Exclusive historical content*

The god Loki became a particularly notable figure in 2017, and certainly made no secret of his intentions during this period. He established his own network of broadcasting and entertainment companies across Europe.

The show *Loki's Lost* quickly became a ratings forerunner due to its unbelievably high prizes and equally high death toll.

The contestants on this high-stakes game show put their own lives in the balance, and often those of their fellow players. This format has proven to be a hit, and the show's unpredictable nature keeps viewers hooked from week to week.

One particularly unforgettable episode on 21.12.2017, the Winter Solstice Special, featured a total of two hundred people losing their lives, as the winner of the show chose to sacrifice all other contestants and then himself in the name of his god (who was not Loki). Unfortunately, due to network regulations, the name of the god was censored in pre-broadcast editing.

To this day the identity of the god responsible for this massacre remains an industry secret. However, Loki was more than happy to oblige whoever or whatever demanded the sacrifice.

Plans for brand new cities also began to be realised, inspired by modes of community living in ancient Germanic, Celtic or Slavic cultures.

2017, then, saw the gradual return of peace to the world.

People generally accepted the gods, no longer seeing them as threats or adversaries. On the contrary: after the battles and massacres of the Great Change, the gods took on a more benevolent role, and were seen to be dealing firmly but fairly with those who had initiated the conflict.

With the new governments came various constitutional changes, for example: legislation surrounding crime and punishment was often altered to incorporate local gods and their corresponding belief systems, changes which largely remained geographically specific.

Another development: the first human children fathered by gods began to be born, and abandoned children, whose mothers were clearly goddesses, were found.

D&D have access to records and data that indicate the extraordinary growth patterns of many of these children, some of whom were recorded as progressing from baby to teenager in the space of a year. Occasionally, overwhelmed human parents would turn to adoption agencies in an attempt to distance themselves from their superhuman offspring.

The demigods were among us, and the fusion of human and godly characteristics was underway.

>>>*Exclusive historical content*

Since late 2017, a young model named Aurora Monti has been causing quite a stir, as her stunning beauty causes anyone in her vicinity to lose their reason. No matter what she wears, be it makeup, jewellery, fur, lingerie, it immediately sells out across the continent.

A model agent commented: 'She could drag a washing machine down the catwalk and people would go out and buy it.'

Rumour has it that the model is a daughter of Venus, a theory which some think is substantiated by the fact that the woman is never seen in public with her mother, only her father.

The woman's birth certificate, dated 2016, lists Jane Doe as the mother.

Authorities are visibly overwhelmed by these new circumstances.

The year **2018** was something of a shock to the new system: in an unexpected move, the remaining Christian and Islamic spiritual leaders called for *Reconquista, Jihad*, or *the modern Crusade*, urging their remaining followers to fight for their respective gods.

Volunteers had been secretly preparing for this action over the past year. In the run-up to their strike they had executed detailed reconnaissance missions in the centres of the new gods, and identified the most important figures in each area.

When the order came, thousands of radicals and fanatics attacked across Europe: shrines burned, buildings were torn down, humans were murdered, and there were even high profile attacks on gods and legendary figures.

(Details on events in the rest of the world can be found in the *D&D Self Study Series: How the World Changed.*)

The response followed immediately, as the gods correctly anticipated that the resistance from the defeated religious minorities would not end at the first wave of attacks.

The gods released a torrent of destruction and extermination – but carefully dosed and exclusively targeted at those who had dared to show resistance. Together with their followers, the gods wiped out the majority of radicals and mutilated the survivors, branding them as examples of the consequences of defying the ruling gods.

There were therefore many remarkable instances of gods who would appear and deal out individually tailored retribution, without causing the slightest damage to their subject's environment.

>>>*Exclusive historical content*

I.

In Munich, in an Oktoberfest beer tent, a Catholic priest was eviscerated by a bolt of lightning as he brought a glass of beer to his lips. However, the glass did not break, and the beer remained unspoiled.

II.

In Stuttgart, a Celtic god personally visited a meeting of the movement *Protestants Against The Idols* – known as PrATIs, struck the leading priest dead and offered the other members the chance to join the ranks of his followers.

Those who refused were killed instantly; those who complied were allowed to join his followers and leave.

Though we would once more recommend the edition *D&D Self Study Series: How the World Changed* as a source of more information on worldwide events during this time, let us take another look across the Atlantic.

2018 was an exciting year in the United States, as Mexico saw its chance to extend its power by reaching not into South America, but towards the North. The country was newly empowered by the appearance of its ancient gods, and claimed large chunks of Texas, New Mexico, Arizona and California as its own territory.

The Mexican president justified the move, which went reasonably smoothly given the widespread political turmoil, by referencing the repressive measures suffered by his country at the hands of those particular states over the last few centuries.

He made the reasonable and ultimately undeniable point that the USA as a whole had been exploiting his country for hundreds of years, and made a convincing case for his seizure of the territories.

Eye witnesses claim that the Mexican troops were led by the gods Itztli, Xocotl and Mextli.

>>>*Exclusive historical content*

The USA was forced to accept the loss of the southern states to Mexico, as these regions had already officially broken away from the United States during the years following 2012 (see *D&D Self Study Series*). But one thing was certain: nobody would make the mistake of underestimating the Mexicans again.

Speculation was widespread in the newly conquered regions and within the ranks of the First Nations regarding the Great Spirit's absence and lack of resistance during the invasion by the Mexicans.

The events of **2018** can be summarised by the following: new turmoil arose across the world, but was quickly extinguished. The gods demonstrated their power over the people.

Gods also combatted the old religions in legal spheres: they demanded that governments issued a blanket ban on Christianity, Islam and Judaism, or at the very least penalise their public practice.

Many restrictions were passed into law across Europe, such as bans on church bells and national denunciations of religious holidays, outlawing practices that, until that point, had been tolerated.

Christianity, Judaism and Islam were henceforth to be referred to as cults, as they could provide no proof of the existence of their gods.

In the current year, **2019**, it is evident that the world is continuing to adjust to life with the gods. Europe is concentrating on finding its feet after the conflicts of the last few years, and though *Reconquista, Jihad* and *the Modern Crusade* have certainly left their mark, the countries involved are largely beginning to recover.

>>>*D&D Safety Notice*

Anyone openly associating with Christianity in any way is considered, by most countries, to be a troublemaker, someone who attracts the wrath of the gods by believing in something that doesn't exist.

For the most part, people in Europe tend to live in harmony despite religious differences, but occasionally there are assaults or lynch mobs targeting Christians, Muslims and Jews. Though the authorities are obliged to step in in such cases, unfortunately their motivation can be clouded by their own religious beliefs.

Should you belong to one of the cults, please pay close attention to your surroundings and attend to your own safety at all times. If you need to pray, do so in a secure, private location, worship quietly and avoid loud songs of praise, etc.

D&D recommends downloading the Cult-App, which can advise on the safety levels of different areas for members of the cults, providing information on the risk levels of both the gods in that region and the activities of its inhabitants.

The Vatican is an exception to the above.

So far the gods have allowed the papal state to remain standing, and even the pope has remained untouched. This move appears partly to stem from a wish to avoid provoking uproar across Europe, and has resulted in the city becoming a sanctuary for persecuted Catholics from across the world.

>>>*Exclusive D&D News*

As long as everything in the city stays peaceful, there will be no action taken against the Vatican.

Should any unrest occur, *D&D* has discovered that there are official plans amongst the Roman-Hellenistic gods to demolish St Peter's Basilica as a warning to the Catholic population.

Unlike the Christians, the Jews were unable to maintain their traditional pilgrimage site.

The state of Israel was dissolved on 1.1.2018 until further notice, as a result of immense threats from the neighbouring states, who were all armed and supported by gods. However, it has not yet been ruled out that the inhabitants may return to this ancient state in the future.

Having fled to all corners of the world, the people of Israel are now scattered and attempting to live normal lives, safe from religious persecution. Many of the Orthodox Jews moved to Masada, which has become a stronghold of sorts. The settlement is currently undergoing extensive renovation and development.

Apart from these developments, the cogs continue to turn in Europe, and people continue to live their lives.

Some gods are very publicly active, some are less so; many are leading construction projects or founding companies, either themselves or through trusted intermediaries.

The assimilation of gods into everyday life has led to calls for special laws to govern non-human beings (see chapter: *People of Note, Malleus Bourreau*). To date there has been no success in implementing any such laws.

>>>*Exclusive historical content*

Today, countless building and renovation projects are underway to restore ancient cities such as Babylon, Sodom, Gomorrah, Nimrud, Assur, Hatra, Nineveh, Machu Picchu, Angkor, Petra, Chichen Itza and many more.

In Europe, forgotten buildings and monuments are being

raised back to their former glory, creating a striking architectural contrast in many places between the modern and the ancient.

Though we have not yet reached the end of the year, **2019** can so far be summarised thus: the world is becoming more peaceful.

The gods are now a part of normality and are increasingly engaging in normal life with humans. More and more demigod children are appearing across the globe, a sure sign of integration.

The line between humans and gods is becoming ever blurrier, which is also evident in the diverse behaviour of the gods: from unapproachable to familiar, from headstrong businesswomen to benevolent miracle workers.

Apparently the gods have reached a mutual agreement regarding their areas of influence: there is no conflict over borders between gods, aside from a few small settlements, or the ambiguities of London and its unusually large Hindu god population (see above, and *D&D's London – A City of Worlds*).

As ever, the gods continue to select loyal followers for journeys to unknown locations, and those who return often tell of foreign planets and dimensions.

The new era is continuing to stabilise.

And yet the question remains, especially for many of our readers from the old faiths: where are Allah, God and Jahwe?

Are they amongst us already, performing covert miracles and protecting their followers?

Or have they chosen not to manifest to their followers, as some form of test?

Unfortunately at this point, *D&D* can provide no conclusive evidence on this subject.

[. . .]

BOOK 1

Episode 1: Sacrifice

> The gods of whom my parents told me, I have reverenced for all the time I lived under their rule, and I have always honoured those who begot my body. I have neither killed any other human being, nor stolen from any what he had entrusted to me, nor done any other unpardonable act.
>
> *The Egyptian Book of the Dead*, c. 1500 BC

It wouldn't have interested me, not even slightly.

Anyone living in these times knows exactly the kind of atrocities being committed by these ancient fucked-up deities, celebrated by blind, dull people. Or sometimes the other way round.

The modern and complex.

The archaic and brutal.

We're trapped in a fucking oxymoron, and it's killing us. Technology, miracles, atrocities. Without vodka I'd be screwed.

Watching the news channels broadcasting from the Via del Sudario, I thought to myself: fuck this.

But then I saw him, caught in a hurried shot panning across the front of the house – the man looking out of the window.

You have to know who he is to recognise him.

He's about forty with a narrow face, not particularly remarkable per se, either in stature or appearance. His black hair is short on the sides, a little longer on top and shaved on the neck. He's recently grown a thinned-out version of the Fu Manchu moustache with a small beard which, combined with his remaining stubble, makes quite a bold statement, like a fucked-up old musketeer, but somehow more masculine. Underneath his right eye runs a barely visible horizontal scar, inflicted by a knife. That much I know.

Together with the black hat and the round sunglasses he was almost unrecognisable.

But not to me.

There was no stopping me: I had to go.

With shaking fingers I filled my hip flask, got dressed and rummaged through the piles of crap in my run-down flat until I found my semi-automatic.

And since then I've been following him.

He doesn't know it, but I'm there.

I'm there . . .

Italy, Rome, November 2019

Malleus regarded the mayor's office, ransacked of all furnishings and objects except for the large, grey stone writing desk, presumably too heavy to move and too sturdy to destroy; instead it had been painted with what a layman might assume were simply red, upward-pointing arrows.

Faded rectangles on the panelled walls showed where pictures had once hung, and dustless outlines on the floors and carpets betrayed the previous positions of looted objects. The stereo, speakers and other built-in electronics including the television had been removed with professional skill, as evidenced by the few remaining cables hanging out of the walls. The door to the safe was open, revealing only a yawning emptiness.

What caught Malleus' eye, however, was a set of three makeshift ropes, which on closer inspection was made from new, sinewy branches. A fresh scent suggested that they had been cut only recently. Three loops wound round the heavy table and trailed out of the open window.

One would assume that the criminals – for whatever reason – had chosen to use natural rather than synthetic materials to escape the scene.

The object hanging on the other end of the rope, however, was far from natural.

The twisted branches creaked softly, moved gently as if someone were pulling on them.

Malleus strode across the room and glanced out of the neighbouring window onto the street outside, bathed in dwindling sunlight and busy with people.

The curious amongst them crowded into the Via del Sudario behind the police barriers. People were taking photographs and chattering excitably amongst themselves, some leaving, others arriving, drawn by the novelty, eager to see what was happening with their own eyes.

Malleus raised his personal digital assistant – PDA for short – and filmed a quick panning shot of the crowd. He captured the looming temples and palaces, restored to new glory, lit with attention-grabbing spotlights; enormous braziers adorned pillars and flat roofs.

The city's dutiful maintenance of its ancient monuments had accelerated after the arrival of the ancient gods into a magnificent restoration project. A new Rome had arisen, in splendid neoclassical style.

Beacons glowed in the Colosseum, illuminating the countless arches and throwing great shafts of light into the dimming sky to greet Jupiter.

The Roman Forum, once a ruinous tourist attraction, was being fully restored. Works were still in progress, and the plans for the new buildings stretched until 2050, Malleus had read in a newspaper on the way to Rome. The gods willed it so.

The gods will a lot of things, he thought.

'Monsieur Bourreau! Come downstairs so we can finish this undignified spectacle,' called one of the plain-clothes detectives. 'They've been hanging there long enough.'

Malleus pocketed his PDA, crossed the room and regarded it one last time before exiting into the corridor and heading downstairs. He was wearing his dark frock coat, cut after the Indian fashion, and a black military coat with an extra high collar. His shoes were plain, flat and black.

On the way downstairs he lit one of his thin, twisted cigars. They smelled terrible and produced enough smoke to be considered a significant source of air pollution. Malleus hated e-cigarettes as much as the smoking ban, so he ignored both. He puffed on a Culebra with a green band. *The green ones are best for thinking.*

He could have corrected the yelling officer: he wasn't a Monsieur, he was neither French nor Belgian. He was German, or at least that's what his passport said. But correcting him would only have raised the attention of the crowd. He didn't like being recognised, though it did occasionally happen despite his sunglasses and hat.

As Malleus came out into the open, the clouds rolled together into a grey-black mass and the first bolts of lightning began to flash across the sky; low thunder rumbled over the crowd and the buildings of Rome.

'Zeus is coming! See, he's manifesting to inspect the crime scene,' he heard a passing woman saying, full of conviction. She was manically snapping photos of the gathering webs of clouds. 'He'll find these Germanic murderers before the police do. Watch for his signal!'

Malleus adjusted his hat. There was much he could have said. For example, he could have said that Zeus couldn't care less who had killed who. That Zeus was almost certainly behind a bush right now having it off with someone just like her. Or that Zeus didn't generally bother to disguise himself as a storm. That, in any case, they were on Roman soil, meaning it would be Jupiter who would turn up, if anyone.

But anyone who wanted to believe in this apparently godly spectacle would believe regardless. This kind of supposed evidence had been turning up for years. All over the world.

Malleus remained unimpressed.

For him there were at least half a dozen explanations for the return of the gods; for instance, that extra-terrestrials understood exactly how to subjugate the human spirit, and had done some extensive reading into our pantheon. Or perhaps mass hypnosis in combination with technology, giving people something to waste their energy on so they'd rather pray to deities than protest against their circumstances. He held these and many other theories to be entirely plausible.

Malleus pushed past the barrier and found the grey-haired detective, appropriately named Romano. Everything about him was grey – coat, eyes, beard.

They shook hands, then turned to look at the house.

Dangling out of the window – fully visible in the glow of the streetlamps – was a man's naked corpse. Judging by the proportions and tattoos it was the mayor, Emanuele Domenico, with a black bag tied over his head. To the right and left of him hung two dead dogs, strung up in the same manner as their owner. Snow-white Labradors, their tongues lolling flaccidly from their muzzles.

The crisp wind played with the three bodies, which had been discovered in the early morning by a passer-by. Dog and man began a grotesque dance, swinging and crashing together, spinning in sinister pirouettes. The legs of the man were caked with dried excrement.

'*Rome, the city which took the whole world, is itself taken,*' Romano read the scrawled runes above the windows aloud. 'And the upward-pointing arrows again too.'

'Tiwaz: the T-rune, of the god Tyr.' Malleus puffed on the cigar dangling from the left corner of his mouth, spilling its acrid smoke up into the night sky. He removed his sunglasses to see more clearly; the blue contact lenses concealed his multi-coloured irises. 'Head of the Germanic pantheon and understood as a son of Odin in later mythology.' He stuck his hands in his pockets, taking care not to crush the sunglasses. 'Master of slaughter and god of war.'

'We already knew that.' Romano jumped as a bolt of lightning flashed across the sky and dissolved with a crackle. A few bystanders clapped and praised Jupiter. 'It displeases our gods when Germanics murder people in their city.'

'Would they prefer it if it was just their followers killing each other, Commissario?' Malleus grinned widely. 'The gods are more similar to each other than they like to admit.'

'What's that supposed to mean?'

'The Tiwaz rune shows a remarkable similarity to the planetary sign of Mars. In fact one might even wonder if Tyr, Jupiter, Zeus and Mars might be—'

Romano snorted. 'No blasphemous lectures today please. I know what you are, Monsieur Bourreau.'

'And that's *exactly* why I'm standing here. Because I can think *clearly.*' Malleus kept his tone polite. He took his right hand out of his pocket and pointed to the sentence on the wall. 'It's a quote attributed to Hieronymus, one of the fathers of the early Christian Church, as he witnessed the Sack of Rome by the Visigoths. That was in 410, according to the Christian calendar.'

'We know.' The grey Romano endured the history lesson with visible irritation.

Malleus savoured it. 'The ransacked office is a reference to the pillaging of Rome.' With his left hand he took the cigar from the corner of his mouth, and spat a few crumbs of tobacco onto the floor. That was the drawback of cutting off the whole cap rather than just punching a hole in it. 'The hanging in a public place, the ropes made of branches, the hood over the head, the dead dogs, it's all reminiscent of ancient Germanic punishments. And they hung him high too, which is especially shameful.'

'They?'

'It would take more than two men to subdue the dogs, hang that lump of a mayor and completely empty the office.' Malleus gestured backwards with his thumb, his cigar swirling more smoke signals as a loud clap of thunder rumbled above them. 'A lot of effort.'

The first stragglers began to leave the area, fearing either the growing storm or the possibility of falling victim to Jupiter's wrath. A lightning strike to the ground would knock a few people off their feet . . . or leave them seriously injured.

'We thought so too.' Romano made a couple of reassuring gestures in the direction of his task force, who were pointing with concern at the corpses and the darkening sky. They were getting anxious. 'All things considered, we're treating it as a murder with religious motives: Germanics who want to announce their arrival and make a show of Tyr's power. Hence killing Signore Domenico according to their old customs. We wanted to get an expert opinion on it. Just to be sure, before we take it to the press and the Pantheon. Do you agree with my assessment?'

'Pantheon. Right. I've always wanted to go there.' Malleus scratched his left eyebrow.

Romano looked shocked. 'You can't seriously want to set foot in the shrine?'

Malleus laughed. 'What do you think's going to happen? Is the whole building going to crumble to the ground as soon as I go in?' He puffed on his cigar and blew the smoke skywards. The blue-grey fog ascended slowly and vertically, unmoved by the rising squall.

The detective quickly checked his tone. 'What you do in your free time is your business. Not mine.' He looked up at the corpses, now swinging and spinning more vigorously, as if dancing gaily in a fresh spring breeze. 'So I'll have them cut down—'

'It's too early for me to give my full opinion. I'll need to take a closer look at the writing and the colour,' Malleus interjected. 'But whoever wrote this, I don't think they were well-versed in Germanic runes.' He pointed with his left hand at the writing on the wall, gesturing back and forth with his cigar, glowing as red as the painted characters. 'Scrawled, uneven, uncertain. And the Tyr runes on the victim's table were painted sloppily too. Whoever did this had plenty of time, so it isn't just that it's hurried work. Someone who wanted to publicly herald the power of his god would make more of an effort. A *lot* more. This painter was just copying from a source.'

'Oh?'

'Hanging was a punishment usually reserved for thieves.' Malleus pointed to the body of the mayor. 'To be truly accurate they should have cut off his head afterwards and put the skull on public display. This isn't about the old customs, it's all about the mayor. A celebrity. The official representative of the Rome they want to break. They strung him up because blood's more impressive when it's dripping from above.' He looked at the detective. 'I'm sure you know that from your temple sacrifices.'

Romano's protruding cheek muscles betrayed his clenched teeth. 'So it's not a religious murder?'

'No. And the fact that these supposed Germanics found the safe and opened it without force—'

'Domenico could have told them where it was.'

Malleus shook his head. 'I don't think so. No marks on the body suggesting torture or beating. At least none that I can see from here. And another thing: they took everything of value with them – but they left the study untouched. What kind of half-arsed pillaging is that?'

'Maybe it's symbolic?'

'Please, Commissario.' Malleus exhaled a cloud of smoke into the wind. 'Germanics showing restraint? At a pillaging? Does that sound right to you?' He took another puff on his cigar and flicked the end. The falling ash lost its glow immediately, curls of smoke surrendering to the gathering winds.

A light rain began to fall, and more onlookers dispersed. The wet ground would conduct electricity better. Many of the laws of physics still applied, regardless of how miraculous the actions of the gods might be.

'Find out where the things in Domenico's office came from,' Malleus recommended, 'because I'm guessing he didn't pay for any of it. *Then* you'll find the real and probably very earthly reason why he and his dogs are hanging out of that window. My guess? Somebody gave a lot of gifts and a lot of money to the mayor in the past, and yesterday they took it all back. Could be an arm of the Mafia. Could be a disappointed industrialist sending his repo-men to reclaim some bribes. And to distract from the real motive, all they had to do was stir up the tensions between the Germanics and the Italians – give the gods a bit of a tease.'

'Like atheists, you mean?' Romano replied cuttingly.

Malleus smiled. 'My dear Commissario! Atheists can't make fun of something that doesn't exist. That would be a paradox.'

Romano dispatched his team, who prepared to retrieve the corpses, muttering various comments as they worked. 'So I should tell the press it isn't a religiously motivated murder we're looking at?'

'Would be wise, Commissario. You'll lose the upper hand, sure, because whoever did it will know you weren't taken in by this little stunt, but it shows you're serious.'

Malleus was about to continue when a bolt of lightning tore out of the sky.

Goose pimples covered the skin of every person in the square as the electric potential in the air became palpable, and the crackling energy coursed straight into the mayor's corpse in a shower of sparks.

The crowd in the Via del Sudario cried out in unison.

The impact of the electrostatic discharge tore the body in two, blood spraying across the walls. The lower body fell to the street with a loud thud, the charred flesh rupturing on contact. The entrails followed, some hanging momentarily from the cadaver like long, thick worms before tearing apart and tumbling into a pile.

The smell of excrement intensified.

The branch holding the body had caught aflame and the fire quickly spread to the hood over the corpse's head, burning the face of the murdered mayor.

The onlookers stared and fell silent, searching mutely for the correct interpretation of this sign from the gods.

Malleus offered the stunned Romano his hand and shook, though the detective barely returned the gesture. 'You should probably give a public statement at a later date interpreting this particular incident as a confirmation from the gods of Signore Domenico's criminal machinations. Retribution from Jupiter or something. But I'm sure you'd already thought of that, Commissario,' he said, giving a casual wave as he walked off.

Malleus put on his aubergine-coloured gloves, slipped under the police tape and pushed his way through the hushed crowds, who were now watching the fire service as they sprayed the glowing remains of the corpse with their fire extinguishers.

He felt drawn towards the Pantheon, like a scientist towards the centre of an epidemic.

* A Ω *

I'm following him.

Even on that first evening after seeing him on the TV. Of course he has no idea.

How freely he walks the streets of Rome – as if nothing and no one could ever scare him. He has no fear, and it makes him conspicuous.

There are many different stories about him, and I've collected them all.

He fought in the Great Change, when Islam, Christianity and Judaism rebelled against the newly ubiquitous gods and actually thought they had a chance of winning.

Those arrogant fools. They were fighting against gods!

And as their own gods still neglected to appear, it ended with a resounding defeat. It got particularly nasty in the larger Christian strongholds – the USA, and Central and South America – and plenty of blood was spilled in the Arabic countries where Muslims had once been strong. Europe, too, didn't escape without its fair share of casualties.

That's just what happens when faith and knowledge are pitted against each other: one of them has to fall by the wayside.

Nowadays the proponents of those once powerful religions are reduced to little clumps of people, scattered over the whole world and ridiculed for their beliefs. The 'Godless People', they call them. Nothing more than cults. United in defeat. Perfect fucking irony given their history, if you ask me.

The churches were torn down or renovated and re-dedicated, and most of the mosques and synagogues went the same way. It varied from god to god how much tolerance was shown towards those mortals who had previously dismissed them as superstition. Most of them simply wanted to watch their former oppressors burn, slaughtering entire communities. Must have been pretty satisfying I guess, letting out centuries of pent-up rage. 'Dechristianisation,' they called it.

At the moment there is peace among the gods, aside from the skirmishes and muscle-flexing and contests to see who can perform the most impressive miracle: healing the injured, conjuring storms and so on. Like little boys comparing dicks. But none of the gods seem to have too much interest in rebuilding their former empires. Good news for humanity.

Before, the international superpowers were worried about the destructive potential of their atom bombs.

These days it's the gods everyone's scared of.

Damn right. I'm sure the end would be much uglier today than it would have been with the nuclear warheads.

So, which side did Bourreau fight on?

I think he was part of a guerrilla force. Did a fair amount of damage, in all directions. Rumour has it he lost someone close to him, which made him all the more unrelenting. Apparently he even managed to kill a couple of the smaller gods, only to surrender afterwards and make use of the amnesty that came with it.

Clever bastard.

Tough bastard.

If you ask me, the gods respect him for it.

He's heading to the Pantheon, the building recently restored for the preservation of the Roman deities, brand new and yet ancient. Extensions, expansions, and all the old tomb stuff has been thrown out. Everything's neo-Roman now. There's always some priest or other sacrificing in there, making sure the gods continue to watch over Rome and Bella Italia.

It's Bourreau's first time in the Eternal City. Makes sense that he'd want to go and see the place where the gods are all collected together, from Jupiter to . . . I can never remember all the names.

It's clearly more than just courage that's pulling him there.

Insanity?

Stupidity?

* Α Ω *

Malleus stood in the Piazza della Rotonda in front of the Pantheon. Measuring 43 metres in both height and diameter, the Pantheon had been known as the largest dome in the world for more than 1,700 years.

He stood for a moment next to the Egyptian obelisk in the middle of the square and let the view sink in.

The rotunda had been built in the year AD 114, and had lived through numerous transformations and alterations. But never had it possessed more significance than now – both for those who devoted themselves to the Roman gods, and those who detested them.

Protruding from the front of the formidable dome was the familiar rectangular building, the pronaos, reminiscent of a classical temple with its façade and pillars. Copious amounts of gold leaf had been applied to the grey marble of the Corinthian columns, and the original gilded bronze tiles on the roof of the dome had been restored in October. The floodlights positioned on surrounding buildings bounced their light off the dome and up into the evening sky.

Splendour.

Wealth.

Godliness, which utterly failed to sway Malleus from his convictions. When others prostrated themselves in fear or devotion, he lit a Culebra and asked people questions. He would gladly question the gods too, if one would ever actually dare to submit to his interrogation.

Fountains had been built in the east and west sides of the pillared hall, with statues of the river gods Tiber and Nile shipped over from the Piazza del Campidoglio and installed above the basins – both were decorated in the same ostentatious fashion as the rest of the building.

Wasteful extravagance.

Malleus walked up the stairs inside the front of the building and through the open, six-metre-high bronze door into the inner Pantheon.

The building had ceased to function as a temple at the start of the fifth century, and later, after its appropriation by the Christians, took the name Sancta Maria ad Martyres, which in time became Santa Maria Rotonda.

It was immediately clear to Malleus, however, that every trace of Catholicism had now been swept away.

He knew that the tombs of the painters Raphael and Carracci had long been removed from the rotunda, along with the heart of Cardinal Ercole Consalvi. The shrivelled relic had been burned at Jupiter's behest, though the remains of the artists and kings had only been moved elsewhere in order to avoid too much outrage amongst the Italians. The Pantheon now belonged solely to the Roman gods.

Malleus removed his hat. He took in the many flickering torches and braziers that burned in the rotunda, lending a mystic air to the immense dome. LEDs and other modern lighting had been deliberately shunned in favour of this homage to the past.

Countless colours of stone from all corners of the former Roman Empire had been used in the building's construction. Huge squares and circles of deep red porphyry, grey granite and patterned giallo antico combined in an intricate floor design; Malleus marvelled at the stark contrasts decorating the great circular wall of the inner chamber.

The interior of the rotunda contained seven niches, some rectangular, some semi-circular and bordered by pillars, each filled with an oversized statue of a god, and each surrounded by devotees standing or kneeling and murmuring prayers and requests.

Priests in traditional togas wandered around, collecting offerings and burning them in great braziers that stood at the feet of the marble effigies.

Malleus watched the smoke, intended to travel all the way to the gods and secure their favour or mercy. It rose in billowing clouds and disappeared through a circular opening at the peak of the dome, nine metres in diameter: the oculus. This and the entrance were the only sources of natural light.

Malleus got his bearings, located the statue of Jupiter and walked towards it. The elaborately designed floor was slightly sloped, allowing the rainwater to drain away along narrow gutters.

In the times before the gods returned, archaeologists and scientists had puzzled endlessly over which deities had actually been worshipped in the Pantheon. Since the Great Change, however, the priests had been given clear instructions on exactly who the gods wished to see represented in the rotunda. The less important gods were given a place in the aediculae, the small shrines built into the walls.

Malleus walked past Mars and Venus, Sol, Luna, Mercurius and Saturnus, and finally ended at Jupiter. He joined the queue of people standing before the statue.

Nobody paid him much attention.

Not even the so-called gods. Smirking, he regarded the walls, populated by empty-eyed marble figures staring indifferently at the crowds. So far, none of the statues had crumbled into dust or come alive to chase him out of their temple.

As Malleus came to the front of the queue, a priest approached him to take his offering.

'All I have to offer are my words,' Malleus said in a friendly tone, holding his hat in one gloved hand. 'Hello, Jupiter. I expect you'll know who I am. You gods claim to know so much, after all. And since you just shredded up the body of Mayor Domenico with a bolt of lightning, or so everybody's saying anyway, I assume we're both of the same opinion regarding the murder.' He spoke loudly and clearly, so that his voice cut through the murmur of the worshippers and echoed around the Pantheon. 'You know me, I'd never pass up an opportunity to meet a god and maybe have a little debate about his background.' He looked around him, registering the appalled faces of the onlookers. 'But apparently your lump of marble's not available for comment today.'

'I must ask you to leave,' said the priest, gesturing with his arms as if trying to shoo away a large, unruly hen.

'Can Jupiter not ask me to leave himself, if he doesn't want me in here?' countered Malleus in a calm, unassuming tone. 'I wouldn't mind if he booted me out personally.'

'Get out!' shouted a man behind him in the queue. 'Jupiter won't manifest just because you want him to.'

'Jupiter will punish you,' a woman assured him. 'How dare you insult him so!'

'You should leave now,' the priest demanded.

'Sure.' Malleus turned to the statue. 'A real shame, though. At least in the Pantheon I thought you might have bothered to turn up. Maybe next time.'

He made his way towards the great doorway.

Somebody spat in his direction as he left.

Malleus ignored this. He was being deliberately provocative and was happy to deal with the consequences – to a certain extent, anyway. It was only fair, he thought. And his military coat was waterproof.

Someone murmured his name, and a flurry of whispers spread through the rotunda. His visit to the Pantheon would be talked about. He'd already been banned from more than a few shrines across the world, always by priests and monks and various relevant authorities. Never by an actual god, though.

That was exactly what Malleus was aiming for, but so far no luck. The deities seemed to be sufficiently afraid of him, or disgusted by him, to avoid him completely.

We'd have so much to discuss. I wonder how they'd react to my questions. Malleus left the temple and made himself comfortable in a small café on the Piazza della Rotonda. He sat in the covered terrace under a heat lamp and removed his silver cigar case from the folds of his jacket.

He selected a thick, twisted cigar with a green band and

punched a hole in the cap, then took a cedar splint from the silver case and used it to light his cigar: the only way to get the taste just right. He exhaled and observed the people scuttling across the square in the inhospitable weather.

The storm had grown; the rolling thunder and crashes of lightning were louder and more frequent. Even the rain was stronger, as if Jupiter were trying to wash away the traces of the mayor's murder.

Malleus enjoyed the drumming of the rain on the ground.

Of course he hadn't expected the god to show himself, but it was worth using the opportunity anyway, while he was still in the city. His next contract, whether it was for Interpol or a private customer, could require him to leave Rome.

Malleus had already seen many places in the world both ugly and beautiful, devastated by war and rebuilt by gods, unadulterated natural beauty and pure human artifice, constructed with steel, concrete and gold. And yet everywhere he went, he was needed, as a provider of expert advice or leader of investigations.

He fell into deep thought.

In 2012, everything had changed.

The majority of prophecies had spoken of the end of the Mayan calendar, the end of the world – people were expecting plagues, volcanoes and earthquakes, comets. In short: the Apocalypse.

A few, however, had interpreted it as the beginning of a new calendar, as a new era. It would appear that they were correct. In 2012 the gods had returned. The cards were reshuffled, and some of them seemed to be marked.

I was clearly dealt a losing hand. Malleus had already ordered a double espresso and a water as the consequences of his visit to the Pantheon began to unfold. From between the pillars of the Pronaos, a man and woman strode out and stood at the top of the steps, looking around at the square. As they spotted Malleus in front of the café, the man took out his smartphone and made a call.

The waiter brought his drinks and Malleus added sugar to his coffee, stirring slowly, as was his habit. He took advantage of the moment of illusory calm to check the news on his PDA.

He had bought the device from a friend who specialised in making bizarre modifications to branded gadgets. A dedicated hobbyist, the guy had added all kinds of extras, from stronger battery life to encryption technology, and a variety of special functions that Malleus had not yet discovered. His friend liked to make a game of it, remotely activating new features every so often.

Malleus stroked his Fu Manchu moustache and read through emails from investigators across Europe. They sent him pictures and reports from crime scenes, looking to his expertise for confirmation that nothing religious or divine was in play. The reigning uncertainty following the return of the gods meant that people wanted to cover their backs.

But sometimes, Malleus found that he was repeating himself endlessly to various officials: a murder was simply a murder, or manslaughter, or an accident.

Malleus was part of the Interpol team based in Paris-Lutetia. In his spare time he freelanced as a private investigator, taking on capital offence cases with suspected godly influences. The widespread uncertainty following the return of the gods meant that the authorities often felt the need to cover their backs regarding the supernatural and metaphysical, a service which Malleus was happy to provide – for a fee.

So far, though, the culprits behind every case had turned out to be simply blind followers of some god or other, or aspiring tricksters, whose crimes – and Malleus found this particularly notable – were met with a distinct lack of divine intervention or retribution. The deities seemed to deem it unnecessary to punish the pretenders themselves. So Malleus delivered the offenders to the earthly authorities.

Shame. No leads. He drank his espresso, and his eyes, disguised by the blue contact lenses, flicked from left to right as he scanned the display.

A shadow fell over his screen.

'If you're *not* the waiter,' said Malleus in a quiet and friendly tone, 'please move along. If you *are* the waiter, please bring me another water.'

A woman's face shoved past the brim of his hat into his field of vision. 'You're that Bourreau. The one who mocks the gods.'

'Never explicitly, signora. I simply invite them to engage in a dialogue. A sadly one-sided affair so far.'

He looked up and noticed two men flanking the woman. She had organised backup.

'It's not my fault they're not getting in touch. They do with other people, apparently. Anyway, I don't believe I've had the pleasure, signora.' Malleus hated being trapped in conversation by people he didn't know. He found it presumptuous.

'You insulted Jupiter!' she hissed, narrowing her eyes.

'I did not, signora. But you were presumably standing behind me in the queue when I said to him that we probably agree about the mayor . . .' he offered as an explanation, hoping to avoid a tangible confrontation by talking so much that she'd leave. He didn't like hitting women. And his knuckleduster could break bones if the punch really hit. He didn't want to do that to her.

'Why should he speak to you?' she said. 'You mock the gods,

you blaspheme. Go into the Pantheon and beg the mighty god Jupiter for forgiveness.'

'Beg the *statue* of Jupiter,' Malleus corrected her. 'The *god* has never shown himself to me, signora. And not to you either, I presume?' He flashed her a winning smile. 'I'll leave you to your faith, and you leave me to my doubt. It's the scientific version of faith, you know.'

'It's not *faith*. It's *knowledge*,' the man on her left cut in indignantly. 'Go and bring Jupiter an offering as atonement for your behaviour!'

'Isn't it up to the priest to stand here and demand that, signore?' Malleus puffed on the cigar and casually slipped his hand into his left pocket, which contained one of his two knuckledusters. With his right hand he took off his hat and placed it on the table. 'Why do people so often get involved in things that don't concern them?'

He slid his fingers through the smooth metal rings, his hand grasping around the thicker middle section, which consisted of a collapsible Derringer and a hellishly sharp flick knife. It was a modern imitation of the Apache Knuckleduster Pepperbox. With luck he wouldn't need to use the inbuilt 9mm revolver.

'I'm a follower of Jupiter, it certainly does concern me!' The woman drew back her arm and threw a hefty punch at Malleus's face.

Malleus didn't hesitate, and countered her attack with a hard kick, so that her fist missed him and flew past his cheek. Her companions caught her as she fell backwards.

'I'm warning all three of you,' he said without raising his voice. 'I will defend myself. And it could end painfully for you. I assure you that I do not intend to insult your religious feelings towards

Jupiter. But I'll say it again: if he thinks I deserve punishment for my behaviour, he'll have to come and tell me himself.'

The woman responded in indignant Italian, but one of the men dragged her away; meanwhile two waiters had appeared at the door, though more out of curiosity than anything else. The second companion strode threateningly towards Malleus. 'Atheists like you will soon be exterminated by the gods,' he whispered coldly. 'You are walking insults to the Pantheon, and you will disappear. One way or another.' With that he turned and left.

I'd love to see that. Malleus slipped his fingers out of the knuckleduster and called to the waiter for another water.

* Α Ω *

Those three idiots, self-proclaimed defenders of Jupiter!

I'm standing next to the obelisk on the piazza and watching the Bella Donna walking towards him in a dark red coat. She's coming from the opposite direction to the god-botherers nearing him from the temple. He's sitting totally relaxed, reading his PDA. Of course he noticed the idiots a while ago.

No idea how much trouble they want to start. In any case, I don't like it. I found him, he belongs to me.

The trio of idiots walks past me towards him, deep in discussion. The woman wants to rip out his entrails, the men are promising at least a public humiliation that he won't forget.

Wonder if they'll sound so convinced with a bullet through the leg or the arm?

No, not from him.

From me.

Hidden in the folds of my coat, I screw the silencer onto my trusty APB, a fully automatic pistol capable of single shots, short salvos or sustained fire. Twenty shots and a detachable box magazine. I lock the steel shoulder rest into place. All in all it's a pretty nice piece, developed by the Russians in the seventies. A little heavy, clunky even, but pinpoint accuracy every time.

It ends with a brief scuffle outside the café, and he comes out on top. No need to use the APB to keep the peace.

The three stooges leave the area in a rage and walk past me again, across the piazza.

The Bella Donna in the dark red coat, who has approached from the other direction, now sits down next to him. I'm guessing she's a new client. I'll soon find out.

'Call the others,' I hear Little Miss Jupiter snapping at her henchmen as they walk my way. 'We can head him off if he goes to a hotel.'

I turn my head towards the trio of idiots as they disappear down a side street. So he's not out of danger yet.

Soon, though. I'll make sure of it.

I leave the cover of the obelisk and glance once more in his direction. He's deep in animated conversation with the woman. He should be fine for two, three minutes without me.

The rain keeps getting heavier, drumming forcefully on the cobbles and roofs. The cumulative roar of the raindrops is enough to swallow or dampen any sound in the streets below.

The three of them are walking about fifty paces in front of me, still deep in conversation, and the woman makes a gesture, dragging her index finger across her throat. Then they stop and stand under a canopy, and she pulls out a smartphone.

I can't let that call happen. Her intentions are pretty clear.

I take a step to the side, into the shadows, and lift the silenced APB, pressing the narrow stock against my shoulder.

Aim, fire, pivot.

Aim, fire, pivot.

Aim, fire – done.

The frantic metallic clack of the mechanism as it clicks forwards and back is the loudest noise; the shots themselves barely make a sound.

The three idiots fall almost simultaneously, their blood spraying against the wall behind them.

I lower the fully automatic and it disappears into my coat as if it had never existed. The woman's smartphone falls onto the cobbles, the display smashes into pieces.

Didn't have to be this way, *I think, and breathe in the smoke curling from the muzzle of the gun and up through the folds of my coat.* If you had just left him in peace, I would have left you alive.

Slowly I make my way back to the piazza to check on him. My coat and hood keep the pouring rain at bay.

The police will find the bullets. Painstakingly inscribed with my sign. And the shells, which I never take with me. Never. Calling cards. Engraved symbols leaving no doubt as to who is responsible.

The cops will be shocked – they thought I'd stopped doing this a long time ago. Then they'll look for connections to the old cases and won't find anything.

Or at least I'd be very surprised if they did.

As I step back onto the piazza I hear the horrified cries of the first passers-by behind me.

A grin spreads across my face.

That's my applause. My reward, my recognition.

And I'm willing to kill for it.

* Α Ω *

Malleus continued puffing on his twisted cigar and looked back at his PDA.

'You stayed very cool,' said a woman's voice next to him. 'Given all the threats she made.'

Malleus had already noticed her perfume, a mixture of ocean and fresh grass, with notes of bittersweet flowers. He turned his head and saw a woman with long brown hair flowing down her back, accented by a dark red streak running from her left temple.

She was wearing a tight, knee-length dress in white, grey boots and a dark red coat; her fingers were covered in black gloves.

He stood and bowed slightly in her direction, laying a hand on the back of the chair next to him.

'Would you like to take a seat next to me, signora?'

She nodded and allowed him to pull out the chair for her. The waiters immediately swarmed around her, and she ordered an espresso and *dolci* in perfectly accented Italian.

Malleus noticed the necklace dangling across her chest. It was made from white gold, with two figures depicting the gods Aeracura and Dis Pater: goddess of death, and the ruler of the underworld. So she was someone who chose not to follow the main figures of the pantheon. He found that exciting.

'You've got my attention.' He gestured towards her jewellery and noticed a red spot the size of a pinhead on the seam of her coat – fresh – and a few coarse, black hairs. 'You should have been more careful at the sacrifice.'

'How did you—?' She looked down at her coat. 'Ah, of course. Good eye.'

'It's how I make my living.' Malleus smiled. 'Which authority sent you?'

She had to smile. 'Is it that obvious?'

'Very.' While Malleus spoke, he stayed vigilant. His gaze wandered past the obelisk to the entrance of the Pantheon, watching for more outraged god-botherers hoping to cause a scene. 'You made a sacrifice to secure the gods' help with something. Perhaps for this conversation with me, signora?'

The brunette nodded. 'There's an underground altar a few blocks from here, dedicated to Aeracura and Dis. It was open for personal prayers. Normally they only open it up for secular stuff.'

Malleus made a note in his PDA. He must do more research on those two gods. 'Black animals as sacrifices?' he guessed, pointing at the hairs on her coat.

'Dis, yes.'

'Cat?'

'A black piglet.' She nibbled at one of the dolci. 'You're analysing me. Are you always in work mode?'

'These so-called gods apparently never sleep, so I have to make sure I can keep up.' He sipped his water as she closed her lips around the biscuit-covered chocolate. 'May I enquire as to who exactly is interested in my services?'

She reached into the inner pocket of her dark red coat and pulled out a card bearing nothing but her name and email address.

'I take it you're Oona Milord?'

She nodded. 'Long O, please. It's Finnish.'

Malleus tucked the card away. 'I'm listening.'

Milord took another dolci and sipped her espresso. 'It won't be anything particularly concrete, Mr Bourreau. You are contacted by international authorities and private clients for investigative services, mostly in relation to the divine aspects of crime – is that correct?'

Malleus made a gesture of confirmation, and reflected on her phrasing: *the divine aspects of crime*. He liked the sound of it.

'We would ask you,' Milord continued, 'to report to us every suspicion you have regarding the origin of a divine being. Location, date, reason for your assessment. Nothing more. For each report, you'll receive one thousand euros, and if your suspicions can be proven, another ten thousand and a contract.'

Malleus considered. Her offer didn't sound like anything he'd expect from the major law enforcement authorities. But she wasn't going to tell him who she represented, he could see that in her eyes. He stroked the tips of his moustache with his thumbs and forefingers. 'What do you mean by "origin"?'

Milord thought for a moment, then took out a tablet computer from her handbag, clapped open the lid and pushed it across the table to Malleus.

The screen was filled with various tiny objects: transparent shards of stone full of sparks and exploding stars, electronic and mechanical objects that looked as though they had been taken from the pages of a steampunk novel, geometric pendants with hieroglyph-like symbols.

'You've heard that there are certain people chosen by the gods to experience the gift of travelling through space and time to unfamiliar places?' enquired Milord.

Malleus nodded absently. He studied the artefacts on the screen, all of which would doubtless be sold for huge sums of money, and for which countless crimes would be committed. Corporations, too, would be interested in these objects and their unknown technologies – and of course, access to those distant other worlds.

'People brought these back from their travels with the gods into other worlds. Devotional objects. There are those on Earth,' Milord added, 'who are thinking very seriously about the consequences of this.'

'I understand what you're thinking.' Malleus gestured at the image of the pendant with the symbols. 'Other . . . divine beings could be made aware of Earth by the presence of these travellers, and seek to establish their own cults here.'

The woman nodded. 'Exactly. We are of the opinion that the

current pantheon of Earth is already sufficiently populated and does not require any further additions. If you, Mr Bourreau, agree to keep your eyes open for us, we can prevent new cults from gaining power.' She raised her cup and fixed him with her brown eyes across the rim. 'Which I believe lies firmly in your interests. Or am I mistaken?'

Malleus pushed the tablet back across the table. 'Is it not up to the gods to defend their own territory?'

Milord placed her cup on the saucer with a loud clink. 'The gods can't be everywhere at once. And they have enough problems trying to keep each other in check, ruling over their people, and/or trying to live amongst them.' She looked serious. 'Imagine what could happen if an unknown quantity tried to push its way into the existing pantheon. A battle between the gods could destroy the world.'

'Or liberate it.' Malleus couldn't resist showing his doubt.

'I prefer not to live surrounded by ruins and mountains of corpses. The Great Change was quite enough for me.' Milord took the last biscuit. 'You can be as atheist as you like, Mr Bourreau, and limit yourself strictly to the observable facts. All we're interested in are your reports.'

'I'll think about it, signora.'

'Fine.' Milord smiled, but her initial friendliness had waned. She seemed to have been expecting an immediate yes. She stood up: he did the same out of politeness. 'I look forward to hearing from you, Mr Bourreau. I won't wish you the blessing of the gods,' she said, absently touching her necklace.

He bowed and waited until she was a couple of paces away before he sat back down. 'Dis,' he mumbled thoughtfully, typing into his PDA. 'Ah, of course.'

It was another name or manifestation of the gods of the

underworld, Pluto and Orcus. Aeracura was believed to be a combination of partly Celtish-Germanic, partly Illyrian deities, similar to Proserpina.

Too many gods. Malleus signalled to the waiter for the bill. *Too much opium of the masses. The overdose will destroy humankind.*

Why was it only he and a small handful of individuals who recognised it?

His PDA lit up and displayed a message from Interpol: there was work in Germania.

Germania, Treva (Hamburg), November 2019

Malleus had thought about sending an email to Oona Milord. Just a short one. To see if she or someone else would answer it.

At the same time he was brooding over the possibility of sending a virus along with his message, one that would trace the route to its recipient and lead him to the server. His techie friend should be able to come up with something along those lines.

He let the BMW i8 find its own way through the maze of streets. The autopilot function was so reliable that it was actually safer to leave the driving to the car while Malleus read through his PDA messages; a twisted cigar with a blue band dangled from the right corner of his mouth, the smoke dwindling.

Aside from the usual reports of godly acts, miracles and manifestations and so on, there were updates on the stock markets, international news, natural disasters and other events that had existed even before the Great Change. The world was in a new era, but not everything had transformed.

Malleus read about a triple homicide in Rome, on the piazza where he and Milord had been sitting. Two men and a woman had been dispatched with precise shots, with no evidence of an altercation. Nothing was missing from their personal belongings.

Really? Malleus looked at the pictures and recognised the woman who had tried to punch him in front of the café. He wasn't shocked, but he was certainly intrigued.

He searched for further reports on the incident and used his PDA to translate them from the Italian. He found an unnamed source who claimed to have overheard some interesting details from the forensics officers who had arrived on the site of the murder: the shells found at the scene were marked with unknown symbols. There was still no statement from the police.

Something in the sidebar of the website caught his eye, advertising the forthcoming completion of two large, ambitious building projects, begun shortly after the return of the gods:

Visit
SODOM & GOMORRAH
The historic pearls of the Dead Sea,
newly rebuilt in all their former glory.
Luxurious hotels,
endless possibilities for relaxation and entertainment.
Book now and receive
free gifts and surprises of your choice.
Everything is allowed.
EVERYTHING.
We look forward to fulfilling your deepest desires!

Malleus shook his head.

Investors and a legion of workers equipped with the newest construction technologies had reconstructed Gomorrah from the remains of Numeira, and the archaeological site of Bab edh-Dhra had been rebuilt into the new Sodom. The locations – centres of pure hedonism in the Old Testament – were now towering combinations of modernity, kitsch and faux antiquity sited on the coast of the Dead Sea, ready to cater to tourists who wanted to indulge without restraint.

All the previous pleasure resorts, from Las Vegas to Shanghai, had become obsolete. Their attractions looked like harmless family holiday destinations compared to what these new cities had to offer.

They were run by *S&G Ltd*, an impenetrable consortium of firms and financiers, apparently including a god whose name had not yet been announced. There were rumours suggesting Marduk, who had also played a large role in the restoration of Babylon, might be involved.

According to unofficial reports, the cities were inundated with beings that were far from human. The end of Islam, Christianity and Judaism had set free powers that were thousands of years old, especially in the Orient.

For Malleus it was not without appeal. Perhaps in Sodom or Gomorrah he would have the chance to encounter Marduk? Though Marduk had begun his career as a mere city god of Babylon, he had now risen to be the highest god of the local pantheon, just as he had risen to power in legend.

Quite the promotion. But Malleus was aware that Marduk's followers were extremely fanatical. As soon as he was recognised, things would get pretty dangerous for him.

The i8 turned left, and his phone rang. The ringtone promised nothing good.

'Accept call,' said Malleus loudly.

The screen in front of him displayed the round, bearded image of his supervisor, Ilja Lautrec, calling from the Interpol central office in Paris-Lutetia. The guy was in his mid-sixties, looked Greek, spoke French with a Russian accent, and was permanently disgruntled. His light blue tie clashed with his pale green shirt. His choices of clothing were not bold, simply divorced from any concept of fashion whatsoever. 'Where are you, Bourreau?'

'I'm letting the autopilot decide.'

Mentally Malleus was still preoccupied with Sodom and Gomorrah, rebuilt by the returned deities, their corporations and followers.

Of course, it had been a slap in the face for the hardened Jewish community, who had retreated to Masada after the voluntary dissolution of Israel, armed to the teeth. Besides its great symbolic significance, the fortress on the plateau also possessed formidable defences hastily constructed by its new inhabitants. The gods let the settlers be, while the settlers upheld the traditional vow: *Mezadá shall not fall again.*

Most practising Jews, like the Christians and Muslims, had spread out across the diaspora and waited for Yahweh to give them a sign. Had they not voluntarily surrendered the Promised Land, the neighbouring nations would have unleashed their arsenals – including the powers of the gods – over Israel.

'You're late, according to your colleagues in Germania,' Lautrec stated admonishingly, brushing a couple of errant dark curls out his face as they escaped the copious gel in his hair.

Malleus threw a quick glance at the dashboard. 'Five minutes.'

'Good. Sounds like there's a press mob there, from what your point of contact in Treva told me. Take the back entrance.' Lautrec hung up.

'Autopilot: head for the back entrance of the address,' Malleus commanded.

'Confirmed,' returned the neutral voice of the navigation

system, and the i8 turned off again. 'Estimated time of arrival: one minute.'

Malleus narrowed his eyes as the car drove past the former rail station and through the quarter known as Altona, now a trendy residential area.

The façades of the skyscrapers were bathed in the light of huge LED billboards that screamed their advertisements into the city air, illuminating the streets below so that no streetlamps were necessary; the images changed every minute. People milled about on the streets below, wandering in and out of the many shops despite the cold temperature and light drizzle. *Heightened humidity*, as they said in Treva.

One billboard was advertising for the god Tyr. An animated film showed the god jumping from scene to scene, performing miracles and giving out beers produced in a brewery in Flensburg, according to the small print along the bottom of the screen. 'Convert now,' said the animated god firmly, and looked into the camera. 'Discover the true religion.' Finally, several addresses appeared on the screen denoting the locations of sacred groves and places of sacrifice that would soon be hosting winter solstice celebrations.

Malleus didn't want to know how many people were on their way there.

The i8 rolled into the pedestrian zone and slowed at the address, pulling through the crowd of media representatives, who sidestepped the car and, of course, tried to catch a glimpse of its driver. Someone pointed at Malleus, who immediately regretted not having insisted on tinted windows.

The BMW drove round to the back entrance and pulled up. 'You have reached your destination,' the automatic voice declared loudly, seemingly proud of its achievement.

Alerted by the sound, the photographers and camera team quickly rounded the corner and encircled the car.

I suppose it's unreasonable to expect intelligence from a navigation program. Malleus put on his sunglasses, pulled his hat down to cover his face and stepped swiftly out of the car, puffing vigorously on his cigar. With the high collar of his military jacket, his face was almost completely disguised.

He was immediately bombarded with shouts and questions.

He knew the game well and walked calmly through the rabble; the smoke spilling from his mouth and from the end of his cigar billowed against the wall of journalists. They coughed, their questions caught in their throats, their photos blurred.

'Problem, gentlemen?' Malleus called cheerily as the police ushered him into the timber-framed building, decorated with Germanic runes. The owner had requested the protection of Thor and Freya.

Another unanswered prayer. Malleus put out his Culebra and placed it back in the case. He showed his pass to the clerk, presumptuously passing him his hat and heavy coat, revealing the kurta-like shirt he wore underneath. *But we're all ignoring that, of course.*

He slipped off his shoes and walked barefoot down the corridor towards the spotlights set up by forensics to illuminate the crime scene. He could concentrate better when he felt the ground on the soles of his feet.

Malleus padded silently into the sales room of a souvenir shop, which also contained a selection of antique furniture, including two bureaus, a kitchen cabinet and a few tables, which he estimated dated from around 1900.

The two forensics officers in white plastic protective suits nodded in his direction, and both detectives gestured brief greetings.

They were standing around the corpse of a greying old man with a large gash across his throat and multiple stab wounds to the left side of his chest. Next to the body was a piece of tongue, secured to the worn floorboards by a long nail. A puddle of blood had spread around the body. The clothing of the victim looked inexpensive: blue jeans, navy blue checked shirt, slippers. Both his watch and his massive gold signet ring were decorated with the emblem of Thor's hammer.

'Good day, Detectives.' Malleus showed his pass, which nobody looked at. 'Is one of you the contact for Interpol?'

They shook their heads, and the white suits rustled the same response.

'That would be Chief Inspector Grenzner,' he was told. 'But he's back at headquarters.'

Malleus looked around the room. The till was open and the counter had been rifled through. The cases were piled high with souvenirs: cups, scarves, shirts, flags, glasses, caps and anything else one could possibly imagine wanting to bring back home from Treva. Statuettes of the new Germanic gods stood on the shelves alongside approximated figures of the ones who had not yet materialised. Some Roman, Celtic and Asian gods were relegated to the lower shelves, accompanied by a brash, handwritten sign spelling out *Final Reductions.*

The deities won't be happy to have lost their value. Malleus turned and scanned the room for more details.

A glass fridge housed a selection of canned drinks and sweets. Old posters covered the ceiling and walls, along with two crookedly hung pictures of historic scenes.

'There won't have been more than a hundred euros cash in the till,' he speculated aloud, and looked at the corpse. He inhaled deeply. 'Has one of you been to a barbecue recently?'

They shook their heads again.

Malleus crouched next to the body and pushed the collar of the man's shirt aside with his fingertips.

A fresh burn wound became visible on the wrinkled skin below the neck. Germanic runes spelled out the word 'Traitor'.

Malleus clicked his tongue. 'Stabbed in the heart, tongue removed, throat slashed, branded,' he summarised. 'Someone wanted to make it clear that this man had earned his punishment – but I can't see the reason they punished him yet.' He looked up at each detective in turn. 'Why the media frenzy? Is the victim a celebrity of some kind?'

'Of sorts,' replied the more corpulent of the two. 'Hannes Hein, seventy-three, has been running the shop for fifty years. He was the guy people went to round here if there was something that the police couldn't, or wouldn't, handle. There are a lot of different cultures living in the new-builds, and depending on their gods that can cause a lot of friction.'

'Plus, he used to deal with a lot of the small-time dealers who were causing trouble,' added his colleague. 'Hannes was a mixture of father figure and peacemaker round here.'

There had still been no mention of anything that justified calling in Malleus. Quite the opposite. *One of the dealers could be behind it, or anyone else he'd brought to justice.* 'Anything else?'

'He was the go-to guy for the yearly rituals,' answered the chubby detective. 'Summer and winter solstices. A druid.'

'Ah, now we're getting somewhere.' Malleus stood up and walked over to the two paintings. Carefully he took them down from the wall, but there was nothing behind them of any interest – for him or the murderer. He knocked on the wall, but found no evidence of a hidden safe or false panels. 'Someone thought he was a traitor. Who was he betraying?' He looked at the pair of detectives. 'His house has Germanic runes on the front of it and he's wearing Thor's hammer on a ring. But the Germanics don't have druids. He could only have been an organiser of festivities at most.'

'Yeah, something like that,' replied one of the detectives, who was suddenly anxious. His colleague looked at him with a bemused expression. 'I . . . don't know much about . . .' He fell silent.

Malleus rolled his eyes. People were still unable to grasp the origins of their own beliefs, even after all these years.

The question remained why Hannes Hein, in spite of all his merits, was being accused of treachery.

Malleus attempted to hang the painting back on the wall, but the hook was small and awkward. So he laid the picture on the counter – and in doing so, noticed an odd mark on one of the painted archways. *As if the colour had faded in just that one spot.*

Carefully he touched it with his index finger and felt a slight resistance.

There was a humming sound from the wall behind one of the forensics team, and a door opened slowly. Light flickered in the chamber behind it.

'Would you look at that.' Malleus pointed to the painting. 'A wireless remote.' He looked more closely at the frame and noticed several integrated solar cells. They provided the expertly hidden sensor with power.

The police officers craned their necks, attempting to see into the cubbyhole that had revealed itself, but they let Malleus take the lead. His bare feet made no sound as he paced gently across the room, passed the exsanguinated corpse, the pool of blood and the officers, and peered cautiously into the chamber.

It was filled with containers, some as small as tea lights, some parcels, some envelopes, bulging at the seams. Some boxes were made of wood, both plain and painted, and some were decorated with inlays or metal fittings. Others were made of stone, seashells, or precious metals.

On a row of shelves, Malleus saw preserving jars containing limbs, fingers, teeth, jaws, a whole hand. Next to these were crucifixes, a Torah, and some Christian clerical garments that were clearly at least a few hundred years old.

Every object, regardless of nature or origin, was labelled with a clearly visible code.

'I believe we may have found the reason this man was killed,' Malleus said quietly. He raised his PDA and took a few pictures, then shot a video. 'Detectives, we need to find the inventory, to . . .'

One of the forensics officers passed him a piece of paper wrapped in a protective polythene bag. The page was covered in codes and spattered with blood. 'Here, Mr Bourreau.'

Malleus took it and saw that the codes were encrypted. An arduous task awaited him. 'Would have been too easy to just write the damn things normally,' he said, and photographed the page with his PDA.

'They're relics or something,' announced the corpulent officer with conviction.

'Indeed, Detective.' Malleus had already recognised one of the two full-sized engraved crucifixes leaning against each other on the back wall. 'The triumphal cross of Aschaffenburg, forged around AD 980. Missing since the abbey of St Peter and Alexander was torn down. It was thought to be one of the few remaining Ottonian sculptures. And where has it turned up, of all places? In Treva.'

'Valuable, I assume?' interjected the second forensics officer.

A treasure trove. Unbelievable. 'Hundreds of thousands, at least.' Malleus gestured towards the receptacles. 'Relics, all stolen or liberated from churches. The exact terminology doesn't matter. Herr Hein was clearly a prolific trader in Christian devotional objects.' Moving around the chamber, he found chests with Germanic and Celtic symbols. 'I take it back.' On the right-hand side of the room he noticed caskets with varying levels of ornament, which appeared distinctly oriental. 'There are sacred objects from other cults here too.'

'Bloody hell,' the corpulent officer remarked. 'So he was fencing stolen goods.'

'He may even have been masterminding heists and robberies.' Malleus counted seven empty spaces on the different boards and shelves, where indentations in the thick layer of dust showed that something had recently been removed.

He accessed the photo of the list on his PDA, and compared the codes with the objects in front of him until he had eventually figured out what was missing.

Now all he had to do was crack the encryption.

'The fun never ends,' murmured Malleus.

He presumed that whoever had murdered this man had also gained access to the chamber and taken those seven objects with them. His curiosity as to which objects they had stolen was immeasurable.

'You should make sure this is all kept under high security, Officers,' he said to the detectives. 'And I'm sure you'll make some museums and communities very happy if you return their lost treasures to them.' Malleus leafed through a nearby notepad, which had clearly been used as rough notepaper.

Additions of large and small sums, percentages. The calculations were shares and expected profits in various relics deals.

'Looks like he made a good living from it,' remarked the other policeman.

'But he paid for it with his life,' Malleus replied thoughtfully. A shred of paper fluttered out of the notepad, with an address on one side; underneath the address was a tick mark. He pocketed the scrap, making a mental note to send the address to Paris-Lutetia for checks. 'Another life claimed by religion.' He laughed quietly.

Nobody joined in.

'Good. I'll join the investigation.' He patted the side pocket of his tunic. 'I'll take care of this address, you keep investigating in Altona. Give Mr Grenzner my warmest regards. I'll be in touch with him soon.'

The officers confirmed with a nod.

Malleus went out and retrieved his belongings from the young officer at the door. 'Are they still outside?'

The man nodded.

Malleus put on his hat, took out the case with the twisted cigars and chose one with a black band. The journalists deserved nothing more.

'Hold your breath,' he advised the young officer. 'Or you'll cough your soul right out of your body.'

He clicked open his lighter and, as ever, lit a splint first.

* A Ω *

I'm following him. I've fitted his car with a tracking device so I don't lose track of him.

Germania, Treva. Been a long time since I was last here. I liked the water, the port. It had a good atmosphere.

In the north they've refurbished most of the larger churches and turned them into residential blocks or temples. In one place they actually tore down a Christian place of worship and replaced it with a sacrificial grove. The neo-Germanics certainly didn't waste any time. Some places have even been repurposed as Roman temples, though they're always kept small and unassuming, in order to keep the peace.

For the most part the different religious sects round here leave each other in peace. That will change, as soon as one belief becomes fanatical. Guaranteed, there are still plenty of secret Christians among them, although they'll probably reduce down in time to the usual tiny handful.

I don't know my way round Altona too well, but streets are streets: if you find your way in, you can find your way out.

They called him in on another murder. A little shop, tourist rip-off and local landmark.

As the cops are leaving, I slip inside.

A glorified religious looter, fallen victim to his own greed. Once a seller of relics, artefacts, sacred objects, relating to every deity and religion, lined up on shelves like a supermarket.

Good analogy. That's how it goes with most people nowadays – they're paralysed by the sudden choice. Before they only had a corner shop of deities to choose from, now they've got aisles full of options.

Gods as products: ingredients, side effects, best before dates. And, of course, the price that must be paid for them.

Most people don't read the small print and only pay attention to the packaging, the label, the adverts. They impulse buy. Sometimes the products are even identical to one another, and nobody notices. Or wants to notice.

Gods and supermarkets. Fits perfectly.

If I'm seeing this correctly, there are seven objects missing from this little treasure trove.

Wait, no.

The light is bad, but . . . two more indentations in the dust, on the left-hand shelf. Two more, that makes nine.

So that's why the guy was killed: to get to his little treasure trove of new and forgotten relics. For free. Like robbers in a supermarket.

Should be an exciting case for him, I reckon.

I take a little something with me, a souvenir from Treva, then I return to trailing him.

He won't escape me.

I see everything he does, everything he leaves behind.

Celtica (France), Brittany, November 2019

The BMW i8 drove along the D780, hugging the coast and occasionally passing close to the tumultuous Atlantic as it churned against the cliffs.

Waves broke against the rocks and crags, and sea spray flew across the windscreen, the wipers working constantly despite the lack of rain. The air was filled with the rumbling and crashing of exploding waves.

Malleus watched the spectacle from the car and drank a tea freshly prepared by the vehicle's integrated hot-drinks machine. The comforts of modernity.

He was on his way to the address he had found in Treva.

A quick data request and enquiries at the authorities in Celtica, formerly known as France, hadn't thrown up anything unusual.

The occupants registered there were a Monsieur and Madame Duhamel, 65 and 59 years old, owners of a small hotel in the tranquil village of Arzon, home to just short of 2,000 residents. No previous convictions, nothing abnormal on their records.

But Malleus refused to be put off by this. Hannes Hein, too, had appeared almost saintly on paper, but his side business had been far from lawful, in the eyes of either the gods or the international courts.

So he had no choice but to take a trip to Arzon.

He had booked a room in the Hotel Fleur de la Mer under a false name. Something told him that it would be wiser not to announce himself as a detective, especially when news of Hein's death was probably already spreading amongst other stolen goods merchants and customers.

Malleus noticed some standing stones on the other side of the road. They reminded him of the huge field of stones in Carnac.

Before the Great Change, the old beliefs had endured in the west of Celtica, despite the Christianisation of the area. Various stone structures stood in their thousands there: dolmens, menhirs and tumuli, upholding the memory of both ancient and later Celtic customs for centuries. The three groups of Carnac stones – the Ménec, Kermario and Kerlescan – had gained new significance in recent years, beyond their former archaeological interest.

A road sign became visible at the side of the road. At the next junction he could turn off and head towards Brocéliande, according to the local tourism office.

Malleus smiled. *Greetings from King Arthur and co.*

Before, it had been called Paimpont Forest, but now it was referred to by its legendary name, Brocéliande. As the largest forest in Brittany, it was home to countless legends, which were now, of course, all considered to be true.

They all centred on Merlin and Nimue, the Lady of the Lake, from the Bridge of Secrets to the Valley of No Return, *Le Val sans Retour*, to the Lake of Comper.

Malleus knew that expeditions had been organised to find

these legendary places – and that they'd been found. Merlin's grave, next to the Lake of Marelles in the east of the forest, had become an important gathering place for druids.

Only things missing now are the unicorns. The i8 took a slight left off the roundabout and continued along the coastal road. Within a few minutes he had reached Arzon.

The little hotel was right by the harbour, perched on a rocky outcrop overlooking the village, with a spectacular view of the surging waves and the crags to the north. It was made of strong stone to withstand the winds, and had green shutters decorated with white and red Celtic patterns. Smoke rose from both large chimneys and was whipped away by gusts of sea air.

Malleus couldn't help but think that she would have liked it here.

His wife had loved the sea. The raw, wild sea, powerful and intimidating. He thought of her often. And the little one.

The thought of those he had lost brought first a smile, then a swell of melancholy. *Not now.*

The autopilot had registered the spaces in front of the hotel and went into parking mode.

The wheels had barely come to a stop and the low hum of the engine had barely ebbed away when Malleus sprang from the vehicle, as if by doing so he could somehow escape the memories of his family. He left his coat on the back seat.

He picked up his briefcase and stepped through the weathered double doors into the hotel.

A traditional Breton song tinkled out of concealed speakers, and a cheery bell above the door announced his arrival. The faint scent of wood varnish and cold smoke hung in the air.

The dark-haired female owner appeared and he recognised her instantly. She looked all of her fifty-nine years, with a sinewy figure and dark tanned skin. She wore a dress resembling the traditional Bretonian costume.

'*Bonjour, monsieur. Bienvenue chez nous. Comment allez-vous?*'

'*Bonjour et merci, madame,*' Malleus replied, slipping easily into French, though without the hard Bretonian accent. He took off his hat. 'I've reserved a suite, under the name Claudius.'

'Very good choice, monsieur.' Madame Duhamel nodded and reached under the counter to take out a key. 'You're not staying long in Arzon, Monsieur Claudius? That is a *very* small case.'

'Sadly not. My holiday schedule is very tight.' Malleus took the key. 'I'm travelling along the coast and visiting all the ancient sites.'

She smiled enthusiastically. 'Very good. So you're getting to know the gods here? I believe yours in Germania are somewhat different.'

'Yes, indeed. Perhaps I'll find myself converted to the Celtic faith, if it speaks to me more than my own.' Malleus gave her a friendly smile. 'Do you have any recommendations of holy places to visit? Any exceptional sites I should see?'

'They are all exceptional,' Madame Duhamel replied with conviction. 'Have you been to the biggest barrow yet? The one where the god Lenus manifested?'

Malleus shook his head and stroked the ends of his beard. 'Where is that?'

'East of Carnac. You simply must see it: over a hundred metres long, sixty wide and about ten high, and the upper platform is huge.' She laughed cheerfully. 'Before the gods returned there was a chapel on it. Then Lenus the Injurer manifested on the first of September and drove them out of there with his axe and spear just as the Christian mass finished and they were all praying to their creator for protection. Lenus was happy to receive their sacrifice!'

'I'm sure that strengthened the faith of many.' Malleus spoke as if he too found this a heartening development.

'Well, it convinced me anyway. The chapel is gone and Lenus' spear is still there – he thrust it into the barrow as a sign of his power.' Duhamel pointed at the stairs. 'Second floor, on your right, Monsieur Claudius.'

'Thank you, for the room and for the recommendation, madame,' he replied and made his way to the staircase.

The wooden steps creaked loudly under his shoes – creeping around the house looking for clues would not be an option. Squeaking floorboards were the best protection against intruders, a fact well known by the Japanese shoguns, who had warded against them with their 'nightingale floors'.

Malleus was itching to drive to the barrow and inspect the spear, supposedly thrust into the ground by a god.

He wasn't closed off to the possibility that it had actually happened. He, in contrast to the blinded, influenced, subjugated masses, simply had his own opinion concerning these beings who had suddenly appeared from nowhere. This opinion remained strictly scientific, and of course highly sceptical. And he still didn't see it as proven that these things were divine.

Malleus could not deny the thousands of people who had been massacred in the Great Change for their beliefs. He'd fought in the wars himself. Against people. Against gods.

Muslims and Christians had been hit the hardest in terms of numbers, their resistance finally broken by the intervention of the gods, whose powers held firm against weapons, tanks and bombs. It had been all over the news channels and the internet: buildings being destroyed by bolts of lightning and natural disasters. Occasionally you'd see one of these supposed gods fighting on the front line alongside the soldiers who followed them. They always won. A wave of conversions followed the fighting.

Well then. Malleus reached his room and went inside.

It was small for a suite, but very comfortable and had clearly just been renovated. Everything was decorated in the Breton style, including the walls themselves, which were painted with Celtic murals. The large window, which stretched to over three metres high, allowed a fantastic view over the Atlantic.

He set down his case and stood in front of the glass, staring out over the swelling and sinking of the waves – as if the sea were breathing.

Why this address? Malleus guessed that either the couple belonged to the same stolen-goods ring as Hein, and had provided him with artefacts from the Breton barrows, or that the Fleur de la Mer had been a meeting point of some kind. He wasn't excluding the possibility that the couple might be completely innocent in all this. *Guess I'll have to find out.*

Arzon lay on the end of a peninsula. This presumably made it easy for the illegal traders to keep watch over the village if unwelcome guests should turn up and start snooping around. On the other hand, the location meant that any criminal could make a hasty escape by boat, should things get dicey.

He took out his PDA and looked up the barrow claimed by Lenus the Injurer.

Certainly worth a look. The barrow reportedly contained a veritable treasure trove of gifts and offerings: thirty-nine original axes made of jade and sillimanite, as well as ten necklaces, a chain with ninety-seven callaïs pearls, and the remains of a beaded necklace made from a substance similar to ivory.

There are people who would pay a fortune for one of those pearls.

Parked behind the hotel were two cars with Celtic plates,

a sleek Lexus and a hefty-looking Toyota SUV. Like the room, they also looked to be new. Money certainly did not seem to be a problem for the Duhamels.

Malleus left his room and walked around the corridors, seemingly getting his bearings like any new guest might after checking in.

He regarded the landscapes and portraits hung around the building, the small sculptures on the sideboards, peeked into rooms that were being cleaned by a charming housekeeper. Everywhere he went he was consistently met with brand new decorations and furnishings.

Then he left the Fleur de la Mer and retrieved his heavy military coat from the i8. They'd been through a lot together, he and that coat. He'd be needing it soon enough, as the evening was getting chilly. With his hat pressed firmly over his black hair and his collar raised, he walked over to the harbour, steadying himself against the buffeting winds and cutting through little alleys where he encountered few people, none of whom looked like tourists.

Malleus selected a cigar with a pastel-coloured band and dipped into a sheltered doorway to light it before continuing on his way.

His thoughts wandered, working through all the possibilities.

It was imperative that he found an opportunity to look through the Duhamels' private rooms. If he found a solid connection to Hein, he could easily have them called in for interrogation. However, if nothing presented itself, he would have to do a little digging. By going through the guest records, for example. Name by name.

An empty yet apparently open café called *Poivre* caught his eye as he walked past. He noted the black rainclouds looming on the horizon and felt the first scattered raindrops as he ducked inside.

Malleus laid down his coat and hat, and chose the table with a view over the narrow street; the slate roof of the hotel towered in the background. The café smelled of warm caramel and wood fire, as if he'd just stepped into an old-fashioned sweet shop.

The one thing that didn't quite fit was the TV wall, with a two-by-four-metre screen blaring out the show *Loki's Lost*, featuring the god Loki.

A small army of contestants, collectively known as *Loki's Lost*, had to complete various challenges; one by one they were whittled down until a single contestant remained, who would receive a prize from the god himself. In accordance with the generally bloodthirsty mentality of Loki's followers, the show allowed contestants to be eliminated by any means. Injuries were commonplace, as were deaths, especially when there were only a dozen contestants remaining. Sometimes the prize itself turned out to be a reward with undesirable consequences, risks and side effects – so typical of Loki.

Malleus found it barbaric, archaic. People sacrificed their own lives and those of strangers' to a god, without noticing that they were dying for Loki rather than for the prize.

A blonde waitress in a white blouse and an apron came over, and he ordered a coffee and a sweet crêpe with Calvados apples, whipped cream and praline. 'And would you be so kind as to turn that off, please, madame?' He said, indicating the TV.

She nodded and disappeared into the kitchen, followed by the sound of clattering pans. Evidently she was also the chef.

The TV wall went black, and peace returned to the Poivre.

As Malleus waited, he read his new emails and messages on his PDA, but nothing caught his attention.

His techie friend had sent him an update regarding the codes from Treva. He'd taken a look at them, but it was obvious that unless they found the appropriate encryption key – he guessed it was probably a book – they would be impossible to decipher.

That's going to be difficult. Irritated, Malleus considered ordering a bottle of cider.

He quickly typed an email to Officer Grenzner, requesting a list of every book in Hein's shop and apartment, including information on the condition of each one. The key could be hidden in one of them. *Could.* Sometimes this line of work took a lot of patience.

'*Voilà*,' announced the waitress cheerily, and placed a sweet-smelling crêpe on the table in front of him. Malleus hurriedly stashed away his PDA. She took out a lighter and ignited the Calvados brandy drenching the pastry. Blue-tinged flames danced across the crêpe, apples and praline for a few seconds before dying out. The sugary scent intensified and Malleus's mouth began to water. '*Bon appétit*.'

'Thank you.'

'Ah, you're from Germania,' she guessed by his accent. 'Where are you staying?'

He gestured towards the window with his fork. 'Fleur de la Mer,' he said, taking the first bite of his meal and closing his eyes to fully appreciate the flavour.

Normally he wouldn't have told her the name of his hotel, but he thought he might be able to get some information out of her. As he was currently her only customer, he suspected she might be willing to chat for a while.

She promptly confirmed his suspicion. 'Ah, very good choice, monsieur. All newly refurbished,' she said, and stayed standing beside him holding the serving tray to her chest.

'It's lovely,' Malleus replied with a mouth full of crêpe. He tapped the edge of the plate with his fork. 'And this is just heavenly.'

She laughed and sat opposite him. 'Thanks. I'm Charlène. I'm afraid I won't be giving you the recipe though, monsieur.'

'Then I'll just have to come back and order one every day,' he replied with a wink. 'Was there a reason for the renovations at the Fleur de la Mer? Usually a bit of old-fashioned charm is a good thing, no?'

'Oh, it was *very* old. And perhaps they were trying to distract themselves from their daughter.'

'I didn't see a daughter,' he followed with interest.

'You wouldn't have. She disappeared about six months ago.' Charlène's face was momentarily grieved. 'I hope the gods are protecting her.'

'Disappeared.' Malleus made a mental note. 'How terrible.'

'While she was walking by the sea. She never came back. Some say she just couldn't handle her career as a model. The pressure, depression and so on.' Charlène sighed. 'But I knew her well. She would never have done that.'

'Tragic,' Malleus said half-heartedly, and continued to eat his crêpe. 'If I were her parents I would certainly have been looking for a distraction from the worry.'

Charlène nodded. 'And what brings you to Arzon in November, monsieur? The sea's rough, there's nothing going on. You're lucky the Poivre is even open.'

'Oh I was certainly lucky to come across the Poivre, madame.' Malleus smiled at her. 'I'm on holiday. A tour of the coast, on the trail of the gods.'

'Then you went to the right place with Madame Duhamel. She knows her stuff.' A door slammed in the back of the kitchen and Charlène got up. '*Oh là là*, my boss. I'd better go and pretend I'm working before he sees me sat chatting with you. You'll be back again soon?'

'Every day,' he answered and pointed to his now almost empty plate. 'To see you, of course.'

Charlène giggled and briefly held her hand to her mouth, then hurried into the kitchen.

Malleus enjoyed the rest of his meal in peace, and searched on his PDA for further information on the missing Duhamel daughter. The light saltiness of the praline was simply divine.

It was tricky finding her at first because she had worked under another name, but he found her soon enough: Elizà Royale.

Malleus stared at the images. *Stunning.*

Never had he seen a more attractive young woman. Seventeen years old, tall, very pale, hair the colour of copper and deep blue eyes. Her features were flawless and so perfectly proportioned that you could assume she had been created by a talented sculptor.

Elizà had walked for a few different designers, and had even made some adverts for perfume and jewellery lines. She was described by various fashion sources as 'heavenly', 'divine', and 'the most beautiful woman in the world'.

He sent off another email to Grenzner in Germania. All the limbs and body parts found in the chamber in Treva, regardless of size or appearance, should be tested for age and DNA.

Malleus leaned back and looked up at the roof of the Fleur de la Mer.

He had an unmistakable feeling, and he didn't think it was the apple brandy: *Elizà Royale is the key to this whole case.*

* A Ω *

I follow him into this shitty little town.

At this time of year you can recognise a stranger a mile off. There's no good reason anyone would be staying here.

Aside from that, I hate the sea. Unpredictable, treacherous, deadly. Not just because of the water, but also what lives in it.

Anyone who has read Lovecraft knows: the further you are from the sea, the better. The Great Old Ones are gods too. If Marduk can rebuild his old Babylonian empire, why shouldn't Dagon give it a try? Innsmouth could be anywhere that's close to the sea.

He's staying at the Fleur de la Mer, the best hotel in town.

I reckon I'll just park my car somewhere outside town and sleep in there.

Arzon. This is going to be a dead end for him.

Unless . . .

Fuck, what if he ends up getting attacked? He'd have no chance against them with that toy gun of his.

I'll have to stay close.

The house on the harbour, right opposite the Fleur, looks good enough. Have to see who lives there. I'll make myself a little base in there, with a good view of the hotel.

I have to keep following him.

* Α Ω *

The weather died down, and Malleus decided to go for a walk on the beach.

It was quite rare that he found himself in such a quiet landscape, without irritating people, without the din of the city, without the stress and cruelty he saw every day in his profession.

He felt he had to take advantage of this weather as soon as the first ray of sunlight appeared, though he knew that being surrounded by nature risked bringing back painful memories of his once beautiful, happy life.

And so it happened that Malleus found himself climbing down a rusty ladder in the harbour and trudging along the hard pebble beach that nestled between the cliffs.

The round stones crunched under his feet, and seaweed and shells lay strewn about by the previous tide. The waves only seemed to be receding; the tide had long reached its lowest ebb and was beginning to creep back up the beach.

Gulls initially circled Malleus with curiosity, hoping that he might feed them, or that he might have something they could steal. As they realised their error, they scattered across the beach and picked half-heartedly at mussels and seaweed.

After a few hundred metres his walk became more of a clamber. The Atlantic coast was rugged, littered with rocks and gigantic boulders, as if left there by giants.

Malleus took a deep breath of the salty air. The wind made a pass at his hat and the cold drove tears into his eyes, and yet he enjoyed it. His high collar shielded him from the gusts of wind, and sporadic rays of sunshine wandered across his face, warming his skin. The grass rustled gently on the looming cliffs, snaked by little paths and roads.

Malleus tramped further along the beach until he reached a wall of rock jutting over a metre upwards.

This was the end of his walk.

If he wanted to carry on, he'd have to wade through the ankle-high seawater beyond it, which would mean drenching his shoes and socks.

He noticed some linear scratches at eye level in the surface of the rock, obscured by a layer of organic grime. He wiped away the algae and shells left there by the tide and they fell to his feet, revealing a series of words.

It was written in a neo-Celtic dialect, and not that long ago by the look of it:

Enter the shrine of Lir,
Whether you bring offerings
Or offer yourself.

Lir. Malleus activated his PDA. He hadn't come across this name yet. *Too many gods, there always had been.*

Lir, his database informed him, was a god of the sea and father of Manannán, as well as the king of the Tuatha Dé Danann.

The scrawled words, undoubtedly carved into the rock by human hands, could definitely be understood as a threat.

And that piqued Malleus' interest.

He waded through the water, which instantly soaked through his shoes and trousers, and reached a small cove in the shape of a horseshoe. The steep cliff faces were dotted with caves and recesses.

Perhaps the missing girl had come to this shrine and fallen into the hands of overenthusiastic cult followers. That would at least explain why the young woman had disappeared. Better than suicide.

Wouldn't the local police have found her in that case? Malleus looked around. *What, when the law values godly interests over human ones?* He knew that from previous cases. That's why people called him.

His eyes, still disguised by his bright blue contact lenses, glanced out of the cove over the shallow water's edge, and he noticed a pole standing high out of the water.

He took out his PDA and used the zoom function, which showed him the wooden construction in full clarity. There were old-looking iron brackets attached to it, perfect for securing human sacrifices until they were claimed by the incoming tide, or *mori*, as the Celts called it. The Celts believed that the sea was its own kingdom, an otherworld, completely distinct from the underworld.

In the sludge underneath the pole was an object, which he identified with some difficulty as a decaying shoe.

Malleus lowered the device and regarded his own shoes. *I guess they're already wet.* He may as well walk out there, retrieve the shoe and look for further clues. He wasn't assuming that the shoe belonged to Elizà, but perhaps the find would lead him to a fresher, more productive line of enquiry. Other than that, he still needed to go through the region's missing-person records for the last few years. He was curious to see how many of them might have been offered to Lir.

Malleus glanced at the alcoves and caves in the cliff faces. The darkness inside them didn't worry him. He asked himself what made more sense: *Check out the pole first, or the caves?* As he had no idea when the tide would be coming back in, he consulted his electronic adviser, which promptly informed him that he had another four hours until high tide; in the area he was standing in, the water would come up another ten metres at least. The beach would disappear and with it the caves.

Malleus decided to walk quickly out to the shallows. Otherwise the sea could grab the shoe and drag it away to deeper waters.

'Hello, stranger! I'm glad you found us. What offering do you bring?' A loud man's voice echoed behind him. 'How do you wish to ask for the grace of Lir and the sea?'

'Or are *you* the offering?' added a second voice.

Malleus turned around. Whoever these people were, he didn't appreciate their tone.

Three men were clambering down towards him between the cliff faces. They wore simple clothing and thick jackets against the weather. Their faces were covered by blue masks decorated with seaweed, fish scales and shells. Apparently they didn't want to be openly affiliated with the cult of Lir.

'I'm just out for a walk,' explained Malleus politely, and stuck his hands in his coat pockets. 'I didn't know this was a shrine.'

'The warning is pretty hard to miss,' spoke the third man, jumping down onto the pebble beach.

Slowly the group walked over to Malleus. They were unarmed, but their hands looked strong and rough. Malleus guessed they were probably fishermen. It could be quite a fight.

'Where was that then?' he asked, acting dumb. 'There wasn't a sign.'

They gathered in front of him, leaving less than an arm's length of space between them.

'Bloody tourists,' said the man on the right. 'No eye for detail.'

'I'm so sorry, messieurs. I don't want any trouble,' began Malleus. 'With you or with Lir.'

'I believe you,' replied the leader, who had striking brown eyes. 'But you have desecrated the shrine. And as you have brought no offering with you, we must offer your life as sacrifice to Lir and the sea.' He pointed towards the pole. 'You'll be held there. If you're not dead by the time the next tide goes out, then we'll know Lir has forgiven you.'

'Eight hours underwater,' estimated Malleus quickly. 'How would that work?'

'Lir could save you, if he wanted to.' The leader grinned visibly under his mask, wrinkles appeared around his eyes. 'Or you could always give money as an offering. As an exception.' His companions chuckled softly. 'Lir is a modern-day kind of god.'

'Oh, then I'm in luck.' He took out his wallet and selected a hundred-euro note. 'That should be enough, I hope?'

The leader nodded and raised his hand to take the money.

But Malleus suddenly crumpled the note into a ball and threw it hard, out into the water. 'Lir, I ask you: accept my offering,' he cried, then looked back at the trio. 'Was that right?'

The men stared at him.

'Not in the sea, you moron,' the leader exclaimed. 'You're supposed to give it to *us*!'

'You never said that, monsieur.' Malleus shrugged his shoulders. 'Now Lir can collect the note himself and go spend it. Maybe on a cruise ship. Or down south in La Baule.' He looked at them innocently. 'Have a good day, messieurs.' He turned and went in the direction of the pole.

'He's taking the piss,' whispered one of the men.

'That was a hundred-euro note. He's just stupid,' responded another. 'He must have more on him.'

'Hey,' Malleus heard them call after him as he left. 'Hey, stay where you are!'

He didn't react, and continued marching straight ahead. His goal was the shoe.

'Lir isn't finished with you yet.' Splashing, rapid steps followed him and drew closer. 'He wants you to give us everything you have.'

Malleus stuck his right hand in his pocket and slid his fingers into the rings of the Apache Knuckleduster Pepperbox, with its combined mini-revolver and double-edged blade.

As he felt a hand on his shoulder, he turned and drew his weapon, dealing the ringleader a short, hard blow under the solar plexus.

All air knocked from his lungs, the man was raised to his full height by the punch before collapsing and falling to his knees, gasping for breath. Seawater splashed around him as he fell.

Malleus did not hesitate, throwing another punch over the fallen man and connecting the titanium knuckles directly with the forehead of the attacker on his left.

The blow flung the man backwards, cracking his mask and lacerating his forehead. He landed on his back in the shallow water.

Malleus swung his still outstretched arm back to the right and caught his third opponent on the temple with the outermost edge of the knuckleduster. The man tumbled to the side with a cry and fell alongside his companions. A few curious gulls hopped squawking to the side.

Malleus grabbed the ringleader by the neck and pressed his face into the cold, shallow water so that his mouth and nose were submerged. 'Where is Lir?' he asked curiously and coolly. 'Is he coming to save you from me?'

The man's screams bubbled through the water and he flailed his arms, trying to escape Malleus' grip.

Malleus allowed him a short breath, then continued as before. 'Where's your god?' he questioned placidly and looked at the other two men, who were slowly pulling themselves to their feet. 'Is he just waiting a while before he rescues you?' Again he pulled the leader up from the water, then threw him to the side, hard; he landed backwards on a pile of seaweed, wheezing and spitting. 'I would say your offerings have been rather a waste.' He carefully rinsed the blood off the knuckleduster in the seawater.

'Arsehole!' shouted the man with the cuts across his forehead and blood running down his mask. He helped his friend to his feet. They seemed to be readying for another attack, while the screwed-up banknote floated past them on the water's surface. They didn't notice it.

Malleus pulled out his Interpol identification. 'That's enough, I think.' He gestured behind him to the pole. 'Did you chain Elizà Royale up there too?'

The rage in their faces was joined by confusion and fear.

'No, of course not,' replied the leader and held his stomach in pain. The knuckleduster had given him quite a formidable bruise. 'Lir doesn't take human sacrifice.'

'So the brackets are just there for decoration?'

'They're just meant to scare people,' the man with the cuts explained, attempting to rub the blood from his eyes. He failed, and the cuts continued to bleed down his face. 'Then people pay quicker.'

'So you, messieurs, are filthy con-artists.' Malleus looked at them contemptuously. 'And you don't give a shit about Lir, correct?'

All three vigorously shook their heads.

'No, no, we pay homage to him and offer him fresh grass and sometimes other things like . . . pearls,' countered the leader. 'Lir is powerful. When we go out with the boats, we need his favour.'

Malleus did not ask them whether they had ever actually seen this god. 'Did Elizà Royale ever run into you out here?'

'We don't do anything to locals,' explained the third man. 'Just tourists.'

'There've been no complaints against you?'

'Well, it says in the warning. It's like with a private beach. If you enter, you have to pay the fee. And the complaints . . . mmh . . .' The ringleader hummed and hawed. 'Henri didn't follow them up,' he said with a cough.

Malleus made a note to lodge a disciplinary complaint against the authorities in Arzon. 'Did any of you see Mademoiselle Royale on the day that she went missing?' He noticed that the water around his feet had risen slightly, and the current was starting to pull at his legs.

The man with the cuts on his face raised his hand to speak. 'She used to come to the shrine now and then. She liked to climb the cliffs and run along the dunes and cliff tops.'

'Was she running on that day?'

He nodded. 'Further up there's the ruins of a signal tower, and from there a path goes to the edge. Where most suicides jump off.' He pulled a handkerchief out of a pocket and dabbed at his injuries. 'We liked Elizà from the start,' he added. 'She was lovely and so beautiful. Not vain at all, though.'

Malleus nodded. 'Is that a shoe out there?'

'Also to scare people,' conceded the ringleader.

'Right.' Malleus gestured towards the beach. 'Back we go, messieurs.' He bent and picked up his hundred-euro note, unfolded it and placed it in his pocket.

The trio skulked up the beach in front of him, fighting the current until they reached dry land.

Malleus sensed that they had told him the truth. 'Monsieur, what did you mean by "from the start"?' he asked.

'What?'

'When you talked about Elizà.'

'Well she'd been living with the Duhamels for ten years,' the man explained obligingly. 'She was a foster child.'

Another piece of the puzzle. Malleus swung round and walked past the wall of rock, up the part of the beach he had initially come from. His shoes squelched, water trickling from the seams. They were probably ruined.

As he raised his collar and left the shrine of Lir behind him, he grew increasingly certain that Elizà Royale's origins were the reason for her disappearance, and for the appearance of the Duhamels' address in Hein's chamber of relics.

There was one thing Malleus was certain of: the young woman had not thrown herself into the sea.

* Α Ω *

I'm following him, along the coast and the cliff tops.

He can't see me, but I keep him constantly in my sights. While he was in the café I went to the hotel and tagged his clothes, so I can find him wherever he goes.

The path along the cliffs is dangerous, and I have to be careful not to slip and twist an ankle, or fall and slide down the escarpment on my arse, landing at his feet like a bloody amateur.

Well look at that: three guys appear, right out of a ruin, and I kneel down so as not to be seen.

As they run they pull some weird hippie masks over their faces. They don't see me. They climb down the slope, right towards where he's standing and looking around.

I lie on my stomach, crawl towards the edge in the shelter of the long grass and screw the silencer onto my APB, mounting the shoulder rest and using the stone in front of me as a stand. Not ideal, but better than nothing.

They try it on with him, blackmail him a bit, and he does his whole your-god-can-kiss-my-arse routine. He's on good form. Then he even beats them up a bit. No need for me to step in.

I can't tell what they say after that, but things seem to get a bit more peaceful. Oh, good. We'll let them keep their lousy lives.

They climb back up and he goes back the way he came.

Could have a quick look at these caves while I'm here. But what for? Just another supposedly godly hole, made by humans.

In all honesty, there aren't even that many people who have spoken to gods. But I don't want to be unfair, obviously it depends on the god. Some of them spend all their time in palaces and skyscrapers or partying in the groves, others leave the odd call sign here and there, or only speak to their followers.

That down there does not look like the work of a god come to earth. So I don't think I'll bother.

I stand up, unscrew the shoulder rest and silencer and hurry off to reach the village at the same time as he does.

Without me is not an option.

I won't stop following him.

* Α Ω *

Malleus sat next to the window in his suite with a cup of strong black tea and perused the list of codes from Hein's chamber, which he now had on paper thanks to his portable printer.

In front of him on the desk was his tablet computer, which displayed the list of books sent by his colleague in Treva. He had also requested a PDF version of each book, with identical dates of publication and editions to those found in Hein's apartment.

The amount of titles was quite considerable once the contents of the small library in the victim's apartment had been added. And *every* book could potentially be the key to deciphering the coded objects.

The light in the large room was dim and the flames in the open fireplace crackled gently, filling the room with warmth and a gentle glow while another winter storm swept sheets of rain across the window.

The quiet, continuous rumbling came not from the storm, however, but from the surf. The tide crashed forcefully against the land and collapsed into great columns of spray on impact with the cliffs.

Malleus had turned on the TV in front of the bed and flicked through to the news channel. He wanted to keep up to date with events in the USA; new laws were being voted on in Congress and the Senate.

When the gods returned, it had been necessary for the 'conservative white man' to accept some difficult changes. For one thing, the wars had resulted in Americans with white heritage falling behind Latinos and African Americans in terms of population. Additionally, the 'First Nations', or Native Americans in North America and Canada now had the protection of the Great Spirit, or Manitou, or whatever else people called it.

And that meant one thing: power.

A lot of power.

It led to a hurried reform of reservation laws and the direct involvement of Native American peoples in the government in an attempt to appease the Great Spirit, who would certainly not be amused that his people's lands had been stolen or bought for cheap trinkets, weapons and liquor.

In parallel to this, the United States had become home to a diverse smorgasbord of religions due to the Celtic and Germanic roots of many of its immigrant populations, despite the increasing proliferation of the Great Spirit's teachings. The South American ancestral beliefs of the huge Latino community also gained great leverage in the ranks of the gods, and many African sects joined them.

Then there were the hardcore islands on the map, veritable city-states of radical Christians and Muslims and crude cults, fighting fanatically for their beliefs. But their numbers were dwindling.

Malleus counted one hundred and forty books.

He stroked the ends of his beard, sipped at his tea and swiped around on his tablet, narrowing down a selection of books and setting aside the editions that Grenzner had described as 'barely handled'.

That left fifty-one. And there was no guarantee that he'd selected the right ones.

Got to start somewhere. Malleus compared the codes with the page numbers in *The Hobbit*.

Well that one doesn't fit.

He was about to exclude the book when he realised that it might match the second code on his list under certain conditions. He couldn't guarantee, after all, that Hein had only used one book.

Combined with the hundred and forty books, this realisation led to infinite possibilities, a wealth of potential combinations that elicited a deep sigh from Malleus. The total list had numbered ninety-seven objects. Seven of them were missing.

Procrastination reared its ugly head and Malleus was suddenly incredibly interested in watching the news.

Or brewing another cup of tea.

Or going for a walk.

Or smoking a blue-banded Culebra.

He looked out into the darkness, filled with howling winds, rumbling thunder and rain. *No, not a walk.*

His tablet and PDA pinged simultaneously. News from Celtica.

He opened the email, which contained a reply from the local authorities regarding his queries.

Thanks to his Interpol status, he had been given access to sensitive information concerning Elizà Royale's background.

Her birth name was Fabienne Azincourt, and she came from Marseilles. Her parents were Robert and Antoinette.

Malleus raised his eyebrows: Elizà had two older sisters, there were pictures attached to the email, both old and recent. The children had been taken away from the parents because mother and father had been involved in organised crime. Antoinette had died six years ago, and Robert was serving a life sentence in prison.

Malleus had to admit that all three sisters were *extraordinarily* attractive: red hair, blue eyes, snow-white skin, not just pretty faces but visions of beauty.

Carmen and Susanne, the other two sisters, lived in Bordeaux and Nantes. The email stated that there was nothing notable about their situations. They were both studying, one law, the other religion and psychology, and were both members of the Celtic faith, *c'est tout.*

Elizà Royale was officially recorded as missing, as her body had never been found. The Atlantic seemed not to want to return such a beauty to land, and the followers of Lir presumably thought she had joined the ranks of the mer-people.

Malleus ruled *that* out at the very least.

The young woman's life insurance wouldn't pay out as long as there was no proof of her death. It would be years still before the foster parents saw a cent of the money.

So where did the Duhamels get all the cash? It was time to have a chat with one of the proprietors and see if he could steer the conversation somewhere useful.

Other than himself there were only three guests, so he hoped to find Madame alone in the little bar downstairs. This plan fitted in nicely with his growing urge to procrastinate.

Malleus stood and threw on his Indo-European jacket, taking his PDA with him as he left the suite.

On the way downstairs he noticed a metallic tang in the air.

He was well acquainted with the coppery scent from his experiences in the war, and at the many crime scenes he had seen in his time: fresh blood had been spilled, and not too long ago.

Malleus slipped off his shoes and slid his fingers into his knuckleduster, folding out the integrated revolver, whose 9mm bullets were deadly at close range; he also flicked open the double-edged blade.

Avoiding the creaking stairs, he slid slowly down the handrail and landed silently on the black and white marble floor.

The scent of blood grew stronger.

Malleus crouched and saw a collapsed body hunched by the entrance of the dark lobby. Judging by the silhouette and clothing it appeared to be Madame Duhamel; a black puddle had gathered at her feet. In the corridor leading to the breakfast room lay a lifeless man, face down in a pool of blood. There was no saving these two.

Malleus listened intently.

He heard a faint clatter from the kitchen, and suddenly the door to the breakfast room swung open, filling the corridor with light.

Malleus saw that the dead man was undoubtedly the other owner, whose throat had been cleanly sliced open. Next to his head was a piece of tongue, nailed to the floorboard. *The same MO as in Treva.*

A woman in black clothing appeared in the doorframe. He guessed she was in her mid-twenties. She bit calmly into a sandwich, then reached behind her and turned off the kitchen light with a click. Darkness returned to the hotel.

Malleus crept backwards, matching the timing of her steps through the lobby so that the creaking floorboards blurred into one sound.

The woman headed for the stairs. She walked right past him without noticing him. In one hand she held the sandwich, in the other a dagger with an elaborately decorated hilt. The dark liquid on the blade was the blood of Monsieur and Madame Duhamel, who would clearly no longer be of any help to Malleus in his investigation.

She climbed the stairs to the first floor.

Malleus didn't wait another second. He stood up, pointed the revolver at her, and turned on the light in the stairway.

'Stand still and turn around slowly,' he commanded. 'Drop your weapon.'

The woman froze.

Her fingers spread, dropping the dagger to the floor where it buried itself point-first in the floorboard.

Cautiously she turned, taking a slow bite from her sandwich as she did so. She was neither pretty nor ugly, an unremarkable face. Her figure was athletic, which made sense given how much time she seemed to spend travelling around killing people. *You'd need to be in good shape for a job like that.*

'Ah,' she said, chewing and looking at him. 'I was just coming to find you.'

'You're under arrest for the murder of Monsieur and Madame Duhamel.' Malleus had left his cable ties in the suite. A cord from the nearby curtain would have to do for now. 'I'm an investigator with Interpol.'

'International cop. Thought so.' The woman remained unimpressed. 'Because of the thing in Treva.'

'Come downstairs slowly, then lie on the ground.'

She carried on eating. 'How did you end up here?'

'A note in Hein's chamber. With this address.'

'Ah! So easy.'

'Right. But still missing some details.' Malleus knew he was being stalled. 'Down. Now. Hopefully your interrogation will fill in some gaps.'

'Or what?'

'Or I shoot you in the leg.'

'Listen very carefully, because this is all I'm going to tell you.' The woman had finished her sandwich and was licking each of her fingers clean. 'Hein was a greedy old bastard. Wanted money or he was going to talk. Just like those two.' She nodded towards the Duhamels. 'She sent me to silence these dishonourable bastards.'

'Who is "she"? Your boss? A goddess?'

'She is she.'

'And the objects?'

The woman looked irritated. 'What objects?'

'In Hein's secret chamber.'

'I never went in any secret chamber. That's not part of my contract.' She eyed him appraisingly. 'I silenced the treacherous tongues. And it ends here.' She made a sudden sweeping motion with her foot.

Her sole flicked the dagger sticking out of the floor and transformed it into a whirling missile, hurtling towards Malleus. Then she jumped at him.

* Α Ω *

Nice place. I've made myself at home in the dark breakfast room, while he sits upstairs and works.

I'm still following him.

Next to me is a glass of grape juice with a piece of ginger floating in it. It keeps me fresh and alert. I was quiet enough when I fetched it from the kitchen. Remarkable how safe people feel, tucked away inside their own four walls.

Nobody sees me in the darkness, I'm just another shadow, an optical illusion in a chair. Neither the woman nor her husband have any idea I'm there.

Nor the stranger who comes in.

She stabs the startled woman as soon as she enters the room, multiple blows to the heart, then slits her throat. Clean and quick.

I drink my juice and watch curiously to see what she does next.

The stranger creeps towards the counter, hears the man coming out of the kitchen and calling after his wife.

She jumps on him, grabs him by the throat and shoves him against the wall, holding the tip of her blade against his heart. 'What were you thinking?' she whispered. 'Demanding more money than she promised and paid you?'

He begins to answer, then sees his wife's blood trickling round the corner. It inspires him to resist her. Idiot.

Of course she stabs him immediately. Four, five quick blows between the ribs. 'Your souls will die. This is for your betrayal!' She releases him and quickly cuts out his throat as he falls, then bends down and cuts out a large chunk of his tongue. She has brought a nail with her, and stabs it through the tongue, stamping the nail into the ground with her heel.

'See, Kostianaia Noga, I do your bidding,' she says joyously. 'Nobody will discover what happened to the one we brought you.'

Her stomach growls loudly, and she goes into the kitchen. By the sound of it she's making herself something to eat.

Tough cookie, this one.

I pull out my APB, screw on the silencer. She'll probably want to kill him too. But I can't allow that. Fuck . . . whoever she mentioned. Noga? Naga? Whatever.

He comes downstairs and notices that something's not right. Now that's what I call timing. And he's got his funny little weapon with him. Good.

She comes out of the kitchen, he stops her, there's a bit of back and forth.

My automatic is already out, I support the barrel with my other hand and hold myself ready. This woman won't surrender. She'd rather die.

As she kicks at the dagger, I fire. A single shot.

I hear the clang as my bullet grazes the flying weapon and throws it off course. I didn't want anything more than that; he can handle the rest on his own.

If not, I'm here.

I'm always here.

* Α Ω *

Malleus pulled the trigger twice and the Derringer spat its bullets at his attacker. Then she pulled him over, already losing her strength. His shots had both hit. On impact he drove his flick knife through her throat, and they both fell to the ground.

He shoved her away from him, only removing the blade from her throat when he had moved out of the path of the spray of blood. *You should have surrendered.*

As she fell, he saw the two holes in her torso, one small and one large exit wound in her back. Malleus always loaded one chamber of his Derringer with steel bullets, and the other with hollow-points. With that combination he was well armed against most enemies.

He retrieved her remarkable dagger from the floor. He couldn't find the blade; it appeared to have broken off when it hit the wall behind him.

He searched the stranger's corpse and found nothing that gave away anything about her identity.

He did, however, notice the numerous tattoos peeking out from under her shirt collar.

Malleus unbuttoned her shirt, bringing more inked designs to light.

He was familiar with this style of tattoo, but it wasn't from Western Europe. The Cyrillic characters confirmed his suspicions. She had belonged to the elite of Russian professional criminals, the *vor v zakone*, 'thieves in law' whose tattoos carried specific meanings. Only an expert could understand them.

I hadn't counted on finding a lead like this. Malleus wasted no time calling his superior and asking him to send some officers from the nearest city. He didn't trust the authorities in this little town, or the surrounding area. Then he took a photo of the woman's face and ran it through the Interpol database in the hope that she might have brought attention to herself elsewhere and been arrested in the past.

He noticed a necklace lying next to her body; his knife had sliced through the leather band.

Malleus picked up the bloody band and looked at the abstract, black-stained figure, which depicted a woman's body. *Are you her contractor?*

At this moment in time, this wooden idol was his best lead. It was becoming clear to him that he had stumbled upon a tangled mess of cover-ups and terrible secrets, orchestrated by an as yet unknown goddess.

And alongside the murders and the disappearance of Elizà, the original, burning question remained: who had stolen the seven objects from Hein's secret room?

Germania, Treva, November 2019

'We've got your girl, Bourreau.' The detective in the chic designer suit approached Malleus, who was perched at a spare desk in the station, and proudly laid two printouts in front of him. He smelled of expensive aftershave and wore his long white hair tied back in a braid. 'I've sent you the file.'

At first Malleus thought he meant Elizà, but on glancing at the pictures he recognised the face: it was the assassin from Arzon.

The authorities from Russia, which was now calling itself Old Russia, had been good enough to send over the woman's file.

Her name was Julia Djomotschka, and she had already had more than a few brushes with the law. It had begun with minor offences in her teenage years, petty theft and fare dodging, followed by a few short cons and later muggings and store robberies.

Djomotschka was wanted in Old Russia for various violent crimes, including grievous bodily harm resulting in death and an attack on an armoured cash transport vehicle. She had been given the death penalty, a sentence that Malleus had unwittingly administered on the lobby floor of the Fleur de la Mer.

'We should send the Russians the body,' said Grezner.

'I'll inform the French,' replied Malleus, leafing through the pictures and notes. Djomotschka had made roots away from her homeland. The Latvian authorities had an address for her in Riga; her religion was stated as 'Orthodox', although the figure on her necklace suggested otherwise.

Malleus was familiar with the difficulties of bureaucracy, the fact that most citizens wouldn't update their details despite being able to do it online. The process of dechristianisation was still very much in progress, despite the success of its initial waves after the Great Change. The Occident had been largely freed from the official influence of the Christian denominations, but that didn't mean that the process had got any easier.

Around eighty per cent of Europeans had been uninterested by the old religions and their customs, but then suddenly the gods had appeared, encouraging adherence to exactly those forgotten cults, or demanding it with threat of force.

Malleus knew that these deities were showing restraint after their massacres of the Christian rebels. But their leniency towards former Christians, with their lax worship, incorrect prayers and unsuitable offerings, would come to an end. *Sooner or later.*

Just as Christianity had been declared the state religion by Constantine the Great after the Battle of Milvian Bridge in AD

312, so it would come to an end: abruptly. *In hoc signo vinces* had been put to rest.

Like so many, Djomotschka had changed her religious allegiances following the Great Change.

Malleus took the goddess figurine out of the drawer and looked at it. The woman's apartment was in Riga, she came from Russia, so it was highly likely that this figure depicted a Slavic god.

The Slavs had a huge variety of deities, nature spirits and cults. Malleus would have to travel to Riga and try to root out exactly which cult she was a part of. It could be dangerous, however, if there were more fanatical followers like Djomotschka, willing to kill on the orders of a deity or a priest.

Malleus turned the blackened figurine in his fingers, then took a brush and magnifying glass and swept away the dirt that covered it. As he did so, he tried to recall what he already knew about Slavic religions.

As was often the case, there were points of similarity with Indo-Germanic mythology. There was the god of thunder, named Perun. To make things complicated, there were also parallels with Persian, Baltic, Germanic, Celtic and classical Greek and Roman cultures, reflected in the appearance of oracles, rituals, cremations and many-headed idols.

Malleus had always suspected that Christianity had only caught on in the first place because there was only one god. *It was just easier.*

And the people of Europe had managed, despite that simplicity, to break off into denominations, isolating any apostates and fighting amongst one another, all in the name of *one* god. Apparently one religion was enough of a precedent to start killing one another – no need for any others to get involved.

Well, that won't be an issue much longer. Malleus compared the figurine with archaeological artefacts from the Slavic period and with newer imitations that had been in circulation for a few years.

The bristles of the brush swept away the darkly pigmented dirt from the figurine, revealing a light, shiny surface. The material was some kind of bone, which had been carved and then crudely painted black.

Human bone? Malleus collected the crumbs of dirt to be sent to the lab and rinsed the talisman delicately in warm water, uncovering the finer details of the engraving.

The writing was in Cyrillic: *Kostianaia Noga.*

He quickly translated it using his PDA: *Bony Leg.*

It took him only a few seconds to look it up and discover that it was an epithet commonly added to the name of Baba Yaga.

Researchers commonly interpreted the legendary Eastern witch as a form of Slavic death goddess who led the dead into the underworld. She was often depicted as the guardian of the water of life and death.

So there was a cult in Riga surrounding Baba Yaga, whose influence stretched as far as Treva and Arzon.

An email arrived on his PDA from the authorities in Celtica, the ones who had given him the addresses of Elizà's sisters.

At his suggestion, they had investigated further into the sisters' whereabouts in Nantes and Bordeaux: Carmen had stopped turning up to her classes and had been reported missing by one of her professors; and a note from Susanne had appeared, stating her intention to commit suicide.

The authorities had begun a state-wide search for the young women, which in Malleus's opinion was entirely unnecessary.

Those women are no longer in Celtica.

He slipped the figurine into his pocket and left the station.

He had a catastrophe to prevent. In Riga.

Latvia, Riga, November 2019

The short journey was not enough to make any headway in figuring out the mystery of the seven stolen objects. Malleus sent an email to his colleagues in Treva, tasking them with another full search of the crime scene in the souvenir shop.

With no leads on the identity of the thief, he was left with only the numbered list, and he was doubtful that the remaining artefacts would turn up anything useful.

He had believed Djomotschka when she said that she hadn't stolen anything. Her mission had been clearly defined: take out the Duhamels and ensure that what had happened to Elizà and her sisters remained a secret.

The first results of the DNA analysis reached Malleus' inbox as he stepped off the plane in Riga.

The disembodied limbs in the containers – both the glass jars and the reliquaries – were human, but of varying ethnicities. There were no mutations or abnormalities in the genetic material, nothing suggesting a connection to any particular deity or religion.

A few of the caskets and boxes had shown up on a preliminary database scan as valuable stolen goods missing from museums and private collections, which did not come as a surprise to Malleus.

Some of the body parts and the receptacles containing them had proven to be several hundred years old, and others less than one year. So Hannes Hein had procured some of the objects and had others freshly manufactured. Only the deciphered list would explain why the newer limbs were ascribed such significance that one would pay money to own them.

Perhaps they belonged to executed criminals. Or maybe they're just anomalies, meaningless lucky talismans. Malleus strode across the arrivals hall and climbed into the car he had rented online. A BMW i8, naturally.

He stated Djomotschka's address and let the autopilot drive him through the foreign city.

He had heard that Riga was beautiful, but he was too tense to take in the view from the window.

Instead he inspected his two Apaches and the two modified Cobray Pepperbox Derringer 410s he also carried with him. The Cobray was a medium-sized Derringer with a long barrel and five chambers loaded with lead-shot shells and full-metal-jacket bullets. Perfect for both crowd control and single targets.

The car had barely stopped moving before he climbed out and walked into the decrepit tower block at the edge of the city.

There was an illegible notice stuck to the door of the lift, which somebody had helpfully decorated with a large, crudely drawn penis. The lift was probably out of order.

Of course, Djomotschka had lived on the top floor.

Malleus stroked the ends of his beard and began his ascent, floor by floor, past countless shabby doors; past doorbells and plaques, some unwelcoming, some completely anonymous, some simply a sheet of paper with scrawled names; past mounds of rubbish, their stink emanating into the corridors.

The higher he climbed, the more squalid the building became. On the last few floors there were doors that had been kicked in and a pervading smell of mould and damp. This was certainly not somewhere a tourist would end up on their trip around the

'Pearl of the Baltic'. This area of Riga was more like the discarded, ugly oyster shell, of no use to anybody.

'DJOMOTSCHKA' had been scrawled on the door with a permanent marker, in both Cyrillic and European script.

Malleus allowed himself a few deep breaths, took off his hat and wiped the sweat from his forehead. Then he reached into his coat pocket, wrapped his fingers round the grip of the Apache and clicked off the safety catch.

Answers, here I come. He aimed a sharp kick at the door.

The entrance swung open and a swell of stale cigarette smoke hit his nostrils. Everything else was quiet.

Carefully Malleus moved through the assassin's apartment, getting a feel for the dimensions of the place, his weapon drawn and half raised.

But the flat was abandoned, and had obviously been half-emptied and cleaned.

Malleus closed the front door and leaned a chair against it, so that he would hear it tip over if anyone tried to enter behind him. He began to search through the furnishings, which could only be described as austere.

Djomotschka seemed to have supported herself purely through muggings and robberies.

There was a fair amount of loose cash in euros, the new Stribog rouble, dollars, British pounds, and some gold and silver coins stamped with the images of various gods. In certain cities and states these were now the only acceptable currency.

Smartphones, tablets, cameras . . . Djomotschka must have had some successful hauls in the tourist centres of Riga. But Malleus had not yet come across anything that could help him to locate the missing sisters.

Shit.

Malleus observed the many posters and drawings of Baba Yaga on the walls, and a small altar outside on the balcony.

He opened the screen door and looked around.

Cold winter air bore down on him. The wind was pretty strong up here. He was glad of his thick military coat.

Malleus found incense, coals, frankincense, dried herbs, bones – all stowed away neatly in a small set of drawers. An altar consisting of a footstool with a water bowl and carved bone figurines arranged on top of it was leaning against the railing of the balcony.

Malleus inspected it closely, removing the objects one by one, searching for clues – until his eyes rested on the markings on the railing.

There were marks indicating the position of the sun, and an arrow underneath.

Malleus raised his head and peered into the distance, towards a forest.

Amidst the dense mass of trees, he saw a small hole.

A clearing. With the help of his PDA he established that the glade was located approximately ten kilometres from his current position, and that there were no roads leading to it.

He marked the coordinates so that he would not end up lost amongst the trees on the walk that awaited him, and left the assassin's apartment.

Malleus hurried down the stairs, left the tower block and began to cut across country towards the forest. He assumed that he would find a shrine of some kind in the clearing. *Why else would the altar be oriented towards it?*

He pulled his collar high around his neck, lit a cigar with a green band and quickened his pace. After a good hour of walking he reached the edge of the forest and pushed his way into the foliage.

Both of his girls, wife and daughter, had always been afraid of mountains and forests, without ever having a concrete reason for it. If they ever went walking together, they would only go through woods that grew sparsely and full of light.

They would never have set foot in here.

Malleus pushed the thoughts of his family to the back of his mind. They were distracting and painful. He knew he would never overcome their loss. Time only opened further wounds, obscuring the older ones with new pain.

After another two hours he had fought his way through the thick underbrush and reached the place marked on his PDA just as dusk was falling.

Found it. Malleus knelt at the edge of the circular clearing and took in his surroundings. Mist rose from the damp grass, billowing in milky clouds around his knees.

The ground was slightly lower towards the middle of the circle, as if something had been carved into it a long time ago; in the centre was a bowl, around a metre in diameter, which was hard to make out in the dim light. The trunks of the oak and birch trees surrounding the glade were carved at regular intervals with colourful markings, which Malleus photographed in sequence.

A boulder lay at the eastern edge of the clearing. It had been decorated with symbols and plant tendrils, and was probably used for worship of some kind, though it did not appear to have been used for regular sacrifices. It could also have been used as a raised area for the priests to stand above their congregation, Malleus supposed.

Malleus was wondering whether it was wise to enter the

clearing and investigate further when a flame crackled into life in the centre of the circle. It burned on the surface of the crystal clear water contained in the central basin. In the dim light, Malleus could see the bowl more clearly, and guessed it was made of bone.

Water is life, and the bone represents death. Malleus listened for voices. *The elements associated with Kostianaia Noga.*

It quickly grew dark, and the mist gradually dissipated. Creatures could be heard running through the forest, now cloaked in darkness save for the glow of the flames. Clouds hung across the sky and obscured any light from the stars. The fire, apparently fuelled by the bowl of water, was the only thing preventing Malleus from being totally enveloped in the dense blackness.

Then a figure emerged from the brush and walked over to the bowl, kneeling in front of it to begin a quiet prayer.

She had barely sat down when a second figure followed, then a third, and a fourth, until eleven people were kneeling around the flickering flames uttering the same words in a language Malleus had no knowledge of. He could make out some of their faces clearly by the firelight; they were all women between the ages of thirty and seventy.

There was no reason for him to intervene yet. Praying to a deity was not a crime.

At the same time, Malleus was sure he had come to the right place. A goddess of death would not be satisfied with offerings of nuts or grass. Perhaps they were planning to sacrifice the sisters from Azincourt.

An hour passed.

Malleus waited, taking pictures and videos from his hiding place.

Then three women appeared, dressed in white with long

red hair worn loose around their shoulders. Their gaits were awkward, as if they were considering each step before taking it.

Malleus recognised Elizà, Susanne and Carmen. Their eyes were open, their gazes empty and their strikingly beautiful faces were expressionless. He guessed hypnosis or drugs had been used to control them.

They drifted towards each other from different sides of the clearing, and the circle of praying women around the bowl expanded by a few metres.

The sisters reached the bowl and laid face down in the wet grass, so that their heads were touching the edge of the bowl; then they joined hands.

The praying women fell silent.

One of the women stood up and went over to the sisters, who lay obediently and waited.

Malleus saw no dagger or weapon in her hand. Nevertheless, he took out his Cobray and held it ready to fire. *And now what?*

If this was the 'she' that Djomotschka had referred to, he was looking at the person who had ordered the murders of the Duhamels and Hein. He would arrest her.

He also doubted that the sisters were taking part in this ceremony of their own free will. That would have to be established during interrogation.

The woman began a chant, peppered with repetitions of the name Kostianaia Noga.

Suddenly the fire in the middle of the water shot outwards in burning lines of flame, towards the heads of the three sisters.

So they are sacrifices! Malleus had to intervene. He clipped his PDA onto his coat so that it would record what was happening, and jumped out of his hiding place.

'Police! You're under arrest,' he said in Russian, and then in

English, pointing the barrel of the Cobray at the woman. 'On suspicion of contracting the murders of Monsieur and Madame Duhamel in Arzon, and of Herr Hein in Treva. And of abducting these three women.' He pulled out the second Cobray to emphasise his orders. 'On your knees, and stay there until I reach you. The rest of you, stay where you are.'

The woman broke off her invocations and looked towards him; her gaze was still detached, from the trance she had been in seconds before.

The lines of fire on the water's surface disappeared – and with them the central flame.

Blackness immediately fell on the glade.

A woman's voice bellowed a command, full of rage. Rage directed at him, the intruder.

Malleus knelt down, heard the rustling of material and footsteps in the grass, moving towards him at speed. 'I'm warning you,' he shouted and shot a single bullet into the air.

For a fraction of a second the muzzle flash illuminated the crowd of women rushing towards him, their claw-like fingers grasping at him, ready to tear him limb from limb. Behind them stood the leader, upright and proud, pointing towards him with an outstretched arm.

Then the darkness returned.

Unfortunately, Malleus was left with no other choice. He slid the barrel of the Cobray across: the next chamber was loaded with lead shot.

* Α Ω *

He's lucky that I'm following him. He doesn't even realise what he'd be up against if he was doing this alone. He's relying on me without even knowing I'm there.

The clearing is easy to overlook from above; I've made myself at home on a branch of a leafless oak tree near his hiding spot. The shoulder rest and silencer of the APB have been set up since I got here.

More and more women are appearing. I change the smaller magazine for a larger one.

The spectacle is nice. I don't fully understand what the old one is murmuring about, but the three girls lying there as if they're trying to eat the grass or start a new sport called 'Lying in Formation around a Bowl' – they don't look like sacrifices.

That tends to go somewhat differently. But that's his area of expertise. He'll have to find out what these women are up to.

Unlike him, I'm prepared for the darkness. My glasses have night vision, so the clearing is as clear to me as if it were daylight.

Of course he intervenes. He has to. It's his job. He does his job, I do mine.

The old one snaps out the light and sets the other ones on him.

Not a problem on my end. I've got enough bullets.

The gentleman even gives a warning shot, very considerate. He's totally unaware that three of them are closing in on him from behind. Their nails, which look as sharp as a hen's claws, would easily shred the flesh from his neck.

The lead shot from his bigger Derringer knocks the first ones off their feet, and I deal with the three behind him in short salvos; each one gets three shots.

Then he's only got four in front of him and the main one, who's quietly keeping out of the fighting for now.

But I can see that she's lost patience and is getting very, very angry. The losses are too high. She's got something planned.

She goes over to the bone bowl and scoops up a handful of water.

Whatever she's planning to do with it – I can't let it happen.

I change the APB over to single-shot mode, wait until he fires another lead shot, and shoot the old one through the thigh.

Shrieking, she buckles, and I fire another shot through her knee to keep her down.

In the meantime he's made himself enough space and is using the light on his PDA to look around at what's happened.

I'm not worried, he's tough enough. He'll be able to cope with it.

Good thing I was there.

I'm glad I'm following him.

* A Ω *

Malleus had used all the ammo in the Cobrays and was sure that the lead shot had pushed back the women. The muzzle flash had thrown a little light on the targets, though aiming didn't play much of a role with that kind of ammo.

None of the attackers had reached him.

Is it over? With the inbuilt, surprisingly powerful torch on his PDA he did his best to illuminate the clearing and saw the women who had been shot; he had already sent off an emergency distress signal. Hopefully the Latvian authorities would be smart enough to send a helicopter to his location. *Yes, it's over.*

The hands of the women looked normal, but he could have sworn that, before, they had looked like the talons of predatory birds or hens. He had made a note of it, in case it turned out to be useful evidence.

The injured were tending to their own wounds, and others were hobbling or dragging themselves across the grass to those who were lying motionless. The smell of blood filled the air, of course, but without exercising self-defence, it would have been him lying eviscerated on the grass.

Malleus reloaded his weapon while he walked, stowing away one Cobray and running his fingers over the ends of his beard.

He headed towards the sisters, separated their hands and turned them onto their backs, one by one. *Let them be alive.*

The Azincourts had their eyes closed, and were breathing as if in a deep sleep. The gunshots and the screaming had done nothing to disturb them. One after the other, Malleus checked their pupils, which were highly dilated and not reacting to light. *As I thought: drugs.*

Malleus stood up and pointed his light towards the leader, who was in the process of standing up on the boulder where she'd fallen; blood poured out of the wounds in her leg. He put her age at around fifty; her shoulder-length, dark grey hair lay tangled and wet across her face, which betrayed the pain radiating from her injuries.

'Going somewhere?' He went over to the stone, the Cobray in his right hand. 'My name is Malleus Bourreau from Interpol. You are being detained for resisting arrest, and on suspicion of soliciting to murder and three counts of abduction.' He took a set of handcuffs from his coat and tied the woman's wrists behind her back. 'I can't wait to hear your explanation for all this.'

'Kostianaia Noga will kill you,' she promised him with a piercing glare through her tangled hair. 'You haven't prevented the coming of the goddess. You have only delayed her!'

Malleus looked over at the sleeping sisters, who had rolled over and were huddled together for warmth. It looked so natural, so intimate, as if despite their separation they had spent their whole lives together.

He was struck by a sudden understanding of what had been planned that evening in the clearing.

Kostianaia Noga, or Baba Yaga, was part of a triple goddess, comprised of the virgin, the mother and the crone. He had read a folk story on the plane in which Baba Yaga lived with two sisters bearing the same name as herself.

Malleus looked over at the Azincourts. *Sisters. The same names.* 'You wanted to bring the goddess into this world, to live in these women,' he speculated, 'with no concern for their lives.'

'They would have become death and rebirth,' she spat back at him. 'We would have made them immortal!'

'You would have robbed them of their real lives.' Malleus shook his head. 'The lives they wanted to lead!'

'I speak the truth. If one of them had died, the others would have anointed her with the water of death' – she nodded towards the bone basin – 'and she would have risen again healed and just as beautiful as before. They would have become divine, filled with supernatural power! And now they will remain simply human.' She spat at his feet. Some of the spit caught in her hair and dripped onto the ground. 'Kostianaia Noga will find you.'

'I will certainly die one day, but not at the hands of a god,' replied Malleus calmly. 'I already have plenty of those as enemies, and I'm still living.'

The whirring of a helicopter grew louder as it neared the clearing.

A powerful searchlight cut through the darkness with a cold, synthetic shard of light, jolting back and forth until it landed on the clearing.

Wind blew up around them, artificial gusts whipped up by the blades of the helicopter. The machine hovered over the clearing as the pilot searched for a suitable place to land.

Malleus breathed a sigh of relief.

The innocents were protected, and the injured would receive medical attention. After that the women would be taken into custody for interrogation, to establish the extent of their organisation.

He took out a cigar. With a red band.

He had earned it.

Germania, Treva, November 2019

Malleus had opened various documents on three monitors. On the central screen he was playing the recording of the interrogations he had carried out with the women in Riga. He was watching them for the tenth time, soaking up every last detail and trying to comprehend the fascination. *What are these people finding in the divine?* Malleus found himself asking this in every case he worked on.

The energy wasted on cults, rules, debates, inter-religious trench warfare, the interpretation of commandments and texts and words that some entity had supposedly said, written or otherwise left behind – it demanded people's full attention.

Other things gave him something to hold on to in life, but not what people considered to be gods.

Malleus concentrated on closing the case.

Inese Šķēle was the leader, and she had made no secret of that during the interrogation. The fifty-six-year-old stood by everything that had happened: the abductions, the murders.

She claimed that Kostianaia Noga had appeared to her in a dream and commanded her to prepare for her arrival as the triple goddess. The death goddess had told Šķēle she wanted to lead humanity. To that end, she needed three sisters, into whom the three facets of godliness would flow.

The other women were enthusiastic followers who had been taken in by Šķēle's promises of a new deity. They wanted to be there for the first hours of the triple goddess' arrival on Earth. They were promised special favour and fortune for life if they served the triple goddess and spread her word.

Malleus had quickly noticed in the interrogations with the survivors that they were no fanatics. They were clearly ready to believe in this goddess, and were convinced that she existed. They had done a lot to prepare for her arrival, but they were quick to assert that they had not done everything.

When he had played them his video footage of the attack, as they descended on him like furies with contorted faces and fingers like claws, they were horrified. They hadn't realised how drastically they had changed in the clearing, how utterly determined they had been to kill him because it had been commanded of them.

Malleus attributed it to the usual mass hypnosis. *That* was the strongest weapon against the human psyche: making people compliant through psychological games, through illusions, through manipulation. It could involve drugs, but it didn't need to. The women had been victims of Šķēle's captivating words and presence.

Four of the women had not survived the fight in the clearing. But if he hadn't opened fire, he wouldn't be sitting at the computer now.

Malleus was a man with no scruples. Compassion, sure. Sympathy, of course. But he excluded anyone who threatened his life – or at least that's what he told himself. He wasn't always fully convinced by his own set of rules.

A call symbol appeared on his monitor: Elizà Royale wanted to talk with him online.

Malleus put on his earpiece and accepted the call; he quickly ran his fingers over his beard to tidy it up.

'Bourreau,' he said in a business-like manner, but accompanied it with a smile as the dialogue window opened.

The young woman with the brilliant blue eyes appeared on his screen, her two sisters seated behind her. 'Hello, Monsieur Bourreau', she said in French. She had put her red hair up in a loose bun. 'Are you well?'

He had to laugh. 'I think I should be asking you that question.'

'We're doing well – thank you,' Elizà replied, slightly embarrassed. 'You saved us from these crazy people.' She swallowed. 'Thank you for not giving up on me. Without you—'

'It's no problem, mademoiselle,' he interrupted her gently. 'You are safe from Šķēle.'

'Really?'

'Yes. She confessed to ordering the abductions and the murder.' He could see that Elizà was still struggling with the deaths of her foster parents.

For that reason he neglected to tell her that the Duhamels had received money in return for sticking to the story about her suicide and covering up her disappearance. They had bartered away their daughter, betrayed her and literally sold her off.

And he also decided not to mention Šķēle's conviction that Kostianaia Noga would come and free her from prison.

'How did this woman know about us?'

'She claims that the goddess showed her your faces in a dream, but I have my doubts. It's proving difficult to investigate because her assassin and her middleman in Treva are both dead,' he summarised. 'I found the address for your foster parents on his body.'

'Was he that awful man?' Elizà managed to describe the late Hannes Heiņ in few words.

Malleus was surprised. 'You saw him?'

'Briefly. I was chained up and gagged in a little room while he ran his business outside, selling some kind of tourist stuff,' she explained, visibly disgusted. 'He would come and check on me, told me I'd better not die. Then they carried me off somewhere else.'

Malleus wondered if she might have seen one of the stolen artefacts. Intrigued, he stroked the ends of his beard. 'Madaemoiselle, I appreciate this might be difficult, but could you describe to me what you saw in that little room?'

Elizà thought for a moment, and described a few different objects at random, until he interrupted her with a gesture and held up a picture of the shelves in the chamber. 'Let's try it this way: what objects were placed here, where these empty spaces are? Do you remember anything, mademoiselle?'

Elizà leaned forward, pressing a couple of keys on her keyboard. She was presumably zooming in on the picture.

'The top right. The ceiling light always lit that one up when he came into the room. And left, underneath that: the light was reflected down there.' She thought for another moment. 'Underneath there was a rectangular brick: five smooth sides and the top was decorated with some kind of illegible writing.'

Shit. Malleus twirled his beard round his fingers, surprised. *I didn't notice anything missing there. So there must be more than seven stolen artefacts.* 'Any details?'

Elizà closed her eyes. 'The symbols on it were arranged in five, no, six rows. And separated by lines carved into it – for easier reading, I guess.' She tapped at her right temple. 'The man mentioned the brick on the phone, I think. At least, he said the words "brick" and "Chogha Zanbil".'

Inscriptions on a brick. Guaranteed to have come from a temple. Of course, he would have to find out exactly who or what Chogha Zambil was for it to be of any use. 'That's a good start,' said Malleus hopefully. 'And the other object?'

'It looked like a crown, but a bit more . . . primitively made,' she explained. 'I think it was gold, but with a green layer underneath the gold leaf – you could see the borders of it where the pieces had been joined together. And there were jewels on it. I think they were red. And there were embellishments with sort of . . . lumpy flowers made of gold. I couldn't make out anything clearer than that.'

Malleus was excited, and thanked her profusely. Many of the details Elizà had described could help him in his search, and perhaps in cracking the codes. 'Are you still in Riga?'

Elizà shook her head. 'We all spontaneously decided to fly to Lutetia and spend a week together. We have so much to talk about after being separated for so long. The memories of our time together in Marseilles are faded, and the things we've been through in the past few weeks and days . . . it's like they're clouded in fog.'

Malleus threw a glance at his right-hand monitor, where he had placed the note with the sisters' blood test results. There were traces of opiate derivatives, which could explain both their behaviour in the clearing and Elizà's description of still feeling blurry. They had drugged the sisters into staying quiet and compliant.

'I'm sure that's the best plan for all of you right now,' he agreed. 'And you know we can offer you psychological support at any point that you need it.'

'I know. They offered it to us before.' Elizà took a deep breath. 'I know I've already thanked you, but . . . if there's ever anything I can do for you, Monsieur Bourreau, please let me know. Money is no object. And please, no false modesty. You know that I'm rich.' She smiled with an air of gravity only seen in people far beyond her years. The abduction had left a deep imprint on her. 'Thank you so much.'

'Live your life, Mademoiselle Royale. You and your sisters,' he replied. 'And no more gods.'

'I promise.' The young woman waved goodbye, and the dialogue window closed.

Malleus added another three to his running total. *Hopefully three fewer people who will fall into whatever bizarre game is taking place on this planet.*

A woman with blonde highlights around his age or perhaps a little younger was striding towards him; she wore a red business suit with white shirt and heels, which might have looked very modern in the eighties, but not now. In her right hand she held a printout and she was looking very pleased with herself.

'I found one, Monsieur Bourreau,' she said in French.

Malleus eyed her. 'You're going to have to give me a little more than that, please, madame.'

'*Familiar Studies of Men and Books*, by Robert Louis Stevenson.' She laid the paper in front of him. 'It was a book that Hein and maybe someone else was using, to build his code. This one' – she pointed with a blue metallic painted fingernail at one of the codes and the translation scribbled underneath it – 'corresponds to the first of the objects that the murderer took with them after killing Hein. The gods were on my side today, giving me a little victory to celebrate so soon after getting here.'

'Djomotschka was the murderer, but she wasn't a thief.' It occurred to Malleus that he hadn't yet finished writing his report to Interpol Central. Lautrec would surely be waiting for it by now. 'So my search continues. But the gods certainly have nothing to do with it.' He looked at her curiously. 'I don't believe I've had the pleasure. Who assigned you to support me on this case?'

The woman looked at him nonplussed. 'You didn't get the memo?' She was visibly embarrassed by her rash enthusiasm.

'Oh, my apologies. They told me you'd be informed as soon as you arrived in Treva.'

'Unfortunately not.' He waited five seconds, giving her time to explain herself, which she did not. 'And who are you exactly, if I may ask again, Madame?'

She held out her hand. 'Marianne Lagrande. I'm your new partner.'

His right eyebrow shot upwards.

'Monsieur Lautrec thought that you would benefit from some support, so he sent me over,' she hurried to explain. 'Before you get annoyed: it's only for this one case with the murder and the missing objects,' she qualified hastily on seeing the discomfort and outrage rapidly spreading across his face. 'But I did suspect I might be more excited about this than you are,' she conceded, thus ending her presentation.

Malleus concentrated his efforts on holding back everything that was going through his head and threatening to come out of his mouth. 'Good work,' he managed in spite of himself.

'Yeah, thanks. Unfortunately Hein was using a lot of different books, though,' explained Lagrande, relieved that he was sticking to business. 'We still have a lot of decryption work ahead of us.'

He looked at the notes and drawings he had scribbled whilst speaking to Elizà.

'It could be about to get a little easier.'

He was still reluctant to accept that he had been given a partner. She was guaranteed to have a different opinion on the gods than he did. *Not one person* he had ever met shared his approach. And it was that arrangement that enabled him to do his job the way he did it.

Lagrande stood hesitantly in front of him, the red of her suit glaring painfully into his eyes.

'Then keep up the good work.' Malleus smiled trivially. 'I'll wait for news.'

She nodded and left.

Malleus would have to find ways to avoid her constant presence. This was exactly what he didn't need.

Indignantly he looked at Lagrande's translation:

Engraved horn (right) of Nandi, in silver casing. Price: 1.9m. Origin: available on request.

Underneath Lagrande had noted:

Nandi, bull from Hindu mythology. Mount and loyal servant of the Hindu god Shiva.

This was a good start, but he wasn't happy about it.

The word 'partner' was as offensive to him as the crudest of profanities.

He had worked with a partner twice, but sooner or later they always ended up prostrating themselves before one god or another, or losing themselves in indecision, doubting themselves and failing to consider the evidence objectively.

I'll just have to keep her tied to her desk. Malleus pushed his bad mood to one side. He had stolen objects to locate, one of which Lagrande had identified, and two more which he hoped to identify with the help of Elizà's descriptions. Using the details she had given him, they should turn up soon.

Those who usually showed interest in such items were the followers of whichever god was involved, or wealthy collectors, or indeed a combination of both.

An email arrived in his inbox and broke his train of thought. It was from Lautrec, and the title read: *Assignment of research assistant.*

Malleus chuckled quietly to himself. *That sounds quite different to 'partner'.* Lautrec enjoyed making himself sound more important than he was.

Malleus could live with an assistant who would rummage through Hein's books for him. She wouldn't get in his way while he was investigating on the front line, and this reassured him greatly.

He looked at the clock.

Before heading back to his hotel, he would make one more visit to Hannes Hein's store. Grenzner had informed him on the journey back from Riga that forensics had not yet begun their second round of checks. There were more important cases in Treva, especially since the assassin had been found and the murder case was officially closed.

Malleus knew that the thefts held no particular interest for the police. The goods had been stashed away in storage and, when possible, packaged up and sent to the other side of the world to whichever collector or shrine had laid claim to them.

But they interested Malleus. Intensely.

There must have been some kind of logic behind the thief's choice to take those nine objects and leave behind so many other priceless artefacts. Even the smallest jade box left behind, missing from the British Museum for years, could have fetched up to two million euros from the right buyer, or even the museum itself.

Why would they leave all these treasures behind?

Malleus left his temporary desk and walked out of the station, climbed into the i8 and programmed the autopilot to drive him to Altona, where he once again entered the little souvenir shop by the back entrance.

Driving through the area earlier that day, he had seen the

flowers, candles and figurines left by locals by the entrance of the little shop. Hein seemed to have been a prestigious member of the community; his other life as a stolen-goods dealer had either done nothing to change that, or had not yet become common knowledge.

Malleus swiped the electronic police lock using the chip in his pass and it opened with a warning buzz. Forced entry would activate the alarm in the nearest police station and simultaneously trigger an electric shock that would incapacitate even a well-built adult.

Malleus went into the shop, turned on the light and wandered around.

His gaze swept back and forth across the rooms without looking for anything in particular, simply aiming to get an impression of the place. He was relying on his subconscious to pick up on anything significant. To help it along, he took out a cigar from the silver case and puffed it while he strolled around the property. Purple band.

At some point he caught himself picking up a nineteenth-century whisky glass that his wife would have liked.

She had loved the stronger varieties, the single malts that they had drunk together by the sea. *And then . . .*

He put down the glass a little too hastily, as if it were in danger of bringing back more painful memories. A torture that surpassed the physical.

His earpiece buzzed gently in his ear.

Malleus accepted the call. 'Bourreau.'

'This is Mischner, Mr Bourreau,' said a woman's voice he did not recognise. 'I'm the assistant to Dr Wunderlich at the Institute of Forensic Medicine in Treva. We're carrying out an autopsy and we've found something that will interest you.'

'And what could that possibly be, Ms Mischner?' He wandered past the shelves of tourist crap, marvelling at how many people had terrible taste and how proudly they displayed it. 'Perhaps a little god inside the body, driving the person like a robot?'

Mischner laughed brightly, genuinely amused. 'No. Something a little less exciting. It's . . . let's say it's an object. It had a label on it with a combination of letters and numbers. When we compared the combination with the investigations database, it led us to your current case.'

'The robbery and murder of Hannes Hein?'

'Exactly.'

Malleus stood up and took a deep puff of his cigar, the tobacco crackling lightly as it burned. 'I'll come over right away. Thanks for calling me.'

'No problem. The address is Butenfeld 34.'

'Great. See you soon.' He hung up and turned around once more to regard the scene that had stubbornly refused him any further leads.

But there was a new clue lying in wait for him on the cold steel table of the forensic institute, one that he had not expected.

* A Ω *

I'm very satisfied.

Really, he's done a good job, and since I've been following him we've been working together just great.

But he still hasn't noticed that there were nine things stolen from Hein. Or has he? I'll have to let him know somehow if he doesn't figure it out himself.

I'm enjoying my new existence.

He belongs to me, only me. I can travel with him for as long as it suits me. And when it no longer suits me . . . well, I'm a very good shot. Nobody can do anything to him.

Nobody except me.

Which is why I'm always there, wherever he is.

* A Ω *

Barely thirty minutes later the i8 pulled up outside the building and Malleus strode through the lobby and long corridors of the institute. Eventually he found the door that led to the white tiled room filled with the smell of disinfectant, raw meat and blood, not dissimilar to an abattoir.

An electric saw screeched and cut through bone as he entered at the other end of the examination room.

A man was working on the skull of a corpse on the table and stood with his back to the door, but his assistant noticed Malleus as he came in and ushered him over. Her apron, protective suit and plastic visor were all sprinkled with red. Such investigations were impossible to carry out without a certain level of gore.

Malleus wondered whether a haruspex – the priests who read omens in entrails – would ever agree to have a forensics team rummage through their own innards after death. As far as he was concerned it was the doctors who were the real clairvoyants: they could learn more truth from the state of somebody's organs, and without having to interpret them in the vague, mystical way the haruspices went about it.

The woman gestured to the man and he switched off the bone saw, laid it to the side and turned to face his visitor. His gloves were smeared with blood, so he didn't offer a handshake. 'Ah, Monsieur Bourreau. I am Wunderlich – though I may as well be called Hades or Hel, given my usual daily activities. Welcome to my underworld,' he said cheerily, his words muffled through the protective mask over his mouth and nose. He pointed at a tray on the table. 'There it is. We cut that out of this young fellow here.'

Malleus gave them both a friendly nod and went over to the table.

In the tray stood an idol, carved from ebony, about the size of a child's fist and, judging by the smell of it, totally clean. Its appearance and design suggested an African deity. That didn't make things any easier.

'May I pick it up?'

'You can even take it *with you*, if you would be so kind as to fill in a little paperwork,' replied Wunderlich, whose only visible body parts were his eyes. 'It belongs to your case after all. My assistant noticed the label. You have her to thank for calling you in.'

'You're certainly helping me out of a dead end here.' Malleus picked up the statuette and observed it closely, turning it and appraising it further. 'It was *inside* him?'

'In the rectum,' explained Wunderlich. 'Wrapped in plastic, that's how it stayed so clean. Seems he was trying to smuggle it into a plane. It's not metallic, so he would have got through the security scanners fine.'

'And yet here he is, lying on your table.' Malleus neared the table to get a view of the body. 'Cause of death is . . .' He fell silent when he saw the head the man had been sawing at as he walked in. 'Ah, I see.'

'Male body, early twenties, Caucasian, etc. Found floating in a dock on the Elbe, near the shipyard. Time of death: less than three days ago, and cause of death you can see: headshot at point-blank range through the right eye. The powder burn and residue are easily visible around the wound and on the face.' Wunderlich folded the two large flaps opened up by the Y-incision back into place across the chest cavity. 'You can see the sheer number of cuts and stab wounds in the chest and lower body, plus the haematoma around the ribs, neck and face,' he reported.

'He was beaten and interrogated,' Malleus surmised, and resisted the urge to stroke his beard.

'It *could* be interpreted that way.' Wunderlich nodded towards his assistant, who helped him to turn the body onto its side. 'Recognise anything?'

Malleus looked along the body's shoulders, back and legs, but saw nothing out of the ordinary.

'He has no tattoos or significant scars,' he said, stating the obvious.

Wunderlich and Mischner returned the body to its former position. 'Excellent! The young man was well groomed, went regularly for pedicures and manicures, and his organs were in great nick. I'd say we must be looking at upper middle class, at least.'

'No identification on him?'

Mischner shook her head. 'His clothes were all from upmarket brands, designer labels worth from about 100 to 2000 euros. That's all we know.'

Malleus didn't yet know how to link this body with the events of the past few days, but was happy to have located the first of the stolen objects.

He looked at the label attached to the surface of the idol. *No doubt about it, this came from Hein's collection.*

He hurriedly filled out the receipt for the artefact and signed it. 'Thanks again for letting me know,' said Malleus, and moved towards the exit. 'May I send you something to take a look at, Ms Mischner?'

'Sure.' She smiled under her mask. 'Do you think we'll be finding more that connects to your case in the future? More bodies?'

Malleus shrugged. 'I don't think so, but I can't rule it out.'

Wunderlich pointed at the bag containing the body's innards. 'I can call a haruspex in if you like.'

Malleus said everything he needed to on that particular subject with a silent wave goodbye.

He had barely left the building when he had to dodge out of the way of a cyclist speeding along the path with no lights. Malleus stumbled against a doorframe and the statuette slipped from his fingers.

Before he could catch it, it landed on the cobbles with a crack – and smashed.

Malleus stared at the pieces, until he realised that they were nowhere near as damaged as he had initially thought.

Predetermined breaking points? He bent down and carefully collected the fragments of the figurine, noticing that each one had markings, notches and holding pins on its interior surface; only one of the pins had broken off. *One puzzle after another.*

His earpiece buzzed quietly in his ear; he had an incoming call.

'Bourreau,' he answered, stowing the fragments in his bag and heading towards the i8. An artefact of unknown origin that could be fully disassembled and put back together again – quite the intellectual challenge. A game of patience, but with high stakes.

'There's been a death. The signs point towards more than just a simple murder,' said the voice of his superior. 'It could fall under your area of expertise.'

'I'm still in Treva,' he explained gruffly. 'The Hein case—'

'The Hein case is closed. Your assistant can take over the loose ends with the missing objects,' Lautrec interrupted. 'This has priority.'

'Where?' Malleus opened the door of the sleek BMW.

'In the Vatican.'

Malleus froze.

The once powerful papal state had suffered greatly under dechristianisation. It was said that the Roman gods only allowed the Vatican to continue existing within the Eternal City as a sort of curiosity.

There were hardly any pictures of the place, which had supposedly fallen into disrepair and decay. And not only in terms of architecture.

Malleus saw this as a smart move: the gods were demonstrating that they were sufficiently assured of their power to allow the representative of the Christian god on Earth to live inside their own city. The Romans were thriving on the obvious decline of the Vatican whilst surrounding it with the construction of new neo-Roman buildings, praising their gods.

So murdering someone within the highest remaining structure of Christianity – regardless of sect or denomination – would be unwise.

Malleus had therefore already ruled out the possibility that the so-called Roman gods had had anything to do with the crime – they had more to gain from the Vatican's slow demise. *Not my department.* 'The Pope?'

'No.' Lautrec cleared his throat. 'His son.'

BOOK 2

Episode 2: The Vatican Riddle

'There will be seen on Earth creatures fighting each other without pause, with great losses and many deaths on either side. Their malice shall know no bounds . . . Once sated with food, they will seek to assuage their desire to inflict death, affliction, torment, terror, and exile on every living thing . . .'

Leonardo da Vinci, *Prophecies*

Italy, Rome, November 2019

Malleus Bourreau ran his thumb and forefinger along the tips of his Fu Manchu moustache and looked thoughtfully out of the plane window.

The Airbus A390 gently curved its path and began to prepare for landing. As the plane tilted, Malleus caught a brief glimpse of the Vatican's last remaining scraps of splendour. St Peter's Basilica appeared then quickly shrouded itself in rainclouds and fog, as if offended by his gaze.

Or ashamed. Malleus hadn't expected his next official Interpol assignment to bring him back to the Eternal City so soon, where the remains of the Papal State lay slowly crumbling, surrounded by Roman prosperity. *Or grieving for what's lost.*

The murder of the pope's son was an unprecedented

occurrence, and the investigation would undoubtedly require the services of a specialist such as himself. The Vatican police were also members of Interpol, so Inspector Bourreau had been an obvious choice. Malleus smirked slightly. *What do you even call the son of God's direct representative on Earth? Is there a special title for that?*

It was clear that the head of the few remaining avowed Catholics believed the murder to be the work of a god. A god, but not *their* god.

The A390 landed as soft as a feather, and proceeded to drive slowly along the winding runways until Malleus and the other two thousand passengers were finally allowed to exit. Many of them had been flying for longer than himself; he had boarded during a layover in Treva, where the aircraft had filled up with passengers from central Europe.

He wheeled his luggage through the terminal into arrivals, avoiding the long security queues thanks to his Interpol pass.

Towering LED boards showed images of various sites in Rome and the surrounding area, recommended by the tourism board as the top places to visit.

The influence of Jupiter and the Pantheon was hard to miss.

Ostia Antica, Tibur, home of Hadrian's Villa, and Praeneste on Mount Ginestro – the famous classical sites appeared on the screens, enchanting in all their renovated glory.

These images were followed by a highly over-produced clip, in which the gods bestowed their blessings on the incoming travellers, and Jupiter encouraged them in a booming baritone to convert and follow him and his godly colleagues.

There followed a series of clips documenting miracles that had been carried out by Jupiter and co., including testimonies from various thankful recipients. Finally a visibly inebriated

Bacchus appeared, advertising the Bacchanalia that took place twice a year. The take-home message was simple: lots of orgies, and lots of wine.

Malleus carried on walking through arrivals, and saw an older-looking man in a black cassock with a small white embroidered crucifix on the chest; his blonde hair was partially obscured by a distinctive headpiece, a cross between a beret and a hat. A slim shoulder bag rested on his hip.

He was waiting at the barrier, flanked by two men in dark suits with colourful insignias on the lapels. Swiss guard. Apparently the cleric felt safer with them than the Vatican police.

The trio was largely ignored by the public, save for a few excitable teenagers, who were imitating the rigid posture of the bodyguards, smirking and taking selfies.

Malleus put on his round sunglasses, raised the collar of his military coat around his neck, strode over to the little welcome committee, and tipped his hat respectfully.

'I assume you are waiting for me, gentlemen?' He spoke to them in English.

'Quite right. Welcome, Mr Bourreau,' replied the man in the cassock, his tone friendly yet restrained. 'I am Father Severinus, personal assistant to the Holy Father. I've been asked to bring you directly to the Vatican.' He stepped to the side and gestured with his right hand to the exit. 'We're parked right outside the door.'

Malleus politely declined the guard's offer to carry his luggage and took out his cigar case, selecting a blue Culebra which he had cut and prepared before boarding his flight.

'If you wish to return to your hotel after the meeting, we will arrange for a driver,' explained the cleric.

'Thank you, Father. But I think I'd rather hire a car.'

The walk through the terminal was without incident, though

increasing numbers of arriving tourists were beginning to gawk at the priest and his Swiss guards.

In other countries it was expected that anyone of Christian, Muslim or Jewish faith would conceal their religious affiliations in public: it was a matter of self-preservation.

In Rome, however, public displays of Christianity were largely tolerated, as if the return of the gods in 2012 had changed nothing. This was, of course, partly due to the fact that the city was home to the most significant monument to the Christian faith, which attracted masses of tourists. The walled city was a curiosity, its archaic inhabitants a fascinating leftover from a previous era. As long as the pope continued to draw in the tourists, the Vatican would survive.

As they walked, Malleus removed a splint from his cigar case, held it to his lighter, and then lit his cigar. He paid little attention to smoking regulations. The air surrounding an airport was already full of every carcinogen one could imagine. *As if a little tobacco would make any difference.*

Father Severinus did not make conversation. The bodyguards, too, remained silent and intensely watchful, constantly checking for potential threats from every direction.

Malleus could feel the tension radiating from the three men. The Vatican was encircled by newly empowered religions, religions they had once competed with, tirelessly battled and oppressed for centuries.

Revenge – some gods had already taken theirs, bloody and swift: others had simply left it to their followers. It could happen at any time. Often at the hands of a particularly zealous tourist from a less Christian-friendly area.

They left the terminal and walked towards an impressive black Rolls-Royce Phantom II, its doors decorated with the pope's coat of arms. At this point things became really uncomfortable.

A pack of audacious tourists, speaking loudly in Russian and clad in an indecent number of backpacks, cameras and khaki shorts, had discovered the Rolls and were gathered around it snapping photographs. Many of them were posing, making obscene gestures towards the vehicle or holding their own religious amulets up to the camera, making it clear who had come out on top in the contest of the gods.

Malleus puffed calmly on his cigar, recognizing the symbols for the east Slavic gods Stribog and Hors on the amulets. *Gods of the wind and the winter sun.*

Of course the crowd was even more excited when they saw the car's passengers walking towards them.

The rabble drew closer, laughing and jeering as they encircled Malleus and his hosts. Insults and obscenities were yelled. More photos were taken.

Malleus found it childish, but he knew that it was impossible to reason with these people. *Or with most people, for that matter*, he thought with a smile.

The trunk of the Phantom II opened automatically and Malleus heaved his hand luggage and small suitcase inside. The first bodyguard slipped into the driver's seat, while the other held open the door for the priest.

At that exact moment, the cleric was hit in the neck by a half-eaten hamburger.

Ketchup and mustard sprayed through the air, staining his cassock with wet flecks of dark red and yellow. The meat fell apart on impact, spilling down his collar and onto the ground.

Malleus closed the trunk and regarded the crowd, noticing one woman at the rear as she drew back her arm to throw a large milkshake.

The cup flew over the heads of the tourists and landed with a heavy splattering sound in the centre of the priest's shoulders, its contents slopping down his back in a cascade of sickly yellow.

Throughout this onslaught, the priest remained calm, not even turning to face his assailants as they filmed their attacks and yelled their abuse. He simply climbed into the car, slow and dignified, as if the banana-flavoured liquid dripping down his body were a holy anointment.

The bodyguard closed the door after his charge, and then signalled through the window for Malleus to enter the Rolls-Royce through the other passenger door. Apparently they had been instructed only to step in when there was a danger of serious physical harm.

One of the hecklers identified Malleus as the last remaining target outside the vehicle, and grabbed a box of chips out of his companion's hand, about to throw them at the detective.

'I'll explain this very clearly,' Malleus interjected in fluent, accent-free Russian, his tone calm and friendly. 'This coat is worth more than your life.'

The man lowered the box, evidently taken aback. 'Are you threatening me, asshole?'

'Not at all. Just an observation.' He turned and climbed into the Phantom II. 'Good day, sir. Say hello to Stribog and Hors, if you happen to see them.'

The door closed, and no further edible missiles followed. His comment had clearly had the intended effect.

Malleus could not help but inhale the scent of banana that now permeated the car's interior. The white leather upholstery was covered with plastic sheeting. He poked at the thin, rustling plastic. 'Does that happen a lot, Father?'

'Constantly.' Severinus smiled weakly. 'Mostly drinks,

sometimes food. I'm thankful to the Lord when it's nothing too hot or icy.'

'Good sense of humour. I suppose you need one as a Christian.' Malleus gave an appreciative nod and looked out of the window, still smoking his Culebra.

'Even more so as an atheist, I think.'

'Touché. But I try only to make fun of ignorance.'

The burgeoning neo-classical architecture of Rome loomed to the left and right of the street. Temples were undergoing renovation, dazzling new builds were rising up all over the city, and every night the Colosseum was illuminated by great spotlights and sacrificial fires.

Volunteers were once again permitted to fight in the arena, just as they had centuries ago, though now they fought to honour the gods rather than the emperor. The popularity of these contests had led to so many people volunteering as *morituri* that there were extensive waiting lists. Survivors received a cash prize. Victors of multiple contests could become very wealthy, and were considered to be 'darlings of the gods'.

There were efforts within the Italian government to reinstate the death penalty, in conjunction with the gladiatorial games. This move would also ensure that the supply of morituri remained constant, should there be a decline in volunteers.

'You turn the other cheek, Father.' Malleus pointed with his crooked cigar at the guards, the glowing tip drawing an orange line in the air. 'But these two can hit back on your behalf?'

Severinus laughed quietly. 'Sorry to disappoint you, but I don't wish to engage in a theological debate.' His bodyguard handed him a handkerchief, and he wiped the remains of the hamburger from his neck. 'Not with you, Mr Bourreau. You believe in nothing. Absolutely nothing. And so you understand nothing.'

'Oh, that's where you're wrong, Father.' He blew a puff of smoke against the roof of the car, where it whirled into fleeting images of faces. 'I believe in myself.'

'And that belief isolates you from all others.'

'Well it's served me well this far. I know I can be relied on.' Malleus fixed his eyes, disguised by blue contact lenses, on the priest. The Rolls drove on through Rome, purring gently. The suspension smoothed out every tiny bump in the road, creating an almost hovering sensation. 'Gods can't be relied on, real or imaginary. People put all their trust in them, offer up their livelihoods, even their countries, and still their gods disappoint them.' *Even if they beg on their hands and knees.* Unpleasant images from the past began to bubble to the surface of his consciousness. From the war. From his other life, when he still had a family.

'The Lord never disappoints me.'

'I know the New Testament God was never that interested in getting actively involved in things. That's why you and the handful of Christians left on the planet are having to show a little extra patience at the moment.' Malleus maintained an amicable tone, internally shooing away the troubling memories. '*God helps those who help themselves* – isn't that a Christian proverb?'

'Just a saying. And not something you'd hear from a true believer.' Severinus remained unfazed.

Malleus chuckled softly. 'So you did wish to engage, Father.'

'What?'

'In a theological debate.' He rolled down the window and flicked his cigar butt onto the street. 'But let's talk about the case. That's more useful for both of us.'

'You mean to say that talking about God is a waste of time?'

Malleus took off his sunglasses and hat, revealing his black hair, cut short on the neck and longer on top. He placed his glasses inside the hat, and the hat on his lap. 'Let's just stick to the earthly plane for a while, specifically the parts where blood's been spilled.' He pulled out his PDA to record the conversation.

'Very well.' Severinus folded the handkerchief. 'The Holy Father found the body of his son yesterday, at around one in the morning, in the Pinacoteca Vaticana, room nine, where the da Vincis are kept.'

'How many people in the Vatican know that he's the son of the pope, Father?' Malleus interrupted.

'Officially: half a dozen. Unofficially' – Severinus looked contrite for a moment – 'I couldn't say. Word travels fast in the Vatican. He was known as Brother Theodorus.'

Theodorus – gift from God. Malleus looked at the two Swiss guardsmen, who were currently separated from their conversation by bulletproof glass, but were doubtless privy to their fair share of gossip during their patrols through the halls of the Vatican. 'Was the body moved?'

'No. We closed off room nine. The Holy Father immediately instructed the Vatican police to get in touch with Interpol and request your assistance.'

'Why me?'

'There was something written in blood on the body, on his forehead: the number 666.'

'Seriously? The number of the beast?' Malleus repressed a laugh. 'A bit dramatic for my taste. Written in *his* blood?'

'No, he was strangled.' Severinus took some photos from his shoulder bag. 'I insisted on photographing the scene immediately, in case anything should change while we awaited your arrival, Mr Bourreau.'

'Good thinking.' Malleus took the photos.

The first was a close-up. The man's throat was covered with

marks far larger than the average human hand. But more strikingly, the marks were red, the skin blistered in some areas, in others black or completely removed, revealing the raw flesh underneath.

'Burns?'

'Yes. It seems that he was strangled by Satan himself.'

Malleus had to grin at that, he couldn't help it. 'Meaning the Christian devil has manifested, but God hasn't?'

'Our Lord is everywhere,' responded the priest graciously. 'He is testing us as he tested Job. The most steadfast amongst us will prove ourselves and be an example to those who are still forced to hide and pray in secret.'

Sure. Malleus examined the photos in silence.

The young, brown-haired man in the pictures wore a black cassock with the sleeves rolled up, as if he had been about to pick up something heavy just before his death.

Next to his body stood a desk, upon which an assortment of brushes, small blades, magnifying glasses and spray bottles were arranged. The painting on the easel, situated just behind the corpse, seemed to be in poor condition. The oils were partly dissolved, partly scratched off, and about a third of the canvas appeared to be blank white space.

'Is that an incomplete work by da Vinci?' asked Malleus, showing the photo in question to Severinus.

'I don't know. Brother Theodorus was our expert in painting restoration. He worked on a lot of different pictures, in most of the rooms of the Pinacoteca.'

'I'll need a full list of them,' Malleus replied.

The priest looked at him in confusion. 'What relation does that have to the murder?'

He smiled softly. 'You never can tell. It could simply be a trivial murder, nothing to do with Satan or any other god for that matter. Human weaknesses and emotions are the most common motive for any crime. Greed. Money, power, recognition, property. And love. Sorry, *carnal desire*.' Malleus looked directly into Severinus' eyes. 'Did Theodorus have any lovers?'

Severinus let out an irritated sigh. 'Ah. That stubborn old cliché. All priests are gay and spend all their time—'

'*I* didn't say a word about homosexual priests,' Malleus interrupted kindly. 'There are men and women living in the Vatican. He would have had plenty of choice. And outside the Vatican, for that matter.' He ran his thumb and forefinger over his beard. 'In any case, Father, I'm heartily indifferent to the victim's sexual preferences. You may have interpreted it as an attack, but my question was a neutral one.'

The priest flushed red. 'Forgive my outburst,' he apologised. 'But . . .'

'So did he or not?'

'I don't know.'

'Is the victim's mother still alive?'

Severinus swallowed. 'I would prefer if you led your investigation in a different direction, Mr Bourreau. And I would certainly advise you not to mention that subject to the Holy Father, should you meet him.'

'So Theodorus was seriously supposed to be a gift from God?' Malleus was struck by a thought: there had never been any scientific test to establish the pope's paternity.

'Let's call him a child of forbidden love.' Severinus' mouth grew thin. 'The mother does not live in the Vatican.'

'But it's one hundred per cent certain that the Holy Father . . .?'

'In his estimation: yes.' The priest cleared his throat. 'As I said: you will *not* be continuing your investigation in this direction.'

Malleus' brain was already hatching various theories on the

origins of Brother Theodorus, who was probably just the child of an affair, a child who was lucky enough to be palmed off to the Vatican to keep it out of the way.

Or it could be a secret adoption. Was the pope even allowed to adopt children?

Either way, it meant a scandal if people found out the truth.

The modern popes were far less renowned for stories of their opulent lifestyles and numerous mistresses than their historical predecessors.

Such a scandal would have the greatest effect on the many Catholics spread across the globe for whom the Holy Father was their final representative on Earth. Aside from the pope, there were no parishes, no priests or bishops, no structures left.

It would shake the church to its foundations. Malleus suspected a political motive lay behind the murder of the pope's son, and he thought it entirely possible that one of the new gods could be responsible. *We'll see.*

But he was ruling out the devil.

Satan, Lucifer, whoever, hadn't shown himself in 2012 or the years since, and Malleus decided it was unlikely that he'd decided to make an exception now.

* Α Ω *

Rome.

Again.

But I'm here, I'm following him and keeping watch.

What? Is he serious? He's going to the Vatican, a refuge for the desperate and abandoned, all sitting around assuring each other that their God is real and that He's listening to them.

Actually it's just the same as it was centuries before. Only this time the other religions have a clear advantage.

I read somewhere that the pope compared the appearance of the gods in 2012 with the Flood: they were sent to cleanse the earth, to flush out everything un-Christian, and they'll disappear again when the Last Judgement comes.

Doesn't really fit though. Desperate.

But what else is the old guy supposed to do?

It's not like he can perform miracles. The others definitely have the upper hand on that one. The Christians in their churches can't even turn water into wine. The other gods could do it in their sleep.

Hard times for Christians.

I heard somewhere that Mecca still exists, and they've left the Kaaba standing. They let the Christians have their holy city, so they didn't want to take it from the handful of Muslims left in the world either. These new/old gods can actually be pretty merciful.

But the Black Stone is gone, I think.

It was always said to be the centre of conflict, that stone, even amongst the companions of the prophet Muhammad. Because people were worshipping a thing, an object.

Nobody knows where it is now. Some ancient cult will probably have claimed it back as their own. Back to the roots, Stone Age and so on.

He drives off, and I take the next taxi. Of course they're headed to the Vatican. Where else would they be going in a car like that?

I've been in places where they used cars as target practice if they displayed a Christian symbol. Stick a Christian fish on the back windscreen and you were guaranteed to see guns within seconds, big ones. Suicides used to just stick a crucifix on their forehead and walk outside into the street.

Three seconds and they were gone.

I wonder who's died.

It's fucking perfect irony, really: the institution which formerly trained its own exorcists is now forced to call in an atheist to clear up a case!

Murder. Guaranteed.

The pope?

That would be the icing on the cake.

I guess I'll find out soon.

I'll just keep following him.

* A Ω *

Malleus knelt down next to the young man's body in room nine of the Vatican Pinacoteca. This was one of the smaller rooms in the art gallery, with paintings from the fifteenth and sixteenth centuries including da Vinci's *St Jerome*, and others by Bellini, de' Conti and Caravaggio.

According to Father Severinus, the victim had just turned twenty-one. Surrounded by such sumptuous artworks, the corpse looked oddly plastic. He seemed almost to have fallen out of the white space of the partially restored painting behind him, only to be suffocated by reality.

Malleus examined the finger marks on the man's smooth shaven neck, holding his hands above the outlines without touching the skin.

Whoever had strangled Brother Theodorus must have been extremely tall, judging by average human proportions.

The burns formed a near perfect outline of the perpetrator's fingers round the throat: blisters, charred patches and raw chunks of tissue, the seared skin torn away when the attacker finally loosened their grip.

'We need forensics.' Malleus was struck by the echo of his own voice. The small yet empty room gave his words space to reverberate, accentuating them as it accentuated the paintings it housed.

He noticed sharp wounds in the neck, inflicted by fingernails digging into the skin. The victim's eyes were wide open; the glassy pupils were empty and lifeless. His facial expression was not one of exceptional horror or fear, though it was contorted by his final struggle for breath. Soul-wrenching terror, such as one would expect to see in a face that had locked eyes with Satan, was certainly not evident. On his forehead was the number 666, and judging by the colour at least, it seemed to be written in blood.

'The Vatican doesn't have its own police department,' answered Severinus. 'And the Holy Father fears that our state colleagues may tend towards indiscretion, Mr Bourreau.'

'I understand. But we can't solve this without forensic assistance. I could contact Interpol . . .'

The priest shook his head. 'If necessary, we should consult with one of our own doctors. But I don't think he'll be of much use to you.'

'Oh, I'm sure he could clear up a few things. A time of death would be helpful, for a start. Then he can run some blood analysis, both the victim's and the blood on the forehead,' Malleus suggested. 'And if he would be so kind as to conduct an autopsy, he could at least give us a rough idea of any further injuries or anomalies.'

'I'll ask the Holy Father for his permission.'

'It would be in his best interest.' The special legal systems of the Vatican were not always to its advantage, Malleus noted. He detected an artificially pleasant scent on the body. The victim had worn perfume, and – aside from the initial signs of decay – looked exceptionally well-groomed. His dark hair was perfectly sculpted and smelled faintly of hairspray.

But there's another smell too. Malleus took off his hat, sniffing the air as he lowered his face towards the scrawled numbers on the victim's forehead.

No doubt about it: nuances of iron, oil and rust emanated from the smeared blood. 'Would you please turn off the smoke alarms, Father?' He stood up and took out a Culebra with a green band. He went through his ritual: light the splint with his lighter, light the cigar with the splint.

Severinus took a tablet computer from his shoulder bag and made a few tapping gestures on the screen. He looked experienced. 'Done, Mr Bourreau. And congratulations: you're the first person in over eighty years to be permitted to smoke in the Pinacoteca Vaticana.'

'I'm truly honoured.' Malleus gave the priest a dashing smile. With his hat in his hand, he stepped closer to the half-restored painting. 'What can you tell me about *this*?'

'You have nothing to say about Theodorus' death?' responded Severinus in disbelief.

Malleus took a few quick puffs on his cigar and blew the smoke directly upwards into the dangling chandelier. 'He was strangled.'

'Anything else?' the priest uttered, his irritation evident.

'*Apparently* strangled. Hence my request for an autopsy and blood analysis. Other than that all I can do now is conduct a closer examination of the crime scene.' He gestured with the glowing end of his cigar towards the painting, the smoke rising into a curling question mark. 'This painting could be the reason for the young man's death.' He studied the desk with its containers, brushes and tools, lamps and magnifying glasses. 'To rule that out, I need more information. Father, if you would be so kind as to explain exactly what I am looking at here.' He turned to the painting, took a puff on his cigar and ran his thumb and forefinger over the ends of his moustache.

Severinus made a swiping gesture on his tablet. 'I've got a list here of the projects Brother Theodorus was working on.' He compared the images on his display with the shabby work on the easel. 'This must be the *Madonna of the Yarnwinder*. There are two copies of it, but this one is the original. Painted by da Vinci himself.'

Malleus recognised by the pride in the man's voice that he had more to say on the subject. 'Any further details, Father?'

'Overall the Pinacoteca is in possession of fifteen original paintings attributed to the *maestro*, either partly or wholly painted by him. Most of them are oil on wood.' Severinus pointed towards the tattered work before them, and held up the tablet for comparison, which displayed a copy of the work. 'The art world had generally accepted that the original had been lost, but we tracked it down and saved it.'

'What makes you so sure?'

'The picture itself. This quote from Pietro da Novellara describes the work while it was still being painted: "*A Madonna, seated as if at work with her spindle, while the Child, with His foot on the basket of spindles, has taken up the winder, and looks attentively at the four spokes in the shape of a cross. As if yearning for the cross, He laughs and holds it so tight that the Mother cannot take it from Him.* The painting was commissioned in 1501 by Florimond Robertet, Secretary of State to Ludwig XII.' Severinus pointed at the work. 'All of those details are evident in this work, even despite the severe damage. The copies all differ greatly from da Novellara's description. And we have additionally analysed the paints used, and verified da Vinci's signature.'

'So the work is presumably of great value.'

'The current market value for this piece, based on the *Mona Lisa*, would be just under a billion Euros, even in this condition.' Severinus seemed entirely unfazed by the outrageous figure. 'If Brother Theodorus had finished his restoration, well . . .'

'If nobody knows it's here, it's presumably also uninsured.' Malleus found it slightly perverse that so much money could be attached to a piece of painted wood from the sixteenth century. 'But given that it's still here, we can assume that the murderer wasn't too interested in the *Madonna of the . . .*' He looked searchingly at the priest.

'*Madonna of the Yarnwinder.*'

'Right.' Malleus puffed pensively on his cigar, enveloping himself in a cloud of tobacco smoke. 'A billion. Simply left on the easel, so he could kill a priest, write 666 on his head and vanish.'

'A particularly *significant* priest,' Severinus felt compelled to emphasise.

'I intend for the moment, Father, to disregard the *significance* of the victim's identity.' Malleus waved his Culebra vaguely as he spoke, the glowing end painting lines that hung in the air for a heartbeat, underlining his words. 'If I were planning to attack my arch nemesis by murdering his son – would I just leave this painting behind?'

'I don't know, Mr Bourreau, would you?'

Malleus laughed softly. 'No.' He surveyed the ceiling. 'No cameras?'

'The system's been broken for months. When we open it to tourists we have two guards in the room at all times.'

It would have been easy. 'Back to your question.' Malleus pursed his lips. 'If *I* were the murderer, I would have taken the Brother Theodorus's body with me to St Peter's Basilica, stripped him naked, covered him in the number 666 and strung him up on the front of the building where the spotlights hit it, so that all of Rome could see my message: Look! Even the devil is more powerful than the Christian god! Then I'd plaster the city with posters telling everyone that the pope was the monk's biological father. And obviously broadcast it on all the TV channels and every media outlet you can think of.'

'That would be . . . effective.' Severinus paled at the thought.

'And I'm not even the devil. He would do even worse. He's far more imaginative than I am, if I've heard correctly.' Malleus pointed towards the body. 'But he didn't do any of that. Theodorus is just lying here strangled, almost like it was an afterthought.' He lifted his head and looked round at the rest of the paintings in room nine. 'Have you checked to see if anything has been taken from the room? Or replaced?'

Severinus swallowed. 'No.'

'Because you've been so concentrated on the murder.' Malleus took a long drag on his Culebra, the crackling of the burning tobacco producing a faint echo in the sparse room.

He exhaled slowly and released the smoke a little at a time, forming curls with his lips. A theory took shape in his mind. 'Brother Theodorus was probably simply in the wrong place at the wrong time – *not* the perpetrator's primary target. We'll have to see what the autopsy tells us.'

Severinus inhaled sharply, even this small sound creating an echo in the hollow chamber. 'I'll go and inform the doctor. Then I'll have to give a brief report to the Holy Father, and after that perhaps we can take an inventory together, if you have nothing against that, Mr Bourreau?'

'Not at all.' Malleus put his cigar in the right corner of his mouth. 'In the meantime I'll stay here and take a look around.'

'Please feel free to call me if you need anything or if you have any difficulty finding your way out of the building. Since the new building works were completed it's rather a labyrinth in here.' The priest gave a parting nod and left the room.

Malleus wandered along the row of paintings, inspecting

the ornate frames, the floor in front of each picture, the wall brackets. He searched for any aspect that could have been tampered with.

Despite his best efforts, even using his PDA to magnify the smallest details, he could find no evidence of alterations to the works or the room itself. Perhaps he would have better results with the help of Severinus, who was presumably far more familiar with the pieces.

Brother Theodorus would have been able to point out any irregularities. He glanced over his shoulder towards the body. But the place where the body had lain was empty – Theodorus had vanished.

* A Ω *

Maybe there's a good reason I've never set a foot in the Vatican.

And now because of him, I'm going there anyway. Because I'm still following him.

People are always going on about it, saying how run-down it looks now. Dilapidated. Fucked, basically.

So I thought I'd be creeping around in a mixture of refugee camps and makeshift hospitals for geriatric Catholics, full of disease and the stink of decay. I was scared I'd catch something.

But it actually looks quite impressive, even if the cleaners could maybe put a bit more effort in.

The Vatican state, though, is bursting at its seams. Refuge. Sanctuary. Like people crowding into a bunker, sheltering from the incessant religious attacks raining down like bullets and bombs.

They've housed people in every place they could find in the Vatican's fractional square mileage, in every imaginable house. Except of course for a few exhibition rooms, like the Pinacoteca or the museums. They don't want to disturb the art. Or in the Sistine Chapel. Though it's not like they're going to need it for a papal conclave anytime soon.

In the gardens they've set up tents, big and small, some for dozens of people, some for hundreds. The holy lawns are taking quite a stomping. Sculpted fountains appear here and there, looking rather out of place amongst the canvas roofs.

I bet the few surviving cardinals didn't see their last few years on this earth ending up this way. In poverty. Sleeping in camp beds, amongst their flock, giving solace and . . . well. Whatever else you can give. Futile optimism. Just like in the war, even when the bombers are flying over for the hundredth time.

I find it uncharacteristically easy to move through the masses of people. They even greet me as if I were one of them.

The Swiss guards and police officers are visible in most areas, but in the hopelessly overcrowded halls, streets, corridors and gardens, it's impossible to operate consistent checkpoints. And the pope himself did decree that the gates should never be closed. Any believer should be allowed to enter and claim sanctuary.

As if there were no such thing as assassins, or drunken idiots who want to kill people in the name of their god.

I climb up the outer façade of the Pinacoteca, as the bug I planted in his clothes informs me that they're in room nine. The climbing is pretty easy, the many edges and ornamental details make it a fairly simple task. I've climbed higher than this before, to get a good view of my victims.

There they are. He and the priest are talking, speculating.

Clear finger imprints on the corpse's neck. Large, fiery.

But not Satan. Definitely not. Beelzebub, the devil, the prince of hell, whatever you want to call him – he couldn't get in there if he wanted to. It's holy ground, and there are some rules he has to stick to.

So we can assume it was a human, at least.

The priest walks off.

He stays, wanders around, examines things – and doesn't notice that he has company. Wow, not bad! Quick and silent, I only see the tail for a second. And just like that the body's gone.

Nice job.

He notices it after a couple of seconds: he leaves room nine. I can finally venture inside . . .

I climb along the edge of the building until I find an open window and swing myself inside; my APB comes out immediately, silencer screwed on as soon as I hit the floor.

Although – I'm not sure what my bullets can do against the thing I just saw, the thing now rushing through the rooms of the Pinacoteca dragging a corpse behind it like a massive ripped-up shopping bag full of innards.

But bullets will have to do.

Because wherever he goes, I will follow – sounds almost biblical.

Well – when in Rome . . .

* Α Ω *

Malleus had pulled out his Apache Derringer and unfolded the 9mm pistol. He didn't plan on getting into hand-to-hand combat with a killer whose hands caused third-degree burns.

The disappearance of the body had caught him totally off guard.

Whoever had taken it had acted in a split second, but the soft dragging sound was easy to distinguish in the deathly silent building. It could only be coming from the body.

Malleus had already slipped off his shoes, and began to follow the sound.

The lights in the other rooms had been switched off; his surroundings were illuminated solely by the small amount of daylight spilling in from outside.

The unknown intruder who was dragging away the remains of

Brother Theodorus seemed to know their way around. Not once did they collide with anything or falter and lose their orientation.

Malleus couldn't help thinking while he pursued the intruder, searching for an explanation.

Why would someone steal a murder victim? To hide any traces that might be found on the body? Or was someone planning to desecrate the body more publicly?

The dragging stopped abruptly.

Malleus immediately stopped running, crouched down, and strained his ears, listening for any sound.

The dark didn't frighten him; he had learned to value it during the Great Change. As long as no frantic, flashing lights were involved, he was fine.

He noticed a quiet ticking, like the running of a clock or the purring of a mechanism full of tiny cogs. Malleus became aware of the nuances of oil and rust that he had previously smelled on the corpse.

The intruder was lurking somewhere in the half-darkness too.

'You won't be able to take the body out of the Vatican,' he called, changing his position in the room immediately afterwards to evade attack. 'Leave the priest here.'

Malleus heard a loud tearing sound in response: the ripping of material.

The cassock. 'Leave the body in peace,' he called again and crept towards the source of the sound.

A humanoid figure was crouched over the body of Brother Theodorus. The figure wore no clothing, and in the darkness seemed to have no sexually defining characteristics; its raw, dark skin looked almost like slate. Theodorus' robe had been ripped down the middle and spread open. Huge, paw-like hands rummaged through his underclothes, pulling and tearing at them.

He's searching him. Malleus raised the Apache. The distance to his target was about eight metres. That was a guaranteed bullseye for the revolver, despite its small barrel.

However, at this range the impact would be so destructive that there would be very little left of the perpetrator. He wanted at least to identify what kind of being he was dealing with. From this angle it could be many things. Malleus thought perhaps a human who had been severely crippled, or mutated somehow.

'Step away from the body,' commanded Malleus, increasing the pressure on the trigger until he felt some resistance.

The paw-like hands paused, and the creature hopped behind a pillar for cover, dragging the corpse with it.

Well it's definitely not the devil. Malleus stepped out of his cover and pulled the second Apache out of his coat, folding out the revolver as he stepped forwards.

As soon as he saw the figure, still tearing at the unfortunate priest and his undergarments, he shot.

Two rounds, one of lead shot and one a full metal bullet, hit his target, issuing a metallic clattering sound like hail on sheet metal. The crouching shadow let out a roar. A deep red, fiery maw became visible, spitting glowing sparks into the darkness. Every hole left by the projectiles glowed red, as if there were nothing beneath its skin but burning embers.

The speedy, high-pitched whirr of cogs arose from the figure, and a tail whipped into view with a hissing sound.

What the . . .? Malleus jumped backwards and raised his arms to evade the attack. The end of the tail whistled past him and grazed across a pillar, scoring a line in the stone as marble and dust flew through the air.

He pulled the trigger again, firing the second cartridge of lead shot.

His attacker was immediately peppered with more glowing red holes.

The creature had had enough. It thrashed around, dragged off a piece of the brother's cassock and let go of the body.

I need to know what it wants. Malleus took up the chase. He ran past the place where the attacker had previously sat. Through his socks, he felt something sharp against the sole of his foot, and heard the clinking of little pieces falling away from it. He couldn't see it in the dark, but that discovery would have to wait until later.

He reloaded as he reached the newly built entrance hall, illuminated only by emergency lighting. He looked around.

The mysterious intruder was running with a stooped posture, as if it couldn't walk upright, and had almost reached the door. Sparks streamed from the numerous holes in its body like jet trails.

Malleus looked through one of the front windows and saw three people were nearing the entrance from outside, two men and a woman wheeling a gurney. Apparently the doctor had arrived to transport the body for an autopsy.

Malleus saw the accident coming. They were going to crash into the creature, it was inevitable.

As a warning, he shot at the window.

The glass shattered with a crash, and the three people outside stopped in their tracks, ducking and shielding their faces.

The stooping creature had reached the door and torn it open, still holding the shredded cassock in its right hand. It saw the three people standing outside, and froze.

The doctor and his companions began to inch backwards, the woman holding up a crucifix she wore round her neck.

'That is not Satan!' shouted Malleus and ran forwards, raising both Apache Derringers. It was clearly possible to injure the creature, so according to logic it should also be possible to disable it completely.

The doctor yelled something in Italian that sounded like *police* and *guard*, stretched out his arms and pushed his companions away from the entrance as he backed away.

The creature hissed. Sparks danced from the holes in its skin, as if its body contained a blazing furnace stoked by a bellows. The whirring and buzzing of mechanical parts continued.

The misshapen head turned 180 degrees and fixed Malleus with its dark eyes as he ran towards it. Then it turned back round to the doctor, and hunkered down, ready to pounce.

Before it could jump, the creature was hit by another round from the Apache, lead shot and steel bullets tearing through its body in a sharp metallic cacophony.

The whirring changed, became arrhythmic.

Instead of jumping, the creature whirled around to face Malleus, its tail whipping out past the door and across the fronts of the three people outside. As one, they cried out in pain and fell to the ground.

Malleus was out of ammo. With a flick of the wrist he snapped the pistols inwards and folded out the double-edged blades.

Apparently it's hand-to-hand combat after all. The streams of white sparks, billowing behind the raging creature like comet tails, demonstrated exactly how much heat was about to rain down on Malleus.

He had intended to avoid this.

At that moment it occurred to Malleus exactly what kind of creature had killed Brother Theodorus.

Unfortunately it made no sense.

No sense at all.

* A Ω *

From the far side of the hall I look over to the entrance, scurry into the hall and crouch down in a corner to get a better firing angle. The pillar is good cover.

He's got out the knuckle-dusters and knives, as if he's picking a fight with the biggest, meanest arsehole at the bar.

It won't be that easy.

A fight with this monster is going to get hot. Doesn't seem to bother him.

I hug my APB close to the pillar, aim at the creature, which just tore a line across the stomachs of the three newcomers with the sharpened end of its tail. They're lying about on the ground, two priests and a nun. Breathing their last. Bleeding all over the ground.

I switch into fully automatic mode, my APB can handle this. The shoulder rest gives it enough stability for full accuracy.

The beast roars towards him, its arms jamming forwards to grab him. The open hands are glowing white with heat.

I pull the trigger before they get too close together and I have to risk hitting him too. I still need him, he still entertains me. Without him I would never have come across this thing – he keeps me busy at least.

The bullets tear through the creature's torso and I let the APB wander upwards, firing constantly.

They rip through the throat, punch holes through the head. Every bullet leaves a long trail of sparks in its wake; chunks of the creature fall clinking onto the marble floor.

I run out of ammo.

Looks like . . . fragments of metal, cogs of all sizes. Whatever killed the priest, it wasn't human. Doesn't make it any less nasty though.

Within a few seconds I load another magazine, but the beast is already on him.

I hold the APB still, totally still, and hold my breath. The sight is aimed at the two of them, locked in struggle. As soon as I get a clear line of sight, I'll fire.

I have to keep following him.

* Α Ω *

The attacker had almost reached Malleus when its torso was racked by a series of spontaneous eruptions.

Holes peppered the slate-like skin as fragments of iron, metal splinters and shattered cogs flew through the air, enveloped in clouds of glowing hot sparks. The internal damage had finally begun to disable the beast; it was collapsing in on itself.

This slowed the creature sufficiently that Malleus had time to plan his attacks. It still had a head – this would be met with a forceful punch; the other hand would ram a blade into its chest and rip it open.

He dodged the white glowing talons and felt the heat graze past his face; bizarrely his first thought was to protect his Fu Manchu moustache, rather than his skin.

His first punch hit home; the titanium knuckle-duster collided with the beast's cheekbone, snapping its head sharply to the side. The impact made an unmistakable metallic sound, and his fist met a resistance far stronger than human bone.

The mouth of the humanoid creature opened as if to scream, sparks billowing out into the air. But Malleus kept his focus. With his second blow, he shoved the knife through the hard metal torso and pulled it upwards.

The blade managed to shear through the metallic skin for a few centimetres, then broke off completely.

Was that enough? Malleus jumped backwards away from the beast, and stared for two heartbeats at what was left of the

Apache: the blade had not simply snapped off – it had completely melted away.

The creature buckled and fell to its knees, sparks spouting out of the wound in a thick stream and hailing onto the marble floor. The smell of hot iron filled the air as tiny wheels and cogs sputtered out of the creature's body. Racked by spasms, it shuddered to a halt, the whirring slowed to a faltering rattle.

With a final loud *ping* the sounds from inside the creature fell silent.

Slowly, rigidly, it tipped forwards and fell onto the tiles, cracking apart like a broken puppet. More sparks gushed out of the beast, cooling like the remains of a dying firework as gears and sprockets rolled across the ground. The glow from inside the shattered body quickly expired, the heat faded abruptly.

Malleus loaded the Apache and hurried towards the door to check on the doctor and his companions.

They lay sprawled across the steps, split open across their stomachs, their upper and lower bodies sliding apart, innards spilling out. Their blood ran together, forming a lake of wet blackness in the twilight.

There was no helping them now. Malleus turned quickly back to the defeated creature, pocketing the Apache Derringer.

The creature was still holding onto the ragged strip of the late brother's cassock. Malleus prised it from its claws and felt it curiously.

He noticed a light rustling.

There's something inside. He unwrapped the crumpled rag, revealing a handkerchief-sized sheet of paper, which looked as if it had been torn out of a very old, unlined notebook. It smelled faintly of paint and chemicals.

Though he could barely make it out in the low light, it looked like a page of ornate handwriting, the letters seemingly mirrored. He guessed the language was Italian.

Why was Brother Theodorus carrying this? The smell pointed to one conclusion – this scrap had been taken out of the destroyed Da Vinci painting.

This also told him something else: the secret notes he held in his hand had been deliberately hidden inside the painting in 1500 by the man himself.

To protect them? To transport them in secret?

Brother Theodorus had probably noticed the papers while he was examining the *Madonna of the Yarnwinder* and removed them.

And it was at that moment that he'd been ambushed.

Malleus looked down at the artificial creature. Clearly the target had not been the man at all, but da Vinci's notes.

Ergo: the mechanical murderer had returned to the scene of the crime because it realised it was missing a page.

'Nothing to do with Satan whatsoever,' murmured Malleus to himself, carefully placing the page in his pocket. *But a god was responsible.*

He bent down and examined the pieces of the creature, finding no batteries or any other energy sources.

He was aware of only one god in the area who was known for creating mechanical servants.

Hephaestus, or Vulcanus as he was known to the Romans. But why?

He took out the page again and tried to make sense of the cryptic handwriting, searching for the meaning of the text.

The mirror writing didn't make it easy, but he nevertheless managed to grasp a vague impression of the Italian words.

Then he saw the word *macchina*, and it dawned on him.

Da Vinci had invented countless machines and devices. These words must belong to some kind of construction manual.

That made sense.

If there was any god who would be particularly interested in da Vinci's inventions, it was the god of fire and forging. According to legend Hephaestus had fashioned two servants for himself out of pure gold. But those ancient robots would have been far less deadly for Brother Theodorus than the spark-filled creature lying in pieces on the tiled floor.

The 666 business was just a distraction, to disguise the real motive for the murder.

Malleus had a feeling he had just pieced together a crucial section of the puzzle.

But he had no proof for any of it.

'Give me what is mine,' breathed a husky voice from the darkness, 'and I'll give you information on the artefacts you seek.'

Malleus looked round. 'I presume,' he responded unperturbed, 'you are Hephaestus?'

Yet again, he was conversing with a god who seemed to have no manners at all. He'd come to expect it, but still.

'Indeed.' An incredibly tall male figure bulging with unbelievable muscles emerged from the shadows into the moonlight. His face was framed with black curls of hair, and he walked with a limp, as described in the legends.

Not the prettiest of faces, thought Malleus, *eyes too small, everything slightly wonky and unappealing.* His clothing on the other hand was a modern redesign of a short toga, with panels of black leather and metal plates decorated with inlays and engraved pictures.

At least he's making the effort to look like the typical images of Hephaestus. But this didn't even come close to convincing Malleus of the being's godliness. He pointed to the destroyed creature, unaffected by Hephaestus' entrance. 'I don't suppose you'd care to fill me in on what happened here? So I can tell the pope why Brother Theodorus had to die?'

'He didn't have to die. My artless servant, created from the sparks of my forge and an intricate mechanical system, seems to have got rather carried away with his assignment, and then tried to cover it up,' Hephaestus said softly, though lacking any genuine sympathy or regret. 'He also managed to take the wrong documents. And then he ran into you. Please pass on my condolences to the pope.'

'He was bringing you da Vinci's secret notes for one of his inventions,' Malleus clarified.

'Indeed, mortal.' Hephaestus nodded. 'Much in this world interests me, as I have been absent for so long. Da Vinci's designs are good. Different. Expandable. I can bring them to fruition in my forge.' His great calloused hand, in which Malleus' fist would easily fit twice, stretched open. 'Give me the notes.'

'Any sympathies you have, you can pass on to the pope yourself. But I'll be sure to let him know who was responsible for the murder of his . . . Brother Theodorus.' Malleus spoke softly, but with great clarity. 'Which artefact are we talking about?' He found it remarkable that a Greek god would be aware of his search for the stolen objects from Treva. Apparently there was more to the artefacts than a back-room business led by the stolen goods dealer Hannes Hein.

'You can pick *one*,' Hephaestus teased. 'Bring me the other two pages, which someone in the Vatican has stolen, and I won't have to let my servants Kratos and Bia loose on the city until they find them.'

'There are more pages?'

'There was a whole notebook, which I consider to be my property.' Hephaestus gave Malleus an imperious look. 'Three pages are missing. I'm offering you a deal. Does all of this' – he gestured around them – 'mean nothing to you? Could you stand by and watch while it was destroyed? The art, the buildings, the people? They would all die. For the sake of two sheets of paper.'

Malleus cursed internally.

He couldn't remember exactly what form of havoc Bia and Kratos were capable of wreaking on the city, but he knew the pope wouldn't like it. Aside from the death of the innocent inhabitants of the Vatican, it could lead to another wave of persecution affecting Christians across the globe – all triggered by Hephaestus.

Malleus hated being pinned down.

'You get three pages, you tell me about an artefact,' he confirmed.

'Yes.'

'Can I trust you?'

'I give you the word of a god, mortal!' he thundered.

Which means precisely nothing to an atheist, even if he's looking right at one of you, Malleus thought to himself. *You're either a figment of my imagination, a product of government suggestion, or an alien. None of which are particularly trustworthy.* He smirked. 'So you'll tell me where I can find the artefact?'

'Any information you wish to have.' Hephaestus beckoned with his massive, calloused hands. 'The page. As an advance payment.'

'Some information. As an advance payment,' he replied in a friendly tone.

The god gave a rumbling laugh, small sparks shooting from his mouth and dancing upwards towards the ceiling. 'Now I see why the others like you: you're very amusing. Makes a change to see a human who doesn't immediately throw themself to the ground at my feet.' He breathed in. 'One of your artefacts is an extraordinary crown, which holds a secret inside it, invisible from the outside. You will find it in a country not far from your homeland,' he spoke with grandeur.

Malleus handed over the page, placing it on the marble floor in front of him. 'Any information on the thief in the Vatican who robbed the body?'

'The pages must have been stolen from inside the painting without Brother Theodorus' knowledge. The poor man certainly seemed rather clueless when my servant asked him for the pages.' Hephaestus looked over to the open door and the three corpses. 'I regret their deaths also.'

'Why? They weren't your followers.'

'Their deaths were meaningless and unintended. Even if they had no god, they could have had some use in the world.'

Malleus could understand this position from a god's point of view: humans as lesser beings, as means to an end, as playthings or something to keep the gods occupied. 'Are their souls on the way to Hades now or Elysium?' Malleus enquired curiously.

'It's none of my concern.'

Exactly the answer he would have expected from an ancient god. 'I'll start the search then . . .'

'I'll allow you two days,' boomed Hephaestus. 'Then I'll send in Kratos and Bia.' He rapped his knuckles against a pillar, which immediately cracked in several places. 'Nothing will remain standing. Few will survive. You should hurry.' He took a step backwards, and a whirl of sparks shot out of the shadows, carrying the page upwards and sweeping it out of the shattered window.

Malleus reached into his coat and took out the cigar case, following his ritual with the lighter, splint and cigar. The band on this Culebra was a sepia colour, and the smoke had a yellowish tinge to it as Malleus exhaled, as if it came not from his lungs, but directly out of an old film.

He adjusted his hat and strode towards the exit, taking a final look at the three bodies outside as he booted up his PDA. He set a 48-hour timer, and made a note to call Father Severinus to update him on the evening's developments.

Two days to track a thief amongst the Vatican's masses was utterly unrealistic.

Malleus hoped for inspiration to strike. Or perhaps an epiphany would better fit his surroundings, he thought with a wry smile. Though he was probably too atheist to qualify for one of those.

Room nine would remain the focus of his investigations. The thief had hopefully left some clues behind. In the room, on the picture, the frame, the tools.

Inspiration, epiphany, flash of genius. He puffed on his cigar and raised his eyes to the clouded sky, obscured by the curls of smoke. *Any one of those would be pretty convenient right now.*

* Α Ω *

Father Severinus stood in the entrance to room nine, his face a study in despair. 'I looked up Kratos and Bia,' he informed the smoking Malleus, who was examining the damaged *Madonna of the Yarnwinder* with a magnifying glass, the embodiment of diligent detective work. He was hoping the thief had left behind a hair or some other trace; his hat was placed precariously on the windowsill.

'The Greeks believe Kratos is the god of power and authority, and together with his sister Bia he bound the hero Prometheus to the mountainside and fought against the Titans.'

'And Bia?' Malleus listened intently. He wore his dark grey

Indo-European shirt; his military coat lay neatly folded in a corner of the room.

'The personification of violence. Both of them are Hephaestus' aides.' Severinus sighed and crossed himself. 'Lord, you are truly testing us.'

'He's in tune with the times,' commented Malleus. 'When he tested Job, everything was at stake. Now the same is true for the Vatican.'

'Except that we're now dependent on the investigative powers of an atheist,' the priest sighed. 'At least Job had his faith.'

'Surely I myself could be interpreted as a test from your god?' replied Malleus with a smile. 'An atheist protecting you from the whims of an Olympian deity. And the whole thing caused by da Vinci's drawings.' Malleus shot Severinus a twinkling smirk. 'Wasn't he thought to be homosexual? That rounds it off rather nicely, don't you think?'

'Lord, your ways are mysterious,' the cleric muttered, crossing himself once again. 'Do you need anything else, Mr Bourreau?'

'No. Except a list of people who knew Brother Theodorus well.'

'You think one of them was the thief?'

'Perhaps. Or there could have been someone orchestrating things, someone in a group of thieves.' Malleus ran his finger along the lower edge of the *Madonna of the Yarnwinder*. 'Someone fallen on hard times who wanted to make a little cash with the help of the master's secret notes? It would be easier than trying to sell such an infamous painting on the black market.' Unfortunately the inspection found nothing, and he stood up straight. 'Can you think of anyone who fits that description, and who would have known about the restoration work?'

'Brother Theodorus had assistants from time to time,' conceded

Severinus. 'Enthusiasts who wanted to see the paintings up close. But most of them are no longer here.'

'Where have they gone?'

'Missionary work, mostly. Long term trips. They travel across the world and establish resistance against the false idols by spreading the Lord's word.'

Or they die as martyrs.

Severinus turned to face the door. 'I'll go and prepare a list, Mr Bourreau. Please call for me if you need anything.'

'Thank you, Father.' Malleus waved the hand holding the cigar as a farewell. 'I don't suppose you have any coffee?'

'Of course.' With another audible sigh, the man left the room, his footsteps fading down the hall.

Malleus had spent the last few hours poring over every inch of the room with a powerful flashlight, and telephoning his boss Lautrec at Interpol, partially to keep him updated on the situation, but also to reassure Severinus, who gave a report of the pope's many doubts and concerns.

Malleus had long been campaigning for a legal system that could hold the gods accountable for their destructive whims and tantrums, but he was basically alone in this mission.

He understood the fundamental problem: only a god could sit in judgement over other gods – who would take on that role? How would justice be measured? How would punishments be meted out? Would the gods merely have to pay a fine?

He paced over to the window, placed his hat on top of his folded coat, and swung open the windows to let in the morning light, the sound of the city and the crisp winter air.

The bells of the cathedral and the churches were no longer in use. The sound was forbidden, just as the muezzins in formerly Islamic areas were forbidden to call to prayer.

Instead, the city was flooded with the clanging of various gongs and bells from the temples of Apollo and Sol Invictus, as their followers greeted the morning sun. A few strains of song could be heard amongst the din, issuing from a distant shrine to Helios.

Together, the various cults created a rich tapestry of religious music, just as the Christian bells of Rome once had, though now the morning chorus was unmistakably dominated by the gods of the new era. That was something that took even an atheist a while to get used to.

Malleus inhaled deeply, stretched and looked out across the Vatican roofs to the dome of the cathedral, as it sat in silence, enduring the ignominy of being surrounded by idolatrous noise.

She would have loved to visit Rome. Yet another place his wife would never see.

She'd had a great interest in architecture, and had even begun to study it, progressing at a great pace despite the arrival of the little one. Her dream: a new kind of skyscraper, entirely self-sufficient. *She would have made it happen.* Malleus took another deep breath, swallowed.

'You ordered a coffee?' an unexpected woman's voice enquired in an Eastern accent.

He turned from the view, took the Culebra out of his mouth. 'I did.'

A young woman stood in the doorway, her long black hair tied up in a bun, emphasising her striking features; a grey bonnet was pinned on top of her hair. The green of her eyes was almost luminescent in the morning light, and the cut of her black habit accentuated her slim figure. In her hands she balanced a tray with a pot of coffee, cups, milk and sugar, and a small selection of dolci.

'What outstanding service. Thank you very much.'

'You're very welcome. If you would like anything to eat, Mr Bourreau, please let me know.' She came closer and placed the tray onto a small table. 'My name is Sister Marina, but here they call me Marinuschka.'

The Eastern European name confirmed what her distinctive accent had already suggested.

'That's very kind of you, Sister.' He guessed she was about twenty, and asked himself silently what had driven her into the arms of the Catholic Church, whose future prospects were not exactly dazzling. A life of poverty and persecution was an odd choice for a young woman.

Malleus poured himself a coffee and added milk and sugar. 'Would you like some, Sister?'

After a short hesitation and an uncertain, fleeting smile, which only made her more endearing, she poured herself a cup.

'Did you know Brother Theodorus?'

Marina shook her head. 'He lived a very private life, the others say. The work on the paintings was his way of serving God.'

'Do you come to the Pinacoteca often?'

She nodded and seemed to pay very close attention to his words. She was probably still in the process of mastering English. 'I love art. Pictures. Everything.'

Malleus sipped at the strong coffee and enjoyed the milky-sweet bitterness as it slipped down his throat. He could feel the hot liquid in his stomach. He hadn't eaten for a long time.

'Father Severinus and I have investigated everything at least twice over,' he began, 'but can you see anything, Sister Marina? Anything different from normal?'

She looked around with wide eyes while blowing softly across the surface of the hot coffee, looking almost childish. Innocent.

She held the cup in both hands, as if warming herself on a cold day.

She walked softly around the room, her habit swinging gently. As she paced, she hummed a melody that sounded more like an Eastern European folk song than a church hymn.

Malleus observed the nun in amusement while he drank and puffed on his Culebra; he was still smoking the sepia banded cigar from earlier.

'That smells good.' She turned to him. 'Do you have another?'

He swallowed his coffee. 'You mean . . .?'

'Yes, your cigar.' Marina beamed, showing her white teeth. 'We don't often come across the finer things round here.'

'And how would a Sister such as yourself know that my cigars are the *finer things*?' Malleus had to prevent himself from laughing in surprise.

'The band.' She leaned her head forwards and gestured with her nose towards the cigar in his hand. 'I've never seen that kind before. They're made especially for you, am I right?'

'Who would have thought? A nun *and* a cigar connoisseur.'

'Don't let my appearance fool you,' she warned quietly and gave him a mysterious look. 'I had a life before this one.' Something intangible glimmered in her green eyes.

For a moment Malleus was reminded of the many people who had lost their minds in the Great Change. It was a common occurrence in the battles against those terrifying new beings, when the gods hunted for human survivors through the trenches and the ruins. The indefinable quality in her gaze hinted at hidden depths of psychic unrest. *Maybe that's why she's in the care of the church.* 'You're twenty years old, at the most.'

'Then imagine, Mr Bourreau, how much I might have experienced already.' Her words slipped coquettishly out of her rounded lips, which were turned up at the corner in an enticing, almost sinful hint of a smile. It was not an expression one would commonly associate with a nun.

Malleus smiled at her. 'I'm sorry, Sister, but I'm not sharing these ones. Should we meet again, which I sincerely hope we don't, as I'm only in these parts when someone has been murdered, I'll bring you some good cigars.'

'Deal,' Marina smiled. 'I could always kill somebody. That would speed things up.' She said it with a smile, but there was a serious note in her voice that left Malleus feeling oddly wary. It fed into his suspicions regarding the case – had she known the brother?

But Marina soon turned to the wrought-iron barrier in front of da Vinci's *St Jerome*. 'The top of the third post from the right,' she said. 'It's lower down than the rest of them.'

Stunned, Malleus followed her gaze.

'You're right,' he exclaimed, electrified. Only someone with an outstanding eye would have noticed that detail; apparently the sister had a gift for investigation.

He set down his coffee on the windowsill, put on his gloves and turned cautiously to the top of the post, gingerly twisting and tugging at it until the cap came off.

Malleus shone the small light from his PDA into the top of the pole.

Inside the metal tube, down at the bottom, the light reflected off something transparent and plastic. He wouldn't be able to reach it with his fingers.

He was about to fetch a spoon from the coffee tray, but Marina stood next to him and passed him a knitting needle.

'That should do it,' she said, peering curiously into the tube.

Where did she get that from? Malleus thought to himself that she had already proved a demonstrably better assistant than

Madame Lagrande, who was sat in Germania researching the stolen artefacts from his previous case. If Hephaestus kept his word, he would soon have at least some progress in that direction. But he wasn't counting on it.

He poked around with the needle until he managed to get hold of the plastic and pulled it carefully upwards.

Wrapped in transparent cling film were two rolled up pieces of paper; the remaining pages of the secret *codici*.

Malleus was naturally curious as to what Hephaestus was planning to build with these designs, but he was also interested to see the stroke of creative genius so important that it warranted such secrecy. *Just how dangerous is this invention?*

'Do you speak Italian, Sister?'

Marina nodded.

Malleus cautiously unwrapped the pages from the cling film and unrolled them slowly, careful to avoid even the slightest tear. 'Could you translate this for me?'

She narrowed her eyes, then opened them wide, then squinted again at the page. 'The handwriting is very, very bad. And . . . it's in mirror writing,' she confirmed. 'Who writes like that?'

'Da Vinci.' Malleus took pleasure in her look of utter disbelief.

'*The* da Vinci?'

'Yes, him.' He couldn't help but enjoy the shock in her bright green eyes. He still hadn't made full sense of her, her mannerisms and behaviour seemed full of contradictions. 'Can you make sense of it, Sister? I can go and fetch a mirror . . .'

'I think I can manage without.' Marina leant forwards over the page, and a black curl of hair loosened itself from her bun and fell around her face. She read:

'. . . this wonder of mechanical artistry continues. I have redesigned the machine and improved upon the initial concept. And all those who believed it was impossible to build a perpetual motion machine will be astounded.

Machines of war will never again stand still, never falter or break down; wars as we know them will come to an end and faster victories will be won.

And as the body is nothing less than a machine itself, it will be a simple task for me to take a mere puppet and transform it into a golem *mechanicus*.

With this golem and the perpetual motion technology I will create an innovative war machine . . .'

Marina stopped. 'That's it.'

Malleus held up the second page.

Rather than handwriting, this page was covered in complicated sketches and countless calculations and formulas, which Marina was unable to translate.

But he knew now why Hephaestus was so keen to get hold of these missing pages: without the calculations and notes, it would be impossible to build the machine.

Golem mechanicus. *War machine.* He took a quick drag on his cigar, drawing in more nicotine to focus his thoughts. In his mind's eye, the apparatus in da Vinci's sketches took form, and evolved into more and more sinister machines, reminiscent of the nightmare technologies of the *Terminator* films.

Why did he want these? A war? Or just because he admired da Vinci? Malleus could imagine that Hephaestus and the famous polymath could have spent weeks and months discussing machines of destruction.

'What are you going to do with them, Mr Bourreau?' asked Marina, taking up her coffee cup again.

Malleus looked into her deep, green eyes, her gaze seemingly filled with hidden messages. Innocence, invitation, curiosity and something else, something lurking. *Like a child with a secret.*

'What am I going to do with it?' He took a deep breath – and dunked the antique pages into her cup of coffee.

The paper instantly sucked up the brown liquid.

Malleus pushed the notes all the way into the milky coffee. He gave them a final stir with his gloved finger.

Marina followed his circling finger with her whole face, like a cat staring at a toy. 'You just destroyed da Vinci's notes, Mr Bourreau.'

'Exactly. And as they were a secret in the first place, nobody will miss them.' He fished the paper out, and laid it on the radiator by the window. 'Now *you*, dear Sister, and Father Severinus, will inform the whole of the Vatican that room nine must be completely cleared, including this iron barrier. To look for clues.'

She grinned. 'And the thief will come back to take the pages out of their hiding place.' Marina threw the rest of her coffee out of the window with great enthusiasm, and placed her cup on the tray. As she walked past, she brushed against him as if by accident, smiled, bowed her head, and disappeared out of the room.

Malleus was genuinely unsettled by the sister. His wife would have been clear on the matter: immature and unstable. *She's better off in the Vatican than outside in the real world.*

His thoughts turned to Severinus, and the possibility that by finding the pages the future of the Vatican had been secured, at least for a while.

Now to close the case all he had to do was catch the thief, hopefully by scrutinising the people close to Brother Theodorus. As soon as the pages dried he would wrap them back up in the cling film and drop the package back into the metal barrier post. The bait.

Thieves in the Vatican. Malleus considered the best place to hide in wait. *It's come to this.*

Though he hadn't yet arrested or questioned his perpetrator, Malleus was filled with a certain satisfaction. *The case was closed, the city was protected from Kratos and Bia, and da Vinci's plans for a devastating war machine had been neutralised.*

The only thing still troubling him was that there was no way to hold Hephaestus legally accountable for the four deaths he had caused. It was merely another example of the capricious nature of the gods, something he had grown to despise.

Malleus assumed that humanity would one day grow tired of their tyranny, and rise up in resistance.

Then the so-called gods would be forced to put something in place, in order to avoid losing their entire following.

On the other hand, perhaps they could simply create new people in their place, less rebellious, better behaved and more obedient – if they had that ability.

There must be a reason why the gods were being so lenient towards their followers, instead of spreading death and destruction.

Who knows if what I'm seeing and experiencing is even real. His thoughts were becoming too complicated even for him. *Who cares. I'll make the best of it as long as I'm on this earth.* He looked around for a vantage point with a good view of the entrance to room nine, puffing away on his cigar. The smoke from the Culebra seemed to spell out a word in the air: *golem.*

* Α Ω *

Well would you look at that.

The little sister's making eyes at him.

She's a cheeky one. Young enough to be his daughter. But I guess if she likes him, who cares?

I'm sitting on the roof of the Casina Pio opposite the Pinacoteca, watching what's going on with the electronic zoom function on my scope.

They've found those last two pages Hephaestus wanted, and he immediately made them unusable.

Clever, fearless. I like that about him.

Let's see how the god reacts when he gets a da Vinci a la Macchiato.

I've decided I'm going to get myself a cassock. It's the best disguise you can wear around all these priests. You immediately blend in, nobody gives you a second look. About the only place in the world where that's the case, of course. Outside it's completely the opposite.

It should be fun, I can get pretty close to him in disguise. And he won't know who I am. That I'm following him.

Oh, what's she doing?

She's in room twelve and . . . wow. She's losing her shit! Kicking the walls, punching them.

Classic tantrum. Either that or she needs an exorcist, poor thing.

Hahaha, oh I get it: SHE was the thief!

And now she's screwed, because . . . no, wait. She was the one who showed him where it was, the hiding place.

Guilty conscience?

Scared the god will come back and destroy her home?

Whatever her motives, I still think it was her.

But anyway, I'm going to find myself a cassock. Might have to make someone disappear to get one. Oh well. I have to stay here, following him.

And if Hephaestus breaks his word or gives him any trouble, he'll be in for a shock: I'll introduce him to a new level of Hades.

* Α Ω *

Malleus had retrieved four micro-cameras with motion sensors from his suitcase.

He placed one opposite the entrance to room nine, one across from the post with the pages in it, one directly above the doorway and another in the hallway leading to the gallery. His PDA flicked between each camera's display at the touch of a button, but if the motion sensors were activated the display automatically switched to the relevant view.

As he checked his reception he noticed the timer he had set earlier: *8h 21min 21sec.*

The message regarding the clearing of the room had been spread across the Vatican, and he just had to hope that the thief wouldn't wait longer than eight hours to come and claim the pages.

It would be satisfying for him to personally apprehend the perpetrator before handing them over to the authorities. He should at least be able to arrest this guy for theft, even if he couldn't put Hephaestus behind bars for what he'd done. At least some mortal justice would be served.

Malleus hid himself away in room seven, sipping more coffee from the flask he had been relying on for the last forty-eight hours. He hadn't slept since before this all started. In order to avoid dozing off in these last crucial hours, he had stirred a couple of pep pills, stimulants, into his drink. From room seven he could see through to room ten, which was the only way to gain access to room nine and the da Vinci notes.

He was itching to light up a Culebra with a tea-coloured band, but the smoke would have alerted any intruder to his presence, so he was forced to wait.

That can be my reward for catching the thief. Malleus checked his PDA screen, put it back in his pocket.

Time passed.

There was no sign of anybody, or anything. The Pinacoteca

lay still, its halls and galleries bathed in the dim glow of the emergency lighting. His contact lenses were sensitive to the red tint, his vision unhindered. There was not a sound to be heard.

Malleus thought about the gods.

Sometimes it took over his mind, wondering what was behind it all.

Super-intelligent aliens?

Mass deception through mind-altering substances pumped into the water and air, carried out by governments trying to keep the population under control?

Or was he just lying helpless in a coma, this entire situation a cruel nightmare, because what could be a worse fate for an atheist than living in a world full of gods?

Sometimes he went through phases of complete indifference. He was trapped in an environment that he couldn't change – so he just had to put up with it.

And very rarely, as he did now, he wished that he could make a deal with the gods, to establish some kind of contract, set out laws that they would obey and punishments that they would submit to.

Of course this was pure fantasy; in principle the gods were untouchable.

Mostly. Malleus thought back to the Great Change, when Christians, Muslims and Jews had been forced to their knees and converted by the old gods and their followers; when he had fought on many different sides, and ultimately only for himself; when he had lost too much – far too much, more than just his faith; when he had gone up against smaller gods and taken them down.

If he thought about it, he had probably just managed to take out some creatures like the servants of the forge god, who appeared godly only to the uninitiated. But against an entity like

Hephaestus, his Apaches or the Cobray would be utterly useless. He may as well spit at him.

His gaze stayed focused, time ticked on, and still no secret visitor arrived.

Malleus opened up his emails.

His boss had been demanding a closing report from him. His assistant Lagrande had some new leads for the missing artefacts from the Treva case.

The news grabbed Malleus' interest, though Rome currently had first priority over his brain power.

Lagrande, the living embodiment of the eighties, was currently gathering information from various sources on a statuette that had been found stuck in the rectum of a young male corpse.

The god it depicted was an African deity, who seemed to be known by various names.

The simplest of these was Oddua or Odùduwà.

Lagrande had quickly found out that this god's origins presented quite the puzzle. He appeared in his creation myth as the first human on earth, taking over the tree of life from the drunken god Obatala, whose foggy state had resulted in the creation of too many misshapen and deformed creatures. In the African tradition Oddua was sometimes worshipped as male, sometimes as female.

Oddua's statuette had not been officially recorded as missing, but there were whispers amongst collectors, some of whom had put out offers for the piece should it be found. *Extremely generous offers.*

Nothing new had been found regarding the body of the young man who had been trying to smuggle the statuette.

Nevertheless, Malleus was pleased to have a few new clues to follow up, should he find himself free of Interpol cases for a spell.

The search for the artefacts had become a personal project for him, generously supported by his assistant, who he knew Interpol would not be paying if Lautrec found out what she was actually researching. He chose to leave his superior under the impression that Lagrande was assisting him on the Vatican murder case.

The camera on the entrance to room nine activated itself; the sensor had picked something up.

A dark figure in a cassock with a separate long pointed hood was approaching the room. It moved through the shadows as much as possible, then passed Malleus' vantage point in the hall. The figure crept towards room nine, stood still and looked around, listened intently, then went cautiously into the room.

The cameras trained on the corner and the iron barrier silently activated.

Malleus watched the figure sneaking purposefully towards the balustrade – towards the second post.

I didn't check that one, he realised, suddenly filled with irritation at his own negligence. He had been so excited to find the pages that he never even considered the possibility of more objects hidden in the posts.

But the shadow, their face entirely obscured by the hood, stepped back from the metal pole, seemed to count on its fingers, and then cursed under its breath. It kneeled down in front of the third post.

Malleus smirked. *I was lucky.* For a second he had imagined a thief for each iron pole sneaking into the room to retrieve whatever prize they had hidden in there.

He stepped away from his hiding place, slipped his right hand into the pocket of his coat and closed his fingers round the knuckle-dusters.

Time to finish this.

Father Severinus, the Vatican police force and some of the Swiss guards were poised in various rooms and outside the windows of the Pinacoteca, ready to appear on Malleus' command and squash any resistance the person might be able to put up. They were also hooked up to the images from the cameras, in case things got out of hand.

Malleus neared the room, following the feed on his PDA as he went. The figure was unscrewing the top of the pole and poking around with a finger, trying to get hold of the plastic package inside.

But despite much visible effort, huffing, puffing and whispered curses, the shadow's efforts were in vain.

Malleus remained standing outside the room for a moment, suspiciously running his fingers over his beard.

The real thief would have known how deep the package was hidden and brought some kind of wire with him to fish it out.

What is going on here?

The figure looked furtively to the left and right, clearly searching for something that would reach down into the tube. They noticed the coffee tray, and quickly cleared it of cups and dolci. With a few powerful smacks against the floor, the intruder smashed the tray into pieces, then selected a long, narrow piece and turned back to the post.

'Should we go in?' Father Severinus came through on Malleus' earpiece.

'That isn't our thief,' he whispered in reply, stepping back into the shadows. 'We need to follow them.'

The figure had fished out the package and stashed it away, without checking its contents. Then it got up and hurried off, out of the room and through the halls of the Pinacoteca.

Malleus followed him in his socks, having removed his shoes earlier to avoid being heard.

They headed through the building and out of the main exit.

Malleus was forced to put on his shoes when they reached the rough ground outside.

The pursuit turned right, in a speedy tour through the tented settlement by the monastery and past the former administration buildings of the now silent Radio Vatican.

'We're on our way,' Severinus informed Malleus.

'Okay, but keep your distance, Father,' Malleus replied. 'We have to wait for the handover. Only then will we know who is really behind this.'

He hurried past tents of all sizes set up in the parks. The square had become overcrowded and he guessed that there were also makeshift beds set up in St Peter's Basilica and the museums.

When they reached the Grotta di Lourdes, the figure turned off into the American Garden.

It was then that Malleus realised they were heading towards the heliport. The thief was obviously letting his messenger bring him the package there so they could make a swift exit by air.

He decided to intervene.

Malleus caught up to the gradually flagging figure before they came into sight of the helipad, and delivered a sharp kick to the back of its legs.

The figure fell and tumbled across the ground. The hood slipped away from its face and revealed the face of a forty-year-old man with sparse, fair hair. The man flailed out in self-defence, but on seeing the barrel of the Apache Derringer pointed at his forehead, he froze.

'I can have you arrested by the Vatican police within seconds,' said Malleus sternly, with a satisfied smile on his face. 'For handling stolen art.'

'It wasn't me,' stammered the man, glancing nervously behind Malleus. Hurried footsteps drew closer; backup was on its way. 'She forced me to do it. If I didn't bring her the pages she was going to do something to my family.'

'Father Bonifacius!' exclaimed Severinus as he reached the pair.

'I had to do it,' the man insisted, his face a picture of despair. 'She was going to make my family's life hell on earth.'

'Who is she?'

'One of the new ones. I don't remember her name.' Bonifacius balled his hands into fists and rubbed his eyes, breathing heavily. 'She really meant it.'

In this state the man would never be able to carry out the handover now, not without the thief noticing something was wrong.

No need for that. Malleus had a better idea.

'Would you please take off your cassock?' he asked, handing his hat, coat and outer shirt to one of the Swiss guards. 'I'll go to the heliport in your place.'

'But . . .' Bonifacius tried to contradict him, but was persuaded by a look from Severinus to follow the command. He stood up and slipped off the pointed hood, followed by the cassock, and passed them to Malleus. 'She told me she'd be waiting in the furthest corner.'

'I promise you' – Malleus looked the hapless messenger in the eyes – 'we will catch her. Nothing will happen to your family.' He threw on the heavy black garment, pulled the hood over his head and held out his hand. 'The package, please, Father Bonifacius?'

He took it out of his undershirt. 'You keep your promises?' he said quietly.

'I do.' Malleus tucked the package away, took both Apaches with him and walked round the corner, past the entrance to the Grotto.

He began to limp a little, bending forwards and holding onto his hip, as if he were injured. That way the woman who was expecting Bonifacius wouldn't notice the slight difference in height.

Malleus hoped against hope that it wouldn't be Marina.

He liked her, but that flash of madness in her green eyes seemed to predestine her for the inexplicable.

'We're holding Father Bonifacius for now,' said Severinus in his earpiece. 'We need him as a witness.'

'Very good,' Malleus agreed quietly as he neared the landing area, which consisted of two landing pads, one circular and the other square with a large H painted on the smooth asphalt. 'After that he's a free man as far as I'm concerned. Interpol is more interested in the real thief.'

He walked diagonally across the grass under a group of trees towards the landing pads, surveying the area from under the hood.

Not on the back wall as the Father had told him, but to his right, stood a woman in a black habit, pressed close against the trunk of a tree. She quickly raised her arm to signal him over. Malleus returned the gesture and made his way over to her.

At each step his relief grew: it wasn't Sister Marina who was waiting for him.

The woman was much older and more heavily built, her face angular with a strong chin. A sizeable wooden cross dangled round her neck over her black nun's garments, and her hair was tucked away under a broad grey hood.

'Over here,' she said. 'Did you find it?'

'Yes,' he replied in a voice tinged with the pain of his fictional injury. 'But I think I've broken something.'

She laughed. 'Be glad that I'm not breaking anything that belongs to your family.' She took two steps towards him, as if she couldn't wait any longer. 'Give me the pages.'

Malleus stood still and pulled back his hood, taking out the Derringer and pointing it at the nun. 'I'm afraid you won't be getting those from me. But I can provide you with a lovely police cell. You could think of it as your cloister. You might even grow to like it.'

Quick as a flash, she pulled a clunky object from inside her habit. 'Like hell I will!'

Malleus aimed and pulled the trigger.

The full-calibre bullet tore through her upper arm, and with a cry she dropped the Beretta semi-automatic. She grabbed instinctively at the wound with her other hand as the blood poured out, then began to stagger and had to steady herself against the tree.

'You bastard,' she spat, the colour rapidly draining from her face.

Severinus and the police piled into the square, some with their weapons trained on the slumping woman.

'I'm Inspector Bourreau from Interpol. May I ask who you are?' Malleus asked the nun politely. 'Sister Clepta might be fitting, but I'm guessing you're not actually a real nun.'

The woman allowed the Vatican police officer to handcuff her as another inspected her wound, staunching the bleeding with a bandage. 'Roberta Mazzini. From Rome.'

Malleus nodded and slipped off Father Bonifacius' cassock. It was becoming decidedly too warm under there. 'As you can see, I do not belong to the Vatican either. Come. We'll have a doctor look over your injury. Tell us when you stole the pages from Brother Theodorus. Things can be a lot easier for you if you cooperate.'

'He was already dead when I went in,' she mumbled in answer as she leant on a policeman's arm. 'I knew what he had found in the picture. He told me one night after sex.'

Father Severinus inhaled sharply.

'He was always talking about it. The pictures, the treasures, his discovery,' she reeled off as she slowly walked away from the heliport.

'You deliberately got close with him?'

'Obviously. I wanted to find out how I could get close to the more expensive paintings, without setting any alarms off,' she admitted frankly. 'When I saw him lying there, I knew all I had to do was take the other papers out of the picture and I'd be able to solve my . . . problems.'

'Your problems?' Malleus picked up on her hesitation.

'Money. I actually wanted to take the *Madonna of the Yarnwinder* out of the frame and take it with me, but I didn't have time and then this ancient-looking night guard appeared.'

Malleus laughed. 'That was the pope, coming to check on his . . . painting.'

The woman gritted her teeth against the pain of her arm wound.

'Then you threatened Father Bonifacius to make him fetch your prize.' Malleus looked at the Beretta, currently in the gloved hand of a police officer.

She nodded. 'If he'd have been caught, I could still have stolen the picture later. Or so I thought.'

Malleus slowed his pace, then stood still. 'Why the landing pad?'

Mazzini looked at him, alarmed. 'I don't understand your question,' she replied unconvincingly.

'Please don't insult me by pretending to be stupid. Why did you meet with the Father at the heliport, Signora Mazzini?' he repeated the question more clearly.

She bit her lip.

'Father Severinus, send out two cars. Quickly. Tell the police to search the area surrounding the external walls. I guarantee you there's somebody waiting there for Signora Mazzini to throw the pages over the wall. The heliport wasn't the end of her mission.' Malleus took his hat, shirt and coat, slipped them on and ran back to the landing pads. 'I'll see if I can spot anything from here.'

Severinus gave the orders over the radio, and the officers immediately moved into action.

Malleus was convinced that Mazzini hadn't been snooping around the Vatican on her own. Further interrogation would be carried out by his colleagues in the Italian police, but he guessed that there was probably a whole band of art thieves operating within the walls of the holy city.

That explained why Mazzini was able to threaten the poor Father Bonifacius and his family, and why she was carrying round a Beretta. Others in the gang would have been working on disabling the alarm systems, and others still would have been observing the routines of the police and the Swiss guard.

The young Brother Theodorus had fallen for the charms of the Signora, who had probably won him over in no time with her body and sexual experience. She had wrapped him round her finger and in doing so discovered a new way to earn some fast cash, by selling the *codici* before the paintings even came into the plan.

Case almost closed. Malleus decided to save his celebratory Culebra until later.

He reached the wall and saw a stepladder leading to one of the lights that illuminated the helipad at night.

He quickly climbed it and found himself on a small platform that gave him a view up over the battlements and across the city outside.

Directly behind the wall was a car park filled with vehicles in neat rows.

Malleus smirked as he watched the police arrive in two black Fiats, blue lights flashing. They were doing their best to give the impression that they knew exactly where to find Mazzini's accomplice.

As if on cue, one of the parked cars reversed out of its space with a screech and made a dash for freedom.

Two policemen burst the tyres with a series of targeted shots. The car skidded along for a few metres, then smashed into a wall. Police surrounded the vehicle; two men were pulled out onto the ground and held down.

That's all folks. Malleus was immensely satisfied, and looked out across the Eternal City, which seemed to be regaining more of its ancient glory every day. Funded by Jupiter and the Olympian gods, cranes loomed throughout the city like the skeletons of ancient dinosaurs, and countless temples joined the Colosseum in its reign over the skyline.

Malleus turned to St Peter's Basilica, which stood veiled in darkness. No spotlights drew attention to the centre of Christianity's last remaining outpost. *Literally a shadow of its former self.*

He stepped back down the ladder into the heliport, and began to make his way to the cathedral.

Hopefully the i8 he had ordered earlier would be parked

in front of it, which he would immediately drive over to the Temple of Vulcanus. The temple had once been located outside the city, but had now been moved to the very centre: the Campus Martius.

Malleus was certain he would meet Hephaestus there. Vulcanus, Hephaestus – the new Pantheon seemed happy to skim over the fact that the Greeks and Romans shared many of the same gods, only with different names.

Of course he could also have headed towards the Lapis Niger in the newly renovated Forum Romanum, the oldest shrine to the forge god. However, the early Roman site consisted of a massive altar built with huge black stones, on which a brazier, five metres across, burned day and night. Malleus' presence there would not go unnoticed. He would rather negotiate with the god in private.

He took out his PDA, checked the timer: *0h 31min 45sec.*

I'm just about on time. Malleus walked past a tree, when suddenly a figure shoved itself onto the path in front of him. It happened too fast for him to react.

Soft, feminine hands cradled his face, pulling him forwards, lips pressed against his.

A warm body pressed against him, and he felt the pressure of her breasts against his chest, her hips pushing into him.

Malleus did not avoid the kiss. Gradually he realised who was behind the ambush. Marinuschka had been waiting for him.

She took his hands and slid them underneath her habit. His fingers met her glowing hot skin, and she moved so that he was cupping her firm breasts.

'Take me here,' she whispered as she caressed him.

Malleus gently pushed Marina away from him as she moved towards him with a sigh. 'No,' he said softly. He didn't want to.

He couldn't. He had no time to tell the young woman about his past. His devastating loss. His pain. The promise he made to himself, never to feel that again.

She shot him a poisonous look. 'You're rejecting me?' Her face was almost predatory, filled with desire, tinged with growing rage and indignation. 'Do you *know* what I'm *doing* here, for you? What that *means*?' Marina stepped back. 'You have no idea! No idea!' She glared at him, outraged, her hands balled into fists, then turned round with a sharp cry of anger and ran off.

Malleus watched her leave. Her behaviour was truly a mystery to him. Exaggerated. Uncontrolled. Being wanted by a far younger woman might usually be flattering, but her desire seemed tinged with a streak of psychopathy.

And the timer was still counting down.

Breaking into a jog, Malleus hurried on and reached the i8, which sped him on autopilot to the Campus Martius.

Malleus looked down at his PDA. *0h 14min 56sec.* It would be tight.

He patted the pocket of his coat and heard the rustle of the plastic package. For a brief second he had feared that Marina's ambush had been a ruse to rob him of the pages. The inspector's scepticism rarely took a break.

Just to be sure, Malleus checked both pages more closely. They were still there, crumpled and coffee-stained.

Relieved, he took out his cigar case. His reward.

* Α Ω *

I was this close to shooting the little lady out of his way. Before I realised who she was, that is.

Temptation in the Vatican – sounds like a bad porn movie. Fifty Cassocks of Grey.

But the man I'm following is a professional, so the girl can look as good as she wants. He has other matters to see to. And there's plenty of women in the world who want to get involved with him.

She swishes off, raging like a fury, and he begins to jog. Probably to the car. He'll either be going to the shrine to Vulcanus at the Forum Romanum, or the Campus Martius.

I don't think they ever really had a chance, those two. Him and a nun, and a pretty crazy one at that . . . what's she doing over there?

She's . . . getting undressed?

She is. Hiding behind a tree, as naked as the day her god made her.

Ah, there's a bag there, with underwear, a long black dress, high heels. She's transforming into a normal woman – to follow him? So that her habit won't attract attention on the streets, I guess.

She pulls her dress up and attaches a narrow dagger with a homemade sheath to her thigh. I can't read the engravings on it but it's certainly nothing Christian.

So things are a little more interesting than I thought. She's certainly more interesting.

She slips on a dark red leather jacket over the dress, takes a smartphone out of her pocket and types furiously on it.

I have to keep moving, I'm following him and yet he's nearly out of my sight.

That nun is not a nun. I'd bet the pope's life on it.

Next time I'll shoot her as soon as she gets anywhere near him.

I can't let someone else interfere with him.

* Α Ω *

Malleus stood alone in the renovated Vulcanus temple.

A priest in a fire-red toga with red embroidered flames along the seam had been awaiting him at the entrance, and silently led him inside, only to disappear through a side door. The god seemed to have given direction for his arrival.

He puffed on his cigar, decorated with a violet band, took out his PDSA and looked through the smoke at the timer: *0h 01min 09sec.*

Right on time. Malleus looked up and around the temple, letting the curls of smoke spill from his mouth; he placed the PDA in his chest pocket, so that it stuck out slightly. He held his hat in his left hand.

The temple interior was decorated in black and red, and by his estimation the restorations were not fully completed; the frescos still required some paintwork. The five-metre wide brazier was set slightly off from the centre of the temple, and blazed with an enormous flame that radiated a powerful heat.

Behind it stood the statue of the god: tall, bursting with muscles, and wearing a short tunic and leather apron, and a sky blue felt cap, as he had been depicted in legend. In one hand he held his forge hammer, the other rested on an anvil; a slight buckle in the right leg hinted at his limp.

The god I met in the Pinacoteca was a modernised version of himself. Malleus noticed the ashes round the edge of the bowl, undoubtedly from sacrifices offered to Vulcanus. He smirked. *I wonder if they'll change the statue when this all comes out?*

His PDA beeped a warning; the countdown had reached zero.

At that moment the fire gave an almighty hiss and a cloud of sparks poured from its centre, sinking to the ground and forming itself into the figure of Hephaestus.

He had decided to manifest as the same towering figure he had chosen in the Vatican, and limped towards Malleus, his head slightly bowed; the leather panels creaked with every step.

'Malleus Bourreau,' he rumbled, glowing dots dancing from his mouth. 'You are indeed a reliable man.'

Malleus nodded and pulled both pages of Leonardo da Vinci's *codici* from his coat pocket. He had half expected the god's patronising tone, but that didn't mean he liked it. 'I have found what you requested.' He laid the pages in front of him on the marble floor. 'Here you are. As a sign of my trust in the word of a god.' That sentence was perhaps the biggest lie he'd told for a while.

'Excellent.' The entity lifted a finger.

Sparks swirled out of the sacrificial bowl and lifted the pages over to the god, without even charring the edges.

'I have decided that to make amends for the deaths caused by my assistant, I shall pay a sum to their relatives in compensation. Do you think that one hundred gold pieces per life will suffice?' Hephaestus held the corners of the pages cautiously between his thumb and forefinger.

'If you believe that life can be measured in currency, sure,' commented Malleus.

'You're right. I will measure their weight in gold and give that to the families. That seems appropriate.' His eyes turned to the coffee-stained pages, upon which no legible words remained.

Only a few letters had survived Malleus' sabotage; just enough to prove that Malleus had indeed located and delivered the originals. As he had planned.

How's he going to react? Malleus couldn't help but puff a little faster on his Culebra.

Hephaestus straightened himself up with a jerk, fixing Malleus with a glowing, furious glare. 'What am I supposed to do with these?' he thundered, so loud that Malleus winced at the pain in his ears.

'I haven't the slightest idea. I don't know what you wanted

to do with the *codici* in the first place,' he answered in a polite, gentle tone. 'I simply fulfilled my side of the arrangement.'

'These pages contain nothing of use!'

'That is none of my concern. It must have happened while they were in the thief's possession.' Malleus took the cigar out of his mouth. 'But those are the two missing pages. Get them tested and analysed if you want. You're a god, you can probably do that with a snap of your fingers.'

Hephaestus inhaled deeply, with a sound like a huge bellows filling with air. 'I will not be defrauded by a mortal,' he boomed, engulfing the pages with a jet of flame in the palm of his hand. Grey flecks of ash fluttered towards the ceiling.

'I had nothing to do with it.' Malleus placed his hand, Culebra between his fingers, onto his heart, the smoke painting a grey trail as he moved. 'I give you my word.' He did his best to conceal his own nervous tension.

Hephaestus' eyes grew narrow, glowing from deep red to bright white. 'I no longer find you amusing or entertaining,' he growled. 'But – I will keep to my word. The Vatican will remain untouched by my hand. And now, tell me which artefact you wish to know more about.'

'The crown you spoke of before.'

'Then listen carefully, Malleus Bourreau. I will only say this once.' Hephaestus stood up to his full height, his muscles twitching.

His lips moved slowly and clearly – but issued no audible sounds. He was revealing the secret, without speaking it aloud.

'Did you get that?' he finally asked, tauntingly. 'I'm returning the favour.' With that he burst into a cloud of sparks that quickly scattered into nothing.

Malleus stroked the ends of his beard, turned round and made his way to the temple exit. *Can't say I'm surprised.*

His excitement fell. The encounter with the god could have ended far worse for both himself and the Vatican, he had to focus on that.

'Wait.' The voice of the priest echoed behind him in the tall chamber. 'You must offer Vulcanus a sacrifice.'

Without looking back or missing a step, Malleus flicked his half-smoked cigar behind him. It curved through the air and landed in the brazier, tinting the huge flame a lurid violet.

The priest cursed loudly.

'That wasn't cheap,' Malleus shouted back, as he put on his hat and left the shrine.

He made his way down the steps and climbed into the i8. After a second of thought, he programmed the car to drive him to his hotel.

He would rather not set foot in the Vatican again. The gratitude of the Holy Father was not important to him; he had simply done his job.

Everything else, the handover of the pages to Hephaestus and his reaction, his confession of guilt in the deaths of the four victims, he would write in his report and send to his boss Lautrec. The chief of Interpol could decide how much of it he wanted to pass on to God's earthly representative. The deaths of four people would be balanced out with gold, though Malleus had no idea how Hephaestus planned to determine their weights.

Of course it would have interested Malleus to find out why the pope called Brother Theodorus his son, and what he would have to say about his son sleeping with a fake nun, but he was fairly certain that Severinus would not be sharing those particular juicy details.

Malleus turned off the video record function on his PDA and allowed himself a quiet chuckle.

Hephaestus might not have said anything aloud – but his lip movements had been captured by the camera. Malleus had intended to use the recording as a backup in case anything had gone seriously wrong, but it turned out that forethought had been a stroke of genius.

You'll live to regret that move, Hephaestus, he threatened with a look, as the BMW silently rolled past the temple. *And the next time we meet, I'll be pissing in your brazier until you show yourself.*

Malleus turned back towards the road and ordered a tea from the automatic drink system inside the car. The tea was strong, the perfect accompaniment to a fresh Culebra with a ruby red band. He was extremely satisfied.

As the i8 stopped at a red light, Malleus looked over at an advertising board on the house opposite the crossing. A lavish advertisement for a new temple to Horus on the eastern outskirts of Rome twinkled in the darkness, encouraging investors to buy bonds. *The Egyptians are getting ballsy. This isn't their territory.*

A lone, metallic silver Mercedes limousine stopped next to them, the silhouette of a woman visible through its tinted windows.

The dark pane of glass glided a few inches downwards, revealing the woman's dark hair, arched brows and piercing green eyes. He recognised them immediately.

Marina?!

The i8 drove on, and the silver Mercedes turned off, the window still open. The woman's penetrating, glinting gaze followed Malleus as they drove further apart.

How can that be? The car wasn't marked with the Vatican's coat of arms.

He could still make out the number plate and noted it down hastily on his PDA. A quick check against the Italian police database told him that the limousine belonged to a chauffeur service.

He must have been wrong.

Malleus sipped at his tea and saw several messages on his PDA, from Severinus, Lautrec and from his assistant Lagrande, none of which he wanted to read.

His attention was grabbed by another email, however, that came through the account he reserved for private contracts.

Malleus opened it, read.

Fascinated by the events described in the message, he leant forwards, stroking his thumb and forefinger over his Fu Manchu.

Line by line he became more engrossed in the report, absorbing the details of a monstrous set of events which would certainly present a welcome challenge for his intellect and investigative powers.

He'd wanted to travel to London for years. The toehold of the Hindu gods in Europe had piqued his interest.

The city alone was an opportunity he couldn't pass up, never mind the eight naked corpses that had been found in a stately home. These deaths were dramatic – and something about it just felt wrong.

BOOK 3

Episode 3: Preta

'Whoever consummates his life dies his own death, victoriously, surrounded by hopers and promisers. Thus should one learn to die.

(. . .) In your dying shall your spirit and your virtue still glow, like a sunset around the earth: or else your dying will have turned out badly.'

Friedrich Nietzsche, 'On Free Death',
from *Thus Spoke Zarathustra*, 1883–1885

Britannia, London, November 2019

Malleus Bourreau sat back as the autopilot of his rented BMW i8 drove him through London's most Indian area – aside from Harrow and Southall, of course, in the west.

With the return of the gods, the city sprawled around the Thames had become a toehold for the Hindu pantheon in Europe. If Malleus remembered correctly, this religion had more than thirty thousand gods and incarnations, making it difficult to keep an eye on all of them – or to fight an invasion, should they choose to advance and try their hand as a new colonial power.

It's almost as if we're not in England at all. Malleus stroked the ends of his moustache and observed the houses of Brent through the window, pressed up against each other in regimented rows, and decorated in true Indian style: lots of colour, with ornaments and cheerful little embellishments, radiating luxury and flair.

A flood of Indian design had swept through the English terraces. The Western infrastructure was still a visible contrast, though even the dull lamp posts had been brightened up with colourful streamers. The Hindu community were making a clear display of their dedication to their gods.

The location of this spiritual centre was no accident. Since the mid-nineties, Neasden had been home to the Shri Swaminararyan Mandir, an enormous Hindu temple, which Malleus was looking forward to visiting. He was intrigued by its architecture, and even more so by its legendary restaurant, which served only vegan food, even avoiding the use of onions and garlic in order to cater for Brahmins.

But it was not the city's architecture or cuisine that had brought him to London.

It was a case.

A highly lucrative and, more importantly, challenging contract.

The transformed terraces glided past the window of the i8. A sign advertising the newly renovated Wembley Stadium went by, where cricket and squash were played almost non-stop and broadcast on the stadium's own TV channels. Malleus had noticed the coverage on the flight in and on the huge screens at Heathrow airport.

He considered whether he should light up a Culebra, but the car's satellite navigation system informed him that he would be reaching his destination in a couple of minutes. He kept the cigar case in his coat.

His PDA beeped its way into his consciousness, alerting him to a message from his boss Lautrec at Interpol headquarters.

Not now. Malleus hoped it wasn't an official commission calling him to leave immediately for a case in Europe. As long as it wasn't urgent, he would stay and carry out the interview with his private client before seeing to any Interpol business.

But on opening the email, he found it was only information – no orders. Information that both astonished and disturbed him.

As soon as the forensics team finished their work at a crime scene, any projectiles found were automatically compared to the Interpol database. During one of these routine checks, something bizarre had turned up: three people in Rome had been shot with the same weapon as three unrelated women in Latvia.

What unnerved Malleus was this: the three Romans were the ones who had cornered him on the Piazza della Rotonda shortly before meeting their sudden end. And the victims in Latvia belonged to the group of Baba Yaga followers who Malleus had found in an abandoned clearing in the woods, and prevented from harming a group of innocent women.

There was more: the extremely precise, non-lethal shots to the knee and thigh of the group's leader had not issued – as he had assumed – from his own Apache Derringer, but from the same weapon responsible for these six killings: an APB Stechkin, an incredibly specialist silenced fully automatic pistol which used 9mm shells. It had been originally developed in Russia for the KGB and Russian special forces.

Six dead, one injured, the same weapon. All somehow related to me. Malleus's amazement grew as he read the notes from the Italian authorities.

The APB was not the only remarkable object involved in these crimes; the bullets and shells left at the crime scenes were also quite extraordinary. They were engraved with markings from an as yet untranslated code, one that made the identification of a suspect far easier for the Italians.

The Roman investigators were convinced that this was the work of the fabled *assassin di glifo*, the Glyph Killer; their message included an attached file containing the notes from the previous investigation.

Malleus opened it up and saw countless records relating to past crime scenes and victims. *Fifty-two*. His mouth went dry.

He didn't have time to read through the reports in detail before the meeting with his client, but a fleeting glance told him that at some point the murderer had simply stopped. For reasons yet to be identified. And now he was showing up again, in Malleus's cases.

I have a homicidal guardian angel. Malleus wondered whether there were any engraved projectiles and shells to be found at the site of his last investigation in the Vatican. Given the Vatican's special legal status, the Italian authorities had not seen it as their responsibility, and consequently no forensics work had been carried out.

Malleus recalled his battle with the mechanical creature in the Pinacoteca, how it had been ripped apart from the inside – without his intervention. He had put it down to defective machinery – but now all signs pointed to someone stepping in with an APB to finish the job.

I need to be certain. Malleus wrote a hurried email to Father Severinus, his contact in the Vatican, asking him to conduct a search for bullet casings in the Pinacoteca.

The i8 turned right down Braemer Avenue.

Malleus shook the disturbing presence of the Glyph Killer from his mind as well as he could. He couldn't be distracted while meeting a client.

The little street led to a lake, just visible through the trees that surrounded the buildings. This area was populated with larger properties, many with several extensions and alterations. Marble pillars and towers created an impressive combination of European and Indian construction styles. His wife would have found it fascinating.

The BMW stopped in front of the most elegant, attractive house, which towered behind a whitewashed wall like a palace, the two slim turrets on either side almost ramming their long points into the grey clouds overhead. An imposing bronze door engraved with Hindu ornamentations closed off the building to visitors.

Malleus guessed from the length of the wall that his client had also bought up the land surrounding the property. The message was clear: here lives someone of considerable wealth.

He climbed out of the car and slipped on his military coat, smoothed down his black hair, longer on the top than the sides, and put on his hat.

He was aware that his clothes, with their light Indian cut, could either be very well received, or interpreted as a rather smarmy attempt to butter up his client. But Malleus liked the style of his shirts, which he had designed and commissioned himself some years ago.

Before, he had always looked forward to those afternoons at the tailor's, being measured or trying on his designs, chatting over tea or a good rum. His daughter had hidden in the workshop under the sewing machine or in the cupboards full of material, and Malleus had searched for her. A playful game between a little girl and her father. For a second he could almost smell the scent of the material, heard his daughter's laughter in his ears.

Before. A long, long time ago. He gathered himself, though he couldn't help but check behind him down the street, alert and watchful.

Malleus wasn't expecting to see his stalker right then and there, but he wanted to reassure himself that he was alone. He had to find an explanation to fit the information Lautrec had given him. For his own sanity, if nothing else.

With an electric buzz, the bronze door swung open behind him.

Malleus turned towards the entrance.

The sight of the property as it slowly emerged from behind the door took his breath away.

The owners must have invested millions. The marble façades, the fountains and ponds, the garden, the plants, the paths and veranda – pure performative opulence.

The building in front of him was a miniature maharajah's palace, and even the grey English weather could do nothing to dull its splendour. In the background was a stunning view of the lake, which looked as if it had been installed exclusively to complement the majestic property.

As the bronze door opened further, it revealed a man with a thick, neatly clipped beard waiting for him in the entrance. He wore a traditional sherwani in bright white with a jacquard print, a white turban, and light-coloured canvas shoes.

Those unacquainted with Indian customs might associate his light-coloured clothing with joy or celebration. But Malleus knew that in India the colour stood for mourning, in contrast to the black preferred across most of Europe.

'*Namaste*, Mr Bourreau.' The man greeted him with a bow, before reaching out to shake his hand. His complexion was dark, his eyes so brown that they appeared almost entirely black. 'I'm relieved that you could make it.'

Malleus walked over to him, finding it remarkable that the head of the house had come to greet him personally rather than sending a servant to guide him through the impressive property.

'*Namaste*,' he replied, shaking the man's hand. 'My deepest condolences, Mr Gautama.'

'Thank you. With your help I hope to find out in which direction I should be pointing my anger.' He gestured towards the snow-white steps leading up to a set of double doors. 'I have prepared some chai. But if you would prefer something else, please let me know.' His client walked up the stairs, his hands behind his back.

With a quiet hum, the bronze door closed behind them.

Malleus followed Shankar Kumar Gautama over the raked gravel to the main building. The Indian-born businessman was amongst the thirty wealthiest people in Britain, and was exceptionally well connected within British politics and society. His family held the Indian aristocratic title *Tazimi Sardar*, though Malleus couldn't say exactly what that meant. Not his area of expertise.

They entered the foyer, also filled with an abundance of marble. The walls were covered in detailed panelling, enormous hand-knotted rugs lay on the ground, and an impressive flight of stairs led up to the second floor, though there was also the option of a lift. Paintings and golden lampshades hung on the walls, and a crystal chandelier hung in the hall, spreading out across the ceiling like the branches of a great tree.

Something hit Malleus immediately: silence.

No quiet noises, no conversations, no music.

Nothing.

The heavy scent of incense and joss sticks hung in the air, so thick that even the smoke of a Culebra would have been engulfed in seconds.

'As you may notice,' said Gautama in his warm, deep voice, 'there is no life amongst all this luxury. I am the only living person in this tomb, and I myself feel dead inside. The last piece of life left inside me is pure hatred. Hatred for those who did this to me.' He gestured towards an open door on his right. 'After you, Mr Bourreau.'

Malleus had to suppress a shudder at his words. He entered the salon, which was decorated in sumptuous colonial style. Red drapes on the walls accentuated the height of the ceiling, which held two large fans, hanging motionless in the heavy air. The room was filled with darkly coloured furniture, rich brown leather Chesterfield chairs and sofas.

Malleus took a seat in the corner by the fireplace, where a small peat fire was burning. He laid down his coat and hat, and pulled his PDA out of his long Indo-European shirt, placing it on the low teak table in front of them. On the table was a large iron teakettle balanced on a small warmer, two teacups and a selection of Indian nibbles and sandwiches.

Outside, the grey-blue lake lapped noisily against the steps that led from the garden into the water; rainclouds rolled across the sky.

Gautama sat opposite him, his face evidently making every effort to appear friendly, yet unmistakably marked by grief. He said something in Hindi and the lights turned on, though kept at a dim level. Then he poured the tea. The aromas of cinnamon, green and black cardamom, honey and cloves rose in gentle clouds from the milky tea.

'Thank you.' Malleus took the cup and sipped the chai. 'It has an outstanding flavour, Mr Gautama.'

The man smiled briefly. 'My wife's recipe,' he said with a

shade of bitterness to his voice, taking another sip of the tea. 'You must be wondering why nobody is here.'

'It had crossed my mind.' He ran his fingers over the ends of his moustache.

'My staff made the decision to leave the property. They believe it is haunted by a *preta*,' he sighed, leaning back in his seat. 'Please feel free to smoke, Mr Bourreau. I've heard you have good taste in cigars.'

'Later, but thank you.' Malleus had never come across the term preta before, but he assumed it came from Hindu mythology. 'A preta is some kind of ghost?'

'Much more than that. The *antim sanskar*, our funeral rites, are very strictly controlled, to ensure that everything goes well for our loved ones after they die. My mother died just over half a year ago, and it would seem that the Brahmans who attended her did not adhere closely enough to the *antim sanskar*,' Gautama explained. 'She has now become a preta, meaning that from the moment of her death until her soul arrives at its final destination, she will wander here.' He sipped his tea. 'I understand that you may feel sympathy for my loss, Mr Bourreau, or perhaps even contempt for my beliefs. But you must understand the gravity of this situation. Pretas belong to Yama, the King of Hell, and they are inherently evil. They seek only to cause human suffering.'

'I'm guessing you've already taken steps to appease the spirit. They were not successful?' His client had not mentioned this aspect of the case in his report. Until now Malleus had been operating on the assumption that it was a group suicide.

Gautama shook his head, his deep black beard brushing softly across his white sherwani. 'We have left various offerings for the preta, but nothing worked.' He gave another command in Hindi.

A section of the wall transformed into a screen, showing a

photograph of a dark-haired young girl in a red and yellow sari. She had Gautama's eyes. The image showed her lying on the ground.

'One of the maids took this with her smartphone just after they found my youngest daughter Anjay,' he clarified, staring out of the window. He couldn't bear to look.

The video began to play.

In the background were various raised voices, the camera was shaky. Anjay's throat was slit open. There was no way she was alive. Malleus estimated Anjay's age at around eight or nine.

The dead child's head turned abruptly to face the camera, her glassy eyes fixing on the lens. Her mouth moved, speaking in a language Malleus didn't understand, but the animosity behind the words was unmistakable.

'You will all die. Every one of you,' Gautama translated flatly. 'Not one life in this cursed palace will remain. My son will suffer just as I suffer! I curse. . .'

Then the people in the video descended into chaotic screaming, and the recording ended.

Malleus exhaled slowly and drank his chai. He quickly suppressed the memory of his own dead daughter. This case could have a decided impact on his own state of mind.

'After that, my staff left me.' Gautama turned away from the window to face the inspector, a tear dropping from the corner of his left eye, though his face did not betray his sadness. The tear rolled down his cheek and into his dense beard. 'I am happy to follow the laws of the gods,' he said quietly, 'but I must know who it was that took everything I live for, and neglected to kill me.'

Malleus was touched by the man's strength of character. 'You don't believe that it is a preta who caused your family members to commit suicide, Mr Gautama?'

'Never.' Gautama's brown eyes deepened in the dim light to become bottomless pits. 'Something wanted my staff to believe there was a preta in the house. And it is this something that must be investigated, Mr Bourreau.' He set down his teacup. 'I trust you have read the police report I sent you?'

'Of course.'

'I wrote that I could not answer any questions regarding the report,' Gautama continued. 'At the time of the event I was staying in Mumbai. But I can show you all the rooms. Nothing inside them has been altered.'

'The bodies . . .?'

'They have already been cremated, in accordance with our customs. Their ashes will be flown to India today, where they will be scattered into the Ganges,' answered Gautama. 'My wife would have wanted the traditional funeral rites.' He tapped on the table with a finger, and an integrated touchscreen appeared on its surface. His fingers moved quickly, and Malleus's PDA buzzed in a matter of seconds. 'I've sent you a program. If you use your smartphone camera as you walk round the rooms, the program will incorporate the images of the bodies as they were found.'

Augmented reality. Malleus was loath to rely on electronic devices, as he would much rather have seen the bodies in front of him, where he could examine them for traces and clues.

'I know what you're thinking. But the photos are extremely high quality. You'll be able to see just as much as in real life.' He rubbed his hands absentmindedly, as if removing specks of dirt from his palms. 'Which room would you like to start with, Mr Bourreau? I have more to tell you as we go.' He stood up.

'Let's work from the top downwards.' Malleus finished his chai and stroked his moustache ends thoughtfully. He could tell already that this would be an exceptional case.

They left the salon together and climbed the snow-white stairs; the quiet echo of their steps and the rustling of their clothes were the only sounds.

'You have a suspicion as to who might be behind the appearance of the preta, Mr Gautama?'

'I do.' Gautama guided him through the corridors, past paintings depicting Indian landscapes and temples, photographs of ancestors, and a few abstract pieces.

Statues of gods and divine creatures stood in alcoves, and large vases full of flowers and orchids adorned the hallways. Gautama seemed – as with the chai – to have seen to the decoration himself.

Of course there was also a man-sized statue of the god Kali, recognisable to anyone with a rudimentary knowledge of Hinduism. The black-skinned goddess brandished a curved blade, balanced with one foot on a human body and held a skull in her other hand. The smell of incense penetrated every corner of the house. Apparently they had tried to smoke out the preta.

'My eldest daughter Narami had a visit from her friend Robin Warwick that day. They wanted to marry.' Gautama laughed emptily. 'Teenage love, that's all it was. The young man is a soldier and a devout worshipper of the Celtic god Barrex. My wife told me that they had an argument.' Gautama stood still in front of a door sealed off with a police notice. 'He wanted her to convert to his religion.'

'And your daughter refused?'

'Of course.' Gautama's dark eyes fixed on the inspector. 'Warwick left the house in a rage. Hours later, everyone I loved was dead.'

'You think that Barrex might have taken revenge for the rejection.'

'Narami was known for her sharp tongue. I can imagine that her words were hurtful. Perhaps Barrex was angered by her, but what he did in return was cowardly and malicious. And he wants me to believe that it was the work of a preta.' Gautama placed a well-groomed, powerful hand on the handle, pushed it down and opened the door. The police notice tore in two. 'Find the true perpetrator, Mr Bourreau, and I can make you a very rich man.'

Malleus nodded and walked inside.

* A Ω *

London.

Home of Jack the Ripper.

The perfect place for a murder, I'd say, and the man I'm following has certainly got plenty to deal with. Eight bodies, eight suicides, eight different methods, if the tabloids are to be believed.

I must remember to hack his PDA when I get the chance. I get the feeling I'm missing a lot of information that he sees on there. The bug I've got on him is nice and all, but if he doesn't read his emails aloud I'm screwed. Annoying.

He's driving out to Brent. Getting a taste of India. Bollywood has nothing on Brent.

It's crazy how much the Hindus have spent on this place, and that temple over there is amazing! Hopefully he'll drop in for a visit, I fancy a look around.

Things have really changed in this nine-million strong city, thanks to these new ancient gods. Tower Hamlets and Newham were almost emptied completely – mosques and other places of worship are left standing around, totally deserted.

But the number of Hindus has shot up, and now there are over a million living in Rippertown. Brent, Harrow, Southall. And they're also moving to Newham and Tower Hamlets, of course. There's plenty of space there now.

The Jews have mostly stayed where they were, in Stamford Hill and Golders Green, and for the most part they're left to their own devices.

The Christians, what can I say? The old rites never really disappeared in Britain, especially on the small islands and in Scotland. The gentlest of nudges from the gods, and farewell Anglican church, hello Paganism! The rest of them still pray to their Lord, but secretly and silently. There are even some priests claiming to have seen omens that he's about to send down a new saviour. I'll believe it when I see it.

The situation with the Hindus could still get a bit tricky. Lots of gods, lots of demands. The British certainly didn't have this situation in mind when they colonised India. Turns out they brought over a lot more than curry.

His client is reasonably well-known. For his wealth. For his businesses. For his ruthlessness.

Gautama.

Sounds a bit like Gotham. Certainly fits his character.

I've heard a few things about the guy that made me want to avoid ever doing business with him. He looks sophisticated, but he's also a master of some obscure Indian martial art. Apparently he rips his opponents into pieces, kalari-something. Indian champion 2014 and 2015.

My old connections informed me that he's implicated in at least four cases back in India; intimidation, assault, and murder – no bribery though. He doesn't do things by halves.

Given how many Indian gods there are I can imagine that at least one is mad enough at him to kill off his family. As revenge for what he did back home in India.

I'll have to keep a close eye on my subject, the man I'm following. Hopefully he knows everything I do about Gautama.

Here we are.

Nice place, Gautama's living like a maharajah. He's reading something on his PDA, seems to have caught his attention. Before he goes through the door he looks round. And right down the street. Almost as if he knows that someone's following him.

I guess forensics have finally done their job and compared the shells from the different crime scenes.

Yeah, it's definitely time to hack his PDA.

As soon as he goes to sleep, I'll get on it.

* Α Ω *

Malleus stepped into the dark room and was hit by the strong scent of incense. The overpowering aroma would undoubtedly mask any other scents in the room that could have helped him in his investigations.

He took his cigar case from his shirt pocket, lit a splint, then the Culebra. Light green band.

The room was dimly lit for a second by his lighter, and dried specks of blood became visible across the walls and floor.

The rapidly flickering light made him nervous for a heartbeat, reminding him of the Great Change, and of that day, the day he had barely escaped with his life. The flame died, and he was calm again.

Malleus took a few puffs on the cigar, the end glowing orange in the darkness, the burning tobacco crackling loudly.

Then he turned on the light and held up his PDA, opened the augmented reality program and watched the screen as he slowly swept the room, activating the camera's record function as he did so.

It was as if the suicide had just taken place, a few minutes ago.

The body of Narami lay naked on the carpet; she had ripped open her stomach with an Indian dagger, which the program identified as a kukri, a Gurkha knife. Further information was also visible on the screen, including the temperature of the body, weight, and other forensic data.

Malleus moved methodically around the young woman's room, investigating both with his PDA screen and without, feeling around in the area where the body had lain, though there was nothing to be found in the carpet. It was strange using the PDA, seeing Narami in front of him one second, empty space the next.

He searched under her bed, and found a pendant about the size of a coin, marked with symbols that were not Hindu in origin: two short swords depicted in parallel, and two crossed spears.

Malleus sat on the ground and examined his find.

The pendant had a loop that would attach it to a leather necklace or a thin metal chain. It was of modern design, with Celtic ornamentation on the back, and the embossed words: *Barrecis the Highest protect me.*

Malleus entered a quick search on his PDA and found that the Celtic god Barrecis or Barrex was especially popular in Northern England. The *Interpretatio Romana* put him on a level with Mars, and the words *mars barrex* had even been found in a dedicatory inscription on Hadrian's Wall at Carlisle.

The pendant must have belonged to the man Narami had been planning to marry. It was after all no secret that he had been present shortly before these terrible events had taken place.

Malleus held up his PDA again and panned across the ghostly image of the corpse in the room. He zoomed in on the neck and throat of the young woman.

A thin line was just visible on the skin.

Malleus stood up. *I was wrong.* So Narami had ripped the pendant from her neck during the argument. Or perhaps her lover had done it for her. *Or someone else, who was angry that a Hindu woman was wearing the talisman of another god.*

He had already excluded the possibility of a preta. Not that he didn't believe in ghosts – they had been around since long before the return of the gods. But even the angriest of dead grandmothers wouldn't have had the power to drive eight people to suicide. If he had understood Gautama correctly, a preta would have dealt out its punishments personally. Lacerations, broken bones, bruises. But none of these were evident on the bodies.

Malleus quickly looked up on his PDA what strategies could be taken to appease the so-called *hungry spirit* if offerings were not effective.

'Of course,' he murmured, and took a drag on his cigar. *Gods, demigods and other spiritual beings can bring the preta back under control.*

He left the room and was met by Gautama, who had waited patiently for him. Not by the door, but in front of the imposing six-armed statue of Kali, his own arms crossed behind his back as if in polite conversation with the goddess.

'Come, Mr Bourreau,' he spoke without turning around. 'Next we will look at my wife's room.'

Malleus caught up to him, looking closely at the impressive statue as he walked past. The goddess of creation and death. Gautama led him to the next room.

Room by room, they made their way through the palatial property, always accompanied by the building's quite literal deathly silence.

He viewed six more bodies through his PDA: coronary arteries sliced open, hung from the ceiling, a knife through the heart, a knife in the right eye, strangled on a four poster bed, suffocated with a plastic bag.

They were always naked, and there was never any sign of external influence, in the rooms or on the bodies themselves. They all seemed to have killed themselves: Gautama's wife, her two sisters, the older children.

Outside the rain had begun to fall in earnest, huge droplets drummed against the windows. Storm clouds rolled grumbling across the sky, peppered with flashes of lightning.

Malleus drew heavily on his cigar. He had seen a lot of bodies in his time, but the quick succession, one after another, was beginning to take its toll.

The worst was yet to come. He walked into the room belonging to the Gautama's youngest daughter, Anjay.

Here, as in many of the previous rooms, a huge lake of dried blood stained the pink carpet. It was the archetypal little girl's bedroom, lovingly decorated with posters, a doll's house, computer, toys and teddies, a four-poster bed and even a swing. An air current caused the swing to rock slightly.

Malleus shuddered and couldn't help but think of his own loss. He lifted his PDA reluctantly, afraid he could be flooded with old memories at any second.

As he panned his PDA across the room, he thought for a heartbeat that he saw the dead girl sitting on the swing.

But the figure didn't appear on the display.

Only when he lowered the device was he met with the image of Anjay, perched on the swing in her bloodstained yellow sari, and fixing him with a curious stare. The curling fingers of his cigar smoke reached across the room towards her – and as they reached the swing, the figure dissolved into thin air.

Malleus forced himself to remain calm, and waited patiently for the hairs on the back of his neck to stop standing on end. He took a long drag on his Culebra.

England did have a long tradition of ghosts. The rise of Hinduism had done nothing to change that.

Celtica, Paris-Lutetia, November 2019

Marianne Lagrande stood forlornly in her small office in Interpol headquarters and looked at the filing shelves in front of her, crammed with documents pertaining to her various colleagues' cases. Opposite the shelves was an air-conditioned glass cupboard filled with hard disks containing all the digital details of each case: reports, photos, videos, witness statements. Diodes lit up and blinked, fans hummed, cables wound round each other like snakes in an artificially cold terrarium.

Lagrande, her blonde hair tied up in a girlish ponytail, tugged her tight red dress down a couple of inches and pouted to herself.

She was sick of the stale air.

She was sick of being cooped up in the office.

She had genuinely enjoyed making enquiries for Malleus Bourreau in Treva, organising his mail and telephone calls, even taking a trip to the crime scene to search for the codes that might help solve the mystery of the stolen artefacts. Despite the fact that it had nothing to do with his case in the Vatican.

Sadly Lautrec had become wise to the situation and ordered her to return to Paris-Lutetia. As long as Bourreau was out on non-Interpol cases, she was stuck here doing admin, proofreading and answering banal internal requests.

Boring. Lagrande sat behind her desk, took out her personal laptop, a USB stick and a Thermos flask filled with what she knew to be the best coffee in the world. So good that she brought it from home, so she didn't have to share it with the scroungers in the office. Screw them. *Mind-numbingly boring.*

Lagrande was in her mid-thirties, but wore heavy makeup in order to appear older, as she had no interest in being chatted up by men of her own age. She poured out her luxury coffee into a cup and breathed in the rising cloud of coffee-scented steam.

She turned on her police desktop, pushing the keyboard to one side.

Opening her personal laptop on the desk in front of her, she cast her eye over the findings she was planning to send to Bourreau – as soon she was one hundred per cent certain she had cracked the code.

Lagrande couldn't just abandon the case now, not when it was so nearly solved. Like a Rubik's cube with only two squares out of place – but she had no idea how to get them into the right order.

A video chat window opened spontaneously on the enormous triple screen desktop in front of her, showing Lautrec's round, bearded face. His sickly pink shirt was almost as offensive as the accompanying yellow and black striped tie.

'Madame Lagrande, would you be so kind as to process the cases from row 32/21B as a priority?' he asked, without looking up into the camera. He seemed to be reading files as he spoke to her. 'We need them asap.'

'Of course, Monsieur le chef,' she replied, accustomed to his disregard.

He nodded absently. 'If I catch you working on those artefacts again, I'll have to give you a warning.'

'Of course, Monsieur le chef. I wouldn't dream of it.'

He let out a distinctly joyless laugh, as if he could see exactly what was on the screen of her laptop, and turned off the video chat.

Lagrande sighed. *32/21B*. Vehicle theft, new cars stolen directly from transporters. But that was so – *boring*.

She opened the Interpol database and began listlessly scrolling through, eyeing it occasionally whilst training her concentration on the laptop. She was working her way through the page numbers of the books from Hein's apartment, comparing them with the numbers on the list of artefacts for the second time.

By Belenos! I've done it!

Lagrande rolled her office chair in front of her laptop, so that she could turn back to her desktop at any moment and act as if she was working normally. Lautrec probably expected those files to be processed already.

She had found the next book that decrypted a code into something legible: '*Treva and its Port at the Turn of the Century*,' she read under her breath.

As an alibi of sorts, Lagrande sent the first few files on the vehicle thefts to Lautrec and then set to feverishly translating the code.

It seemed to refer to the brick previously described by the French girl, the witness who had been imprisoned in Hein's chamber of stolen artefacts. She had been able to identify how many objects were missing: nine. *Elamite brick from the ziggurat of Chogha Zanbil*, Lagrande spelled out, translating one letter at a time. She was electrified by the discovery. *Baked and glazed clay, huge, probably from the wall of the ziggurat at Dur-Untash. West Iran, 1260 BC.*

She clapped her hands excitedly and took a sip of her drink. Screw Lautrec – him and anyone who had ideas about scrounging her coffee. She was working knee-deep in history, unearthing its secrets. What she was doing right now was big. Really big!

The next few lines were a translation of the inscription on the brick:

I, Untaš-Napiriša,
Son of Ḫumban-numena,
King of Anshan and Susa,
Wished to extend my life and my noble reign,
And wished to avoid any discontinuity of my prosperous royal line,
And thus I erected this temple of baked bricks,
And the high temple of glazed bricks.
I gave it to the god Inšušinak of the temple Siyankuk.
I consecrated the temple tower as a ziggurat.
All that I did and created
I gave as a gift to the god Inšušinak.
To the one god,
Of whom there is only one, and yet many worship him,
Without knowing.
Honour him,
For he is all and everything.

Lagrande poured herself more coffee and didn't notice as the chat window opened up again on her desktop, showing Lautrec's face once again.

'You're slow today, Madame,' he said impatiently. 'We need the cases from 2017 to today, all the ones marked *Juri*.'

She quietly rolled her chair into view of the webcam. 'I'm working on it, Monsieur le chef. I had a problem with my computer.'

Lautrec nodded. 'One hour.' He hung up again.

Lagrande swore, the way people used to swear in the eighties, and turned on the private sound system she had installed despite office regulations. 'Love Missile F1-11' began to blare out of the speakers – perfect for her current mood.

Her fingers danced across the keyboard at lightning speed, and swiped deftly across the touchscreens on her desktop monitors, her blue metallic fingernails tapping lightly against each surface. After thirty minutes she had sorted and extracted the correct files and sent them over to Lautrec. *Slave driver.*

Sighing, she turned back to her research on the brick.

Lautrec raced through exhibition catalogues and museum reports, quickly finding what she needed.

The stone belonged to a group of Elamite bricks that had been dug up over a few years in West Iran.

This particular brick was of special interest, and had been found in 1936 in the ancient city of Dur-Untash, near the modern city of Susa. Various other inscribed bricks had been found in the temple walls – but this was the only brick dedicated to the *one* god.

'Inšušinak, or Inshushinak, was one of the main Elamite deities,' she murmured fascinated. *God of the underworld and judge of the dead.*

Lagrande also found out where the brick had been stolen from – after its original removal from West Iran, that is. It had been housed in the British Museum in London. Apparently its absence had only been discovered during an inventory check. Its estimated value was around £80,000.

She didn't wait any longer, and emailed her findings to Bourreau.

Her greatest hope was that Bourreau would somehow manage to convince Lautrec to let her search for the artefacts on an official basis, that she could work round the clock as the inspector's assistant. Her success had only fuelled the fire – she wasn't about to give up now.

'One of these days I'm going to find one of these things,' she swore, and dove back into her research.

Britannia, London, November 2019

Malleus sat back as the i8 drove him through sheets of rain and growing fog to the address where Robin Warwick lived when he wasn't stationed with his regiment.

East End, in south Hackney.

The autopilot promptly made him aware that the area was far from safe, and that he should be ready to defend himself at all times. The change in religious climate had done nothing to improve the rates of crime or poverty in the East End. The British economy was in tatters after the Great Change and the loss of Scotland to independence. The recovery so far had been sluggish at best.

But Malleus was fine with a little danger.

He would have been less fine with having to visit the young man at his headquarters, as he belonged to the *Royal Regiment of Fusiliers* – based at the Tower of London. The military police would undoubtedly have attempted to obstruct his investigations. So the fact that Warwick happened to be on leave was, frankly, a relief. His investigations of the crime scenes had given Malleus nothing to move the investigation forwards. He was hoping that in questioning the young man he would at least solve the puzzle of the talisman found in Narami's room.

Malleus pictured Gautama's face as he had seen him off at the front gate. Ever the gentleman, his expression had been stoic, but permeated by hate. Anyone who came into contact with that hate would surely lose their life. *More than that. They would lose everything they loved.*

He did not doubt for a second that his client would go into battle with anyone, even gods, to avenge the deaths of his family.

Malleus took a second look through the forensics files for the case, but nothing unusual caught his eye. The notes simply detailed the fatal wounds had been dealt with great force. The will to die must have been extremely strong. *Toxins, drugs, alcohol: nil.*

The i8 informed him that he was now entering Hackney, and locked the doors with a click.

The driving rain obscured Malleus's view from the window. But through the sheets of grey he could make out cramped rows of small, simple houses, run-down and in need of considerable renovations. Clearly a working class area fallen on hard times, with too few jobs for those who could only work on the bottom rung of the ladder.

House-sized billboards appeared on every other street, most defaced by thrown stones, bullet holes or graffiti. Mockingly they advertised expensive products, property developments, luxury cars, and a host of other things that nobody in Hackney would ever be able to afford. There were gods too, giant and smiling, advertising their cults. It seemed the Egyptians were showing an interest in establishing themselves in England.

The i8 slowed down.

'In one hundred metres you will reach your destination,' the female computer voice informed him. 'In the last twenty-four hours there have been – *zero* – crimes reported in this area. However, please remain cautious and pay attention to your surroundings, sir.'

The BMW pulled up.

Malleus put on his hat, folded his collar up to cover his neck, and climbed out of the car.

The raindrops fell heavily, splashing against the waterproof material of his coat without penetrating it. The water streamed off the brim of his hat.

Malleus looked up at the four-storey brick house on the corner of Downs Park Road and Ferncliff Road, where Robin Warwick lived with his parents and two sisters. He walked silently through the downpour and rang several of the bells at once, hoping to increase his chances of being let in.

His plan worked. He stepped into the hall and began to climb the stairs to the third floor, leaving a trail of wet footprints behind him.

The hall smelled of food, wet clothes and old cleaning products. The steps were smoothed out by years of footsteps, and the walls were covered in scratches, graffiti and flecks of dirt. It had clearly been years since the landlord had invested in any renovations or repairs. From behind one door he heard the deep barking of a dog – by the sound of it a very large dog.

On the second floor he came across a large group of teenagers in tracksuits sitting on the stairs, smoking and chatting loudly, each holding a can of beer. They stared at Malleus as he walked in front of them, and turned to continue staring as he passed between them with a polite greeting.

He came to a door with a sign reading *The Warwick Family* and rang the bell.

A few seconds passed, then the door opened a crack to reveal a woman in her fifties. She was wearing an apron over a plain white blouse, looked at him with obvious suspicion and shoved a foot behind the door.

'We're not converting,' she said curtly.

Malleus couldn't help but smirk. The slightly Indian-looking cut of his shirt could give the impression that he was recruiting for the Hindus, he supposed. 'No need, Miss Warwick.' He took off his hat and brushed off the last few droplets of rain. 'I have some questions about your son Robin. It's about the death of his fiancée.'

'Fiancée?' she screeched, turning sharply back into the hall. 'Were you engaged to that curry-muncher?!'

Lovely. Malleus guessed that Robin and Narami's romance had involved more than a few secrets. He was having problems following their English – the slang in Hackney was on another level.

'The fuck are you on about?' came the gruff answer from a back room.

'There's a policeman here telling me you were engaged to that dead rich curry-muncher,' she squawked back. 'Get your arse out here and sort it out!'

Robin appeared in a vest and tracksuit, his dark blonde hair shaved close to his skull. He had a striking, somewhat pointed face, and a lean body: conventionally attractive, but not exactly your traditional English gentleman.

'What the fuck are you on about mate?' He squared up to Malleus, hanging an arm round his mother's shoulders.

Footsteps shuffled up the stairs. The teenagers from the floor below had come to see what all the noise was about.

'Could we possibly discuss this inside, Mr Warwick?' Malleus responded in a friendly tone. 'I just need to clarify a few details.'

'Oi, Rob?' one of the teenagers interrupted threateningly. 'Is this bloke bothering you?'

'He sounds like a Hun,' added a girl from the group. 'He's not from round here.'

'Maybe he's a foreign exchange policeman,' sniggered another kid.

Malleus gestured inside the door with his hat. 'May I, Miss Warwick?'

She shrugged off her son and shooed him past. 'In,' she said and gestured towards the kitchen.

'Thank you, Miss Warwick.' He followed Robin, who was giving the distinct impression that he did not enjoy surprise visits.

The young man sat at the table in the smoke-filled kitchen. Pans and bowls filled with leftovers cluttered the countertop.

His mother leant against the doorframe, folding her arms across her chest and following the proceedings with the scrutiny of a high court judge.

Malleus took off his heavy coat, hung it on the back of the door and took a seat opposite Robin. He carefully placed his hat on the back of his chair.

'Weird-looking policeman,' Robin commented, fixing him with an intense stare. 'Running round looking like a half curry.'

'Mr Warwick, I've been commissioned by Mr Gautama to investigate the recent events at his house.'

Robin looked at his mother. 'Fuck's sake, Mum! He's some sort of Hun spy! I'm not telling him anything.'

'Shut up,' she replied resolutely. 'I didn't know, did I?'

Malleus took the pendant out of his pocket and placed it on the table. 'I found this under Narami's bed. Looks like it was on a chain or a necklace round her neck.' He pushed it towards Robin with one finger. 'Did you rip it off her neck, or did she do it herself?'

Robin's face changed, momentarily coloured by uncertainty and guilt.

There was a knock on the door. 'Everything alright in there?' called a voice from outside. 'You want a hand with that police, mate? We can throw him down the stairs for you if you want.' Laughter echoed in the stairwell.

'Mum, can you tell them to shut up?' Robin asked.

She turned her head and screeched a resounding 'Fuck off!' towards the door.

'Your fiancée—'

'She wasn't my fiancée,' Robin butted in, his eyes darting towards his mother.

'Your *girlfriend* died a horrifying, pointless death, along with seven members of her family. You may be able to help me piece together what happened, Mr Warwick.' Malleus tapped the pendant with his index finger. 'Was this yours?'

Robin nodded weakly.

'Did you rip it off her neck?'

He shook his head.

'Did you have an argument?'

Another nod. 'But I didn't kill her,' he said quietly. 'Or the others.'

Malleus noticed that the colour had drained from the man's face. The appearance of the Barrex pendant seemed to have had quite an effect on him. 'Should we talk privately in your room?'

'Nope. No way,' the mother interjected. 'I want to hear this.'

There was another knock on the front door. 'Oi! What's going on with the Hun?'

'Mum, please, can you get them to leave?' Robin said exasperatedly, and his mother disappeared into the hallway with a snort. 'I didn't want this to happen,' he whispered as soon as his mother left. He ran a hand over his shaved head.

'What happened?'

'We really wanted to get married,' he whispered hoarsely, 'but she would have had to convert, to follow Barrex and the Celtic gods. Otherwise my family would never have accepted her.' He pointed to the pendant. 'I gave that to her. But Narami went mental when I told her she'd have to convert. Ripped the pendant off her neck and laid into me, called me a coward, insulted Barrex. So I stormed out and . . .' Robin looked despairing for a second, tears welling up in his pale blue eyes. 'I threatened her. I said Barrex would show her how powerful he is. Said he was stronger than her Hindu gods with all the arms and the elephant heads and all that. And then she'd have to come back to me and say sorry.' Tears sprang from his eyes and rolled down his smooth-shaven cheeks, collecting at the point of his chin. '*He* killed her. All of them,' he said quietly, his voice breaking. 'I never wanted that. I never wanted that!' Sobbing, he sprang up and left the room.

'Mr Warwick!' Malleus followed him. 'Mr Warwick, calm down. I—' He stopped at the kitchen door: the young man was holding a gun and loading it methodically. As a soldier, he knew how to handle firearms. 'Wait, Mr Warwick, please!'

'What are you doing?' shrieked the mother angrily, striding through the hallway and shoving past Malleus. 'Fucking hell Robin, put that thing down! Nobody's getting shot, alright?' she snapped, and turned to Malleus. 'What have you said to him? Have you threatened him?'

'Call an ambulance,' he replied calmly, not taking his eyes off Robin for a second.

'Don't be ridiculous, he's not going to shoot you,' she spat.

'I never wanted this!' Robin shouted through his tears and lifted the semi-automatic towards the unflinching Malleus, then in one swift movement lodged the barrel under his own chin. 'I never wanted Narami and her family to die. I'm sorry!' He looked over to his perplexed mother. 'I'm sorry.'

'No!' Malleus took a step forwards and reached for the gun, but the shot had already been fired.

The bullet tore through Robin's throat and straight out of his skull, blood spurting out of his nose and open mouth, his scalp exploding into tattered rags of flesh. Shreds of tissue and bone splattered across the wall behind him. In a fraction of a second everything was covered in red.

The young man collapsed, and another shot rang out as he hit the floor, his lifeless finger still squeezing the trigger. The bullet missed Malleus by a couple of inches and tore a chunk out of the doorframe.

Miss Warwick let out a piercing scream. 'My boy! My boy!' she sobbed, grasping desperately towards him.

At that moment the front door flew open. One of the teenagers was still kneeling, he must have picked the lock.

His friends rushed inside, two holding revolvers, both barrels pointed straight at Malleus. Despite the thick Hackney slang, he could tell they were shouting curses and death threats.

There was no time to explain: the gang was worked up and looking for Hun blood.

Malleus lowered his head and ran into the kitchen. Shots hit the walls around him, spraying him with dust and chunks of plaster.

He slammed the door shut and jammed a chair under the handle, then headed straight for the landline and called 999. The local police would know better than he did how to diffuse the situation with this mob of teenagers. He didn't want to have to injure anybody, or worse.

More shots rang out, holes exploding through the woodwork, bullets tearing through the kitchen cupboards and destroying the china inside.

'We have confirmed your emergency, sir,' a voice crackled

through the receiver. 'We have located your call. Two officers will be with you in a few minutes.'

Minutes. Malleus looked over at the chair. *Let's hope it lasts that long.*

He quickly snapped up the pendant, then his coat and hat, before they could be hit by the bullets ricocheting round the kitchen. This wasn't how he'd envisioned his visit to the Warwicks.

But – he had a lead.

He rubbed the pendant thoughtfully between his thumb and forefinger. Barrex apparently took insults very personally. *Suppose he has to, as a god of soldiers.*

'Fucking Hun!' one of them shouted through the door. 'We're gonna fucking have you!' He rattled the door violently, and the chair began to wobble under the handle.

Malleus said nothing, and took out his two Apache Derringers.

* A Ω *

This has to be one of the most fucked up areas I've ever followed him to. This place is home to some of the biggest victims of the Great Change: the economic victims. In debt, unemployed, usually drunk and constantly pissed off.

People round here are just waiting for someone like him to show up, and on top of it all he's Germanian. This area was hit badly in the Blitz. They still haven't forgiven the Krauts.

Things seem to be going badly.

I go over to the house, sneak inside and run up the stairs until I reach the landing. The lock's already been broken, how handy.

Put together the APB, attach the long magazine. I'm dealing with a pro here. Warwick is with the Fusiliers, so he presumably knows his way around a weapon. Hopefully the guy I'm following is bearing that in mind as well.

With a few minor acrobatics I make it out onto the slippery, wet roof and lie flat against the edge using the gutter as a support. Carefully I attach the scope to the APB. Doesn't hurt to have a bit of extra kit every now and then.

The rain is unpleasant, spraying like quicksilver across the silencer and making it impossible to aim.

He's with the boy, they're sitting in the kitchen, talking . . . what's he doing . . . shit, no. Put the gun away, or I . . . oh. OK. The threat appears to have eliminated itself.

Cars buzz round the corner, skidding over the wet, potholed asphalt and stopping abruptly outside the flats. Young men jump out, bomber jackets and tracksuits, football shirts. Baseball bats, chains, guns.

They shake hands grimly, go inside, up the stairs.

The first of them come through the hallway of the flat, and he has to barricade himself into the kitchen. I can only see a few segments of the hall through the window. The tacky glass bricks in the flat obscure a good portion of my view.

All I need to do is take the safety off, aim, shoot.

The guy with the neck like a bull and the shotgun – deep breath, shoot.

Classic headshot. He falls to the floor like a collapsing building.

They bellow in confusion, I can hear it from all the way over here. They think it was my guy who shot him. The guy currently crouched in the kitchen calling the police. Idiots. How could he have done that? Nobody sees the hole my bullet left in the window pane.

Now they're shouting amongst each other, one of them going for their fallen comrade's shotgun.

Hang on, did I say you could do that?

Deep breath, shoot – another one down. He falls on top of his dead friend, brains dripping down the wall next to him.

Ah, they've noticed now.

Some of them run down the stairs, spilling out of the entrance and search the rooftops for my hiding spot.

I guess I can afford to give them a clue.

Deep breath, shoot – lovely shot, right through the knee. The APB really is a fantastic piece of kit, you can't beat it for accuracy.

Meanwhile, up in the flat they've been trying to get through the door. Not with me around.

Deep breath – wait until a target presents itself.

Two guys in West Ham United shirts are trying to walk through the hall. One is jumping around excitedly like a mad kangaroo, the other is creeping theatrically. That might work in your action films, boys. Reality looks a bit different.

Shoot, move, shoot. And . . . silence.

A police siren howls in the distance, colourful lights blinking frantically through the dull grey rain. Those will be the police he called earlier.

I think I'll stay at my post until I know he's safe.

Oh, someone's feeling brave. One of the kids left upstairs is holding a gun, something military, kneeling down and pointing it in my direction. Alright, kid, I'll let you have one shot.

A series of bangs, and a gorgeous red-gold explosion surrounds the barrel in perfect symmetry; the window pane shatters completely, falling from the frame in tiny shards.

The bullets come pretty close, ripping chunks out of a couple of the bricks nearby, sending brick dust trickling downwards.

My turn.

Switch over to burst mode, deep breath, shoot – chest shots, four bullets right in the centre. He falls backwards, arms out and motionless.

Here come the police, parking up and running, three of them, weapons drawn, into the staircase; a second van follows them round the corner, four more officers jump out as backup.

I can probably leave it now. My subject is safe. Although he's definitely realised by now that he's not alone.

* A Ω *

Malleus had positioned himself next to the door, ready to eliminate any of the attackers who made it into the kitchen with his trusty knuckledusters.

There were a few cries of confusion, then silence; followed shortly by more shocked, furious shouts.

Footsteps clattered out towards the landing, and he heard hushed voices. The mob seemed to be reconsidering their tactics.

'Oi, you fucking Hun,' someone shouted. 'Call your fucking sniper off. We'll let you go!'

Malleus ran his thumb and forefinger over the ends of his moustache. Until recently he would have had no idea what they were talking about. But the Interpol update about the bullets in Rome and Riga had given him a good idea of who might be watching his back.

He said nothing and waited.

There was a short pause, then he heard a heavy thump as another body fell to the ground.

'Hey! Hey you fucking Kraut! Listen: I swear,' screamed a woman's voice, 'I will throw this fucking Molotov cocktail into the bloody kitchen right now if that bastard doesn't stop shooting my fucking mates.'

Malleus looked round the kitchen.

There were two windows he could potentially escape from. His guardian angel was apparently perched on one of the roofs opposite, taking out his attackers with startling accuracy. *Assassino di glifo.*

He ignored the questions for now: why was this person following him, protecting him? He pushed them to one side and focused. Right now he was just happy not to be fighting alone against a mob of angry kids who thought he had murdered Robin Warwick. Unfortunately for them, they were paying for this misunderstanding in blood.

Cautiously he looked through the net curtain down onto the street, where a handful of cars were parked haphazardly, having arrived seconds ago. Nobody dared to venture out into a potential line of fire in search of the hidden shooter.

'It may initially appear that I was responsible for the murders of those eight innocents.' Malleus was startled by a voice coming from inside the kitchen. It sounded like metal scraping against metal.

He turned round to face the source of the voice.

On the blade of a cleaver hanging on the wall, the blurred reflections of the kitchen formed themselves into the image of a human face. Malleus couldn't make out any details other than some vaguely masculine features and a beard.

'I am Barrex,' the blurry head introduced itself. 'I came to inform you that you are travelling the wrong path, mortal.'

Straight to the personal stuff again. No manners, these gods. 'And you didn't feel like manifesting a few minutes earlier to save Robin Warwick's life?'

'Through his death, his soul came to me. It told me what occurred in this house.' Barrex's voice remained level, and seemed to be emanating from all four corners of the room. 'Know this: Robin's account of the events in the Indian's house was false.'

So Warwick's soul had appeared before the god to whom he had sworn allegiance. It sounded almost plausible, if you subscribed to the most widely held model of the afterlife. Not that Malleus did.

Malleus set his PDA to record. 'And why do you feel compelled to correct that mistake? Worried about your reputation?'

'I am greatly respected amongst those who fight for their nations and beliefs. My followers would question me if you were to report that I was responsible for the deaths of eight Indians. And supposedly because one of them had merely insulted me.' Barrex's face remained an undulating shadow in the cleaver's blade. 'Search further, human. Find the one who must truly answer for their deaths, and now also for Robin Warwick's. I will be watching.' The silhouettes dissolved back into vague reflections of the kitchen.

From the neighbouring room came a series of shots that sounded like they came from an automatic rifle. They ended abruptly. The muffled thump of another body collapsing, the weapon clattering to the ground.

Malleus heard the howling of the sirens, and blue lights flashed through the window, illuminating the kitchen. The police had arrived.

It was over.

But for Malleus the search was about to begin again from scratch, as soon as he was released from the inevitable interrogation that would follow, that is. His status as a well-known officer of Interpol should get him a free pass, even if he had not been here on official Interpol business.

He would keep his guardian angel of death to himself for now, or feign ignorance if questioned. They would undoubtedly discover eventually that it was the Glyph Killer. *I could make my stalker into an official Interpol case.*

So Barrex claimed innocence.

Malleus would turn his attention to someone who he had not yet had the chance to speak to: the housemaid who had recorded the video footage of Anjay's body.

Her witness statement could be crucial. He needed the details that the camera wasn't able to record: smells, sounds, feelings.

He sincerely hoped that the maid was still alive, and had not fallen victim to the preta. Sometimes simply the fear of a curse was enough to bring it to fulfilment.

'Police!' came a bark from outside. 'Everybody down! Down, now! And you, Lilly! Does your dad know what you're up to out here?'

Here we go. Malleus slipped on his military coat and put on his hat. *Let's get this over with.*

Celtica, Paris-Lutetia, November 2019

'No way!' Marianne Lagrande had promised herself that she would stop dramatically exclaiming things out loud, but the information on the next stolen artefact from Treva was even more shocking than what she'd found on the ancient Elamite brick.

Bourreau had sent her his reports from Rome, complete with all his personal notes, the cryptic information given to him by Hephaestus, plus the recording of his lip movements.

The Interpol video analysis software had initially produced nothing more than garbled nonsense, but Lagrande had swiftly realised that an ancient Greek god would probably also be using an ancient language.

She had set the input language to Greek, as there was no option for ancient Greek, and immediately the program had begun to spit out words that made some kind of sense: *crown, nail, iron, master, long*. Lagrande had combined these key words with the description given by the Royale girl of the stolen crown. She had reached a conclusion even before the video software had completed its analysis.

Lagrande looked at the image on her screen: the Iron Crown of Lombardy, created at the beginning of the ninth century. Every detail matched the description given by the witness.

The crown was a golden band, a few inches tall and made up of six sections, decorated with rich green enamel. Circling the inner rim was a thin strip of iron, which according to legend was beaten from a nail of the True Cross. This was the source of its name, the Iron Cross: the twenty-two priceless jewels on its golden exterior did nothing to change this.

Crazy. Lagrande was still sitting in her office. She couldn't tear herself away from her research, forbidden though it might be.

Apparently this nail had been in the possession of Emperor Constantine the Great, who had received it as a gift from his mother Helena. And that Emperor had gone on to make Christianity the state religion of Rome. So the symbolic meaning attributed to this object was far from negligible.

Lagrande read that the crown had been found in the Cathedral of Mona in Northern Italy, but had gone missing during the chaos and lootings of the Great Change.

Its value: three million euros.

Now I just need to find the corresponding entry on the list. Lagrande was beaming. She sent the newest information directly to Bourreau and got her things together to leave the stuffy office.

She hid away all the requisite papers, and had just packed her bag when she received a message from Chief Inspector Grenzner from Treva.

The body of the young man from which they had extracted the African statuette had been identified. Its owner had sent out a Europe-wide report of its disappearance.

It fit perfectly with their existing intelligence: he was the son of a British art dealer based in York, in the north of England.

Lagrande sent that to Bourreau as well. *We're making progress.*

Britannia, London, November 2019

Nightfall, and Malleus found himself standing in front of the entrance to a new-build concrete block of flats on Southall Broadway in Ealing. On the eighth floor lived Sushmita Chopra, the housemaid.

Everything, literally everything, was written in two languages: once in English and once in Punjabi. Illuminated billboards on the squat office buildings blared their offers into the gloom, people with bags and trollies buzzed along the pavement, dragging their purchases home. The looming tower blocks dominated the skyline, masters over the smaller buildings.

Malleus heard a little English, but the language overwhelmingly spoken around him was Hindi or another Indian dialect. European-looking faces were few and far between. Ealing seemed to be more or less populated by various immigrant groups. Asian people, black people, Jewish people, all mixed together in a localized melting pot.

A Christian priest stood on a corner in his black habit, quietly reading out verses of the Bible in Latin. People tolerated him. On an LED screen behind him Hecate advertised the Wiccan cult; she placed great emphasis on her status as a *magna mater*, who had wandered the earth long before the advent of the Greek gods. Many British people had been turning to Wicca.

Especially the Christians. Malleus stepped into the tower block and took the stairs. The exercise would help him to gather his thoughts.

The interrogation by his English colleagues had taken no more than half an hour. As soon as he'd mentioned the name Gautama, there had been no problem. The dead and injured in Hackney left behind by his mystery sniper had been put down to a gang incident. Apparently the police were assuming that Gautama had sent some private backup along with Malleus. Robin Warwick had shot himself, that much was obvious: nobody was interested in his motive. No further questions.

By the fifth floor Malleus was beginning to break into a sweat.

Since Barrex had appeared to clear his own name of the eight apparent suicides, and Gautama himself had ruled out the workings of a preta, Malleus assumed that there must be a third god at play.

But what would a god want with eight dead Indians?

Is someone trying to torture Gautama? To drive him out of England? To undermine his business empire by taking everything he loved?

Though he was sure he had only scratched the surface when meeting Gautama, he understood him well enough to know that he would never allow himself to be driven out of the country. The deaths had seeded a deep hatred in him, a hatred that would not stop until it had found its target and destroyed it, mortal or otherwise.

As soon as the police had released him, Malleus had sent a request to Interpol and their colleagues in India for a background check on his client. He didn't see Gautama as a player in the murders, but there could be something hidden in his past that would provide him with a lead. Had Gautama made an enemy somewhere amongst the thirty thousand Hindu gods?

He also sent the video from the housemaid's smartphone to his friend at Interpol, asking him to enhance the images so that every detail in the background could be seen.

At the seventh floor, Malleus took off his hat; by the eighth he had removed his coat.

Wheezing lightly, he stood on the neon-lit landing outside Sushmita Chopra's apartment door – and hesitated. The sign on the doorbell read *Singh.*

He rang anyway and waited.

A few seconds later a man with a turban and an impressive beard answered, both of which clearly denoted him as a Sikh. The Sikhs believed in a single creator deity, and went to great effort to distance themselves from Hindus and their many gods at every opportunity. Malleus didn't want to consider the possibility that their god might have turned up and got involved in the whole situation as well.

'Yes?' The man appraised him with dark eyes.

'*Namaste.* Please excuse the disturbance, Mr Singh, but I thought' – Malleus looked at the sign again – 'a Ms Chopra lived here?'

'She did. We're still getting post for her.' He waited.

Malleus waited too.

'My dinner is ready,' said the man after a second. 'I'd like to go and eat it, if you don't mind. Sorry I couldn't be more help.'

'Would you mind telling me when she moved, sir? It would be very helpful to know.'

A woman called something in the background in Hindi. He answered Malleus' question: 'We've been living here for two days.'

'May I see the post, Mr Singh?

'It's not your post to see,' responded the man in an unfriendly tone. 'Who did you say you were again?'

He wasn't technically supposed to do this on unofficial business, but he did it anyway: Malleus pulled out his Interpol badge.

'But please be discreet, sir. Thank you for your understanding.' He passed him a business card. 'If Ms Chopra should get in touch, please ask her to contact me.'

Singh nodded, pocketed the card and disappeared for a few seconds into the flat. He returned with four envelopes. 'Here you go. Namaste.'

The door closed.

'Enjoy your dinner, sir,' Malleus called through the wooden door and smirked.

He was struck by a sudden craving for Indian food, which he was sure he would be able to satiate in this area of the city. Indian food and a Culebra. One that would help him think.

The housemaid's hurried departure seemed something of an overreaction. Did she really believe that the preta would follow her to her home?

Malleus took the lift downstairs, flicking through the post: the end of tenancy agreement from the landlord, the final bill from her energy provider, a notification that her visa was soon to expire, and some advertising for a travel agent.

Using his PDA Malleus pulled up the contact details of the remaining employees of the Gautama household, and it soon become clear that another three were not answering calls to their mobiles or computers.

Ahmir Khan, Rajesh Jankat and Rakish Sahid Kapoor.

To stave off his hunger, Malleus stepped into a busy little restaurant next to the tower block, *India's Finest Cuisine.*

He sat by the window, laid down his coat and hat and ordered a mango lassi and a mixed platter of grilled meats with various Indian sauces.

He filled the time until his food arrived by looking through the files on each of the disappeared staff.

They had each worked for Gautama for differing lengths of time, from four years to six months. Sushmita had worked there for around half a year. *Loyal, discreet, punctual, not a single mistake or slip-up.*

Malleus scrolled down.

All of the other employees had at least one or two reprimands or deductions from their pay.

These four, though, had perfectly clean records.

He used his Interpol credentials to access the database and ran a check on Khan, Jankat, Kapoor and Chopra.

Khan and Jankat had been born in England, Kapoor had lived here for ten years, and Chopra had turned up about half a year ago. Again, there was nothing on their records.

They're perfect employees. Malleus's food arrived and he savoured every morsel: the grilled meats, the refined flavours of the marinades, and the sweet spices of the dips. He wrapped the chunks of meat in a naan bread that made his fingers greasy and his stomach full.

He decided that after his meal he would go and canvas the addresses of the other three employees, though he didn't expect that any of them would still be living there.

Why were they disappearing? He was sure that there was another reason for their secretiveness, besides the threat of the supposed preta.

As he ate, he looked through the window onto the lively street outside and observed the scenery. He could easily be looking out onto a street in Mumbai if it weren't for the recognisably English facades of the buildings.

His chewing slowed.

A thought pushed through to the front of his mind, one that he had previously been keeping to one side. It occurred to him that this very second, amongst the crowds of Southall Broadway, his stalker was almost certainly stood watching him; the person who had protected him from the bloodthirsty Hackney teenagers, who had shown no hesitation in killing them – who had been following him since Rome, at least.

Malleus didn't know what he had done to attract the attention and protection of this person. And he didn't want either of them.

This has to stop. It was putting innocent people in danger, people were dying. *I have to trap this person.*

His PDA beeped: he had an incoming message.

Malleus cleaned his fingers on a napkin and opened the email, which contained the files regarding Gautama's past.

His eyebrows wandered slowly upwards as he read, and his craving for a Culebra became ever more urgent.

Shankar Kumar Gautama had been involved in many investigations in India, all of which had come to nothing. He had been suspected of commissioning intimidation, blackmail, grievous bodily harm and even murder.

He had also broken the wrists and jaw of a guest at an event in New Delhi, who had apparently dared to inappropriately touch his daughter. The guest never testified.

Two of his competitors in a bidding war for a new build in Bangalore had been found dead in a brothel, full of cocaine and alcohol, despite having never previously taken any drugs.

Malleus considered the image Gautama had managed to build for himself in England. The man was squeaky clean, none of the events in India were ever so much as alluded to in the press.

He pushed his empty plate to the side and looked back out onto the bustling street.

This explained the rage in his client's eyes. Gautama was used to having the last word on things. *Perhaps I should have done a little more research before I took this case.*

Malleus stood up, placed a few notes plus a generous tip on the table, and left the restaurant, heading for the i8.

He had another three flats to visit. Hopefully soon the suicides would start to make some sense.

Malleus was not surprised when nobody opened the door to him in Harrow, even as he rang the doorbell for the fourth time.

However, the name next to the bell gave him hope that this time, at least, there might be someone inside worth talking to. The two addresses he had previously checked had both come to nothing: the employees had clearly made a dash for it like Sushmita Chopra. Rakish Sahid Kapoor, however, seemed to still be in residence in this modest little building, which had a decidedly less Indian feel to it than those surrounding it.

Malleus ran his fingers over his moustache and looked around. It was a quiet little residential street, with as few people walking about as one would expect at this late hour. One or two dog walkers were taking their pets for a midnight stroll, nobody else was around.

Malleus found it pleasant not to be surrounded by the illuminated billboards for once, to experience something close to true darkness in this part of town.

In fact, the darkness put him at an advantage, as he wasn't intending to leave without having a proper look around.

Malleus pulled out his electric lock pick and placed it against the lock on the front door. Vibrating quietly, the machine did its work. There was a series of clicks as the lock cylinder was cracked. The door was open.

Malleus stepped quickly inside the dark house, listening carefully and looking around intently.

A tiny LED light blinked on the ceiling opposite him, first green, then switching to red. Kapoor had installed a home security system, and Malleus was probably now making a live appearance on the display of his smartphone.

No time to lose. Malleus went quickly through the room and deactivated the cameras, of which there were an impressive number, before turning on the light and hurriedly searching through the objects around him.

It didn't take much imagination to put the clues together: by the looks of the clothes and documents scattered about the room, the three disappeared staff had congregated at Kapoor's house. He had obviously been offering them a hideaway of sorts.

What's going on here?

It could have been the fear of the preta that had united them.

Or something quite different.

Malleus opened a cupboard expecting to find supplies and quickly realised his error. Inside was a life-size statue of a ten-armed deity, whose five pairs of shrugging shoulders seemed almost to betray its own cluelessness at the situation.

The figure seemed to have been carved from dark ebony, and was surrounded by a large bronze ring. It wore an expansive necklace of decapitated heads, and a skirt-like garment made from disembodied arms. In one hand it held a sickle-like blade, in the other a bowl of blood; on its forehead was a prominent third eye, and its outstretched tongue seemed to mock Malleus. With one arm held high, either in victory or consolation, the figure danced on one leg, atop a man's corpse.

Kali. Fresh flower petals lay underneath the statue, flecked with drops of blood. It smelled of opium, and there were white crystals scattered around, like crumbs of sugar. *Goddess of death and much more.*

Even Gautama prayed to her.

A notification pinged from his PDA, another incoming message.

Malleus glanced at it, deep in thought.

The email was from his friend at Interpol, the one who had been working on the background details in the smartphone video.

But to his surprise the specialist had uncovered something else: the film had been edited. The original film had been painstakingly transformed into the preta version, and the audio showed inconsistencies that pointed to post-film editing and dubbing. His friend wanted to know if he should continue analysing the footage.

Malleus thanked him and replied – further analysis would not be necessary.

An artificially created preta, a Roman-Celtic god who doesn't want anything to do with it, and three disappeared staff holed up with Kapoor. He turned to face Kali. *The connection to Gautama is this god . . .*

Something flapped past his ear. In a flash, the thing wrapped itself round his throat and pulled tight.

Malleus was dragged onto the tips of his toes by a powerful force, pulling his upper body backwards while the pressure round his throat increased. His constricted arteries stopped pumping blood to his head within a few seconds, and his Adam's apple made an audible crunching sound.

Malleus's attempts to stamp on the toes of his attacker did nothing to free him, though he clearly heard a couple of foot bones breaking under his heel. He grabbed towards his pocket to pull out the Apache Derringer inside, but his hand was pulled to the side.

The method with which he was currently being murdered

made him sure of one thing, though perhaps his realisation was more than a little overdue: he had uncovered a gang of Indian Thuggees – professional robbers and murderers, who worked in large family groups or fraternities. Unconsciousness overwhelmed him as he struggled for breath.

Kali's tongue stretched out mockingly as ever, the upheld arms of the unmoving statue conveying what looked suspiciously like a celebration.

* Α Ω *

The guy I'm following is getting cocky.

While he's searching Kapoor's house, he doesn't even notice that he's no longer alone. I can't see who it is, but he came right in through the side door.

Shit. I can barely see anything from out here. I'm sure I had one somewhere . . . ah, the balaclava.

Here we go. While I run I screw the silencer onto the APB.

The sounds I'm hearing in my earpiece from the bug I put on him are not good! He's wheezing, rattling, retching.

The door is still open, I can just go in through the front, across the hall into – there! There's his attacker, he's got a silk scarf round his throat. Well-built, this guy.

I crouch down, stalk up to him and stand up straight next to this brick shithouse of a man, pressing the muzzle of my gun to his temple.

But he just lets my guy go, pulls his head away and whips the scarf round so quickly that he manages to get the weighted end round the silencer on my APB and pull it off target.

My shots miss.

He plants a solid kick into the centre of my body and pushes me backwards, pulling a dagger from a holster on his back as he does so, and jumps on top of me.

I hit him with the APB, the silencer cracks him right across the mouth, and I raise my knees to keep his dagger away from my chest.

My right elbow smacks him square across the face and he tumbles over to the side, crouched over. His pupils are massive, he must be on something.

I raise the arm holding the automatic, smacking the barrel as hard as I can against the bastard's knees. I switch it over to burst mode, the gun stutters slightly as I fire. Two bullets right, two left.

Screaming, his knees shattered, he falls before the statue of Kali, whining and writhing around so pathetically that I have to laugh.

'What, Thuggee?' I whisper, to disguise my voice. An easy trick when you don't have a modulator to hand. 'You lousy prick. Go kill your own people. It'll be much better for your health.'

He raises a hand to the statue, says something. All I understand is one word: Kali.

He smears his blood on the foot of the statue, kisses its toes.

'What is this shit?' I taunt him, and crouch down next to him as he squirms. 'Do you really think that she . . .'

I suddenly have a strange feeling, and push myself sharply backwards, landing on my arse. Something moved past the top of my head.

Directly in front of me, a sickle is jutting out of the man's skull. This wooden goddess hacked at me with her bloody sickle – and instead managed to stab one of her loyal followers right through the head. What a fuck up!

I stand up, listening for more footsteps.

But he seems to have come alone.

The guy I'm following is still breathing. He still has much to do.

So much to do.

Good thing I'm following him. Hopefully this little episode will teach him a lesson.

* Α Ω *

Malleus quickly returned to consciousness, but it took a while before he could open his eyes. His throat burned, and he could feel a band of swelling exactly following the outline of the silk scarf.

In front of the statue lay his attacker.

The statue's arm holding the large sickle had somehow come loose or broken off, and in falling had split the man's head clean in two before burying the tip of its blade into the ground. There was an enormous pool of blood in front of the statue, and another emanating from the man's kneecaps.

Malleus's eyes panned across the bullet casings strewn across the carpet, then the holes shot into the wall, and a couple in the statue of Kali; a stray bullet had clearly shot right through its now absent tongue.

Malleus knew who it was that had saved him. *Again.*

Whether he liked the fact that he had a stalker or not, things in Hackney and now here would have gone very differently without his mystery follower.

That would have been quite the abrupt ending. Atheist found dead in front of Kali statue. He was glad to have spared the British press that salacious headline.

Malleus stood up and searched the man's body, who he was almost certain was Kapoor, though the two separate halves of his face made it slightly more difficult to identify.

He found an ID card, car keys, another knife strapped to his calf under his trouser leg, and a smartphone with an unread message on its homescreen: *When are you coming? The others are waiting.*

The sender of the message was Sushmita Chopra.

Waiting. Malleus looked at the statue of the death goddess, rubbing his wounded throat. *Waiting to strike.*

They had killed the eight people in Gautama's estate, and this time they were waiting for the final member of the household. Because he had been in India during their first attack, which they probably hadn't expected.

They must have noticed the mistake in their plan too late. Malleus put on his hat, stroking the ends of his Fu Manchu with his thumb and forefinger.

He guessed that the Thuggees had come up with the preta distraction so that they could still have access to Shankar Kumar Gautama after the initial attack, without the added security that would have come with a standard, non-mystical mass murder. Now he could be killed and counted as just another victim of the *hungry spirit*, albeit with a slight delay.

He tried to reach his client, but nobody responded to his messages or calls.

So he informed the police, instructing them to send vehicles to Braemer Avenue. He received another email from Lagrande with more information on the Treva case. *Not right now.*

Malleus ran outside, climbed into the i8 and sat behind the steering wheel. Breaking the speed limit wasn't an option on autopilot.

He raced at breakneck speed through the streets of London, thankfully relatively empty at this time of night. A couple of times he had to warn an unsuspecting pedestrian with the horn and headlights – they jumped out of the way.

Is Gautama a Thuggee himself? In his mind's eye Malleus saw the impressive man in his huge property, kneeling before the statue of Kali in prayer. *I've stumbled into a war between two families of professional liars and murderers.*

* Α Ω *

Some pretty crazy driving he's doing.

I risk it and use my own route. I know where he's headed. He's going an awkward way because of the car. With my motorbike I'm faster than he is.

I make it to Braemer Avenue before he does, park my bike a few houses down and make my way through the neighbour's gardens, wading a few metres through the lake at the back of the Gautama property. Of course there are cameras everywhere, but . . . they're turned off.

That means they're already here.

Three murderers, in a palace like this. They could be hiding round any corner.

Should be interesting.

I pull out the APB, screw on the silencer and wait in the bushes until he arrives.

I wouldn't want to miss him.

* A Ω *

Malleus pulled up outside the bronze gate and climbed hastily out of the i8, his Cobray Derringer in his left hand. Its shotgun shells were the only appropriate ammunition against these three attackers, clearly trained killers.

As there was no way of opening the heavy bronze gate, he climbed onto the roof of the i8, jumped over to the wall of the garden and pulled himself up, landing in the gravel on the other side a few seconds later.

The enormous property lay shrouded in darkness, the blinking LEDs of the security cameras were absent. Malleus saw this as a definite sign that the Thuggees were already inside and on the hunt for his client. He moved quickly towards the entrance.

The back door leading to the large park and the lake was not closed.

He darted inside and held the Derringer ready to aim.

Cautiously he slipped off his shoes, let his coat slide quietly to the ground and set down his hat on top of it. It would make it easier for him to stalk around unnoticed.

Malleus moved slowly, soundlessly through the ground floor of the property.

Again he found himself enveloped by silence and the penetrating scent of burning incense.

Neither the Thuggees nor Gautama betrayed their locations with any sound, not a breath or a rustling of material could be heard. Malleus, on the other hand, was convinced his shirt was rustling as loudly as if it were made of tinfoil.

Before he gave up completely on the search, Malleus decided to make his way to the corridor where he'd seen the statue of Kali. If he had figured out the head of this family correctly, he would be waiting for the intruders by that statue. Gautama would certainly make it much more difficult for the trio to reach him than the eight sleeping innocents they had already killed.

Malleus pushed his rising ruminations to one side. His priority right now had to be his own survival, and that of his client.

He reached the top floor, slowing to a cautious pace the further he progressed along the hall. The goddess of death and resurrection stood in the darkness at the end of the corridor, alone and abandoned.

He's not there.

Soft, golden light spilled from a narrow crack under the door, though there was still no sound to be heard.

Malleus took a deep breath, raised his Cobray and opened the door, striding inside and holding the weapon ready to fire. He closed the door behind him immediately and silently.

He found himself in the library, where the walnut bookcases on the walls and throughout the room spanned from floor to ceiling. Endless books were crammed together, old and new literature, thick tomes and ancient atlases. A collection of old maps were displayed with a waist-high globe in the centre of the room. The room was illuminated by a great number of candles, and a fireplace provided additional warm light.

Gautama sat sleeping in a comfortable winged armchair, a book open on his stomach, as if there were no danger to his life at all. His smartphone lay on the table next to him with a glass of chai. It was lighting up and vibrating.

Malleus moved closer.

He managed about four steps towards the man before a floor-board creaked loudly, betraying his presence more effectively than if there were some kind of deliberate alarm mechanism located around the chair. Gautama's eyelids shot open, his dark eyes fixing immediately on the detective.

'Good evening, Mr Gautama,' said Malleus, positioning himself so that he had the door in sight. 'Is that the only entrance into this room?'

'It is.' He rubbed his bearded face with his hand. 'How did you get in?' He picked up his smartphone and looked at the display. 'Oh,' he grumbled inwardly as he read the messages.

'Sir, I've notified the police that your life is in danger. I suspect that the remaining three Thuggees aim to murder you,' Malleus offered as explanation. 'The power in your house is out. They are already here.'

Gautama picked up the glass of chai and drank the last few sips. 'Can you explain what has led you to the conclusion that the murder of my entire family was carried out by a gang of *Thuggees*, Mr Bourreau, rather than by a preta or the god Barrex? Those kind of criminal gangs were stamped out over a hundred and fifty years ago in the colonies.'

'In my eyes the evidence points solely to that conclusion.' Malleus was struck by the man's calm countenance in the face of his own potential murder.

He gave a brief but clear account of everything he had experienced over the last few hours, from Hackney to the edited video footage, to the attack in Kapoor's house, which had served as a meeting point for the gang of assassins.

'The method with the silk scarf, weighted on one side to make it easier to swing around a victim's neck, it's unmistakable. Plus the statue of Kali in Kapoor's house. And I'm certain that more evidence will appear once we interrogate the remaining members of the group.' Malleus looked at the man, attempting to gauge his reaction. The British police would not be amused to find out that a branch of Thuggees had managed to establish itself on their soil. 'I didn't anticipate that this contract would put me in the middle of a war between criminal families.'

'You think I'm involved in some sort of gang war? You are mistaken.' Gautama smiled emptily. 'I have enemies, Mr Bourreau. As do all rich and powerful people. Apparently one of them, a particularly cowardly one, has set this band of professional murderers after me. I believe you are right concerning the murder of my family: I survived because I happened to be on an unplanned trip to Mumbai.' He nodded slowly, his long black beard shimmering in the candlelight. 'You have given me names and details of those responsible. The case is solved, and as far as I can see the murders have been explained.'

'But the police should—'

'The police have ruled that they were suicides,' Gautama interrupted him. 'Let's allow them to believe that. I will take care of the rest.' He took his smartphone and opened an application. 'I'm transferring you a million pounds. Does that sound right,

Mr Bourreau? Fitting compensation for your experiences over the past few days in London, I hope. And of course a recognition of your services and your discretion.'

'My daily rate will be enough, sir.'

'Not for me.'

Malleus knew that Gautama was attempting to buy his silence regarding the events he had uncovered. There was no way he could explain away such a huge sum as payment for what essentially amounted to a few hours' work. Plus he was still an Interpol investigator – he couldn't accept it.

Gautama held his gaze and finished the last swiping gestures on his touchscreen. 'It's an honour to be able to generously compensate you for your shrewd detective work, Mr Bourreau. I'll be sure to recommend you in the future.'

Malleus decided to donate any money remaining after his usual fee to charity. This money was clearly drenched in blood and sourced through countless crimes in India. 'Glad to be of service.'

Gautama nodded graciously and picked up his smartphone, making a quick call to the police. He called off the van that was heading towards Braemer Avenue and explained that there had been a misunderstanding.

'You really want to deal with this yourself.' Malleus couldn't endorse his client's taking the law into his own hands, but he was fairly certain that he could do nothing to stop it – other than by playing his Interpol card. *I should probably do that.* To assuage his growing conviction that Gautama was part of the Thuggee network, if nothing else.

He made his decision within three heartbeats: he would tip off his British colleagues regarding Kapoor and Co. Gautama could try to play the victim if he wished.

Then the door to the library opened.

* A Ω *

There he is! He jumps the gate, winds quickly through the Thuggee palace and finds the open back door.

Then I follow him. He can't get too much of a lead, otherwise I might lose him in all the rooms and corridors.

I've barely made it inside and he's already disappeared. Damn it, he's left the coat with the bug behind. Is he starting to suspect?

But after the events in Hackney he must be aware that I'm his guardian angel, that he needs me. Why would anyone want to get rid of me?

I begin the search. Start with the ground floor, probably in the room where he first met with Gautama.

The night vision on these glasses is invaluable, the darkness makes no difference to me.

Here's the room, and . . . what?

A section of the wall panelling is folded outwards, and there's an open safe behind it. Full of money. And documents, some hand written in Hindi, some printed. A lot of debt certificates. Hard drives, USB sticks. And photos of people.

The next victims?

Blackmail?

At first glance I'd say the Thuggees were looking for something.

In any case, the guy I'm following isn't here.

Keep looking.

* A Ω *

Ahmir Khan and Rajesh Jankat strode into the library one after the other, each holding a long dagger. They wore black clothing and light shoes that completely masked the sound of their footsteps.

'Leave, Bourreau,' Khan commanded, pointing at the door.

His pupils were immensely dilated, there was no doubt that he was under the influence of something very potent. 'This has nothing to do with you.'

'Since it's fairly obvious you plan to murder this man' – Malleus raised his Cobray – 'I'm afraid it has rather a lot to do with me, sir.'

The two men stood still as Gautama slowly stood up from his chair.

'You want to protect a man guilty of multiple murders?' Jankat spat reproachfully. 'As a policeman?'

'If that is true, Mr Gautama must stand trial in a court of law.' Malleus cleared his throat. 'You do not have the right to murder him, regardless of any crimes he may have committed.'

'It's *retribution*. Not murder.' Kahn gestured with the tip of his blade towards Gautama. 'He's as much a Thuggee as we are, he leads a huge criminal fraternity. He commanded his people to murder our entire families.'

Gautama gave a quiet, furious laugh. 'Such nonsense. Thuggees are professional liars. That's where the name comes from, the Hindi *thugna*: to deceive. We should be thankful to the British Empire for wiping them out a couple of centuries ago.' He stood next to Malleus. 'Except for these ones, of course. But we should be able to take care of that, don't you agree Mr Bourreau?' He turned his head to face the inspector's. 'These men just confessed to eight counts of murder, Inspector.'

Malleus listened and considered the fact that he could not currently see any sign of Sushmita Chopra. Were these two here as some kind of distraction, while she carried out some kind of ambush?

He was beginning to really hate the direction this case had taken. He would almost have preferred to be hunting a preta.

The barrel of his Cobray remained trained directly on the two men. 'I'm afraid I'll have to arrest you. For murder and attempted murder.'

Khan and Jankat laughed and said a few words in Hindi.

Gautama repeated their words scornfully and pulled open a drawer in the table next to his armchair. In one hand he picked up a long, asymmetric kris dagger with a wavy blade and ivory handle. In the other he held a chrome-plated Browning semi-automatic.

'Think of me as your assistant, Inspector Bourreau,' he said in English, clicking the safety off the gun. 'If these murderers should show any resistance during their arrest, I will intervene.' He pointed with the end of the gun towards the two men.

'I'd like to clarify one thing, gentlemen: where is Ms Sushmita Chopra at this moment?' Malleus added. 'I assume she's watching the corridor?'

Gautama raised the gleaming metallic pistol and aimed. 'Jankat,' he said coldly. 'Kali will find you and all those who helped you to murder my family. I swear it.' Before Malleus could stop him, he pulled the trigger.

Four shots rang out.

As the bullets made contact, Jankat took a small step backwards, before collapsing to the floor, gasping for air. Blood poured from the deadly wounds in his head, throat and chest; it spattered and smeared across the wooden shelves and floor.

'Gautama, no!' yelled Malleus.

'It is my right.' He aimed the Browning at his next target.

Khan jumped to take cover behind a set of shelves. 'Kali will find you first,' he called from behind his makeshift shelter. 'I am her arm, her sword, her will.'

'You take right, Mr Bourreau, I'll go left.' Gautama moved

swiftly, still stretching out the semi-automatic in his right hand. 'If you hesitate, you will die.'

Malleus went in the opposite direction, disobeying Gautama's command. 'You will not shoot this man,' he commanded sharply, whilst making another call to the police with his free hand. 'You called me and commanded that I get involved. That's what I'm doing.'

'I intend only to defend myself,' he responded, cold and disingenuous.

Malleus saw Khan in front of him, kneeling behind the shelves and holding the dagger. He paid Bourreau no attention, his eyes trained solely on Gautama, waiting to pounce. 'Stand up,' he ordered. 'Slowly. The dagger—'

A shelf of books suddenly fell from a great height towards Malleus's head.

The heavy, leather-bound volumes made painful contact with his head, shoulders and arms, knocking the Derringer from his hand.

Malleus took a hurried step back and reached into his pocket for the Apache.

In the middle of the avalanche of books landed a small figure, which immediately threw itself at him, clutching a katar fist knife in its left hand.

The blade slashed towards his face.

Malleus recognised the black-clothed Sushmita Chopra, who had clearly been hiding on top of the bookcase.

In one movement he dodged the attack and knocked the blade from her fist with his knuckledusters. A metallic clang rang out as the steel blade met titanium.

Though he didn't savour doing so, he gave Chopra a sharp knee to the stomach and stepped backwards. He didn't like hitting women, but when they were trying to kill him there was no alternative.

'You're under arrest, Ms Chopra,' he said clearly and flicked the Apache so that the revolver was facing the tiny woman. 'Put the dagger on the—'

Chopra held her stomach and stood up, wheezing. 'You should have left when you had the chance,' she spat, and raised the katar.

She sprang forwards, the dagger moving in a perfectly straight line towards him. She clearly aimed to plunge the tip of the blade straight into his solar plexus.

At that moment, the outline of Barrex's face appeared on the blade, and the dagger spontaneously changed direction in her hand, heading wide, away from Malleus.

Chopra stopped, astonished, unable to explain her weapon's sudden disobedience.

Malleus kicked at her knees, hoping to take her down.

But this time she escaped his foot, and rallied with a solid punch to his kidneys, her hand moving to pull the blade across his throat.

But the god's face appeared again: the blade once again changed direction.

Malleus shot twice with his Apache, deliberately targeting the air next to Chopra's head. The deafening shots should stun Chopra and hold her back.

She jumped visibly, startled enough to break off her third attack. She stared at the rebellious blade. 'Kali does not wish your death?'

Malleus took another step back from her. 'That's enough,' he said. 'Put down the—'

There were two more gunshots – and Chopra collapsed in

front of him with a sigh. Blood streamed from two holes in her back.

'No!' Malleus turned his head to Gautama, who lowered the smoking semi-automatic and sank another two bullets into the lifeless body of Khan, who was lying in front of him, the kris dagger sticking upright out of his chest.

'You can thank me later, Mr Bourreau,' he responded coldly and fired once more into the man at his feet, the shells tinkling softly as they hit the floor. 'I just saved your life.'

I'll have him charged. For murder. Malleus knelt down next to the young woman as she gasped for breath. Her lungs had taken damage, and judging by the red pool gathering underneath her body, one of the bullets had hit an artery. 'You could have . . .'

'Only his death will secure the lives of all those people in India,' she whispered, her words jerking as she gasped for air, swallowing the blood that was welling up her throat. 'It is complete.'

Malleus looked up at Gautama, who was slowly walking over to her. 'No. He's alive.'

Chopra laughed and fell into a coughing fit. 'Kali will find him. The chai . . .' She pointed over at the bookcase. 'I was already here when he came in. I wanted to be sure. Poisoned . . .' Her body tensed, her eyes became glassy . . .

Gautama reached them. 'There they all lie. The people who murdered my family,' he commented, his voice devoid of emotion, but the hate in his gaze ever-present. 'Thank you, Mr Bourreau. Without you I would have been their next victim.'

For a brief moment Malleus thought he might snatch the Browning from Gautama's hand, turn it on him and pull the trigger. He readied himself to use his Apache if necessary. 'For you, this isn't over, I presume?'

The man laughed like a merciless god of revenge, like the Indian version of Barrex. 'You can leave now. You've had your payment.' Then his facial expression changed. He laid his free hand on his stomach, uttered a groan of pain and retched.

Malleus looked over at the glass that had contained the chai.

Gautama followed his gaze – and understood.

'No,' he grimaced, kneeling down next to the woman's body as he began to lose his breath. He rummaged desperately through her pockets until he found a small plastic bag, still containing a few black crumbs.

Gautama vomited blood and greenish-black liquid over Chopra's body, swayed on his knees, and fell onto his side, racked by muscle spasms. The gun clattered to the ground.

He tried to speak, but his chattering teeth bit into his tongue, blood ran in rivulets out of his mouth into his beard and from there onto the floor of the library.

Malleus stood up and observed the man in his agony, which would end only after a few torturous minutes. His red-soaked beard smeared designs into the wooden floor as his body convulsed in pain.

Malleus took his cigar case from his jacket and picked out a Culebra with a light blue band. He lit it with a splint, and sat down in the armchair Gautama had been sleeping in a few minutes ago.

Malleus puffed a few clouds of smoke, and slowly began to work through what had just happened.

The case – solved.

The murderers – brought to justice.

A Thuggee leader – eliminated.

Further killing – prevented.

And yet he had never before experienced such a feeling of dissatisfaction at the conclusion of a contract.

He would inform his British colleagues of the Thuggee gang details, so that they could carry out the necessary investigations themselves. It was possible that further bands of professional murderers existed, and the potential threat if they spread outside the borders of London was significant.

Through his personal cloud of cigar fog, he saw the ghostly silhouette of little Anjay, standing next to the bookcase and looking down at her dead father, before she disappeared with another curl of smoke.

Malleus put it down to his active imagination. And England.

* A Ω *

I missed it.

When I finally find the source of the noise, the library, it's all over.

I look through the door.

He doesn't see me, just sits in the chair like it's a throne, smoking a Culebra, I can't see which colour band this one is. He likes to change them depending on his mood. This one presumably has some special meaning to him.

All dead, shot, stabbed and . . . poisoned?

Except him.

I make a silent oath to him that this will never happen again. If the Thuggees had killed him, my life would have no meaning. I found him first, after all.

He's too important.

Far too important.

I have to take better care of him.

Follow him like his shadow.

Celtica, Paris-Lutetia, November 2019

Marianne Lagrande sat in her tiny living room on the twenty-first floor of a tower block in the Paris banlieue and stared at her computer screen.

It was five in the morning. In the next flat over the man was screaming at his wife again before work, and she was screaming back. This little scene played out every day except for Saturdays and Sundays.

Lagrande's eyes burned, she could barely think clearly anymore – and yet she had cracked another code.

Firstly she had found the entry in the encrypted list, along with the corresponding book, that confirmed she was correct about the Iron Crown. The work *A Heart and A Crown* had been the key to proving without a doubt that the artefact had been in Hein's stash.

And now *The Art of War* by Sun Tzu had given her access to information on yet another stolen object.

It was some kind of Japanese fan, associated according to the list with an entity named Susanoo or Susanoo no Mikoto. Lagrande had initially hastily translated it as *Susanne*, until she later realised her mistake.

As much as I want to carry on, I don't think it's physically possible. I'll do the rest . . . tomorrow. After sleep. In a few hours. She rubbed her tired eyes and pushed the laptop to one side, sending one last quick email to Bourreau. He should know how much effort she was putting in, and against the direct orders of their shared boss.

If he doesn't want me as his personal assistant after this, he can kiss my ass. She shuffled across her flat, doing her most convincing impression of a zombie, and flopped into bed. Lagrande fell asleep before her head even touched the pillow.

She slept so soundly that she didn't notice when a key moved in her front door, and the handle slowly began to turn.

Britannia, North of London, November 2019

Malleus sat in the i8 and let the autopilot drive, while he used the external keyboard attached to this PDA to write up his final report to Lautrec.

The initially private contract had become a case for Interpol. He couldn't ignore a network of Thuggees, it was a matter of British national security.

MI5 had thanked him profusely. Nothing more.

Before the police had arrived, Malleus had found stolen files on the bodies of the Thuggees, which had clearly originally belonged to Gautama. Inside had been masses of photos and information on some of the most influential people in Britain. Perfect blackmail material.

Malleus had destroyed it all in the fireplace. The hard disks and USB sticks had gone up in flames too. He stoked the fire vigorously to remove every last trace, so that nothing could be salvaged.

He was not naïve enough to believe that there were no copies of this data elsewhere. But he hoped that he had at least made life a little more difficult for the Thuggees who would follow in Gautama's footsteps.

The route he had programmed into the i8 was not taking Malleus back to Heathrow airport, but to York. There he would find the father of the young man who had been fished out of the

Elbe in Treva. Dead. With a mysterious African artefact hidden in his rectum.

Malleus was hoping he could at least get some information from the man's father regarding the statuette itself. Best case scenario, he might even know something about some of the other objects that were missing from the dead dealer's collection in Treva.

He took his double espresso from the car's integrated coffee machine and pressed *send* on his PDA as he stirred in a sachet of sugar.

Lautrec would receive his report within seconds, though it only contained details on the part concerning the Thuggees. He had left out the part about the guardian angel with the APB, who shot people as if they were simply target practice. *That's my problem to deal with.*

Outside the north of England flew past, all hills and meadows with a few trees. Great pillars of cloud were gusted across the landscape by the Atlantic wind; seemingly as a protest against this treatment, they emptied their grey droplets onto the ground below. Grey curtains hung as a foreboding backdrop to the shower and cast a dull pallor over the right side of the motorway, while the other side was lit by a shaft of light, bursting through the gloom.

His wife would have enjoyed this view. *She would have loved it, in fact. We didn't do enough together*.

Malleus looked in the rear-view mirror, half expecting to see his stalker sitting in the back seat of the i8 – though whoever it was seemed to have kept their distance from the events in the library. He had observed the initial investigations by the British police at the scene, and no additional bullet wounds or shells had been found. They had all been killed by Gautama's weapons.

The question as to whether Barrex had really diverted Chopra's blade, or whether it was merely some psychological phenomenon, was of little interest to Malleus. He would have escaped her attack regardless of the intervention, simply by virtue of his combat training. Whatever these beings were, he wasn't about to rely on hand-outs from them.

He was about to check the latest message from Lagrande when he received an email on his private investigations account.

Malleus saw the subject of the message, but didn't open it. It was regarding the accidental death of a child, considered by the mother to be the work of a jealous god.

He didn't need to open the message. His empathy was secured within the first three words of the title, there was no question of his turning down the case. There was a child involved – he couldn't say no.

But first: York.

BOOK 4

Episode 4: Star Child

> 'Death and beauty are two things profound, so of dark and azure, that one might say that they were two sisters, terrible and fecund, possessing the one enigma, the one secret.'
>
> Victor Hugo, 1802–1885

Britannia, York, November 2019

Malleus Bourreau sat on a couch covered with reindeer furs, opposite the man whose dead son had been dragged out of the Elbe. It was quiet in the art dealer's office and the only sound in the antique-filled room was the echoing tick of a tall grandfather clock. The walls were wallpapered white and decorated with old paintings and historical weapons. Lights embedded in the green panelled ceiling filled the room with a warm, harmonious glow. A fire crackled in the corner, staving off the biting cold for which Northern England was so notorious. An iron screen surrounded the fireplace, protecting the luxurious carpets from the occasional spitting sparks.

Even the strong tea he'd been handed by one of the dealer's employees was doing little to cut through the encroaching sleepiness he felt in the warm room.

He was wearing his dark frock coat, and a long, high-collared white shirt, black trousers and shoes underneath. In front of him on the table lay his PDA, from which he had just read out the precise details surrounding the death of Stephen Ryan Crick.

Malleus observed the elderly man sitting opposite him. He was in his early sixties and, true to his artistic trade, wore an expensive suit in an outlandish black-and-white checked print; topped off with a crisp white shirt and a black tie in a double Windsor knot. He made an elegant impression; not everybody could carry off such an ambitious look.

The silver-haired Marcus Roy Crick had been silent for some minutes. His grey eyes stared at his powerful, well-groomed hands folded in his lap. The weighty signet ring on his right middle finger bore the sign of two ravens, *Hugin and Munin* – the dealer was a devotee of the Nordic gods, not that unusual in York despite the strong Celtic and Roman influences there. Malleus guessed by his tanned skin and strong hands that Crick spent a lot of time outdoors, maybe sailing; or something similar.

The man raised his head suddenly, looking Malleus in the eye, the light from the ceiling illuminating his dark grey beard. 'Thank you for making the trip to inform me personally, Inspector,' he said evenly, his knuckles whitening as he pressed his fingers together. 'He never took my warnings seriously.'

'Warnings, sir?' Malleus discreetly switched on his PDA's recording function.

'Our family has collected and dealt in art for four generations – it began with colonial art, which laid the foundations for the Crick family fortune.' He took a short breath. 'My son wanted to resurrect that side of the business. I'd spent the last few years specialising in paintings and Viking artefacts. I followed the legal route; he . . . followed the risk. And the higher profits.' Crick inhaled, unclasped his hands and reached for a whisky bottle standing on the table. 'We often argued about it.' With a practised grip, he poured himself a generous glass. 'For you, Inspector Bourreau?'

'A small one, thank you.' Crick passed Malleus a cut crystal tumbler filled with about sixty ml of the amber liquid. *If that's a small one, what does he count as a large?*

'I'm telling you this, Inspector, because I want you to find the person who killed my boy,' Crick continued. 'In order to do that you need to know what he did and what connections he had.' He lifted his glass. 'To those we've lost.'

'To those we've lost,' Malleus repeated, raising his glass in kind.

A small sip told him that the art dealer had outstanding taste in whisky: this one was mild, aromatic, minimal burn on the tongue, notes of caramel and a little salt.

The toast didn't take him back to thoughts of his dead family; instead it took him straight back to the wars of the Great Change, back to the front line, the trenches, the crashing of falling grenades and the howling of ash-coloured creatures as they tore through the trenches, bringing death to every soldier they encountered. It took him back to the carnage and death.

To those we've lost. Malleus took another drink and tried to shake off the flashbacks. Panic was not a useful emotion.

'My son was in contact with various shady characters; stolen goods dealers and so on,' Crick said, swirling the whisky round in his glass.

'Like Hannes Hein in Treva?'

To Malleus' surprise, the man shook his head. 'I've never heard that name come up. In one of my last conversations with my son, he told me proudly that he'd found the statuette of Odùduwà. A dealer by the name of Mohr had called him from Treva.'

'Did Mohr often call him with tips?'

'Mohr is a small-time player, more of a petty criminal than anything else. He lifts poorly secured artefacts from museums and flogs them on the black market,' Crick answered with more than a hint of contempt. 'I wondered at the time how on earth he'd managed to come across Odùduwà. I warned my son it could be a fake, but he was absolutely convinced it was the real thing.'

'How many people are looking for the artefact?'

'Must be a good dozen. I know three customers myself who would buy the statuette in an instant if I had it.' Crick sipped at the whisky. 'When I last spoke to my son he was with Mohr and a few other people, viewing a couple of different objects.'

'Do you know what else the dealer had on offer?'

'My son told me about four other artefacts that he was particularly excited about.' Crick thought for a second, and listed, 'A Japanese fan, a mediaeval crown, an embossed Indian horn and a small golden beetle from South America – one of a series, he thought. He sent me some pictures he took with his smartphone. I'll forward them to you, Inspector.'

'Thank you. But your son only bought the statuette, sir?'

'For ten thousand euros,' grumbled Crick in disbelief. 'Mohr had no idea how much these objects were really worth.' He emptied his glass and poured himself another. 'Of course, I know now why he was so eager to get rid of them. They weren't fakes. He had stolen them from another collector.'

Malleus ran his fingers over the end of his moustache. He didn't agree with Crick's theory. People in possession of expensive items were usually only in a hurry to get rid of them when their lives were in danger. Not when he had stolen them from one of his fellow dodgy dealers.

That led Malleus to one conclusion: Mohr had ripped off someone else – someone higher up. Someone who had ordered and paid for those five artefacts, and who had not received their expected deliveries. If he was correct, there would soon be more bodies found with connections to the break-in at Hannes Hein's place in Treva, and he suspected Mohr would probably be among them.

Malleus shared his conclusions so far: 'I believe your son, Mr Crick, was taken by the person who ordered the break-in in Treva, after they realised Mohr had ripped them off. I believe this person captured your son, interrogated him, tortured him and killed him. Mohr was out of his depth, selling the artefacts way under their actual value so that he could get rid of them as quickly as possible. It won't be long before they find his body too.'

'If you're right, the other four dealers at the viewing along with my son are in serious danger as well,' followed Crick.

'I fear so. Which makes it all the more urgent that we track down the person who contracted the break-in, as well as your son's fellow dealers. They may have committed a crime in handling stolen goods, but death is certainly too severe a sentence.' Malleus sipped his whisky. 'You are an art dealer, Mr Crick. Your connections to collectors and dealers in the scene would be incredibly valuable to this investigation. Would you be willing to advise Interpol on this case?'

Crick showed willing. 'By Odin, I want you to find the bastard who did this to my son, Inspector Bourreau. Bring him to justice.'

'With your help, we have a better chance.'

'I'll do anything. *Anything.*' Crick stood up and paced over to the window, fixing his gaze on the view of York's streets through the falling snow. 'Tell me what you need to know.'

'Well, it would be a good start to know what kind of objects Mohr was selling.'

'I'll take a look at the pictures my son sent me and let you know what I think.' Crick made a beckoning gesture towards Malleus. 'You said you thought my son was trying to smuggle the statuette?'

'I believe so, yes. Transporting it openly would have led to questions at customs, and without the proper paperwork it would have ended up in a police evidence locker.'

'Where is Odùduwà now?'

Malleus stroked his beard again. That was a good question, but one he couldn't answer right now. He stood up and went to join Crick, who clearly wished to show him something. He had taken the statuette with him to Paris-Lutetia, in order to store it there, but it was entirely possible that his would-be assistant Marianne Lagrande was currently playing around with it, trying to solve more of its mysteries.

'In a safe place,' Malleus answered. He was slightly concerned about Lagrande, come to think of it. The newspapers would certainly have reported on the statuette, as it was mentioned in the official police reports on the Crick murder. Whoever had ordered the break-in would surely be on its trail by now, presumably starting in Treva, and then moving straight to Lutetia. *I must tell Lautrec that he needs to keep an eye on the statuette. And Lagrande.*

'That's good. My son was convinced that it contained something extremely valuable.'

Malleus' breath caught in his chest. He thought back to the moment he had dropped the object outside the forensics building, smashing it into pieces. He had definitely found all the pieces – but he had no idea if there had been something inside it. *It was too dark.*

'Valuable in the material sense, or in the . . . *spiritual*? Or some kind of note with a message?' Malleus tried to narrow it down.

Crick shrugged his wide shoulders. He held the glass in one

hand and rested the other in his pocket. 'There she is: one city, three names: York, Jórvik, Eboraceum. We are now Nordic, Celtic and Roman: that's a lot of gods to get your head around.' He clicked his tongue. 'None of them came to help my son. Not even the one who was shoved up his arse.'

Malleus sipped his whisky.

He could have easily contradicted the old man, but tact won out. He stayed silent and looked out across the old town, an almost impenetrable sea of roof-tiles.

On his way into the old town, his i8 had driven past Clifford's Tower, the former keep of York Castle.

There had been a massacre here in 1190: the city's entire Jewish community had been wiped out. But the burn marks on the formidable castle walls were much more recent.

During the Great Change, history had begun to repeat itself as Christian attacks against Jews, and later followers of the Celtic and Nordic gods, rose sharply. The Jewish community in York had once again fled their attackers and sought sanctuary in the ruins of the keep, only to die in a hail of gunshots and improvised grenades. At the height of the chaos, a bolt of lightning seared down into the centre of the keep. There was no doubt that it was Thor's work.

York Minster, once the second-largest Gothic cathedral in Northern Europe, had also been destroyed, falling prey to the flames that had sprung up from the countless lightning bolts that peppered the city that night. An *unearthly* amount of lightning, as the Nordic community in York had proudly proclaimed – Thor and Odin had made their mark on *Jórvik* twice that night.

'I like living here,' said Crick quietly, placing his glass on the windowsill. 'As a boy I used to run through the Snickelways, playing hide and seek with my friends.'

Malleus had heard of the Snickelways: narrow streets from the late Middle Ages that wound round the market places, the upper storeys of the buildings crammed so tightly together that their roofs touched above the streets to form makeshift arches. Today these tiled vaults had become something of a tourist attraction, nicknamed the Shambles for their ramshackle appearance.

'It's totally dark there on some days, especially in winter, and there a few places where you'll see a ghostly figure or two hanging around,' Crick continued. 'Did you know that we have hundreds of ghosts here, Inspector?'

'No.'

'I've seen a few myself. Do you believe in ghosts?'

Malleus had to smirk. 'Sometimes they certainly seem more real to me than the gods.'

Crick nodded almost imperceptibly. 'Perhaps we should be praying to ghosts instead of gods. We expect less from them.' He looked at the tiny depiction of Hugin and Munin on his ring, then kissed it delicately, as if asking for forgiveness. 'Thank you for your time, Inspector. You'll hear from me as soon as I find out more about the objects, and I'll send you anything I have on Mohr.'

'Would you be so kind as to send the information to my assistant, Madame Lagrande? I'll give you her contact details.'

'Of course.' He turned to Malleus and went to shake his hand. 'From today you can consider me a new colleague in the search for my son's murderer.'

'As long as you can assure me that you'll let Interpol handle the manhunt. No going off on your own to seek personal revenge.'

'That's their job, Inspector. I'm not getting involved.' Crick gestured into the grey, snowy sky with his other hand. 'But if

Odin or Thor choose to strike the bastard down with a bolt of lightning, you can rest assured I prayed for it.'

I'd bet my salary that won't happen. Malleus shook Crick's hand and left.

* A Ω *

A nice little alliance forming there, between him and Mr Crick. That's good. Should help him out with the whole artefacts thing.

And here we are in York, city of ghosts and spirits. I should come here on holiday, I like it. Old buildings, old stories, a lot of history.

He's even more heavily bugged than before. But I still can't get into his PDA. He takes better care of that than he would a girl, if he had one.

Shit, he could have any girl he wanted. Like that little nun. Except of course, she isn't a nun at all.

I found out that there had never been a Sister Marina or Marinuschka in the Vatican. It wasn't cheap, but I delayed my flight for a couple of days after that whole business and had a look around.

The car she had rented was under the name of a Marina Dotch. Dotch – or daughter, in the correct Russian pronunciation. Seems the girl had come all the way to the Vatican just to be close to the guy I'm following.

I still need to check out the knife she carried hidden on her thigh.

Was she meant to use it on him?

Is the fake nun genuinely infatuated with him? Or does she intend to eliminate him?

I should probably have just shot her. I probably will. As usual.

Anyway, he's in York, she isn't.

He walks out of Crick's house, stamps through the snowdrifts to the i8. But he won't be going back to Germania. I reckon he's got himself a new contract.

I wonder how this thing with the artefacts will pan out.

I guess I'll see.

Because I'm still following him. Where would he be without me?

Celtica, Paris-Lutetia, November 2019

Marianne Lagrande lay awake in bed with the distinct feeling that she was no longer alone in her small two-bedroom apartment.

Her sleep had not been interrupted by her unconscious without good reason.

Living in a less-than-harmonious banlieue, she had to be aware of her environment, and this awareness couldn't be switched off for something as inconsequential as a good night's sleep. The city suburbs could be much more peaceful than the media would have people believe, but only for those with a certain level of street savvy. If you weren't careful it was easy to simply be swallowed up by the shadows of the immense skyscrapers with their solar panels and LED billboards.

With the return of the gods, life in the ghettoised areas of Paris-Lutetia had changed drastically. The overwhelmingly Muslim inhabitants had at first fought to keep their beliefs – indeed, the stricter denominations had even threatened their own members with death, should they renounce their faith.

Whole building complexes had gone up in flames, collapsing in great towers of fire and dust, together with those who chose to remain and die for Allah. After that many fled, though never escaping the new spiritual reality unfolding around them, and most of the others converted, just like the majority of Christians. There was no arguing with gods who could shoot flame and lightning from their hands. By the end of 2019, the banlieue was inhabited by a huge range of different religions, though none of them brought any greater wealth or prosperity to the area.

Lagrande closed her eyes, listening.

From the other room she could hear a murmured exchange between two men and a keyboard clacking. She realised immediately that they were on her laptop. They must be looking for something specific.

Lagrande ruled out burglars. They would have just taken the laptop, maybe the stereo system too, and left.

Drawers were opened slowly and quietly; they were searching the room. It was only a matter of time before they found her.

Lagrande opened her eyes and looked around. They hadn't been into her bedroom yet – her cupboards were all still closed. Apparently they wanted to turn the first room upside down before moving onto the next.

She slipped quietly out of bed, reached under the mattress and pulled out the taser she kept wedged between the slats. It could be discharged directly into the body through skin contact, or at range through the four darts attached to thin conductive wires: just the thing for unwanted guests.

Lagrande activated her silent alarm through the telecommunications panel in her wall. That would inform not only the police, but more immediately, building security.

She was wearing black underwear and a long, baggy T-shirt. Her long blonde hair was tied in a loose ponytail.

Soft footsteps slowly came towards her room and the door began to inch open. A masked head appeared through the gap.

Lagrande shoved her full bodyweight against the door.

The front edge of the door cracked against the intruder's head. Blood sprayed out from under the balaclava and he fell to the ground with a groan.

Wanker! She opened the door sharply towards her, the taser grasped in her other hand.

A second masked intruder was sitting, visibly shocked, at the kitchen table, fingers still poised over the keyboard of her laptop. Like the other guy, he was dressed in normal street clothes, with a leather jacket that looked a little baggy around the shoulders.

'Don't try anything, bitch,' he warned her.

'You started it,' she replied coolly. She could see that he had been reading through her emails with Inspector Bourreau. *It's about the artefacts!* A USB stick was poking out of the slot on the side of the computer, a tiny LED on its casing blinking steadily. 'What's going on?'

He stood up in an instant, swinging his weight towards her and grabbing at her arm.

Lagrande took a step back and in a moment of panic fired her taser.

Two darts shot straight into the man's chest, followed by the obnoxious crackle of electrical current – but the electrodes had buried themselves into a bulletproof vest, causing the man no damage whatsoever.

His weighted-knuckle glove came barrelling towards her too fast for her to dodge, and the fist connected with her left cheekbone.

The force of the punch slammed her against the small kitchen dresser. Plates, cups and glasses crashed to the floor. A sharp stabbing pain radiated across her jaw and the coppery taste of blood spread through her mouth.

Lagrande grabbed one of the shelves and swung it round to crack across her attacker's skull.

The man countered the blow with a powerful right arm, smashing the wood in two. He spat a loud curse through his gritted teeth, but he remained unmoved.

In the couple of seconds it took him to recover, Lagrande held the contacts of her taser against his arm and pressed the trigger again.

This time his Kevlar couldn't help him. The current coursed through him and he collapsed in a twitching heap.

Lagrande stamped her heel directly into his groin to give him something a little more permanent to remember her by. The pain in her jaw was excruciating, and she silently hoped it wasn't broken. As she thought about the possibility, she kicked him again in the scrotum.

'Stop it, you dumb bitch.' A blow hit her square in the back and sent her flying over the crumpled man in front of her, and face first onto the couch. A third man had emerged from her bathroom.

Lagrande spun onto her back and was about to fire the two charged darts left in her taser – and found herself staring down the barrel of a large, silenced semi-automatic. She froze.

'Where's the fucking statuette?' the masked intruder said in a low voice.

'I've no idea what you're—'

He pulled the trigger, the slide clicked back, and a bullet fired into the cushion beside her. Cheap foam padding burst out and sprinkled across her T-shirt.

'In the evidence room,' she answered hastily.

'Do you have access?'

'No,' she lied. 'I'm just an assistant. Only the investigators have access.'

The man on the ground outside her bedroom heaved himself up against the doorframe, breathing heavily. He kicked at Lagrande, the tip of his shoe cracking painfully against her side. 'You'll get another one in the mouth later,' he hissed, poking tentatively at the wound on his temple.

'Get William on his feet,' the man with the gun muttered behind him. 'Search the other room.' He looked at Lagrande. 'We're taking her with us. Bourreau will have to get the statuette out of the evidence rooms, or we'll start sending him pieces of his "assistant".'

The third man was dragged upright. Wheezing heavily and holding his crotch, he slowly sat with his legs wide open, breathing deeply in and out. He was of no use for now, but the looks he shot in Lagrande's direction held the unequivocal promise of a long, painful death.

'He broke the statuette,' William finally managed to squeeze out.

'What?' The one with the gun looked at him questioningly, the barrel still aimed squarely at Lagrande's torso.

'In the last email. She was supposed to go and search for pieces in front of the forensics department in Treva,' he managed between deep, wincing breaths. 'We can back off.' He gasped. 'Shit, I think my ball's exploded.'

There was a knock at the door.

'Madame Lagrande, building security and police here,' someone spoke loudly behind the door. 'You activated the—'

The third intruder swung his gun around and fired the entire magazine at torso height through the door. Screams erupted outside. When the chamber clicked empty, he loaded a new cartridge and continued firing. 'Move out,' he ordered the others as he shot. 'Take the bitch with you.'

'Wankers!' Lagrande kicked William square in the face as he began to heave himself up off the couch, and shot her taser at the third man, one dart connecting with his leg.

The charge wasn't enough to fully incapacitate him, but it was sufficiently strong to drop him to his knees in front of her.

Lagrande rammed her knee against his nose and lunged towards the bedroom, slamming the door shut behind her, locking it, and jumping away immediately, rolling under the bed for cover.

Not a second later bullets began to punch through the thin wooden door, which offered no resistance whatsoever. They whizzed past her head, ricocheting off her bed, clanging against the metal frame.

Her heart pounded in her chest as she lay under the mattress, her breathing shallow and rapid from fear and adrenalin.

The shooting stopped. There was the sound of raised voices outside the apartment, then bullets began to fly in through the front door. The squeaks and static of police radios could be heard in between shots – they were calling for backup.

After a while – Lagrande couldn't tell exactly how long – everything went quiet.

She ventured out from under the bed and peeked through what remained of her bedroom door into the kitchen. The men had disappeared.

Lagrande crept out of the bedroom, looking cautiously around her for signs of movement.

There were a few bullet holes in her front door and in the window. The laptop was still on the table but the USB stick was gone. Blood was splattered everywhere.

She looked out to the hallway where two police officers and a security guard were lying on the ground in a lake of blood. One of the police was groaning softly, writhing to and fro in agony.

Lagrande pulled her ponytail tighter and hurried into the corridor to administer first aid until the emergency services turned up. Just to be sure, she picked up one of the men's radios and called for backup herself, but was reassured that forces were already on their way.

She turned her attention to the injured man. The other two were definitely dead.

While she opened his shirt to reveal his wound and removed the man's belt to bind together what was left of his arm, she calculated the quickest route to Treva, to the front of the forensics department, to the pavement where Malleus thought he might have lost whatever was inside the statuette.

There was no way she could let it get into the hands of these wankers – whatever it might be.

Tunisia, Tunis / New Carthage, November 2019

Malleus was sweating – in November.

He had slightly underestimated the temperature difference between York and North Africa. He had long since folded his military coat over his arm; at least his hat and sunglasses were providing some protection from the bright heat of the sun. Luckily he had packed a lighter-coloured version of his usual black jacket.

He parked his car – a sand-coloured Range Rover; there had been no i8s available for hire – and walked up to the house of his client, who lived within spitting distance of the archaeological excavations of ancient Carthage. As in so many cities since the return of the gods, the ruins were being rebuilt; once complete, they would stand as a symbol of the resurrected power and glory of the gods, who took great pleasure in such displays of worship.

Malleus pulled his handkerchief from his pocket and dabbed at the sweat on the back of his neck. A few hours ago he had been tramping through snow – minus two degrees – and now a mild sea breeze was wafting the scent of ripe citrus fruits into his nostrils. He hadn't yet decided which circumstance he preferred.

From the street he was able to get a good look at the progress being made on the former excavation sites. The pillars and buildings and temples had already been constructed and the finishing touches were well on their way to being complete. The Roman gods had a strong grip on Carthage now; a kingdom that had once cost Rome dearly in blood and battles, until they had finally managed to flatten the city. '*Delenda est Carthago* – Carthage must be destroyed,' he said quietly. Someone important had said that at the end of his speeches. *Plato? Cicero?*

Everything here had been rebuilt, mostly more beautiful and ostentatious than before, including his current surroundings, the more upmarket area of Tunis. On his way here he had passed the Tunisian presidential palace. The people round here had more than enough money to live comfortably.

Malleus had almost reached the entrance of the modestly decorated two-storey building before him. The exterior looked like ancient clay walls, but he guessed this was a homage to the region's heritage. What did impress him were the clearly recognisable Egyptian hieroglyphs surrounding the door. His client worshipped Ra and his consorts.

Malleus found that intriguing. North Africa certainly had an entirely different pantheon from Europe.

He took a photograph of the symbols with his PDA, which informed him that they referred to the god Sokar.

'One of the oldest Egyptian gods of death,' he read on the display. 'Once a fertility god. Human body, falcon head, depicted partly in the mummified form of Osiris. The tombs of Saqqara are thought by many scholars to derive their name from the god Sokar.'

A god of death. He suddenly craved a Culebra. A blue band.

As he reached the door, it was opened by a man and a woman, both wearing long, airy black robes. The pair attempted a welcoming smile, but their expressions were so crooked and empty that Malleus was immediately flooded with pity. He knew how it felt to lose a child. That's why he took cases like these.

He took off his hat and sunglasses. 'Madame and Monsieur Tameri,' he greeted them politely with a gentle bow. Cool air hit him from inside the house, as if from a tomb.

'Welcome, Monsieur Bourreau.' The man nodded, his wife following suit. 'Please, come in and cool down. It's far too hot outside.'

'Thank you, that's very kind.' Malleus stepped inside and handed his coat to a servant who appeared beside him. He slipped off his heavy shoes and was handed a pair of light indoor sandals. He could hear soft string music, and the tinkling of a wind chime mixed with the gentle babbling of a fountain standing in the entrance hall. Again, he smelled the scent of citrus fruits.

'Shall we go into the atrium?' M. Tameri directed them gently with one arm.

His wife let out a sob and steadied herself on his arm. 'I'm sorry, Monsieur Bourreau,' she said waveringly. 'I don't think I can . . . My son—' She held a hand in front of her mouth, but it didn't hide the tears running down her cheeks.

'I can discuss it alone with your husband, if you'd prefer,' offered Malleus, exchanging a glance with Tameri, who accepted gratefully. 'Please, get some rest, Madame. There's no need to put yourself through this.'

She hurried away immediately, her sobbing cutting Malleus to the core as he silently followed Tameri through a series of generously appointed rooms decorated with both Roman and

Egyptian elements, the seal of Sokar displayed in each and the prominent hieroglyphs cementing the impression of the householders' devoutness.

They took a seat on some loungers surrounding a low table. On the table stood a bowl filled with the ripest, most beautiful fruits Malleus had ever seen. During the Great Change, soldiers would have killed for fruit like this.

'As you may have seen,' Tameri began, clapping his hands together to summon a servant who brought plates, served refreshments and adjusted their cushions, 'the Egyptian community is building a small sun pyramid to honour Ra, as well as a temple to Sokar.'

Malleus remembered having passed a large mound of earth on his journey where works were clearly underway. 'I believe so, yes.'

'The Saint Louis Cathedral used to stand there, on Byrsa, the citadel hill. But the Christians no longer need it. Their community dissolved and converted, partly to us, partly to the Romans, and some to the old cults, of course.' Tameri lifted a decorated glass of lemonade and took a long drink. 'You may be wondering what that has to do with my son Snofru's accident.'

'I assume it will become relevant.' Malleus sipped his drink and realised his error. *Not lemonade.* Sweet and fruity, with orange blossom water and bitter almond extract. *Almond milk.* It was delicious.

'I am one of the architects overseeing the build. For practical reasons we are repurposing much of the stone from the ruined cathedral itself.'

'How did the cathedral end up on top of the hill in the first place, Monsieur?'

'The French built it in 1890, because they thought the grave of Louis the Ninth – a king from the Crusades, one of their saints – was situated there.' Tameri set down his glass. 'Up until the mid-sixties it was the largest North African church, and an important centre of culture. With the help of the National Museum of Archaeology, we relocated it to the city and started our construction.' He wiped his mouth. 'My son used to love accompanying me to the building sites.'

'How old was your son, Monsieur?'

'Three. A good runner already, and climbed like a little god.' Tameri ran his fingers across the ornamental details on the table.

Responding to his touch, part of the table's surface became a monitor, which raised and tilted to face them on the low lounging chairs.

A child with dark, curly hair appeared on the screen, climbing over small and large stones in nothing but his nappy, lifting himself up ledges and laughing with construction workers. He appeared to have a very sunny disposition.

'Very sweet.' Malleus noticed a mark that stretched right across the little boy's back. It looked almost like a tattoo in dark brown, but the skin was slightly raised. 'May I ask what this mark is, Monsieur?'

'The reason he had to die.' Tameri paused the video with a small gesture and zoomed in.

'It's the sign of the god Sokar,' Malleus realised aloud. 'And I presume he had it from birth?'

Tameri nodded. 'My wife and I were priests of Sokar when we travelled to New Carthage. The god bestowed upon us the great honour of allowing my wife to bear his child.'

Malleus took a long drink of almond milk and tried not to imagine how a falcon-headed deity might have sex with a human woman. Although now that he thought of it, they did say that

Roman and Greek gods transformed themselves into bulls and swans in order to have their way with mortals. 'Were these circumstances known to the community?'

'Why should we keep it a secret?' Tameri sounded genuinely confused. 'It is the sign that our god is close to his followers, so close that he left behind a gift of flesh and blood.'

'There must have been plans for the boy's future, Monsieur?'

'Of course: we built the pyramids for him. He was going to lead the Sokarians as a demigod and show us how close our god can be. How close he *is* – that he is a *part* of us.' Tameri pressed play on the video.

It was now abundantly clear that the child was moving with a coordination far too advanced for his years. He was beyond gifted. It was arresting, the discrepancy between his tiny size and his behaviour. He was even talking fluently with adults.

The screen went dark for a second, only to be filled seconds later by a close-up shot showing the burned body of a child. No grisly detail was spared.

The boy lay in a charred metal bowl, his limbs twisted at grotesque angles. The camera panned out and it became clear from the scenery and the nature of his injuries that he must have fallen from a scaffold at the pyramid construction site. The base of the metal vessel was blackened, and the little body was surrounded by ashes and burnt shards of wood.

Malleus leaned forward and made the same gesture that Tameri had previously used, zooming in on the image. *Yes – I thought I saw something.*

Though the child's body was heavily charred, his bones broken and skin blistered from the fire, the heavy wounds couldn't conceal the fact that the sign of Sokar on the boy's back had been heavily lacerated with some kind of blade.

Someone did this deliberately. Malleus leaned back. 'May I have a copy of this video, Monsieur Tameri?'

'I'll send you all the footage and files. Or if your PDA has a Hyper-Infrared Interface?' – a red LED lit up – 'just wave your device over the table.'

Malleus transferred the data; he would look over it all in private, each and every image. 'I understand why you don't believe this was an accident,' he said carefully. 'Do you have any suspicions as to who may have killed your son?'

'Someone who didn't want Sokar to become established in New Carthage.' Tameri looked helpless. 'But we've never been openly opposed – *that's* what I don't understand. Otherwise I would have done everything in my power to keep the boy protected, I wouldn't have let him out of my sight . . .'

Malleus nodded thoughtfully, stroking the ends of his Fu Manchu moustache with his thumb and forefinger. 'Has Sokar communicated with anyone since it happened? A promise of vengeance, or anything similar?'

Tameri shook his head. 'He is full of grief.'

'He told you this personally?'

'No. I just believe he is.'

Malleus stood up. His clothes were already drenched with sweat, but there was nothing to be done about that. He had to go and look for clues. 'I'd like to take a look at the crime scene, Monsieur Tameri. Would you accompany me? You would be a great help in preventing any misunderstandings as to my intentions at the site.'

'Of course, Monsieur Bourreau.'

'Since the . . . *accident* . . . have any people left the community of Sokar?'

'No. They have stayed loyal to their god and brought us great comfort through their continued faith.' Tameri walked him to the front door, changing his clothing with the help of his servants as he walked, in the brisk manner of a Grand Prix pit-stop. He now wore a white robe and was holding a light-coloured hat.

'The authorities don't share your suspicions regarding the accident?'

'No. For them it's a case of neglect. They began an investigation into myself and my wife.'

'They seriously claim that the injuries on his back were caused by the fall?' He found that extremely odd.

'They did, Monsieur Bourreau. Lacerations caused by the shards of rock that fell with him.'

'The investigator wouldn't happen to be the priest of a rival god?'

Tamari stopped walking. 'No. But his sister converted to Sokar. She had previously belonged to the Temple of Poseidon. It's a new build, down by the old Carthage harbour, from the Punic times.'

Malleus noted the fact, but guessed it wouldn't be important. It was too obvious.

There were already plenty of suspects and motives amongst the ranks of the Sokarians. He could well imagine that more than one woman in the community dreamed of bringing a demigod into the world. Malleus would look into this line of questioning later. *Probably endless rumours to trawl through.*

He remembered an old Germanian phrase, used to describe children who died at an early age: *Sternenkinder*. Star children. For Snofru it was doubly true – not only was he very young, but also the child of a 'divine' being.

A servant handed him his shoes and he noticed they had been freshly polished.

The door swung open and the midday heat bore down on

them like a starving wild animal, panting at them with its sandy, glowing breath.

Malleus left his coat in the house and put on his hat. This was turning into his hottest case in a long while. And his socks were definitely too thick for this weather.

* A Ω *

Just my kind of weather! The guy I'm following has done me a huge favour: sun, warm temperatures. And the sea.

It wasn't easy to follow him here. In fact, he caught me a little off-guard, flying with his chartered jet to Carthage. But anything he can do, I can do too.

Good thing the little airstrip is right round the corner from this new client's house. I caught up on his couple of hours' head-start, and luckily he hadn't travelled any further once he got here. Otherwise things could have got hairy.

There they are, on the building site, Tameri and him.

Pyramids and temples. Egypt. Looks wrong somehow, stuck in the middle of all the old Roman crap. Impressive, yes, but not right.

As soon as the priest passes the workers he is greeted with subservience. Show-off. But despite that he does still have something sympathetic about him.

The two of them are talking about the progress of the building projects; they should be complete in a year – the murdered Sokarian boy will be immortalised in a temple alcove. The Egyptian community is growing; many people from Central Africa are converting and helping to spread the cult of Ra.

Fucking hell, I bet the Pharaoh of Egypt is pretty happy about that! It'll be interesting to see how big his territory gets.

The Pharaoh's done nothing, and yet they follow him in droves, just another self-proclaimed god. He's got a pretty easy ride – as long as Ra and his buddies are happy with the job he's doing as their representative, anyway.

Actually, now that I think of it, being Pharaoh is a bit like being the Pope.

Yeah, round the Mediterranean, they're all a bit scared of the Egyptians nowadays, even the Romans and the Greeks.

Personally, I kind of enjoy the variety of religions that've cropped up since 2012. It's not like there's been any more injustice or conflict than there was before. Obviously, the Great Change had to happen to break the chains of the old regime, but since then, a lot of peace. All the great critics and naysayers back then certainly didn't see that coming. They were so used to how things ran under the sign of the cross, the half moon and the star of David.

But I could be wrong, maybe things are about to kick off again. Like before.

Since the Great Change the gods have been playing nicely. My guess: to give the populations they decimated a chance to repopulate. Nice of them.

I wonder which cult will be the first to armour up for battle. Whoever it is will have to come up with another name for their holy war – you can't have crusades without Christians.

He's climbing the pyramid.

He'd do well as Pharaoh, I think. He's surveying the town as if it belonged to him. As if he were a god himself.

His trick is that he denies everyone. It makes him a kind of anti-god. An antidote.

They should fear him, instead of finding him entertaining, just like Hephaestus told him back in the Vatican.

Pride always comes before a fall.

Always.

* Α Ω *

Malleus immediately saw something at the site that he'd been unable to confirm from the video recordings. He stroked his moustache in thought.

In order to land in the metal bowl, the boy would have to have jumped. But Malleus doubted that a three-year-old could have jumped that far, even taking Snofru's extraordinary development into account. The place where the child had landed had been cordoned off with police tape that had already been ripped off by the wind and was fluttering noisily, wrapping itself round scaffolds and curling though the air.

Something else occurred to him as he eyeballed the site from the top of the hill: the temple and pyramid were surrounded by Roman temples and building works, and directly to the south lay the Amphitheatre, in all its newly restored glory.

The fact that the Sokarians had selected this specific hill had surely made them a great deal of enemies. Secret ones.

His PDA told him that this hill, Byrsa, had once dominated the city and its harbour. The Phoenicians had founded the colony around 750 BC, and it had survived until 146 BC, when it had been besieged and defeated by the Romans. The citadel acted as a defence for the developing city within, which had had more than four hundred thousand inhabitants at its peak.

Malleus looked out to the glittering sea and the intricate structures of the Punic harbour, now dotted with neo-classical new builds. He smelled the salt on the wind. Carthage was certainly the place to be if you liked the heat; it really was the perfect location, on a peninsula with the Gulf of Tunis to the east, the lagoon of Sebkhet Ariana to the north, and to the south, a lake.

His PDA was unable to find any information regarding the potential influence of Egyptian cults in the area at any point in history, so it was beginning to look as if Sokar was the first god from the other side of the Mediterranean ever to make his mark in Carthage – and not only that, but on the most exposed and strategically positioned location in the whole city. Everyone would be forced to look up at his temple and pyramid. *Every single day.*

North of Byrsa loomed the necropolis of old Carthage, an area much more suitable for Sokar as a god of death, Malleus thought.

He's staking a claim to the city, he surmised, patting his pockets for the cigar case full of Culebras. The fact that he had fathered a demigod here would have done much to strengthen Sokar's ministry in the region.

Malleus picked out a crooked cigar with a blue band, lit it with a splint, puffed on it a few times and focused on the view, his thoughts wandering as his eyes roamed across the landscape. He took out his PDA and shot a quick video of the panorama, then pointed the camera downwards to capture the scene of the accident.

A notification popped up from the PDA's translation function, still activated from its use on the hieroglyphs at Tameri's house: *TANIT.*

Tanit? Malleus vaguely recalled his client having mentioned a local cult – was that their name?

He tapped the screen of his PDA, focusing the camera on the image it had registered as a hieroglyph: a triangle underneath a horizontal line, all topped by a round disc. The program had interpreted the metal bowl as the disc, the triangle was formed by a pile of rocks and an iron bar imitated the horizontal line.

When Malleus looked up who or what Tanit might be, the stream of results prompted him to take several long drags on his cigar, one after another.

Bingo!

Tanit was a Punic goddess, the chief deity of Carthage, a symbol of fertility and responsible for the protection of the city.

One detail stood out: worshippers of Tanit were thought to have engaged in child sacrifice, and more specifically, child immolation.

That would explain a few things about the boy's death. Malleus clambered hastily down the planks, steps and ladders that led back to the ground to take a closer look at the bowl that had contained the body.

Inside the cordoned-off area, Malleus knelt down and picked up a fragment of wood. He scratched around in the ashes and charred remains until he found something.

Carefully, he dug out the objects from the ashes. He was left with a pile of what looked like the dried out, half-burnt remains of fruit peel – and a handful of tiny bones.

A glance at his PDA confirmed that the proper sacrificial offering to Tanit included pomegranates, ears of corn, figs – and a single dove.

Malleus stood up, pushed back his hat and mopped his brow with a handkerchief. Someone had offered up Snofru as a sacrifice, though this was more than a standard bid for Tanit's blessing. Someone wanted to show the Sokarians who held the real power in Carthage.

This won't have been the only murder. He left the cordoned-off area and dictated his notes into his PDA as he walked back across the construction site towards his car.

The Tanit symbol at this scene had been hiding in plain sight, laid out as if by coincidence, but next time it was certain to be more obvious, more prominent. But was it even possible for the murders to escalate any further? They had already killed a demigod. The only place to go from there would be exterminating the entire community.

I need to get Tameri up to speed on this. Precautions need to be taken.

Malleus kept coming back to the question of how Tameri had managed to secure the deeds to the citadel hill, especially in the name of an Egyptian deity. Who had sold Byrsa to the Sokarians? What were the conditions of the deal, and what was the price?

At that moment it became abundantly clear to Malleus who the next victim would be: Tanit had reasserted her ownership of the hill, and whoever had brokered the deal that sought to take it from her would be the next subject of her revenge.

Before he spoke to Tameri, he needed to scope out the size of Tanit's following in New Carthage – did the forgotten fertility goddess have a large group of devotees or just a single, cowardly fanatic?

He feared that the killer would be successful in provoking some form of retaliation from Tameri, which would be counterproductive.

After a short rest at the *Grand Carthage Hotel*, he resolved to continue his investigations. He had to get ahead of this mess. But first, he really did need to change his socks.

* Α Ω *

He seems to be making progress, and now he's headed for the old town.

Shit, I really need to hack that PDA. I'm so cut off without it, just blindly running around after him like an ignorant prick.

There must be some way of getting in to it while he's in the hotel. I need to get inside his head. All he has to do is get a spontaneous flight when I'm not close by and bam, *I've lost him. Then he'll end up running into some more nasty pieces of work like the Thugees and it'll all be over.*

That isn't going to happen.

I won't let it.

I—

What's that? In one of the temple alcoves the shadows are getting darker. They're gathering into the figure of a man with a white suit, a hat and a briefcase. Looks like a lawyer or some kind of insurance broker, but with an air of . . . death.

One of the workers catches sight of the figure and immediately throws himself to the ground in devotion, but Mr Lawyer picks him up and puts him back to work. The man is awestruck, in total ecstasy.

Seems like maybe there's a god taking an interest in the legal aspects of the case. I wonder what that means for my guy.

Shit. I left my god-killing bullets at home.

This could be interesting . . .

* A Ω *

'Mr Bourreau,' said a soft voice. 'One moment, please.'

He turned and saw a small man standing behind him. His suit was clearly made from the finest linen, and he wore a panama hat and espadrilles. In his left hand he held a brown briefcase.

'Yes?'

'My name is Kek al Hadiri,' the man continued, tipping his hat as he approached. 'Mr Tameri asked me to act as your guide whilst you're in the city. I'm the family's lawyer, and friend, of course.'

A lawyer as a friend? Malleus puffed on his Culebra, the smoke forming a question mark in the air as he considered this development. He had been assigned a babysitter, that was obvious; Tameri wanted to know what direction his investigation was taking. *Every step.* 'Is the family under the impression that I require legal aid, Monsieur?'

'Let's just say things tend to move a little faster round here if you can not only threaten to involve your lawyer, but also immediately introduce him.' Al Hadiri smiled, but his kohl-lined eyes remained cold and expressionless. His forehead was marked with a symbol, a black hieroglyph.

Malleus didn't want to point his PDA in the man's face. *I can check it later, more discreet that way.*

'Very well. Could you give me a lift back to the Tameris' house? I left my coat there, and I think a change of clothes is in order before I carry on with my investigations.'

Al Hadiri gestured towards a white Toyota SUV, embellished with tasteful advertisements, all in French, for his law firm. 'My time is yours, Monsieur Bourreau.'

'And how much is your time worth?'

'Around 250 euros per hour.' He walked alongside him. 'And worth every cent.'

Malleus no longer needed to ask any questions about the Tameris' wealth.

Germania, Treva, November 2019

Marianne Lagrande felt incredibly conspicuous, creeping around in front of the forensics department in the pouring rain whilst pointing her torch into every nook, cranny and crack in the pavement, but there was simply no way around it.

She wore an outstandingly visible yellow raincoat made of a waxy synthetic material that was doing a great job of protecting her from the wet and dirt. The water ran down in rivulets from the rim of her large hood, missing her face completely as she hunched over the ground.

Occasionally a passer-by would offer to help her in her search, thinking she might have lost a key, a wallet or a ring, but she declined; *she* didn't even know what she was looking for.

Hidden in her jacket was a veritable treasure trove of cigarette butts, corks and other assorted pieces of litter, each carefully removed from the ground with a long pair of tweezers and placed in a plastic bag. Lagrande panned her torch around slowly and methodically, tirelessly searching.

The three men who had attacked her in Lutetia were dead. Whilst fleeing the banlieue they had run into the requested police backup, and the officers had made short work of them, at least partially motivated by revenge for their fallen colleagues.

The policeman whose wounds Lagrande had tended at the scene was still alive, but the building security guard and the other officer never had a chance. Lagrande tried not to think too hard about how close she had come to dying herself.

Bourreau had already received her report by email, and Lautrec had given her a day off, 'to deal with the shock'.

So far, she had spent that day flying to Treva and meticulously searching a stretch of pavement.

She had also received an email from Mr Crick in York; Bourreau had told her he would be working with them on the case – the father of the young man whose rectum had played host to the statuette was desperate to find those responsible. She had already sent him her latest findings, and he was working on answers.

We're going to crack this. Lagrande sniffled. She was frozen through, and beginning to go slightly numb. Her fingers were growing stiff. *Why couldn't this have happened in summer?*

She stood up and stretched. Her back was in pain, and she was in need of a long trip to the sauna, followed by a swim and an hour or two in the Jacuzzi. She doubted her battery farm style hotel would be able to cater for those demands. Everything in the building could be folded out or tucked away, Japanese style.

Even the tiniest corners had been put to use. But she wasn't complaining – it was very comfortable to stand in.

Lagrande caught sight of a coffee machine inside the forensics department. A beacon of hope. It didn't even have to taste good, it just had to be warm.

She turned towards the visitors' entrance and noticed a twinkle of light out of the corner of her eye.

Immediately she sank to her knees and started probing with her torch until she had found the exact source of the light: a spark in a tiny crack between two paving slabs.

Excitedly she set the torch aside and used her hands to shift a loose slab, giving her just enough room to dart in and grab the glittering object with her tweezers.

It's . . . a diamond! Lagrande held it in the light of the torch. Simply cut, but even in that light, incredibly clear and pure, except for a tiny imperfection deep inside the diamond itself. *Is this what I've been looking for?*

She decided to mull it over somewhere a little warmer.

She went inside, ordered a coffee from the machine and leaned against the radiator, slurping the drink; it tasted vile, but it went some way towards defrosting her insides while the caffeine and sugar gave her circulation a much-appreciated boost.

After a while she peeled herself out of her coat, beneath which she was wearing black jeans with silver embroidered pockets and a white turtleneck jumper – an incredibly discreet outfit, by her standards. She carefully placed the diamond in her purse for safekeeping, then untied her blonde hair to let it dry out.

There was a beep from her smartphone: someone was calling her.

'Lagrande?'

'Chief Inspector Grenzner here.' The chief investigator for the Hannes Hein case. 'Hello, Madame.'

'Oh, hello, *Monsieur le Commissaire*,' she said cheerfully. 'You received my email?'

'Hence the call.' He briefly gave instructions to someone in the background. 'I'm currently at a crime scene that I think might interest you, or rather, Mr Bourreau. The victim's name is Mohr, Hektor Mohr, and from what I can see here, it looks like he was dealing in art *objects*. Could be a connection to the thefts in the Hein case.'

Mohr! That was the name Crick had mentioned. 'Monsieur Bourreau is currently indisposed,' she said in a friendly tone, 'but I'll be right there.'

'You?'

'I'm his assistant – and I have my Interpol pass with me.' He didn't need to know that she was technically a secretary and definitely not an investigator of any kind. After all, she had already introduced herself to him as Bourreau's *partner*.

'If you say so, Madame. But it's not a pretty sight.'

'I'm used to it,' she replied, and was struck by a sudden memory of the policeman she had saved. *I'm from the banlieue.*

As soon as the address pinged through onto her phone, Lagrande threw what was left of the hideous coffee into the bin, gathered up her waterproofs and called a taxi.

She was excited: she was working on a real case, and leads were appearing thick and fast.

Tunisia, Tunis / New Carthage, November 2019

After a quick shower in the room Tameri had reserved for him in the Grand Carthage Hotel, Malleus finally pulled on fresh clothing.

The light colours combined with the oriental cut of his clothing rendered him almost indiscernible from the local residents, save for his dark-coloured hat. He dumped his dirty clothes in the laundry bag, to be seen to by one of the hotel's many electronic devices programmed for such menial tasks such as cleaning, shoe-polishing or dusting.

A few minutes later he arrived in the lobby, where the lawyer was waiting for him. He was talking to a hotel employee, a porter in classic livery, who was handing him a set of print-outs.

Al Hadiri passed them on to Malleus. 'Here you are.'

'Thank you.' He glanced at the pages: a collection of all the press cuttings covering the accident at the pyramid, including two large Egyptian papers. Clearly all eyes were on the events in New Carthage.

'Are you from this area, Monsieur al Hadiri?'

'No. Why do you ask?'

Shame. He might have been able to tell him where he could find someone familiar with the rites of Tanit. Malleus spotted a small table across the lobby, with a plaque that read *Concierge.* 'Excuse me. I'll be right back.'

He strode past the marble pillars lining the hallway, his hat balanced on the cuttings. The building had air-conditioning, of course, but his hair had not yet completely dried from the shower. 'Excuse me, sir?'

The light-skinned man stood up from his chair as Malleus approached. His polished gold name-badge read *Mr Boulanger.* 'How can I help you, Monsieur? Restaurant, club, trips to—?'

'Tanit,' Malleus interrupted with a smile.

'Tanit,' the man repeated, with a puzzled expression. 'You mean the patron goddess of the city?'

He knows what I want. How convenient. 'I read that the goddess was once worshipped here and I was wondering if the practice has begun again, since the return of the gods?'

'Of course, Monsieur.' Boulanger sat down and looked around for a pen and paper. 'Have I understood correctly – you would like to visit a shrine?'

Malleus smiled even wider. 'One hundred per cent correct, Monsieur.'

'Then you should go to this address in the old town, by the Punic harbour,' he explained. 'In the courtyard there is an ancient cemetery – a tophet, as the priestess calls it.' He passed Malleus the piece of paper. 'There's no need to call ahead. Open until sunset, Monsieur.'

'Is photography permitted?'

'As far as I know, yes – but the priestess there will be happy to give you any information you need and answer any questions.'

Malleus nodded and gave the man a ten-euro note. 'It's astonishing, really, how little you hear her mentioned around here.'

'Her?'

'The goddess.'

'Well, yes, Monsieur. That's mainly to do with the Roman gods, I presume,' Boulanger replied, clearly full of opinions on the subject. 'I must admit, I did briefly consider joining Tanit's followers.' He lowered his voice. 'But she doesn't really have that much to offer. Fertility's one thing, but I already have four children and no garden to look after.'

Malleus laughed and tucked the note into his pocket. 'Thank you, Monsieur.' He turned back to al Hadiri. 'Feel free to take the night off, Monsieur. I don't believe I'm in need of a lawyer at present.'

'One never knows until it's too late,' replied the lawyer earnestly. 'The Tameris are paying me to accompany you as a local contact and translator. Not everyone here speaks French or English – and please, correct me if I'm wrong, but I assume you are not fluent in Arabic?'

Malleus had to concede that point, but he still felt resentful about the man following him around everywhere. Apparently there was nothing much he could do to prevent it. 'No, I'm afraid I'm not.' He put on his hat. 'Then you shall be my guide, Monsieur.'

'Gladly.' He started towards the door.

'You don't know where I plan to go yet.'

'I saw the address on the note.' The lawyer smiled falsely. 'Forgive me my curiosity, Monsieur Bourreau. An occupational hazard.'

'One I'm all too familiar with.' Malleus walked beside him as they left the hotel.

Though the day was drawing to its end, the air in New Carthage was still exceedingly hot. Songs could be heard issuing from the temples, though they were only faintly recognisable above the clamour of the city. Tourists from a whole host of nations were buzzing around the harbour area, taking photographs and gawping.

Malleus and al Hadiri pushed through the crowds, past cafés and pubs spilling out onto the streets, their patrons eating and drinking and smoking shisha in the balmy evening atmosphere. Traditional dancers moved from bar to bar, performing for customers and passersby; Malleus thought they probably earned decent money on a night like this.

He consulted his PDA as they walked.

There was an update from Lagrande, which caused him to stop suddenly, ignoring the bustling crowd, and read it through, top to bottom, twice. Bodies everywhere, a diamond in the pavement in front of the forensics building and another victim who appeared to have a connection to the artefacts.

She's good. Malleus wrote back, congratulating her on her progress and expressing his regret that he couldn't be at the scene right now. He assured her that he would make it back to Treva as soon as possible.

But he was a little concerned for her safety. Anyone willing to send three heavily armed men to their deaths in an attempt to recover a statuette and a diamond would not give up at the first sign of failure.

'Monsieur Bourreau?' the lawyer said softly.

'Just a second,' he replied absently and added something to the bottom of his message: that she should not put herself in danger.

That might not be enough.

After a short pause he sent another message, this time not to Lagrande.

Then he stashed his PDA and caught up to al Hadiri, who was loitering in a souvenir shop in order to avoid the throngs of tourists. He caught a glimpse of the citadel hill above the rooftops – Byrsa was visible from almost everywhere in the city, meaning Sokar was perfectly positioned to loom over everyone.

A few minutes later they reached the address he'd been given, and they were greeted by an illuminated sign of Tanit swinging precariously from a couple of wires. It was flanked by a number of laser-projected images of doves, ears of corn, figs and pomegranates, which Malleus found a little tacky – but it was, he supposed, the year 2019.

They entered the front courtyard, which had distinctive clay walls and a two-metre-high central pillar carved from a single stone. Malleus recognised it as a *stela*, reminiscent of the ancient monoliths that had been erected to honour the goddess before the reign of Christianity. There was no inscription, save for the symbol of Tanit, not even a depiction of the goddess herself.

A priestess dressed in a white sleeveless robe appeared and tipped a small bowl of grain into the huge fire-basin at one end of the room. The flames devoured the grain and husks flew up into the air, dissolving into ashes as they rose. The woman sang softly as she walked over to the stela and bowed in front of it. She took three steps backwards before she turned round to face them.

'Good day, Madame,' said Malleus, taking off his hat respectfully. 'What type of ritual was that, if I might ask?'

She came closer, eyeing the two men and performing a gesture that presumably conveyed the blessing of the goddess. 'How wonderful that you take an interest in Tanit, even if' – she glanced at the lawyer – 'one of you has already chosen another direction.'

'He is just my guide,' replied Malleus with a wide smile. 'It was something to do with the harvest?'

'Correct. Tanit has watched over Carthage for thousands of years and blessed us with much prosperity, even when the credit for her gifts is taken by others.'

'Since you mention it' – Malleus took out his PDA – 'would you mind taking a look at this photograph, please?' He opened the image of the child's burnt body.

Bemused, she took the PDA from him – and gasped in shock, holding her hand to her mouth. 'Are you with the police? You think I had something to do with what happened to that poor boy, for Tanit—'

'I'm a private investigator, Madame. Malleus Bourreau is my name,' he reassured her. Her fear and horror at the image were clearly genuine. 'I presume you recognise the symbol of your goddess at the scene of Snofru's death. The boy was murdered, and it looks like the perpetrators were followers of Tanit.'

She walked a few steps away from the entrance, the men following beside her. 'I noticed the symbol as soon as the story broke in the papers,' she admitted. 'I prayed to Tanit that nobody else would recognise it.' Her eyes darted back and forth between Malleus and al Hadiri. 'We had nothing to do with it – our community is small, and peaceful. But you're here to talk about the burnings that used to happen under the tophet – the child sacrifices.'

Malleus nodded in confirmation, a few strands of his dark hair falling across his face. He brushed them back. 'Convince me I've reached the wrong conclusion.'

'The tophets are just cemeteries, nothing more. Of course it's more exciting to make up stories about murder and burning children,' she explained firmly, 'but Tanit never demanded human life. She is the goddess of fertility and the hunt, not of violence.'

'So how did she come to have such a violent reputation?'

'The propaganda spread by the ancient Greeks and Romans has stuck, even to this day. Specialists analysed the contents of the urns here and found only the remains of foetuses and stillborn children buried under her symbol – but they were never sacrificed.' Her words were tinged with a note of resignation and disappointment. 'Look around at what they're building – Jupiter, Apollo, Poseidon. Even the Egyptians are building a shrine on the citadel hill.' She gestured towards the stela. 'And she, the protector of this city for generations, is stuck in this tiny courtyard. The tour guides don't even tell the tourists about her. The city is full of corruption.'

'And yet we still have a dead child lying in the centre of the symbol of Tanit,' Malleus said, stroking his moustache. 'How do you explain that?'

'Sabotage. Someone trying to tarnish the goddess' reputation, to finally make her disappear, and her entire cult with her,' the priestess speculated. 'What better way than something as horrifying as this?' She looked at the PDA again. 'That poor boy.'

Malleus had to agree. *It was too obvious.* 'Why do the other gods see Tanit as competition?'

'Our cult has some branches in Malta and Ibiza,' she said, her voice thoughtful. 'Quite successful ones. On Ibiza, Tanit was worshipped until as recently as AD 200, and we've just begun repairs on the old shrines there – with modest resources, of course, but still . . . Our centre in Europe is the Cueva d'es Cuieram in Ibiza. It's near Sant Vincent de sa Cala, in case you're considering becoming a follower of Tanit – it might be more convenient for you than New Carthage.'

'Probably not, Madame. But thank you.' Malleus found her arguments fairly logical. 'Answer this question as frankly as you can: who do *you* believe could be behind the murder?'

'All of them,' she said almost before he could finish the question. 'It's all just part of the fight to see which god gets control of New Carthage. What do you think?'

Malleus looked at al Hadiri, who was writing a message on his smartphone with one hand. 'Your assessment, Mr Lawyer?'

Al Hadiri pulled an expression of vague regret without moving his kohl-lined eyes from the screen.

The priestess laid a hand on Malleus' right arm. 'Monsieur Bourreau: please solve this murder before someone else sees what you and I can see in that picture. Otherwise I fear they will soon come to destroy Tanit with pitchforks and burning torches.'

'I'll do my best, Madame. May I have your name? And a number I can reach you at, if you'd be so kind.'

'Alexa.' She gave him a phone number and an address. 'Tanit will thank you for this, Monsieur Bourreau.'

He didn't reply – he didn't want to be impolite. For an atheist, the gratitude of a god was a hollow promise.

'Monsieur Bourreau!'

He turned to al Hadiri, whose voice was serious and more than a little alarmed.

The bald-headed lawyer was holding up his smartphone, upon which was displayed the local headline: PRIEST OF POSEIDON FOUND DEAD. The image showed the mutilated corpse of a man, almost unrecognisable as such, and next to him the bloodstained body of a child no more than a year old.

Malleus looked more closely. *They're in a bowl! And underneath, the triangle.* This time the journalists would surely be able to see it too.

He took the lawyer's device and showed it to the priestess. 'Tanit's enemies are on the offensive,' he said, handing the smartphone back to al Hadiri as he turned towards the exit. 'Pray to your goddess, if you think it will help. I'll deal with the facts.'

He headed straight for the place where the two bodies had been found. It irritated him that he had not yet found out whose symbol his guide was wearing on his forehead.

Germania, Treva, November 2019

Marianne Lagrande found the sight of the corpse less horrifying than she had feared. Chief Inspector Grenzner had either exaggerated, for some reason, or simply had no idea what level of gore she'd already been exposed to in her capacity as Interpol secretary. She'd photographed plenty of crime scenes in her time – not to mention the scene outside her own front door in the banlieue.

The victim, Hektor Mohr, was naked and looking very much

as if he'd been beaten and tortured in the same way as the young Mr Crick, before having his throat cut open.

The perpetrator had put him in the bath to bleed out. Perhaps they had intended to dissolve the body in acid but had been interrupted or called off.

Lagrande left the bathroom, where the forensics team was already hard at work, and wandered through the pokey flat in the Harbour Odin Complex.

It had been newly built in 2017: forty floors of four hundred apartments, around two thousand people, all of the same religion – only those who had openly and contractually committed to worshipping Odin could rent an apartment here, and anyone who neglected their religious duties was thrown out. The god touted it as a 'social housing' scheme, with availability strictly limited to his own followers.

Mohr had been one of those followers – and he was the person who'd sold the statuette to young Crick. *So no doubt he was flogging other objects too.*

The apartment was as good as empty. The building administrator had told the investigators that Mohr had not fulfilled his duties to Odin and was about to be evicted; they had a full waiting list for the apartment.

Lagrande had looked through the victim's smartphone and found an email receipt for a self-storage facility at the harbour and messages from a few different women and two men to whom Mohr appeared to owe money.

As she scrolled through his photos, she came across a blurry video of a woman with long black hair and a red coat. Her face was difficult to make out, but she looked to be of Asian origin. In her left hand she was holding . . .

It's a pen, no . . . a folded-up fan. Lagrande zoomed in as much as she could, and recognised a couple of blurry Japanese letters.

The fan of Susanoo no Mikoto!

It looked as if Mohr had tried to covertly record his attractive customer, but the autofocus of his camera looked to have been overwhelmed by his quick movements. *Or the woman had noticed and protested.*

Lagrande sat on the single chair remaining in the flat and studied the video millimetre by millimetre, her blue-green eyes intently scanning the screen.

Half hidden under the folded fan was a printed piece of paper, visible for a second. It was bordered in purple and bore an image that resembled a stylised lily.

A luggage tag, she realised.

On her own smartphone she searched for airlines that flew from Treva to Asia, comparing their logos to the picture on the tag, until she came up with FujiSan Airline. The young woman had obviously checked in her luggage early and taken a quick trip into the city before her flight – during which time she had run into Mohr and purchased the fan.

The video had been taken three days ago, so the woman would be back in Japan by now. *It's a big country, a lot of islands – not the easiest place to track someone down.* Lagrande used every bit of charm she could muster and managed to convince Grenzner to request the passenger list through the Germanian authorities.

Within an hour she had received the data, including names, passports and pictures of every passenger on the flight.

There she is! She was at least ninety per cent sure. *Keiko Kitashima* – and the address wasn't in Tokyo, but Kyoto. The woman had been doing business in Germania, so hopefully she would speak a little English.

It took Lagrande a mere ten seconds to find Kitashima's phone number and press the call button.

'Good evening, Miss Kitashima,' she said in a friendly tone as the call was picked up. 'My name is Marianne Lagrande, I'm calling from Treva. I'm with Interpol. If you activate your camera, I can show you my pass.'

On the screen of the smartphone a small dialogue window popped up and the woman appeared, dressed in a kimono, her face very pale. She was halfway through putting on her makeup, and her expression was one of concern. She bowed slightly as a greeting. 'Interpol? Police?'

'Correct, Miss Kitashima.' Lagrande showed her secretary pass to the camera, assuming that the woman would be unaware of the differences between her ID and that of an official investigator. 'We're aware that you were in Treva recently; that you purchased a fan from a Mr Hektor Mohr. I'm currently in Mohr's apartment. Well, I'm afraid he's been murdered.'

'Oh, oh that's . . . dreadful!' she exclaimed, visibly shocked.

'Do not worry, Miss Kitashima, you are perfectly safe. My colleagues and I are concerned about the fan that you purchased. Unfortunately it is a stolen artefact, and it must be returned as soon as possible. I realise Mr Mohr may have shown you certificates of authenticity, but rest assured, you were not the only customer who Mohr managed to deceive in this way.' Lagrande found a balance between brisk and friendly, carefully steering her away from the possibility of asking any questions.

'Yes, that's . . . yes, there were other people there too,' Kitashima managed. 'I . . .' She sounded unsettled. 'How terrible.' Her face had paled noticeably beneath the makeup. 'Of course I will return the fan, Miss Lagrande.'

'Kyoto is a little far for us to travel—'

But Kitashima was shaking her head. 'The fan is still in Treva. It was a gift for my former mentor. I am a geisha, Miss Lagrande, and my *okasan* – my geisha mother – lives with her Germanian husband in Ottensen. I was visiting her.'

Lagrande's mouth suddenly felt very dry. 'Please tell me the address. I'll send an officer immediately to pick up the fan.'

'Of course.' She sent through the details on her phone. The address was on the Elbchaussee. 'Is she in danger?' Kitashima asked.

Lagrande could not rule out the possibility that the murderers were also able to get hold of information on Mohr's customers.

She stood up and left the apartment. 'No,' she lied, but added, 'it's very unlikely. I don't suppose you have any information on the other buyers?'

'I have one – I'll send it through now. A nice old man who works in a museum. We got talking at Mohr's place. His name is Hermann Wilkmann; he's from Mannheim.'

'Please do not tell him anything about this conversation, Miss Kitashima.' Lagrande felt the grip of excitement tightening round her chest. 'We will deal with it. Thank you for your cooperation, and have a good evening.' Then she hung up and began to run in the direction of the Elbchaussee. Grenzner called out that he could order her a patrol car from base to take her there.

Lagrande didn't think that the *okasan* was in danger.

But it couldn't hurt to hurry.

Tunisia, Tunis / New Carthage, November 2019

Malleus had almost reached the latest crime scene, which had been easy to find, thanks to his PDA's navigation system. And he had managed to lose his guide in the crowded streets, a situation he was more than happy about.

According to his device, he was now on the west side of the Punic harbour. Four narrow streets intersected in a small square with a fountain. The surrounding houses towered three or four storeys high, with large awnings at the top that had been furled up at dusk. Instead of street lamps, strings of lights crisscrossed the streets.

Finding the scene of the crime had presented little difficulty – the real problem was the mass of gaping onlookers blocking the street in front of him.

Malleus did his best to inch his way through, but the bodies around him were pressed together so tightly that he thought he'd have had more luck shoving himself through a brick wall. Every neck was craned forward, head weaving from side to side to get a better view.

He could hear a voice coming from the centre of the little square, a woman calling out in French and Arabic while the dense crowd around her applauded and shouted.

I suppose I'll have to take a detour. Malleus looked around and walked into one of the tiny shops along the street. He casually greeted the inhabitants as he headed straight for the stairs, disregarding the shopkeeper's indignation. This was no time to stand on ceremony.

He made his way up to the second floor and strode into the room with the small balcony he had spotted from the street below. *Perfect.*

Flinging open the window, he jumped out and took in the view of the clogged street.

The shouting woman had climbed onto the fountain in the square. Malleus realised that her face was familiar: *Madame Tameri.* Her words were loud and urgent, her face full of rage and fury. The crowd around her shook their fists, calling out threats that Malleus could not understand, save for the word *Tanit*. His client looked ready to take the law into her own hands, just as he had feared.

Malleus wondered for a moment whether she could have gone as far as killing her own son to gather enough sympathy and outrage amongst the citizens of New Carthage for an uprising against the old cults.

No. He didn't get that impression from her; even now, Madame Tameri radiated only grief and helplessness: the unspeakable pain of a mother mourning her dead child.

He still had to stop her. Murder could not be atoned for with further violence, especially when that violence was likely to be directed at the wrong people.

Malleus eyed the other small balconies and windowsills dotted along the street.

The last time he had done any kind of extreme sport had been during the war, if you could call running for your life across battlefields and through ruined cities 'sport'.

No way around it. He stepped onto the railings and leaped across to the balcony of the next window along. His landing was somewhat disrupted by a hanging basket, but he gathered himself and continued forward, stepping quickly onto a small canopy that swayed ominously under his weight.

Using the momentum of the swinging awning, he took another jump onto a crumbling ledge and ran the length of it until he finally lost his balance and went sliding down a first-floor canopy, landing on the cobbles below – just a few steps away from Madame Tameri.

* A Ω *

What the . . . how the hell am I supposed to follow him up there?

This entire day has been a shambles. I'll never get through that mob; they're rammed together too tightly. I can't exactly shoot them all.

Ah. He's taking the balconies.

Good. I'll take the roof.

I'm going into the house next door, up the stairs, looking out of the window to see what he's up to. One big jump to the next balcony and – something drops out of his coat. His PDA!

Change of plan. This is my best chance to hack his wonder gadget.

Back downstairs, under the balcony, and . . . there it is, next to a smashed-up hanging basket. I stay crouched under the balcony so he can't see me and slip the device into my pocket. I've got it.

He's reached the woman and is interrupting her speech.

Okay, back to the old plan: up onto the roof, find the best sniping position.

Although looking at the crowd now, pushing and shoving around . . . I think maybe I need to do more than just protect him. Helicopter – that would do the trick.

So, a few decent roof jumps and I'm on the house closest to the square, right above where he's standing with that Sokarian woman.

No, they'll never get out of there alive. Bad idea on his part. Too many people, too many feet ready to trample everything into mush.

Holy shit, what killed this priest? Looks like a pack of dogs or wild cats or something. Baboons, maybe. They're vicious, actually, and basically wild now. Saw it on TV once. Not pretty.

Anyway, how do I get him out of this?

Ah, there's some kind of antenna cable here. Cut it off, tie it to one of these strings of lights and we've got a rope – I can throw that down for him if things look bad. Good, so let's get out the APB for now. Silencer, shoulder rest, ready.

Anyone else who comes near that rope gets a bullet in the skull. That goes for the Sokarian as well.

I'm following him, and him alone.

* A Ω *

'Madame Tameri, please get a hold of yourself,' called Malleus, elbowing his way through the front few rows of onlookers.

'This has nothing to do with you!' she spat at him.

'It does, Madame. Taking matters into your own hands is not the answer.' He looked down at the body of the priest next to the child as he spoke – and stopped in his tracks.

The body looked as if it had been torn to shreds by a pack of hungry lions, but the child – the child was alive. *Unharmed.* The photos online had led him to think that the tiny naked little girl in the fire-bowl had been killed, but now he could see that the blood splattered across her body belonged to the eviscerated man next to her. Nobody seemed to be taking responsibility for the child. Malleus ripped a turban from a bystander's head, ignoring his cries of indignation, and laid the material across the girl.

The tunic on the mutilated priest's body bore the embroidered sign of Poseidon. Chunks of flesh hung from the man's bones, his head had been caved in and half-wrenched off. One eye dangled from its socket by the nerve. Bones jutted from his extremities, splintered and broken, and a huge gash had opened up the man from the belly to the chest. For Malleus it looked less like a sacrifice and more like the work of a creature that was very, *very* angry.

Three iron bars had been placed under the bowl in a triangle, creating the symbol of Tanit. The baby girl looked around, wide-eyed and terrified. Judging by the colour of her skin one of her parents was black, but her eyes glowed ocean-blue.

Where the hell are the police? Malleus remembered Alexa's description of the city's corruption. Were the police taking their time on purpose? Were they giving the mob time to reach the shrine of Tanit and destroy it?

'We have found the people who murdered my son,' Madame Tameri said beside him, her words drenched with hate. 'Tanit has always demanded the lives of young children—'

'No, you're wrong, Madame Tameri,' he said softly. 'I have another lead. This' – he gestured towards the body and the child – 'was *intended* to be found. *You* were intended to find it and to bring people here to destroy the shrine of Tanit.'

She looked suddenly uncertain. 'But . . . *who*?'

'That's what I'm trying to find out.' Malleus looked at the furious crowd. People were pushing towards the square from all four of the surrounding streets. The front of the rabble was dangerously close to the fountain, their feet almost touching the body of the priest and the defenceless child next to him. 'Send the people away, Madame,' he told her urgently as he bent down to investigate the body.

He was shocked to find several objects amongst the shredded hunks of tissue: a smartphone, a lighter, an empty parcel of what looked to be fire accelerant, and a small knife, the type used for skinning animals.

The priest was going to kill the child? Astonished, he dropped the evidence into a plastic bag as the shuffling feet of the crowd edged closer. No matter how much the front rows pushed back against the crowd, the pressure from the rows behind them was stronger.

Quickly he picked up the blood-spattered child in her improvised swaddling and lifted her out of harm's way. Stepping back onto the fountain, he shouted to Madame Tameri, 'Send these people away, now! You raised the mob, only you can get rid of them.'

Madame Tameri lifted her arms and spoke in Arabic and French, her tone appeasing yet desperate.

But the woman's rage had spread through the crowd like an unstoppable virus, and it could no longer be contained. Slowly, inexorably, the mass of people continued forward, despite the protests of the front rows as they were pushed over the remains of the priest.

Malleus was reminded of the huge crushing machines at landfills, the ones that can't be switched off – only instead of rubbish, there were bodies tumbling forward, compressed by the force of the crowd. Things were looking bad. Aside from the threat to his own life, there were hundreds of people here in danger of being hurt – suffocated, trampled, crushed. His Derringer would be of no use to him.

All at once, the lights about the street went out and the square fell into darkness. The dim light from inside the surrounding houses went out next, extinguished so that only the stars were left to illuminate the scrabbling throngs.

The crowd fell quiet, looking around in confusion, searching for an explanation for the sudden blackout.

Some of them took out smartphones, bathing the street in a cold blue glow, just enough to see – until Malleus saw an inky cloud of pure darkness rolling along the street towards the square like a silent black sandstorm.

He looked around hastily.

The darkness flooded the square, lapping across the rows of people in waves, engulfing them and hiding everything from view. The houses were swallowed up around him. The stars disappeared.

* A Ω *

What's—? Why can't I see anything? The night vision function is . . . No.

It's like I'm blind. It must be some kind of god . . . ha! Mr Lawyer! The guy who manifested out of the shadows at the temple. This has to be him.

Not a bad idea: if you take people's sight, they stand still, like animals. That's all we are, after all.

The street has gone quiet. His trick has worked.

But I'm worried. I've got no target, nothing. If someone takes this chance to stab him in the ribs, I'm going to be really pissed off.

I swear, I'll leave New Carthage nothing more than soot and ashes. Wouldn't be difficult. I know how to make that happen.

No, just . . . breathe, wait for the darkness to pass, APB at the ready.

* A Ω *

Malleus didn't know why, but he held his breath. He didn't want the darkness to reach his lungs.

The initial shock and outcry rippled through the crowd and fell to a whisper. The shuffling of feet stopped, and nobody moved.

The darkness was absolute – there was no up, no down. Only the contact with the floor and the feeling of gravity assured Malleus that he was still standing upright.

'Move back,' he called out in French. 'Move backwards, slowly. Then—'

The darkness evaporated like fog in the sun and the stars returned, twinkling faintly over the heads of the silent masses as they collectively breathed out. Malleus had never heard a sound of such unadulterated relief. *They're just happy to be alive.*

The men and women gathered in the streets looked around

at each other, shaken yet happy, and without a word, without pushing or hurrying, turned round and trickled out of the square like running water.

Malleus breathed in and swallowed, sweat trickling down his back under his shirt. *That was too close.*

Someone touched his arm. 'Come with me, Monsieur Bourreau,' said the lawyer next to him, linking arms with Madame Tameri. 'Let's leave the rest to the police.'

The woman took the child from Malleus' arms, stroking its head protectively. 'Poor girl,' she said softly. 'Your hotel is closer than our house, Monsieur Bourreau. We'll clean up there. She can't stay like this.'

How did he get through the crowd? Malleus nodded in agreement and looked down at his bloodstained shirt, then at the remains of the priest of Poseidon, now trampled by hundreds of feet and reduced to a pile of debris. Forensics wouldn't even be able to take fingerprints.

But the evidence is clear. He just needed a little more to be certain. And he would find it in the temple of Poseidon.

* A Ω *

I need to take a closer look at the PDA, take it apart a bit and hack into it. I need to be its second master. I've got the equipment for it in my car.

Off the roof, then.

I follow the trio at a distance, already taking a look through the PDA. Looks home-made, or at least highly modified. From far off it looked like he'd just bought some weird phone at a flea market or something, but . . . cover off, and . . . wow!

What is all this shit?

The guy I'm following clearly has some very inventive friends. Technologically gifted, even.

They walk through the lobby and disappear in the direction of the lifts. Good. Then I'm off to the car.

This PDA is pretty impressive. Extra parts soldered on, elements stuck into extra ports . . . is that a battery? No, a . . . Fuck, no idea what that is. Something you can't just buy at the local techie shop, that's for sure. Crazy. I'll take some pictures so I can go over it more closely later.

Here we go. First crack the passcode. My little computer can do that, no problem.

Then upgrade the spyware, pull the newest info out of storage – aha. An ID code that leads to an online storage facility. I have a feeling that might be where I find the information on all his cases.

I have a real treasure trove here.

So, mission accomplished. Cover back on, done. Now this gadget is ready to go back to his master and be a good little spy.

Just like I am.

I have to know what he's doing. Everything.

* Α Ω *

Germania, Treva, November 2019

Marianne Lagrande sat in the back of the police car as she and the two armoured officers sped through the rich part of town. *You'd have to earn a lot of money as an okasan to live in a villa on the Elbchaussee, or at the very least, have a lot of savings from your life as a geisha*, she thought.

As a kid from the banlieue she knew such places only from hearsay or from watching soap operas online; she'd never set foot in such an opulent house.

The police officers had been permitted to use force to retrieve the fan, but she doubted this would be necessary. The geisha-mother would probably have been informed by her former student, and in any case wouldn't be too keen to hang on to the object when she found out how much death was associated with it.

Lagrande kept Bourreau updated by email: according to the legend, the fan belonged to the Kami Susanoo, the Shintō god or spirit of the wind and sea. He was said to be stormy and quick-tempered, and often played tricks at the expense of others, which led, so the myth went, to him leaving the heavens. During his time on earth, he changed his colours and guarded farmers against pestilence, becoming the patron saint of farming and teaching the people about civilisation and culture.

Lagrande found a Susanoo very sympathetic character; he appeared to have a lot in common with Loki, even if her Nordic gods and the Japanese Shintō had basically nothing to do with each other.

The police car stopped in front of the villa, which looked out onto the river and the harbour opposite.

The armoured officers stepped out of the vehicle and Lagrande followed. Their body language made it clear that this was their call; she was there merely to accompany them and not the other way round.

Since the Great Change, the Germanian police force had beefed up its security considerably. No officer went out without at least a bulletproof vest, so now almost every policeman looked like they were on their way to shut down a demo: impressive, demanding of respect.

She followed them through the garden gate, the only entrance in the front wall, which was lined with long wrought-iron spikes. She looked around.

The villas lining the street were in starkly contrasting styles;

though some were clearly imitating the style of their neighbours, they were twice as large.

Lagrande couldn't comprehend how one person could need so much space. There would be so much cleaning, and it must be such a long way from the couch to the fridge. She pulled her blonde ponytail a little tighter and caught up with the officers, who were already ringing the doorbell. *Or maybe they all have servants.*

The traffic on the busy Elbchaussee came to a stop for a few seconds as a couple made their way over the zebra crossing, forcing the cars to stop.

Lagrande regarded the expensive vehicles parked bumper to bumper along the street. Marques with stars or rings looked to be particularly popular in this area of Treva.

Only a grey VW campervan with a dull, tarnished paint job on the other side of the garden wall looked a little out of place.

As the couple reached the other side of the street, the side door of the VW van slid open and the long barrel of an automatic firearm became visible, pointing straight at the entrance to the villa.

Lagrande threw herself with a shout towards the police officers behind the wall just as the deadly staccato of automatic gunfire began. *It must be a large-calibre machine-gun*, she thought, as the bullets tore chunks out of the stonework around them.

Lagrande scrambled away from the place where she had landed, fearing the mystery attackers had already spotted her hiding spot. She looked up at the officers as the door they had just rung was opened.

They were caught in a hail of bullets, their Kevlar vests shredded as they fell forward into the entrance hall, surrounded by flying splinters of doorframe. Blood sprayed in all directions, spattering across the outer wall and the hallway inside.

The small, elderly Asian woman standing in the doorway was instantly riddled with bullets, the projectiles ripping her flesh into tatters. The falling policemen took her down with them.

The shooting went on for some seconds after the three people in the doorway hit the ground. From where she was, Lagrande could see a cupboard in the hall shot to pieces, shards of mirror spinning like confetti through the air, and countless tiles shattering under the continued fire.

Merde! Her heart pounded in her throat. She had always managed to avoid this kind of trouble in the banlieue. The police officers' weapons were too far away for her to reach, and all she had on her was her smartphone, a notebook and a pen.

Not much help against a machine-gun. The pen was perhaps mightier than the sword, but she didn't have much faith in a Biro against a few hundred rounds per minute. *They must have followed me – either since Lutetia, or from the crime scene in Treva.* Lagrande managed to crawl another few metres and then she stood up and peered out from her cover behind the top of the wall.

Two masked men with Steyr AUG assault rifles stepped out of the campervan while a third stayed behind in the darkness of the van, maybe to change the magazine of the automatic weapon they had stashed in the back. Empty shells rolled out of the van, landing with an eerie tinkling sound on the asphalt.

Just as Lagrande was readying herself to sprint into the villa and search for the fan – which she refused to let her attackers get hold of – another masked man stepped out of a nearby BMX. He immediately knelt and pointed a weapon with a long, wide barrel, directly at the open door of the transporter van.

That's a grenade launcher! Lagrande stared at her mystery saviour, who clearly did not belong to the brutal raiding party that had just murdered her colleagues.

The man fired, and the explosive shot into the campervan.

The detonation blew the windows out of the van, and the man inside was thrown out in several pieces. The force of the explosion brought the other two men to their knees. Car alarms rang out along the street and lights started flashing madly.

Before the two men on the ground could get up, the man kneeling by the BMW reached for a shoulder holster and pulled out a Glock 18. With the ease of someone who had done this a thousand times, he calmly aimed and dispatched them both, each with a single headshot.

Lagrande stared at the heavily built man as he stood up, looked over at her, tapped his fingers to his forehead in a casual salute and stepped back into his car. The BMW – an X7, she noted – drove off down a side street, leaving behind the smoking remains of the VW, and two bodies on the Elbchaussee.

Police sirens wailed in the distance. The first few cars in the street screeched off, fleeing the chaos. Nobody got out of their car to check she was all right – the battle might not be over.

Lagrande ran over to the entrance of the villa.

For the second time in a week she stood over a couple of policemen full of bullet holes, though this time neither of them was alive.

The *okasan* also lay on the ground, her body riddled with bullets. Only a miracle would save her now. In her hand she was holding the fan. It looked like she had been quite happy to hand the stolen artefact back to the authorities.

Lagrande climbed over the bodies and picked up the fan. It had piled up quite the body count.

She had no idea who her mystery protector was, but she suspected Bourreau might have sent him. She looked out at the wreck of the VW and the bodies of the masked attackers strewn across the road – the attackers who would otherwise have killed her. Ruthlessly.

All because of an old fan.

Tunisia, Tunis / New Carthage, November 2019

Malleus sat in his bathrobe on the balcony, which was at least ten metres square, and smoked a Culebra with an amber band. On the table stood a glass of the best Venezuelan rum, which perfectly complimented the taste of the cigar.

After arriving back at the Grand Carthage he had showered and given his blood-smeared clothes to the laundry service. He hoped the stains would come out, otherwise he would find himself in urgent need of a tailor.

I really ought to fly back to Germania and pick up a different set of clothes, anyway. He could barely remember what his own house looked like – not that it was important; it wasn't what other people would call home. He stored his things there, that was enough. It had to be enough.

It wasn't always like that.

The rum was making him melancholy, he realised with dissatisfaction, but the case was not yet closed, so moping would have to wait.

Plus he was missing his PDA.

He guessed it must have been stolen in the crowd, or maybe it dropped out of his pocket while he was jumping from balcony to balcony. His techie friend would be heartbroken. *Me too.*

His case files were all safe on a server: the device always uploaded everything onto a remote hard drive as soon as it connected to the internet. But the PDA was unique, and irreplaceable.

It had to happen one day. Malleus sighed.

He was staying on the top floor, so there were no balconies above his to obscure his view of the night sky. In front of him lay the Mediterranean, lapping quietly and constantly at the shore, as if it were breathing. It spread from the foaming waves all the way back to the horizon, becoming a huge black nothingness crowned by the star-filled sky.

The waves glittered in the starlight, rolling onwards as if mysterious beings were tumbling around below the surface, observing the humans from their element.

He heard the little girl laughing through the door as Madame Tameri played with her. The priest had bathed the child and soothed her dry skin with moisturising cream, finally wrapping her in a towel and singing to her softly.

She can't become another star child. Though he assumed he would have been told if there was another demigod child in the Sokarian community, Malleus nevertheless stayed present while the child was bathed, inspecting the girl's cocoa-coloured skin intently. But there was nothing out of the ordinary, no birthmarks or semi-tattooed lines. She was a totally normal child.

The darkness that had spread over the streets to save them was still at the back of his mind. He assumed that it was probably Tanit making herself known. Regardless of the cause, without the quietening power of this darkness, a lot of people would have died.

'Quite an exciting day,' he heard al Hadiri saying next to him. The bald lawyer, whom he was seeing now for the first time without his briefcase and hat, sat down next to him. He opened a button on his suit jacket. 'You handled it well.'

Malleus was too old to be flattered by the well-meaning praise of a stranger. He puffed a few times on the Culebra, then reached for his glass. The smoke rolled in on itself as he breathed out, imitating the waves of the Mediterranean. 'Tomorrow will be even better,' Malleus said.

'What makes you so sure, Monsieur?'

'Are you asking that as a lawyer?' he responded, drinking the rum. He had drunk no more than a couple of shots' worth, but after a few swallows he could already feel its effects.

'Pure curiosity, Monsieur Bourreau.' He rubbed his bald head thoughtfully, the dim light of the street lights outside reflecting off his smooth skin. 'You searched the body of the priest?'

Malleus nodded. 'Tomorrow I'll take the evidence to the police.'

'Meaning you have plans for it before then?'

Malleus nodded; it didn't matter if the lawyer knew his plan. 'What does the hieroglyph mean, Monsieur al Hadiri?'

'It's the sign of the god Kuk.'

The name meant nothing to Malleus, and without his PDA to quickly look up the deity, it was no more than a meaningless word. 'Has your god ever appeared to you?'

'More than once. He manifests in front of his followers once a year, to relieve us of our wishes and our troubles.'

Malleus gave a disparaging laugh. 'A fun family day out, no? Heal your cancer and grow back your amputated limbs.'

Al Hadiri pressed his fingers together and leaned back. 'You do not have a god, correct?'

'I don't believe in them, Monsieur. I'm too suspicious of them.'

The lawyer broke into a laugh that ran through Malleus like a shudder. It was knowing and confident, as self-assured as a soldier before a battle that he knew was already won. 'Do you know what people like you are called?'

'Atheists,' he responded laconically.

'The principle of atheism worked while there was no

knowledge of gods. Atheists believed, too. They *believed* that there was no God.' Al Hadiri smiled cunningly. 'But now, you're a revisionist. You deny the reality in front of you.'

'Oh, I don't argue that these beings exist. Or that they have power over people.' Malleus puffed out a smoke ring that looked remarkably like a hand giving the middle finger. 'But they are not gods. Not heavenly beings.'

'Instead—?'

'Fantasy – beings from another universe. A collective drug trip. A governmental experiment. My nightmares while I'm lying in a coma in the real world,' he counted off casually, sipping at the rum. 'This topic of conversation will not get you anywhere, Monsieur al Hadiri. And besides, whatever beings they are, they don't seem to need a lawyer.'

The man laughed good-naturedly. 'You're right. But would you not agree that religion gives many people a sense of purpose in their life?'

Malleus had no desire to engage in philosophical debate; right now he wanted to solidify his plan of action for tomorrow, and work out how he was going to gain access to the temple of Poseidon and obtain a confession from the priests.

'Another time, Mr Lawyer,' he replied graciously. 'I think I've earned a rest today.' He downed the rum and ran his fingers through his dark hair. 'But I can guarantee you, anyone who needs to ask permission or forgiveness from a god has gone wrong somewhere along the line,' he added. As al Hadiri went to open his mouth, Malleus lifted his cigar to his mouth, the glowing red end crackling audibly like a growling animal. 'No. Another time.'

'Surely you'll allow me the chance to respond?'

The hotel room doorbell rang.

'You may prepare your speech in private, Monsieur.' He grinned, standing up and walking through the hotel room, cigar in hand. He opened the door.

In the doorway stood a girl of no more than fifteen years old. She looked at him with an expression of embarrassment. She wasn't wearing the hotel uniform but a black dress with several cut-outs revealing sections of her dark underwear. Her mid-length dark hair was streaked with bright white, and a light-coloured line led from her hairline down across her face, as if she had been cut in half and stuck back together.

'I didn't order anyone, Madame,' he said in a friendly tone, thinking to himself that she was far too young to be working as a prostitute, though some of the pleasure tourists would probably disagree.

She took hold of his free hand and kissed its palm. 'You saved my daughter's life,' she said in English. She had an accent he couldn't place.

'Oh.' Malleus felt stupid. 'I'm sorry, I—' He stood to the side. *She could easily be the child's sister.* 'She's inside.' While he scrabbled to think of a way to undo his *faux pas*, he realised that he needed some kind of evidence that she was the mother before he could just give away the little girl. The temple of Poseidon would not give up easily, after all.

But the girl pressed a credit card-sized pass into his hand, which showed a picture of the little girl. There was no mistaking the hologram. It was her child.

As the young mother walked into the room and the baby began to gurgle in delight, stretching out her arms towards her, Malleus needed no further proof.

He felt a lump in his throat. The nameless mother's joy moved him, waking painful memories of his own, and leaving him with a stale kind of happiness.

Madame Tameri stood next to the bed and smiled, equally happy to see the reunion of mother and daughter. Malleus saw in her face that she was touched by the same pain he was feeling, though hers was fresher, more raw.

The young woman thanked Madame Tameri profusely, then walked over to Malleus, her daughter on her hip.

Malleus held the Culebra to one side, keeping the smoke away from the child. He gave her back the pass, which she stashed in one of the cut-outs of her dress.

'See, Bala? This man saved you,' she said, and spoke some more words in a language he only vaguely knew. She turned to him. 'I told her to remember your face. When you meet again one day, she should recognise the man who saved her life.'

Malleus swallowed, his eyes prickling slightly. 'Thank you, Madame. But I don't think I'll live to be old enough that Bala and I will meet again.'

The young mother looked at him incredulously. 'You? You will surely live to be a hundred years old. You saved the life of an innocent child – the gods will not forget that.'

Malleus cleared his throat.

Again, the girl took his hand and kissed his palm. She bowed, and spoke again in the unknown language.

Bala stared at Malleus for a long moment, her ocean-blue eyes apparently taking in his features, before grabbing hold of her mother and giggling.

The girl left the room and walked out into the hallway. She turned back as she left, then hurried down the corridor with the child in her arms.

Something good did come of this trip, then. Saving a life instead of just explaining a death. Malleus raised his cigar as he watched the woman leave, and was about to take a drag – then held his breath – just as she entered the lift he noticed the brand mark on the woman's neck.

A flood of images raced through his mind, images that in normal conditions he could keep under control: rain, an endless system of trenches, the screaming in the night, the tearing flesh and cracking bones, the cries of the men, the sound of constant gunfire in a bunker, strobe lights flashing, screaming and dying, screaming and dying . . .

'Stop!' he yelled, his voice suddenly desperate. Malleus started to run, his bathrobe flying behind him. 'Who is your god?'

As the lift doors closed, he saw the girl turn round, her face in profile, her head slightly bowed. Her expression had changed; now she looked frightened.

'Who is your god?' he screamed frantically.

The lift headed downwards before he could reach the call button.

I have to know! Malleus looked around and found the stairs. Tearing open the fire-door, he ran as fast as he could, jumping down as many steps as he could. The belt of his robe snagged on a banister edge and he lost his footing, tripping over his own feet until he could brace himself against the walls and regain balance.

On the fourth floor he finally lost control and tumbled head over heels down a couple of flights. Dazed, he could do nothing but lie on the ground and wait until his head stopped spinning. Aside from a nasty graze and a throbbing in his temple, he had survived.

* A Ω *

Fuck, he's seen me! He—

No, he hasn't.

But why the sudden madness, then?

I thought I'd blown my cover. I was lucky.

I squeeze into the corner as he runs straight past me, heading for the lift where the young mother just disappeared.

Is she important? For him? Pretty interesting brand she has on her neck, there. Wait, that's— Oh. He'd be better off staying away from this one. He won't though. Idiot.

He's running down the right set of stairs.

I take the left and reach a lower floor before the lift does. I press the button and the cabin opens. The girl is inside with the child. She looks as me mistrustfully, gives a weak, distancing smile.

I step inside and lean against the wall by the door.

Yep, it's definitely the symbol I thought it was. But what is she doing in New Carthage? Shouldn't she be in Sodom or Gomorrah, somewhere like that? I know my way around there.

The little girl's eyes are amazing. How did they happen? Is she another demigod?

Judging by the symbol on Mummy's neck, things could still get pretty interesting.

I wonder if they sent her to set up a new den of iniquity in Carthage?

The lift reaches the ground floor, the doors open.

The young mother walks out very quickly, adjusting her hair to cover the symbol. No doubt she realises that it's not a good idea to wear it openly. She steps into a limousine, which drives off.

That was all very unexpected.

But why is my guy so freaked out? Screaming and losing his mind about a god he technically doesn't even believe in?

I need to do some more research on his history. I know his present pretty well, but his past still has some . . . gaps.

I have a feeling there's something bad lurking round the corner of all this. And if he starts a fight with it, I'm going to need some different equipment. Armour piercing ammo, weapons of mass destruction. Big guns.

As I walk past the concierge's table, I quickly drop off the PDA, with the remark that it belongs to the man I'm following.

* A Ω *

Malleus saved himself the rest of the trip downstairs after his fall. The woman would be long gone, and with her, the prospect of solving a mystery that had plagued him for years.

He limped back up to the top floor and returned to the room, where al Hadiri and Madame Tameri waited with questioning faces. On the table lay his PDA, a little battered but apparently still functioning.

Malleus readjusted his bathrobe with fumbling hands, hiding the scars that crisscrossed his chest. Those were his business alone.

'This was given in at the front desk for you, Monsieur Bourreau,' Madame Tameri explained, obviously expecting some form of explanation for his bizarre behaviour. 'Some honest person left it with the concierge . . .'

He nodded and headed straight for the minibar, where he took out the rum and poured a fresh glass almost to the brim. With a fresh Culebra, red-banded this time, he walked past them and out onto the balcony, drinking as he walked.

Hands shaking, he took a long, deep drag, followed by a large mouthful of rum, pacing up and down the balcony.

'Monsieur Bourreau, what—?' al Hadiri ventured.

Malleus gestured him away with his hand. 'I'll call you tomorrow, Madame Tameri,' he said.

'Is there anything I can—?' she began to ask, but he waved the question away.

'Tomorrow, Madame.' He pulled the balcony door closed, to make it clear that he needed peace, did not wish to entertain visitors and that they should leave.

Malleus put them out of his mind and continued to pace around the balcony, staring out at the waves. They didn't care what was happening to him, or indeed, anyone else on the earth. They just kept rolling in and out, as they had for millennia.

His shaking wouldn't stop. The war had found him again.

The sight of the unknown symbol had been enough to awaken in him the horrors he had lived through, to break open the wound in his soul that he had spent so long stitching together, cauterising and bandaging.

Malleus threw the rest of the rum down his throat and smoked frantically until he felt dizzy and his blood became more nicotine and alcohol than human.

That colossal, ash-coloured humanoid born from nightmares, with giant, whip-like arms, the creature that had wiped out his entire unit, shredded them, devoured them, mutilated them – that creature had worn exactly the same symbol on its forehead as the one on the girl's neck.

Malleus' research had never found anything. Nobody recognised the symbol. He tried to remember the name or the address on the pass, but his mind was blank.

I wasted my one chance. With a loud shout he hurled the rum glass over the balcony into the night, his bathrobe falling open and exposing his scars to the night air. They suddenly seemed to burn.

That night, when his unit had been exterminated, he had prayed to die. But he had been spared. And he didn't want to kill himself. There were people who needed him, even if he wasn't able to be with the people he had loved above all others.

Wasted. Malleus pressed his hands around the railing, gripping it until the wood creaked in his grip. *Wasted.*

Tunisia, Tunis / New Carthage, November 2019

Malleus woke up on the balcony. The sun was shining mockingly down on him. The rum bottle was still in his left hand and his right was burned and covered in ash. *Cigar kiss.*

Wheezing, he stood up and ran his thumb and forefingers over the end of his moustache before walking to the bathroom, standing in the shower and dejectedly turning on the water.

Freezing cold water rained down and robbed him of his breath before he managed to fumble his way to the temperature control.

But Malleus was awake.

He straightened up and let the water run down his body, washing himself and then brushing his teeth as he showered.

A flashing light on the shower control panel indicated he had an incoming call, which he picked up with the press of a button.

'Monsieur Bourreau, this is al Hadiri,' the lawyer said, his voice tinged with concern. 'I take it you're awake and amongst the ranks of the living again?'

Malleus felt ashamed for his meltdown in the night, but without the rum and chain-smoking he would have lost his mind in a far more permanent manner. His self-administered anaesthesia helped to repress the images, the memories, the pain of his loss, and the knowledge that things would never again be like they were before 2012.

'I'm working already,' he responded, turning off the water. 'In an hour we should have the names of the people who killed

Snofru Tameri.' He looked through the glass door at his battered PDA. He would need it to get his confessions.

'I'll come with you.'

'No, thank you, Monsieur al Hadiri. That would have the opposite effect.' Malleus used the control pad to order breakfast in his room, which was promptly confirmed. 'In two hours I'll be at the Tameris' residence. The police will already be informed by that point. Have a good day, Monsieur.' He hung up the conversation.

Feeling a little more awake, he left the shower, donned his bathrobe and ate his breakfast in a shady corner of the balcony. His gaze fell automatically on the citadel hill, where works were continuing uninterrupted. The workers and volunteers had apparently doubled their efforts in honour of little Snofru.

Half an hour later Malleus placed a phone call as he walked through the streets of New Carthage, dressed in his light-coloured clothes, hat and sunglasses. He breathed in the warm sea air. His path led him along the harbour to the temple of Poseidon. In his pocket was the plastic bag of evidence collected from the crime scene yesterday.

His morning coffee had left him a little more upbeat, but last night's alcohol was still having an effect. His mouth felt like it was coated with fur. He couldn't even stand the thought of a Culebra.

The latest information from Treva suggested that his plan to protect Lagrande's life had been successful. Meanwhile, the authorities there were busying themselves with investigating the identities of the masked attackers in the VW campervan; Grenzner thought they were probably mercenaries.

Lagrande had already sent him a photo of the fan, together with a single word: 'Thanks.' She knew it was he who'd sent the mystery shooter.

You can count on him, Malleus thought. *I did, during the war.*

Malleus entered the building, which was constructed entirely of roofed pillars. It led down, one level at a time, to the sea. *Probably best that he becomes her official bodyguard, at least as long as we're working on this artefacts case.*

The light blue waves glugged against the marble, seaweed bobbing against the steps as two priests with long tridents fished it out.

The oversized statue of Poseidon, wearing only a loincloth and holding a trident, was made entirely from coral. It towered on the western side of the temple, dappled with the morning sunlight, its pearl eyes fixed on the sea. A few people sat praying on the steps, scattering red and yellow flower petals into the water.

Malleus took off his hat and stood in front of the statue. 'Poseidon, you must already be aware,' he spoke loudly in French, so that the priests and people around him could hear. 'Yesterday one of your priests was killed. Something ripped him to pieces while he was attempting to murder a small child and frame the goddess Tanit for the murder.'

The people on the steps looked over at him, aghast, then turned to each other and started whispering.

Malleus reached into his pocket and pulled out the bag with the evidence inside. 'I found this on your priest, Poseidon. I'm about to give it to the police, to aid them in their investigations surrounding the death of the young Egyptian boy. I assume you know who else is involved in all this, and that you will not allow any further—'

'That's enough,' thundered a man's voice, and Malleus turned his head to see an old man hurrying towards him. His white tunic was decorated with blue edging and the small embroidered image of a trident. His white beard swayed with every energetic step. It looked like his little performance had successfully summoned the high priest. *Just as I planned.*

The man grabbed Malleus by the arm and pulled him away from the statue, behind one of the many surrounding pillars. 'You dare to enter the temple of Poseidon and—?'

'I am a private investigator, Monsieur,' he interrupted the man coldly. After all, he was the one being seized. Malleus held the bag in front of the man's face. 'On this smartphone there are calls and messages that lead back to you. The dead priest was working on your orders!' This was a guess on Malleus' part, but he hadn't had time to take a closer look at the phone. His own PDA sat in his breast pocket, silently recording. 'This evidence is going straight to the police.'

The high priest went white as a sheet. 'That cannot be!' He laid a hand on the trident stitched on his chest, as if trying to prevent Poseidon from hearing their conversation.

Malleus bared his teeth in a malicious grin. 'You thought you hadn't left a trail?'

'I never told Petros to kill a child,' the man sputtered. 'We wanted to drive out Tanit – her return wasn't good news for anyone. And the Sokarians, too. The last thing we wanted in Carthage was an *Egyptian demigod.* He would have attracted followers in their hundreds.'

'So he had to go? And while you were at it, Tanit too – am I correct, Monsieur?'

The high priest realised his mistake and bit his lip. He looked around hastily. 'Surely we can come to an agreement. The temple cannot be involved in this. And besides, don't forget: the priest has already been punished with death. I'm sure it was Poseidon who came himself and saved the child . . .'

'You genuinely mean to claim that Poseidon prevented the

second victim from murdering the girl?' Malleus' thoughts froze for a second as he saw the scene again in his mind's eye. *The man's wounds, they . . .* Whatever had spared the child from a fiery death, it could be the same creature that had obliterated his unit during the Great Change. *Could be.*

The high priest nodded. 'You make the smartphone disappear and we'll make it out as if Petros was just insane, blinded by madness. Then I'll announce that Poseidon showed deepest displeasure at Petros' actions, and that he put a curse on him and cast him out of the temple – *before* he attempted the second murder,' he added thoughtfully. 'That could go a long way towards keeping the unrest in New Carthage in check, and the temple would still come out of it unscathed.'

'What do I get out of it?' Malleus shoved his conscience to one side for a moment. He was morbidly curious as to how much someone would pay him for such a cover-up.

'Money,' the man said without pausing for breath. 'Who's paying you to investigate? The young whore?'

Now he was listening. 'You mean the mother of the child who was meant to die yesterday?'

'Oh, not her then.' He looked at Malleus searchingly. 'Ah, the Sokarians! Petros should have known that they wouldn't let the boy's death rest. And this so-called police force, who won't even—'

'What do you know about the young woman?'

'Zohra?' He looked confused. 'She was born here, sold by her parents when she was two years old and sent to Gomorrah. One can only imagine what she gets up to there, and who the father of the child is, for that matter. She brought the kid back here when she returned.' The high priest was clearly uninterested in this line of conversation; his only concern was the reputation of his temple. 'So, do we have an understanding?'

Malleus grabbed the man by his collar. 'Listen closely. Your deceitful practices here will no longer be swept under the rug by the authorities – I'll see to that myself,' he spoke clearly and forcefully, directly into the man's face. 'And if the citizens of New Carthage decide, upon hearing the facts of the matter, to tear down the temple of Poseidon and its child-murdering priests, I will not stand in their way. Gods come and go. The more who go, the better.' He breathed in deeply. 'Where do I find Zohra?'

'You don't want money?'

'No. You will go to trial, High Priest – unless Poseidon decides to do us all a favour before then and kill you himself, you cowardly piece of shit.' Malleus let him go. His PDA had recorded their entire conversation. The man's complicity in the murder was clear, and the rest was for the court to decide. A glance at his PDA told him that the police would be arriving any second to make the arrest. *Good timing.*

Malleus heard a soft scratching noise behind him, and instinctively dodged to one side.

* Α Ω *

New day, new start for the guy I'm following.

Off to Poseidon's temple to bring the bad guys to justice. Good boy.

It won't be easy to stay unseen here; these bloody pillars don't give a lot of cover. But at least they have flat roofs.

Up I go!

A minute or so and I'm perched up top with a decent view of the temple and the sea outside. Not a lot of cover up here either, so I'm pretty much fully exposed. Anyone could see me if they looked up. So let's hope he gets a move on.

His little show has already begun, and it's obviously going well. But . . .

shit, I can't see any more. I'll change positions. The amount of bird shit up here, ugh.

No, I can't see him from here either. These fucking pillars. Always one in the way. I can hear, but I can't see anything. The hacked PDA camera is showing me the asshole priest, but that's not much use.

Further to the right, and . . . fuck. That's—I need to get back to the ground. Getting up here was—

What's that priest doing? Nasty-looking trident, clearly not intended for fishing.

He moves so quickly – the fucking pillars are in the way, shit!

I slide over to the edge and set up my APB, but – where is he?

* A Ω *

A shadow hurled itself forwards.

The trident stabbed past Malleus and directly into the high priest's chest. One of the temple priests who had been fishing seaweed out of the water had obviously tried to come to his superior's aid.

Malleus drew his Apache Derringer from his pocket, ready for further attacks, but at that moment the young priest's shoulder spontaneously exploded, blood spraying in all directions without any visible cause.

The man dropped the trident with a loud cry and fell backwards onto the steps. 'I . . . didn't want—' he stuttered.

The high priest swayed towards the injured man, then fell. The trident still lodged in his chest jarred loudly against the marble as he slid down the steps and into the water. His body sank immediately beneath the waves, as if pulled by a force from below.

Malleus pointed the Derringer at the second priest, who had collapsed into a heap and was staring speechlessly at his bleeding shoulder. 'Stay,' he commanded coldly. Apparently there had been another accomplice in the plot against the Sokarians and Tanit. The police who were about to turn up would be happy that there was someone left alive for them to arrest.

Malleus fixed his eyes on the ceiling, scanning and searching – and briefly caught sight of a figure crawling away from the edge before vanishing from sight. His guardian angel had struck again – though not a moment too soon.

He took a final look out at the sea that had engulfed the body of the high priest.

Malleus guessed they wouldn't find the body – or the trident.

Tunisia, Tunis / New Carthage, November 2019

Malleus sat on the couch where this case had begun and concluded his report. The Tameris sat opposite him, and behind them stood al Hadiri, all listening intently to his account. He had already sent his report via PDA to the lawyer.

'It seems that only one of the priests of Poseidon was not involved in the plan,' he finished. 'The police arrested two men, and it is assumed that by doing so, further violence has been prevented.' He took a sip of the almond milk, which was doing wonders for his still pounding head. 'And with the deaths of Petros and the high priest, I suppose you could say your son's murder has been avenged, if you wish to interpret it that way.'

He took another sip and sighed contentedly. He had taken credit for the bullet wound on the priest's shoulder – self-defence, he had claimed – and they had accepted his explanation without question. They hadn't even run ballistics tests.

'Monsieur Bourreau, I am so grateful to you,' said Monsieur Tameri after a moment. 'We always knew that it was not an accident.'

'And I,' his wife added, 'will go today and ask Alexa for her forgiveness. It was not right that in my grief I called for the destruction of Tanit's shrine.'

Malleus agreed; without the sudden cloud of darkness which had fallen over the streets of the old town, the night would have ended with countless dead and injured. 'I believe she will understand,' he said.

'There is enough room in New Carthage, and any god who lacks in followers will grow weak of their own accord,' Monsieur Tameri prophesied. 'I think the next few years will be difficult for Poseidon.'

'People are quick to forget,' Malleus pointed out. 'They will happily lay the blame on the priests and continue to pray to Poseidon – people who live by the sea will always worship a god who has power over the waves.' He stood up. 'Monsieur and Madame Tameri, I must leave you now.' He held out his hand.

'You have our thanks. You showed the world the true nature of our son's death. Sokar is grateful, and the pharaoh will hold your name in favour.' Madame Tameri spoke softly. She looked more composed, now that she knew the truth and the murderers had been brought to justice. 'And there will soon be a new demigod in New Carthage.' She took her husband's hand. 'We have great faith that it will come to pass again.'

Malleus cleared his throat and did his best to push the image of the woman having sex with a falcon-headed god out of his mind's eye. There was already enough so-called erotic literature out there about the gods. He didn't need to think about it. 'I wish you all the best.'

Al Hadiri gestured towards the exit. 'I will drive you to the airport, Monsieur Bourreau.'

'Surely there's a taxi driver who will charge less than 250 euros per hour?' he had to ask with a smile.

The Tameris laughed politely. 'Your services are worth every penny, Monsieur. Don't worry about the money.'

Malleus didn't tell them he never did. He put on his hat, collected his luggage and went outside with the lawyer, back into the sunshine and the heat.

'Ah, Monsieur Bourreau, one more thing: did the police find out what killed the priest of Poseidon in the square?' al Hadiri asked as they stepped into the white Toyota.

'They haven't told me. They simply thanked me for solving the murder of Snofru. The high priest seemed to be implying that it was Poseidon himself.' Malleus took off his hat in the car and selected a Culebra with a green band from his cigar case. 'Do you have any ideas?'

'No.' He started the car. 'But it must have been *very* angry.'

Malleus considered the fact that he had found nobody at Zohra's address. Immediately following the encounter at the temple of Poseidon, he had hurried over to speak with the young woman, with no success. Neighbours told him she had been picked up by a limousine.

Wasted. He had no splints left in his case and looked around the dashboard for a cigarette lighter, to no avail. He hated non-smoking cars.

He shoved the unlit cigar in the corner of his mouth anyway and looked at his PDA.

New updates from Germania and Lagrande. The case of the stolen artefacts was picking up momentum.

They now had both the fan of a Japanese god and the statuette of an African deity which had hidden at least one diamond.

On top of that, they also had leads on an ancient tile from

Persia, the horn of a holy Indian cow, the crown made with a nail from the cross of Jesus Christ and a set of some kind of beetle statues. And now apparently a clue had come up in Mannheim.

A nice little case we've got going. Malleus took a drag on his unlit cigar out of habit, tasting only the light aroma of tobacco.

There was a message from Lautrec: he had officially assigned Lagrande to Malleus. She was too clever and too deep into the case to waste her talents on office work which could easily be taken over by 'officers less imaginative'.

Since there had now been multiple murders surrounding the artefacts, and according to Malleus' predictions there would soon be a lot more, Interpol was now justifiably keen to solve the case quickly.

Al Hadiri stopped the car. They had reached the terminal of the tiny airport. 'Here we are, Monsieur Bourreau.' He stepped out to help Malleus with his luggage.

'Thank you.' From here he would take a chartered flight all the way to Frankfurt, and then the next plane to Treva. *I guess I won't go home to change clothes just yet.* At least the hotel had managed to get the stains out of his shirt.

Malleus got out and took his bag and case. He held out his hand to al Hadiri. 'I prefer not to say goodbye,' he said with a smile.

'Me too,' replied the lawyer, equally friendly. 'If I may give you a piece of advice: take care of yourself, Monsieur Bourreau. The gods have indeed returned, but not always, and not everywhere.'

'I hope you're right, Monsieur al Hadiri.' He lifted his suitcase. 'And I also hope that they go back where they came from.'

The lawyer winked and stepped back into the Toyota, which drove off.

Malleus strode through the departure lounge, went through the various security procedures, showing his licence for the Derringer and his Interpol pass, and fifteen minutes later, was sitting comfortably in the jet.

* A Ω *

Wow, the updates are really flooding in. This artefact thing is really entertaining. I never would have thought.

But how am I going to get to Treva as quickly as him? I don't want to miss his meeting with his secretary.

Hm. The next flight to Frankfurt goes tomorrow, and he's managed to squeeze himself onto a chartered flight. Can I risk getting on the same flight as him?

Did he see me on the roof of the temple? Could he recognise me?

When I check online it says there's no room left on the plane, I can't book a seat. Probably just too close to the departure time. There aren't that many people walking across the airfield onto the plane.

Fuck, I can't do it. But I can't lose him.

I'll think of something else. That business in the Poseidon temple was too close; he almost saw me. Though it shows how good he is.

He should consider himself lucky he didn't end up seeing the kid's mother again. That conversation would definitely have taken a turn he wouldn't be expecting. The whole situation is pretty unforeseeable.

I'm standing here at the airport. I can see him getting on the plane. I have to think of some way to keep on his tail.

His path is my path.

* A Ω *

Apart from Malleus there were only seven other passengers on the plane. They had distributed themselves around before the plane rolled onto the runway, maximising their personal space.

Malleus paid no attention to the safety announcements; he flew too often.

Oh yes – the symbol. Malleus clicked his tongue, opened his PDA and drew the hieroglyph from al Hadiri's forehead onto the touchscreen.

The result appeared promptly.

'Kuk, also Kek,' he read quietly out loud. 'An ancient Egyptian god, known since the Middle Kingdom. Later depicted as half of a couple with Kauket or Keket; both gods were part of the Ogdoad of Hermopolis.' According to the legend of the Ogdoad, before the creation of the world, Kuk and Kauket had been two of the eight gods – four couples – who had ruled. *They represent the primal darkness.*

Malleus immediately thought back to the darkness that had swept through the streets in New Carthage. *Kek al Hadiri.* Had the god manifested in order to keep an eye on the competition in the city, or was it just a total coincidence?

'Bonjour, Monsieur Bourreau. May I ask you to fasten your seatbelt and switch off your device?'

He looked up to see a brunette stewardess in a smart yellow and green uniform standing in front of him. One hand was folded behind her back like a waiter, the other offered him a glass of mineral water.

'Ah, of course. Sorry, I wasn't paying attention.' Malleus put down the PDA on the empty seat next to him and fiddled with his seatbelt. The message that had just come in from Mr Crick in York would have to wait. He was still parched after his rum-fuelled episode the previous night, but he didn't want water. 'I don't suppose you have any almond milk, Madame?'

She made a politely regretful face. 'I'm afraid not, Monsieur. But I have something much better.'

'Oh, fantastic.' The metal buckle slid together under his fingers with a click.

She took her hand from behind her back and thrust a taser directly onto his chest. 'Voilà.'

Malleus went to raise his arms in defence, but too late. Thousands of volts surged through him and as his vision dimmed, he heard the jet turbines whirring into action.

The jet took flight, and Malleus felt his ears pop with the change in air pressure as he slipped out of consciousness.

BOOK 5

Episode 5: Turbulence

Addendum December 2012:

Turbulence can sometimes be caused by gods, the works of gods or entities associated with gods. In this update to the flight manual, we will provide an overview of the areas most likely to be affected by reoccurring god-related turbulence.

All pilots MUST be acquainted with the altered technical demands presented by these new airspace parameters and must remain informed about all updates to air corridor regulations.

ATTENTION!

During the flight you will receive reports every sixty seconds regarding sightings of gods, entities, etc., in your area and around your flying altitude. You must be ready to change your flight path AT ANY TIME, in order to avoid aircraft damage or destruction.

Pilot Training Manual

Updated edition published 18.09.18

* Α Ω *

Unknown airspace, November 2019

Malleus Bourreau was woken by the pain of his teeth grinding together and by a metallic scraping sound.

Slowly and deliberately, he unclenched his muscles, relaxing his jaw and relieving the pulsating pain in his head. His chest also throbbed, right at the point where the stewardess had unexpectedly jolted him out of action with a taser.

A hijacking! Malleus looked around the cabin of the jet, which was clearly flying at a reasonably high altitude. The metallic scraping sound was coming from the set of handcuffs attaching his wrists to his armrest – he couldn't lift his arms more than a couple of inches.

He twisted around in his seat and craned his neck to look around. Aside from himself, he could see there were four other passengers cuffed to their seats: two men, two women. One of them, an older man, was just waking up; the others were still passed out, probably from their own taser shocks. The passengers had chosen to disperse themselves around the cabin, so it wasn't possible for Malleus to make contact with any of them without alerting the hijackers. He would have to speak to them if he wanted to try and coordinate some kind of plan, but that would draw too much attention.

He turned to face the aisle that led to the crew area and the cockpit. Strands of his dark hair were hanging in front of his face; he blew the hair from his eyes with a sharp exhalation.

The blue curtain that sectioned off the front of the plane was closed and quiet voices could be heard behind it.

There were eight of us at take-off. He could just about recall where the other three passengers had been sitting, but they were no longer in their seats and, for now at least, he couldn't see any blood splatters or signs of a struggle.

The stewardess was obviously one of the hijackers – but the other three people? Were they in the cockpit? Had they been taken down to the hold? Why?

Too much speculation. Malleus tried to stretch his hand into the pocket of his light-coloured coat, checking to see if his Derringer had been taken, but the handcuffs were fastened too tightly. He could only fumble around under the armrest, where he felt the metal tube the cuffs had been attached to. He doubted that he could get free without some seriously impressive manoeuvring, and he had no idea how long he'd been unconscious. He couldn't get to his luggage, or to his coat, which he knew contained spare weapons.

I'll have to wait. Malleus hated being compelled to do nothing.

He made himself as comfortable as possible and listened out for signs that any of the other constrained passengers behind him were stirring. While he listened, he mulled over the potential motives of the hijackers.

A Learjet was an expensive machine. If someone with sufficient means were to steal such an aircraft and land it in certain countries, they would need only to remove the transponder and rename the plane and they would have successfully acquired a private jet for a relatively low price.

Or the hijacking could be an attempt to kidnap a passenger, or a group of passengers, or their luggage.

Or something being transported in the hold.

Or me.

And of course, there was always the possibility that the unknown attackers were planning to use the plane itself as a weapon.

In the past it had mainly been fanatical Christians, Muslims or Jews who had ended up on the news for their willingness to die for their faiths by attacking the shrines of the returned gods. Flying a jet into a temple or a holy site would usually get them a decent amount of press coverage. Followers of other returned gods tended to abstain from that particular form of protest.

There was also the organisation *GodsEnd*, who aimed to bring about the fall of the gods by demonstrating their weaknesses and lack of omnipotence, usually in fairly drastic displays of violence or destruction. They could also find a lot of uses for a jet, Malleus speculated.

The curtain moved and the brunette stewardess popped her head through the gap into the passenger section. She was still wearing the neat green and yellow uniform, but her jacket was open, displaying the shoulder holsters she was wearing underneath. On the right was a revolver, on the left the taser with which Malleus was already acquainted.

'Ah, Mr Bourreau,' she greeted him in a friendly tone. 'Please forgive our methods, but it was in everybody's best interest that we subdued the passengers as quickly as possible.' She stood in front of him. 'Is everything alright? No heart problems from the electric shock?'

'No,' he responded. 'I'd like to smoke, though. A Culebra, blue band.'

She laughed politely, just as one would expect from a flight attendant. 'I'm afraid I can't allow you to smoke. But would you like something to drink?'

Malleus nodded. 'What's the purpose of this hijacking?'

She winked at him, disappeared through the curtain and returned with a full glass of water and a straw. 'I'll be making an announcement shortly, when the other guests have woken up, so that everyone's on the same page.' She set down the glass elegantly on the tray table in front of him and placed the straw between his lips. 'Try not to get impatient. We have a long journey ahead of us yet.'

Malleus drank as she carried on down the aisle and checked on the other passengers.

One of them raged at her and swore a lot, another cried and complained. The third demanded to go to the toilet, and the fourth asked for a beer and a cognac.

A long way, she said. How far can this jet even go?

After a short while, the stewardess made her way back to the front of the cabin, picked up the receiver for the tannoy system and pressed a button. There was the usual two-note tone signalling the beginning of an announcement.

'Ladies and gentlemen, I'd like to welcome you to your journey with our newly founded Airline, Con Air, on board this chartered flight 08-15 from New Carthage to who-knows-where,' she said proficiently, without skipping a beat. 'My name is Tiffy. As you may have noticed, there have been a few changes to your flight today. We will inform you of the exact reasons for this on an individual basis, in the comfort of your seats. Our safety expert is currently checking your luggage for forbidden objects and substances, and he will then be making his way round the cabin to consult with each of you personally. Until then, we ask you to remain quiet. Toilet visits will be offered later in the flight. Finally, the captain and I would like to wish you a very pleasant flight.' She hung up the receiver and disappeared through the curtain with a chuckle. 'I've always wanted to do that,' Malleus heard her giggling quietly to an accomplice.

So I know about as much as I did five minutes ago. Malleus emptied his glass and leaned back in his seat. A glance out of the oval window next to him confirmed that they were flying over the cloud-layer; there was no land or sea to be seen.

The sun was shining from behind them – so they were heading north. Their course didn't seem to have changed much from the one he'd originally intended to fly.

A muscular man wearing a black set of overalls and a black balaclava came through the curtain and sat next to Malleus. His eyes were disguised by sunglasses, and he was carrying a Beretta 92FS in a shoulder holster.

'Hello, Mr Bourreau,' he said in English, with a noticeably eastern European accent. He smelled of liver sausage and sweat. 'The passenger list says you're an inspector with Interpol?'

'Correct.'

'Then you will probably be even more annoyed than the others that you are unable to do anything about this hijacking.' He looked down his nose at Malleus.

'It would have annoyed me more if you were a god,' replied Malleus, catching sight of his own reflection in the man's glasses. Usually he would have stroked his moustache to great effect at this point, a mannerism he enjoyed. But the cuffs prevented him from doing so – and from smoking the Culebra that he so desperately craved. A green band instead of the blue he'd asked the stewardess for, perhaps. Green helped him think. 'Or are you one?'

'I do currently have the power of life and death in my hands. But people have that power far more often than gods.' The masked man laughed quietly to himself. 'What were you doing in New Carthage, policeman?'

Malleus was glad to find out they hadn't done any significant background research on him – unless they were deliberately giving that impression to lure him into a trap. 'Investigating. For a private client.'

'You take private cases for extra cash?'

'Yes.'

'Is that allowed?' The man sounded intrigued. 'In our country it is called bribery if a policeman receives extra money on the side.'

'Bribery is different. And my contract allows me to take other jobs.' Malleus feared that he would have to wait a very long time for a cigar to calm his nerves. He needed it for more than that, in fact: it was an addiction, after all, and one that he was only consciously confronting now, for the first time ever, now he had no choice. Even the thought of being forced to abstain from his Culebras was causing him physical distress; the seeds of panic were beginning to take root in his chest. 'You obviously didn't hijack this jet for my sake, so I'm guessing it's a little inconvenient for you to have an Interpol agent on board. Right so far?'

'Right so far.' The black sunglasses prevented him from getting a look at the brawny man's eyes. He couldn't get a read on his reactions. 'You'll want to know what I intend to do with this plane.'

'You don't give me the impression that you'll be sharing that information.' Malleus nodded towards Tiffy, who had just poked her head through the curtain and was casting a watchful eye over the other passengers. 'I've already given it some thought, but there are too many possibilities to narrow it down.'

The man raised his hand and patted Malleus on the left shoulder. 'I'm glad. Surprise is the spice of life.' He stood up. 'Keep quiet, officer, and no harm will come to you.' He went over to the next passenger, taking the liver sausage aroma with him.

Tiffy had marched along the aisle and disappeared through another curtain on the other side of the cabin, followed by the clicking of a door mechanism. She was either going to the toilet, or on her way to the hold.

What could she be doing in there?

* A Ω *

Not the most comfortable way to travel, I'll admit.

Especially not in a plane that's over thirty thousand feet up.

But since I'm following him and can't afford to let him out of my sights, I can deal with it. There's no other option.

There are two air-masks back here for emergencies. Makes life easier for stowaways like me. Not that much luggage, even though the flight was fully booked – maybe they all just brought hand luggage: travelling 'express'?

I bet there are some pretty expensive outfits in these cases, maybe some delicious lingerie. Private charter flights aren't cheap, there have to be some ladies of luxury up there. Let's take a closer look.

Uh. Weird. Just normal clothes, average stuff, no designer brands. And . . . ammo?

Shit, a lot of ammo. This case is full to the brim with magazines, fifty rounds each. Unusual calibre, shells without casings. Nine millimetre. And those look like . . . five millimetres.

There's only one weapon I know of that's been tested with such tiny calibre shells: the G11.

There must be some decently armed bodyguards upstairs. Good to know.

So what's in the rest of these bags?

Zip, click, click

Aha. Money. Old Euros, old Russian Roubles, gold coins. About five hundred thousand, by the looks of it. A lot of gold, but decidedly average clothing – using understatement to avoid attracting any unwanted attention? And if they do attract any attention, they've got the guns to deal with it.

Quite a few packages lying around in the hold: air freight travelling to Frankfurt I suppose. I wonder what—? Shit, the door!

I've got a visitor.

A brunette stewardess comes in, with . . . a taser and a Walther PPK under her jacket. I might be wrong, but I'm pretty sure that's not standard uniform.

I duck down between the few cases and carefully push the largest one across the floor so she can't see me behind it.

She's checking the storage compartments with – a skinning knife? Unusual, that's a pretty technical blade to have just lying around. The way she's handling it . . . well-practised. She could cut someone's throat with that. I think I'm in love. I bet she's got some delicious lingerie on.

She's cutting open case after case, uncovering boxes of champagne, reinforced safe-boxes, presumably filled with jewellery, packages of incense. She looks disappointed. Clearly she was expecting more.

A voice crackles from her jacket pocket. 'Where are you?'

She pulls out a radio. 'Inigo, it's not here.'

'It *is* there. I put the container there myself.'

'It's not in any of the storage cases. And it hasn't slipped down between the packages.' *She's evidently pissed off. She's looking at a bottle of Champagne as if she's considering popping the cork and necking half of it in one go. I'll join you for a glass, sweetie.*

'Not in the storage cases,' *grumbles Inigo,* '*next* to the storage cases. Make sure it's still standing upright. The client wanted it upright.'

'Shouldn't I—?'

'No. Just leave it there for now.'

The stewardess pockets the radio, curses to herself and finally heaves out a smallish hard case bearing the words HUMAN ORGAN.

She opens it and takes out a container with – is that a heart?

Shit, yes, that's a heart in a plastic bag.

Small, fresh. From an animal, or . . . a child?

She inspects it briefly and puts it back in the case. Then she disappears.

Ha, what kind of nightmare flight is this? A Learjet transporting a tiny little heart, together with a ton of ammunition for old-fashioned guns, not to mention the— Ugh, how do I get into these situations?

I follow the trolley dolly without her noticing, up to the curtain leading into the cabin. I want to check on him.

The man I'm trailing.

I have a sneaking feeling it was the right call to follow him on this flight.

He's going to need me.

* Α Ω *

Malleus concentrated hard in an effort to make out the masked man's conversations with the other passengers.

The hijacker was speaking very quietly, and his voice was somewhat muffled through his woollen balaclava, but the men and women were answering loudly enough that he could get an impression of who his fellow hijackees might be.

It was quite the illustrious crowd.

The young blonde woman diagonally behind him was the daughter of a rich industrialist; the thirty-something-year-old in cheap clothing appeared to be a hacker responsible for cracking some seriously complicated systems; the older man was joint head of a corporate group whose name Malleus couldn't quite make out, and the other woman was a multi-millionaire.

Definitely some high-value targets, judging by bank balance alone.

Malleus realised that he was by-catch, unintentionally caught up in a net full of very valuable fish. The hijackers had very little use for him, even as a hostage. The others would all attract far more attention, and higher rewards.

He also realised where by-catch usually ended up – overboard.

While he was listening to the others, Malleus had also been examining the handcuffs with his fingers, figuring out their model and manufacturer. He knew most handcuffs had a weak point, but without the right tool, it would be impossible for him to exploit it.

What he hadn't managed to deduce from the conversations was the *reason* for the hijack.

All four? Just one? Anything he came up with was just speculation.

His mouth grew dry, despite the glass of water – anxiety was taking hold. His body was making polite yet insistent requests for a drag of a Culebra – not in an hour, not in thirty minutes, but immediately. He began to sweat.

The masked man's footsteps came towards him and passed him by, his huge figure disappearing behind the curtain.

The hostages were alone in the cabin.

'You're police?' Malleus heard before he could even turn round. It was the hacker, his voice already racked with panic. 'Do something!'

Malleus slid to the side of his seat, as far as the cuffs would allow. The light material of his coat tugged uncomfortably at his throat. 'I would do so immediately, if I had the opportunity. But unfortunately I find myself in exactly the same situation as you, sir.' He shook another strand of dark hair from in front of his eyes. Without his hat to keep it in place, his hair did as it pleased.

The older man laughed. 'The law in handcuffs. Could be the title of a book.'

'Could we please introduce ourselves? So we know who we're dealing with?' suggested the millionaire woman. 'I'm Eleonore Haviland.'

'Theodor Smythe,' replied the older man.

'Ryko,' the hacker added.

'Ivanka de Bonde,' offered the other woman.

'And my name is Bourreau.'

'Seriously? *The* Bourreau?' Ryko laughed. 'I've read about you online. You're the atheist who investigates gods.'

'Right now the god stuff isn't important,' Malleus replied in a friendly tone. 'Everyone, I'd ask you to pay close attention. You all just spoke with the masked man – is there any reason why he might want to kidnap one of you?'

'Why wouldn't *you* be the target, Inspector?' Haviland responded. 'Can't you police get access to files and so on? Or are you investigating something sensitive at the moment? Or maybe this man has been contracted by a god who wants to kill you without getting their hands dirty?'

Good theories. Someone's still using their brain. Malleus wasn't unimpressed with her suggestions, but disregarded them within moments. 'If someone wanted me dead, I would be already, Madame. For access to the Interpol server, Mr Ryko here would be able to provide far greater services than I would, and as for sensitive cases – that would describe almost everything I've worked on.' He awkwardly attempted to look round at the passengers. 'I'm looking at a collection of rich and powerful people. If the masked man isn't planning to use the jet for a terrorist attack, which I would doubt, given his behaviour so far, I'd say it probably has something to do with you – either all of you, some of you, or only one.'

The four hostages looked pensive.

'What would it even matter if we knew the reason?' Ivanka de Bonde asked. 'It wouldn't change anything.'

Malleus didn't agree. 'Knowledge always brings power. Sooner or later.'

'Well let's hope it isn't *too* much later,' commented Smythe with a dark laugh. 'I'll start: no idea why I'd be interesting to him. Aside from my being a member of Watermark. Chairman of the board.'

Watermark. A series of scandals ran through Malleus' memory as he heard the name, mostly related to environmental concerns. It would certainly make a serious statement against the firm's practices if the chairman of the board were kidnapped or harmed. Thinking was beginning to be painful. *What I would give right now for a Culebra!* 'Mr Hacker?'

Ryko thought for a second. 'I was working on something,' he admitted reluctantly. 'It was basically trying to—'

The back curtain opened sharply and Tiffy reappeared. 'Ah, our guests are getting to know each other.' She walked slowly down the aisle. 'That'll be enough of the chatting, if you don't mind.'

'You can't prevent us from speaking,' Smythe said coldly.

'Yes, but I can make you regret it,' she answered with a glare. 'One more word without my permission and you'll be a lot more uncomfortable than you are now, sir.' Tiffy cleared her throat. 'So, would anyone like to use the facilities?'

Malleus observed the fake stewardess. Her uniform was slightly dirty at the knees: she must have been crawling around in the hold, looking for something, perhaps. He had a thought. 'I would, please.'

'But of course, Inspector.' With an assiduous air, Tiffy came over to his seat, reached into the right pocket on the outside of her jacket and took out a small key.

That was all Malleus needed to know.

Germania, Celtic Electoral Palatinate (Baden-Württemberg), Mannheim, November 2019

Marianne Lagrande entered the foyer of the museum and immediately spotted the white-haired, elderly man in the blue suit. He was standing next to a museum employee, organising a stand of brochures. *There he is.* She raised a hand to get his attention.

He saw her and nodded hesitantly – he clearly had only a very vague idea of why a blonde-haired woman in a white dress straight out of the eighties might be walking towards him.

Of course, it had been something of an exaggeration when she had described herself to Hermann on the telephone as an *investigator* for Interpol. It was true that she *was* investigating, but sadly there was no official job title for a secretary who was conducting field research other than, well, secretary. She had no special authority.

As Wilkmann was unaware of this technicality, she hoped the conversation would go smoothly, with no need for further fabrication on her part.

He exchanged a few quick words with the employee and left the brochure stand to greet Lagrande.

'Hello there. How may I help you?' He smelled of aftershave intended for elderly gentlemen and the polish from his shiny black shoes.

Lagrande showed her Interpol pass, intentionally obscuring the section that detailed her status and description. 'Marianne Lagrande. We spoke on the telephone, Mr Wilkmann.'

He looked moderately pleased and slightly guilty. 'Of course. Please come with me.' He led her through the staff area into one of the as-yet empty galleries. *Holy Gold – Cursed Gold* was the title of the exhibit. 'You said you had a few questions about my stay in Treva?'

Lagrande nodded. 'It's regarding a murder.' She had concealed this fact on the telephone in order to keep him in suspense. He didn't seem to be your typical law-breaking type, and his record was completely spotless, so she couldn't count on him having the kind of guilty conscience that would motivate others to talk or negotiate. She wanted to make things as easy as possible for Malleus Bourreau, and didn't want to get the authorities involved every step of the way. *Far too much fuss*, she thought.

'You know a Mr Hektor Mohr?'

Wilkmann thought, fiddling nervously with something in his right trouser pocket as he did so, probably his keys, from the jangling sound. He looked like a nice old grandpa being forced to rat out his grandchild. 'No,' he answered after a while. 'Where would I have met this man?'

'When you bought stolen goods from him,' she replied in an entirely friendly tone.

'Oh?' he said with surprise. 'Not possible.'

Lagrande had to stifle a smirk. Wilkmann was beginning to remind her of a cartoon character she remembered from her childhood. 'I'm afraid so.'

'That was stolen? But he was such a nice young man.' He adjusted his museum jacket and name – further evidence of his discomfort.

'You will have noticed that no certificate was provided to accompany the object. Or receipt,' she added, concealing her amusement. This was going even smoother than she had expected. She ran her metallic blue fingernails lightly through her long, backcombed hair: pure eighties power. 'I'm afraid your excuses are useless, Mr Wilkmann. We have witnesses who were present when you met with Mohr. We've already questioned them.' She batted her eyelashes.

Wilkmann sighed and slumped slightly. 'I'll admit it – but the museum had nothing to do with it! I paid for it with my own money and put together the exhibit myself.' He stood in front of a display case. 'And you're wrong about the certificates and receipts. I insisted on them, because the museum management needs them in order to display a piece. It was no problem for him to provide them.'

'Do you often do that?'

'Purchase exhibits? Yes, when I'm abroad. I'm a trained historian and archaeologist and I've taken part in many digs in my time, lots of historical sites. Until the gods returned, that is.' He laughed. 'Then it was a bit . . . well, pointless. At least in the most famous places. Most of them have been reincarnated, so to speak.'

'So the museum often works with exhibits of questionable origin.'

'No, goodness no!' Wilkmann exclaimed with considerable outrage. 'I swear by Odin and Teutates, this thing with Mohr was an exception.' He laid one hand on his heart and took the other out of his pocket to honour his oath. 'Of course, I noticed something wasn't right. But you have to understand, Inspector, I would rather have seen these gold pieces end up with us than with some private collector who would just hide them away, or – even worse – melt them down into worthless lumps.'

'I doubt one could ever call that amount of gold worthless.'

'They would have lost their value for me as a historian and archaeologist. What is gold without culture, anyway? Just expensive metal.' He looked pained. 'Mohr is dead?'

Lagrande nodded. 'We know it wasn't you,' she lied, 'but we're going through all our leads and questioning the witnesses to see if they saw anything useful. And of course we're collecting the stolen artefacts,' she added hastily.

Wilkmann nodded softly. 'I thought as much.' He placed one hand on the glass of the case in front of them. 'Here they are.'

Lagrande had to smile. *He already knew he was going to confess when he led me in here.*

She turned her head, her full hair falling over one shoulder, curious to see what Mohr and the others had lost their lives for.

Behind the thick glass glittered a dozen thumb-sized golden figures, carved to resemble insects, birds and crocodile-like creatures. As she looked closer, she could see that their structures were incredibly precise and exact.

'I believe,' commented Wilkmann, 'that these are all from the same source as the golden insects in the Museo del Oro in Bogotá. The Colombians have more than thirty thousand of them.'

'What do they represent?'

'There are a few theories. Many believe they were created by indigenous people who had a deep belief in their gods of creation. They wanted to pay tribute with objects like these, but also to forge a connection with them – to be closer to them. As close as we are now, I'd guess,' the man spoke with the air of an enthusiastic teacher. 'You see this figure on the left-hand side?'

Lagrande turned her blue eyes to follow his pointing finger. 'They look a bit like . . . primitive aeroplanes,' she said in surprise. 'The insect head distracted me at first.'

'Well spotted. You are a talented investigator.' Wilkmann looked pleased. 'That's the reason some people also call them the ancient American aeroplanes.'

The way he spoke suggested to Lagrande that there was more he wasn't saying. Her excitement was growing. *First the diamond in the statue, now this.*

She turned to face the man, who was smiling at her like a fatherly priest. 'There's more to these artefacts?'

'There are many theories—' Wilkmann began.

Lagrande looked across his shoulder and caught sight of a very muscular repairman, wearing a boilersuit and pulling a sledgehammer out of a duffel bag. It occurred to her that it might be quite difficult to use a sledgehammer to repair a glass display case. *You'd generally use it to do the opposite.*

'—listening, Inspector?' she heard Wilkmann say in a slightly bemused tone.

'No,' Lagrande said under her breath as she reached into her bag to pull out the combined taser and pepper-spray. 'Get help.'

The repairman spun round and slammed his hammer towards the case – but before he made contact, he was hit with a stream of biting liquid from her tiny spray can, right in the middle of his face.

With a yell, he lost momentum and missed the display case, instead hitting the perplexed Wilkmann, who was moving too slowly to avoid the blow.

The impact propelled the elderly man across the floor of the room and into a plinth that was holding a vase. The object was well secured, but it shuddered enough to set off a loud alarm throughout the building.

Not a problem. Lagrande shoved the taser against the repairman's chest as he tumbled to the ground, dodging his elbows as he lashed out, and activated the current.

There was a loud crackling sound and the man collapsed into a gasping pile in front of her.

Lagrande turned to face Wilkmann and instead found a second boilersuited attacker, aiming a hefty-looking revolver straight at her.

She dived behind the nearest case and curled into a ball, her bomber jacket softening the impact as she bumped against the corner of the case.

Shots rang out, the bullets smashing through the case and barely missing her. Splinters of toughened glass flew through the air.

Lagrande looked at the charge status on her taser: still enough for two attacks using both electricity and pepper spray.

She heard footsteps as another person entered the room and received some kind of direction from the second attacker. *These have to be the same contractors as in Lutetia and Treva.* She slipped off her shoes and crept hastily to the next case, which contained another set of golden objects that she didn't recognise. *I hope things don't go as badly as last time.*

The unknown attacker rounded the corner of the case with a Ruger Super Blackhawk and covered his companion. 'Stay where you are,' he said coldly in Lagrande's direction. 'If I see your head, I will shoot it.'

There was a dull cracking noise, then a loud smash as the pane of glass finally gave under the impact of the hammer and fell into hundreds of tiny fragments. They fell like hailstones onto the polished stone floor and skidded as far as Lagrande's hiding spot.

'Come on, Jeff. Up you get,' she heard the second man saying impatiently. 'It's just a bit of electricity.'

Cursing, the third man got to his feet.

The alarm had grown louder, and there were scattered cries from the few guests in the museum as they ran to safety.

Lagrande watched the men in the reflection of a polished gold plate as they gathered up all of the golden objects and, after a second's hesitation, turned to the other exhibits.

I got here in time, but still a few seconds too late.

'Now go,' their leader yelled glancing back into the room. He caught sight of her reflection in the polished metal. Laughing, he shot at it, the large bullet punching a hole in the glass, which cracked without shattering. The plate inside the display case wobbled in circles until it fell still, the artefact now perforated with a perfectly round bullet hole. 'Stay where you are.'

Branleur! Lagrande wasn't going to be intimidated by these guys again.

She hurried from case to case, following the trio as they rushed towards an emergency exit and out of the building. Her knee-length white dress had proven to be less of a hindrance than she'd anticipated – the split up the side allowed her more freedom of movement than the designer had perhaps intended.

She followed them out of the building and found herself right next to the car park. She crouched behind a hedge. Dense droplets of rain were pouring from the sky, soaking her hair and clothing within seconds.

The men jumped into a beaten-up Toyota Hilux, the sledgehammer was thrown carelessly to the ground and the pick-up growled into action.

As their exit was blocked by a parking truck, the pick-up screeched backwards and was sent into a 180-degree spin by its driver. The robbers were heading for the entrance.

Sirens wailed in the distance. Apparently the police, already on their way, were not too far off.

You're staying put. Lagrande looked at the sledgehammer and set off running. She grabbed it as she sprinted up to the Hilux, ran round the side and using her full momentum, threw the tool right into the windscreen.

The iron head of the hammer crashed through the glass,

disappearing into a huge hole and crisscrossing the windscreen with so many cracks that Lagrande could no longer see through it.

The Hilux careened off the narrow road and ran into the barrier machine, mowing it down and finally beaching itself on the remains of the machinery. The front wheels spun impotently in the air and the engine gave a spectacularly unhealthy sound before dying altogether. It looked as if the driver had been hit by the hammer and lost consciousness.

I'm the sister of the mighty Thor. Lagrande took a deep breath and hurried over to the car, her combination pepper spray and taser in her right hand.

Passers-by stood around, stunned and clearly considering rushing to the aid of the car's passengers.

'Step away,' she yelled, pulling out her pass, 'police! Keep away from the vehicle!'

The back door swung open abruptly and a blond man stepped out. Blood was spurting from a hideous wound on his head and his nose was broken.

'What did I say to you, bitch?' He raised the Ruger Super Blackhawk and aimed it at Lagrande. In his other hand was the small bag stuffed with stolen gold.

Lagrande dived into the bushes as the gunshots began.

The bullets appeared to have missed her – at least, she didn't feel anything hit.

Where is he? She peered over the neatly trimmed hedge—

—right down the barrel of a revolver.

'Go to your car,' the man commanded her, wiping the rain and blood from his eyes with the back of his free arm.

'I came by train,' she replied.

'Shit, you're fucking useless.' She saw the tendons on the back of his hand move a few millimetres as he flexed his index finger.

The shot was louder than she'd expected.

The man was slammed to the right, as if he'd been hit by an invisible car. The weapon flew from his hand and into the hedge.

Lagrande looked around.

Diagonally across the car park, she saw a masked man – the one who had saved her life in Treva. He was holding a large-calibre gun; she couldn't tell the model. He tipped his fingers to his forehead in the same greeting she'd seen in Germania.

You again! Lagrande snatched the Ruger Super Blackhawk from the hedge and jerked it upwards. The man froze, but she pointed it past him and aimed at the Hilux, pulling the trigger several times, aiming at the second thief as he clambered out of the pick-up. The barrel jerked sharply upwards with each shot, pain shooting through her wrists.

The bullets poured through the rear windscreen and into the car body, almost certainly missing her opponent. Then there were no more.

Her mysterious saviour seemed to understand: he turned to the side and fired one single, self-assured shot.

It hit its target, who dropped to the ground. Lagrande could just about make out his crumpled silhouette through the wheels of the Hilux.

But as she looked back towards her rescuer, he had already vanished.

She used her rain-soaked dress to scrub her prints off the empty revolver and then threw it onto the body of her attacker. She snatched the bag full of golden artefacts. *Saved. From whom? By whom?*

Unknown airspace, November 2019

Malleus felt the fingers of the brunette stewardess on his wrist, and heard a series of clicks.

'If you try anything funny,' she said as she unlocked his cuffs from the armrest, 'I will shoot one of our less important hostages.' She helped him out of his chair. 'And then I will shoot you, Inspector. That's not an idle threat.'

Malleus didn't say anything, just nodded. He stood up, his hands now cuffed behind his back, and together they walked down the aisle towards the toilet. He used the opportunity to take in every detail of the other four hostages: their faces, clothing, expressions, and anything else he could make out.

The millionaire Eleonore Haviland was around fifty, wearing expensive clothing; she looked like she'd come to terms with her circumstances admirably quickly. She eyed him as he walked past as if trying to read his intentions from his face.

Theodor Smythe appeared to be equally resigned to his position, his resolve no doubt strengthened by years of tedious board meetings and shareholder conferences. He was around the same age as Malleus, his face angular and smooth-shaven, his hair combed back close to his skull. He too was making an attempt to figure out the inspector's next move. In the pocket of his jacket, Malleus caught a glimpse of a pack of cigarettes.

Ryko the hacker looked almost childlike in his panic. He was breathing heavily and sent Malleus a long, pleading look. Perhaps his blinking was in code, maybe binary – sadly Malleus had never bothered to learn it.

The rich heiress Ivanka de Bonde was staring out of the window, as if waiting for the long-overdue arrival of a god or a rescue team to pull up alongside the plane. Her eyes were fixed on the world outside the cabin, apparently uninterested in Malleus.

This was obviously a potent combination of important people, and yes – theoretically, any one of them could be the hijackers' intended target.

But which one is it? His thoughts were currently occupied with the insignificant, the smallest details he'd noticed while passing each of them.

Tiffy opened the toilet door, revealing a surprisingly roomy cubicle. 'Think about it, Inspector: a hostage, then you,' she said, uncuffing him. 'Shout when you've shaken off.' She turned to leave the cubicle.

Malleus noticed a smartphone hanging out of from her jacket pocket and quickly grabbed it as she turned. To his relief, Tiffy didn't notice anything as she closed the door.

Quick, before she notices. He looked at the smartphone, a compact satellite model with no connection to the usual terrestrial-based networks – meaning no carrier restrictions or locks to outsmart. *Perfect.*

He quickly dialled Lagrande's number, but she didn't pick up. His calls to other contacts at Interpol wouldn't connect – the signal was too unreliable.

Too good to be true. His only remaining option was to write a text message to Lagrande and Lautrec.

> Flight from New Carthage hijacked, Learjet to Frankfurt, flight number unknown. Please take action.

Malleus' thumbs flew across the tiny keyboard, adding the names of the other hostages whilst pressing the flush with his knee as he typed.

No reaction from Lautrec, but an SMS came straight back from his assistant.

Lagrande: What can I do?
Malleus: Call Lautrec – inform authorities in Germania and Celtica. Contact air traffic control.
Lagrande: Will do. Is it related to the artefacts?
Malleus: No. Something else.
Lagrande: Sure? What should I do with the objects? Are we still keeping them in your hiding place?
Malleus: For now, yes.

There was a knock on the door.

'Out you come, Inspector. You've had plenty of time – there's no way you could have eaten or drunk that much,' Tiffy said with irritation. 'The others need to go too.'

Malleus made some fairly convincing retching sounds. 'I think I ate something bad,' he called out in a pained voice, pressing the flush again.

Lagrande: Tell me where I need to take them, Chief.
Malleus: Got to go. More later.

He switched off the phone and dropped it into the rubbish bin, splashed his face with water and patted his clothing to check for anything useful. Nothing – his kidnappers had done a thorough job while he was unconscious.

Not even a Culebra.

Malleus looked at his tired face in the mirror. The scar under his eye looked redder than usual. His eyes, obscured by the blue contact lenses, were shining almost feverishly. He wet his hands and smoothed back the long black hair falling across his face. Adjusting his clothing, he opened the toilet door.

Tiffy stood in front of it, evidently incensed. 'I was just about to shoot one of these four,' she said, cuffing his wrists behind his back again.

Malleus walked down the aisle back to his seat, stumbling as he went as if he were dizzy from his supposed vomiting. He grabbed onto Tiffy for balance and finally slumped down into his seat.

She unclipped one of his wrists and attached the empty cuff to the armrest, turning to the other passengers. 'Anyone else?'

Nobody volunteered.

'I could have taken my time,' Malleus noted.

Tiffy flounced through the curtain and the door to the cockpit banged shut behind her.

He opened his right hand to reveal the small key he had fished out of the stewardess's pocket.

I could almost believe that was down to the luck of the gods. A moment later, his hands were free.

But Malleus didn't move.

He had to prevent the other passengers from reacting in surprise and alerting the hijackers through the curtain. And there were sure to be cameras monitoring the cabin, even if he couldn't see any from where he was sitting.

He needed to think – and without the aid of his customary Culebras. His mind was preoccupied with the messages from Lagrande and the details he'd observed when passing his fellow passengers. His temples were beginning to pound and his body was aching for the cigar he didn't have. He broke into a flop sweat.

'What were you doing in the toilet?' Ryko asked. 'Presumably you have a plan to fix this?'

'Obviously,' Malleus replied absently, looking out of the small window next to him. His mind was churning out details about his fellow hostages, which he was diligently sorting, one by one, forming a profile of each player in the game.

The flight path had not changed, and the jet was still flying north, although it was difficult to judge how long they had been in the air. He guessed they would keep to their original course for as long as possible, to avoid drawing attention from air traffic control.

If Lagrande had managed to raise the alarm, the hijacker's strategy would be in vain. Interpol's report to air traffic control would be swiftly followed by the appearance of interceptors alongside the jet – they wouldn't try anything dramatic whilst flying over the open ocean, but as soon as they reached a national airspace over land the fighter pilots would take action.

If. Malleus could almost feel the cogs whirring, each synapse lighting up. *If Lautrec is informed.*

After a few minutes, he had settled on a plan which would either end in catastrophe or in finding out the truth.

Or both. How it would work out for *him*, he wasn't so sure.

Malleus slipped off the handcuffs and slowly stood up from his seat.

'You got free!' Ryko blurted out in surprise, breaking into a laugh. 'I knew this guy had something up his sleeve.'

'You idiot! Sit down!' hissed Haviland. 'You heard the woman, they'll kill you *and* one of us if we try anything.'

Smythe leaned over in his seat to get a better view. 'Leave him to it. He can free us, and then we can take out the hijackers together.' He gave his handcuffs a demonstrative rattle. 'Come on then, Bourreau, let me loose.'

'They have cameras,' de Bonde correctly observed. 'They

probably already know he's out of his handcuffs.' She looked slowly from one to the other. 'The question we should be worrying about now is which one of us is going to get shot for his sake?'

Malleus allowed them to continue, interested to see what this quasi-philosophy experiment would reveal about his fellow passengers.

The excitement disappeared from Ryko's face. 'Fuck. I . . .' He fell silent, shrinking back into his seat.

'Well, I'm too rich,' Haviland said grandly. 'Mr Smythe is also far too valuable, thanks to his position in his company, and Mr Ryko's computer skills make him the most useful person here.' She fixed her gaze on the young heiress, who she had just hypothetically sentenced to death.

Ryko stared at the motionless Malleus. 'Don't you want to *do* something?'

'Yes.' His cravings were making him so jittery and irritable that he would even have settled for a cigar with no coloured band at all. 'I would like very much to do something.' He went over to Smythe and tapped on his jacket pocket. *There they are.* With a quick movement, he pulled the crumpled cigarette box from the man's pocket. Judging by the weight, it probably contained a lighter as well.

'Cheap brand,' he commented. 'And nobody here smells of expensive perfume. Those are the details that don't add up. And not one of you has asked about the three other passengers that are missing.' The group looked at him in bemusement as he shoved a cigarette in his mouth, lit it, made his way back to his seat and sat down. He crossed his right leg over his left and looked casually out of the window. 'Could do with a drink to go with this, but it would appear Tiffy is conveniently busy right now . . .'

'Inspector, what are you doing?' Ryko almost shouted. 'Didn't you—?'

They're not giving up. 'I'm smoking a cigarette,' Malleus replied with amusement, blowing the smoke up to the cabin ceiling. 'If you want one' – he waved the pack in the air – 'just take your handcuffs off and come and get one. There're still five left.'

'He's gone mad,' stammered de Bonde.

'He thinks this is a game,' Haviland added icily.

'I don't know exactly *what* this is,' Malleus answered, his gaze drifting across the landscape of clouds surrounding the jet, enormous in scale and almost solid. This situation would be far less stressful if it were possible to just run off across the clouds. 'But I know none of you are who you're claiming to be.' He took a long, unsatisfying drag. 'You're all part of the hijacking team.' The grey smoke poured from his nose and mouth, too thin to form the billowing shapes he enjoyed making with his cigars. Vile, bad-tasting, cheap tobacco – but it was helping to push back the dreaded withdrawal headache. 'My guess: this is about the artefacts that were stolen in Treva, nothing more.'

The silence in the cabin proved that his assessment was correct. Nobody objected, nobody laughed – nobody had anticipated him seeing through the scheme.

Then the curtain swung open and Tiffy appeared with a friendly smile. And of course with the crackling taser.

Germania, Celtic Electoral Palatinate (Baden-Württemberg), Mannheim, November 2019

'It all happened very fast. He just turned up and shot everybody.' Marianne Lagrande sat in a meeting room at the museum that was usually used for informative talks about obscure archaeological objects and patiently answered the Germanian investigator's questions. She was wearing a uniform borrowed from the museum, her soaked dress hanging up somewhere in a back room to dry. Her wet hair hung down her back, uncharacteristically smooth, her careful backcombing undone by the rain.

She was managing to avoid giving any specific details regarding the whereabouts of the golden figurines that were currently hidden in her handbag, around three feet away from the officer asking the questions. 'I can't really add anything else.'

The police hadn't found the stolen objects in the car and were therefore assuming that they had been thrown from the vehicle during the collision with the barrier, or taken by Lagrande's unknown rescuer.

The investigator turned off the camera and nodded. 'Thank you, Miss Lagrande. That's all for now.' He wagged his finger exaggeratedly, faux-reprimanding her. 'But try not to run after any more criminals with sledgehammers. That was a close call.'

Lagrande smiled guiltily. 'I promise, Inspector.' She stood up, shook his hand and left the room. Her handbag felt like it weighed forty pounds, but she tried not to let it show. *Please don't make a clinking sound.*

Wilkmann was waiting for her in the corridor. He had a bandage on his head, having sustained a nasty cut in the earlier chaos, but he was wearing his own clothes, which looked almost exactly the same as his museum uniform.

'You are genuinely . . .' He searched for the right word. 'A hero.'

'Thank you, but I only did what I had to.' *Got in far too much trouble for my secretary pay-grade, though.* Lagrande smiled and took the old man's arm. 'Let's get a coffee and recover a little bit, shall we? And you can tell me why you think these guys wanted the gold figurines – then maybe we can figure out their next targets and get there before they do.' None of this was technically untrue.

'That sounds wonderful.' Wilkmann let her support him as he walked, limping slightly. The hammer-blow had done nothing to help his bad hip. 'I'm glad nothing happened to the vase I fell onto.' He looked at her curiously. 'Why didn't you draw your gun?'

She had been expecting the question.

'I didn't have it with me,' she replied.

'But you had a taser with pepper spray,' he said questioningly.

'In a small room like that, guns can do more harm than good. Ricochets . . .' She trailed off intentionally, quickly changing the subject and pointing out of the window towards a small café. 'Shall we meet there? I'll just go and get back into my clothes.'

'Or we could go to the museum cafeteria? You don't have to get changed. The uniform suits you well.'

'I'd rather not. Too many reporters.' In fact, Lagrande was hoping to get as far from the police as she could. It was possible that they were just receiving the information that a similar shootout had occurred in Treva, with another two officers and an elderly Japanese woman mowed down in the street.

Wilkmann accepted her suggestion and Lagrande made her way to the back room where her clothes had been draped over a radiator. She quickly slipped back into her dress, noticing with a pang of regret a long, ragged tear, then threw on her bomber jacket. She hurriedly fixed her makeup, redrawing the thick black liner round her eyes.

She and Wilkmann left the museum through the side entrance, dodging the throng of regional, national and international press that had gathered round the police barrier at the front. This kind of thing didn't happen every day in Mannheim, especially not with such a blockbuster ending.

They entered the little café and settled into an alcove near the back, ordering coffee and mineral water. Aside from the two of them, there were around a dozen other customers, some reading the newspaper or typing on laptops or tablets, others following the news on the small TV in the corner. Naturally, it was tuned to the coverage of the events at the museum.

'I'm just disappointed that he got away with the gold figures,' Wilkmann commented after a sip of his coffee.

'Yes.' Lagrande subtly pushed her bag further underneath her chair. 'It looks like the miniatures were their priority. Why was that?'

'Small, heavy, gold,' Wilkmann summarised bitterly, readjusting his bandage. It was so neatly wrapped that it could almost have been an accessory; there were certainly a couple of customers in the café trying to guess what religion he belonged to. 'And easy to melt down.'

'Are they particularly collectible?'

'They're beautiful and interesting, but not *unique.* The police asked me that too. I told them there's another thirty thousand just like them in Bogotá.' Wilkmann took another sip of coffee.

Lagrande wasn't giving up so easily. 'Heavy though,' she repeated to herself, thinking of the huge diamond she had found concealed inside the African statuette. She had yet to investigate the Susanoo fan, but perhaps there was a stone hidden in that too? 'And weren't you telling me before that there was something else about these figurines in particular? The shape of them?'

'Very heavy.' Wilkmann pushed his empty cup across the table slightly and called to the waiter for a schnapps. 'But you're right, they are special. Some researchers think those figurines are more than just the shapes of insects or animals.' He took out a small tablet from his bag and brought up an image on the screen. 'I would much rather have demonstrated with the originals, of course,' he apologised.

'This will do fine,' she said reassuringly, with an awkward smile. The gold figurines under her chair seemed to be crying out to her like a bag of lost kittens.

'So, some people call them the ancient American aeroplanes, because some of their features are more reminiscent of constructed aerodynamics than what one might find in the natural world. People have even tested out scale models in wind tunnels,' Wilkmann began to explain. 'These wings here? They're especially striking – and nowhere to be found in the animal kingdom. And that's' – he pointed – 'thought to represent a tail stabiliser, with the two perpendicular rudder pieces, and so on.' He thanked the waiter for the schnapps and knocked it back. 'Some scholars have compared this structure with air-freighters, or even with ancient American depictions of spacecraft.'

Lagrande had heard the theory that the indigenous peoples of South and Middle America had based their pantheon on the previous visitations of extraterrestrials, but the gods who had returned in 2012 certainly didn't resemble any space-travelling beings she'd ever heard of. 'You think these are stylised models of spaceships?'

Wilkmann shuddered as he began to feel the alcohol's effect. '*I* don't,' he emphasised, 'but others do. I personally just find them beautiful in their symmetry.'

Lagrande wished she could just pull out one of the pieces and examine it immediately, investigating its surface for moveable sections or seams, x-raying and scanning it so that she wouldn't be left to find out its secret by coincidence, as she had been with the diamond on the rainy pavement in front of the forensic institute.

The artefacts she'd managed to recover so far were officially being kept in a vault in the evidence storage facility at Interpol: the fan supposedly belonging to the Japanese god Susanoo, the broken African statuette of Odùduwà, and the diamond found inside it. *Officially*.

But on Inspector Bourreau's instruction she had instead hidden the objects in a safety deposit box rented through a private security company. For safety reasons.

'I hope you find the guy soon,' said Wilkmann, drinking his water. He was about to say something else when the head waiter turned up the volume on the flatscreen TV in the corner.

'—the discovery of the business card makes for an unexpected turn in the Mannheim museum attack,' a reporter said earnestly into the camera. In the background was the main museum building, and a little further behind her, the café they were sitting in. 'We have just received reports that the Federal Police are on their way to Mannheim, as well as the State Security Service. At this point, nobody is considering this discovery a coincidence, as the card appears to have been deliberately placed on the body of one of the thieves. In recent months little has been heard from the militant group *GodsEnd*, but suspicions have been raised that the attacks here in Mannheim might be intended to gather funds for upcoming action from the group. This would present a new way of doing things for *GodsEnd* . . .'

Lagrande watched open-mouthed as the news reporter gave a brief summary of the activities of *GodsEnd*, whose aim was to destabilise the religions supporting the new gods by providing evidence of the ungodly. Their members were not shy when it came to demonstrating the flaws of gods, and they were well known for making attacks on shrines, as well as kidnapping priests and other high-ranking figures.

'You were lucky to escape, Miss Lagrande,' she heard Wilkmann saying next to her.

'We were *both* lucky,' she insisted. Her mind was working overtime. She didn't believe for a second that her guardian angel had been sent from *GodsEnd* to protect her from harm. She still put his appearance down to Bourreau, who must have hired a secret bodyguard he trusted more than his own colleagues.

Did he put the card there just to create confusion and divert attention away from himself? That card now meant that she would almost certainly be hearing from the federal and state police.

But not today. Lagrande finished her coffee and held out her hand to Wilkmann. 'I have to get back. It was lovely to meet you. If you think of anything else that might be important about the gold figurines, please call or email me. And where you got them from in the first place? That can stay between the two of us. Get well soon, Herr Wilkmann.'

He nodded, thanked her once again for her help and understanding, and they parted ways.

Lagrande immediately headed in the direction of the nearest taxi stand, her handbag, heavy with gold, digging into her shoulder.

She would be happy to help the Germanian authorities with their investigations, but a closer examination of the gold figurines took priority. Inspector Bourreau would surely agree with her.

Speaking of whom. Lagrande checked her smartphone. *No new messages from him.* A distinct feeling of worry began to fill her chest.

Unknown airspace, November 2019

A quick peek through the curtain.

The passengers are standing around and talking quietly. Only the guy I'm following is sitting in his seat, sleeping, as far as I can tell.

They all look pretty wealthy, for sure, but . . . something isn't right. Can't quite put my finger on it. Oh, yeah: the guns. They're all carrying guns.

The young one they're calling Ryko has a P7 in a belt holster, and the man in the suit does too. The older lady and the one in the especially expensive-looking outfit both have Glock 17s.

No bigwigs here then; a team of soldiers playing dress-up. But who – or what – are they protecting? The heart? And why is the stewardess—

I'm an idiot. They've *hijacked the fucking plane.*

Because of him?

Or are they trying to take the heart, to—

A big masked guy in overalls has come in carrying a tablet. He exchanges a few words with the stewardess and points to the monitor.

'Be quiet,' *she shouts at the cabin, and the conversations immediately die.* 'The client wants something from us.'

Mr Muscles holds the tablet so that everyone can see the display, and the indicator LED for the camera attachment flicks to green.

'You've fucked it up,' *the unknown speaker says stroppily. I can't make out who it is; he's made sure he's only visible as a silhouette.*

'He's a detective. He's clever. What did you expect, sir?' *the stewardess counters.*

'More effort,' *he responds with a snarl.* 'Inform me as soon as he wakes up. I want to speak with him myself. Perhaps he has something interesting to say.'

'Yes, sir.'

'Is the artefact safe in its packaging?'

'Yes, sir.'

'I'm still waiting to hear exactly how you located and verified the harpoon tip.'

Harpoon tip? I didn't see one of those. But she checked the heart – oh, the tip is IN the heart!

The stewardess nods eagerly, looking almost excited. 'We haven't had time to explain yet, sir. It was more difficult than we thought to take the jet without the pilots raising the alarm at the airport.'

'Then tell me now. Don't add to my anticipation.'

The stewardess looks nervously at Mr Muscles, who is holding the tablet as if he's advertising it in an infomercial, and then over at the guy I'm following, slumped in his chair. 'I'll make it brief, sir, and I'll send you the full report in writing straight away.' *She lowers her voice.* 'We found a total of six Miocene Inuit harpoon tips made from walrus ivory, some with art dealers, some in small museums. Then, as you requested, we acquired the Inuit girls' hearts – all five years of age. Five of the tips did nothing, but the sixth one reacted just as you required. You will see it yourself, sir.'

The man in the display is beside himself with excitement. I can hear it in his breathing. He couldn't give a shit about the six little Inuit girls. I mean, perhaps I'm not the one to be judging when it comes to murder, but kids? Never. Okay, there are always exceptions, but still: bastard!

'Excellent!' *the client says in a rough voice.* 'Then continue with the plan.'

The display goes dark and Mr Muscles disappears again through the front curtain.

* A Ω *

A fucking artefact. Another one.

I can guarantee it's on the list from that bloody murdered dealer's place. And the silhouette guy is behind all of this.

The guy I'm following is in danger, but not immediately. They still want something from him.

I disappear for a moment into the little storage room and get a better look at the cabin. Then it's time to clean up.

He's never been so in need of my help.

* A Ω *

Malleus woke again, this time without the gritted teeth and with the taste of cheap-brand smoke in his mouth. It felt like his body might be getting used to this taser lark.

I've ruined their little play. A glance out of the window told him that the jet was still on course. *What's next? A tragedy: Act Two?*

In front of him Tiffy was currently in conversation with Haviland, while Ryko walked past him and behind the blue curtain.

Someone behind him laid a hand on his shoulder. 'The inspector is awake,' called Smythe, and the women turned to look at him, both with angry expressions. They were clearly unhappy that he'd seen through their charade.

'Tell us, what gave it away?' Haviland greeted him, her arms folded across her chest.

'We tried so hard,' Smythe added and stood next to the two women.

'What was the point of the whole deception?' Malleus replied. The burning across his chest was painful, but his mind was growing sharper in its efforts to shake off the dull ache. The pain in his head, however, was purely down to cigar cravings and would not be leaving anytime soon. *Not without a Culebra.*

They didn't answer. Instead, the wide-set, stocky man in overalls and a balaclava emerged from behind the curtain. He held a tablet in his hand; it had an extra camera attachment clipped to the side. Without saying anything, he stood in front of Malleus and activated the tablet, showing the silhouette of a man from the chest up. He could just make out the lack of hair on the man's head, but little else.

'Inspector Bourreau,' the silhouette greeted him in a nondescript voice. 'I expected some resistance, but never in my wildest calculations did I foresee my plan being disrupted by an atheist, of all people.'

Malleus realised he wasn't dealing with another crap actor this time, but with the mysterious contractor who was responsible for the deaths of Hannes Hein, Mohr, Crick and many others. *And there will be other bodies we haven't found.* 'You hijacked a plane and hired these idiots, just to speak to me. That's a lot of effort.'

'The circumstances were fortuitous, Inspector. On board there is another artefact, which I hired these idiots to acquire,' the man responded coolly. 'From *you,* I want only information. And my objects, the ones you've stolen.'

Malleus laughed softly. 'You are overlooking the small fact that the artefacts never belonged to you in the first place.'

'I have no interest in their origin. I gave people a lot of money to acquire these objects, and as I was betrayed by a certain colleague, all I am doing is gathering the products for which I have already paid.' The man drummed the fingers of his right hand on a wooden surface and a ring flashed in a beam of light for a second, showing a coat of arms featuring a pyramid. 'You may be an inspector in your world, Bourreau, but in mine you are nothing more than a thief.'

'We evidently differ in our understanding of the law.'

'As long as the law is in agreement with my requirements, there is balance and order. Otherwise, I achieve things by my own means.' The unknown speaker gave a self-satisfied laugh. 'As you've seen.'

Malleus knew this type of person: he was dangerous, lived by his own rules and never hesitated when going for what he wanted. 'At least that's how you *want* things to go.'

'That's how things *are* going.' The man on the screen drummed his fingers again and another ring was visible for a second, this one engraved with an eye. There was a mechanical noise in the background. 'The ladies and gentlemen on board this jet are soldiers, hired to retrieve one of my objects. The first one I received was a forgery, so I had to take things into my own hands in order to get the original. When I found out you were in New Carthage, I booked out this entire flight, including your seat.'

'I didn't really get the whole theatre aspect of it, to be honest.'

'You saw through it so quickly. How?'

'The way these supposed millionaires were wearing their clothing was too sloppy. I could have accepted that on its own, but I also noticed Mr Smythe's fake watch. The original is far more carefully finished. Plus the cigarette packet sticking out of his pocket was a little too cheap. Even for someone with bad taste,' he added. 'There was something that gave each of them away, to someone with a trained eye. The supposed super-hacker Ryko has calluses on his hands, which makes no sense for someone who spends all his time on computers. Not one of them is wearing expensive perfume, just cheap deodorant.' He looked at the screen as he spoke, trying to recognise more details from the background behind the mystery speaker. 'Then the fake SMS from my secretary? She would never call me *Chief*. That's how I deduced that everything around me was fake.'

'Unfortunately, yes. My idea didn't come to fruition. I was hoping to build up a bond between the hostages so that you might later be persuaded to give up some information by threats against them,' the man explained. 'I didn't fully believe Mr No when he said that pain was all anybody needed to start talking.'

'Mr No?'

'He's standing in front of you, holding the tablet. He prefers not to share his real name, or his real face, for business reasons,' the man continued. 'Unfortunately, I must now ask him to make you talk, Inspector. His experiences in the Wars of the Great Change have given him quite the skill-set. I had hoped to spare you from it – and your friends. And your family.'

Malleus felt relieved for a moment that he had nobody he cared about, nobody anyone could harm in order to get to him, apart from Lagrande, and she had the best guardian angel anyone could wish for, wherever her work led her.

Despite that, his thoughts immediately snapped back to his wife and his child, the irreparable losses he had suffered, and he felt a tugging in his chest. His headache began to throb as a surge of heat ran through him, followed by another wave of sweat.

I can't afford to lose it right now. 'I don't think Mr No will have much success,' Malleus replied.

'If you can assure me that the artefacts will be brought to a location of my choosing, at a time of my choosing, I might spare you the entire procedure. In fact, you could even just tell me where to find them,' the unknown man suggested, quite the generous blackmailer.

'You'll never get into the evidence locker.'

'The objects aren't in the evidence locker. I've already checked,' the man butted in gleefully.

I knew he would have access. Malleus smirked. 'They haven't somehow been stolen?'

'Like the gold figurines in Mannheim?' He laughed loudly.

'Neither you nor I believe a word of that. Those are some lovely red herrings you're throwing about. But the people from *GodsEnd*? A little far-fetched.'

Malleus didn't know what the man was talking about, but he assumed there had been some kind of attack and another set of objects from the list stolen. *How did they end up in a museum? Was Lagrande tangled up in that, too?*

It was highly likely, since *GodsEnd* had an link to the bodyguard he'd arranged for his secretary. *He couldn't help himself; he had to make it into a bloody propaganda opportunity.*

'Just to make clear exactly what the future holds for you, Inspector, this flight ends for you in one of two ways: with your full cooperation, or with the death of everyone you hold dear, including yourself. You should know, I have other ways of retrieving my property. Your life is not sacred. But the first option would be far more pleasant for everyone.' The silhouetted man took a deep breath. 'So, Inspector Bourreau – I would like you to tell me the location and access information for my artefacts: the fan, the statue and the figurines.'

'Tell me what you intend to do with them.'

'As soon as I have them.'

'No deal.'

'I see.' The man on the screen sighed impatiently. 'You would prefer to get to know Mr No. We'll speak again in a few minutes.'

The image on the screen disappeared.

The huge man in front of him laid the device to one side and gathered himself, sending another waft of liver sausage smell towards Malleus' nostrils. 'If I were in your position, Inspector, I would have told him.' He pointed down the aisle to the toilet. 'I'm going in there. And when I get back, I'm going to make my client a *satisfied* client.' He walked past him.

'Take the bodies with you,' called a voice from the cockpit. 'I don't want them in the front, there's something trickling out of one of them. It's gross.'

Mr No stood still for a second, then disappeared through the curtain. He returned dragging three bodies, all tied together with a luggage strap: the two pilots and the real stewardess. By the look of the thin lines across their throats they had been strangled with a garrotte.

Tiffy and Haviland watched the bodies being dragged past without any trace of sympathy. Smythe pulled a cigarette from the packet he had retrieved from Malleus and shoved it between his lips. It was their job to kill people, after all.

Cigarettes. For smokers with no style. 'Where are my Culebras?' Malleus asked. 'They were very expensive.'

Smythe tapped the jacket pocket that Malleus hadn't checked, then sat down in the seat next to him. 'Confiscated.' He reached into another pocket, took out an expensive-looking bottle of beer and opened it with his keys.

I hope you choke. Malleus tried the fit on his cuffs, which had been reinforced this time with cable ties. *No way to escape.*

'How are you planning to land in Frankfurt?' he asked Tiffy, who was playing absentmindedly on her smartphone. 'You've got a pilot, I assume, but by the time you reach the terminal . . .'

Haviland laughed and disappeared through the curtain. A series of clicks followed, then the sound of a bag being ripped open. There was a waft of freshly baked bread. 'Oh, pastrami,' she said joyfully.

'Who says we're landing?' Tiffy responded with an exaggerated smile, as if admonishing a smart kid in the classroom. 'Aeroplanes have accidents. And people with no parachutes who are cuffed to their seat and probably unconscious don't tend to survive them.' She stuck a hand in her pocket and took out a small plastic packet. 'Peanuts, Inspector? They could be the last ones you ever eat.'

Smythe laughed and glugged a mouthful of expensive beer.

* Α Ω *

Who do we have here? Mr Muscles with his mask on, a huge lump of a person, and he's brought me his rubbish. The hold is small enough without these three corpses taking up space. Can't have this.

The lines on their throats are clear. Clean kills, professional work.

But what's with the mask? Who's going to recognise him here? The bodies? The luggage?

I think it's high time I head to the front and sort some things out – or maybe not. I could play my own little game with this lot. I've already had an idea.

The big guy seems to be in a really bad mood. He's shoving the three bodies under a shelf with his foot; I can hear the bones breaking with each kick. After a final glance into the room he goes over to the door, gives the box with the heart in a little pat and goes back out.

Good.

* Α Ω *

Before I let loose, I check the rest of the soldiers' boxes. Express freight for Frankfurt – or that's what it says on the outside anyway.

Ah, parachutes. Our friends are planning to leave the aircraft while it's in the air.

Not good news for my guy.

Shit, the door!

Masked Man comes in and throws himself on top of me. He's a heavy guy. The punches to my kidneys are extremely painful; the elbow stabs to my face start my head throbbing.

I fall back against the boxes and kick him square in the ball sack, stopping his next attack in its tracks. With one leg I pull his feet out from under him and he falls backwards on to one of the transport boxes.

Within a second I'm back on my feet, ignoring the pain in my back and face, blood running down my cheek.

I reach for my knife and he grabs his. Okay then – let's play hardball. At least there'll be no messing about with bullets, accidentally shooting holes in the jet and losing cabin pressure.

It's been quite a while since I stabbed someone to death, now I think of it.

Fuck, turbulence! – the plane wavers and swerves to one side. I lose balance and smash into a set of shelves, then suddenly I'm falling towards the ceiling, boxes flying around me as if there's no gravity at all. The jet is flying in a steep curve, the turbines roaring into action, and suddenly we're rolling over the right wing and going into a nosedive.

There's a deafening rattle, as if a line of goblins were performing Riverdance on the shelving units.

It occurs to me more than once that these idiots clearly put no effort whatsoever into properly securing the luggage. Better keep my— Oh, there's Mr Muscles again!

He hasn't let go of his knife and he's coming right at me with it, the prick!

And he's fucking quick!

This is—

* A Ω *

The seatbelt prevented Malleus from sliding out of his seat, and perhaps more importantly, prevented his arms being torn from his body, securely fastened as they were to the back of his seat. But he didn't escape a painful tug in both arm sockets.

The turbulence began unexpectedly; there was no forewarning

from the pilot. Various warning signals and alarms could be heard from the cockpit.

The hijackers flew around the cabin like plastic toys. They hadn't had the foresight to wear their seatbelts.

Smythe crashed into the table next to Malleus and folded around it, his eyes rolling backwards as he fell unconscious.

Tiffy wrapped herself around a seat with both arms and Ryko copied her. Haviland lay trapped between a seat and the wall, while de Bonde flew around like a leaf in the wind, amassing various cuts and bruises as she collided with the furniture.

The jet finally rolled over its right wing and shot downwards, triggering the oxygen masks to fall from the ceiling. They dangled wildly around like miniature nooses.

What happened? Malleus looked out of the window.

The plane was diving nose-first through the grey clouds. Through the speeding cotton wool he thought he could see shapes on the wings, trying to reach the landing flaps.

Finally the jet raced out of the clouds and into a grey-black atmosphere. The nosedive slowed and smoothed out – the pilot had control. The rattling and shaking continued and raindrops hammered against the thick plastic windows.

They had flown right into the middle of a storm, and less than half a mile below them, he could see the tumult of the ocean.

With an almost sardonic ping, the seatbelt sign lit up.

There was nothing on the wings – Malleus must have imagined the shadowy figures.

Smythe wasn't moving, clearly passed out. Ryko was vomiting loudly and de Bonde was heaving herself into a chair, wincing in pain and holding her right arm, which looked to be broken. Tiffy cursed loudly and stormed through the curtain to the cockpit.

Malleus stretched his feet towards Smythe, who was leaning

against one of his legs, but he was still cuffed, his hands attached to the arm of his seat, and there was nothing he could gain from the chaos around him. *Damn it!*

Tiffy came back. 'Air pocket', she told her injured comrades with a growl. 'Some kind of turbulence, god-related. The flight control warning came too late.' She looked at Smythe and heaved him into the seat next to Malleus, then checked his pulse.

'My arm is broken,' said de Bonde with a ghostly-white face. 'I can't feel my fingers. I've torn a nerve or something.'

'Probably just trapped.' Tiffy walked over and inspected her injury, while Ryko helped Haviland to her feet. Suddenly their mission seemed to be of secondary importance. Throughout the jet, the realisation was setting in that they had avoided death by a wing's length.

The loudspeaker clicked on.

'That was close,' came the tense voice of the pilot. 'The jet lost something – I have no idea what it was, but due to the weather and the condition of the aircraft we're going to have to stay at an altitude of three thousand feet and take a different route to avoid – whatever that was. As soon as we're out of the storm, I'll take us back to twenty-five thousand plus. And—' The man stopped suddenly and only his quick breathing could be heard. 'What the hell is that?' he shouted in panic. 'Hold on! HOLD ON!'

The Learjet rolled upwards and to the left, speeding up and pressing Malleus firmly backwards into his seat.

Thanks to the pilot's warning, the hijackers were prepared this time and didn't go flying round the cabin. The jet started to fly in a kind of slalom pattern and the passengers rushed to fasten their seatbelts.

Something impacted heavily with the underside of the jet, it juddered upwards and there was a loud grinding. With a gurgling of metal, one of the turbines died.

Malleus saw a sheet of water spraying past the window. *We're three thousand feet up, and we got hit by a wave?* At least now there was no doubt that a god was involved in this somehow.

Someone wants their artefact back, Malleus realised in a flash. The unknown collector had persuaded these people to rob something that a god didn't want to let go of. If they had managed to hold more or less to the same course, they would be flying over the Mediterranean, so . . .

Poseidon or Neptune?

'What did you steal for your client?' he yelled over the din.

'None of your business,' Tiffy answered, her face pale.

'You have to throw it out of the jet,' he continued, 'or this thing's going to take us down with it.'

'That doesn't change things for us. The client would have us killed anyway if we gave up his property,' Tiffy replied. She sounded stressed, but not afraid. The hijackers were all reasonably calm.

'I'm pulling the jet high,' reported the pilot. 'Fuck, how are there waves over half a mile high?'

They felt another impact, and another sheet of water sprayed against the windows, as if the Learjet were a cliff or a sea wall.

This god isn't going to give up. 'What are you transporting?'

Ryko passed Tiffy the tablet, the display cracked but still functioning. A call was connected. 'Where is Mr No?'

'In the hold,' she answered. 'Haviland, go and find him.'

The older hijacker shook her head. 'I'm not taking my seatbelt off. He'll be fine.'

The faux stewardess threw her a scornful glare, then turned to the tablet. 'Sir, he's currently indisposed,' she said into the camera. 'We're flying through a storm, it's—'

'The god wants the property you stole back!' Malleus shouted in their direction. 'The waves are half a mile high!'

'Impressive,' said the silhouetted man, not quite managing to hide his concern. 'But that can't be true. You're nowhere near Sedna's area of influence. You must have flown into some other divine happening by coincidence.'

Sedna. Malleus had never heard the name before, so it wasn't one of the standard gods, as he understood them. 'I disagree.'

The man on the screen leaned forwards, still obscured by shadows. A tie-pin flashed into visibility for a second: it had some kind of coat of arms. 'I know what I'm talking about. You're not the only expert in the world. Or the only sceptic.' There it was again, the soft, self-assured laugh. 'Did Mr No make you feel any more cooperative?'

'Sir, due to the current difficulties Mr No has not yet had the opportunity to discuss matters with the inspector,' Tiffy explained.

'Where is he?'

'In the hold.'

Malleus noticed that the grey clouds were whizzing past the window again. The pilot had managed to pull them back up to a higher altitude.

One of the turbines was still silent; it didn't appear to have recovered from the drenching by the enormous waves. But the Learjet was able to continue its journey, though its speed was significantly reduced. *Hopefully the slower flight will interfere with their plan.*

The shape on the screen made an unsatisfied noise. 'Good. Then I'll call again in ten minutes. By then I expect you to have begun the interrogation. In the meantime, Inspector Bourreau, I'll be sending some friends to check up on Mademoiselle Lagrande. No harm will come to her – until I order it, of course.'

The screen went blank.

The constant rattling subsided and the flight smoothed out its slalom course. The seatbelt signs pinged off.

As if from nowhere, Mr No suddenly appeared between Tiffy and Malleus. He had sustained a few scratches, his overalls were dirty and the right lens of his sunglasses was cracked. The nose-dive had clearly been even more chaotic in the hold.

'What the fuck was all that?' he hissed.

The stewardess gave him a quick summary of events.

'So we're safe again now?'

'Yes.' Tiffy took off her seatbelt and held up the tablet. 'The client is calling back in' – she looked at her watch – 'eight minutes. By then you need to have all the information out of this bloody policeman.'

'Should be doable,' Mr No said curtly, rubbing his evidently injured shoulder. 'We had a stowaway,' he added. 'Arsehole attacked me while I was dealing with the bodies.' He pulled out a gun from his back pocket, complete with silencer. 'He had this with him. Old Russian model. Haven't seen one for years.'

The hijackers exchanged hurried glances.

'Was that your partner, Inspector?'

'I have no partner.' Malleus could guess who the muscular man had run into in the hold. *My mysterious shadow. He actually followed me from New Carthage in the jet!*

'What did you do with him?' Haviland asked.

Mr No turned his head, directing his sunglasses at the woman. 'Disposed of him. We're flying pretty high, after all.' He held out his hand; the knuckles looked bruised and deformed, as if they had suffered during the fight with his opponent. 'The key for the handcuffs.'

'Why?' Tiffy didn't look happy.

'I need to be able to move him around if I'm going to hurt him.' He took the key and unlocked Malleus' cuffs, then squatted in front of him to unfasten his seatbelt. 'You heard,' he said quietly, 'what I have to do to you now. So let's talk about the fan of Susanoo and the statuette of Odùduwà. Where will it be possible for our client to pick them up? Because they are *his* property.'

Malleus wasn't afraid of the pain. He was more concerned about Lagrande. *I need more information.* 'Let's make a deal,' he suggested. 'You tell me what happened in Mannheim, and I—'

The masked man grabbed Malleus' right hand, held his thumb and bent it painfully backwards, causing Malleus to gasp in pain. 'The fan of Susanoo, and the statuette of Odùduwà,' he said calmly, pulling out a bloody knife. 'From now on every question that I have to ask without receiving a sensible answer will cost you one finger segment. Then we'll move on to the toes.'

Malleus stared at the sunglasses but couldn't get a look through them. 'Start with my little finger. Then people will think I'm a Yakuza,' he offered.

The masked man gave a dark laugh. 'It's up to you whether you end up looking like a Yakuza or just someone who had a serious accident with some heavy machinery.'

Malleus raised his free hand and ran his thumb and finger over his Fu Manchu moustache. *I have to do something before we get attacked by the god again. Or before I lose my fingers.*

Atheism was no help against the laws of physics and a Learjet falling into the sea was, quite simply, a death sentence.

He carefully tensed his muscles and prepared to make a desperate attack.

* Α Ω *

Celtica, Paris-Lutetia, November 2019

Marianne Lagrande sat in the tiny, isolated office where she usually carried out paperwork and research for her Interpol boss Lautrec. She stared at the small collection of golden figurines.

What is your secret?

She had positioned her three huge monitors so that anyone entering the office would not be able to see them, just in case one of the cleaning staff should unexpectedly unlock the door and come in.

On one display was all the information she'd been able to collect on the fan of Susanoo, plus the legend of the god himself, and below this was the X-ray Lagrande had requested at the lab.

On another screen was a rotating image of the statuette, the pieces of which were being systematically combined in infinite patterns by a computer program, to test whether they fit in an alternate configuration.

On the third screen was everything she had managed to find on the Horn of Nandi, the Iron Crown of Lombardy and the Elamite tile from Chogha Zanbil, all open in different windows.

There were still more artefacts on Hannes Hein's coded list awaiting transcription, but Lagrande had had enough to deal with recently and hadn't yet found the time.

She glanced at her smartphone. Bourreau hadn't been in touch since his last message from North Africa. He was probably still on the flight.

Sighing, she unscrewed her Thermos, filled with the world's best coffee, and poured herself a cup. She was wearing distressed leather trousers and a white shirt, a black vest top barely visible through the material. Her long blonde hair was tied in a ponytail, as she'd had little time to attend to her usual style. Combined with the unique jewellery she wore on her fingers, wrists and ears, her style was once again unmistakably eighties.

Lagrande inhaled the aroma of her coffee as it drifted up from her cup, holding the drink with both hands while she eyed the files on her screen. Her metallic blue nails made a light clicking sound against the side of the cup.

Nine objects stolen, all from totally different cultures, she mused. *What's the connection? Maybe there just isn't one, aside from their huge market values.* She focused on the Elamite tile for a second. *Is it the text that makes this one special?*

The online call icon appeared on her central monitor.

Mr Crick! Lagrande accepted the call and switched on her camera. She had sent a message to the antiquity dealer at his home in York, informing him that she was in possession of the gold figurines. She trusted Marcus Roy Crick as she would a colleague – after all, he was working with them to find the man who murdered his son during his attempt to smuggle the statuette of Odùduwà. While she was on the case, he was to be considered a brother in arms. Or at least, that's what Monsieur l'Inspecteur had decided, faced with a lack of alternatives.

The silver-haired Brit appeared on the monitor, set against the backdrop of a mosaic window depicting his family crest. The crows Hugin and Munin featured heavily. He was incredibly well dressed, as always, in a white shirt, checked tie and black waistcoat.

'Bonjour, Mademoiselle Lagrande,' he said in a painfully northern English accent. His lips were slightly obscured by his short, dark grey beard. 'I received your message.'

'Good to hear from you, Mr Crick,' she switched into English for everybody's sake. 'Thank you for calling me back. This line is safe, totally encrypted. Anything we say here is completely private.'

Crick nodded. 'I hear the man who killed my son has sent his minions after you,' he began without hesitation. 'Glad to see you got out safe and sound.'

For the second time, Lagrande thought. 'It wasn't easy.' She took one of the gold figurines and held it in front of the camera. 'What can you tell me about this?' As she held it up, she noticed two lines on its surface. She had almost mistaken them for scratches, but – *an engraved symbol?*

'Nothing more that what you've already sent me, I'm afraid,' Crick admitted. 'South America isn't my area of my expertise. But I do have something else for you and Bourreau.' He clicked his mouse and a message appeared in her inbox. 'There are sources that suggest a similarity between the structure of the diamond you found in the statuette and the stones in the Iron Crown of Lombardy.'

'That can't be true,' Lagrande said involuntarily. *Is this the connection I've been looking for?* 'What sources?'

Crick was unmoved by her disbelief. 'A collector with whom I've done business made me aware of it. I wanted to keep you informed, since we're looking for potential connections. To be sure, though, we'd have to take the stones to the lab and have them analysed.' He typed something on his keyboard. 'I also contacted a friend in Tokyo and asked him to send me everything he has on the wind god, Susanoo.'

Another message arrived on her screen. *At least he's giving me a lot of information.*

'The reason why it's so valuable, aside from supposedly belonging to a god, is outlined in this legend describing its origin. I thought there was a possibility it could lead us to something.'

'Nothing on the gold figurines?' she asked again.

'Unfortunately not, Miss Lagrande.' He leaned forward. Have

you managed to decipher any more of the artefacts on the list that I could begin to research?'

'I've been fairly preoccupied for the last few days, I'm afraid.'

'Wouldn't it be easier if you sent me Hein's list and the books?' he offered. It must have been the fifth time he'd attempted to get that information from her. 'I can take it off your hands for a while.'

Lagrande declined with a charming smile. 'Ah, thank you Mr Crick, but I'm afraid Inspector Bourreau would rather it stayed with me.'

At least that's what she was claiming. Despite what the inspector said, she didn't fully trust the art dealer. He could still have an ulterior motive in wanting to track down the artefacts, alongside his desire to find his son's murderers. The one desire did not negate the other.

The man looked as disappointed as the last time she'd declined his offer. 'Then I'll keep my ear to the ground. Stay safe, Mademoiselle.'

'And you too, Mr Crick.' She hung up the call and opened the file he'd sent on the stones, then set to reading the legend of Susanoo and his wife Kushinadahime.

Time passed quickly as she read, coffee in hand, and she had just come to the part with the fan when there was a knock on her door. 'Mademoiselle Lagrande?'

Lagrande froze and said nothing.

'Mademoiselle Lagrande,' she heard a woman's voice saying in French, 'my name is Wertheimer, I'm an investigator with Germanian State Security. We have a few questions concerning the attack at the museum in Mannheim. Would you be so kind?'

'Of course.' Lagrande could not have been any less enthusiastic. 'One moment.' She hurriedly dropped the golden figures into the bag and hid it in a lockable drawer, switched all of her screens to unrelated documents and images and walked over to open the door.

In front of her stood a 'classic Germanian', as Celticans liked to say: a robust figure, prominent chest, blue eyes, and blonde hair tucked away in a bun at the back of her head. Her makeup was modest, so as to avoid looking too attractive. Her trouser suit looked good on her.

'Hello there – please do come in,' Lagrande greeted her guest in Germanian, gesturing towards a wobbly chair that currently held her laptop. She quickly moved it onto her desk. 'What would you like to know?'

Wertheimer sat down and took out her pass. Everything according to regulations. 'Please excuse the interruption. I realise Interpol already has a lot to deal with.' She looked briefly at the monitors, which displayed nothing of interest. 'You returned to Lutetia very soon after the attack. Did you not receive my message at the hotel?'

Lagrande shook her head, her blonde ponytail swinging behind her. 'I'm sorry. You should have called me.'

Wertheimer smiled. 'I would have. But some things are better discussed face to face.' It sounded almost threatening. 'I understand you were recently the victim of another attack. In your own apartment.'

'Yes.' Lagrande cursed inwardly, disguising her annoyance by taking a swig of coffee. The Germanian investigator had clearly done her homework.

'The perpetrators were heavily armed.'

'Mm-hm,' she managed in agreement.

'And when I read the report, I realised there were parallels with the attack in Mannheim: masked men, recklessness, use of deadly weapons in a public space.' Wertheimer fixed the secretary with a look. 'And of course, yourself.'

Lagrande saw the trap that was being laid and did her best to portray an image of calmness. 'I can imagine how it looks, but the only connection between the attacks is related to an Interpol case, and I'm not authorised to discuss it further without my superior present.'

'You're referring to Inspector Bourreau, to whom you're currently assigned to as an assistant?' Wertheimer said. 'Quite the personality.'

The two women eyed each other, the tension rising with every second.

'That coffee smells divine.'

'Thanks. Unfortunately there's none left.' Lagrande batted away the woman's attempt to gain common ground.

Wertheimer gave her a penetrating look. 'How well do you know Inspector Bourreau?'

So the woman was moving the focus away from her. 'He's my boss.'

'That wasn't my question, Mademoiselle Lagrande.' Wertheimer didn't lose her Valkyrie smile, which gave the impression that it could evolve at any moment into a physical attack.

Lagrande wasn't intimidated. 'We don't know each other that well.'

'Have you ever spoken about his activities during the Great Change?'

'No,' Lagrande responded, baffled. She noticed that the woman's mannerisms had become less affected than before. 'What does that have to do with the attack in Mannheim?'

Wertheimer took her smartphone from the inner pocket of her jacket and opened a photo showing a man in a filthy uniform.

He was firing a heavy mini-gun in one hand, holding it almost playfully, as if it were weightless. 'Ove Schwan, 4th Company of the Guerrilla Light Infantry Battalion Røkkr. Combat name: *Exitus.*'

'And? Was he one of the robbers?' Lagrande studied the chiselled face, etched with determination and ruthlessness. She wouldn't want to mess with this man. And at that moment, she realised who she was looking at. *Is that – my bodyguard?* She hoped that her poker face was still convincing.

'Do you recognise him as one of them?' Wertheimer held the phone up in front of Lagrande's face. 'Or have you just recognised the face of the mystery man who killed those men in cold blood and ran off with the gold figurines? DNA analysis of the business card we found on the body is being carried out as we speak.'

'He was wearing a mask,' Lagrande answered, inwardly resenting her voice for coming out so cracked and squeaky. *Idiot.* 'I couldn't see his eyes. He was too far away.'

Wertheimer lowered her voice. 'Witnesses from Treva, where two police officers and an elderly woman were murdered, have described a muscular man getting out of a BMW X7 and killing the attackers: perfect headshots and a *grenade launcher*.' She smiled at Lagrande. 'I take it this is the same man who was in Mannheim?'

'I couldn't say,' she replied in a friendly tone. 'I was lying behind the garden wall.'

Wertheimer said nothing, and put her phone away. 'Thank you for your time, Mademoiselle Lagrande. You've been very helpful.'

'Have I?'

'More than you realise.' Wertheimer gave her a nod. 'Pass on my regards to Inspector Bourreau. Tell him to keep his past in the past from now on. If he lets it get mixed up in the present, it will become a problem in the future.' She stood up and energetically adjusted her jacket. 'Good day.' As she walked away, she added, 'You should plug in your laptop.' Then the Germanian investigator was gone.

Why? I didn't have it switched on. Lagrande turned to the computer and saw the low battery light blinking red.

She opened the lid and was taken aback at the completely blank screen. No status message or any other sign that the computer was even running.

Carefully she bent forwards and listened to the innards of the laptop as she pressed a few keys – until the computer finally gave an error sound, protesting an excess of open applications. The display, however, remained blank.

Shit. Lagrande remembered the attack in her apartment, when one of the intruders had managed to get hold of her computer. *The USB stick – I totally forgot!*

If he had installed a bug on her laptop, whoever had sent them would have had access to a lot of things.

Her hard drive.

Her emails and phone calls.

Her location.

Basically anything that had come into contact with the infected computer.

Lagrande packed up the laptop and ran out of the office. The data technicians at Interpol would have to take a closer look at it. She had to limit the damage.

With a little luck they might even turn the tables on the hackers; they could even trace their location. It could lead them straight to the mystery person at the centre of all this, the person responsible for so many deaths. Even the Trojan horse must have left tracks in the sand.

Unknown airspace, November 2019

Malleus was given an unexpected advantage: the seatbelt sign lit up again, and a split-second later the Learjet lurched downwards.

Now! He snatched the weapon from the masked man's shoulder holster and kicked him square in the chin.

But his opponent had outstanding reflexes. He didn't manage to dodge the attack completely, but he deflected it sufficiently to avoid the brunt of its power. He stumbled into Tiffy, who had lost her balance in the latest turbulence. Mr No landed in the aisle and growled furiously, his cracked sunglasses falling from his face.

Malleus clutched the arms of the chair tightly, preventing himself from being thrown about as the plane careered through the air. He pointed the gun at Smythe, who was reaching for the P7 semi-automatic under his jacket. *You should not have stolen my Culebras.* He pulled the trigger twice, aiming at his upper body and hoping that he wouldn't hit the cigars.

He had no time for caution. The hijackers had signed up for violence the second they murdered the jet's real pilots and stewardess. And in any case, the man behind it all had made the terms of engagement very clear: *cooperation or death.*

Smythe was hit once in the lower throat and once in the shoulder; the wall and window behind him were spattered with red and he slumped to the ground. Thankfully the bullets stayed in his body, rather than puncturing the wall of the cabin. *Now . . .*

But Mr No was already on his feet, raising the Stetschkin in one hand.

Malleus went to attack him, but before he could move, the metal gun butt collided with his temple and he fell back into his seat, unconscious again.

Fate clearly did not want him to escape his torturers just yet.

* A Ω *

'Shit!' Tiffy cried, looking frantically from the slouching detective to the blood-soaked body of Smythe. 'Whose fucking idea was it to take off his handcuffs?' she spat, pointedly stamping on the sunglasses of the guilty party.

The Learjet steadied itself and Haviland hurried over to Smythe, examined him for a second and shook her head. 'Nothing to be done. Unless we've got a god or goddess on board.'

'They should have one in every first-aid box,' Ryko commented sarcastically. 'Reanimation. Even Jesus could do that. Would really help the Christians out if he turned up and did a bit of magic for us.'

'What the fuck just happened?' Tiffy screamed at Mr No, pulling her semi-automatic and waving it at the unconscious investigator. 'Fuck, Smythe was our best explosives guy.'

Mr No pushed her arm to the side. 'Leave it,' he muttered. 'We need the policeman alive until he tells us where the artefacts are being kept.'

Tiffy pushed him back and gave a screech of frustration. 'This wasn't the plan!'

De Bonde looked up at the seatbelt sign, which had just switched off. 'Bloody on and off, on and off.'

'How much longer?' Tiffy yelled into the cockpit.

'French airspace and mainland in less than ten minutes,' came the reply. 'You need to hurry if we're going to pull this whole thing off.'

'Circle the plane and tell the French we've got a problem with the instruments. They'll buy it,' Tiffy barked. 'No, wake up the policeman and pull bits off him until he tells us where the stuff is.'

'We shouldn't have taken the second job,' Haviland said half to herself, pulling a bottle of spirits from the minibar.

'Too late. We're in this now.' Ryko looked out of the window. 'We're in the clouds again.'

'No waves, just a mild storm,' reported the pilot. 'The god seems to have calmed down.'

'Thank Hades,' murmured Ryko. 'I was this close to throwing that fucking artefact out of the plane. Honestly.'

'Right.' De Bonde blew him an exaggerated kiss.

Mr No jostled Bourreau's lifeless body upright in his seat and took back his weapon, eyeing the others as he placed it back in his shoulder holster. His brown-green speckled eyes looked alert as they scanned the remaining men and women in the cabin.

'Do you need help waking him up or something?' Tiffy asked incredulously. 'Come on, get going!'

De Bonde returned Mr No's stare. She froze – then dropped down behind a seat to take cover. 'That's not Mr No!' she shouted. 'The eyes!'

'What?' Tiffy stammered, turning to the wide-built hijacker beside her. 'The eyes?'

'The eyes.' Mr No confirmed quietly. 'She's right.' In one lightning-fast movement, he pulled out the Stetschkin and shot her twice in the face.

Tiffy fell into the aisle in a cloud of blood. Ryko cursed and jumped behind a seat. Haviland tried to take cover behind Smythe's still warm body.

'Here are your options,' said the man who wasn't Mr No

calmly, pointing his weapon at Haviland, who was doing her best to stay still behind the corpse. 'You all get off the plane, and then you can do what you want. You've got parachutes.'

'Or?' Ryko queried from behind a seat.

'You all die.' The fake Mr No nodded towards De Bonde. 'Go to the cockpit and tell the pilot. If you try anything interesting, I'll set off the bomb I've put in the hold.'

'Okay.'

The hijacker scurried through the curtain and disappeared.

'So,' the fake Mr No said to Haviland. 'Decision?'

'I get off the plane,' she said meekly.

'Weapons,' he ordered down the barrel of the APB, which had not moved a millimetre since he'd pointed it at her. 'Slowly.'

Haviland pulled out her Glock 17 and laid it carefully on the ground, along with a knife and a Derringer. Then she stood with her arms raised in surrender, kicked Smythe's body away from her and stepped into the aisle.

'Ryko?' he said, edging his body over the top of the seat to get a better look over the cabin.

'I would like to get off too,' the hijacker replied from his hiding spot. His weapons arced across the cabin, bouncing off a seat onto the floor. Two hands appeared in the air, followed by the rest of him. 'Whoever you are: have fun with the plane.' He moved cautiously into the aisle, following Haviland through the curtain into the front of the plane.

The fake Mr No pulled out his second weapon and pointed it towards the curtain that led to the cockpit. After a few moments he heard them leave the plane. He waited patiently, his breathing steady.

Ryko reappeared, a G11 assault rifle in his hands and determination on his face. He pulled the trigger immediately.

The *click* that followed resonated throughout the cabin.

'I removed the firing pin.' Mr No explained, firing two shots from his own APB.

The bullets flew through Ryko's nose and left eyeball. Blood, brains, and fragments of skull spattered the blue curtain.

A rush of gunfire issued from the front of the jet. The curtain was shredded as bullets tore through it and into the seat in front of Bourreau and the man who wasn't Mr No.

De Bonde moved forward and to the right, sheltered behind her own gunfire, while another man appeared, changing his empty magazine with a slick, practised movement

Mr No returned fire and shot him down with three bullets to the upper body. He fell with a gasp.

'Get out,' de Bonde commanded. 'Leave Bourreau here, take your parachute and leave.'

'If I wanted to leave, I would have done so a while ago,' replied the false Mr No.

'What do you want with Bourreau?'

'Everyone has their calling,' No replied calmly. 'Mine is to make sure that nothing happens to Monsieur Bourreau. Unfortunately, that stands in direct opposition to your aims here. But I'm giving you the chance to leave. Ryko was unwise. Haviland has already left.'

'If we let him go, our contractor will kill us anyway.'

The man who wasn't Mr No gave a curt laugh. 'According to my careful observations, there should only be one person remaining in the cockpit: the pilot. So there's just you and him left. Two people.' He leaned forward and saw de Bonde's knee poking out from behind the seat she was using as cover, along with the barrel of a G11. He aimed and pulled the trigger three times.

The first bullet tore the weapon from her hands. The next two shattered her kneecap. Screaming, she fell back against the cabin wall.

Not-No sprang up and around the seat, firing both of his weapons.

Not a single bullet missed. De Bonde slid bleeding to one side.

'And then there was one.' Not-No tossed the Beretta to one side and reloaded the Stetschkin, making his way into the cockpit.

'Is he dead?' the pilot asked in panic, turning halfway round before seeing the answer to his question. Cursing, he tried to kick the door closed.

Not-No kicked back and the door flew open.

The hijacker made an attempt to draw his weapon but stopped as the APB was pointed directly between his eyes. 'No, wait! Don't! I— You need me to—'

'You can stay,' whispered Not-No, 'and I'll have to shoot you. Or you can go into the hold, take a parachute and follow your colleague Haviland.'

The man stood up slowly, dropped his weapon on the ground and hurried away to the hold.

Not-No watched him scurrying away, the Stetschkin trained on the nape of his neck. Only once he was through the curtain and the sound of the plane door opening had reached the cabain did he lower his weapon. He didn't hear it close.

Malleus opened his eyes and saw Smythe, dead, in the seat opposite him. Smythe's eyelids were wide open, as if accusing him of his murder.

The plane was quiet, except for the whistle of wind coming from the open plane door.

Too quiet. Cautiously, he looked up, and saw the masked man slowly lowering his APB.

'Inspector Bourreau,' the man said in a low voice. He was not as powerfully built as the man he was impersonating. He must have been sticking out his stomach to complete the illusion. 'There were differences of opinion within the group regarding its future,' he explained levelly. 'But a solution was found.' His striking, colour-speckled eyes fixed on Malleus. 'We are now the only living people on board this Learjet.'

'And what is my future?' His head was pounding from the blow to his temple and from tobacco-withdrawal. Concentrating and ordering his thoughts was a struggle.

'You're an important man. And you clearly have something left to contribute to the history of humanity. I won't allow your story to be cut short by some random idiot.' He picked up the tablet and threw it over to the inspector. 'He's going to call again. See how much information you can get out of him and you might be able to track him down. If you want.' He stepped backwards slowly. 'I'll make sure we have a soft landing.'

Malleus looked back and forth between the tablet and the man. *I don't understand any of this.*

Tiffy's body lay on the floor. De Bonde was slumped in the corner and a man's body was stretched across the aisle in front of the cockpit, which stank of blood. *Differences of opinion. Quite the solution. And I have the feeling that the only remaining hijacker is actually—*

'Don't try to parachute out of here, by the way. I've sabotaged them all.' Mr No walked into the cockpit and closed the door. With a click, he locked it from the inside.

The call symbol appeared on the tablet. It was the unknown contractor.

Malleus accepted the call, holding his thumb over the camera.

'Has the inspector said anything?' the silhouette demanded, clearly irritated. He was evidently not in the mood for any further complications.

Malleus removed his thumb from the lens. 'I have something to say to you personally,' he replied, hearing the man stifle a gasp on the other end of the line. 'You will never see the artefacts that I have recovered again. And I will not be intimidated by you.' He leaned forward and brought his face closer to the camera. 'One day we will meet face to face. And in the meantime, I will find every artefact you are searching for, before you find it. I promise you.'

'Inspector Bourreau, be reasonable,' the man answered. 'I can give you a lot of money'

'You can stick your money up your obscenely wealthy arse.' He went over to the dead Smythe and retrieved his Culebras. He opened the case with one hand, and stuck a cigar with a sepia-coloured band in his mouth. Already, he felt the first pangs of relief. 'You have too much blood on your hands for me to let you walk away from this.'

'Then you will no doubt be aware that a little more blood will not make much difference to me,' the man replied coolly. 'You. Your friends. Anyone who prevents me from completing my collection and setting into motion the—' He stopped before he could talk himself into a rage. 'Don't do this, Bourreau.'

'Do what?' Malleus sensed just how important these objects were to the silhouetted figure. *What more will he do to get his hands on them?*

'Don't make me your enemy.'

With a click he opened his lighter, lit a splint, and with it his Culebra. 'You've got it wrong.'

'How so?'

'You' – he gestured with the glowing end of his cigar towards the lens – 'have made an enemy of *me*.' He puffed a cloud of smoke at the camera. For a second it took the shape of a skull. Then he hung up.

He noticed the tingling in his fingers and toes first. A clear indicator.

We've flown higher . . . and . . . the hold door is . . . Dizziness clouded his thoughts. *Air! I need . . .*

He stretched his hand up towards the dangling air masks, but his fingers grasped at nothing. Once again, Malleus passed out into the comfortable cushioning of the Learjet's seat.

The Culebra stayed between his lips, giving him the tiniest amount of nicotine before it too faded out.

Celtica, Paris-Lutetia, November 2019

Marianne Lagrande strode back into her office a few hours later, staring furiously at the laptop in her arms. 'Traitor,' she hissed at the inanimate computer.

The IT specialists had only needed a few seconds of impressively speedy keyboard manipulations to confirm that very cunning, outwardly invisible spyware had been installed on the machine, making it possible for a third party to get access at any time to her hard drive, emails, camera and microphone, without her noticing a thing. Her laptop had been working as the perfect spy for the enemy, though, thankfully it appeared its efforts to infect her smartphone via Wi-fi and Bluetooth had failed.

The IT department had explained that this kind of infection was only possible by connecting a USB stick – the kind the intruder had used during the attack in her apartment.

It was impossible to tell exactly how much information they had managed to access. But the artefacts didn't seem to be in any more danger than before; she was sure she hadn't mentioned their hiding place in any telephone calls or emails.

But how sure can I be? Lagrande breathed out heavily, furious. If she wasn't one hundred per cent certain, the artefacts weren't one hundred per cent safe.

There was only one solution. She would have to go to the hiding place and check, and, ideally, find another one. She would take the gold figurines with her and store them with the other artefacts, until the inspector returned.

She looked at her watch, at her smartphone, at her pigeon-hole. Nothing from Bourreau.

He can't possibly still be in the air by now. She looked up the weather details for his flight online. *Delays?*

No reports of meteorological disturbances – but there were mentions of some divine turbulence spreading across the Mediterranean from Marseille. Priests of Poseidon and Neptune had already been called out and had sacrificed to both sea gods, and Celtic priests were also attempting to assuage the mori.

Hence the radio silence? Lagrande searched for the flight from New Carthage to Frankfurt and found several chartered flights, but only one corresponding to the correct time. It had been reported that the aircraft was flying a divergent route, the pilot presumably trying to avoid the risk of turbulence.

Slightly less worried about the safety of her boss, Lagrande let her fingers rest on the keyboard for a second, then started a new search.

The Interpol database had nothing to say about Ove Schwan, but the internet at large certainly had enough information on the Røkkr Battalion.

Røkkr is ancient Nordic for 'darkness'. Contrary to her first impression, which had painted the battalion as a voluntary group fighting on the side of the gods, Røkkr appeared to be a collection of defectors who had fought against the gods to the bitter end.

Since then, the unit had disbanded, some of its members claiming amnesty, some killed, others disappearing and continuing to fight underground.

Like the people from GodsEnd *who left their card at Mannheim.* Thanks to the information they had gleaned from the card, the state police, or at least Wertheimer, appeared to have their targets set on Ove Schwan.

Lagrande found photos of the soldier, mostly on social networks, some from reports on the war. He didn't look like the kind of guy who would be held down by moral scruples, or who would hesitate in a difficult situation.

She leaned back and poured the rest of her hot coffee into her cup. There was no way she would have shared it with that Germanian woman.

The question about how well she knew the inspector had got her thinking: what connection was there between these two men? There were plenty of rumours about Bourreau's past – everyone had heard something different, but nobody knew anything for certain, though everyone had an acquaintance who supposedly knew the full details.

By Belenos! Was the inspector in the battalion? Lagrande realised in an instant that he *was* one of them. *Everyone has their secrets.* She certainly had a few herself.

So she was working for a highly interesting, clever and good-looking investigator, who had no respect for gods, denied their very existence, and demanded real explanations for the things that happened in the world. Savouring the coffee, she constructed a plan. She would check the artefacts and then, together with the newest objects, take them to a new, safer hiding place.

Even more secret than this one. Lagrande stretched her head backwards and felt her ponytail touch her back. She drank the last few drops of her coffee, then she opened the drawer, locked by a fingerprint scanner, and felt for the bag with the gold figurines. *Nobody's getting their hands on these.*

She felt . . .

And felt . . .

No! Panicked, she looked into the drawer, which held nothing but the usual files and papers.

Cursing she rummaged around inside, emptying its contents onto the floor and searching madly through the rest of the cabinet, then through her entire office, as if some trickster had just appeared out of nowhere and hidden the figurines as some kind of cruel joke.

But there was no trace of the bag.

A cold shudder ran through her. Bourreau had kept reminding her that their unknown enemy had good contacts. *Very* good contacts.

Or is Crick behind this? She trusted that man completely when he claimed that he wanted to punish the people who murdered his son, but she also believed him capable of playing his own game, cooperating with her only when necessary. This was about more than a handful of stolen artefacts. She remembered Wilkmann's warning, that more surprises lay in store for her. *Like with the fan of Susanoo.*

Whoever had taken the gold figurines had made it past the security checks, the retina scan on door and the fingerprint scanner. People couldn't just get into the office spontaneously. This had taken preparation.

She packed her things into her laptop bag and prepared to leave. *The artefacts are waiting for me.*

First, Lagrande went straight to Lautrec to fill out the application to carry a firearm. The time for tasers and pepper spray was over.

Unknown location, November 2019

Malleus woke up and immediately regretted it. *For the fourth time.*

But this time was different. He could feel the cold wind and rain on his face.

As he opened his eyes, confused, he realised he was lying on an abandoned runway. Despite the cold, some persistent weeds were growing in tiny cracks in the concrete and in the grooves of the asphalt. Dusk was beginning to fall, light grey was turning dark, and further in the distance had already faded to black. Light wisps of fog strayed across the area, providing a kind of natural soft focus.

Well, this is unexpected. Groaning he sat up and saw a burnt-out building not far from where he was sitting. Nearby was a destroyed tower, a partly torn-down security fence and a variety of rubbish being blown about by the wind. *Where the hell am I?*

Then something tugged sharply at his back, jolting his entire body. He heard the billowing of fabric.

Malleus looked down at the parachute surrounding him. Someone had put it on him over his heavy military coat. The powerful breeze was playing with the light plastic material attached to the long lines behind him, blowing it into a sail.

Before it could drag him across the empty runway, Malleus undid the fastenings and left it to the wind.

His hand luggage and case were clipped to a belt round his waist, along with a box from the hold: the masked man had made sure he had all his belongings before leaving the jet.

He didn't land it. The cold rain was beginning to revive Malleus' powers of reasoning. *Did he jump out too? Or did he carry on flying?*

Malleus knew that he had finally come face to face with his mysterious guardian. He had suspected it as soon as he saw the Stetschkin APB. *At least now I know what his eyes look like.*

With that knowledge, he was already far ahead of any policemen before him. Being repeatedly saved from murder by a serial killer was irksome; he certainly wouldn't be lenient towards the *assassin di glifó* on account of it.

He unfastened the carabiner hooks and stood up, gathered his luggage and walked towards the shelter of the ruined terminal. As the rain grew stronger, the drops splashing heavily in all directions, a few hailstones appeared for good measure. He found his Derringer, his Culebras and his PDA. He switched it on to check his location, and to see if he could get hold of Lautrec. As he waited for it to load, his glance fell on the unknown box. It was labelled *HUMAN ORGAN.*

There was a handwritten note on it:

Contents: something no longer needed.

Malleus chose a cigar with a green band, to help him think, and opened the catch on the front of the container. Cautiously he opened the lid.

Inside was the tablet, slightly damaged, from the Learjet, and a small heart lying on a bed of ice. Inside the organ was an object about the size of a middle finger, glowing blue-white through the muscles of the heart.

This was the artefact the silhouetted man had been speaking about. *So that's what their special sacrificial heart looks like.* Another blow to his opponent. Malleus couldn't help but smile.

But his good mood vanished instantly as he remembered who he had to thank for this generous gift.

My shadow. He stroked his Fu Manchu moustache and lit his cigar. He didn't like being watched. *Even if I do owe him my life.*

He took the tablet out of the box for later inspection. As he touched it, the screen lit up and displayed a page from a book: *The Legend of Sedna.*

* A Ω *

Sedna has many names, and lives up to all of them: not only Mother of the Deep and Storms, but also Mother of All Sea Creatures and Queen of the Sea.

Before Christianity alienated the Inuits from their own true religion with its false monotheistic theories, they worshipped Sedna. The Mother of the Deep told them which ocean creatures they could catch and eat. Disobeying her orders had dire consequences, as she would send a storm or pull the offending hunter and his entire family to the bottom of the sea.

Long ago, Sedna was a beautiful but conceited girl who turned away every man who sought her hand in marriage. One day, her father could not bear it any longer and gave his daughter away to the next hunter who asked, although the man had refused to show his face.

As the man paddled his kayak away with the beautiful Sedna inside, the young woman noticed that he was actually a raven, who was planning to carry her up to his cold, draughty nest on the top of a cliff.

Sedna cried and screamed into the wind until her father

heard her. Struck by his guilty conscience, he set out to rescue her and bring her back home. His plan worked, but on the journey back, the raven followed them both and beat his wings until a great storm began to blow. The waves were so high that Sedna's father became terrified, and threw his only daughter out of his kayak.

Sedna grabbed the edge, but her father smashed his paddle against her freezing fingers until they smashed like icicles. Her fingers were taken by the raven and magically transformed into seals, whales and other sea mammals.

But the unfortunate Sedna sank to the bottom of the sea.

To this day, she waits on the ocean floor. Her rage at her father's betrayal transformed her into a powerful, vengeful goddess, and her anger at humanity stirs the ocean into great waves and storms. The only things that can calm her angry waters are respect and flattery. Since the Inuits recently abandoned monotheism and returned to their original religion, shamans have been diving down to the ocean floor to find Sedna, and combing her long black hair. This pleases Sedna, and in return she ensures the Inuits have bountiful catches and successful hunts.

Anyone who does not abide by the custom of pouring water into the mouth of their catch as thanks to Sedna can expect to be harshly punished.

* Α Ω *

Since the silhouetted man had himself mentioned the name of the goddess, Malleus guessed that the object in the box must have something to do with Sedna. He shoved the tablet into the exterior pocket of his suitcase for the IT team at Interpol to take a look at. Combined with the background noises from the video calls, and the ring and tiepin he had seen, he should be able to come up with some ideas about the identity of his mystery opponent.

Perhaps Crick will be able to identify him.

His PDA beeped to notify him that it had found a satellite signal. He checked his location; after a few seconds the screen displayed: *Hahn (Hunsrück), Germania, Celtic region.*

Immediately there was another notification, warning him that this is a former war zone from the Great Change, where he was likely to find unexploded munitions and mines; he didn't read the rest of it.

Malleus glanced back over his shoulder at the ruins. *The old airbase.* Before its use as a civilian airport, it had been used by the Americans, but it had changed hands many times during the course of the Great Change. A lot of military aircraft had been launched from this base, he recalled. Bombs and artillery had been used until the Resistance broke and the base was finally destroyed.

That's what some people say. Others spoke of divine interference, and yet more believed that the company running Frankfurt Airport had used the opportunity to finally stamp out their competition and hired a troop of soldiers to do their dirty work.

Whatever you choose to believe. Malleus had never been here before, and he didn't have enough information to make his own guess.

His attention shifted to the object inside the heart. Using the clingfilm that wrapped the organ, he carefully pulled it out. As he removed it, the glowing faded. *I'll have to find out which entry you are on the list.*

He pushed the bloody harpoon tip through the thin plastic film and held it out in the rain to clean it. After a few seconds, he could make out a set of fine etchings.

Ivory. He turned it over and examined it from every angle. *Not from Africa, by the look of it, more like First Nations. Combined with the Sedna story, it's most likely Inuit.*

He carefully placed the object in his cigar case, and puffed on his cigar as he wrote messages to Lautrec, and then Lagrande. He had to tell her what had happened to him, and ask her to send a local police officer to pick him up.

And now the jet.

At that moment his news app notified him of a crashed Learjet in the forest near Frankfurt Airport; it had disintegrated amongst the trees before going up in flames. All passengers were presumed dead, the media were reporting. The emergency services were searching the area.

Not all passengers.

He also found hundreds of reports and commentaries online regarding the events in Mannheim. His relief at finding that Lagrande had escaped unharmed, however, was cut short.

What was he thinking? Malleus was irritated by the business card. Now other parties would inevitably get involved, parties who wanted to get closer to *GodsEnd. This makes things so much more complicated.*

Malleus realised he was thirsty. He cupped his hands and caught the rain, pouring it into his mouth until it was no longer dry.

Lautrec replied to his message, briefly expressing his relief, and promising to send a specialist team from Frankfurt to fetch him. 'Hold on,' was his advice.

Malleus was puzzled by his phrasing. *Does he think I'm going to starve or something?*

Somewhere in the ruins behind him, a metal rod fell to the ground with a jarring sound. A swarm of crows flew upwards, squawking with fear, swooping in a circle through the grey sky and refusing to settle. They blotted out the dying daylight. The forest radiated a darkness that was slowly creeping towards the airport.

The flapping of feathers cut through the hiss of the rain. Malleus looked out at the crows and puffed on his Culebra. A lot of people would see those crows as a sign. *Odin's birds. An omen of death.*

Another metallic clang issued from inside the ruined building. Then another.

And again and again – until they found a rhythm and became a drumbeat.

Like they're being driven out for a hunt. Malleus felt a shudder run through him. *By whom?* Cautiously he stood up and checked both his Apache Derringers were loaded; the smoke from his cigar formed another skull, one that the wind could not blow away.

Malleus did not doubt that he was the prey in this hunt. *I should have read the rest of that warning notification.*

Between the ruined walls, around a hundred yards away from him, a human figure emerged and raised its head to sniff the air. The figure was flanked by three large animals, around hip height, that looked a lot like wild dogs.

I really should have. Malleus squinted, pulled out his Derringer and prepared to fire.

BOOK 6

Episode 6: Proof of God

'There is no race so rude, no man so savage as not to be imbued with the belief in gods. Though many have depraved notions about the gods in consequence of their own defective characters, all admit that there is a divine nature and power; nor has this belief been brought about by the conference or consent of men, nor established by institutions or enactments. But on every subject the common sense of nations is to be regarded as the law of nature.'

Marcus Tullius Cicero, *Tusculan Disputations,* 45 BC

'You must wager. It is not optional. You are embarked. Which will you choose then? Let us see. You have two things to lose, the true and the good; and two things to stake, your reason and your will, your knowledge and your happiness; and your nature has two things to shun, error and misery. Wager, then, without hesitation that He is. Your reason is no more shocked in choosing one rather than the other, since you must of necessity choose. This is one point settled. But your happiness? Let us weigh the gain and the loss in wagering that God is. Let us estimate these two chances. If you gain, you gain all; if you lose, you lose nothing.'

Blaise Pascal, 'Pascal's Wager', *Pensées*, 1670

'The foundation of irreligious criticism is: Man makes religion, religion does not make man.

The struggle against religion is, therefore, indirectly the struggle against that world whose spiritual aroma is religion.

Religious suffering is, at one and the same time, the expression of real suffering and a protest against real suffering. Religion is the sigh of the oppressed creature, the heart of a heartless world, and the soul of soulless conditions. It is the opium of the people.

The abolition of religion as the illusory happiness of the people is the demand for their real happiness. To call on them to give up their illusions about their condition is to call on them to give up a condition that requires illusions. The criticism of religion is, therefore, in embryo, the criticism of that vale of tears of which religion is the halo.'

Karl Marx, Introduction to
A Contribution to the Critique of Hegel's
Philosophy of Right, 1844

Germania (Celtic region), Rhineland-Palatinate,
Hahn (Hunsrück), November 2019

Malleus Bourreau stood under a canopy at the destroyed airport, peering out from his position of safety against the driving rain at the humanoid figure emerging from a caved-in section of the terminal about one hundred yards away. Three wild dogs were at its side, rising up to the level of its hip, their heads bowed and turned towards their master, who was clad in torn apparel.

The almost rhythmical metallic drumming of dozens of iron

bars continued to pound out from the ruins, maintaining a synchronised beat as they struck the concrete and illuminating the shadows that had previously occupied the vast expanse.

The figure looked over at Malleus, sniffing as he lifted his sunken features once again to face him.

Hold on, Lautrec had said – now Malleus understood what he had meant by that.

In the collapsed, ruined buildings, magnesium torches were burning with a smoky red glow that added a perilous urgency to the gloom.

I really should have paid attention to the warning outside. He resisted the impulse to draw his Apache Derringer and to take his PDA from out of his pocket as a way of making amends for his oversight. It was better to have a clear picture of the surroundings in his mind's eye.

A special unit was on its way to pick him up, his boss had told him.

How long will that take? Malleus' eyes wandered over the ruins through their blue-tinted lenses, but they could discern no other figures.

The vast murder of crows continued to circle unabatedly through the dark grey sky, cawing down at Malleus and the shadows he occupied, as if daring him to complain about their rasping cries.

The darkness could be impenetrable at night, this far away from human settlement. The forest and the clouds acted as a shield against any speck of brightness, appearing to Malleus as black holes that could suck him in without leaving a trace.

The figure raised his left arm high, signalling for the drums to cease. They stopped.

'What are you doing in my kingdom?' thundered the stranger

through the inky darkness of the ruins, conducting wisps of smoky fog to dance before his words, then retreat to one side in deference to their lord.

Malleus could hear the man as clearly as if he were standing directly in front of him. He took several lengthy puffs on his Culebra, wishing that he had chosen a red band instead. He took the crooked cigar from his mouth and drew a deep intake of breath for his reply.

'Don't worry, you won't have to put up with me for much longer,' he called back as he watched his breath turn to vapour. The pounding rain swallowed up his words; they never reached their unknown recipient

'Speak up. I can't hear you,' came the retort in a steady voice. He raised his right arm and pointed directly at him. The three dogs the size of calves raised their heads, pointing their long, powerful snouts at him. Each pair of eyes burned with a different colour, like LED lamps: white, red, green.

'Try a little harder this time, or I'll let my pets have their fun with you,' said the voice in an almost playful manner.

I need to get closer. Malleus really didn't want to, but it seemed preferable to incurring the wrath of those monstrosities. Neither the man nor the dogs were of human origin. As for whether his friends Apache and Cobray would be of any use, that was another matter altogether. *Ideally that's not something I'll have to find out.*

He raised his collar, regretting the absence of his hat as he stepped out of the protection of the half-ruined canopy and moved slowly towards the unknown figure. He left the Culebra on a stone in the dry. It could do no more for him and Malleus didn't want it to suffer unduly in the rain.

'I said,' shouted Malleus with his arms raised in a placatory gesture, the Derringers still concealed, 'I shall soon be gone. It was not my intention to disturb you and your friends.' Judging by his body language, Malleus could see that the stranger was now able to hear him properly. 'I had to parachute down because my plane was about to crash. Please forgive the intrusion.'

When he was about fifty yards away, he stood still, and immediately revised his previous estimation of the size of the man. *He's nearly seven feet tall!* The shoulders of the three hellhounds stood as high as Malleus' chest.

Despite being built like a brick outhouse, the man was still rather difficult to make out. A tattered poncho was draped over him like an aura, while his long hair was blown about by the wind to form a wavy black corona. His face itself was immersed in shadow. The red light of the magnesium torches flickered anxiously over the figure.

'Whoever enters my kingdom may leave once they have presented me with a gift,' the man announced generously.

'What kingdom am I in, and what is your name?' enquired Malleus, still attempting to be friendly. Every second gained could well be valuable.

'My name is Adamastos, and this is my realm,' he said with visible pride. 'It bears my name.'

Malleus recalled that Adamastos was another iteration of Hades, the god of the Underworld according to Greek mythology. He had not counted on this. 'An unusual name to come across in the Celtic part of Germania.'

'I did not seek this place out myself.' Adamastos slowly lowered his arm and the hounds sat down. 'Had it been up to me, I'd have chosen somewhere else to live. Perhaps Koroneia or Olympia, so that I could be near my father – any country, really, where it doesn't rain all the time. No cold. No ruins. All of us who remain hidden away dream of a more beautiful life. But man and the gods do not want us.'

He thinks Hades is his father. Malleus wiped away the water from his eyes and rubbed his Fu Manchu moustache, which had begun to feel unusually soft as a result of all the rain. 'All of you?' He hoped he would not regret the question.

'All of us who have been rejected by mortals,' said a woman's voice suddenly from behind him. 'In legends of old we were hailed as heroes and heroines. Now we are nothing.'

Malleus had expected one of the drummers to creep up on him. He stayed calm and continued to look at Adamastos; at the same time he could feel the heat emanating from the unknown woman. She had to be standing very close to him. 'You're demigods and goddesses.'

'Precisely.' She walked around him and stood before him, naked. Being looked upon by Malleus was clearly of no concern to her. He judged her to be barely sixteen; a waterfall of long, black hair partially covered her breasts and pale skin. The unsteady red light of the magnesium torches submerged her in the colour of blood. 'I am Brigantia, daughter of Brixia and wife of Adamastos. So tell us, mortal: what do you wish to give? What is your life worth to you?'

What entities would be produced if their bloodlines were mixed? Malleus found the idea exciting, as long as one cast aside all atheistic thoughts. Brixia was part of the Celtic pantheon, but he didn't know what she was responsible for and he had no desire to get out his PDA to check at this stage. Of course, it was already starting to happen: children of divine origin were being abandoned, unflatteringly referred to as hybrids or bastards. They grew faster than normal offspring, becoming adults within a year or less – as must have happened to the two in front of him.

Either that, or they're insane: mad people, living in ruins, creating their own kingdom and surrounding themselves with a retinue of fellow lunatics. There were some territories where, after the end of the Great Change, belief in the End Times prevailed. It was mainly in very remote regions, miles away from civilisation . . . and in parts of Germania. 'I could offer you money,' he suggested, 'or the clothes in my suitcase.'

'What about your cigars?' Adamastos asked. 'How many of those have you still got left?'

Malleus pulled out the empty packet. 'My last one is under the canopy.' He suppressed a laugh. He didn't want to become the next challenge for the dog pack, especially as they were obviously under the impression that this was no ordinary tobacco. He felt it best not to let the giant know that he had more packs in his case.

Brigantia laid a hand on his right cheek. Malleus let her. Another second gained. 'A lie, my love,' she said aloud. 'He's still got some. I can see it in his eyes.'

'You sought to *cheat* a demigod?' Adamastos snorted. 'Your life is now forfeit.'

'I've heard that a lot. And from proper gods as well.' Malleus pushed the woman's hand to the side, without any haste or anger. 'Or from beings who claim to be such.'

'You doubt us?' Brigantia laughed, raindrops sparkling off her lips. 'He doubts our lineage, my love.' She took two, three steps backwards away from him. 'Now he *really* deserves to die!'

Malleus felt the rain running under his coat collar, underneath his shirt and kurta. It would appear that negotiations were over.

The first of the magnesium torches went out with a hiss and the red light faded, giving way to a mystical gloom.

Adamastos and Brigantia weren't carrying any weapons, leaving aside the three gargantuan dogs that were probably descended from Cerberus, if you were to ask their master, that is. There were also a still-unknown number of other opponents lurking in the halls. Whether these were demi-deities or not was irrelevant at this stage. He contemplated how quickly he could reach his luggage, which contained more ammunition for the Cobray. Shot and full metal jackets would come in handy.

Lightning blazed out from the stormy sky through the sea of crows overhead and, with a shower of sparks, struck a towering metal support.

Malleus heard Brigantia cry out, and Adamastos ducked instinctively to avoid being hit. White sparks and glowing ingots of hot metal shot in all directions, illuminating the rest of the building with an overpowering, flickering light that refused to be broken. It appeared as if the steel had captured the discharge and was now greedily sapping energy from the clouds as a way of charging and operating an old machine deep within the earth. Malleus couldn't tear his eyes away from it.

The flickering light was reflected on his blue contact lenses and impressed deep into his retinas, through his optic nerve and into his brain, dredging up long-discarded memories.

Fear.

Hate.

Anger.

It brought them all to life, like Frankenstein's monster, then released them – *unleashed* them – and the chains that Malleus and his therapist had painstakingly fastened around his psyche were suddenly broken. Malleus' breathing accelerated sharply; his heart began to race, chasing adrenalin into every cell of his body.

One of those mysterious ashen beasts suddenly appeared in front of him. The monster looked like nothing else on earth – but something like this had brutally ravaged and killed his entire unit in the wars. Its mouth opened, revealing a phalanx of teeth, and the beast howled at him, tentacled arms twitching belligerently.

Malleus' thoughts switched to automatic, and pulling out the Derringers, he faced his foe and opened fire at the hellish visage opposite him, downing it in an instant, before turning to engage the next monster, which had appeared alongside it immediately afterwards. From the corner of his eye, he noticed yet more of these abominations pouring out from the ruins and rushing towards him, but he remained undeterred. *Nothing* could frighten him at this very moment: if he died now, all the suffering he had been forced to endure in this life would cease.

An indeterminate liquid splashed over Malleus; he spat out the warm blood of his enemies and ignored the blows that had been raining down upon him. Instead, he let out another cry and, whirling around, began to shoot again, cutting down anything that came near him. Everything around him – the metallic smell, hot steel and molten asphalt, dust clouds and the roars of his enemies – had merged.

And Malleus, imbued by the storm, fought fire with fire.

* Α Ω *

In a shitty forest somewhere.

And it's still pissing it down.

Nothing on me apart from what I need to survive: my APB and ammunition. Let's just keep following him and see where we end up.

I bet he thinks I threw him off with a parachute . . . that would have been far too dangerous, though. He could easily have ended up hanging from a tree somewhere, unconscious and strangled.

A quick landing, bundle him out and on we go. Easy.

But the ejection after my descent had taken me far further than planned. Fuck wind, fuck the gods! They continue to toy with us and get away with all sorts of shit.

My tracker tells me he's . . . well, he's still at the airport. And he's booked a taxi. Hacking into his PDA has really paid off.

Fine, fine, so he'll soon be in—

Hang on. A warning sign outside the area?

The map says it's a restricted area – highly dangerous, out of bounds unless you've got a permit.

Shit, I've really put him in it here. And in this weather I'll definitely need an hour or so to make it through the forest, even if I run.

If only I'd checked to see why no one was interested in the bombed-out airport any more. Who would have thought that this bunch of lunatics, nut-cases and hybrids that nobody wanted would be romping through there, of all places? We don't want to shoot the retards just yet, because the Germanian government is still afraid of the gods' retribution. An angry entity is difficult to appease, and it's not easy to get your hands on human sacrifices.

Fuck, fuck, fuck.

Hopefully the taxi will pick him up before the bastards show up.

Now then, what's this?

Double fencing, barbed wire, high-voltage warning, a minefield.

My night's getting better and better. The only way to get in there waid be flying.

Or felling a tree.

A mixture of the two will have to do.

I was the one who got him in this mess, so I've got to be the one to get him out of it.

Because I'm following him. And his time is not yet up.

Because only I decide when he dies.

I alone.

* Α Ω *

Malleus stood, blinking blood and rain out of his eyes; he could feel his rapid breathing and his chest was expanding as if it were about to burst. He gradually began to regain control over his senses.

He was standing in the open between the towering wreckage, soaked through to the bone; the rain continued to pound down, beating percussively on the ruins of the airport. Yet a persistent, rhythmical whirring at his back was also at work, induced by the same omnipresent noise of the raindrops.

What happened? He looked down at his hands, which were holding a long-barrelled assault rifle with a fixed bayonet.

Before him lay the enormous corpse of Adamastos and the remains of his three hounds; man and beasts alike had been *torn* apart. The rain pounded down upon the eviscerated entrails as the bravest of the crows began to hop over the carcases to feast on the still-warm flesh.

Fresh red magnesium torches gave off their ethereal light, accompanied by an artificial beam whose bright illumination slowly floated down on a parachute towards him.

Malleus couldn't remember a thing.

Where did the gun come from? It was the latest version of the Germanian Heckler & Koch G3T.

He glanced back over his shoulder. Beyond the broken concrete was a transport helicopter, parked on the tarmac. Its rotor was ticking over, hurling water like a whisk. The light from the instrument panel lit up the pilots, who were slumped over; one of the windows was stained red on the inside. One door hung open, the rosy light revealing a sniper armed with a large grenade launcher with a round magazine; large empty cartridges rolled down from the interior of the helicopter and onto the asphalt.

Malleus could see the body of another soldier in front of the helicopter, equipped with an exoskeleton, a six-barrelled mini-gun and a rucksack heavy with ammunition.

These must be the specialists Lautrec had been talking about: an army taskforce.

He tottered cautiously out from the ruins, towering over bodies that had been riddled with the soldiers' bullets.

The inhabitants of the area appeared to have fought fiercely enough to eliminate much of the taskforce. Malleus passed through the remains of the troops, their bodies scattered and torn, burnt and split apart. Some sort of irresistible force must have been applied, meaning at least one of the protégés in Adamastos' deranged sunken empire had possessed rather special powers.

The powers of a demigod. Still in a bit of a trance, Malleus pressed on, stroking the magazine of the G3T as casually as he had done so many times during the Great Change. Not all enemies had met their end then.

He suddenly realised precisely *what* he was holding in his hands and quickly let the rifle drop to the ground. He *never* wanted to handle this sort of fully automatic weapon again. *I swore an oath.*

Malleus rubbed his rain-soaked face and looked around; he felt slightly more invigorated now, more focused. His luggage remained untouched underneath the canopy. Smoke rose intermittently from the ruins of the terminal, giving off the unmistakeable stench of burning.

He estimated there were three dozen or so dead hybrids, their clothes torn to shreds, lying on the expanse between the helicopter and the buildings. Some had simple clubs, iron bars and homemade cutlasses. Between them lay the remains of the soldiers.

The only sound came from the idling rotors and the raindrops that were washing away the blood and other bodily fluids, letting the earth absorb it all from the asphalt. *Just like a sacrifice.*

Malleus shivered, from cold, from shock, from downright necessity.

As he approached the canopy where his case was still lying, his gait becoming increasingly steady, he started to look for another box of Culebras. He felt a sudden need to light one with a red band. Abandoning convention, he inhaled deeply as he let his eyes wander over the battlefield.

I can't remember a thing. His eyes landed on the steel beam that had been struck by lightning, which had triggered his mental blackout. *Nothing about the taskforce arriving, nor the battle itself.*

He surmised that the intense flickering light had brought back the post-traumatic stress disorder that he had suffered from since the Great Change, ever since those desperate nights when those bestial creatures had ambushed his unit. He'd already had one brief flashback in New Carthage, when he saw the mark on the neck of a young woman; he'd successfully fought that one off.

That was nothing compared to this.

I've always had it under control . . . until now. Malleus felt the soothing effect of his special Culebra and began to feel calmer, more awake, more active. His tremors dissipated. He would never find out what he had undergone and survived during his little blip. His doctors and therapists had all warned him that he might experience partial amnesia. In their experience there was a very good chance that he might develop schizophrenia, primarily as a coping mechanism against the images, emotions and events that would otherwise be burned into his memory.

Well, I haven't got it yet. Malleus carried on puffing as he inspected his tenebrous environment, the darkness permeated only by the miniscule slit of light from the helicopter, which made the scene look even more unreal.

Were Lautrec to find out about this, his entire future at Interpol would be in jeopardy. The wisps of smoke emanating from his lips formed a poignant question mark as they wafted away on the light wind around him.

No one must ever know. He withdrew his PDA from his coat pocket to check the time: barely half an hour had passed. The recording function on the device was switched on – it had been filming the entire time. After some hesitation, Malleus deleted the file from the PDA. He didn't want to see the carnage that had obviously ensued. It might set off a relapse.

No one must ever know, he repeated for his own sake, and then deleted the file from the server. *Leave no trace.*

He noticed a movement in the cockpit of the helicopter. One of the pilots sat up, staring out of the window with a visibly shocked expression. The spotlight underneath the fuselage lit up, casting a wide circular arc of light over the bodies, the debris, the buildings. Meanwhile the roar of the turbines increased and the rotors began to whirl faster, whipping up the air.

He's trying to leave!

Malleus jumped up. 'Stop!' he shouted, knowing full well that the pilot was never going to hear him.

He grabbed his suitcase and hand luggage and hurtled through the rain towards the machine that was preparing for its ascent. The glowing tip of his Culebra hissed violently as it made contact with the moisture in the air.

On his way towards his ticket out of the depressing sunken kingdom of Adamastos, the raindrops suddenly rearranged themselves, forming a curtain of water in which the face of a woman could be discerned, blocking Malleus' path.

'You killed my daughter,' growled the apparition. 'I'll remember your face all too clearly, Malleus Bourreau. And I swear before the gods that I will not spare you. I will have my revenge.'

Malleus charged through the centre of the watery face, breaking it apart. No doubt this was Brigantia's mother appearing through the veil with her threats of vengeance. Either way, he didn't care. *We can add her name to the list of entities who hate me.*

The helicopter was approaching.

Malleus struck out in a wide arc so as to be spotted in the glare of the headlight; the pilot looked over at him and he brandished his suitcase.

But the goddess' features appeared anew from the rain. 'I curse you!' she swore at him. 'Never again will water be succour for you when it is under my control. And if ever you try to swim, you will sink like a stone. Fear me! *Fear a mother's wrath!*'

Malleus smashed the barrier once again. He knew that an entity could react with anger, although he had never before been subjected to a tangible, explicit curse. But he had remained alive for far too long to ever take that sort of thing seriously.

The pilot could see him approaching. The bright light underneath the fuselage was directed directly at him, dazzling him, before moving to the side.

'Go to the side door,' came the instruction through the loudspeaker, 'and keep your head down.'

Malleus nodded and ran to the entrance; he threw his luggage inside and leaped to safety within. He pulled the grenade launcher back, secured it and closed the door, then the helicopter took off and rose quickly into the night sky.

The soldier's body jerked back and forth in the harness as if it were an oversized puppet whose master had grown tired of it.

Malleus could smell the blood clinging to his clothes, as well as that of the dead soldier, which continued to drip from his lifeless body. A powerful sense of nausea suddenly overcame him and he hastily took a deep draw from his cigar, grateful that he'd successfully managed to keep from being extinguished.

'We're flying back to base,' said the pilot over the loudspeaker. 'Are you hurt?'

'No—' Malleus looked down at his body and noticed the long cut snaking its way down his thigh for the first time. Pain arrived on cue, as if the wound had been waiting to be discovered. 'Actually, yes I am', he corrected. 'I'm afraid I might need stitches.'

'I'll let them know.' The pilot left the radio link to the hold open, possibly out of excitement, as he made the call. 'Valhalla, this is Hugin One. Returning from deployment. Target on board. Entity destroyed, monitors show no signs of life. We need a doctor. Target and I are both injured. Come in.'

'Roger, Hugin One. Understood,' crackled the reply. 'We'd better hope that fucking atheist was worth it. Come in.'

'Roger, Valhalla. Arriving in T minus fifteen minutes. Over and out.'

Malleus puffed away and closed his eyes, rubbing his mustache. *I really hope I* am *worth it.*

Germania (Celtic region), Chattia (Hessen), Frankfurt,
November 2019

Marianne Lagrande had elected to dress like someone from the eighties so as not to draw too much attention to herself. She had contented herself with black leggings, a long white turtleneck and boots; her bleached blonde hair was held firmly in place with a clip and a pair of sunglasses rested on her nose. Catching a reflected glimpse of herself, she considered herself to be dressed perfectly normally. She put the fact that other people were staring at her down to her somewhat striking make-up.

Lagrande entered the arrivals hall of Terminal 1 at Frankfurt Airport, where she was due to meet Inspector Bourreau. The atmosphere was leisurely – nobody ever seemed to want to fly anywhere on a Sunday morning.

Apart from the inspector. She looked around, searching for him and eventually spotting him in a café one level below her, just before the entrance to the security area.

He looked tired as he stared at his PDA and casually ran his fingers over the end of his black beard and his goatee. In front of him was a tray containing a cup of coffee, a plate with the remains of a sandwich and a fruit salad; the dark brown object next to him was a half-smoked cigar. He clearly took no notice whatsoever of the smoking ban in airports.

He looks thin. Lagrande let out a long, deep breath and allowed herself to consider precisely what effect the sight of this lost and lonely man had on her.

She liked her boss because he was different, not only because he was an atheist and because he had an elegant yet unconventional dress sense. He had given her the opportunity to prove that she could do more than just write up reports, sift through data, do research and carry out grunt work. The girl from the banlieue was blonde, not stupid, and he had recognised that.

Even if he did need a bit of a nudge to make that discovery. Lagrande smiled to herself and headed towards the escalator to meet him.

Three days had passed since his plane had crashed and Bourreau had been saved so remarkably. He had been held in a military hospital to answer questions about who exactly had brought about such an event, but that was all she knew. Lautrec had been stubbornly silent about the rest.

Lagrande hoped she would find out a fair degree more from Malleus himself.

Bourreau looked up and noticed her, his face breaking into a warm smile, tinged with relief. 'Madame, what a pleasure it is to see you once again.' He rose to pull out her chair, black strands of hair falling carelessly over his eyes as he did so.

That was another reason she liked him: he was a man who would pull out a plastic chair for a woman in an airport café. Manners. Attentiveness. 'The pleasure's all mine, Inspector.' She sat down. 'I can see you've been through the wringer a bit.'

'Only for the last few years now,' he replied with an air of dark humour. To her great astonishment he put his finger on her lips before she could reply. He then took out his PDA, switched it off and placed it in a foam-padded metal box, which he closed carefully. 'You are to take this to an address in Lutetia,' he said conspiratorially, before giving her the district and street address. 'Drop it off in the letterbox with the name *Connoisseur.*'

Lagrande drew the box inquisitively towards her. 'Is that it?'

'That's it.' Bourreau summoned a waiter and let her place her order. She opted for a coffee and a croissant – cliché or not, that was what she fancied. 'A friend of mine is going to take it apart and check it for bugs.'

Her arched eyebrows rose. 'You too?' She had written to him to say that their unknown friends had had infected her laptop with a spyware program during the raid.

'I didn't think of it until it was too late. It could be that someone had prepared the whole thing in New Carthage.' He reached into his coat pocket and pulled out parts of a tiny electronic device. 'The experts at the army base found this during a routine check: tracking bugs, audio transmitters, the works. They had been concealed within various items of clothing. Someone wanted to know where I was and what I was saying.' He pointed to the box. 'And I think he wanted to know even more.'

Lagrande unleashed a barrage of rather unladylike curses, before blushing as Bourreau laughed out loud. *Banlieue girl.* 'The Collector really makes use of every opportunity.'

To her astonishment, he shook his head thoughtfully and brushed the long black strands of hair from his face, drawing attention to the old red scar under his eye. 'This has nothing to do with the Collector. I'm being followed by an unknown quantity. What I don't know is why.' He lowered his voice. 'What I am telling you, Madame Lagrande, is for your ears only. It's the Glyph Killer, who caused so much mayhem in Italy a few years ago. Now it looks as if he thinks of me as his best friend.'

'Since when?'

'Since I started carrying out research in Italy after the death of that mayor. Or at least, I think so. The killings with the registered murder weapon began on that day. Before that, he'd disappeared, for years – a lot of people hoped he'd met his end.' Bourreau rubbed his goatee. 'He has saved my life at least twice. Most recently on the jet.'

Lagrande sipped her coffee carefully. 'Could we play him off against the Collector?' The question left her lips before she'd had time to think.

Yet again he had to laugh. 'You are highly pragmatic, Madame.'

'That I am.' She grinned briefly before her concern for the inspector increased again. 'Should Lautrec be . . .?'

'No,' he said immediately, 'I'm cutting my shadow off from all information and getting away from him. If he wants anything else, he'll have to come to me'.

'Then what?'

'I'll arrest him.'

'Without knowing what he looks like? Wouldn't it be better to trap him somehow?'

'I know what his eyes look like. And his stature. At the moment I haven't got the time to lay a trap. The Collector is my priority.' He quickly summarised what had happened on board the jet.

The incident was officially listed as an unsuccessful hijacking attempt, and he impressed upon her the need for her to conceal any personal connection to him – that would attract more attention, and more attention meant more difficulties in their investigations.

'I spoke to the Collector over an internet connection, and believe me, Madame Lagrande, *this* man will leave as many dead bodies as he needs to until he has achieved his goal. He's much worse than my shadow.' 'Bourreau lifted the Culebra towards his lips and puffed on it. 'That's why I need to catch the next flight to Japan. It's a private job: a statuette has been stolen, and I'm pretty sure it's one of the artefacts he's looking for. There's a suggestion it's connected to the pre-aeronautics, just like the gold figurines from Mannheim.'

Lagrande continued to drink her coffee while she listened and ordered another when she had finished, so she could have something to dip her croissant into. She could feel some doubt stirring within her, but she didn't want to express it. She was still feeling guilty about the loss of the figurines, which contributed a little to that.

But Bourreau could see it in her. 'Have you got a different

theory?' he asked in a friendly tone, not at all condescending. 'I'm all ears, Madame.'

'It doesn't really seem to . . . fit,' she replied cautiously. 'We've already got an artefact from Japan.'

'So?'

'As it stands, the missing objects all come from different cultures or continents.' Lagrande counted on her fingers. 'So far we've got the fan of Susanoo no Mikoto from Japan, the statuette of Oddua with its diamond, from Africa and . . . until recently the gold figures from Bogotá, South America.' She cleared her throat, thinking of the loss. 'We know about Nandi, the horn of the mount of the Indian gods, the brick from the East, and the Iron Crown of Lombardy. And this artefact you got hold of on the jet.'

Bourreau reached into his other jacket pocket and withdrew his cigar case, opening it up as if to offer her something, but instead revealing a carved tip that looked as if it could fit on the end of an arrow or harpoon. 'Inuit,' he said, and snapped the case shut. 'I'll give it to you as soon as I leave to catch my plane. Take the artefact to where the others are.'

Lagrande's hypothesis strengthened. 'I can't think of a single reason why the theft in Tokyo should have anything to do with the stolen objects in Hannes Hein's cubbyhole.'

Bourreau considered her objection thoughtfully. 'It can't be dismissed entirely, my dear.'

Lagrande was deriving a great deal of pleasure from working the case with him: the thrill of the chase. The airport environment took a back seat; she was no longer taking any notice of the announcements, or the people around her. 'Why do you think that it could have anything to do with it?'

'The customer said the bought the figurine during a visit to Hamburg, and he gave Mohr's name.'

Lagrande had to admit that *that* was a good point. 'Then I suppose you will have to fly to Japan to rule out a false trail.'

He nodded, letting his fingers drift over the dark ends of his beard. 'Tell me precisely what happened outside the museum in Mannheim.'

This is what I was afraid of. She gave him a detailed report, mentioning the visit of Madame Wertheimer from the State Security Office, as well as the subsequent theft of the figurines from her desk.

As she was telling her supervisor this, it struck her that Madame Wertheimer might have been behind this most brazen of thefts. She looked at Bourreau and could see that he was thinking the same thing.

'Either way, they've disappeared for now,' he said with sudden focus. 'What's more important is that nothing happened to you – at home, as well as in Treva and at the museum.' He leaned forward. 'Have you spoken to Ove Schwan?'

So that's that then. She said she hadn't, and pushed all her questions about her protector and his shared past with her boss to one side. It was of no relevance to the case. 'So far he's only really said hi.'

Bourreau clicked his tongue with dissatisfaction. 'I'd really like to know what that nonsense about the visitor cards from *GodsEnd* was all about.'

You and me both. Lagrande dipped her croissant into her coffee and took a bite. 'What's been stolen in Japan?'

'A terracotta figurine called a Dogū. As I said, it fits with the gold winged statuettes and the theory of pre-aeronautic navigators,' he replied. 'Some people view them as being more than mere trinkets and offerings.'

'Pre-aeronautics,' she muttered to herself.

'It's the theory that aliens visited mankind in ancient times and helped them found civilisations, or even built them themselves,' he elucidated patiently, 'which is also an explanation, by the way, for many of the strange depictions of the gods. I am rather more inclined to accept that theory.

'I know, sir. I just thought that this would be the first connecting element – but one that applies to only *two* artefacts,' she interjected, chewing vigorously, her elbows resting on the table. Coffee dribbled down her chin, which she wiped off impatiently with one hand. Bourreau handed her a napkin and she suddenly felt like an absolute yokel. 'Surely we need something that brings *everything* together?'

'That's *your* job,' he replied with wink. 'You are my treasured personal research assistant.' All of a sudden, he made a face as if to suggest that something had just struck him. 'Have you got a secure smartphone on you?'

She handed it to him. *Treasured?. You never know when he's being serious.* She looked around the terminal, observing the incoming travellers who were heading towards their gates after a brief detour via the departure board.

With the return of the gods had come new airlines, of course, like LokiFlight and Ehecatl Airways, operated by entities, or so they claimed, and guaranteed never to hit turbulence. Advertisements for holiday destinations looped round on the information screens. Just as Egypt campaigned aggressively for seeing the wonders of the Pharaohs with your own eyes, an unpronounceable Mexican entity was inviting passers-by to a spring holiday by the sea in some equally unpronounceable location. Offers were everywhere; even Sodom and Gomorrah was selling itself as a 'hotbed of hedonism', with the advertisement remaining about halfway friendly to youngsters. At least in Frankfurt.

Malleus connected to the airport's secure Wi-Fi and barely a minute passed before Crick's face, complete with grey beard, appeared on the small display. 'Oh, it's you, Inspector!' he said, surprised. 'And hello, Madame Lagrande.'

She raised her half-eaten croissant by way of acknowledgement.

'My dear Mr Crick, I have some more information about our unknown Collector,' began Bourreau in his friendly, calm manner. 'He is male, estimated to be over sixty, is practically bald, sits at a hardwood desk which is, if I may I venture a prediction, made of teak.'

At these words, Crick let out a snort of derision. 'That hardly narrows it down.'

'He also wears a signet ring on his right hand containing a crest, in the centre of which can be seen a pyramid, and has another ring made from polished gold, with an eye engraved in it and with an embedded gem,' continued Bourreau. 'It might be an emerald fragment. His voice is unremarkable, and he must be very full of himself. One might describe him as being a strong character.'

Lagrande finished off her pastry, fascinated by the calm exterior her boss was displaying. One would never guess how close to death he had come recently. *What happened at the airport?* They hadn't discussed it at all. *Probably not intentionally.*

Crick nodded as he took notes.

'He also uses a tiepin that has the same crest on it. Apart from the pyramid, it was chequered, and had two crossed antlers and a mountain. Or so I think,' he added. 'That's all I know.'

'Well that gives us something to go on at least. I'll ask around.' Crick looked at his watch. 'I've got to see to a customer. How can I get hold of you?'

'My PDA is broken so everything's going through Madame Lagrande for the time being,' replied Bourreau.

'Good. I'll be in touch soon. I should be able to give you updates about the artefacts as well.' Crick broke off the connection.

'Japan waits, Monsieur l'Inspecteur. Lagrande wiped her fingers on the serviette. 'I'll have cracked the rest of the codes by the time you're back. We'll be amazed at what has been stolen and we'll see that *my* theory was right after all.'

'What a sporting proposition.'

'Well, that's me. We banlieue girls are like a dog with a bone when there's something they want.' She smiled at him, feeling that she had perhaps put a little more flirtation into her gaze than might otherwise have been expected of an underling. She quickly lowered her blue-green eyes. *Idiot!*

'Where are the artefacts?'

'Currently in a thick steel safe at *Tresoriale*, a company specialising in high-quality security for valuables. Nobody can get in, not even a deity.' She didn't dare look at him again, though she made things worse anyway by blushing deeply. *That was stupid.*

'How can entities be stopped from entering?'

'They say the owner is one himself.' She coughed and took her phone off him. As she did so, their fingers touched briefly, which was not altogether unpleasant. But when she looked down at her poorly painted nails, her heart sank. *What a shame . . .* She pocketed the device and drank the final sip of cold coffee out of desperation.

'Good. They can stay there for the time being.' Bourreau's expression gave nothing away as he fiddled with his Fu Manchu moustache. 'Madame, you will see to the codes, deliver the PDA just as I said, and otherwise stay well out of the firing line.' He stood up, threw his coat on and placed a black hat on his head. The hat looked very new.

'As well as I can, anyway,' she replied, smiling, and rose as well.

'Give me a hug goodbye?' he asked mischievously.

'Sorry?' she replied instinctively, surprised, 'I mean, sure. With pleasure.' Lagrande placed her hands on his shoulders and kissed first his left cheek, then his right. At the same time she could feel his fingers on her hips, while his other hand worked its way clumsily up her torso before landing on her breast. That wasn't altogether unpleasant either – unusual, but not unpleasant.

'Forgive me,' he murmured, 'I've given you the harpoon tip. You'd better take that to the safe as well.' He straightened up and bade her goodbye again, doffing his hat and turning on his heel; the thin, bent Culebra hanging from the left corner of his lips.

Her insides churning, Marianne Lagrande stood stock-still in the café and looked at the investigator, who was moving towards the security checkpoint.

Something had changed in her as far as this man was concerned. She couldn't really categorise it, but she could feel it nevertheless.

But *that* was *definitely* not on.

She felt a hard jolt in her right arm and shoulder, which made her take a couple of steps to steady herself. '*O là là*, careful!' she exclaimed, annoyed.

A young woman with a large silver suitcase had underestimated the distance and collided with her as she was approaching the counter. She was wearing a simple yet elegant charcoal-coloured sheath dress, ornamented around the collar. The pale-coloured trenchcoat she wore over the top was trimmed with fur. Her long, silky black hair was pinned together at the back, drawing attention even more to her exquisite face and green eyes that were glaring at Lagrande.

'You were in my way,' replied her unknown assailant. 'No

one gets in my way.' She turned to the waiter and ordered a takeaway coffee.

Bitch! Lagrande pondered briefly whether she ought to reply, but this sort of encounter could quickly get out of hand. Devoid of decency and manners, the *nouveau riche* would get their come-uppance eventually, without having to be pushed. She couldn't exactly call upon the next French Revolution.

Instead, she checked to see if the apparently wealthy lady had stolen anything from her. Lagrande knew the push trick all too well. But nothing was missing.

Right, let's go. I've got my orders.

* A Ω *

Did he really think he could get rid of me just because he found the bugs?

Error.

Huge error.

I can see everything from the gallery. Him, and the Eighties woman.

They're talking, but sadly I'm too far away and he's put my ears in the box. He's found out that it's been tampered with.

Now I've got to start all over again by traipsing around after him. How annoying.

Is this really the thanks I get for saving his arse twice? Kicking me out of his life?

Actually, I think this calls for a penalty of some description.

The last thing I was able to read was 'job in Japan'. Toyko: that's where he'll be going.

His flight's been booked – he's on the last seat. Yet again, I've got to think of something but doing this at Frankfurt Airport is far harder than it was in New Carthage. Fuck.

They've been talking for quite a long time, but I can't make out anything. Beyond irritating. Perhaps I should learn to lip read – especially upper lips. Though the Eighties woman's leggings are so tight I'm rather distracted.

The Eighties. What a horrible period. Like an accident that everyone was involved in. Or an orgy in a nursing home, where everyone feels crippling shame after the lights have been switched back on.

Soon I'll watch the video that he deleted from his PDA and the cloud on a big screen. The one of the battle in the airport ruins. It would be twice as good with Dolby Surround Sound. Add some popcorn and Coke and you've got the perfect action film!

Forwarding a copy of everything on his PDA to myself really did have its benefits.

I think he'd be rather surprised to know the truth. The pilot in the cockpit appears to have passed out, and apart from him, nobody saw how the carnage really played out.

I must confess, of all the deities on the fucking earth – I would never have thought THAT one capable of it.

But now I know a secret.

At least one.

What's the betting that he knows even more? As well as the cigars, the smoke that does whatever he wants it to: it forms little shapes and so forth.

Or that he's still alive, despute the fact that the gods should be able to eliminate him with the click of a finger because he's starting to get on their tits.

There's something else going on.

Ah, he's standing up – and hello, what's this? Quite the intimate goodbye they're sharing there. Cute. Almost like a Casablanca *goodbye. Humphrey Nogod and Leggingrid Bergman.*

The woman seems to need a bit of time before she can tear her gaze away from him and . . . bosh! *what a hit that was!*

Miss Elegance has cleared the way with a rather impressive body check, even though she could have easily got through. My, she in a mood must be, and— Hang about . . .

Her face!

I know that face!

Let me just magnify it a bit with my glasses.

By Bacchus, that old poof: That's HER! The mad nun! Well, the not-nun. The one who batted her eyelashes at him and offered him a ticket to ride.

I definitely hadn't counted on her. Merely removing her from the picture as I'd promised to do isn't something I can do on this occasion. That would be a terrible idea at an airport. Pigs everywhere.

Miss Eighties is moving up the escalator and walks straight past me.

She smells good. A bit like powder and vanilla.

What am I doing?

I need to think of a punishment for him. Being excluded was NOT nice.

Ungrateful.

No: cheeky.

Actually, no: shameless. Yes, utterly shameless!

But first of all I've got to work out how I'm going to keep him in my sights.

Nippon (Japan), Honshū (Main Island) November 2019

Despite his exhaustion after having spent thirteen hours on a plane, Malleus was still able to focus on what his counterpart had said about the theft. He drank his sweetened matcha thoughtfully, hoping the traditional Japanese green tea would live up to its reputation as a restorer of spirits. *It tastes of death.*

The flight had taken longer than intended. Although aeroplanes were capable of making journeys far more quickly than they had previously been able to, the other activities of the entities meant that there would sometimes be all manner of spontaneous detours. The airspace over Asia was – depending on the route taken – in a realm lying somewhere between tricky and difficult. The combination of India with its thirty thousand entities and Japanese Shintō with its various Kami always ensured a rather exciting trip.

Given Malleus' brush with death on the last flight, he'd decided to adopt a somewhat fatalistic approach on board on this occasion.

He was met at Kokusai Kūkō International Airport in Tokyo by a uniformed chauffeur, driven to Shibuya in a limousine and taken to the penthouse suite of a towering skyscraper in an express lift. He stood there, surrounded by cabinets and display cases containing all manner of *objets d'art*.

Malleus looked out of the window absent-mindedly, breathing in the perfumed air that evoked the scent of cherry blossom.

Tokyo by night was an impressive sight, in particular the fashionable Shibuya area, its neon advertisements illuminating the surrounding darkness.

Along with India, Nippon was certainly one of the places that had benefitted most from the return of the gods. It was somewhat of a belated vindication for proud Japan, which had been dealt with far more favourably than Europe when contact was first made. Their beliefs had been confirmed, and the handful of Christians living there almost immediately converted to Buddhism or Shintō. Nippon flourished with the good intentions of the Kami.

Mr Satō's outline was reflected in the window. He was a short man of around fifty, wearing a black suit with a white shirt and dark tie – business uniform for most Japanese men. His black hair was cut short and combed through with gel to reveal a centre parting.

To his delight, Malleus could see that he still had all ten of his fingers. He had no desire to have a member of the Yazuka, the Japanese Mafia, as one of his clients. He turned towards him and cast his eyes once again over the exhibit room where two of the many display cases lay in ruins. The stolen Dogū figurine had apparently been in one of them.

Malleus had bought himself a cheap and cheerful replacement PDA from the airport and had quickly set it up so that he could have something to record his activities and report back to Lagrande with. He used it to quietly film the scene before him.

He considered the remaining Dogū, with their geometric patterns of jewels, to be rather ugly, almost grotesque. They measured between six and twelve inches high and mainly represented a female figure with a squat face, stunted arms, protruding legs and frog-like eyes. Their sexual features were greatly emphasised, an allusion to a mother goddess and a fertility cult. One could be forgiven for thinking they were stylised aliens in spacesuits.

The second case had to have contained something particularly large.

Far too big for a Dogū. Something's not right here. 'Would you do me the courtesy of telling me the truth, Mr Satō?' asked Malleus, pointing the lens towards the businessman's face and zooming in closer on the steely smile that didn't shift one iota. 'That's the only way I'm going to be able to help you here.' He didn't like being messed about with.

'So you know?' Satō sighed.

'I know, sir.'

Satō performed a typical Japanese bow. 'Forgive me for trying. But I was afraid you wouldn't take on the job otherwise.'

'You didn't buy the statuettes in Hamburg, did you?'

'Correct, Mr Bourreau.' He pointed to the various *objets d'art* in his private collection. 'I am primarily concerned with pre-aeronautics, as you can see. But that's not all.' He went over to the second of the big smashed cases. 'I collect anything that is of divine origin but cannot be . . . categorised.'

Malleus' ears pricked up and he lowered his PDA. 'What was in the second case?'

The Japanese man bowed once more. 'I do not know.'

'You're in luck. I usually just cancel my jobs with clients and keep the deposit. It's an excellent con,' he said in an attempt to make Satō feel guilty. It was still exciting, though. 'How did it happen, then, Mr Satō? At least tell me that, please.'

'I acquired the artefact quite a while ago, but the delivery was delayed. The authorities in the Ottoman Republic—'

'The Ottoman Republic?' Malleus was astonished at this confession. He had expected it to be a larger, obscure Dogū figurine or perhaps a statue of an *oni*, but not an object from a completely different culture altogether. He could hear Lagrande's triumphant laughter all the way from Paris.

'That's right. Experts had to be brought in before it could be cleared for export,' explained Satō.

'But surely you must know what you bought, sir.'

'I do. Indirectly.' Satō was standing by the broken shards like a schoolboy being given a dressing-down by his headmaster. This was obviously uncomfortable for him. 'They regularly carry out excavation work on the Dülük Baba Tepesi mountain in Turkey. Along with all the typical findings from Roman times, a stela was discovered underneath that had no link to any known god. *That* was what caught my interest. The team of archaeologists sent me some 3D images, on the basis of which I decided to buy it.' He sighed. 'Just imagine, Mr Bourreau: a relic from an *unknown* god! In my collection! That is *unique* . . . it would be an absolute dream come true!'

Malleus smiled wryly. 'So you *did* know what—'

But Satō gestured otherwise. 'The delivery was made while I was away. And my employees who took in the delivery and set it up have been murdered. I think a Kami broke in, out of jealousy for a god who has lost nothing in Tokyo. That's why you are here.'

Malleus pointed to the smaller of the vandalised display cases. 'And what about the Dogū?'

'I removed it so that you'd have a reason to come to Nippon.'

This story still doesn't add up. How did Satō know enough about Mohr's murder to lure him here You couldn't just read about it in the press or on the internet. Malleus needed to catch his adversary red-handed on his next lie. The story his client had woven together was about as fragile as the Dogū figurine. 'Look at me please, sir.'

Satō met his gaze, giving a noncommittal smile.

'How many cabinets are in the room?'

The man visibly hesitated. 'Mr Bourreau, I . . .'

'Please: how many?' he pressed on, maintaining his friendly demeanour. 'And don't take your eyes off me.'

Satō started calculating. 'Thirty-seven.'

'And for how long have you been a collector, Mr Satō?'

'Since . . . well . . . for a very long time.'

'What is your most expensive object?'

'Can't you just—?'

'Mr Satō, please.'

The businessman stared at him.

'You don't know. You know far too little.' Malleus smiled. 'You are not the owner of this collection, Mr Satō.' He stroked the ends of his Fu Manchu moustache, looked around and ambled across the room. Figurines, vases, antique weaponry, all supposedly touched or even used by demigods and gods, if the tags were to be believed. 'What's going on? Is your boss, whose assistant I presume you are, afraid that he might lose face in the presence of a foreigner?'

He stopped in front of the case that had contained the mysterious object and bent down. *Let's have a look at one of these.* His eyes latched onto a chipped fragment of greyish-black stone secluded between the shimmering shards: he picked it up very carefully with one of his leather gloves. 'I do not believe that there ever was an export licence for the artefact from the Ottoman Republic. And *that* is the real problem for you and your boss.'

Satō closed his eyes and bowed deep and low, this time apologetically. 'I did warn him that you'd see through it, Mr Bourreau. But he insisted.'

'How about we carry on as if you'd never tried this little trick and had never invented such a poorly thought-out story?' Malleus held up the fragment for him to see. 'I presume this comes from the object I am meant to be looking for?'

'Yes.' He bowed again. 'Would you like another matcha?'

'You haven't got any coffee, have you? A mocha would be ideal, to match the object.' Malleus couldn't help himself and headed towards the tatami mat, where there was also a small table next to the comfortable seat cushions against the wall.

'Of course. I'll be right back.' Satō bowed and hurried towards the door.

Malleus sat down and laughed softly. *This whole affair is far more interesting than I had anticipated.* The alleged inter-cultural rivalry between the entities had its own appeal. Yet the question of which story was to be believed was still very much open.

Malleus was fully aware of how much honour and losing face

meant in modern Japan. Tradition had been taken to altogether different levels.

It looked like rather a lot had gone wrong with the purchase of this particular archaeological object. Two men and three women had died; Satō had presented them as the burglars' victims, without showing him the bodies. There were also no traces whatsoever in the penthouse of there having been any sort of police investigation.

Malleus concluded that if whatever the hapless Satō's boss was doing in his fancy penthouse in Shibuya ward were to come to light, he would draw his *tantō* and commit *seppuku*.

The job had acquired a second, and very human, level.

Satō returned; he had arranged an apparently original Ottoman coffee service on a lacquer tray. Various types of sugar were placed in small bowls, alongside a jug of milk. The aroma was heavenly, and it became even more intense as the man began to pour, overwhelming the cherry blossom.

Satō handed him the small cup with a bow. 'Mr Bourreau, I have been instructed to tell you everything you need to know in order to help us.'

With a feeling of delight, he took the coffee and began to drink, before adding sugar and taking another sip. *This is how it ought to taste!*

'What I told you about the excavation in Turkey was true.' Satō clapped his hands twice and the room went dark. The wall opposite transformed into a 3D screen displaying the Dülük Baba Tepesi mountain near the town of Gaziantep, according to the overlay.

A bearded archaeologist spoke to the camera. 'Welcome to one of the most special places in Asia Minor. Mesopotamian gods had their temples here; the Romans later built the main sanctuary of

Jupiter, which was followed by a Christian monastery that stood until the Crusades,' the researcher declared enthusiastically. 'We have managed to secure six hundred stamps and cylinder seals of various origins.' He waved to someone out of shot and the camera panned across. 'The first thing we found was a stela in the ruins of the Christian monastery. Five feet tall, discovered in fragments. Just imagine: it was used as a supporting pillar in the monastery wall – Christianisation literally walled in the foreign gods.'

The stela faded as the audio was cut. Satō gestured with his hand to stop the report.

'I need the pictures on my PDA, please,' Malleus said, and looked at the relief of a bearded deity growing out of a leafy cradle. The stalk stretched out of a cone containing various astral symbols; from the sides of the cone rose a long horn and a tree held in the god's right hand.

Satō unpaused the video and the voice of the archaeologist continued offstage: 'This is unbelievable! This is ancient Oriental iconography, as you can see from the style of the beard and the position of the arms. Iron Age, probably. We are looking at a piece of art dating from the early first millennium BC. And no one knows which god is depicted. My colleagues are stumped! The astral signs certainly aren't from anything we can see in our skies.'

Satō uttered something in Japanese and the screen duly switched to an Ottoman state television news programme showing the excavation site. Bodies were lying scattered around the pits, all of which had been slain: pierced, slashed hacked with tools.

'This happened a few days ago,' explained Satō. 'The authorities are working on the assumption that it was grave robbers, or maybe even one of the local entities who was starting to feel threatened by the presence of the archaeologists.'

Malleus immediately thought of the Curse of the Pharaoh; during excavations in the early 1900s everyone had believed in it, despite there being no reasonable *scientific* explanation.

That changed for most people in 2019, though. He drank from his coffee cup. *There really are curses.* The threat of the goddess Brixia filled his head.

'Were they grave robbers sent by your boss, sir?'

'No.' Satō clapped again and the lights came back on, while the screen retreated to the wall. 'The day before, the archaeologists had discovered a statue that was incredibly similar to the stela: highly detailed and unusually precise. The team leader got in touch with us and we quickly came to an agreement about how much we'd pay for it.'

'Forgive me for butting in again, but you hadn't even *seen* the statue?'

'My boss was sent a live feed of it, but the files they sent over were corrupted and unusable.' Satō gestured towards the remains of the large display case. 'It was delivered and set up. Whatever it was.'

By now Malleus had realised what was panicking the influential owner of the penthouse. 'So you believe the statue was actually the unknown god, and it's now on the loose in Tokyo.'

'What I believe is irrelevant, Mr Bourreau.' Satō's expression was anxious and desperate. 'Find out what has happened and how to stop it – otherwise Tokyo could be subject to countless murders.'

Or the Kami have appeared, out for jealousy or vengeance. Malleus now understood the explosive nature of the case he had undertaken. *This could have dire consequences for the city.*

He would also resolve the final inconsistencies in the story that Satō had fed to him. *After I've taken down this unknown entity.*

Nippon (Japan), Honshū (Main Island), November 2019

Malleus gratefully received another mocha from Satō and set himself up in the small office next to the private exhibit room. He needed to sift through the recordings of the CCTV cameras that had been installed at the entrances and exits of the penthouse, and all the way up the building to the roof. He had, in keeping with Japanese tradition – and also because he rather liked it – taken off his shoes, though he'd avoided doing it before because of the shards scattered around the showroom. *Quite the relief after such a long flight.*

Even though Lagrande was guarding the artefacts with her life, he had also tasked her with finding out everything she could about the excavation at Gaziantep and gathering everything that their colleagues in the Ottoman police force had released. Mainly because he was harbouring a suspicion that he needed the recordings from the crime scene investigators at the excavation site to confirm.

Details. The devil was always in them. So it was for Houdini, for Holmes and for everyone who sought the truth and was prepared to ask questions.

Malleus had sent the stone fragments by express cargo to his friend at Interpol to have it examined, its real age and whether it contained traces of any other material. He was now puffing on a green-banded Culebra which had had fine, neat holes drilled into it.

It turned out that when nobody knew what something looked like, it was rather difficult to find out anything about it. He had examined the recordings several times: once in fast-forward, then in slow-motion, then at normal speed, but he couldn't see anything out of the ordinary that could give him any insight into the whereabouts of the statue.

Had the entity metamorphosed into human form when it awoke?

Would it then look Asian or Central European, or altogether different?

Or is it not an unknown god, but rather, a new interpretation of a known entity whose sanctuary had been on the mountain and who was rebelling against its kidnapping?

So many questions; no tangible way of answering them.

Even the Bible had its problems with alternative deities.

Paul wrote in Acts:

Then Paul stood in the midst of Mars' hill, and said,
Ye men of Athens,
I perceive that in all things ye are too superstitious.
For as I passed by,
and beheld your devotions,
I found an altar with this inscription,
TO THE UNKNOWN GOD.

For the sake of simplicity, Paul had interpreted the unknown entity for whom the Greeks had erected a sanctuary as a matter of precaution as the Christian God, without providing any evidence for this.

I can't just reinterpret this like Paul did. Malleus switched off the monitors with a grimace. Given that this collection squirrelled away by Satō's employer was illegal, or at the very least, secret, there were no cameras in the room itself. And the four employees who had been charged with guarding it had become its first victims.

He drank his mocha, still piping hot, savouring the interplay of flavours on his tongue, and turned towards the window to gaze once more upon Tokyo at night, which had woken from its slumber in the intervening hours.

Streetlights shone everywhere and the fronts of high-rises looked even more colourful than those in Treva and were lit up more brightly than Piccadilly Circus and Times Square. The faces of geishas advertised products; shopping centres invited you to peruse their wares; karaoke bars vied for visitors. The return hadn't changed anything architecturally, mainly because the Kami had always remained steadfast throughout. Temples and shrines were everywhere, so nothing had to be rebuilt from scratch in between, bombastic images of Emperor Tennō proliferated on the glowing walls; he had regained power since the return and, as the highest Shintō priest and the direct, god-like intermediary between the Kami and the people, had become even more important than before. He took over the role of head of state once again – Parliament had been kept on, but demoted to a primarily advisory function.

Malleus observed the young man whose role it was to lead Nippon and maintain the delicate equilibrium between man and Kami. The insignia of the emperor, a stylised chrysanthemum with thirty-two petals, could be found everywhere and the Chrysanthemum Throne awaited the much-longed-for king to come. The dynasty remained strong; there was soon to be another link between mankind and the gods.

This country truly belongs to the winners. Malleus let his mind wander.

His gaze remained focused on the blend of darkness, gaudy

light and the steady flickering of moving images as he thought about the bodies of the guards that he had inspected. The attacker had killed them – caved their heads in with blunt force – to such a degree that their skulls no longer had any discernible shape. Bone had been shattered, flesh obliterated. Their heads looked more like limp calzone which had had all its filling trampled on and cast aside.

Great anger, or great weight? It could be that the Ottoman entity took a rather dim view of being kidnapped and taken to another continent or island. But clearly it had been unable to escape. *Why?*

Malleus rubbed his moustache in contemplation.

Satō had said that the penthouse had been searched, without success. But there were no reports in Tokyo of a string of murders that had any sort of parallels with any of the more archaic means of instigating death.

An unknown god. He remembered a poem he had once had to learn at school, by Friedrich Nietzsche.

The Unknown God
Once more, ere I move on
And send my glance forward,
Lonely, I raise my hands
To you, to whom I flee,
To whom I, in the deepest depths of my heart,
Have solemnly consecrated altars,
So that, at all times,
His voice would summon me again.
Deeply inscribed upon them glows
The words: To the Unknown God.
I am his, though up 'til this hour

I've remained in the company of sinners:
I am his – and I feel the noosèd ropes
That pull me down in the struggle
And, should I flee,
Still force me into his service.
I want to know you, unknown one,
You who have reached deep within my soul,
Wandering through my life like a storm,
You incomprehensible one, akin to me!
I want to know you, even serve you.

This type of literary deification had been and remained completely alien to him.

I will never serve an entity. His eyes turned their blue-tinted attention to the tops of the skyscrapers surrounding him. An idea began to build in his mind: what if this enigmatic deity was still *in* the skyscraper?

Deities tended to set up or look for dwellings far above or below the realm of mortals. Hardly any of the entities who had returned ended up residing in the middle, among their followers.

Shouting for joy, feared to death. Or both. Malleus turned back to the monitor and switched on all the cameras on the roof. The Culebra remained in position in the left-hand side of his mouth.

He could see the helipad from various perspectives, two massive masts with rod antennae, as well as an enormous parabolic antenna, several panoramic views of nocturnal Tokyo, all manner of staircases and some iron walkways extending over the edge of the roof that were designed to be used by maintenance teams. A rigged-up gondola for window cleaners was suspended from a crane.

Plenty of choices there if you want somewhere to hide and think. Before Malleus began his pointless foray into the nightlife of Tokyo on his quest to find the statue, submerged in the ocean of buildings and skyscrapers, he first wanted to rule out the simplest option.

He slipped into his shoes, stood up and tapped his glowing cigar butt into the empty cup before placing them both on the table. Then he threw on his coat and set his hat upon his jet-black hair, headed to the staircase and hurried up, taking them two steps at a time.

As he passed by, he took a large axe from the emergency box on the wall, which also contained a fire hose, a first-aid kit and a defibrillator. A heavy weapon would be far more suitable against a statue than the small blades of his Apache.

It was only when he reached a locked door, thereby ending his ascent, that he rang Satō over the radio transmitter. 'I am standing at the entrance to the roof, sir,' he said, still maintaining his friendly manner. 'The door is locked. Would you be so kind as to open it for me? I want to have a look around.'

'Just a moment, Mr Bourreau.' He could hear Satō tapping away at the other end of the line. 'No, the system says it's open – whoever was last out must have forgotten to enter the code when he picked up our guest from the roof. What are you looking for up there?'

Malleus pushed hard against the door and it swung open. 'It hasn't triggered any alarms, has it?' He could see that the brackets had simply been pulled off as if the bolts were made of thin aluminium. *I was right.*

'No. There's no reason for it to.'

Malleus stooped to crouch down in front of the destroyed mechanism and observed it closely. The contacts that were supposed to trigger the alarm were still connected to the bolt. He took his Apache out of his pocket, folded the knife out and touched the fuse.

A warning tone promptly sounded.

'What are you doing, Mr Bourreau?' Satō's voice rang out, filled with agitation.

'Just a test,' replied Malleus, straightening up and gripping his emergency axe even tighter. 'There's a flaw in this design. You'll see it for yourself, Mr Satō.' He continued slowly, 'Would you care to come to the roof, armed? Your runaway statue appears to have hidden himself away here, sir. I recommend a sledgehammer.

Malleus slipped the PDA into his coat pocket with a warm feeling of familiarity and pointed the lens of the recording device forwards so that he could re-examine what had happened afterwards.

The cold wind howled, whistling through the narrow staircase; the door leading outside was open.

Finding yet more small chips of stone as he climbed, his senses heightened and he clasped the axe with both hands. A stone statue of this size would laugh in the face of his Derringer – but if, contrary to his expectation, the entity had transformed into flesh and blood, he could always draw his revolver again.

Gusts of wind announced his arrival in the narrow hallway, tugging at the brim of his hat, which managed to resist and cling to his head. He cautiously approached the grate that led out into the open, and to a catwalk beyond. There were various branches to the walkway, leading to the helipad, the antennae, and to several large spotlights and power cabinets, while the main path wound around the edge of the roof; to the left and right there was nothing apart from gravel and girders.

On his first circumnavigation, Malleus was unable to discern anything that hinted at the presence of the fugitive. He was even spared the trouble of eavesdropping, for the howling wind sang out far too loudly, breaking into oblique, staccato melodies that reeled and played and danced on their journey through every corner and cable of the walkway.

With every step he took he looked around in every direction, not forgetting to examine the towering masts above him. They stretched at least sixty feet into the night sky, punctuating the darkness with the warning lights affixed to them to prevent collisions with unwitting aeroplanes.

If the entity's here, what will its next step be? Malleus groped further forward. *Think. Think about what it'll want to do. And about where it would be.*

A rather unpleasant incident came to mind, which, unfortunately, didn't appear to be completely improbable.

It's waiting for its followers to come to it!

From the corner of his eye Malleus noticed a movement as a shadow flitted past the base of the large antenna.

Then a cloud of pebbles suddenly rained down upon him like mortar-fire.

Celtica (France), Paris-Lutetia, November 2019

Marianne Lagrande sighed as she wrote her tenth email.

Although she had a certain flair for languages, she had very little experience with Turkish. This made talking to her Ottoman colleagues somewhat more difficult, as she attempted to explain to them the combustive nature of their current situation. She'd decided to present the investigation as being linked to Interpol, which she hoped she'd be able to justify retrospectively. If not she could always just say she had been mistaken. Either way, she needed to get her hands on the information Bourreau was waiting for.

She had barely sent off the email when the update she had been waiting for from Ankara arrived in her inbox. It contained photos of the crime scene and the initial rapid autopsy results.

'*Et voilà*,' she murmured, clicking through the attachments to be forwarded to the investigator.

The wounds on the dead bodies were all deeply unpleasant to look at, but Lagrande was undeterred. Excavation equipment had been crammed into, and indeed right through, all manner of body parts, and some of their heads and all of their hands had been cut off.

'All hands cut off: traditional punishment for theft,' she whispered, and wrote in her message to the inspector. This certainly wasn't the work of mere grave robbers.

The wounds, according to the initial report, had been made with a great degree of force and strength, meaning the attacks were most likely carried out by men. All the team's equipment had been destroyed and rendered completely unusable. Nothing had been taken apart from the stela.

She knew precisely which stela this was: the depiction of the unknown god.

Bourreau had sent her the link to the interview with the leader of the expedition, so the conclusion was obvious – even the Ottoman investigators knew that the most prominent object was the one that had been taken by the robbers.

Various fragments of reliefs from the Roman and Christian eras had been found scattered along the access road to the mountain, thoughtlessly cast aside once the attackers had realised that they weren't part of the primary loot.

Value is of no interest to them. Lagrande came to the conclusion that the attackers had not been looking for gold or historical works of art that could be sold at a profit. The unknown god appeared not to be entirely unknown after all – at least to a small group of people. However, they'd reached Dülük Baba Tepesi too late for the statue. Only the stela had remained for them to take.

Lagrande sent off the reports and images to Bourreau in Tokyo.

How can I get my hands on information about its disciples? she pondered. *I can't,* came the unsatisfactory answer, because the investigations being carried out by the Ottoman authorities were barely off the ground. None of the perpetrators had been caught so far. No arrests; no information.

Nevertheless, she passed on the warning to the inspector that the killers could be on their way to Tokyo to recover the statue in the same way that they had acquired the stela: using all means necessary, and with unspeakable brutality.

Lagrande checked her watch and stood up. She had a few things to attend to if she wanted enough time to have something to eat later. She acknowledged her colleagues as she passed them on her way out, and was soon leaving the building and striding purposefully towards the nearest Metro station. You'd be mad to go by car in a city like Lutetia. Autopilots gave you a great deal of freedom but they weren't much use in a traffic jam.

Lagrande started to rush, checking the next train connections using the voice activation function on her smartwatch – she was running late and she really didn't feel like waiting around fer the next one, so she switched into endurance mode in her leopard-print ankle boots – she could do it in less than five minutes.

As she was striding forward, she thought about how she had already completed her main task. The PDA was now in a letterbox with the name Connoisseur on it; everything else would follow.

But she hadn't made any progress on the theft of the winged statuettes.

But she had almost completely translated another text about a stolen artefact. It appeared to be about two objects, though the terms they used to discuss it were entirely unknown to her. She'd have to check the code once more.

Tomorrow at the latest. Bourreau will be proud of me. Lagrande arrived at the stairs leading down to the Metro station and trotted down them. Most people tended to underestimate her athletic stamina, mainly because they considered her to be a bimbo who was good for little other than dredging up the ill-advised fashion of the eighties. But she took good care of herself.

The platforms were full; the trains thundered in and out every minute or so. In rush-hour it was obvious that the city was bursting at the seams.

Lagrande pushed her way through the throng and found a spot from which she'd be able to embark without too much difficulty.

With beads of sweat starting to form on her brow, she waited to board her train.

* Α Ω *

My quarry has cut me out of his life, and worse, I can't even follow him. That was certainly his intention!

How dare he?

How very dare he, now he knows that I exist and that it was I who saved his life on so many occasions. In Riga, in Rome, on the plane . . . his arse owes me a debt of gratitude, the number of times I've saved it.

I am HIS god! He ought to believe in me!

Cast aside, isolated, robbed of my eyes and ears. He needs to be taught a lesson to stop him from doing the same again. He has made me angry, very angry, and that does not bode well. Not good for me.

I can feel old patterns emerging again, patterns I thought I had left behind long ago. This overwhelming filth of emotion is turning me into an idiot. I can feel it.

Stay calm. Take a deep breath.

Calm . . .

Oh for fuck's sake, no! I. Expect. Gratitude.

GRATITUDE! He must be made to understand.

Oh, then *he won't try to escape again.* Then *he'll let me back in. Willingly.*

The Eighties woman – she's the key.

She's my path, and if I can scare her and send him a message, well, he'll be very sorry indeed . . . and then . . . then my calm shall be restored. I'll be able to think more clearly. I'm usually rather good at that, thinking. But not when I'm angry.

Metro station. Full. Good! I can slip in unnoticed, never straying too far from her. You can't really miss her with that white hair of hers.

Fifteen feet.

Push this chap to one side; this kid as well; have a read of the board and look casual.

Ten feet.

Head for the little news stand in the corner; give the woman a little shove and look at her angrily so she doesn't kick up a fuss.

Six feet.

The train she's waiting for has just been announced. Her punishment will be his punishment. He'll understand that, without a doubt.

Press further forwards and . . . the chap on the other side of the platform, the one with the hoodie and his hands in his pockets . . . he's staring over at me. Not even his sunglasses can hide that. I've clocked it.

Three feet.

Turn to look back at the board – keep my head facing the other way.

Is he a cop?

Surely he hasn't grassed me up? Is this a trap that Blondie's laying for me?

The Metro pulls in; she gets on, but I stay where I am. Like the waves crashing against a cliff face, the network of human rats rub past me on all sides, jostling me, but I stay stock-still.

I grip my hand tightly around the handle of my APB. If they're stupid enough to try and arrest me here, fuck it, I'll take them all down with me.

The train has gone.

And . . . fuck it. That prick on the other side has vanished as well.

I've got a bad feeling about this, a very bad feeling indeed. He definitely wasn't a cop. A cop would have . . . he'd have . . . moved or started towards me or tried to look uninterested. Could it be that this tramp is some sort of guardian angel for Little Miss Eighties?

I need to get out of here.

I need to make a plan.

Well, a new plan, in any case.

Think. Be calm. Nothing but calm.

Nippon (Japan), Honshū (Main Island), Tokyo, November 2019

Malleus dropped to the floor, curling up into a ball with his head turned away from the incoming rocks, which pelted down all around him, clinking and chattering against the walkway and the railings. Some of them struck him painfully on the back and neck, though his thick coat prevented any more serious injuries.

The hail had barely ended when he looked up at the parabolic antenna.

No one in sight. He stood up cautiously, ran to the grate yet again and took a diversion towards the helipad, where he knelt, clutching the axe in his right hand and peering around once more.

His assailant still didn't show himself.

The shower of stones had made it perfectly clear that he was not dealing with a human. Yet the powers of this entity seemed limited compared to the overwhelming force of the likes of Hephaestus or Thor. The thought of this made Malleus feel confident that he could actually achieve something with the axe, or even his Derringers.

Where's Satō? He risked a brief glance into the passage leading to the stairwell, but could see neither his Japanese accomplice nor any other form of assistance. *Does he really want to leave me to fight this battle alone?*

As if summoned by his thoughts alone, two men and a woman appeared unannounced from the door, armed with light submachine guns; he couldn't make out the manufacturer from such a distance. They were dressed in black business suits, like everyone else in Nippon, with white shirts and dark ties, capped off by gloves.

However, their faces weren't Asian, but European.

This gave Malleus pause and he decided not to draw attention to himself for the time being. He touched the radio transmitter in his ear, which put him straight through to Satō via the PDA.

His call was answered after a few seconds.

'Mr Satō, was it you who sent these fine folk to the roof?' he whispered.

'Mr Bourreau,' came the reply, his speech resembling a groan more than anything. 'I'm so sorry.'

Malleus saw two more men emerging from the passage, brandishing Uzis with unusually long box-magazines. The determination etched on their faces made it perfectly clear that they knew they'd be encountering an adversary of some description.

'I managed to get four of them,' Satō continued, falteringly.

He sounded as if he were in a great deal of pain – his composure was admirable. 'They are looking for the statue. My boss has said that you have free rein in how you deal with them, but . . . no police. The reward is high—'

He heard a blast erupting at the other end and the line was disconnected.

Malleus' mouth contorted. This was not a wish he felt inclined to comply with.

The unknown figures spread out after a brief discussion, ran along the edge of the grating but then took the more direct route across the gravel. It didn't matter whether they were looking for the statue or him.

As soon as they discover me, I need to shoot faster than them and hit my target. He withdrew a Derringer with his other hand – the Cobray, which had larger bullets in its barrel.

However, Malleus knew someone who was better suited for assisting him on the roof, who was certainly not sitting all that far away from him in a hiding place of her own.

He slipped silently away from the grate and curled up under the edge of the helipad, which offered him more protection from being spotted by the gunmen. There he took out the PDA, retrieved the battered and stained business card that he had had stashed away in his coat during his trip to Rome, and sent an email to the address written upon it. *I really ought to have done this a long time ago.*

A few seconds later, he received a reply in the form of a number.

He entered the number speedily, but without haste. His call was answered, but before the other end had a chance to say anything, he whispered quickly, 'I thought I'd inform you personally, Miss Milord, that my search has been successful. I have managed to track down an unknown entity for you.' He could see the shoes and legs of two men crossing the gangway. 'Including a fanatical group of followers. Would this be of any interest to you?'

Her reply was preceded by a light chuckle. 'Are you sure that this is an *unknown* deity, or are you just saying that to get me to come and rescue you?'

'Well, I know you think it is as well. After all, it *was* you who made sure that Mr Satō's employer hired me.'

'Me?'

'But of course. You heard about the stela, arrived too late, learned about the sale of the statue and its disappearance,' he said, drawing his summary to a conclusion, 'and because you weren't sure whether this was really an unknown entity or whether it was just an esoteric Roman or Mesopotamian one, you gave Satō's employer information about me and my cases. How else could he have known about a dealer by the name of Mohr?' Malleus checked the chambers of his Cobray with his other hand. 'I assume you've been watching our Japanese friend for some time now because of his collection. But you were waiting to see what I'd find.' He looked out at the attackers rushing past him on their way to the helipad. 'Miss Milord, I have completed my task. Now would you be so kind as to do what is customary on these sorts of occasions.'

'Of course, Mr Bourreau. But tell me quickly, what it is that makes you so sure that this is truly an unknown entity?'

'Come here first. Then I'll tell you.'

'You're bluffing.'

'Do you really want an unknown entity to escape, replete with an army of earthly fanatics? Or risk a Kami appearing, triggering a war that would make a battle with Godzilla look like child's play?' Despite his situation, Malleus found time to appreciate that the national monster of Japan contained the word *god* in its name. 'I am *highly* certain, Miss Milord.'

Suddenly a pair of shoes and two black trouser legs landed next to the platform. The man attached to them crouched down and shone the light of his Uzi, attached like a bayonet, directly at Malleus.

Without hesitating, he opened fire and unleashed a full metal jacket through the chest of his unknown assailant luckily the helipad dampened the sound of the shot.

'So you mean to say you have no proof for me?'

'Sorry, afraid I have to go now, Miss Milord.' As the man was collapsing, Malleus grabbed hold of his foot, dragged him under the landing platform and helped himself to his submachine gun.

Then he hesitated.

The memory of the battle in the airport ruins came back to him abruptly. The chains acting as prison for all the pain in his psyche had suddenly come loose. The frantic, flickering muzzle-flash of the automatic weapon could easily trigger a second attack.

This would be followed by deeds that could never be explained afterwards.

Blackout.

I need to keep this out of reach. Malleus placed the Uzi carefully alongside the dead body and crawled along underneath the platform; he kept the axe with him in case he encountered the statue.

Yet another pair of shoes and trouser legs appeared, wandering around the heliport. Malleus' hideout was occasionally illuminated but he managed to remain out of sight of the careless attention of his unknown predator.

This is all rather too exciting. He adjusted his hat and waited, keeping his breathing shallow and quiet, even though he knew it would be drowned out anyway by the whirring and whistling of the wind.

Then a shout suddenly erupted from the gloom.

He could hear the sound of feet from all directions, hurtling over the gravel with rhythmical crunches and clanging on the metal of the catwalk. It sounded as if even more people had joined the fray.

They've found their god. Malleus' curiosity was piqued. *What are they going to do?*

Above all else, he wanted to see what Oona Milord was going to do. She surely *had* to intervene if she wanted to prevent a potential war from spreading across the capital of Nippon.

Malleus snaked his way forward on his elbows, holding the axe out in front of him.

One of the large masts came into his line of sight, antennae protruding from it and towering high into the night sky as if to eavesdrop on the gods' conversations.

From behind the mass of steel emerged an enormous, humanoid figure, which must have been hiding there since the attack on Malleus. It was far more heavily built than the precise statues of ancient Rome or the neoclassical perfection of Renaissance figures, and looked as if it had been crudely hewn from ore by a clumsy child. But similar lines to those on the stela could clearly be seen on it and the astral signs were obvious to the naked eye.

The attackers were kneeling before it on the gravel, singing unintelligibly, their hands raised slightly. Their weapons were lying all around them, apparently unnoticed.

Malleus noticed that the entity's left arm was missing; it had either been broken off amid the haste of its escape or had gone missing during the excavation – then two women stood up and with great effort started hauling the missing limb behind them. They approached the living statue while the song of the men around them began to swell.

The stone entity turned its head, making a profound grinding noise. It beckoned the women over with a movement of its finger and turned its body to allow them to affix its arm.

Milord really needs to get a move on. Malleus suspected that the transformation would take place immediately, as soon as the limb had been adjusted. He tried to reach the agent once more, but no answer was forthcoming.

Whether this was a foreign entity or not, any deity who had to rely on people to bring about their resurrection couldn't possess much power at all.

Or perhaps its full power is only fulfilled when it's complete? Malleus shifted a little further forward.

He was barely twenty-five feet away from the statue now.

The men and women would notice him immediately if he left his hiding place, and this fossilised entity made matters worse as his coarse, weather-beaten face was pointing directly at him.

Nevertheless, he'd have to intervene. He was particularly concerned about those unknown astral symbols.

He was certain that Milord and her team were in reach, and waiting because they still thought he was bluffing. If Malleus made *no* attempt to stop whatever it was the group was doing, they'd definitely consider their distrust of his message justified.

He slid out from under the edge of the platform and stayed crouched down in the shadows, packing away his Cobray and holding the axe in his right hand.

Twenty-five feet was certainly far enough away. Added to that were eleven fanatical opponents, each with automatic weaponry

– Uzis and MP5s, if he was not mistaken – with the potential for hundreds of deaths in their magazines.

The women lifted the stone arm and guided it with great reverence towards where it had broken off, just below the shoulder. Small arcs of lightning flitted back and forth between the arm fragment and the statue itself, exchanging and transferring increasingly violent energy. The symbols on its stony skin darkened, before beginning to glow with a yellowy-green tinge.

Malleus could see the fingers on its loose arm moving, forming a fist and stretching out as if to test that they still worked. Stone turned to flesh from the head down, even though the arm was not yet resting in its correct position.

The singing swelled yet further, penetrating the hue and cry of the wind. Malleus couldn't make out anything; the words didn't appear to belong to any language currently spoken.

St Elmo's fire appeared abruptly on the masts and parabolic antennae, the flames growing longer and stretching out before arcing back and bowing before the new god who stood in their midst.

The women let go of the arm and fell to their knees in front of the entity.

At the same time, the fiery offshoots of blue light smashed back into the entity. The symbols flared brightly as stone became flesh, armour, skin and hair.

The being emitted a mighty roar of triumph, causing the roof to judder while the gravel danced with a macabre, exultant rattle. Only its face remained battered and bruised, with its eyes rolling wildly and a maniacal grimace.

At least now the Kami will be well aware that there's a new kid on the block. Malleus swallowed hard.

His mind was made up.

He stood tall and took two or three quick steps while the men were still occupied with their act of worship.

Be you an unknown god or not. Malleus wielded the axe high above his head and swung it around behind his back so as to hurl it with all his might at this being who so basked in the glow of St Elmo's fire, savouring his rebirth. *There are far too many of you already.*

Celtica (France), Paris-Lutetia, November 2019

Feeling a fair bit calmer now – it's a good feeling.

So, here's the plan: grab the eighties woman. Not today, but tomorrow. Then my quarry will receive his punishment and my message, through her. But who knows, maybe I'll think of something better.

I fucking hate losing my mind.

It's rather nice here in this café.

Celtica. Haven't been here for an eternity. Why's that, though? Ah yes, because I can't stand the language. And as soon as you start speaking English they spit in your coffee. I know them all too well, these frogs. New gods, old habits.

Nothing through from his PDA. He's completely cut me off.

Ah, perhaps not! Looks like I've got a signal. Distorted though, as if it's been jammed. Nope, nothing I can use. Just looks like a system test. I've lost all access, to his servers and everything else.

His friend must be quite the tinkerer. Admittedly a rather insane one, though. I still haven't got a clue what sort of components he fitted to that thing. But one thing's for certain: they're not of this Earth, the old Earth. I'd bet the life of this fucking useless waiter on it.

There he is again. Yes, I know, table turnover.

'Monsieur, voulez-vous quelque chose d'autre?'

'No thanks.' *And now you can fuck off.*

What can he be doing in Japan?

Something for Interpol, or a private client? What have I missed? And what am I going to do if he kicks the bucket out there?

I'd really hold it against him if he were to go and do that. And then of course I'd have to go and hunt down his murderer, if there really is no God.

'The bill, please.'

Chuck a bit of money on the table and away I go. Have a little look around and do a recce of Blondie's home. I'll certainly get some fresh information there.

So, once more unto the Metro and onwards to the banlieue.

. . . Oh Holy Mother of Fuck. Is this a ghetto?

Right, the banlieue. I've heard about these. Tower blocks of misery for the forgotten and the poor: a mixture of gaol and an utterly shitty life.

Basically, it is its own city that bears no resemblance to Lutetia at all. Tower blocks all the way up to the cloud; tattered posters; broken billboards; graffiti and meaningless slogans sprayed on the walls; unheard prayers. Private shops; all manner of small temples. It stinks of a hundred different types of food at all once, of incense, of filth.

Oh look, they've got a playground. What do we reckon the kids do there, apart from learn how to be street-fighters?

Yeah, there they are, down a side street: steel barrels burning. Ah, they're grilling something on them. Whatever it is smells brilliant.

I guess this is where my new best friend lives . . . oh fuck, hoodie alert.

Behind me, with his hood pulled down low over his face.

So you want to play, do you?

It'll be the last time you ever do. And that's a promise, whoever you are.

Nippon (Japan), Honshū (Main Island), Tokyo, November 2019

The axe whirled through the air, bearing down on the statue playing in the St Elmo's Fire, which was increasingly resembling a man with a deeply bruised face. The astral symbols were shining brighter and brighter.

Malleus' attack had succeeded in capturing the full attention of both the unknown god and his followers, all of whom had turned to face him. The singing had ended.

He drew his Cobray and ran to take cover by the base of the antenna, firing at the group while doing so, alternating between shot and full metal jacket bullets, which rained down upon men and women alike.

He saw that the axe had not struck with its blade, but instead with its long, pointed tip. The blow hadn't been enough to completely sever the arm, but it was now dangling uselessly at one side, and the top of the statue had started to turn back to stone.

I've managed to buy myself a bit of time at least. That was all Malleus could do for now; he threw himself behind the base of the antenna and reloaded the Cobray. *That should be proof enough for Milord.*

He knew he was too far away for the shot cartridges to inflict lethal wounds and there were still plenty of enemies to return fire after his opening salvo.

The familiar, almost chirpy rattle of MP5s was promptly unleashed; the roar of the Uzis was somewhat deeper, raspier. Bullets chipped away at the concrete around him and the grey dust rising from his makeshift shelter was immediately carried away by the wind.

Malleus could hear the being roaring with ire, intermingled with the panicked cries of its followers.

What on earth is going on?

He carefully raised his PDA to record what was happening with its built-in panoramic lens. Several men wearing clothes riddled through with holes were rushing in a wide arc towards his hideout. Three more were lying motionless on the gravel, while another two writhed in agony, unable to take part in the hunt.

The female followers were attempting to calm down the entity and remove the axe, but it growled and clamoured with rage, then stamped its feet and turned back to stone in its agitation. The roof shook in response to this violent outburst as waves of vibration rippled across the gravel – it was as if the stones were themselves swimming through water.

Malleus was pretty pleased with the result of his intervention. *But it really is Milord's turn now.*

Another volley of gunfire whistled over his head.

He hastily put his PDA away again and went to change his position. One of the control boxes, or whatever they were, looked as if they'd be a decent alternative. He should be able to keep his assailants at bay from there.

Malleus ducked down and sprinted towards his chosen hiding place.

He was spotted immediately and shots rang out after him, peppering the gravel underneath his feet. Sharp splinters of stone and shrapnel stung him hard on the neck and face.

He rounded the corner of the control box, narrowly avoiding the hail of bullets, and leaned against the metal for a couple of seconds, panting, before glancing around the edge.

To his surprise, the women were lying down in front of the statue as if their heads had been buried in the gravel – but in fact, their skulls had been crushed, just like those of the Japanese guards.

The axe was still stuck in the entity's arm. Two men were attempting to remove it, but it was roaring and resisting their efforts. The rays glinting from the astral signs continued to shine bright, but it looked like the St Elmo's fire was being absorbed.

This unknown god doesn't have much of a brain. He appeared to be wild, rampant and filled with an archaic recklessness that couldn't be stopped.

The symbols lit up with an audible hiss.

The St Elmo's Fire rose up abruptly from the deity like a beacon, chasing its way through the night sky and making it impossible for anyone in Tokyo – or indeed any of the Kami who happened to be in the area – to ignore.

Malleus shot back at the men who had followed him, succeeding in driving them back to the base of the antenna. *What is Milord waiting for?* He called her once again on the PDA.

Nothing happened.

The entity finally managed to knock the axe out of its body, awkwardly tearing off his arm in the process. The piercing cry of anger that followed swept around those surrounding him, whipping up the gravel into a frenzy and hurling it towards the gunmen, cleaving their legs from their bodies.

The stones also rattled violently against the control box in a seemingly irresistible force, and dents began to appear, but the steel was just about holding firm. A disconcerting medley of electrical noises could be heard from inside.

Alarmed, Malleus began to distance himself from the box, which had suddenly started to shudder and whirr. Something rang – an unknown ringtone – and it took him a few seconds to realise it was his PDA; he hadn't had a moment to change the settings on the replacement device.

Milord! He put in his earpiece as he answered the call. 'Please tell me you believe me about the unknown god, Miss Milord.'

'I do, but we're stuck,' came her voice, sounding strained. Shots could be heard in the background. It sanded like a second wave of fanatics had blocked their access to the skyscraper. I can see something on the CCTV monitor that you absolutely must to prevent, Bourreau. The beacon of light coming from the entity must be stopped.'

'That's not my job. You're the agent.'

'And you are an inspector at Interpol and have a responsibility to the people.'

'Yes, but I'm not responsible for stopping wars between gods. For all I care, the Kami can smash this thing into a million pieces.' He wanted to provoke her. 'You've screwed me over. I've given you all the proof you needed. Now it's over to you.' He was still thinking about his next move. 'If this all goes tits-up, you'll be the one responsible.'

Malleus looked back at the mast.

The entity's hapless worshippers were laid out on the roof. The stones had incapacitated them, either for good, or for long enough to stop them getting in the way.

The being continued to stamp around, undaunted and St Elmo's fire continued to pour out from it, rising infinitely high into the aether and forming a rapid succession of cryptic signs.

Cracks began to form on the roof from absorbing such powerful forces; columns broke off and crashed down onto the gravel below like a waterfall. Finally, even the mast that was overlooking the unbridled rage of the unknown deity began to oscillate violently.

'We've got to pacify this thing,' came Milord's urgent voice in his ear. 'Immediately! Otherwise it'll be an absolute catastrophe—'

Malleus assumed she didn't just mean the potential collapse of the tower or the mast. 'Tell me off for what I destroy afterwards,' he said with a tone of finality, and hung up.

He began to run, leaping over the increasing number of yawning cracks.

He didn't have a plan. The axe would have to prove its worth yet again.

Malleus came closer and closer to the erratic entity. The night sky around it had changed colour, as if the darkness itself were retreating out of fear. The sun shone from nowhere, compelled by divine authority and trying to reach the zenith above. One of the last universally valid laws of physics appeared to have been broken.

So THAT'S what Milord meant. Malleus grabbed the axe lying on the ground. The handle had been snapped in half. No less than thirty feet separated him from his target. As long as the god continued to ignore him, he'd have a chance. He liked it when people underestimated him.

We mortals are more resourceful than you think. Malleus jumped over the dead bodies and ran forwards, the blade aimed directly at the stone neck of the statue.

Celtica (France), Paris-Banlieue, November 2019

Turn off to the left, through this Asian archway. It looks rather DIY, this thing does. They've really tried to build some sort of Indochinatown here; over there we've got . . . Okay, I've no idea what that's supposed to be. Something Tunisian, maybe?

The shadows between the makeshift garages or whatever are more than suitable for my purposes here.

APB, silencer and crouch down. I'm already reaping the rewards from the night-vision function on these glasses.

Now, where are you hiding?

. . .

. .

.

Have I lost him?

'So, are you just some sick fuck who likes to stalk women, or do you have a special interest in Madame Lagrande?'

Bugger. The cold pinch in the back of my neck appears to be from a muzzle.

'Now slowly raise your arms and lean up against the wall.' *The man laughs in surprise.* 'Oh, an APB? Large one, top end. I didn't know you could still get those.'

Not a cop then. A friend of my prey?

Right, up we get slowly; he's in for it now.

He reaches for the Stechkin and – here we go: swivel and dig in with your elbows . . . BANG!

The prick actually pulled the trigger! What a noise it made as well – my left's ear ringing and I can't hear a thing. I turn dizzily in the direction of his balls.

But he kicks my attack to one side; the sole of his boot slams into my stomach and catapults me across the bonnets of the cars around us.

Land in a sea of mopeds, turn over some crates as I fall and sink straight in among them. The jungle of handlebars and spokes grabs hold of me; I'm mercilessly entangled in them now. Glasses gone. APB gone. Fuck it!

He kneels on the car bonnet half-over me, looking like a fucking Jawa from Star Wars *with his hood still down, albeit one who's been to the gym a bit.*

Coeus will be pleased,' *he said, holding up his hand with MY fucking gun!* 'Here, let me show you just how it feels.'

I'm greeted by the sound of two muffled pops.

Small, fiery termites with pointed, glowing teeth bite me violently on the shoulder and in my side. This prick has actually shot me with my own weapon!

I lift my right leg, twist myself around and make as if to escape. Mopeds fall all around me, clattering to the ground. Their owners will be back soon. I've got to get out of here. Hopefully there's a camera up there somewhere . . .

'Oh, don't you worry, we're well out of their field of vision here.'

'Wait! Wait – there must have been some sort of misunderstanding. I only wanted to . . .' *I reach for the shurikens in my pocket and pull two out. Those ninjas really knew what they were doing.*

Now, throw them at this wanker. Yes, they've hit him!

He curses, slipping off the bonnet, and falls backwards between the cars.

I am a fucking god!

Look at him crawling around. He's lost a lot of blood as well. I am a fucking super-ninja! And I've still got a couple of stars left to play with.

Bosh, right in the middle of his back!

And bosh, one right through his hood!

Ha, it's embedded in his skull – it looks rather funny! Not sure he'll be able to get that out any time soon.

He fires wildly back at me; my own bullets ricochet around me and I'm struck again on the arm.

Dizzy. Really rather dizzy now.

It's just the shock from being hit. Better go to ground.

No, I can't lie here and rest.

I've got to . . . Everything's spinning like a carousel.

Sirens! Those Indochinatown dickheads have only gone and called the cops. There's no sense of decency in the banlieue any more. Before, they'd have just bumped both of us off and had done with it.

* Α Ω *

Marianne Lagrande hadn't been able to let it go. The enigma of these artefacts was like catnip to a confident, ambitious woman like her.

She was sitting in shorts and a baggy shirt at the small desk in her new flat in the same tower block as her old one. The window was open; the cool night air would keep her awake if the delicious coffee in her mug didn't do the trick. Her long, bleached blonde hair was tied in a ponytail.

She had the text files of the next books belonging to Hannes Hein open in three different windows, searching for codes in the list to help her decipher the mystery of another artefact.

Faint noises could be heard outside; it was quieter than usual for two o'clock in the morning in the banlieue.

Using the information Bourreau had given her, she had first checked the legend of Sedna, which was as sad as it was tragic. The Inuits clearly didn't like their stories to have happy endings.

Starting with the fact that Sedna's hands and fingers, which had been cut off by her own father, turned into sea creatures, Lagrande turned to the statements of various marine biologists who, together with prehistorians and ancient historians, had been searching for discoveries in the depths of the sea.

Included among them was a piece of fossilised ivory from a very old male walrus, which clearly predated the Miocene epoch.

I've got a carved Inuit harpoon-tip which is probably made from incredibly old ivory. There's no way it could have been carved by a human – it's far too old for that. If her theory were to hold true, this tip came directly from Sedna herself, perhaps as a present to the natives.

Unfortunately, Lagrande had to admit, logic didn't get you very far, not where the gods were concerned.

But if it were so, then this artefact was somewhat of an anomaly, and one that perfectly matched Oddua, with its polished diamonds and its inlay. They were stashed away together in the thickest safe at *Tresoriale*, waiting for her or Bourreau to be struck with inspiration about what connected them all.

Lagrande's anger at the theft of the golden figurines reappeared periodically, but there was nothing she could do to change that as she still hadn't found the culprit. She had examined the drawer and the entrance to her office for fingerprints to no avail. She had resigned herself to the fact that this case would remain a mystery. However, she could see how the next two artefacts corresponded to each other – and they really were *two* objects, as suggested by the order of the encrypted codes that she had managed to decipher.

'Tlingit?' She slowly read the translated word back. She had checked the code several times now, but the result remained the same. *What on earth is that supposed to be?*

The internet made finding the solution simple: the Tlingit were one of the First Nations, and spoke a Na-Dene language. The indigenous settlements stretched from the coastal region of southeastern Alaska across the outermost points of British Columbia and the Yukon territory. There were roughly twenty thousand of them and they had clear rights in both Canada and the United States.

An influential tribe. Lagrande was hooked. So two artefacts belonging to the Tlingit appeared to have found their way to Hein's cubbyhole. *Which ones they are, however, remains to be seen.* She drained the last of her coffee and stood up to brew some more.

The wail of sirens could be heard from outside; the police were moving into a settle some dispute or other in the banlieue. Nothing new or unusual.

Nonetheless, she went to the window and looked out into the depths below, shivering in the icy wind. She could see several people waiting for the arrival of law enforcement, then leading the four heavily armed officers straight to the makeshift car park.

She couldn't tell precisely what had happened beneath her.

She turned away and glanced at her rather futuristic-looking Beretta U22 Neos, which was loaded and secured on the table next to her laptop. The gun made her feel safe, even though she hoped she'd never have to use the semi-automatic weapon. Unfortunately, past experience had shown her that the probability of this being the case was very low indeed. The Collector wanted to get his hands on the artefacts.

And I'm the one finding out the similarities between artefacts. Lagrande shut the window and headed back to the machine. *For the inspector.* She thought about Bourreau and allowed herself a smile as she let her mind drift off in a way she hadn't done for quite some time.

Nippon (Japan), Honshū (Main Island), Tokyo, November 2019

The entity turned around lazily and raised its remaining arm in an awkward defensive posture.

Bollocks!

Instead of striking its neck, the axe clattered into its outstretched hand. The blade hacked into it and made its way upwards, splitting its forearm, wrist and upper arm before coming to rest in its shoulder. The limb broke off into dozens of tiny fragments that fell ungracefully to the floor.

Malleus bounced off the hard body of the statue and fell through a gap in the roof, into the exposed roof insulation. The gravel that had spread everywhere else was missing. Only a sudden twist of his body saved him from being crushed by the entity's stone foot as its sole crashed through the ceiling, which had become increasingly fragile. The entity lurched forwards and burst down through it.

No! Malleus was dragged down by one of the slabs that had been torn off in the process.

Things went rapidly downhill in a cloud of dust and debris.

After the impact he got to his feet, coughing and wheezing, and looked around him.

They had landed in the exhibit room, causing more devastation than the unknown entity had during its initial escape.

The deity rose from the rubble with a great roar. The St Elmo's fire and the glowing astral symbols had not been extinguished, however, and they snaked their way beneath the penthouse ceiling and rose through the hole above.

I'm not done yet. Malleus looked around him again. There was a heavy-looking mace in one of the cabinets to his right – he hadn't read who it belonged to; the most important thing was for it to do its job well when it was in his hands.

He quickly smashed the glass with an elbow, grabbed the weapon and ran towards this entity who had some strange elemental force that could summon the sun in the middle of the night.

The light of three torches flickered in from the other side of the room, though Malleus couldn't make out the faces through the backlight.

'Bourreau,' Milord's voice rang out, 'get out of the way! We've got something far better.'

But the entity began its stamping again, and focused its furious hatred on the newcomers.

A swarm of debris swept the agent and her colleagues off their feet; the woman cried out and then fell silent.

Malleus leaped to the next cabinet along and continued jumping from glass case to glass case until he was at head height next to the deity, who had no intention of allowing the hailstorm raining down upon the trio to abate.

You can stay right there. He flailed the mace around behind his head like a baseball bat. *Just like that!*

As the weapon struck the entity's head, the inlaid elements within the mace suddenly lit up, pulverising its skull as if it were made of weak plaster and sending fragments flying in all directions. Its torso tilted forwards; it was still solid, and didn't break apart. The St Elmo's Fire and symbols went out.

Night returned in the blink of an eye and wrapped itself back around Tokyo as if to promise it would never do such a thing again.

It is done. Malleus threw down the mace and hurried over to Oona Milord and her companions, who were buried underneath large pieces of concrete. As quickly as he could, he pushed them aside, using as much force as he could muster. The trio were wearing black combat gear and bulletproof vests that had all manner of bullets lodged in them.

The brunette was lying helpless and bleeding from her nose, which made him think she might have a head injury, but otherwise it didn't look as if she'd suffered anything too serious. Her white gold talisman of Aeracura and Dis Pater hung in front of her vest as if to offer additional protection.

One of her team had broken his arm, while the other had a torn-off piece of armour lodged in his abdomen; both were unconscious.

'Miss Milord, would you be so kind as to open your eyes?' said Malleus loudly, slapping her cheeks. 'Miss Milord!'

He heard more footsteps heading up the stairs and the display above the lift heralded the arrival of yet more people. The voices coming from the stairwell sounded Japanese.

Her eyelids flickered and finally opened. Her brown eyes looked at him inquisitively; with a groan she tried to get up, but then clutched her neck in pain. 'Is he dead?'

'You owe me a favour, Miss Milord,' he replied calmly. 'If my ears do not deceive me, we are about to be subjected to a little visit. You don't happen to speak Japanese, do you? As I really don't fancy being shot as a burglar.'

Her colleague with the broken arm had woken up. Clenching his jaw in pain, he checked the pulse of his injured companion, then shook his head.

The footsteps of the advancing forces were drawing ever closer, and it looked like lift was due to reach the penthouse at the same time.

'We've got to get to the roof,' ordered Milord, straightening up with a cry of pain. Long, dark strands of hair had come loose from her braid and shards of concrete, stone and dust were falling from her body. 'We can be picked up from there.'

Malleus rubbed his Fu Manchu moustache and suppressed a sigh. It looked like dust was emanating from every pore. 'Don't tell me you didn't discuss your . . . *intervention* . . . with the authorities? It's not a pretty sight in here—'

She shook her head. 'Didn't have the time. And officially' – she looked at him pleadingly – 'there's no such thing as the DEM.' Milord put one arm around his shoulder. 'Take me up there. The pilot will only move from where he's parked if he sees me.'

Malleus was unwilling to beat a hasty retreat, especially as he hadn't done anything illegal – in fact, quite the opposite. And he had his official pass on him as well.

But how would the Tokyo police react to me carrying out investigations without asking? He couldn't rule out the possibility of diplomatic complications.

'Let's go, now,' hissed Milord.

In the light of her insistence, Malleus acquiesced and carried her over the debris, up to what was left of the roof. As soon as they had taken up position, the wind swirling around them, an unilluminated helicopter appeared out of the semi-darkness and hovered with its skids barely above the helipad.

It was far too loud to allow for conversation, or any sort of explanation, so Malleus had to content himself with heaving the injured woman into the craft and climbing in with her, before turning to help her injured colleague in as well.

The helicopter immediately rose into the sky and twisted its way through the thicket of high-rises, concealing itself between the Geisha faces, karaoke flyers and beer advertisements. Tennō himself seemed to be personally looking out for them; he laughed and waved as if to wish them a safe journey and thank them for all their efforts.

It took only half a minute for them to abandon their zig-zagging path, which made for a far more peaceful flight. The interior light came on.

'So, everything went smoothly then,' the pilot asked over the loudspeaker, though he could barely be heard over the drone of the turbine and the rotor.

Milord took out one of the helmets that were attached to holders on the wall, placed it over her head and adjusted the microphone in front of her mouth. Malleus followed suit.

'Thank you, Bourreau,' she said over the radio, before taking some gauze from a first-aid kit and pressing it against her bloody nose. Her companion gave himself an injection to quell the pain. 'I am all too aware that you have just saved my life, along with gods know how many other people living in the city. But none of them can *ever* know how close they came to disaster.'

Malleus could feel every bone in his body. As the adrenalin subsided, so came the pain. 'What's the explanation then, Miss Milord?' He fumbled in his coat for the case, took out a blue-banded Culebra and lit it with a lighter and a small chip of wood. No one protested. 'And what agency has the abbreviation DEM?'

She nodded at him. 'Ask whatever you will. I—'

Malleus felt his PDA vibrating. A message had come through. It could be important, so he gestured to Milord with his cigar for her to hold that thought and took out the device; the glowing tip formed a vaguely recognisable exclamation mark.

The message was from Lautrec, his superior at Interpol: a new case.

An urgent case. Malleus puffed several times on his Culebra in anticipation, which certainly did not go unnoticed by the dark-haired agent. 'You're going to have to answer my questions rather quickly,' he said in a friendly tone. 'My boss has just despatched me to solve another mystery.'

'Do you need someone to give you a good reference?' she replied with a weary smile, then, 'Ah, no. I don't exist.'

'You do. But your agency doesn't.' Malleus read the message a second time.

The death of a politician had given Interpol great cause for concern. According to eyewitnesses, a god was responsible.

Under rather hairy circumstances. In Gomorrah.

Deaths were commonplace in the ultimate city of sin and debauchery, but they had never caused ripples of this kind before.

The death of a prominent politician could cause far more uproar than most. And if the witnesses were not mistaken, the murder was being chalked up to an entity who had no business being in Gomorrah whatsoever.

If. Malleus turned to face Oona Milord. My first question to you is—'

He stopped mid-sentence.

He remembered the young mother he had met in New Carthage and whose daughter's life he had saved.

Zohra. Who lived in Gomorrah. And who had that tattoo on her neck, the one Malleus had feared since that fateful night during the Great Change.

BOOK 7

Episode 7: Death and Debauchery

'Then the LORD rained down burning sulphur on Sodom and Gomorrah—from the LORD out of the heavens. Thus he overthrew those cities and the entire plain, destroying all those living in the cities—and also the vegetation in the land. But Lot's wife looked back, and she became a pillar of salt.

Early the next morning Abraham got up and returned to the place where he had stood before the LORD. He looked down towards Sodom and Gomorrah, towards all the land of the plain, and he saw dense smoke rising from the land, like smoke from a furnace.'

Genesis 19:24-28

Bible, New International Version

Nippon (Japan), Honshū (Main Island), Tokyo, November 2019

'I'll take you back to your hotel, Mr Bourreau,' said Oona Milord over the radio built in to their helmets as their helicopter surged onwards through a crepuscular Tokyo. Her black combat gear was covered in dirt and had sustained a substantial amount of damage, although the Kevlar vests she and her companion were wearing had managed to withstand most of the impact from the fallen debris.

They continued their journey through the gully of high-rise

buildings, the bright lights of the billboards snaking their way through the small windows.

Malleus Bourreau cast a forlorn eye over his own dirty clothes; he had paid a handsome price to his tailor for them but they were in tatters, unwearable. He now only had one spare set of clothes, after which he'd have to deal with the ignominy of buying off the shelf until such a time as his tailor could supply him further. The encounter on the rooftop with the unknown god had taken more out of him than he'd thought. Only his military-style greatcoat had withstood the confrontation.

The agent laid aside the gauze she had been using to soak up the blood streaming from her nose and set about inspecting her companion's broken arm; they had left the third man for dead in the high-rise. 'We're going straight to hospital as soon as we've landed.'

Malleus nodded as he puffed on his crooked Culebra, trying to push aside any thoughts of his new job in Gomorrah for the time being. *I need to get a lot more out of her first.* 'Right then, Miss Milord, let's start with something nice and simple. What is the *D–E–M*?'

'It's an authority the public knows nothing about. It's a bit like Interpol in that it operates across the continent, but it doesn't get involved in any deals with other authorities,' she replied brusquely. 'I can't tell you much more than that – I hope you understand.' Before he had a chance to react, she snatched the cigar from his lips, puffed on it briefly and gave it back to him.

Malleus failed to suppress a grin. *This will be quite the surprise for her.* The band was blue, meaning it wouldn't be life-threatening for a unseasoned smoker such as Milord, but it had a somewhat different effect compared to other forms of tobacco.

Milord's eyes widened suddenly; her pupils expanded with alarm.

'That is . . . really rather strong,' she croaked, smoke mingling with her words and writhing over her lips like earthworms.

He didn't bother to tell her that the blue-banded cigars were among the most harmless in his collection. 'The abbreviation, Miss Milord?'

Reaching under her seat to withdraw some bottles of water she replied, '*Deus ex Machina*.' She handed her companion and Malleus one each. 'I told you what we do in Rome.'

'I remember it well: you protect the world from foreign deities.' Malleus unscrewed the cap and took a sip. It was just what he needed after that tussle in the dust. 'So it really looks as if I've been doing *your* job.'

'You just got there before me,' she corrected him with a smile as she splashed water on her face. 'The god you encountered is considered by us to be one of the *salutatori*, which means something along the lines of caller in Latin. The astral signs glowing on his skin were beacons for other beings, showing them where they needed to go. We're still yet to decipher what it is they mean precisely. Our experts are on the case, though.' She raised her bottle with a nod of appreciation. 'Congratulations. You stopped a salutator from sending out his signal for too long.'

The helicopter banked around, dropping as it braked. They had arrived at the hotel; the vehicle started to land.

Something still didn't sit right with Malleus, though. There were far too many things that still needed clearing up. 'So the salutatori are a group of some sort?'

Milord nodded, dust falling from her dark locks. 'At least as far as we're aware. I wasn't entirely sure whether this entity was a copy or an original. There are *Salutatori* all over the world, and what they have in common is that they are all ancient and forgotten. That's why you hardly ever come across one of them, and usually only after excavations.'

The runners of the helicopter touched down gently.

Malleus looked out of the window to see a liveried hotel employee running across the roof to greet their guests. 'But they've got a following.'

'Yes, unfortunately so, and they want to set the salutatori against the ruling pantheon and liberate Earth from the grip of the known entities. They will not tolerate any other forms of divinity.' She took another sip of water. 'You prevented a new attempt today, Bourreau. And *no one* can ever know about it. Understood?'

Malleus saved himself the trouble of responding. He, the atheist who rejected the gods as a mere fantasy, a twisted form of government experiment, or some other as yet unknown explanation, had perhaps ensured their ongoing presence.

Quite the paradox.

He took off his helmet and replaced it with his hat. 'I'll send the DEM an invoice for my fee and my clothes,' he said as he opened the door. 'Don't even think about screwing me over. I'll notice it far more quickly than I did last time.'

Milord smiled guiltily.

Malleus stepped out of the helicopter. He'd walked only a few yards when he felt a fingertip on his shoulder. *Have I left something in the cabin?*

He turned around to see the agent standing close to him and looked deep into her dark brown eyes before feeling Milord's lips brush against his.

To his surprise he felt a momentary tingle coursing through every inch of his body.

She kissed him long and hard before moving away from him yet again. Her black hair fluttered in the wind of the rotor as she smiled at him. 'Thank you, Bourreau,' she shouted over the loud humming behind her. 'Thank you for saving my life.'

Before Malleus could say anything in response, she turned on her heel, climbed into the helicopter and pulled the door closed behind her.

He could still feel the velvet sensation of the kiss on his lips as he watched the helicopter take off. The warm, pleasant feeling inside him lingered for a while, spreading through him further before slowly dissipating as the helicopter disappeared behind the high-rises.

'Have you got any luggage, sir?' asked the hotel clerk loudly; he didn't appear to be thrown in the least by Malleus's haggard appearance.

'No. I'm already a guest here.' Malleus stroked his Fu Manchu moustache and headed towards the lift alongside the porter. 'Thank you.'

He went straight to his suite and took off his dirty, tattered clothes.

Milord's perfume still clung to him, which he hadn't noticed before through the wind and the smell of blood. It was a nice little souvenir but he'd have to wash it off – collateral damage in his quest to rid himself of concrete dust. Swings and roundabouts.

Malleus entered the glass-walled shower gratefully, taking in a surreptitious view of the colourful, busy streets of Tokyo, safe in the knowledge that no one could see him.

He let the water cascade down his back and began to lather himself leisurely, enjoying the panorama of a lively, modern city that had been saved from certain disaster.

Is this even being reported? He uttered a brief command and the television news appeared on the glass wall of the shower.

The various channels showed images of the damaged high-rises while reporters spoke in unison of a gas explosion, subtitles in English running across the screen. Drones could only get as far as the helipad, meaning interior shots of the probably illegal – or at the least, legally questionable – collection of artefacts would never be made public.

An elegant lie. Malleus changed channel.

A spokesperson from *Tanaka High Level Living*, the company managing the skyscraper, was speaking at a spontaneous press conference on the roof, in front of dozens of cameras, describing it as a regrettable accident that had been caused by human error when operating a open gas fireplace. Structural engineers were already working hard to ensure the stability of the masts and antennae.

Malleus's sense of calm was restored. His name hadn't been mentioned, nor had any likenesses of him been shown. Tokyo would surely never know the truth. At the very worst, a few salutatori might have guessed what had been happening on the roof.

He left the water running and, stroking long strands of hair out of his face, he returned briefly to the suite to retrieve a Culebra – this time one with a green band. In doing so, he realised that it was not just his wardrobe that was being slowly eaten away, but his smoking paraphernalia too. He was dangerously close to running out.

I really must contact my supplier. It was no easy feat to get one's hands on the curved cigars he required.

Malleus cut off the tip, lit it with a splint, then, with smoke rising from his lips, returned to the shower and opened up the nozzle, spraying water over his scarred torso. His thoughts drifted to cases, to the war, to battles he had survived.

Still puffing away, he watched the news, then switched over to look for a European station.

He let his mind return to the subject of his case in Gomorrah, where Lautrec was sending him to find out whether or not the murderer was an entity.

But he avoided concentrating too hard on the young mother with the tattoo on her neck who lived there, as he had found out in New Carthage. *Now is not the right time for that. Not when I'm on official business.* He had to keep private and professional matters strictly separate.

Malleus came across several television programmes that contained reports, albeit discreet ones, about the circumstances surrounding the politician's death. What was known was that, Gunnar Olof Hansson, the Home Secretary, had been killed four hours ago during a 'goodwill visit to the Swedish government'. It had been labelled an accident and great effort had been made to point out that Gomorrah's criminal investigation department had ruled out any sort of third-party involvement, though the precise sequence of events for this tragic accident was yet to be completely clarified. No more than that.

Denial in advance is never a good sign. Malleus knew the Swedish government would have no interest whatsoever in playing up the death. A murdered minister would bring unrest, and the more opaque the circumstances became, the more dangerous the situation would become for the state's leaders.

I didn't realise there were any policemen there at all. Malleus had the screen display information and images of Gomorrah.

Together with Sodom, it formed a single state, which was

recognised by the surrounding states. There was a consortium, *S&G Ltd*, which had undemocratic control over their destinies, and was turning a substantial profit in doing so.

Those profits had been published, and in 2018 alone they had secured a turnover of one hundred and fifty billion euros, with an estimated profit of thirty billion.

Sodom and Gomorrah were home to every imaginable form of entertainment: art, culture, concerts ranging from achingly beautiful classical pieces all the way through to death metal – but they also hosted casinos, brothels, clubs and various other places where the word *bizarre* could do no justice to the hedonism on display.

You could get anything here if you had the means – including things that would get you imprisoned or killed in other countries. The word 'taboo' didn't exist, and there were only a handful of laws; even death was allowed, if the victim had authorised it in advance in writing. The cities offered to cater for every conceivable fetish.

The death of the minister Hansson would be an even less appetising affair if it transpired that he had not exactly been an enthusiast of high culture and had not fallen to his death while enthusiastically applauding a particularly stirring aria from his box.

Absolute sin and debauchery could break the most honourable of men and women, or could arouse desires that ensured they would be loyal customers of the sensual cities for ever after. The power and influence of the Consortium grew with every new addiction.

Malleus could already see himself in a situation where he would be envied by no one. *No one at all.*

He smoked his Culebra gently, savouring its taste as he surrendered to thinking once again about Oona Milord's kiss, the likes of which he hadn't had for quite some time. It had triggered something deep within him; and he knew it would have a lasting effect.

Celtica, Paris-Lutetia, November 2019

Mon Dieu. My coffee's already empty. Marianne Lagrande had allowed herself barely any time for sleep; she was already up at six o'clock in the morning, despite having gone to bed at 2 a.m.

Before heading to the office she dedicated a good hour or so to the translation of the text about two Tlingit artefacts that had been stolen from Hannes Hein's cubbyhole.

Lagrande looked down at the items she had discovered.

A frame drum and a mask. The roughly twenty thousand or so members of the First Nations tribe had territories in both Canada and the USA, which meant they exercised a considerable degree of influence on the government.

Hannes Hein's notes about the two objects read as follows:

TLINGIT
Inv. no. 231:
Mask (A) and drum (B), Indian (Tlingit)
A) a shaman mask
•*spirit depicted – unknown or many*
•*material: wood, bone, string, human hair, leather (bison)*
•*age: approx. 800 years*
•*price: >40,000 euro*
B) a frame drum
•*cover: human skin (owner unknown)*

•material: wood, bone, string

•painted, used, still working

•price: >40,000 euro

Caution: both objects are on the list of cultural assets of the First Nations.

Origin of both: Tlingit.

A special case – once-in-a-lifetime. Frame drum can banish various spirits into this mask or can summon any spirit. Only ONE mask is needed.

From her research, Lagrande now knew why the artefacts were so unique: the further away from the Arctic circle they went, the less often the shamans used the frame drum to assist with their incantations or oracular activities. The Tlingit shamans were mentioned explicitly, along with the fact that they could summon and bind all manner of helpful spirits to their will. The mask was key to this: as long as a shaman was wearing it, he was, to all intents and purposes, possessed by the being he had called upon and could act as its mouthpiece. Each spirit had its own mask.

This combination of mask and drum could summon any spirit. She would first have a quick trawl of the internet and then look through exhibition catalogues. *I bet there's more information out there somewhere.*

The description of the incantation made for rather sober reading: the shaman would chose the spirit whose name he wished to invoke and would then go into a trance. Striking the drum, he would start singing and dancing around a large fire.

'Signs: eyes rolled back, ostensibly possessed, no longer able to control movements,' Lagrande said aloud, squinting at the screen, still reading as she went to brew some more coffee. 'Then he stops, stares at the drum and lets out a great cry. From now on his words will be those of the spirit he has summoned.'

A video call popped up on her laptop: Monsieur Bourreau, ringing from Japan.

She quickly accepted the request and while the video was still loading and the camera carried her likeness to the other side of the world, she felt herself turning red at the prospect of being seen in shorts and a baggy T-shirt with her long blonde hair plaited and resting on her chest.

It was too late to run away. Bourreau's face had already appeared.

'Bonjour, Madame,' he greeted her in a friendly tone. To her relief he was dressed just as casually in a kimono, even though it had to be gone midday in Tokyo. 'It would appear we're almost matching.'

Lagrande laughed. 'I've just finished my research.'

'And I've just saved Tokyo, so we both deserve a little comfort.' He smiled mischievously. 'In truth, I'm just waiting for my clothes to come back from the dry cleaner's. They had a bit of a dirt-related incident.'

'Aha,' she exclaimed, looking back at the latest text to be translated and the rest of the information there. 'You certainly pull it off, Monsieur l'Inspecteur.'

Her coffee had finished brewing, which was the best thing in the world at this time of the morning, frankly. She poured herself another cup and sat down at the kitchen table. Flats in the banlieue offered few creature comforts; quite the contrast to the suite she could see behind Bourreau.

'I've managed to translate information about a new artefact,' she announced with pride, and proceeded to give him a detailed report on her latest findings concerning the Tlingit. 'The mask and the drum have been considered lost for two hundred years. Some sources claimed they had been destroyed in a fire,' she read from one of the tabs she had left open on her laptop. 'Shaman Crowspeaker perished, along with his family.'

'And both objects suddenly turned up at Hein's. This man must have been quite phenomenal at acquiring these sorts of things.' Bourreau nodded as if to honour the deceased procurer and stroked his dark beard in a familiar gesture. 'Very good work, Madame Lagrande. Has Mr Crick come back with anything regarding my descriptions of our unknown collector?'

'You seem to be forgetting you're in Tokyo. In England it's' – she glanced at her watch – 'barely gone five. But I'll get in touch with him soon.' She saw a message pop up on the banner at the bottom of her screen, which she began to read. 'Inspector, I think I might have something that will be of interest to you,' she said, failing to contain her surprise.

'What do you mean, Madame?'

She turned up the sound on her microphone so that he could hear the speaker at his end.

'*. . . the French police have struck a blow in their attempts to defeat the extremist terrorist group* GodsEnd. *Officials were summoned to a confrontation in a suburb of Lutetia and found Ove Schwan, suspected to be one of the leading members of* GodsEnd. *Mr Schwan was reported to have suffered serious injuries.*

'*Mr Schwan is also suspected of having been involved in an attack on a museum in Mannheim, where priceless gold figurines from South America were stolen and several perpetrators were shot. Unconfirmed evidence from investigators suggests that Schwan had been carrying a Stetschkin APB, a Russian automatic pistol with special ammunition, which had been used to commit a series of horrific murders in Italy several years ago. Ballistic investigations are underway to determine whether this is in fact the same weapon used. What is not disputed, however, is that Schwan fired his pistol several times before being arrested.*

'The French authorities are also on the hunt for the extremist's assailant. Blood-splatter evidence indicates that one other person has been shot and injured. The authorities are reporting that their search in the banlieue is proving to be extremely difficult, and witnesses are encouraged to come forward with any information they might have.

'We will keep you informed of developments as and when they arise.'

Lagrande thought back to the police operation the night before. *So that was what that was.*

Bourreau's expression was stony; the scar beneath his eye suddenly seemed more prominent. He stroked his Fu Manchu moustache repeatedly. 'I've got to go to Gomorrah,' he said, as if he hadn't heard the reporter at all. 'A high-ranking politician has been murdered and they've asked me to work out precisely what happened.' He shifted forward, his blue eyes piercing her through the screen. 'Madame Lagrande, now you have to be even more careful than before. You know what Ove Schwan's arrest means.'

Lagrande gave a curt nod and reached for her Beretta U22 Neos, brandishing it in front of the screen. 'I'm well-armed, Inspector.'

'That's not a bad start, but we don't know what the Collector has up his sleeve.' Bourreau looked down and started typing. 'I'll ask Lautrec to give you some protection until we've apprehended the Collector. He'll also be getting a report from me about our findings so far. The artefacts are now a priority for Interpol.'

'But I don't need it—!'

'You don't know that, Madame.' Bourreau looked directly into the camera and gave a weak smile. 'It would be beyond a tragedy if anything were to happen to you.'

Lagrande's heart skipped a beat; she started to blush like a teenager. 'I'll take good care of myself, Inspector. And I'll keep digging.'

'Marvellous, Madame Lagrande. The least I can do for all your hard work and professional instincts is to take you out to supper as soon as I'm back in Lutetia,' he promised her with a twinkle in his eye. 'I'll be in Gomorrah in about three hours. Hold the fort until then, Madame. *Au revoir!*'

'*Au revoir*, Inspector.' Lagrande's heart fluttered once again at the thought of the two of them having dinner together.

Romantic. Candlelit, perhaps? He in a suit, she in a dress. Red wine, with a breathtaking view of Montmartre.

And then . . . Lagrande looked at the empty screen. *That'll never happen. A banlieue girl could never get a guy like him.*

She sipped her coffee and set about cracking the next code. She had soon managed to decrypt all the stolen artefacts.

Middle East, Gomorrah, November 2019

Malleus sat in his rented car, a black BMW i8, and started his journey from the airport to his final destination. The autopilot knew exactly where it was going.

The legendary cities of Sodom and Gomorrah were mentioned in several places in the Bible, the Koran and the Torah. None of them painted them in a good light, instead presenting them as hotbeds of decadence, xenophobia, depravity and corruption.

Malleus sipped his tea and looked out at the barren landscape.

He had done a substantial amount of research in order to prepare himself for this particular trip; in doing so, he'd discovered that Lot had not exactly behaved like a gentleman when he'd offered his own daughters to be raped. Strangely enough, in none of the three holy texts did a reprimand appear for such an act.

The cities, however, had been razed to rubble and ash.

But this was not what Malleus was looking at today, if one were to ignore the fact that the area remained as dry and barren as ever. Pools of water in the distance glistened in the sun from time to time, blinding him.

The cities had changed with the Return of the Gods.

It was not just places like New Carthage, Babylon, Palmyra and other historical sites that had risen up again. The impenetrable corporate consortium had bought the land on the Dead Sea and using the time-honoured tools of modern slavery and construction technology, had, indefatigability and downright inexplicability, created a city of bleak, fascinating splendour that had cast a powerful spell on grown men and women throughout the world.

It didn't matter which god or goddess you followed: everybody wanted to go to Sodom and Gomorrah – supposedly even entities . . . in secret.

Neutral territory.

Malleus read the rules of entry; its extraterritoriality demanded that there be at least *some*, albeit not many.

There was a large checkpoint through which every visitor had to pass before entering the cities for security checks, bag searches, instructions and currency exchange – Sodom and Gomorrah had their own currency, if visitors were disinclined to pay by credit card.

Weapons were forbidden, along with missionary activities. Anyone who was caught preaching in the name of his or her entity was subject to corporal punishment and exile from the cities.

Malleus was familiar with the rumours that the entity Marduk personally led the consortium *S&G Ltd.* If he recalled correctly, the Bible spoke of a King of Gomorra. *The perfect title.*

As the i8 approached the checkpoint, LED displays made it clear that he was to wait there for verification, and reminded visitors once again that weaponry was forbidden in Sodom and Gomorrah.

Malleus had his Cobray and Apache Derringer on him of course, and he had no intention whatsoever of relieving himself of them.

If the excited narratives of some of the visitors were to be believed, mysterious beings prowled the streets, and there were also stories of tourists going missing in Sodom and Gomorrah. On each occasion the Consortium had denied it heavily, and provided evidence that their departure had been recorded – but what had happened to those people thereafter was still a mystery.

Malleus took the wheel and threaded the i8 into the security lane for cars, passing underneath a station that resembled a tollbooth. Behind it, he could see access roads to underground car parks that would allow their guests' vehicles respite from the desert sun.

And all this took just a few years to build. Malleus looked at the spectacular architectural effect created by the two cities, which glistened their way inexorably into the aether as if attempting to conceal the gloom and corruption below their peaks.

He stopped the BMW, got out and nodded at the two men clad in camouflage gear and pith helmets, one light-skinned, the other appearing to be of Arabic descent. He pulled on his coat to cover his light robe and white linen trousers, which had come in particularly useful in New Carthage. The dry heat meant there was next to no humidity.

He put on his hat and sunglasses. 'Good day, gentlemen.' He presented his Interpol ID. 'Inspector Malleus Bourreau. I am here to investigate the death of the Swedish Home Secretary,

Gunnar Olof Hansson. I presume you have been informed of my imminent arrival?'

'We have indeed, sir.' said the man whose lapel badge bore the name *Spencer*. 'Welcome. We'll let the Consortium know you're here. Until then we must ask you to wait here with us.' He pointed to the i8 with a friendly, half-hearted gesture. 'Please could you open the boot, sir? My colleague Aziz will have to check your luggage.'

Malleus had expected something like this. 'May I ask why?'

Aziz went to the rear of the BMW and waited. He appeared to have no problem with the heat, nor was he sweating as much as his partner.

Spencer activated his headset and exchanged a few words in an unknown language. 'You'll want to be going to Gomorrah, sir. I trust you are familiar with the instructions for entry, if you'll excuse the formality.'

'Even for police officers in the middle of an investigation?'

'Unfortunately so, sir.' Spencer continued with the whole *I don't care who you are* act. 'I'm assuming your superiors haven't been so kind as to inform you that the cities have not signed *any* agreement with Interpol, sir?'

Malleus stared back. Lautrec had indeed neglected to mention that.

Spencer read the surprise on Bourreau's face and gave a knowing smile. 'You are welcome here, sir, but your presence is based solely on the goodwill of *S&G Ltd*.'

So it would appear. Malleus pressed a button on the car key and the boot opened with a click.

Aziz carefully unloaded the luggage and took it to the table to check its contents, once with an X-ray machine and then with his eyes and hands.

This also meant that he wouldn't have any special powers while he was in Sodom and Gomorrah. 'What about my service weapons?'

Spencer's expression turned regretful. 'I'm afraid, sir, that we'll have to keep them here until you've left these fair cities of ours. Besides, the case doesn't sound as if you'll be having to defend yourself against a horde of assassins, if you don't mind my saying so.'

Malleus could see Aziz taking out first the Cobray, then its ammunition, as well as the cartridges for the Apache, and placing them in a steel crate.

No matter how hard he tried not to, he still thought about the beasts with their ashen hair and glimmering eyes. *What if I come across some of those in Gomorrah?*

All that was available to him now was the glowing tip of a Culebra and, if he was lucky, a glass bottle that he could knock them to the ground with.

Spencer produced a thin plastic wristband, gold on one side and silver on the other, from a casket. 'Your wrist please, sir.'

'Why?'

'It's a guest wristband. All your data is stored on here and we'll be able to find you more quickly in case of emergency. An alarm will also be triggered if it is damaged in any way.

'No thanks.'

'I'm afraid this is mandatory, sir. It's part of our duty of care towards you.'

Malleus reluctantly submitted to his surveillance bracelet.

A silver helicopter chased its way through the city. According to the insignia on the side, it was a VIP Copter.

'Your taxi, sir,' said Spencer carefully.

So he wouldn't be allowed his i8 either. Moving around on his own was becoming more and more difficult.

Aziz brought over his luggage and presented the confiscated weapons and all their ammunition. 'Your Derringer, sir.' Malleus placed it in a box, which Aziz then shut. 'Please enter an eight-digit code, sir. This along with your fingerprint on the top of the box will ensure no one other than you is able to access these weapons. You can have them back, along with your car, when you leave the cities.'

Malleus put the keys of the i8 on top of the box. 'Don't scratch it, please. It's a hire car.' Lautrec would be hearing from him afterwards. He felt as if he had been thrown naked into the middle of jungle, surrounded on all sides by beasts of prey. Unfortunately, he couldn't turn down the order. *Interpol duty.*

The helicopter landed a few yards away from him, sending yellow dust whirling all around it.

A woman in a white business suit with an elegant cut and Far Eastern ornamentation alighted as if this were routine for her. She wore a brightly coloured turban on her head and a pair of reflective goggles that were enclosed on all sides to protect her from sunlight and sand; her pedicured feet were enclosed within a pair of sandals.

She moved towards Malleus with an assured elegance. Spencer and Aziz adopted a military demeanour and saluted.

'Mr Bourreau, you are most welcome here.' Her greeting was friendly; she had perfect lips and teeth. She couldn't be more than forty years old, but her elegance surpassed her beauty. 'You arrived very quickly indeed.' She extended her hand towards him. Gold rings adorned each of her fingers and he could make out traces of tattoos on the back of her hands, which looked both playful and serious at the same time. She smelled of incense. 'My name is Marduki. I am the Consortium's representative.'

Malleus shook her hand. 'You have my thanks. Before we take

off, would you be so kind as to allow me to bring my weapons with me, Miss Marduki?'

Her refusal contained the same degree of friendliness-cum-certainty that Spencer's had. 'I'm afraid not. No exceptions, Inspector. Not even for you.' She gestured by way of invitation to the helicopter. 'Come with me. You won't be staying here long, but I can promise you the greatest possible comfort and cooperation. The Consortium has no interest whatsoever in having this investigation drag on any longer than it needs to.'

Malleus liked clarity, but *this* sort of announcement sounded more like an order than a desire. For this reason alone he thought he'd take his time a little more. 'Of course.'

He forged ahead, with Marduki following behind him.

The VIP copter was designed to be just as home in the cities as in the desert. To his surprise, the interior cabin was fully sound-insulated, meaning he could have a conversation with the woman at normal volume.

At the same time, Malleus's eyes were fixed on the approaching skyscrapers, which were very different to those in Tokyo and London. They incorporated a mixture of modern, Mesopotamian and Oriental architectural elements, yet they never became too twee or kitsch. Gomorrah announced itself majestically with whites, gold, steel, glass and masonry; with domes and towers; with elaborate skyscrapers which, thanks to the open structures, presented a light, filigree effect as if made only of components that had been blown away by a light desert storm. The Dead Sea sparkled and glittered all around, making the whole place look like the perfect holiday destination.

'I see you are surprised. Perhaps you thought this would be more like Gotham City?' said Marduki. 'Gargoyles, black concrete, a never-ending stream of rain and blood, bodies in the street, that sort of thing.'

Malleus looked at her. She was still wearing sunglasses, so he kept his on as well. They observed each other from behind the protection of their glasses like poker players. 'Something like that, yes,' he admitted after a while.

Marduki smiled as if she had just won the first battle. She pressed a button on the panel next to the door and the floor turned completely transparent.

Malleus struggled to catch his breath for a second or two as his brain became convinced that there was nothing solid under his feet.

Beneath them passed the beautiful buildings where princes and princesses lived in opulence, but no tourists trod. Domes were clad in gold; imposing statues of desert warriors crossed scimitars with stylised flames: Malleus was unable to take in all the details.

Other helicopters occasionally flew above or below them – trips seemed to be popular. Then the VIP copter descended towards the flat roof of one of the tallest buildings; the helipad announced it as *Burj al Sodom*.

'Your lodgings for the next few hours, Inspector,' explained Marduki. 'Feel free to freshen up and we'll meet in the restaurant. It's got the best view and the best food.'

Malleus merely nodded. It appeared the Consortium had mistaken his investigations for a sightseeing tour. *I'll make them see the difference as soon as I start asking questions.* For he had quite a few of them.

Malleus looked at his luggage. It was also obvious that they had seriously underestimated him. *Not the worst conditions under which to conduct a successful investigation.*

Somewhere in Celtica, November 2019

'He's too fat. Too fat and too old.'

Where . . .? Don't open your eyes! Just try to stay calm.

There's some sensation, just a bit.

Am I chained up? Yes I'm chained to some fucking metal stretcher or a bed or . . .

'I don't give a shit how old he is.'

'Hey, have you had a look at him? He's clearly had a pretty unhealthy life. His blood results are . . . my dog's got a better blood count than him! And that mutt only ever eats shit.'

Two blokes: one with a deep voice, the other high-pitched. Empty room. Stuffy air. I reckon I'm in a basement of some sort.

'He's disease-free, no HIV and no hepatitis. So we can use him.'

'Sure, but he won't last much longer. Even if we cut him up, his innards are worthless.'

'It doesn't matter. We'll sell them anyway. Sorted.'

What the—? Oh yes, the shoot-out with that twat in a hoodie. The loyal little watchdog for the Eighties woman. I must have passed out and these two idiots found me and took me with them like fresh meat – like butchers finding a dead cow in a ditch.

'Okay, so let's make a list of what we can sell.'

'I'll do it.'

One of them has gone; the other's still here.

Click, electric fan, laptop. He's writing, muttering to himself. Faint music in the background – earphones, I reckon.

It would appear I'm just fucking stock for some organ dealers. I bet I'm still in the banlieue with the frog-eaters. Or maybe some other clan. Perhaps the Chinese? The Indo-Chinese? The Moroccans?

Banlieue.

No one's got any money and everyone wants something.

There are about ten organs that are useable as food. No one cares in the slightest whom they cut up like game.

'Yo, Yasin, my brother. Listen up, you little *ya gazma.*'

He's on the phone. Let's see how much I'm worth.

'I've got some top roadkill here. I'll send you over the blood-count. White dude, shot, no ID. Maybe a neo-hobo.'

I can hear the other bloke laughing down the phone.

'Afraid I can't tell you who he is. Found him after a shooting. It doesn't matter anyway: we'll take care of it. He's lost a lot of blood, but the rest of him is fine.'

He's pulling each of my eyelids up individually.

'Nothing wrong with either of his eyes. Corneas could be used as well. The full works. Do you want us to chop him or . . .? No? Leave him in one piece? Okay.'

I've been around the block a bit, but ending up the hands of organ dealers is the final straw. Fucking looters.

'How's that my fault, eh, *ya gazma?*'

A brief silence, he's pacing up and down; the other one's roaring.

'Yasin! Yasiihiiiin! Shut up! Shut up, bro, and listen: how could it possibly be my fault that the doctor's hands were shaking so much?'

Another short silence.

'Yes, and? We had expenses as well!'

He's walking around, losing control, pacing back and forth again.

I don't want to know how much they're putting on the table for me. Speaking of which, I hope they've disinfected it.

I'm being bumped off.

I swear they'll get no good organs out of me! They'll go through the shredder. Alive. I'll start with my toes.

'Understood, Yasin, my brother. Are you going to come and get him? Good. When – an hour? No, we need to make him pretty for you first. Wash him, disinfect him and so on. Yes we'll infuse him with salt as well. See you later.'

He's hung up, cursing. Now he's leaving.

'Hey! Hey, Kazam! Come back down,' *he shouts from outside.*

Eyes open, look around.

It looks like a butcher's: tiled walls, tiled floor, tarpaulin by the exits. There, on the stainless steel sideboard: surgical instruments; infusion welding equipment; dressing material; ice bags; two chests, probably full of ice cubes.

And what about me?

Lying on a metal welding table in handcuffs. Naked. I'll tear these wankers limb from limb. And they've sewn me up like beginners. Fuck's sake, that's going to leave some serious scars!

Stay calm. Think.

THINK!

One hour.

One hour, that's what he said

I've got to think of something.

I always think of something.

...

I'VE GOT TO THINK OF SOMETHING!

Middle East, Gomorrah, November 2019

'You haven't made me too many promises, Miss Marduki.' Malleus sat with her at a restaurant table, right by the window, overlooking the city from a great height.

Even though he could hear the chink of crockery and the hum of conversation from the other guests in the adjacent room, their privacy was guaranteed. The waiter had assured them that the other ten tables would remain empty until the meeting had finished. Marduki had considered that a matter of course. Members of the Consortium appeared to be allowed anything they wanted.

Even things that would be bad for business.

Marduki smiled at him.

The woman had taken off her turban, revealing short black hair. She had left the sunglasses on, however. An eye condition, she explained.

Malleus thought she wanted to stop him being able to read her expression. The pupils and muscles around the eyes could betray an awful lot, regardless of body language. Anyone who feared being read hid their facial expressions.

She had chosen a light meal: soup with hummus, accompanied by oven-baked bread and followed by fresh figs with a side of caramelised nuts and an orange-honey sauce: as simple as it was stunning.

This did not stop Malleus from withdrawing a Culebra from his case. Green band. He opened the tip, lit the chip and then the cigar.

With a puff he brought the tip to a glow; the cloud of smoke appeared to be trying to draw the skyline of Gomorrah.

Marduki followed his elegantly steady hand movements. 'Those are extraordinarily exquisite works of art,' she said, casting an expert eye over the smoke, fanning it and breathing it in deeply. 'That's something we could use in our club lounge.'

'Now that I do believe.' Malleus pushed the smoke towards the ceiling, where it formed a large squiggle. 'But they've been made for me alone.'

'Is that so?' Her right eyebrow shot upwards. 'By whom?'

He gave her a defiant smile. 'Interpol hasn't sent me here so we can talk about Culebras.'

'I'd much rather do that.'

'And that I can believe as well.' Malleus pointed the glowing tip towards Marduki. 'Tell me what happened – because I hardly think there are any *official* cameras at the place where Home Secretary Hansson was staying.'

Her eyebrows retreated behind her glasses. 'Hansson was always a highly welcome guest with us. He had finished a good-will visit in Tehran with Shahenshah Khishur, then come here to reaffirm his friendship with Gomorrah.'

'You've already cleared up the crime scene,' concluded Malleus in a mocking tone.

'We couldn't just leave the scene of the *accident* as it was,' Marduki emphasised, her voice as fine as silk but as cold as ice. 'The death of our good friend is regrettable, but life goes on – especially in these two cities of ours.'

'Turnover and profit,' came Malleus' corrosive response.

'*Life* goes on,' she insisted, her tone now friendly as she took out her phone and pressed a series of buttons; his PDA vibrated shortly thereafter. 'Of course we took photographs of everything; the measurements and documentation were all done by the book. We suspected we'd receive a request from Sweden to have an external investigator sent over.'

Malleus produced the device and looked at the bundle of data she had just sent over: pictures, reports, even the assessment of a doctor regarding the cause and time of death. Hansson was lying naked on a bed, but there were no wounds on his body.

'He was suffocated,' he read aloud, looking at Marduki. 'I can see a two-finger-wide trace all the way around his neck on the photograph.'

'The tool used in the *accident* has been determined.' She gave a cool laugh. 'You know precisely what it was. But we have no intention of informing the public of the surrounding circumstances, not least the Swedish government and its citizens. That is, unless a highly ambitious investigator from Interpol wishes that it be so.' She folded her hands and laid them delicately on the white tablecloth.

A sex accident. 'Alone? Or with other people? Did he go full Michael Hutchence or did somebody strangle him with a belt for too long?'

Marduki snapped back at him disparagingly. 'Please, Inspector. Our people know what they're doing and what they need to look for in this game. Room service found him.'

'Room service?'

'He had ordered oysters, champagne and caviar. Nothing out of the ordinary.'

'So Hansson was alone in his room at the time of death?' Malleus didn't believe Marduki's claim.

'I didn't say that. His first appointment had already gone, and he no longer needed the second one,' she replied nonchalantly. 'On this particular evening Aphrodite and some African goddess started him off – I can't remember her name.'

'Would you please explain what you mean?'

'Home Secretary Hansson had a particular penchant for fucking very young goddesses, Mr Bourreau. From all sides. It was his fantasy. And he was also a connoisseur of various substances that aren't illegal here. Sometimes he'd just fuck the goddesses; other times he'd have one, two, three or even four with him. You could say his fun in Gomorrah was *divine*.' She ordered coffee loudly. 'He was one of the harmless ones, Inspector. Incidentally, women are just as keen to be mounted by gods. It appears to be a very common fantasy.'

'Just *how* young are these goddesses?'

Marduki gave a politician's winning smile. 'It doesn't matter how old an entity is. They do not inhabit a temporal plane.'

'I want to speak to the girls he was with that evening.'

She gave a slow, meaningful look at her watch. 'I'm afraid that won't be possible. They are working.'

'Then the head of your security service.'

'She's sitting in front of your, Inspector.'

Malleus wondered whether he ought to call Lautrec and request to be withdrawn from Gomorrah. It was painfully obvious that Marduki had been ordered by the Commission to answer his questions without actually saying anything. 'I'm starting to get the impression that you are actively hindering this investigation.'

'We don't need an investigation. Accidental death has been confirmed. Take Hansson's body with you and go,' she suggested as she stood up. She took the coffee from the waiter and drank it, standing. 'Come.'

'Where?'

'To the mortuary. Do you still want to see the body or not?' Marduki moved towards the door. 'I've also asked the maid to attend. Should you wish to ask her any questions, that is.'

It was clear to Malleus that his research was going to be undertaken in the same manner as the food offered to him: selective.

He stood up and followed the woman in her white business suit, once again noticing the intricacy of its pattern.

On his way to the lift, he looked out of the window into the crepuscular city that appeared to be straining to catch every last ray of the ever-dwindling sun, as if to mirror its descent into secrecy and mystery.

The architecture was clear in the daylight, but now it was beginning to cast shadows, out of which something dangerous, something seductive, something fascinating could arise. This was a city of Dorian Gray and Mr Hyde, where the glow of a thousand lights radiated on every face scuttling through its sunken streets. By night, even less would be as it appeared. Night would make every light cast a shadow.

Malleus stood spellbound, watching as the great red sun disappeared, heralding a wild, undisciplined, unrestrained place, as light from stars and moon alike lit the streets. He even thought he could hear the strains of classical music swelling up from some unknown location, as if it were the soundtrack to Gomorrah's descent into night.

Highly impressive. Malleus tore himself away after a while and headed to the lift.

Marduki was holding the door open for him with a knowing smile. She would have seen this fascination hundreds – thousands – of times on visitors' faces. No one could be immune to it.

They rode in silence all the way down to the basement, where they got into a small electric car, which Marduki steered through a labyrinthine system of tunnels.

'This is something we learned from the cities that have a lot of snow in winter and have to contend with temperatures in the minus degrees,' she explained. 'For us, having a maintenance level allows employees to get from A to B without tourists and guests seeing what's going on.'

Malleus stroked his beard. Murderers would be able to escape easily if they were to use this route. 'Is there also a tunnel linking the two cities?'

'Yes. Logistical operations can be carried out far faster down here than above ground. We leave our guests to move around beneath our sun and our night sky without disturbance.'

'How well secured are the tunnels?'

'No one can pass through here without our system noticing them. Everyone who has authorisation to be here has a chip implanted in them which is automatically detected; they contain various levels of access,' she continued. 'There are cameras as well as retina and fingerprint scanners at every locked door.'

That certainly sounded halfway safe.

It wasn't surprising that Sodom and Gomorrah would have the best surveillance network in the world. First of all, they needed to keep an eye on their guests when they descended into total debauchery so that they didn't pose too much of a threat to themselves and others; secondly it was always useful to have something to blackmail people with; thirdly, they were always vulnerable to shock attacks by religiously motivated fanatics who didn't like to see two cities that had been destroyed by supernatural forces suddenly come back to life again.

Malleus was aware of two spectacular attempts that had been thwarted: one with a tanker and one with an aeroplane that released its fuel while flying over. Tons of kerosene rained down upon them, but Sodom and Gomorrah withstood the inferno: they simply didn't catch fire.

'What about the witnesses who described an entity leaving the scene of the crime?' This was the weak point in her beautiful storyline.

'Just rumours,' she replied laconically.

'Rumours that have been reported by news channels,' he added. 'You may not see it quite like this, Miss Marduki, but the state of Sweden will want to know what actually happened in Gomorrah.'

'You know what happened, Inspector.'

'I *know* nothing whatsoever, apart from the fact that hummus tastes better than I had remembered.' Malleus puffed on his Culebra as interlocking walls whizzed past them, while red LEDs occasionally turned from red to green as soon as their vehicle approached.

'Everything else is merely what you have told me. The most important thing is for me to be able to verify these rumours: whether Hansson was strangled by one of your employees or by the room service staff; whether he asphyxiated himself or it was all one big misunderstanding; whether I can believe what the head of the cities' security service tells me. The fact that Hansson is a member of the Swedish government means that any participation by an entity has to be ruled out *or* confirmed.' After taking another draw of his cigar, he added, 'A *real* entity. Not some whore in fancy dress.'

'I understand, Mr Bourreau.' Marduki turned into a side tunnel. 'That being said, I still don't know where these rumours have come from.' She turned her head towards him, giving him a look that he couldn't interpret thanks to her goggles. 'I can only give you the photographs, the body and my staff. The Consortium is convinced you'll come to the same conclusion as I have.'

Malleus knew that the word *bribe* would never cross her lips, but a single suggestion of it would suffice; his wildest dreams could be fulfilled: gold, drugs, material objects . . . a tempting prospect for those of a less stable disposition.

Malleus flicked away the glow of ash from his half-smoked Culebra, which drifted off into the tunnel behind him; he put the rest of it back in its case. *Not for me.*

Celtica, Paris-Lutetia, November 2019

'Kazam? Kazam, where's the—? . . . ah, got it – I can see the key.'

The collection party is here. I still haven't been able to think of anything.

What else?

Naked, handcuffed to a steel table. Unless Father Christmas rocks up with a miracle up his sleeve, it looks as if I'm well and truly buggered. Ah, fuck, he doesn't exist any more. One of the victims of dechristianisation.

Stay calm. Breathe in, breathe out.

Four different stride-lengths: three men and a woman.

'Is Fatty awake?' *asked the woman.*

'He's got to be, surely.'

I am. But you won't get me to open my eyes.

'How are we going to kill him?' *the woman wants to know.* 'He's heavy. Must be at least 15 stone.'

'Yasin, you old *ya gazma*, you wanted him alive,' *came the reply from the prick with the high voice by way of defence.* 'We would have chopped him but . . .'

'Who? You, François? You can't even carve a fucking turkey,' *interrupted the other man. Definitely Yasin.* 'Okay, wake him up.'

Smack—*!*

Oh, a slap. Thanks for that. Really innovative.

'Hey, Fatty,' *says the woman, before I feel her hand on my balls, which she proceeds to squeeze.*

Fuck, that's . . . 'Get off, you bitch!'

The men laugh and the bitch gives my scrotum another tug to piss me off even more. 'He awakes, gentlemen.'

They're all wearing masks so I can't recognise any of them. As if that's important given they'll be cutting me into little bits any minute now.

'We kidnapped you,' *lies the wanker they called François.* 'We're taking you somewhere else. Then you can call someone for a ransom, okay?'

So you want to play, do you? Then play we shall. 'Yes, yes, thank you!' I pant. 'My family can pay you whatever you want.'

'Just a sec,' *said Yasin, sounding curious.* 'What family is this?'

'This guy kidnapped me; I managed to escape but then he shot me.' *I start to sob a little.* 'You're a bunch of wankers but you still saved my life!'

'François, did you know this?' *Yasin is looking me up and down with business-like greed.*

François shrugs his shoulders, then looks at Kazam. 'Shit. No.'

'He's just fucking with us,' *says the bitch.* 'He's just shitting himself about what we're going to do to him.'

'No, it's true! I . . . how much do you want?'

'Ten million,' *Yashin demands immediately.*

'Really? Is that all?' *interjected Kazam, still with a serious expression on his face.* 'We want twenty million, you old sack of shit!'

'I can get you . . . ten million, yes I can manage that,' *I say, and I carry on whimpering and sobbing to make them feel in control.* 'Please, just give me a blanket – and something to drink. I'm dying of thirst here.'

'Fine.' *Yasin gives me a friendly nod and pats my stomach.* 'No problem at all, my little tub of lard.'

'The . . . goods,' – *this bitch just gets better and better* – 'will fetch us at least a million. Without having to deal with all this handover crap. There are too many things that could go wrong.'

'Worth it for ten million, though,' *replies Yasin.* 'We'll check out who he is and take it from there. If you're dicking us around, Fatso, you'll die in more agony that you can possibly imagine.'

'Of course, of course,' *I say gratefully.*

'Good.' *Yasin looks back at François.* 'Give him a bit of Propofol to keep him drowsy, then untie him and bring him a blanket and something to drink. Then he can tell you who he is and who we need to call.'

Fuck.

'Okay, Fatty.' *The bitch has her hand on my bollocks again.* 'Tell me your name.'

François raises the syringe; Kazam produces the key for my handcuffs.

I'll think of something.

I've always been able to think of something.

...

I'VE GOT TO THINK OF SOMETHING!

Middle East, Gomorrah, November 2019

Malleus looked around the lavish hotel room where Gunnar Olof Hansson had died. The suite was adorned with velvet, silk, ebony, hand-woven carpets, crystal chandeliers, a king-size bed; luxury down to the finest detail exuded from every inch of the room. He removed his shoes and arranged them neatly by the entrance.

Examining the corpse had proved to be a fruitless endeavour; likewise his questioning of the room-service girl – she had found the body on the bed with a belt tied around his neck and to the bedstead. The discovery didn't appear to have had much of an effect on her; there were obviously far worse things to stumble upon in hotel rooms in Gomorrah.

Marduki sat at the desk reading incoming messages on her phone. She appeared to be managing the whole night operation, meting out instructions, praise and admonition to her security team. There seemed to be a lot to regulate to ensure their guests experienced the services they had booked. She conducted her calls in a language Malleus couldn't understand.

It was fundamentally of no interest to him; his task here was solely to ascertain whether an entity had been involved in this affair or not.

But that might not be possible. He looked over at his dark-haired overseer. *She's obstructing me at every turn.*

He could feel his Apache Derringer in his coat pocket; he had reassembled it in his room from the parts he had dismantled and stashed in his suitcase. The cartridges were hidden in the heels of his shoes. So at least he didn't have to go around Gomorrah completely unarmed.

Malleus knew there'd be no more clues available to him in this room. The cleaners had done an excellent job; there was no dust, no specks of dirt, not a hint of bodily fluid left behind by their ill-fated guest.

He looked at the rows of windows of the surrounding skyscrapers.

You'd be able to get a good view of Hansson's suite from there. The City of Sin was more likely to play host to eavesdroppers and peeping Toms than anywhere else – and they almost certainly had the right equipment for it.

Good enough to be able to see through the tint in the windows? Malleus wondered what you would see if you were to use an infrared camera or thermal imaging device. He sat down on the bed and opened the drawers, going through the motions.

Nothing.

He flicked through the images of the crime scene on his PDA once again – and noticed a small detail he hadn't seen before. In the mortuary, the dead man had been lying flat, but in the photographs, Malleus could see parts of Hansson's back. He zoomed in further. *These are outline sketches for a new motif.*

The angle wasn't particularly helpful, but Malleus was able to recognise that Hansson had a tattoo: a rune flanked by gentle flames that produced a soft, feminine effect.

The sign of Freya. She was Odin's consort, also known as Frigg or Frija, depending on what language you were speaking. She was also the goddess of marriage and motherhood, considered the guardian of the hearth and home.

Malleus tried to make out the fresh outlines, to see what Hansson had been trying to fill in around them.

Or perhaps over them? The thought galvanised him and he stroked his beard with his finger.

Let's assume that Freya wasn't particularly keen on a prostitute wearing her outfit from top to bottom, so he'd be literally conquering and humiliating an Ásynja; let's also assume she would have held him accountable as a member of the Swedish government who had sworn allegiance to the Norse-Germanic pantheon – and in doing so, had discovered the fresh outlines on his back – would the goddess of motherhood and marriage have been reduced to murder?

Divine retribution. The oldest of all motives.

'What reason could a goddess possibly have to kill a man?' asked Marduki without turning her eyes away from her phone. 'That's what concerns me – assuming the rumours are true, of course.'

Malleus was not at all surprised by this sudden understanding offensive. She would act as if she were suddenly interested in finding a reason for the deed, before concluding that there wasn't one, and hoping he'd simply follow along. Consortium auto-suggestion.

Let's see how far she's willing to take this.

'What do you mean by that?' he asked, as if delighted to have forged an alliance with her. Two actors. *We'll see who's better at it.*

There came a brief knock at the door, which opened without waiting for an answer.

On the threshold stood a man wearing a white business suit, this time without any ornamentation, but with a black shirt and tie. He was about sixty, with a perfectly trimmed beard, which he had left a little shorter around his cheeks and longer under his chin, as if in mimicry of ancient statues or pictures. His hair cascaded in waves down to his nape, while his dark-brown eyes fixed themselves attentively on Malleus. Large gold rings adorned his fingers and his right hand rested on an ivory walking stick with a spherical handle made from silver and ebony.

Marduki froze, lifted her head slowly and immediately prostrated herself before him on the floor of the hotel. '*Namtillaku!*'

Malleus suspected that a very, very important man had just entered the scene. *An exciting development, or the second act in a farce designed to rid Gomorrah of me?*

'Get out,' ordered the man softy, strolling into the suite.

Marduki leaped up and with her head still bowed, pushed herself along the wall without turning her back on the unknown man, until she reached the corridor and fled.

The man was followed by a large animal that, at first, Malleus thought resembled one of the dogs from the airport ruins – until he noticed the differences. Its head bore part of a horn and rested on a long, slender neck that reminded Malleus of a serpent. The light danced off it, playing tricks on the eye, meaning he couldn't tell whether its body was smooth or scaly or short-furred. Its front legs undoubtedly resembled the paws of a lion, while its powerful rear legs were akin to the claws of an eagle. A barb gleamed through the ends of its tail with a magnificent tassel.

Welcome to Gomorrah.

'I hope this night is full of insights for you, Mr Bourreau,' the bearded man said with equal amounts of kindness and nobility. His beast sat beside him and cast a watchful eye over Malleus. 'I am Ramzi Abbas Hakim Amarud. I am a sort of . . . mayor . . . of Sodom and Gomorrah.'

Malleus rose slowly from the bed and pocketed his PDA. 'Good evening, sir.' He started to adjust his clothes without knowing why.

'You must be surprised at my sudden appearance at the scene of the crime.'

Malleus remarked to himself that Amarud had used the term *crime*. 'We are in Gomorrah. Surprise isn't on the agenda.'

'And you're clever to boot.' Amarud gave a light laugh and rubbed the throat of his pet, who batted his head against the man's hip, letting off a loud noise of contentment. 'The Consortium sent Miss Marduki because we wanted to ensure you left Gomorrah with a specific conclusion in mind. That cannot have escaped your notice.'

He remained ostensibly calm, though it was possible to hear resentment building up in him.

'I am here because I want to know what's *really* going on, Mr Bourreau.'

'Forgive my scepticism, Mr Amarud. The Consortium . . .'

'Is a body that has a commitment to business and *S&G Ltd.*' The man, who must have been a shah or a great leader like Alexander the Great in another era, placed a hand on his heart. 'My commitment is to *justice*.'

'That's not the same thing as the law,' remarked Malleus.

'In this city we have our *own* law, Mr Bourreau, even for immortals. And that is the law of justice, though it is rarely applied.' Amarud reached into his suit pocket and withdrew a black card decorated in gold and silver. 'This, sir, is your access card to anywhere in Gomorrah. Nothing and no one will get in your way, for precisely twelve hours. Then the sun will rise and you will leave our city. As you have already been told: there is officially nothing to report.' He placed the card on the desk. 'I want to know the *unofficial* story. Everything there is to know. Make good use of the night, Inspector. Find out who killed Hansson and report your findings to me. *To me!*' His voice darkened. 'I don't care if you are able to provide any evidence or not. Your convictions will suffice.'

Malleus tried to keep his astonishment under control. 'That, sir, is a very far-reaching authorisation indeed.'

Amarud ran his fingers over the horned head of his beast. 'No god enters Gomorrah and breaks its laws. This is neutral territory, where no one may be killed without their permission. Otherwise there'd be far more murders and that in turn would be terrible for business. Or at least that's what the Consortium would say.'

'You want to settle this score yourself?'

'No. It must be done strictly in accordance with the laws of this city, to which everyone must submit the moment they enter. Whether they be here in secret or on official business.' Amarud bowed his head slightly and at the same moment Malleus's visitor wristband came loose. 'You ought not to know this, Inspector, but I am a great fan of your approach. Please don't change it.' He turned away. 'The bracelet hasn't triggered any alarms. You're free to go wherever your investigation leads you. Until sunrise, that is.'

He disappeared from the suite.

However, the curious beast resembling some sort of forbidden genetic experiment remained.

Its cruel eyes bore into Malleus from the top of his head right down to the soles of his shoes, as if contemplating whether there was anything better to eat than a man who smoked too much.

Malleus felt his heart start to beat faster, beads of sweat forming on his palms, despite the animal's relaxed posture.

It gave a hearty yawn, ears stretching back behind him and baring terrifying rows of teeth that alternated between those of a lion and a snake; Malleus could also see two glands inside his mouth, clearly capable of releasing something unpleasant should the need arise.

Even the most half-witted observer could tell that this was by no means a cuddly toy. The creature could tear a grown man into shreds in a matter of seconds with its paws, claws and teeth, before drilling or cutting through him with the concealed barb in its tail. *Just like a priest of Poseidon in New Carthage!*

With one last rumble erupting from its mouth, the beast rose gracefully and silently followed its master, its tail swishing left and right.

Malleus exhaled deeply. He swept the wristband under the bed with his foot and picked up the black card; it was made of very thin wood and contained not only gold and silver ornaments, but also a very fine chip. *The possibilities are endless.*

He looked pensively at the photographs of the deceased Gunnar Olof Hansson on his PDA; the enlarged tattoo was still displayed on the screen.

In a new window, Malleus opened the politician's provisional bill, checking the entries that had accumulated, though the only items listed were generic terms such as *Services* and *Food & Drink*. No details whatsoever.

Discretion. He looked back at the card in his other hand. *Can I use this to throw off my mantle of silence? I guess I'll soon find out at reception.*

He set the timer of his PDA to ten hours, slipped back into his shoes and left the suite. He looked around the spacious hall. There was no trace of Marduki at all. It would appear Amarud had done him a favour and removed her from the picture.

He waved the elaborate wooden card and summoned the lift. Matters had taken an unexpected turn.

His mood had improved but his distrust remained.

Middle East, Gomorrah, November 2019

Malleus stood in front of the entrance to a tattoo parlour. He could have kissed Amarud's black card, several times over.

He now knew about every service Home Secretary Hansson had booked, which was a veritable list of misconduct, insofar as it was connected to the government of a Western state. Even half of them would surely have led to a resignation, had the gutter press got wind of it.

Of course everybody knew Sodom and Gomorrah had much to offer, but as soon as someone in the public eye turned up, people would rather assume that they were there for relatively harmless exploits: too much gambling; too many drugs; perhaps a couple of prostitutes too many, in true Gomorrah style.

The other options the cities could provide – where *other options* really did stand for *anything* – were not activities that one would wish to assume a public figure capable of.

The Swede had certainly let off some steam.

Hansson had belonged to the *harmless* category, at least according to Marduki.

Malleus would definitely endorse that viewpoint so far. *At least compared to local conditions.*

Malleus refused to allow himself to pass judgement. It was not his job to judge people for their preferences or inclinations. He restricted himself to the relevant matters at hand, that would lead him closer to finding out the circumstances surrounding the murder.

Using the little card of miracles, he had managed to track down the witnesses who claimed to have seen a goddess leaving Hansson's suite. The description didn't match the first two whores, nor the one who was due to meet the politician an hour later.

So, someone unknown; perhaps another prostitute, or perhaps someone more familiar.

At least Malleus now had a description, but apart from that he hadn't made many inroads. She hadn't signed in at the hotel and was apparently not one of the guests. Nor was she wearing one of the guest wristbands that recorded her movements – this fact alone led Malleus to presume that what had happened in the suite had little to do with earthly matters.

That brought him back to the tiresome point that there was no way of bringing entities to justice. Malleus would have liked to know why Amarud was so confident that justice would be done.

Too much so. Everything operated so differently in these two cities. Malleus stroked his Fu Manchu moustache and entered the shop. It smelled of disinfectant and air freshener, which combined to create a sharp, unpleasant odour. From the back, separated from the reception area by a series of screens, came the sound of at least four machines performing their inky duty on human skin.

Malleus walked up to the counter, behind which stood a young blonde lady dressed in monochrome – something you could only get away with if you were very young or very stylish; in all other cases it just looked stupid.

He could make out various slogans on a display on the wall behind her, including such gems as *I survived Gomorrah*, *Fuck 'n' Play* and *Once is Never Enough*, as well as silhouettes of the two cities.

'Good evening to you,' he greeted her in a friendly voice, producing the black card.

'Good evening, sir.' She pointed to the number dispenser. 'Please come in, take a pad and in the meantime choose a design. You're about' – her eyes wandered over to the clock – 'one hour back in the queue. If you want to use your own design, that's fine by me.'

'I'm not here for me.' Malleus showed her the ornamental wooden card, waving it like a conductor's baton, before placing an enlarged photograph of the outline of Hansson's tattoo on the counter. 'I would like to know what the complete design of this was going to be.'

'Of course,' she replied solicitously, calling out a name.

The noise from one of the machines subsided and a tattooed older lady appeared in a grey suit with protective foil over the top of it. 'What can I do for you, sir?'

Malleus showed the slim black card once again and asked the same question as before. 'Ah, him. I remember him. He wanted the old Frigg rune to be written over, sir. We made a booking, but after a few days he rang up to cancel and make a new appointment.'

'What did he want then?' Malleus wondered whether he could get away with calling her 'master embroiderer' but thought better of it.

'Something Aztec. Or Mayan? Inca? Cosiquetchal? Something on here, sir,' she replied, turning on a tablet and scrolling and swiping her way through until she had found what she was looking for. 'This one here.' She pushed it across the counter to him.

It took a while for Malleus to work out what the Swede had wanted tattooed on him. Cosiquetchal was clearly a joke, but it contained a clue: the Norse goddess was going to be replaced by Xochiquetzal, which translated as *maiden.*

The Aztec goddess of the Moon, the Earth, flowers, love, dancing and games, claimed his replacement PDA. *Goddess of women's craft-work and the goddess of the twentieth day of the month; twin sister of Xochipilli. Spouse: Tlaloc. Note: Tezcatlipoca kidnapped her and made her his goddess of love.*

Every eight years there had been a festival where homage was paid to her; they danced in masks representing all manner of flora and fauna. It was being held for the first time this year, and the date was drawing close.

A Swedish Home Secretary secretly getting a tattoo of an Aztec god in Gomorrah. Malleus stroked his moustache and goatee before removing the case containing his Culebras and choosing the half-smoked one with the green band. *Half of the penultimate one. It's a good thing I haven't got to stay here much longer. I really must stop by my supplier soon, as a matter of urgency.* 'Did the customer say anything, madam?'

'He didn't stay here for long, sir, but he seemed to be happy with the tattoo. He went on and on about this goddess, saying how much he worshipped her and how she was so much better than the others,' the tattooist recalled precisely. 'And this was all in ten minutes. A recent convert, if you ask me.'

The other lady at the counter nodded in agreement.

'Thank you. You have been most helpful.' Malleus was gradually beginning to shed some light on the matter.

The witnesses *hadn't* been wrong: the entity alleged to have been seen coming out of Hansson's suite couldn't have been Xochiquetzal, because of the lack of Meso-American features, so he had to assume that it was an offended Frigg who had punished this apostate who had once been such an avid follower of hers – and she did so far from home, so as not to attract attention.

She could never allow a government minister to convert to the Aztec religion. Malleus knew that the entities had a sort of inter-territorial protection arrangement, with the exception of a few historical anomalies.

If a man like Gunnar Olof Hansson broke away, however, rejecting the Norse-Germanic gods of his free will and without any conversion attempts, and even went so far as to praise and celebrate Xochiquetzal, well, that could easily lead to a rush of emigrants, depending on what the Central American entity had to offer her followers.

Emergency brake. In a moment of inspiration, Malleus stopped and turned back to the reception desk. 'Tell me, do you know this symbol? Is it part of your repertoire, perhaps?' He drew the symbol on the pad with a DigiPen.

The two employees of the tattoo parlour, who had been so friendly and open, looked as if they'd turned to pillars of salt.

'Sir, I don't believe the card authorises you for that,' replied the receptionist, her features pallid, as the tattooed older lady disappeared hastily into the back room.

'You cannot know that, my dear lady.'

'I can.' She pointed to the drawing. 'This is much older than the case you're investigating.'

Malleus opened his mouth, trying to form a reply that might

elicit the information he was looking for, but he could see the fear in the receptionists' eyes. He remained silent and placed his hand soothingly on the counter. *She's afraid of dying.*

He turned around again – and before him stood a pretty young woman with long, curly black hair. She wore boots, an expensive, high-slit dress made of dark red velvet, over which she wore a waist-length leather jacket decorated with appliqués and rivets.

While her face looked immediately familiar to him, it was the piercing green of her eyes that finally led him to recognise her.

Marina!

'Hallo, Herr Bourreau,' she said to him in her native tongue, with a strong East Germanian accent. 'I thought you might need a bit of assistance.' Her eyes lingered on the black card for a few heartbeats. 'I know where we can find someone who'll be able to help you with the symbol. Without having to flaunt your little badge.'

The offer from this enigmatic woman was rather tempting, but the last time he had seen her had been at a traffic light in Rome – and the time before, she was a nun in the Vatican, where she had desperately, almost obsessively tried to seduce him in the park outside. After he had pulled away from her, she had charged at him in a foaming rage. Her parting had made little sense: *Do you know what I'm doing here, for you? What that means? You have no idea! No idea!*

Malleus stroked the ends of his black beard. *There's definitely something not quite right with her.*

'A nun in Gomorrah,' he said at last. 'Are you the Fist of the Holy Father?'

Marina laughed gaily, throwing her head back and taking a step towards him. 'Oh no. I was *never* a nun. Just a little trick of mine.'

'To what end?'

'Who knows?' She gave him a provocative wink. 'To be close to you, maybe?'

Malleus could easily imagine the other half of her answer: *to seduce you, and urgently, at that.* But people don't sneak into the Vatican just for that.

He wanted to find out more about her, as soon as he left Gomorrah – alone – so he would be better prepared for her appearance in the future.

But as he was the one in possession of the black card, he thought he'd take a chance. 'Okay, let's go then, Miss . . .?' From the corner of his eye he could see the interested expression on the receptionist's face. She had already heard quite enough, and there was every chance she might understand a smattering of Germanian. *Let's get out of here.*

'Marina. Marina will suffice.' She headed towards the door and stuffed her hands in the pockets of her leather jacket. 'Let's go. I'll take you to the Wise Men.'

Malleus walked past her and opened the door, allowing her to go ahead at first before drawing alongside her. He placed his hat on his black hair. 'Who are you?'

The young woman chuckled and stretched out her arms as if she had just woken up. Her leather jacket allowed him a good view of her exceptional figure. 'You can find that out for yourself, Inspector.' She walked into the alleyway of the bazaar as if she had lived there all her life. 'Oh, one other thing: I've forgiven you for rejecting me.'

'That puts me at quite the advantage.'

'Indeed. I wouldn't be helping you otherwise.' Marina took the lead again as he checked their route on his PDA to get a better idea of where they were heading. 'Come on then, out with it!' she demanded, her green eyes lighting up. 'This is our next case together.'

'It's a case for Interpol,' he emphasised, his voice resolute, as he lit his half-smoked Culebra.

'One where, if it weren't for my help, you'd have run out of ideas by now. Just tell me quietly.' Marina appeared to have adopted another role: after the nun came the snotty little brat who had just as little in common with her true nature. 'So what's the symbol got to do with Hansson's death?'

She is far too curious for her own good. 'I still haven't found that out yet,' he lied.

'Aha.' Marina bent down to smell some caramelised ginger at the candied fruit stall and blew a kiss at the irritable merchant dressed in Arabic clothing, who began to shout after her. He laughed and waved her away. 'But you must have some idea about who killed the Home Secretary? You're basically the King of Gomorrah with that black card.'

Malleus looked at his watch. *For precisely another eight hours.* 'So where are we going then?'

'Oh, I'm not going to make it *that* easy for you, Inspector: you've got to follow me.' Marina laughed proudly, like a child on her birthday gazing obliviously at an area teeming with unknown dangers. 'I can read you like a book, Inspector – you know perfectly well what this murder's all about.' He felt like her green eyes were penetrating his pupils, absorbing his every thought. 'It was a *real* goddess, wasn't it?'

'That doesn't concern you, Marina.' He wasn't going to be provoked into a reaction. He kept his distance a little in case she tried to kiss him again. *She's absolutely insane. Remarkable, but insane, nonetheless.* There was no way he could possibly trust her.

The cloud of smoke above him formed a question mark by way of approval.

Celtica, Paris-Lutetia, November 2019

Kasam does me a favour and doesn't close the right handcuff before I get the full dose of Propofol in my veins.

Ha, what a fucking idiot!

I grab the key and thrust my clenched fist straight into his balls, haul my upper body up and slash the bitch across the face, making her stumble across the room and crash into the workbench.

François tries to empty the rest of the syringe into me, but I pull the needle out of my arm and ram it through his right eye, banging it in with my fists curled into a ball until it strikes the back of his eye socket. He gives a girly scream and falls to the ground, twitching like a spastic. The cannula and his grey matter can get to know each other a bit better. Oh look, is that brain juice dribbling out?

'Yasin!' *bawls Kasam,* 'Yasin, Fatty's escaped—'

Unlock the other handcuff, grab the drip stand and bury it in that prick's skull, bosh. Off you fuck – you didn't count on copping a right hook to the head from some bucket of lard, did you?

Right, feet free, get off the stretcher.

Fuck, the Propofol has started to kick in . . . I'm starting to feel drowsy . . . but I'll be fine. Take it steady . . . slowly.

There, scalpels and a bone saw. Decent combination, that.

Yasin comes down the stairs, sees me and raises a taser. He shoots, he misses! Wanker. Here, try and catch these scalpels!

Got him: chest, hands, face, bleeding like a stuck pig. He pulls the little blades out of his flesh – I bet he wants them out!

I'm up close to him now, and he tries to fire the taser at my face again. I hit him with the blunt side of the bone saw and he collapses like a sack of potatoes.

I drag him over to the table where the handcuffs and the bitch are.

Safe now.

Okay, clothes, let's see . . . ah, a doctor's coat. Better than nothing. Everything hangs loose when I walk and it fucking hurts because of that dumb bitch giving me a good squeeze. Still, I can hold everything together with tape so it doesn't rub.

Let's wake up these pricks.

The best thing for the job would be . . . ah, a bucket. With blood left over from their last operation or whatever it was. Stick a few ice cubes in, add some water and chuck it over these two little doves.

'What's happening? What's happening?' *yells the bitch, spluttering and spewing like a small volcano.* 'That's disgusting! I can't see a thing!'

Yasin is shaking, staring at me. This prick looks really angry, as if I'm *the evil one in this story.*

'Pretty shit, isn't it?' *I say, laughing; then I throw the coat to the side where the compresses are and pick one of them up.* 'Do you reckon your face needs to be sewn up? Where did you learn that, camel-fucker? You're just a . . . oh never mind. It doesn't matter. Where have you brought me?'

'Don't tell him anything,' *yelled the bitch.* 'Rutgar will kill us.'

How many times do I have to explain to people that defying me won't make things any better? It's a straight choice between getting fucked and getting double-fucked. Either way they're fucked. We'll see what we've got left in the tank for Rutgar.

I wave the bone saw around in front of her eyes for a bit. 'So, let's begin, shall we?' *I hit my head theatrically with my other hand.* 'I almost forgot.'

The disinfectant is under the cupboard: first, I disinfect my hands, then I pour the remaining two gallons over the two of them and head slowly to the door. There's a box of matches lying next to an overflowing ashtray – perfect.

'Right, I'm going to ask you one more time: where am I? Who is Rutgar?'

'Next time I'll rip your balls right off,' *screams the bitch, while Yasin makes a series of surreal noises like a Spartan warrior:* 'Aahuuu, aahuuu!'

From the staircase, I flick the first match towards the two of them.

The burning match swirls, phosphorous igniting with a red hiss, then goes out, extinguished in combustible alcohol.

'Where am I? Who is Rutgar?' *I say again, peering into the little box for a long time.* 'Sooner or later one of these will set you alight, as I'm sure you're well aware.'

Flick, hiss – out again.

'Where am I? Who is Rutgar?'

'Stop, stop!' *cries the bitch, as Yasin, Warrior Prince continues to glare at me angrily as if to kill me with his gaze.*

Idiot.

Everybody knows it's only gods who can do that sort of thing. And Jedis. Well, something similar, in any case.

'We're in the banlieue, in the basement of an old doctor's surgery. And Rutgar is—'

Yasin cracks his elbow into her temple; she falls unconscious.

What a colossal prick.

I quickly rifle through the bodies, stashing their IDs and cash, as well as the key from the most expensive of the cars on the key rack, before turning my attention back to Yasin and the bitch. More money, fine, fine.

Ah, a house key. I think I might pay them a visit, do a little house-keeping. Right, jacket over the doctor's coat, shoes on. Kazam doesn't need them any more.

'Let us go and we'll let you live.'

I laugh at Yasin and strike all the matches I can hold at the same time, then hold the bundle of flames against the pool of disinfectant, which promptly catches fire. 'Look at that. It appears I won't be releasing you, and you won't be alive for much longer.'

Turn around, exit stage left.

I've got to get back to my prey. That won't be easy now, without a tracker or his hacked PDA.

But I'll get him.

Yasin and the bitch are blending beautifully with their chorus of screams. Burning alive isn't a pleasant experience, after all.

I'd have gladly shot them but my darling APB's been taken.

But I'm out, free, released. And here's a BMW X7, all for me.

The journey continues.

The journey to him.

Middle East, Gomorrah, November 2019

Marina had managed to get him so lost in the darkest recesses of Gomorrah that they hadn't come across any guests or tourists, only locals. They could be recognised immediately by their clothes: dull and inconspicuous, looking like frightened mice scurrying through the streets of Moloch; this district contained no splendour or mystery, just imprisonment for the soul.

Malleus noticed that their posture had changed as well: some people were just hunched over, but others appeared to be suffering from misalignment of various bones; some stared into the distance with glassy expressions, while others cackled and giggled away to themselves, stuffing food down their gullets with alarming haste. Some had fingers missing or crushed; nearly every one of them bore scars.

They're the ones paying the price for the opulence of the cities and the Consortium's actions.

The high-rises all had blinds drawn, which failed to conceal the drab grey concrete behind. Huge lift-platforms, as big as a house, were picking up entire lorries and moving them downwards.

This entire operation is being held up by slavery. Malleus remembered the tunnel system that he and Marduki had travelled through. *Sodom and Gomorrah are built on blood and broken bones.*

Marina turned into a soup kitchen wedged between two lifting stations. It looked as if it had been squeezed in there by force. There was a long queue of men, women and children, all with vacant expressions and lifeless eyes; they handed over food tokens and received what looked like a mixture of ramen and hummus in return: it smelled of stale sweat and herbs, with the occasional hint of disinfectant and piss.

Malleus knew nothing would happen to him, not even here, while he had Amarud's black card on him. A vest made from two layers of Kevlar and a battalion of entities couldn't safeguard him more than that. But he still felt uncomfortable, especially as he had the distinct impression he was being watched.

As he passed by the hovel to catch up with Marina, he read a name on the wall: *Enkišar.* He looked up the name on his PDA for fun.

Enkišar

One of the doors to the Underworld.

The others are: Ganşir, Nedu, Endašurimma, Enuralla, Endukuga, Endušuba and Ennugigi.

Malleus suspected that the Consortium's slaves lived there, in the Underworld: in Kurnugia, the Land Of No Return.

Cynical, contemptuous – but that's not my job. But the atheist in him rebelled, insisting the world would be better off without *any* entities.

He naturally agreed with himself, but nothing came of it. Until he could find a neutron bomb to use against the gods, he'd find it difficult to eradicate them in one fell swoop. *GodsEnd* was essentially powerless, despite how eager they were.

Marina waved at him. She was sitting on the curb between three workers, with her beautiful dress pooling effortlessly around her. The legs of her heavy boots reached all the way up to her knees and appeared to be incredibly stable. 'They're sitting here.'

Malleus couldn't differentiate between the three modestly dressed Arabic-looking men and any of the others; at least there was nothing that made them look like Wise Men. They chewed their food in silence. *What the hell, let's give it a go.*

'Forgive the interruption, gentlemen,' he said in a friendly tone, doffing his hat by way of salutation.

'They can't speak English.' To his surprise, Marina began to talk to them in an unknown language, and they stopped eating and looked at Malleus as if following an inaudible command. Their eyes were filled with wonder and . . . compassion.

Then one of them fished some noodles out of his plate and threw them down on to the street. With the end of his spoon he began to create a shape from them, creating the symbol that had been tattooed on the neck of the young mother and on the ashen beasts from the trenches.

'*Namtarú*,' muttered the old man, before destroying the mark with his heel and carrying on eating as if nothing had happened.

'Ha!' Marina leaped up and linked arms with Malleus before he could stop her. She clung to him in the same way as she had done in the park at the Vatican. 'You're in my debt now,' she whispered to him. 'I'll be sure to call in the favour.'

How could she have known that? He laughed, puffing on his Culebra. *It's surely got to be a trap – Marduki's, perhaps?*

'They gave me the information voluntarily. And apart from that – what is it? A name? A title?' Malleus didn't allow himself to show how excited he was. For years he had searched in vain for a clue – and now he had one, thanks to the soup-noodle oracle.

Marina pointed to the PDA with her index finger, where the countdown was still running. 'Enter it.'

'Later.' He put the device away and looked around the neighbourhood with more awareness this time; it could easily have been used to depict an end-times scenario. *Or an even gloomier, bleaker* Bladerunner, *only without any flying cars.* Even the advertisements were limited to hygiene products, with slogans being beamed out in different languages by LED walls and repeated by quiet, whispering voices, all accompanied by a soundtrack of soft, beautiful music.

How surreal. Malleus knew that only a mile away was paradise, with its package-holiday and luxury tourists drowning in excess and decadence, all undermined by Kurnugia, the Land of no Return, which expanded at the same rate as the skyscrapers did.

He shuddered.

'Do I detect an emotion, Inspector?' Marina giggled. 'Is it not fascinating?'

It most certainly was, but his sense of duty remained at the forefront of his mind. *I've got to clear up the Hansson murder*, he instructed himself in an attempt to restore order, *safely and reliably – but how?*

He had no evidence against Frigg, only his assessment that Odin's wife had killed this religious renegade before his beliefs could gain traction in Sweden, and Aztec entities started to build a following.

Malleus assumed that the entire Norse-Germanic pantheon had given the murder their blessing. *This is a goddess we're talking about, after all.*

But he didn't like the fact that Amarud had said he'd act based solely on his word. *So, a murder without any concrete evidence.*

But logically, there could be no other conclusion.

He looked at the timer. He still had six hours, plus the two he had left in reserve.

This meant he could search for Namtarú wherever it might be necessary. It was possible that no one would be willing to talk to him about it, but they wouldn't attack him either. Shortly before the end of his deadline he would tell Amarud that he was convinced it was Frigg, for all those reasons.

Malleus closed his eyes; his inner sceptic didn't make it easy for him. *What if this was an entity masked as Odin's consort? Loki, for example?*

He cursed.

Marina looked at him in surprise. 'What's up, Inspector?'

I need proof for—' Malleus broke off. It had nothing to do with his insane accomplice. 'I'm afraid I'm going to have to ask you to leave me to my work now, Marina. Thank you very much for your help. Now, take yourself off to a casino, a massage temple or anything else you wish to do.' He tapped the pocket that held his card. 'Otherwise I'll have you locked up by Miss Marduki until I've finished the Interpol investigation. For obstructing the course of justice.'

Her eyes now flashed with green rage, just as they had done in the Vatican Park. 'Are you absolutely sure you want me to be angry with you?' She stole a brief kiss from him and leaped back, as if fearing an attack, then she let out a cocky laugh. 'I bet you one night with me that I'll find evidence before you.'

'Evidence for what?'

'For Hansson's death. That's the reason you're here, right?' Marina put her hands back into her jacket pockets. 'Feeling brave? Up to the challenge of a woman?'

A mental woman. The thought never crossed Malleus's mind, even in his worst nightmares. He had no time for this childish nonsense.

He turned away from her and set off back down the road from where they had come.

'Are you serious?' Marina shouted after him, bewildered. 'You're really going to leave me here?'

'*You* were the one who ran off last time,' he replied without turning around. 'Now it's one all.'

To his great pleasure she did not reply.

A great cry rose up from several voices all around; plates rattled on the floor and footsteps could be heard running over the asphalt.

Malleus whirled around.

He could see the older man, the one who had given him the clue, being dragged through the thronging crowd – he couldn't tell by whom, but he had to be strong and fast. Then he saw the strong, ashen back.

One of the beasts! They had come to silence the witness who had betrayed them.

Malleus drew an Apache Derringer, stretched his black card out in front of him and set off in pursuit.

The workers scattered apart like drops of water falling on a hotplate as the creature and the investigator tore their way through them, though they continued eating – they appeared to be more frightened than interested. This sort of thing must be a regular occurrence.

It's too fast! After a few yards Malleus realised he didn't stand a chance. The shadowy outline of the beast disappeared down a side street.

'No!' he cried in anguish, hurrying forward to look for traces of blood that might possibly give him an idea of its whereabouts. He wandered through the maze of passages, courtyards and overgrown streets that formed this city within a city. The slaves had even built improvised bridges over the roads, using slatted planks made from bamboo and wood, so they could move faster from house to house. This turned the district into a dark jungle where the enemy could conceal himself and from where he could strike at any moment.

Damn it! Malleus finally stopped, panting, and lifted his hat a little. He was inches away from throwing it away out of sheer frustration.

Then he heard a faint yet familiar childish laugh. His head swivelled as he searched around himself in desperation. *There!*

From one of the windows, about ten feet above him, he could see little Bala: the child he'd saved in New Carthage. She looked at him with her enormous deep blue eyes and waved, before disappearing back inside the room.

Wherever she is . . . Malleus started to climb over the unstable scaffolding, working his way towards the window in a matter of seconds and swinging in over the edge.

Bala was wearing a colourful tunic and was being carried by a girl of about twelve years old, dressed similarly. She looked frightened when she saw Malleus, though the little girl laughed brightly and gave a joyful squeal.

'Hello, you adorable ladies. Don't be afraid! My name is Malleus Bourreau and I'm an inspector with Interpol, as well as being an investigator for Mr Amarud. Little Bala and I know each other, don't we?'

The girl laughed again and tried to struggle free; the adolescent continued to hold her back.

'May I ask where I can find Bala's mother?' He showed her the card, assuming this would eliminate any difficulties. 'I need to ask her a few questions. Urgently.'

The girl's face changed seamlessly, becoming a vision of pure horror as a shadow appeared behind Malleus, casting the entire room into darkness.

It was much easier when the enemies decided to turn up one by one.

But the timing wasn't right.

And he didn't suppose the black card would be of much use to him here.

Celtica, Paris-Lutetia, November 2019

'So you've figured out who was going to buy the brick.' Lagrande looked at Crick the antique dealer through the video-chat window open on her monitor. 'But that doesn't mean we've got our unknown collector.'

'I'd be inclined to agree with you, Madame, if this were not the same gentleman who was making a bid for the Crown of Lombardy. And during my discussions with one auction house, they let slip that he was particularly interested in cultural objects from Africa, asking after specific statuettes.' His silvery hair shone in the light. He drew his strong sailor's fingers together so that the signet rings could be seen more clearly. 'Don't hold me to this, but I reckon he's an excellent candidate for our opponent.'

Lagrande was afraid that Crick would try to deal with it all by himself. 'Sir, the inspector told you some fundamental things about the man who had spoken to him. Have you matched the two up?'

Crick's face turned from overly confident to uncertain. 'Have you not been listening to me?'

'I have, and I agree that there are coincidences – no, similarities. But this isn't solid evidence,' she said with a friendly smile.

'Let's just have him arrested and we can find what we need when we carry out a search.'

'Supposing I *were* to send a team, or ask our English colleagues to do so, and your suspect isn't actually the one we're after, the Collector will be given even more of a warning about our investigation,' she replied in an attempt to assuage her British counterpart's desire for immediate action.

Crick pressed his hands together; she could see his knuckles turning white. 'I must say I'm finding it hard to agree with you.' With his hands clasped in front of his face, it looked as if the words were coming directly from his fingers. 'I'll make some more enquiries.' He took a deep breath, reached for a glass and took a sip of the amber liquid within. Lagrande guessed it was whiskey. *Or whisky.* 'I couldn't find the coat of arms – that's almost certainly just one part of a larger piece. The pyramid was of no use either. Your classic suspects would be the Illuminati and the Freemasons, but these symbols have started to crop up all over the place since the Return of the Gods.'

'I understand, Mr Crick. I've found out more about the harpoon tip, and I've come across some evidence of a mask and a frame drum that once belonged to the Tlingit tribe.' Lagrande was happy to have been able to appease him somewhat. 'A First Nations tribe that settled in the USA and Canada.'

'The harpoon tip of Sedna,' Crick responded immediately, to her astonishment. 'A myth that was recently the source of great cruelty.'

'How so?'

'Murder. Some little Inuit children.' He said, and started typing. 'It caused a great uproar, because they removed their hearts so that they could jab fossils of walrus-tusk harpoon tips through them.'

'They opened up children's chests while they were still alive?' A shiver ran down her spine as she felt her rage at the unknown Collector rising with every breath. The inspector had said that the artefact had been hidden in a heart muscle. 'But what for?'

'A test: if it was the same harpoon tip that Sedna herself forged from the first walrus tusk, using nothing but her hands and teeth, to give to humans to bring them luck when hunting, it would light up when placed inside the heart of an innocent child. Such an artefact requires a worthy sacrifice: the life of a child would be given to make sure the village had enough animals to hunt the time next, thereby ensuring they wouldn't die out.' Crick sighed. 'Sedna is not known for her kindness, Madame.'

That much was obvious to Lagrande. She cared little for gods and goddesses; they were too similar to politicians: a hatful of promises, rarely kept. But nonetheless, she prayed to Belenos – she considered him one of the good ones . . . or at least one of the acceptable ones.

'In the meantime, have you found everything that was stolen?' Crick persisted, warming the glass in his hand as if to coax a stronger aroma out of the alcohol. 'You've been almost unstoppable. I have a great deal of respect for what you've achieved, Madame.'

She smiled, and thanked him. 'It's just my job. But there's

still *one* artefact I haven't manage to decrypt – after that, we'll know everything the Collector has managed to get his hands on.'

Crick cast his eyes over a print-out. 'These objects are so vastly different from one another,' he said, still puzzled. 'Nothing fits together: Japan, the Far East, South America, mediaeval Europe, Africa.' He raised his silvery head and looked into the camera, giving her the impression of looking straight into her eyes. 'Care for a wager, Madame?'

She grinned. 'I suppose you're thinking about our ninth object?'

Crick nodded enthusiastically. 'A thousand pounds!'

She laughed loudly. 'Ten euro, Mr Crick. I'm not quite in your income bracket.'

'Please forgive the presumption. Okay then, *you* can bet ten and *I* will bet a thousand. Agreed?'

She laughed again. 'Quite the sporting gesture, Mr Crick. We have a deal.' She pointed to the pad next to her. 'In that case I'd better get back to work. What do you suppose it is then?'

'Something from Eastern European culture – a weapon of some sort. That's something we're still missing.'

'Then I'll say . . . a dagger. Celtic. *Pure intuition.* She waved to the camera and switched off the video.

She rose immediately and took out her handbag, put the Beretta U22 Neos into her holster, threw her jacket on over her white dress and left the office.

She had a date.

A date with the artefacts they had gathered so far, hiding out in *Tresoriale's* steel-and-concrete bunker. Lagrande packed a flask of her best coffee and a sense of fierce determination to wrest the remaining secrets from the objects: to find the key to all the efforts the Collector had made to gain possession of them.

She left the Interpol office building and greeted the two policemen following her at Bourreau's request.

Let's hope the two of them are just as good as the commissioner's friend.

Lagrande got into the police car and told the officers where she wanted to go.

Middle East, Gomorrah, November 2019

Malleus turned around, fearing the worst.

History repeating itself.

Before him stood one of the oversized ash-coloured humanoid creatures with eyes the size of his fist and a mouth that consisted solely of teeth. At least ten black tentacles were growing out of its rudimentary armpits, each moving as if it had a life of its own. The beast had placed them carefully, almost lovingly, on the window frame in order to pull it self into the room, but he knew they had the ability to crack like a whip; they could make light work of metal plates, let alone a human body.

The smell of burning liquorice assaulted Malleus's nose, reigniting his memories of that nightmarish evening when his friends and comrades had died. The black mark on its forehead looked particularly prominent against its grey skin; its white eyes glared at him as they blinked slowly.

Malleus was all too familiar with this approach; the stroboscopic effect was confusing and debilitating in the darkness.

'Get out,' he shouted at the girl, hurriedly tearing the Derringer out of his bag despite the relative absurdity of pointing such a short-muzzled weapon at a beast such as this. Even heavy-calibre ammunition had been incapable of stopping these foes. They regenerated, their wounds healing too quickly.

He raised the black card like an exorcist; it quivered in his shaking hands as if in an earthquake.

'I'm here on Amarud's orders,' he shouted, resisting the urge to turn on his heels, close his eyes and await a deadly blow that would end his life once and for all, to allow decapitation. He stood up to both this desire and the beast before him, who was slowly pulling itself into the room before standing up to face him.

Its eyes blazed like headlights; they were blinking faster now, though not yet as fast as on that fateful night. Black tentacles glided left and right past Malleus and the girl cried out as the door slammed shut before she could escape with Bala.

'You have no right to attack me, or any of the people in this room,' he shouted, holding the card out in front of him. Its ornamental decoration glowed. 'I am here in the name of Gomorrah.'

The beast opened its mouth and a voice that was neither male nor female rang out, a sound resembling an ancient, distorted transmission device. Someone else was speaking through the beast. 'Get out of my way, Malleus Bourreau, or I'll finish the job I started in the trenches. I cannot show you any consideration any longer.'

Consideration? A litany of questions raced through his mind, temporarily distracting him from the panic that had been sweeping through him. Images from times past began to occupy his senses, and he began to believe that he was back in the trenches with the beast.

'Nothing will happen to the child,' he demanded, holding out the card even further in front of him. 'This is just between you and me!'

'Amarud may rule over these cities, but I am the Vizier of the Underworld,' boomed the voice. 'He has no authority over me.'

'This is Gomorrah and you are subject to the laws of the

Consortium and Amarud,' Malleus replied, with more conviction this time.

The ashen monstrosity with its elephantine feet, capable of crushing skulls and bodies alike, stifened; even its tentacles slackened, hanging from its arms like thick power leads.

He wanted me to get out of the way. Only now did the first demand trickle into Malleus' mind. *This is about the girl!*

He glanced back over his shoulder.

The girl was holding Bala tightly, staring at the black arm that was trapping her against the door. There was no escape.

You won't get your hands on her. He would protect this little girl as if she were his own daughter – the one he had lost, along with his wife and the rest of his former life.

Thinking about never seeing the people he loved ever again gave him yet more resolve against his terror and panic.

'Why do you want the child?' asked Malleus. His courage grew with every heartbeat. *I will defeat this beast.*

'She belongs to a different place,' replied the voice. 'Now be gone, Malleus Bourreau. My servant has to finish his task. Your time as protector is over.'

The tentacles sprang to life suddenly; the older girl gave a shrill cry of alarm in an incomprehensible language.

Not while I'm alive. Think of Bala. Think of your family. Malleus unloaded his Derringer, firing in quick succession at the beast's glowing white eyes while it was still standing, unmoving, before ducking down and grabbing the side table with both hands. He discarded the pistol, letting it fall to the ground.

The creature let out a cry of hate and anguish, though its eyes had easily withstood the nine-millimetre projectiles. He took advantage of this brief moment of distraction to ram the pointed table legs through the beast's chest, with all his weight behind it.

His physical attack surprised the monster, who was unable to get its legs down in time to repel his attack. Its gelatinous yet powerful black arms lashed out, twitching this way and that, reaching for anything that would give it stability: lights, floor lamps, chairs, a chest of drawers; nothing held. The objects either fell over immediately or were simply torn off.

I won't give up. Malleus pressed his shoulder against the table, withdrew his pocket knife and flicked it open. The sharp blade cut off several of the tentacles, casting a spray of dark blood; they landed wriggling on the floor.

The beast let out another, more piercing roar and finally managed to balance itself by stretching its arms straight across the room. With one of its leg secured in this way, it rose to its full height.

Malleus stepped back, but the side table that had been viciously cast aside by the beast caught his waist and swept him off his feet. He landed on the floor and rolled over several times, narrowly avoiding the arm that had reached out to grab him.

The tentacle left behind a distinct imprint; the surface of the floor was torn apart, sending fragments flying all around the room. Small hooks protruded from its arm, cutting through the cheap laminate.

That's the idea. In a flash, Malleus crawled over to one of the cut-off tentacles and grabbing it with both hands, wielded it like a whip against the ashen beast.

The beast's hooks had an effect on its own body: with a crack, the improvised weapon left a long welt across his opponent's face, causing its eyes to burst, before he turned to the beast's stomach, which bulged and tore open. Its innards began to fall out; several inches of guts protruded from the screaming creature, and its tentacles started to flail around blindly in agony.

It can be killed! Malleus dropped to the floor, making himself as small as possible, trembling with fear and with joy. *It doesn't regenerate when attacked by its own flesh. I can kill it!*

The small apartment disappeared around him as the black, serpentine arms whistled around him, tearing down the very walls. Dazed and blinded, its coordination was gone.

The child! Malleus squinted behind him.

The girl had taken her chance to escape through the hole where the door had once been.

As the tentacles were flailing in another direction, Malleus struck another blow, aiming at the creature's throat. *Die!*

The arm hit its target, tearing away half of the creatures powerful neck and sending a clear dark liquid through the air, spraying against the wall and windows.

The beast collapsed with an agonised gurgle. Its tentacles withdrew, twisting into thick strands before retreating into their sockets. The ends supported the body on the remains of the floor like fingers. A reddish-yellow mucus oozed from its injured eyes.

Water sprayed from the dismantled walls, turning the dust into a paste while the bare beaten steel of the support beams gleamed through.

Malleus remembered the power of these creatures all too well. He stood up carefully and raised the tentacles to strike the decisive blow. *It's struggling with death.* He could hardly believe his luck.

Its fanged mouth opened. 'I spared you, Malleus Bourreau. I killed all the others, but kept you alive. And this is how you repay me?' cried the voice. 'I will not forget this.'

'I'd gladly do it again any time.'

The beast broke off suddenly and leaped towards him; its innumerable rows of teeth would easily enclose his head. Its tentacled arms broke apart in flight, forming a cage from which he couldn't escape. It had been waiting to hear his voice, so it could have some guidance before launching its final attack.

A shadow the size of a calf suddenly sprang up, throwing itself against the monster and pushing it against the cage, tearing it open, then landing alongside it in the corner of the room.

The impact was too much for the floor; the ground sagged under the weight of the bodies before Malleus could discern who had come to his rescue.

But he had his suspicions.

Malleus dropped the boneless arm and ran out of the room to look for Bala.

A great hue and cry was afoot in the corridor: many of the residents were attempting to get themselves to safety, while others stood in their doorways, gaping at what was taking place before their eyes. Through the confusion Malleus could see the little girl's carer and her mother, whose neck bore the same tattooed symbol as the monster whom he had just killed. The last time he had seen her was in New Carthage.

This time she was wearing a stunning white and grey evening dress, expensive jewellery and high-heeled shoes, a combination that was entirely incongruous in her current surroundings and served to make her appearance all the more unreal. She held little Bala in her arms and gave her a comforting kiss on her forehead, making the child's deep blue eyes gleam with joy.

Malleus made his way towards her, took her arm and pulled her into a window alcove. For the life of him, he couldn't remember her name. *Something beginning with Z.* 'Forgive me, Miss.' She recognised him immediately, but gave no indication of wanting to escape. 'I've got a few questions for you – about that sign on your neck.'

'You've saved my daughter's life. For the second time.' The greyish-white streak remained unchanged in her mid-length black hair, the narrow strip extended all the way up from the tip to her dark skin. 'Whatever you ask of me, Mr Bourreau, I'll do it. Nothing is taboo in Gomorrah.'

The way she emphasised her words led him to believe that she was proposing something of a sexual nature. 'I want only answers.'

She looked anxiously around her; the hubbub was gradually subsiding as the noise from the fight slowly ebbed further away from the flats. 'Ask away – but quickly! I need to go.'

'What's going on with your daughter? Who wants her dead? And what does the symbol mean?'

'She's the daughter of a rival god. The name of the entity who wants to kill her is Namtarú: it is his sign that has been given to me, binding me for ever to him. In both life and death.' She stood on tiptoes and kissed him softly on the cheek. 'I cannot say any more than that. Have a good life.' She turned around.

'Wait! What will become of you?'

'I've got find somewhere where we'll be safe. I thought Bala would be protected here, but it— I was wrong,' she replied, hurrying away.

'Is there anything I can—?'

'No one can do anything for me. Namtarú is Namtarú.'

'Stop!' Malleus followed her and handed her the black wooden card. 'You can use *this* to escape from Gomorrah. You've still got a few hours before it runs out.'

The young woman looked at the shimmering ornaments; her eyes widened. '*Amarud?*'

'Don't delay, Miss.' He gave her a warm smile and stroked

the little girl's hair, thinking about his own daughter. His throat started to constrict. 'Take this opportunity,' he said roughly.

This time she kissed him on the lips.

She tasted of fruit, of sweetness tinged with seriousness, of experiences that would be remembered for ever, of ecstasy, and boundless devotion.

'I would bless you if I were a goddess. But Bala will reward you one day.' Then she dived into the river raging beneath them to make her escape and disappeared beneath the water.

Malleus swallowed. *I still don't know what she's called. Zara?*

Security forces made their way hastily along the dusty corridor, their golden armour based on that of ancient warriors. They carried long weapons he didn't recognise.

Two of them stood before Malleus without lowering their weapons; the rest stormed through the devastated flat.

Another figure appeared through the dust, resembling an aethereal being in her white business suit. Malleus could make out the trademark dark glasses on the woman's face. Marduki didn't want to miss the great spectacle, and the Consortium finally had an occasion to allow her to intervene. A cool smile tipped up the corners of her mouth.

'Sir, you have no authorisation to be in this part of the city,' came a voice through a loudspeaker from the mouthpiece of a police helmet.

'I'm working for Amarud,' replied Malleus without moving to challenge the nervous policemen. 'Miss Marduki knows me.'

'Then you will of course be carrying authentication to that effect, Sir,' said the woman with relish. 'And your guest wristband is missing.'

'They . . . must both still be in my hotel room,' he responded apologetically.

'Oh – what a pity.' Marduki drew a deep breath and sighed with delight. 'Good, sir. Then please lie down with your face flat on the floor.'

Her way of getting revenge. Malleus looked unenthusiastically at the dusty, dirty plastic floor, which would completely ruin his clothes – he'd never be able to get the dirt out of the expensive fabric.

'Sir, I'm going to count to three.'

'All right, all right.' He knelt down obediently, then put his hands behind his back. The dust tickled his nose as the armoured men walked around him, wrapping cable-ties around his joints and searching him.

Malleus suddenly had an idea about his actual case: the death of Hansson.

Why didn't I think of that before?

Middle East, Gomorrah, November 2019

'Sir, I do apologise for the state of my clothes.' After being released at sunrise, Malleus had had a shower at the hotel and sent his clothes to be cleaned and mended, so he had to face Amarud wearing nothing but a hotel dressing gown. 'Unfortunately, this is all the circumstances will allow.' He smoked his penultimate Culebra, the one with a sepia-coloured band.

Amarud was sitting back in the leather chair opposite him, one hand holding the silver and ebony grip of his ivory walking stick, while the other rested on the head of the imposing being sitting beside him. It followed him everywhere like a dog, but its behaviour reminded Malleus more of a cat. Its horned, snake-like head remained still under its master's caress as its eyes flitted from side to side, a tinge of boredom evident.

'Yes, it has come to my attention that you had a few *complications*, Mr Bourreau,' agreed the bearded man, his beard twitching.

He's enjoying himself.

'Marduki was perhaps a little overzealous with the relish with which she conducted proceedings. The Consortium will no doubt be issuing an apology.' His manicured fingernails drifted from the right-hand side of the handle to the left. 'Have you anything to report to me?'

'I most certainly do.' Malleus gave him a summary of what his research in the tattoo parlour had revealed. 'Then I managed to get some information from Sweden about Hansson's private life: they told me that over the last few months, he'd stopped taking part in cult activities in honour of the Norse-Germanic entities – his reasoning was sometimes plausible, sometimes spurious.' Malleus puffed on his crooked cigar.

'I understand. So your conclusion is that Hansson wanted to convert. The witnesses saw the real Frigg, who sneaked into Gomorrah to kill the man *here* and make it look like a sex accident, as does occasionally happen, regretfully. It's all terribly embarrassing for everyone involved, so it's kept quiet and the convert is no more.'

Malleus painted an exclamation mark in the air with the glowing end of his Culebra; the smoke lingered in the room as a ghostly echo for a few seconds, before disappearing. 'That would have been my theory, Mr Amarud – until the *complications*, as you say, arose.' He tapped his nose. 'Dust.'

'Dust?'

'Miss Marduki had a great deal of fun trying every trick in the book to have me arrested. While I was lying with my nose in the dirt, I got the idea that I urgently needed to investigate the filter in the vacuum cleaner that had been used to clean Hansson's suite after his death.' Malleus leaned over the side and produced the glass containing his findings.

He shook out some dry petals, a few specks of dirt and a couple of crumpled strands of moss onto the table in front of them. 'It was still in there. I asked Miss Marduki to have them analysed. She was happy to do it – even without my black card.'

Amarud leaned forward, deeply curious. "Not Norse,' he guessed.

'Exactly, sir. Neither Home Secretary Hansson nor Frigg brought the material with them to Gomorrah.' Malleus took the print-out from the desk next to him and passed it over. 'Origin: Central America. I'll spare you the details.'

'Aztec territory. Xochiquetzal,' continued Amarud. A thick vein began to bulge on his forehead, clearly visible under his skin. *Anger.*

'I should say at this point that this is purely a hypothesis,' Malleus said, backtracking somewhat, stroking his Fu Manchu moustache. 'We haven't got *any* evidence of the entity being in the suite – only a strong suspicion. Thanks to your band system' – he gestured to his own empty wrist – 'it is usually only gods or goddesses who are able to move around Gomorrah unnoticed, even if I don't completely understand how.'

'So Xochiquetzal kills this influential man who could otherwise have given her a foothold in Scandinavia – why?' interjected Amarud.

'If you think about the consequences of a conversion of this scale, it could well be that Xochiquetzal heard about his desire to cross the floor and killed Hansson herself, in order to avoid any more furore or unrest.'

'Quite the exciting thesis you've got there, Mr Bourreau. But what was it that Frigg did in secret in the suite, without reporting to the authorities?'

'If she was indeed the entity who had been spotted: perhaps she just wanted to talk to Hansson?' Malleus puffed a question mark into the air. 'Maybe she felt threatened and came to try to warn him off his plan.'

Amarud leaned back in his chair again, holding his pet close to him. 'All this because a mortal wanted to change religion,' he concluded.

'Not just a mortal – the Swedish *Home Secretary.* Dying under such ignominious circumstances in Gomorrah was the best thing for world peace that could have happened, at least as far as Frigg and Xochiquetzal were concerned.' Malleus gave the man a friendly look. 'Or would you be interested in a new religious war starting, sir?'

Amarud shook his head absentmindedly. 'I can see the clues. And I have listened to your suggestion.'

'It was obvious, wasn't it?' Malleus gesticulated with the Culebra still in his hand. 'Let's leave it like this: Gunnar Olof Hansson died of auto-asphyxiation, which will still remain an *accident.* Officially confirmed by Interpol.'

'Agreed, Mr Bourreau.' The mysterious man lifted his hand from the animal, who immediately rested its head on the armrest without once taking its eyes off Malleus. 'As for the incident in the workers' housing: you said you managed to stop an attack?'

Malleus wondered to what extent he ought to tell the truth. After all, it was possible that Amarud could provide yet more information. *I should.* He'd leave out the details about Bala and her very young mother. 'A creature serving Namtarú appeared and attacked me – it was one of the same beings that destroyed my entire unit during the Great Change. I was the only one spared. I assume it was there to finish off what it had started.'

'Interesting.' The man's eyes narrowed. 'How do you know it had been sent by Namtarú?'

'The symbol on its forehead.' Malleus painted it in the air with the glowing tip of his cigar – but this time Amarud made a barely noticeable gesture and it came to life in a shower of sparks. 'And it spoke to me – it called itself the Vizier of the Underworld.' *He knows far more than this*, he thought, seeing the vein on the man's head bulging further. 'Fortunately, no one was hurt, according to Marduki. The incident is officially being recorded as a *dispute between the workers*.'

Amarud's expression was impenetrable. 'I assume you know who Namtarú is?'

'First I wanted to close the case, and Marduki had unfortunately taken my PDA with her, sir. I've only just got it back.'

'According to mythology, he is one of the seven gods of the Underworld, and serves as the Vizier for various beings down there,' Amarud summarised, barely concealing his rage. 'Some fear him as a god of pestilence with a mouth full of poison, bringing about disease and death wherever he goes. He has made many enemies, but he cannot be harmed as long as Ereškigal is there to protect him.'

'Has he caused trouble in Gomorrah before?'

'Let's just say he has a hard time recognising the authority of others while he is pursuing his own goals.' Amarud rose. 'This time *you* were his goal, Mr Bourreau. But I will punish that as well. I thank you for your exceptional work in this matter, Inspector. You have done the world a great service.' He reached into his jacket pocket and withdrew an envelope. 'Consider this a token of recognition. Neither of us has any need for a bribe.'

Malleus took the envelope, concerned by what he had heard about these religious myths; it was difficult for him to accept it all as an atheist. But because the beast had almost killed him, it became a curious fact. 'Thank you for getting your pet involved when things got a bit sticky.'

'Is that what she did?' Amarud patted its snake-like skull; the beast purred begrudgingly, resting its head against the man's waist. 'I'm sure the pleasure was all hers, Inspector Bourreau. I, however, did not order her to do so. For some reason Mušuššu likes you.' He raised his cane and proceeded majestically towards the door, disappearing through it along with his chimeric creature.

A very special friend. Malleus played with the belt of his bathrobe and drew deeply on his cigar.

He still wasn't satisfied that he had been unable to find any evidence for Hansson's murder, even though he had no doubt whatsoever that Xochiquetzal was the guilty party. He could be sure, however, that Amarud was already working on an improved security system that would register whenever an entity entered Sodom and Gomorrah.

Malleus clamped the Culebra in the corner of his mouth and opened the surprisingly heavy envelope. Apart from a personalised one-year pass to Sodom and Gomorrah, including accommodation and spending money, it contained ten thousand euros in five hundred euro bills, wrapped around a small gold bar.

Mr Amarud is indeed most generous.

He accepted the money calmly. That would do nicely to replenish his cigars and a new wardrobe.

Malleus hoped the girl had managed to escape with Bala. Whether or not she'd evade her enemy for ever, however, was a different matter. He wished for both of those things.

'Namtarú.' He said the name of his new enemy aloud and took out his PDA. He had a large amount of research to catch up on.

First of all, though, Malleus wanted to check the messages that had arrived while he had been stuck in the prison cell. And he had to arrange a lawyer for Ove Schwan without it getting back to him. Money was of no concern now, thanks to the envelope. He thought it utterly absurd that people considered his friend to be the Glyph Killer.

I've also got to get back into Bala's flat.

He switched on the television and left it on in the background, choosing a news channel. Information was at a premium.

Lautrec was asking about the status of his investigation; Lagrande had written to tell him about the latest developments regarding the artefacts, which she wanted to discuss with him alone, and Crick had also contacted him, narrowing the list of suspects in the matter of the Collector more and more. Other than that, it was merely the standard maelstrom of requests for private investigations.

As he scrolled through, firing off the occasional brief reply, a banner with *Breaking News* from Mexico City flickered onto the screen.

What's this? Malleus raised his eyes to follow the story more closely.

At the feast of Xochiquetzal, which was due to take place for the first time in millennia, the goddess had been found dead in her box.

Speculation was running wild and all events had been cancelled. Her husband Tlaloc called on her followers and the people of Mexico to pray for the goddess. *These returning gods can definitely be killed then. Just like the ashen beasts.*

Without the broadcaster making a connection, another report

from the *Divine News* section came in: at a temple dedicated to Frigg, an incident had taken place in the presence of Odin's wife in which the goddess had allegedly been severely injured. More details would soon be provided, while Hugin and Munin had already been sighted, enquiring about Odin.

Amarud doesn't waste any time at all.

Malleus looked back at the PDA and opened his requests from private clients. He had to read one of the messages twice in order to be sure that he had understood it correctly: there was a lady who wanted him to get some of her property back for her. She was accusing a hostile collector of a clever, insidious theft.

The item in question was a horn.

'The Horn of Nandi,' he read, sucking hard on his Culebra. It was one of the stolen artefacts from Treva.

A hostile collector.

THE Collector?

BOOK 8

Episode 8: The Feint

Feint fānt, n. a false appearance: a pretence: a mock assault: a deceptive movement in fencing, boxing, etc.
– v.i. to make a feint: Loki made a feint to the left before striking with his right fist.
[Fr. Feinte]

Chambers English Dictionary, 2019 Edition

Germania, Free State of Saxony (Germanic quarter), Lipsk (Leipzig), November 2019

Malleus Bourreau made his way through the snowstorm along the Hainstrasse, not far from the little bolthole he had nearby, and turned into Barthel's courtyard for his second meeting of the day; in his right hand he clutched a metal suitcase.

The biting wind abruptly broke off, the snowflakes beginning to coast their way towards the cobblestones slowly and calmly, as if the snow itself were offering protection.

Malleus had a great affection for the four walls that he had so surprisingly inherited all those years ago. They were concealed within a beautiful old building with high stucco ceilings and a lavish floor plan that suggested more than a hint of opulence. He sometimes had occasion to withdraw there when the noise in Lutetia became too much for him.

Though his actual Germanic roots were not in Saxony,

Malleus had fallen in love with the city from the moment he'd first come into contact with it. Despite the numerous new developments and large building projects that had sprung up over the course of time, it had somehow managed to maintain its inherent charm.

People had never really taken a great deal of interest in the east of the country, meaning there had been relatively little excitement – or indeed, consternation – when the entities appeared. The Leipzigers considered it little more important than a change in weather and, since the gods hardly interfered there at all, there was almost nothing to observe as far as a shift in the spiritual landscape of the region was concerned. The only major change was the incredibly expensive church in the heart of the city, currently being converted with little ado into a block of affordable flats. No one was protesting.

True neighbourly love. Entirely selfless. Malleus crossed the courtyard and swung into the alleyway at the back, home to his favourite shop; the place where he was due to have his next meeting.

The small façade had been intentionally designed to resemble the style of the Golden Twenties of the previous century, above which was written in an elaborate script:

Karak et Frères
Men's Clothing

Underneath was written in the same old-fashioned gold lettering:

Leipzig/Paris/London/Milan
or anywhere in the world on request

Malleus was rather looking forward to the fitting he had arranged.

He liked clothes that fitted him perfectly, disdaining anything that was derivative, too fashionable or prohibitively exceptional. The Karak brothers also had at their disposal the best tobacco products and alcoholic wares money could buy, including the wondrous Culebras that Malleus couldn't do without.

The bell above the door rang discreetly as he entered, its bright tone on the melodic side of intrusive. His spirits buoyed as he walked onto the shop floor, which felt more like a gentleman's club than a men's outfitter. Karak had had the ceiling moved two floors up, which gave the shop a breathtakingly expansive effect when you turned your head to look up.

It was an informal setting, with armchairs and sofas combining elements of leather and metal. Illuminated bottles of spirits and tobacco products of every provenance were displayed in three-foot-high cabinets and humidors, opposite which could be found shelves with a wide variety of hats, walking sticks, gloves, scarves, ties and all manner of items associated with difference and the upper class. A slender wooden staircase and a lift led to the gallery levels.

'Well, if it isn't my favourite customer,' came the gentle voice of the tailor from the studio next to him. 'Just one moment, Herr Bourreau. I'll be with you as soon as I can.'

'No hurry.' Malleus breathed in the aroma of tobacco, leather and oud that permeated the shop. It was a true treasure, an island of the exceptional in a world of ubiquitous monotony.

He shook off the last of the snow from his coat, put his hat on the stand next to the counter and placed the suitcase alongside the armchair where he usually sat.

An almost dainty, brown-haired man who appeared to have next to no muscles whatsoever appeared through the curtain, giving Malleus a warm, friendly smile. Dressed in black trousers, a white shirt and a dark green waistcoat, with a yellow tape measure around his neck and a spiky pincushion on his wrist, he was the perfect image of an archetypal tailor.

He extended his hand to greet Malleus. 'Sir has returned. And may I say what a pleasure it is to welcome him back into the fold.' His critical gaze fell on the worn-out military coat with the remains of the snowy residue melting on it casually. 'Still wearing this monstrosity, I see? Oh dear, oh dear. I really do hope you'll take me up on my offer one day to make you something a little more . . . befitting.'

Malleus laughed. Even this antiquated form of address was perfectly in tune with the shop, where the customer was truly king. 'Thank you, my dear Herr Karak. But I think I'll stick with the one I've got. Its service has been more than faithful so far.'

The tailor helped him out of his coat, wiping away the snow with brisk precision. 'Be it as you wish.' Karak overcame his disdain and placed it carefully on a hanger, as if out of respect for their mutual past. 'I received your emergency call – I do hope you don't mind my having done a little advance preparation. Assuming, of course, you've managed to maintain your figure.' His gently mocking glance struck Malleus, who opened his arms and turned around slowly on the spot. 'It would appear I was right, even though you do look a little thinner to me. We'll measure you up afterwards, Herr Bourreau.'

'I also have a few new suggestions,' he said, allowing himself to be guided towards the chair in the corner before sitting down.

'It would be my pleasure. But first there's the small matter of the initial orders you placed.'

With the speed and dexterity of a squirrel, Karak climbed the small ladder and was almost immediately six feet up, whereupon he opened a small glass window and took out three cases, before gliding back down with his feet on the outsides of the ladder, as if in a submarine.

'Your Culebras, sir,' he said with exaggerated solemnity, placing the wooden boxes alongside one another, then opening them one by one; a quiet hissing emanated from the integrated humidor, which ensured that humidity and temperature remained at the specified level.

Malleus could see the characteristically crooked cigars with different bands around them. He looked at them with barely concealed delight. The small inserts between the colours ensured the contents did not become mixed up in any way.

'Blue, black, grey,' said Karak, pointing at the Culebras as if reciting a menu in a restaurant, 'and here we have sepia, red, violet, green, teal and ruby. And last but not least: amber.'

Malleus looked at the collection with joy in his heart. He felt as if nothing could ever possibly go wrong again.

Then Karak produced a small aluminium tube as if from nowhere and placed it in front of Malleus. 'Voilà. Something new for you.' He disappeared back through the curtain. 'Try this delectable acquisition out for size, Herr Bourreau. I'll just get that package that came for you.'

Malleus knew the package he was referring to was his old and sorely missed PDA. His friend had sent it to this address because he knew it would be safe there.

He took the metal package in his hand and unscrewed the lid.

A smell of the Arabian Nights sent his senses into overdrive, as if the Middle East itself had been squeezed directly into this Culebra.

Malleus carefully slid the cigar into his hand. *Dark purple.* 'May I try it, Herr Karak?'

'Please do, I beg of you,' came a muted voice from the back. The heavy curtain prevented any tobacco residue from entering his studio, lest any undesired smoke permeate his customers' clothes. 'I had this one made especially for you, having heard rumours about your various peregrinations for Interpol. And if you approve, I'm sure we can arrange for the supply to be replenished. You know me, after all.'

Malleus cut off the ends, then taking the chip and match in his hand, lit the Culebra, which burned with a remarkable aroma. The first puff was enough to tell Malleus what flavours the creators had woven in to the leaves. Four puffs later, the full taste had developed, leaving him with an impression of the mild intertwined gracefully with the aromatic.

He began to feel slightly dizzy as the effect made its way to his temples.

'Could it be that the tobacco in this one is stronger than in the others?' he asked, running his thumb and forefinger over his Fu Manchu moustache.

Karak returned and handed over the parcel containing his PDA. 'It's from the latest crop, and this one is supposed to be of the absolute highest quality. Which is why there are so few of them. It is now just a question of price.' The thin tailor looked openly delighted at the fact that his customer was so enamoured of the goods. 'Suppose I were to anticipate, my dear Herr Bourreau, that you were to wish me to procure some of these for you.' He sat on the sofa opposite Malleus, sinking into it, making him appear small and almost lost.

'Anticipate away, Herr Karak.' He leant back and waved the Culebra around in the air, painting red lines with the tip and creating echoes with the smoke. 'You are, of course, correct. One box will be enough.'

'Very good.' Karak smiled contentedly and gave Malleus a knowing look. 'Now, as for your outer garments: I've made four kurtas for you, two in bright colours and two in black. I've reduced the embroidery considerably so that it no longer stands out, just as you requested last time.'

'Marvellous.' Malleus continued to smoke, savouring the flavour. *It's almost impossible to stop.*

'We've also got four pairs of trousers and two jackets with the same Indian touch.'

'Fantastic, Herr Karak. Truly fantastic.' He pointed at his hat on the stand. 'As you have clearly noticed, this is rather an urgent purchase. The hat you can see here is looking rather . . . haggard.'

'Yes, your assignments do always seem to incur losses, especially where your wardrobe is concerned.' Karak smiled. 'We'll sort out a hat for you later, good sir. As for the fabric I used for your new clothes, I've tried a so-called "spider" material.'

Malleus peered through the smoke that he had created like a bank of fog between him and the tailor, distorting his perception. The man looked somewhat unusual through the haze, as if not from this world; the smoke added a beard to his shaven face. 'Because of my weight loss?'

'Hmm, it's more in the manner of Kevlar armour, my esteemed Mr Bourreau. The fabric is completely new. This is the first time I've used it at all.'

'Do you mean to tell me that my clothes are bulletproof?'

'More or less. They'll withstand rather a lot, at least against normal calibres and blades.' Karak looked even more pleased with himself. 'That way your wardrobe will take a bit less of a pounding, I hope.'

Malleus was looking forward to seeing the bill he'd end up

with from *Karak et Frères.* For what other reason did he earn money?

'Will you be paying cash on this occasion, Herr Bourreau?' Karak pointed jokingly at his aluminium suitcase.

Malleus laughed, releasing a mouthful of smoke that formed conspiratorially around his lips, as if it knew what the man was thinking. 'Can I take it that you are a friend of the unusual, Herr Karak?'

'But of course!'

'Then I've got something to show you.' Malleus, still somewhat elated by the effect of the grandiose Culebra, took out the case, flicked open the locks and lifted the lid. There, in clear foil, lay the cut-off, rolled-up tentacle of the ashen beast. The foil and the adjustable temperature of the case had had a similar effect on decomposition as the humidor. Malleus placed the suitcase on the table and turned it around.

'Oh, how fascinating!' came Karak's reply as he took in the sight before him. 'A . . . *bad* tentacle.'

Malleus choked on his cigar. 'You know what that is?'

'My brother and I have a bit of a weakness for mythological beings. We've always been on the look-out for fashion inspiration, even before the Return of the Gods,' explained the tailor. 'Apart from the Cthulhu myth, there aren't that many tentacled beasts. The *bad* are from Sumerian mythology, literally meaning *wall*, because they can withstand anything.' He looked at the tentacle. 'Apart from you, it would appear, Herr Bourreau. Because *you* get the better of everyone and everything you come across. Impressive, to say the least!'

Malleus had to grin. 'Why am I not surprised?'

'Because you are incredibly astute, my good sir.'

'I don't suppose you happen to know anything about Namtarú?'

'A god from the same area, but I can't remember much more off the top of my head.' Karak pointed to the limbs. 'Another addition for your trophy cabinet?'

'I wanted to have something made out of it.' Malleus stopped to consider how talkative he was being, putting it down to the unfamiliar cigar. *I've got to be careful to only smoke these when I'm able to be silent.* He briefly entertained the idea that Karak had slipped him something at the behest of the Collector. *No, he's a man of integrity.*

'As a whip?'

Malleus blinked with astonishment. The idea had never crossed his mind. He replayed the battle with this monster in his head, recalling the damage the tentacle had done. *That would be perfect.*

'That's not a bad suggestion at all, my dear Herr Karak.' He adopted a more comfortable position in the chair, slinging one leg over the other and admiring the glowing tip of his Culebra. 'The only thing is: who could possibly make me something out of the tentacle of a *bad*, all the while retaining the effect of the small blades embedded in it?'

Karak rose hastily and bowed subserviently. 'My dear Herr Bourreau, it would be a great honour and pleasure to do this deed for you as a gentlemen's outfitter. I have a number of good contacts who know how to keep a secret. If you leave this exquisite piece with me, you'll get it back as a whip. I swear this to you by . . .'

'Let's not start invoking entities, now. Your word is enough.' Malleus grinned. 'It's all yours, Herr Karak.' He got out of the chair, feeling as light as a feather. 'Let's start the fitting.' With a single movement of his hand, he shut the lid of the suitcase and rolled the glow from the remainder of his Culebra, stopping him from endulging further. 'And after that I'd like a new hat, please.'

Miles Karak bowed respectfully once more, as if Malleus were not simply an inspector at Interpol and a good customer, but instead a gentleman who was on the same level as the gods.

Celtica, Paris-Lutetia, November 2019

There was another reason why Malleus hadn't immediately started looking for his client with the stolen artefact.

This reason was in strict police custody at Grannus Hospital, through whose corridors he found himself walking. He had used a trick to gain permission to visit Ove Schwan, despite the serious reservations of Germania State Security. They had demanded that he be extradited immediately – they felt that they were being dominated by Interpol – but when Malleus explained that he wasn't there as part of the *GodsEnd* investigation, but rather, looking into the whereabouts of the gold beetles, they settled down somewhat. But his Germanian colleagues wouldn't stay out of it for much longer.

Malleus could see the two heavily armoured policemen equipped with FAMAS at the entrance to the corridor where the quarantine station was located. However, the bullpup-style assault rifles and Kevlar were not designed to guard against infectious diseases but rather dangerous extremists.

'Bonjour, Messieurs,' he said in a friendly voice, doffing his hat and showing them first his ID card, then the permit issued to him by the chief investigator.

They let him through with a curt nod. One of them radioed ahead to say that an authorised visitor was approaching, while the other held the door open for him. Behind it was yet another corridor with hermitically sealable glass doors, where four more FAMAS-armed men were standing. The Celtica security forces knew Owe Schwan had a military past and they were clearly taking no risks whatsoever with him. The man and his friends from *GodsEnd* were still dangerous.

Malleus passed them and waited outside the door, indicating that he wouldn't enter without their express permission. *As if they could possibly refuse me*. The door swung open before him and a brown-haired detective in a wrinkled suit beckoned him in with a short gesture. He looked as if he had been sleeping in his clothes.

Malleus entered, and saw Ove Schwan chained to the bed with iron clamps; they allowed a certain degree of movement without giving the possibility of escape. There was a bandage wrapped around his light blond hair, and thicker compresses were visible underneath his surgical gown.

The room smelled of disinfectant and the remains of lunch, a rather unpleasant combination. Aside from the bed, he could see a side table, two spare chairs and a table. There was nothing else in the whitewashed room, apart from various sockets for hospital equipment.

The giant man remained calm. He gave Malleus a look of contempt. His acting was perfect; no one would have guessed that they knew each other – let alone that they knew each other *well*. Another armoured policeman was stood next to the bed, holding an HK UMP diagonally across his body. He looked closely at Malleus and relaxed.

'My colleague,' said the young man in the rumpled suit, his bulletproof vest showing clearly over his shirt. 'You wanted to talk to Schwan?'

Malleus nodded. 'Please would you wait outside?'

The detective frowned. 'I'm not sure about that.'

'Well, now you are, my esteemed colleague,' he replied politely.

'This is a matter of Interpol – nothing to do with *GodsEnd*, and nothing to do with the *Sûreté* either.' Malleus could see that the man was part of the recently founded secret service, which explained his hostile expression. 'And please take the guards with you.'

'I'll need to check that first—'

'I've already done that for you.' Malleus handed over the letter giving him the authority to question Ove Schwan.

'Mm,' muttered the *Sûreté* official, summoning the armoured officer. 'Well, he's your responsibility now. And don't get too close to him. He's a dangerous bastard.' Then they disappeared through the door.

Malleus withdrew his PDA and switched it on – not the recording function, but the jamming device his friend had installed. No radio signals or electronic devices would work within a two-metre radius around it. Then he placed his hat on the table.

Schwan laughed. '*A dangerous bastard.* What a cute little Frenchman.' He raised his arms slightly and the chains tautened with a jangle.

'Thanks for taking care of her,' said Malleus in a low voice, putting his hands into his pockets.

'I see you've still got *that*,' replied Schwan, nodding at Malleus' heavy military overcoat.

Malleus looked at the muscular, highly trained man lying imprisoned before him. 'So what happened?'

'I caught someone following her,' he snarled. 'Unfortunately for me, he had an APB Stechkin, which I was able to deprive him of. Just as I was about to finish him off, the prick threw a load of poisoned throwing stars at me.'

Malleus laughed. 'Throwing stars? That's pretty retro.'

'Yeah. What an arsehole. The doctors had their work cut out containing my blood poisoning. They still haven't found out what he had smeared on them. The real problem, however, is the APB. It turns out it's the weapon of a known serial killer. In Italy. And now they're trying to pin it on me. You didn't say anything about this – just that your little friend was in danger.'

Malleus' blood turned to ice. *I've got to tell him who he is.* 'Did you manage to kill him in the end?'

'The police turned the whole area over but couldn't find a body. He's probably still out there somewhere.' Schwan noticed Malleus' lack of surprise. '*Where* do you know him from?'

'I didn't think he was the one threatening Lagrande. Just like the last two cases.' Malleus gave a quick summary of what had happened over the past two weeks and how the Glyph Killer had been stalking him, sometimes even protecting him – though he had no idea what the killer's true intentions were.

He stroked the ends of his beard and flicked away a strand of black hair from his eyes. 'I managed to lose him, so he was probably hanging around close to Lagrande on the assumption that I'd be in touch with her soon.'

'To my mind it looked more like he was about to push her onto the Metro tracks.'

There was no way Malleus would have been able to explain such an attack on his secretary. *Killing and maiming her . . . why? As a punishment? Because he felt left out?*

So it's not just the unknown Collector who's after her. It's a good job I decided against police protection. 'I'll get you a lawyer. The best money can buy.'

Schwan grinned. 'That could be rather expensive. Especially with *these* sorts of accusations.'

Malleus resisted the urge to place a comforting hand on his

comrade's shoulder. He trusted the jamming device, but there was still every chance someone could come back in.

'Did you get a look at his face?'

'Only half of it. I'd recognise him if I saw him, though.' Schwan gave him a rough description and Malleus opened a phantom image program on his PDA to help his friend draw the features of the man who would one day be held accountable for his actions.

After ten minutes they had created a face that Malleus ran through the Interpol database with a few short clicks. The face itself was inconspicuous, harmless, even a little on the chubby side. *So that's my insane, murderous shadow.*

'Good.' Malleus smiled at Schwan, then cleared his throat. 'Ove . . . do you remember the beast which did for so many of us that day?'

'How could I ever forget the flickering eyes and ash-like skin with all those symbols on it?'

'I'm hunting down their master.' Malleus gave a brief account of what had happened in Gomorrah. 'But I still haven't got any explanation as to what those monsters were looking for in Germania and why they were fighting during the Great Change,' he concluded.

Schwan looked at him with a dark expression. 'What culture are they from? Babylonian?'

'Sumerian-Akkadian.' Malleus stroked his Fu Manchu moustache once again. Thinking about the beasts always made him nervous. 'In any case, they were a long way from home.'

'We've got to find out who we're up against!' The enormous fighter suddenly appeared to be filled with energy. He straightened up and glared at the chains around him wrists as if he were trying to release himself by sheer force of will.

'Careful now,' said Malleus, pacifying him. 'You can't even

go five yards. There are half a dozen policemen out there with assault rifles. Let's get you a lawyer first, then we can deal with the rest afterwards.'

Schwan dropped back onto the pillow. 'Will they extradite me? Do you know anything about that?'

'I think that it'll be passed back and forth between the authorities once they find out that the weapon has also been used to kill people in Italy, in Riga and . . . well, probably in other cities as well.'

Schwan gave Malleus a worried look. 'And always places where you've just been, Malleus. They'll be checking you next, and then me again and sooner or later they'll realise we fought together in the same unit.'

'I had perfectly good reasons for being in all those places.' Malleus remained calm. 'But at the moment that's irrelevant.'

'What should I say if they ask me about the gold figurines?'

Malleus turned towards the door and picked up his hand in his right hand. 'Nothing. Silence from now on.'

Schwan let out a wicked laugh. 'That won't be a problem.'

Malleus winked at him. 'You'll regret not cooperating with Interpol,' he said loudly as he opened the door. 'We could have offered you a deal, but that's not going to happen now. Tell the *Sûreté* as soon as you change your mind.'

'Go fuck yourself, pig,' replied Schwan with faux anger. 'You'll never break me, not you or any of these other bums. Not even the holy fucking false gods themselves! *GodsEnd* will triumph. We are legion, and we will not stop until we have awoken every last person on this planet—!'

Malleus closed the door and searched his jacket for his cigar case, choosing one with a green band despite the strong allure of the purple one. 'Wanker.'

The suited officer stood by the door, leaning against the wall with his arms crossed over his chest, looking at him. 'A tough nut to crack, eh?'

'You're telling me.' Malleus put on his hat and lit his Culebra without any regard for being in a hospital. 'But I'm sure you'll get there.'

He walked past him, puffing away. The smoke immediately dissolved into nothing, as if it knew it would set off the smoke alarm otherwise.

Malleus looked at his PDA, switched off the jamming device and checked the travel information, wondering when he could head off to see his next client. His flight to Buliwya, as it was called in Quechua, Wuliwya in Aymara, Bolivia in English, was due to leave in two hours.

He had cigars and a new wardrobe.

Malleus felt stronger than ever, and he was hot on the heels of Opponent Number One.

* A Ω *

Fucking organ dealers!

They've robbed me of the link to my prey. Now I've got to work out how to find him again without any of the bugs and trackers I took so much time and effort to plant.

Fuck! Well at least I've managed to get some money from those idiots, plus some guns and some clothes. That'll have to do for now.

I can forget all about finding him, not without somewhere to start.

But I'm smart. Back on Blondie's trail, and this other wanker is completely out of the picture now. You could say he's a little . . . deflated.

I heard about it on the news. Ove Schwan – what the fuck kind of name is that? OVE?

It sounds like an abbreviation for a formula. Or a disease. OVE has got HIV. Like that.

He's in hospital and is being interrogated by the police. I'd love to pay that little prick a visit. Blow him away. Get rid. Squeeze myself between the door and the frame to get to him. Because of him they've got my APB. MY *APB!*

Just about stop myself from skidding. I can't lose control, neither through my choice of words nor through any lack of composure.

What's done is done: my good piece is gone and I've got to forget about it. I'll never be able to find one like that again on the market, not in fucking Lutetia at any rate. There aren't any Russians here I could trust to find me one.

Maybe in Berlin . . . Or have they renamed that as well now? Whatever. The sort of Russians I need are in Berlin.

Ove, you fucker, you're dead meat. Not just because of my APB. You'd have killed me if I hadn't had my ninja stars on me, wouldn't you, you old dog-fucker?

And for that shall your life be forfeit, O odious terrorist. I've been known to bear a grudge or two. You'll see.

There goes the Eighties woman, accompanied by two cops. Again. Looks like he's put her under police protection. I suppose he had to while his shadow was elsewhere.

Apropos elsewhere*: I've got to buy and prepare some more throwing stars. They're great, those things. Ha, what a sight it was to see them go straight through his hood and stick in his head. Great craic. As if a shooting star had decided to make a beeline for his skull.*

Okay, starting to calm down now. Good. That'll make it easier to think.

Oh, where are we going then?

Tresoriale. *What's that, a vault?*

Right, so what . . .? Okay I can see it now. It looks good with all its security controls.

But I'll still get in. I've already sorted out clothes and an ID badge from one of the guards; did it so quickly he hardly even noticed.

Okay, I'm right where I need to be. Here she comes.

I've got to get over to her sooner or later.

I'll be pleased to see her, my little Casablanca Ingrid. No, Ingrid doesn't do her justice. This girl's tough.

Nevertheless, he still needs to be punished for cutting me off.

Quite the to-do list I've got now – longer than a Leonard Cohen song. Well, it doesn't matter. I've got nothing else on apart from that.

Mirror, signal, manoeuvre.

Buliwya (Quechua) / Wuliwya (Aymara) / Bolivia (English), Departamento La Paz, Tiwanaku, November 2019

Malleus gazed in wonder at the resurrected city as he passed through in his hired BMW i8. It had been one of the most significant archaeological areas in the country until a few years ago, declared a UNESCO World Heritage Site in 2000.

It was quite difficult to breathe at thirteen thousand feet, but his body would have to become accustomed to it, allowing Malleus would not forego his Culebra. Blue band this time.

Even as an architectural novice he noticed it immediately: there was a striking difference in the style of the buildings, as if two different architects had been commissioned to create something new out of the ruins.

His PDA gave him the reason for this: the former Tiwanaku, or Tiahuanaco, was the religious and administrative capital of the Aymara, a culture that had lived at this altitude before the Incas and was known to have reached its peak between 900 and 600 BC, though they'd settled there much earlier than that.

At the time, their sphere of influence reached as far as the coast, the Atacama Desert and Argentina, but the inhabitants had to give up much of this due to climatic deterioration. The emergent Incas, who had previously been oppressed by them, found only ruins.

Aymara and Inca. Two cultures, and literally, the oldest of enemies. Malleus remembered that the Return of the Gods had occurred with far less friction in Central and South America than it had in the USA or other primarily monotheistic countries. It was true that Catholicism had considerable influence there, but even before the entities reappeared it was starting to lose its power over the indigenous people, who had already been turning back to their former traditions.

When the Incan deities suddenly appeared for real, the shift had been fast and automatic. It never crossed the native people's minds to question whether it was the right thing to do, to turn away from the god of their European conquerors. In fact, they grew resentful that they had been forced to worship him in the first place – and they began to tear down the churches.

As he had instructed, the i8's autopilot drove him around Tiwanaku's special features to give Malleus a better overall impression of the place. Thanks to its irrigation system and proximity to Lake Titicaca, the entire city was a luscious green, with large fields scattered across the surrounding area, just as he had seen as he'd flown over the place. Step pyramids stretched upwards, the traditional stone edifices interspersed with modern ones made from glass and steel, while connecting bridges with moving walkways crisscrossed above the streets, allowing pedestrians to move around more quickly above the traffic. There was an Inca statue at the entrance to the Sunken Courtyard, right in the centre of the city, with the main attraction being the

Kalasasaya Platform, the mound with standing stones over three hundred feet high, surrounded by monoliths. There was also a temple, half underground; some experts believed the Kalasasaya to be a solar observatory from pre-Inca times.

Malleus was particularly excited by the enormous three metre-square Sun Gate, hewn from a single rock. It came from Aymara culture and had been restored to its former glory. The impression it made on him was hard to define, and not just because of the frieze emblazoned with the image of a god cradling the heads of two serpents in its hands.

Malleus' client lived in the district that had been built above the ruins of Puma Punku, whose exquisitely carved monoliths belonged to an incomplete structure from Aymaran culture.

The i8 drove past the titanic stones that stood to attention in a closed-off space, waiting to be given orders for deployment.

How unusual. None of the gods who had returned so far were hesitant when it came to demonstrating their power. Malleus was curious about why this wasn't the case this time.

The car turned in to a freshly asphalted street that had been made to look like stone paving by adding various patterns and colours to it. Ana Carmen Tejada's house was on the right-hand side, a traditional box house with a beige stone exterior, just as their ancestors had built.

The BMW stopped; Malleus put on his hat and climbed out. It was a warm day so he left his coat in the car. The new clothes Karak had given him were light and airy, yet fitted him as perfectly as a second skin.

The beautiful reliefs on the front of the house were unmistakable, for they bore a striking resemblance to the decoration on the Sun Gate. His untrained Western eye was unable to immediately understand the precise details of the ornamentation.

His PDA was able to give him substantially more detail when he waved it over the façade to give him a better idea about its classification. *Motif: original reproduction of the Chavín de Huántar Raimondi Stele* came on the screen. *Depiction: a beast with the teeth of a carnivore and the claws of a bird of prey. The sceptres in its hand are made from an amalgamation of cats and snakes; belt jewellery: two snakes on each side. It wears a strikingly large headdress with cat-like faces overlapping it, with strands of hair, feathers and snakes shooting out to the sides. Similar representations of entities: later Andean cultures and Tiahuanaco culture, depicted on the pillar of the Sun Gate.*

Malleus found the abstractly anthropomorphic image altogether confusing. *Surely they're asking a lot of your imagination here.*

There had been many attempts to interpret it, from dragon gods to *felino volador*, a sort of flying feline god. It would appear that the gods' return hadn't solved every little puzzle.

He walked across a short path to the door, which was overshadowed by a canopy, but he had barely started his approach when an older lady in Incan-style clothing in white and natural colours opened the door.

To look at, Tejada appeared to be one of the Indios; she wore her black hair down, kept away from her face by various golden chains and clips. Large earrings dangled down her neck, while a necklace of silver and lapis lazuli rested elegantly across her wrinkled brown shoulders.

She gave Malleus a warm smile and beckoned him inside with a small wave of her hand. Inside it smelled of citrus fruit and freshly baked bread. 'I was getting worried about you, Mr Bourreau,' she said, her penetrating voice strongly accented.

If Tejada were to scream, it could cut away the very stone from this house.

He took off his hat and bowed low, wiping the sweat from

his brow with a handkerchief. 'The autopilot brought me safely here from the airport. But the delay was my fault, Miss Tejada. I wanted to take in a few of the sights as I was passing by. Who knows where your case might take me.'

She laughed and led him through the small hall and into the living room, both of which were tiled with terracotta. The paintings on the walls all bore a certain resemblance to the motif on the front of the house, adding to Malleus' confusion. The woven wall-hangings and rugs were bursting with colour and wild patterns.

'Take a seat,' said Tejada, indicating the small chair next to the window, out of which could be seen a barren garden of cactus and stone. Unlike the places he had passed on his way over, there appeared to be very little water here – either that, or Tejada had a penchant for these rather sober plants.

For an art collector she doesn't appear to have very many pieces. To be precise, Malleus could see only an old bowl sitting on the cabinet, looking as if it was waiting to be filled with nibbles.

'Please tell me why you want to take my case, Mr Bourreau.'

Malleus hadn't expected that. 'What do you mean?' He turned his blue-lensed eyes on the woman.

'It can't be for money,' said Tejada. 'The fee isn't all that high. Plus, you're an atheist and you are known for only taking on cases that have links to gods.' The Indio sat down and looked at him. 'Yet here you are, and this is only a robbery.'

Malleus found it odd having to justify his acceptance of a commission to the person who had specifically requested him. He stroked his Fu Manchu moustache. 'Let's say the object in question piqued my curiosity,' he replied honestly. 'After all, you've got to admit that the Horn of Nandi doesn't really have all that much to do with Bolivia. So I suppose what I'd really like to know is how an alleged bullhorn with links to a Hindu god managed to find its way to this country.'

Tejada nodded like a psychiatrist whose patient had just made a breakthrough. 'That's what I thought.'

'Why does it matter to you, Miss Tejeda?'

'I'm suspicious of your motives.'

'Am I right in saying you think I'm playing both sides?' he concluded with surprise. 'Ah, of course! You think it's possible that the Collector has ordered me to steal even more from you.'

Tejada sighed in agreement. 'It's one of life's great tragedies how quickly you lose faith in the goodness of mankind once you start getting old.' She gestured to him. 'But the last few years have given me little to be confident about. I am one of the descendants of the Aymara, the founders of Tiwanaku. But the scions of the Incas haven't given up their claim.' Her brown, wrinkled palm rested on Malleus' right hand. 'Everyone's talking about how the Christian god and Allah and Yahweh have disappeared and the gods who have come back are wreaking their cruel revenge. But no one is willing to discuss the hatred that's breaking out in their own ranks. The area I live in is nothing more than an upmarket ghetto. But I know the Incas want nothing more than to use us as sacrifices.'

Malleus had to admit that this wasn't something he had ever thought about, at least not as far as the indigenous peoples of Central and South America were concerned. In Europe there were differences between new converts and the Neo-pagans who had been praying to the old gods for a long time and considered themselves to be superior believers. But that didn't really have anything to do with nationality.

'You're right,' he said, starting to think about what it was she really wanted from him. *Help in the face of the coming hostilities, or just to look for the horn?* 'Europe's a long way away.'

Tejada nodded, then apologetically, 'Oh, listen to me, wittering on and on at you, and the reason you're here is for something different entirely.' She clasped his hands in hers for a moment, then drew them away; her earring jangled and clanked lightly against her necklace. 'Please forgive the lamentations of an old woman.'

Malleus smiled at her. *She's had a hard time, but I've got to get her to tell me more about the case.*

Tejada took the tablet lying on the side table and brought up a picture before handing the device over to him. 'The Horn of Nandi. That's what it looks like.' Malleus knew exactly what it looked like, but still he examined it in detail. 'What a beautiful piece.'

'Do you know the legend behind it?'

'That it's supposed to come from the gods' bull? Yes.'

'No. I mean how it got lost.'

'Oh, no, I don't know that legend at all.' Malleus zoomed in further and could make out some of the details that had been engraved into and carved out of the horn. *Finally, information!*

'Pity. Neither do I.' Tejada looked at him, her brown eyes worried. 'Dear oh dear! I didn't ask you if you wanted something to drink. Can I get you anything, Mr Bourreau?'

Her somewhat erratic nature was beginning to irritate him, although that was also partly due to his own innate impatience. He still had no idea whether he was hunting the unknown Collector or whether this was a red herring. *Steady now. Don't be a dick to her.*

'Why don't you tell me where you got the horn from,' he suggested, taking out his cigar case. 'I'd like to make a start on my research. And' – he tapped the digital photo – 'I also need some proof that you are indeed its rightful owner.' He opened the case and let the aroma rise out tantalisingly before choosing a Culebra with a green band.

'Yes of course, of course,' she replied. 'When I was a girl, I married a very rich European man – I knew hardly anything about him, apart from the fact that we were very much in love. That was enough for me at the time.' Tejada laughed. 'It turned out that he had an art collection, which he left to me after he died, much to my astonishment. There were a hundred objects in it, from all manner of cultures and eras: paintings, sculptures and artefacts.' She swiped the screen and brought up a photo gallery. 'You can look at these if you get a moment.'

From the way she was speaking, Malleus concluded that the collection was not in this house. 'And where did you keep this treasure trove?'

'I had given it all to a museum on permanent loan because I thought they'd be the best people to take care of it, being professionals and all. And that way I could give something back to the people as well.' Tejada sighed. 'The other thing I inherited from my husband was this damned Collector: I'm absolutely certain he had a hand in my husband's accident. Then he made me an offer, first for the horn, then for the whole collection.'

That sounds like him. Malleus swallowed. 'That must have been rather a large sum.' He cut off the end and lit his cigar. He wished Tejada would finally get to the point. The Culebra would relax him, and would hopefully stave off his impatience.

'I'm not interested in money, Mr Bourreau. I can't stand that man!' She leaned back in her chair, her eyes lingering on the cactus garden outside. 'Barely had I rejected his offer when I heard that the museum had been broken into. Despite all the treasures it contained, the only thing that was stolen was the comparatively unspectacular Horn of Nandi.'

'How did they get in?'

'The director didn't know. They found the empty cabinet the next morning when they opened the exhibition.'

And because the Collector was insistent that he wanted the horn, you concluded that he was the one behind it?' added Malleus. 'I don't suppose you've got a name for me?'

'No.'

'No?' he repeated in astonishment. *Now I really am beginning to lose patience.* 'Miss Tejeda, I really must say—'

'My husband never mentioned him by name, and he came to me via an intermediary,' she explained, looking for a document in the folds of her garment. It was written in both her native language and English. 'This is the certificate attesting to the legality of his will. That's what you wanted, isn't it?'

Malleus took the multilingual document and cast a quick eye over it. At first glance everything appeared to be in order, with an index containing a list of the works of art that had belonged to her spouse. When he reached the line with the horn, he stopped and puffed hard on his Culebra. 'There's nothing about it being the Horn of Nandi here,' he said, turning to the Indio. 'It's listed as the *Horn of Alexander the Great.*'

Tejada nodded sharply. 'I know. That was a trick. My husband didn't want Hindu fanatics to appear out of the woodwork and start dragging him to court on religious grounds. Or even worse, Shiva to show up.' She threw her arms in the air. 'Imagine, Mr Bourreau, what would have happened – here, in the middle of Tiwanaku, where there are already far too many gods and people not getting along with one another, if another god had shown up out of the blue.'

Malleus could imagine it very well indeed, though he found

the idea more amusing than disturbing. What he was less impressed by, however, was the uncertainty remaining about the artefact. It could be a copy – and who was to say there wasn't someone with dirt on Tejada? Malleus pinned his hopes on his conversation with the director or curator.

'Then I'm going to need confirmation from you that you have commissioned me, as well as the museum's address and the contact details for this intermediary,' Malleus told her. 'I need to start my research right away.'

Tejada gave a relieved sigh and her necklace and earring jangled lightly together.

Celtica, Paris-Lutetia, November 2019

'Back to *Tresoriale*?'

'Of course, Jean-Luc.' Marianne Lagrande felt good as she once again drove through Lutetia with two policemen accompanying her, leading to a destination that would be her crowning glory. The question made it sound as if she were a great lady, flanked by two assistants on her way to the best club in town or about to set foot in the poshest restaurant around.

In fact, Lagrande was on her way to work. She'd be successful this time – she could really feel it.

Then the inspector has to take me out to dinner. She grinned like a Cheshire cat. *And it's going to be a lovely evening. The banlieue girl and the atheist.* She suppressed a giggle.

Her flight had been authorised.

During the night, she had managed to crack the code and work out the last of the artefacts.

Hannes Hein had written this:

Inv. No. 699

BRONZE DAGGER (England), also 'Goibniu's Dagger'

with a sheath made from wood, ivory & bone (original)

•origin: Athlone, Co. Westmeath

•discovered in: bed of the River Shannon

•material: Bronze

•length: 6.5 inches

•age: Approx. 2500 BC

•price: >50,000 euro

Shows atypical features for the period, such as several blood channels in the blade, gold and silver inlays in the handle.

Symbols on it, possibly of Celtic god Goibniu.

You can still see fingerprints embedded in it!

At least she hadn't lost her bet with Marcus Roy Crick. Lagrande had wagered on the final artefact being Celtic, while he had settled on Eastern European. You couldn't really call the Bronze Age Celtic, though, even if Shannon would definitely fall into the Celtic region geographically. *We'll call it a draw.*

Jean-Luc was driving the Peugeot to *Tresoriale*, while his colleague Jonathan was looking out the window at their surroundings.

Lagrande had opted for a simple pair of ripped jeans with black tights showing through, a white roll-neck jumper protecting her from the cold and her parka; her blonde hair was shielded by a red cap.

She was rather pleased to have these two armoured and heavily armed bodyguards with her; she could remember only too well the sort of force she'd had to deal with on several occasions. For that reason there was also a second team following them, out of sight, responsible for providing protection from the rear.

All this because of a few artefacts and a hysterical Collector thumbing his nose at the law. Lagrande could see the perimeter fencing of the airport approaching.

Jean-Luc took over from the autopilot, passing through the security checkpoint without any problem thanks to their police ID badges. They knew each other rather well by now.

They parked the Peugeot in front *Tresoriale's* Hall 2, a high-security facility attended by several guards, and her two bodyguards waited in front of the only entrance to the building, which contained row upon row of steel containers sitting on top of concrete ones. Once built for the most valuable of goods and for items that had been confiscated from flights or at customs, these virtually indestructible cases could be hired out discreetly for rather a lot of money: like a bank vault, only significantly larger. There was the choice of having them air-conditioned or not; Lagrande had chosen the hermetically sealed variant with *special equipment*.

Equipped with a Thermos flask, a large amount of knowledge and her computer, she set about exploring the similarities between the stolen artefacts from Hannes Hein's cubbyhole. She felt very safe in this immense hall. No one could step foot in here without having a very good reason to do so. Without a valid pass proving you were renting space here, there'd be no way past the armoured security detail with their dogs and automatic firearms.

Lagrande found her vault and opened the door using the keypad and a finger scanner. The thick bulkhead swung inwards with a hiss; the bolts used to lock it were thicker than a finger. It would take a god at the level of Hephaestus to make its way through these obstacles.

She sat down at the small table where the artefacts were lying neatly one alongside the other and started once again examining every single detail of the objects under the lamplight with a magnifying glass and a scanner.

Belenos be with me. I'm so close to a breakthrough. In fact, she had discovered something that baffled her in the Japanese fan, the Inuit harpoon tip, the African statue – as well as the diamonds embedded in it – and even on the gold figurines before they had been stolen from her. Apart from the fact that there would have been no way for anyone to polish a diamond in such a way in Africa at that time, she had found a curious symbol on all of the artefacts. It was well concealed, sometimes hidden in the smallest details. It was a tangible imprint on the fan, a tiny impurity in the diamond and a visible burnt piece on the inside of the statue.

The measurements were exactly the same, without any deviation.

Lagrande had had the materials examined in secret in a laboratory to ascertain their original age, including any signs on them, and from this she was able to conclude that some joker had decided to add his own symbol to the artefacts retrospectively in an attempt to instigate an artificially generated puzzle.

And quite the puzzle it is. Lagrande was willing to bet that this symbol would also be present somewhere on the objects that were still missing.

Look, Belenos: I've worked out the common feature – and the reason why the Collector's after them. She unscrewed her Thermos and poured herself a cup.

But the meaning behind it all refused to appear to her. She sat down once again in the container.

* Α Ω *

Quite well guarded. At least from the outside. But here . . .

It looks like a city of containers in a warehouse.

Sometimes it's far easier than you'd expect. I managed to take out a particularly dopey patrol guard and commandeer his clothes, pass and gun. Until they find the body, I'll be Ingo Rittmann. A foreigner. A Germanian. I wonder what sort of life he had in Lutetia. I got his address for free as well.

* A Ω *

Steel crate upon steel crate upon concrete bunker upon concrete bunker. What is all this? Certainly jewellery and trinkets and . . . well, pretty much anything you could imagine as far as treasure goes.

There she is: Blondie.

The pigs have dropped her off outside the entrance, but they won't be able to see me from here, following her along the top of the containers.

No cameras. Right, this is a private place. Obviously no one wants to be filmed while they're admiring their loot, or . . . no idea . . . maybe there are fifty-pound bags of coke kicking around or something.

Okay, so she's staying here. Looking around, still not seeing me – good – and back into the container.

And there goes the steel door again.

Right. Wonderful. Now I've just got to hope she'll come back out.

No doubt she's examining the artefacts.

It's pretty naïve though, taking two cops with her. Now they at least know where she's got something stashed away.

I suppose I could always go and see to them . . . hang on a minute. Two, three, four guys have just come in, all with massive guns. You can bet your life they're after my Eighties woman!

Well, excuse me for taking this as a personal affront. She's become a little bit like Bourreau Mark 2: no one else gets to decide when she dies apart from me.

The rules are the same for everyone, even those idiots below.

Ye gods, what would I give for my APB.

I'll have to do without it.

And I will.

Right, so lie back down, get out this boring little P7 semi-automatic, use the edge as a rest and secure it there.

Right, which one of you mugs wants to be first?

Buliwya (Quechua) / Wuliwya (Aymara) / Bolivia (English), Departamento La Paz, Tiwanaku, November 2019

Malleus passed through the city, marking as he did so how empty it felt. Most of the shops had already shut, their blinds and shutters lowered. As he couldn't read any of the signs in the local language, the reason for the somewhat conspicuous absence of people was a mystery to him – but that all changed when he came to a crossroads where police were diverting traffic away from the main road. Ahead of him he could see hundreds of people bearing placards and banners, gathering in a large square in front of an enormous step pyramid.

A demonstration. Malleus stroked his Fu Manchu moustache and followed the mimed instructions of the policeman; his satnav immediately showed him the new route he was supposed to take.

If the shops were shutting early, that surely meant they were expecting violence. Malleus guessed this was a dispute between the Incan and pre-Incan descendants. The entities appeared to be exercising a great deal of restraint, allowing people to come and go as they pleased.

Malleus handed over the reins to the autopilot and looked

around him, gathering his thoughts about the old – yet very new – states in Central and South America.

There was a cult of the sun here, at least in Tiwanaku. In addition, there had been further attempts in Bolivia to reintroduce the administrative system of the Incas and bring it in line with the modern world, which would take a considerable amount of time and effort to convince people of its merits. After all, you needed to have some very good reasons if you wanted to turn away from democracy and set up what was essentially a rather backward system of governance.

The traditional cult of the Sun God Inti did not forbid the worship of other gods, but rather restricted it. However, entities such as Viracocha, the God of Creation, and Pachamama, the Goddess of the Earth, would surely have some following, otherwise they'd have found a way to expand their power off their own bat. Animistic elements also played a significant role in this culture.

They used to at least. His knowledge about this part of the religious world was proving to be rather incomplete. Although a period of peace had fallen across most of South America, he knew there were still some rather turbulent matters that had yet to be resolved in the eyes of the people.

There was also the question in Tiwanaku of how to deal with the previous cultures and their gods, who had something of a popularity problem. *It wouldn't surprise me at all if Milord's troops were around somewhere in this area.*

Malleus suppressed his pleasant memories of the brunette agent who had kissed him goodbye the last time he'd seen her.

The i8 drove towards a large building resembling a town hall, on the front of which could be seen an imposing symbol of the sun. Various exhibitions were being advertised on the LED wall and the flags hanging down, all about the Incas who had assimilated back into the new development.

Malleus set up the autopilot to look for a parking space down a side street, put on his hat and got out of the car. It was only then that he heard the incessant noise of whistles and countless drums emanating from the demonstration all the way up to the museum.

As he was walking he wrote a message to Lagrande, asking her to give him more information about his client and her late husband. She was also to look up the name of the intermediary, Eduardo Juaréz, in the Interpol database, straight away, please.

Malleus wasn't exactly brimming with enthusiasm for this case.

He didn't know precisely how to classify the old Indio lady, and how much of her 'elderly lady' persona was an act.

When he returned, he promised himself he'd ask her a few questions and observe her reactions. That was not least due to the response from the museum director, who had replied to his email request for a meeting to investigate the robbery with a series of smiley faces, which didn't quite fit the seriousness of the matter at hand, nor the loss of a valuable piece of art.

I'm afraid I might have got my hopes up too quickly. Malleus had to walk around the block once more because he could see the first of the protestors jostling their way through the intersecting road: he was so obviously European that he had no desire to have an encounter with them. Most of them were wearing traditional Incan costumes, with enormous masks and jewellery made from feathers, clearly displaying their cultural affiliations. Slogans were being chanted and the noise of the crowd rang out with cries that were both proud and demanding.

I don't fancy getting caught up in that. But fearing he'd be late for his meeting, Malleus broke into a slow jog.

Suddenly, two breathless people ran out from a side alley and collided with him. He managed to stop himself from falling over by taking a couple of quick steps to steady himself, but the man and woman both collapsed to the ground.

They were both locals, though neither was dressed in particularly striking clothes. The woman had lost her large straw hat in the fall and had grazed her knee, but Malleus could also see other bruises she'd already had. Her companion got up in disgust, his jacket also revealing a tear and several dirty patches.

I'm hardly in danger here. 'Wait – I'll give you a hand.' Malleus reached out to the woman before a strong blow to his back knocked the air out of his lungs, almost buckling his knees; he saw a large stone bouncing on the ground next to him.

He quickly helped the Indio up and turned around.

A group of about thirty or forty people had slowed down and were giving him a look of pure hostility. Some of them were carrying stones the size of their fists and clearly intending to throw them at the couple, although the unexpected appearance of a stranger appeared to be giving them pause for thought. Two members of the group were grasping placards, probably from the demonstration. There were barely ten yards between him and the throng.

'Don't get involved,' implored the injured woman, who was only able to put her weight on one leg. She must have sprained her ankle. 'Get out of here – save yourself.'

'Don't worry about me, Miss. Call the police,' Malleus ordered the man, never letting the approaching pack out of his sight.

'They won't come. Not for Aymara like us.' He gathered

the woman in his arms and set off as fast as his legs could carry him.

We'll see about that. Malleus took out his PDA and made an emergency call. Law enforcement would have to come for him. Then he held his arms out in front of him. 'Stop,' he shouted at the crowd. 'You are . . .'

'Get out the way,' shouted back a young man in English, raising his stone threateningly. 'You lot have no right to order us around.'

You lot. He means Europeans. 'I can assure you that was never my intention.' Malleus smiled wryly, despite the increasing deterioration of the situation. 'Please let these two people be on their way in peace.'

'Go fuck yourself!' The young man threw the rock at him.

Malleus dodged the attack easily; the stone clattered harmlessly across the road. He suppressed the impulse to reach into his pocket and produce his Apache Derringer. He was still holding out hope that the police would be on the scene very soon.

More stones flew over his head.

The couple cried out, while the crowd cheered. You could see from their body language they were getting ready to attack, no matter what this European was telling them.

I won't let this turn into a lynching. Malleus braced himself.

A blaring siren heralded the arrival of a large motorbike as a policeman in black and white leathers came to a halt alongside Malleus, his front wheel swinging with the suspension. The mirrored visor of his helmet gave him an air of Judge Dredd. 'You rang about an emergency, Sir?' inquired the man without getting off his bike. The engine cut out with a deep bubbling noise.

The crowd remained, hesitant.

Malleus pointed towards the throng. 'Yes, Sir. These people

were threatening' – he turned his finger to the couple, the man kneeling down, holding his head where he had been struck by something, his wife trying to support him – 'these two people here.'

'They're Aymara,' hissed the crowd, remaining close together.

The policeman looked back and forth between the two opposing parties and then asked Malleus, 'And what exactly is that to *you*, Sir?'

Has he really just said that? 'People are getting hurt, Sir. That's something that should affect everyone.'

'It's happening all the time across the whole world. Often with good cause.' The policeman turned his visor to face Malleus. 'Am I right in saying that *you* have not been threatened, Sir?'

'They threw a stone at me.'

'Liar!' shouted the young man. 'We didn't do anything to him. He's making it up.' The people around him nodded in agreement.

'Sir, I understand that you are rather . . . overwhelmed . . . by what is happening here,' said the official, his voice icy. 'Please follow me and I'll take you to . . .'

'I'm sorry, Sir, but I'm not overwhelmed in the slightest. My only concern is your blatant unwillingness to protect these two victims from the whims of their assailants,' interrupted Malleus. 'And since it doesn't take a genius to work out that you yourself are not Aymara, the only thing you're planning to do is take me away so I can't be a witness to what's about to happen.'

The policeman cleared his throat. 'Are you suggesting I'm breaking the law, Sir?'

Malleus knew the man was looking for any excuse to arrest him. *Resisting the authority of the state.* That would seal the couple's fate.

He was shocked to see how strong the aversion to Incan and

pre-Incan descendants was, and the extents to which people would act on it – and under the eyes of law, which had been blinded by the reflection of a visor. *Under the eyes of the entities.*

Malleus reached into his trouser pocket and pulled out his wallet containing his service badge. 'My name is Bourreau, Sir, from Interpol. Which makes us colleagues,' he said in a loud, clear voice. 'Should you refuse to intervene on behalf of the victims, *I* will have to do it myself, and then report you to your superior. And to the authorities above them as well.' He tapped the PDA in his breast pocket. 'I'm recording all this, by the way.'

The policeman turned his head to the crowd and spoke to them in their own dialect, resulting in an argument. Malleus used this to his advantage and rung for an ambulance to get the injured couple to safety. 'It's all under control now, Sir,' said the policeman, turning back to Malleus. 'You may go.'

'I'll be delighted to do so, as soon as the vehicle has arrived.'

'Vehicle, Sir?'

'The ambulance. These two people need to go to hospital to be checked over.'

'Are you a doctor?'

'No, I can't say I am,' Malleus retorted, his voice still friendly. 'It's for precisely that reason I've called for an ambulance.'

A clamour rose up again from within the crowd; the policeman made a resolute yet appeasing gesture. 'Sir, you are a very prudent man. I'm sure these two Aymara will be incredibly grateful for that. Beyond that, I'd advise you to be incredibly careful for the rest of your visit, especially when walking through the dark streets of this beautiful city of ours.'

'Is it really all that dangerous?'

The policeman pointed to the pack behind him, who were

moving away slowly, gesturing contemptuously in Malleus' direction. Some of them were taking photographs of him on their phones. 'It will be for you from now on, Sir.' He started the ignition on his motorbike and roared off.

The ambulance arrived almost immediately and stopped in front of them; the paramedics got out and took care of the injured parties without hesitation.

The limping Indio gave Malleus a grateful look as one of the paramedics helped him into the ambulance.

He tapped the brim of his hat with relief and hurried onwards to meet the director.

Malleus had no doubt whatsoever that what the policeman had said was true. And that was all without a single entity getting involved. *It looks as if I can get in trouble with mortals as well.*

Celtica, Paris-Lutetia, November 2019

Lagrande took a large gulp of coffee, which tasted to her of unalloyed joy: she was still immensely proud of having discovered the symbols on the artefacts. Yet both the vastness of the internet, as well as conventional directories from libraries, were so far proving unhelpful in her search to work out their significance.

She was afraid she'd end up searching through ancient, dilapidated archives, bathed only in weak artificial light, where they still had microfiches and yellowed index cards that fell apart to the touch, teeming with silverfish and spiders and all manner of other creepy-crawlies.

Her ambition, however, made her determined to take this route if she had to, so that she could present virtually the whole solution to the case to the inspector upon his return.

If the worst comes to the worst, I might have to go to the Vatican. They've got an enormous collection.

A message popped up on her laptop. *The dove must fly.*

She froze for a moment, the blood draining from her face. *It's time!*

She hastily grabbed her computer containing everything she had researched, downed the last of her coffee and screwed the lid back on her Thermos.

Then Lagrande went over to the concealed second exit to the vault, looked around one last time and scurried out; her Beretta U22 Neos was loaded, with the safety off and in her right hand. In case of emergency.

* A Ω *

Mm.

No, I'll wait a bit longer. Let's see first whether these aren't just some Colombian drug lords here to store some of their produce.

Going from container to container, checking the numbers.

Now they're just standing there . . .

What's the Eighties woman doing now?

She . . . Ha ha, she's got a second exit! She can sneak out while these fuck-knuckles hold station at the front.

Good little trick, that.

Right, shall I get rid of four morons?

One of them turns towards me and . . . Oh shit. His glasses have got something a bit like my old ones had – maybe heat sensors or something. Anyway, they know I'm here now.

He shouts something and they dive to the floor.

Okay, let's find out who's the better shot now, shall we? But firing my P7 at a distance may mean I come out worse here.

Then it struck me: I've now become Blondie's guardian angel because I bumped off her old one.

Ha!

What's she actually doing?Almost certainly calling for backup and letting the wankers shoot it out among themselves.

Buliwya (Quechua) / Wuliwya (Aymara) / Bolivia (English), Departamento La Paz, Tiwanaku, November 2019

Malleus politely waited for museum director Adolfo Soto to stop laughing.

He stroked his Fu Manchu moustache and examined the Indio with his well-fitted suit with traditional Incan patterning. Jewellery and precious stones adorned his hair, striking a balance somewhere between being underdressed and excessively ridiculous, making him look utterly sublime in the process.

The cause of all this hilarity was his question about what was going on regarding the stolen Horn of Nandi, or the Horn of Alexander. Soto didn't look as if he was about to calm down any time soon. And unfortunately, his laughter was genuine.

In the meantime, Malleus began to suspect that either there had been no incident at all, or something remarkably different to what his client had asserted had happened.

The director eventually calmed down, clearing his throat and wiping away tears of mirth from the corners of his eyes. 'I beg your pardon, Mr Bourreau. I'm sorry you had to come all this way for nothing.'

'Forgive me for my confusion, but do you mean to say that the Horn of Nandi hasn't been stolen?'

'Well, yes and no. There was a rather amateurish attempt at stealing a few works of art. The perpetrators' interests lay primarily in Incan objects and exhibits originating from foreign cultures, such as the Horn of Alexander,' he explained. But when our security forces arrived, they dropped their loot. I'm having the horn restored as we speak, as it had a few scratches on it.'

Malleus put the Culebra in his mouth: a sepia band this time. 'May I possibly see it, Sir?'

Soto rested his elbows on the table and smiled. 'Why so sceptical?'

'The story my client told me is rather different.'

Soto's expression gave way to contempt. 'That's probably because Tejada is insane.' The director paused, then reached into the cabinet and took out a folder, leafing through it until he came across the paper he was looking for. He passed it over to Malleus. 'That's the will and inheritance certificate granting the museum sole custody of her husband's entire collection. No doubt she told you that *she* was the rightful heiress?'

I guessed as much. Malleus pulled the folder towards him and cast his eyes over the lines, which had been written in both English and an Indio language.

In fact, his client's husband had left the treasures to the museum *for better care and safekeeping* – which had been appended as the second page of the will. In the same handwriting, the corresponding paragraph that was in favour of Tejada was now void. At the same time, the final provision dictated that his widow might have access to it at any time.

'I didn't know that, Mr Soto,' confirmed Malleus thoughtfully. 'Thank you for looking at the files for me.'

'My pleasure. The last thing I want is for us to us to have an argument because all the facts aren't on the table.' The director shut the file and put it back on the shelf. 'You will of course have noticed that there's quite a lot of unrest in Tiwanaku at the moment.'

'As a matter of fact, I have.'

'Miss Tejada is one of the Aymara, who settled here before the Incas and left behind these imposing ruins. My ancestors built over it after they had shaken off the yoke of the Aymara. And that' – Soto's face took on a hostile expression – 'is not something we have either forgiven or forgotten. After the European *conquistadores* did everything they could to ensure we lost our identity, they came back even stronger with the arrival of the gods. You can't please everyone.'

Malleus understood what he was trying to say. 'What's that got to do with Tejada and the Horn?'

'As an Aymara, Miss Tejada is keen to stir up trouble. She will have come across to you as a scatterbrained old woman, but I can assure you, Mr Bourreau, that she is plotting to return the Incas to oppression. Rumours, paying for campaigns, announcements, that sort of thing. This poisonous woman is making no effort to hide the fact she thinks we'd be better off living in the good old days.'

'So she's not hiring me to investigate a failed robbery?'

Soto shrugged. 'I have no idea what her intentions are. Help, maybe? Because of the way she acted, we had to ban her from the museum.'

'But that's in breach of this will—'

'Miss Tejada broke the rules: that's something I cannot accept. Her presence in these halls is an act of provocation and there have already been a couple of scuffles in the exhibition rooms as a result. She's turning people against one another.' Soto pointed out the window, the stones in his hair gleaming. 'This demonstration is all Tejada's doing. Before you arrived, she handed out flyers in Tiwanaku to remind people of the glory days under Aymara rule, and how progressive her ancestors had been compared to the Incas. She makes demands, urging donations from non-Aymara, which is excessive behaviour I'm sure you'll agree.'

Malleus estimated that he did indeed have a case, though he didn't have a clue as to where it was leading him. *First the artefact.* 'Please may I still see the horn, Sir?'

Soto rose. 'Of course.'

They left the office area together, passing through the attractive exhibition room. The central point of the room, which was easy to work out, even without knowing the language or reading any of the signs, was dedicated to the Inca period. There was nothing about the Aymara who had once built a mighty city on the high plateau. They had been completely silenced, struck from the record, though their remains, such as the Sun Gate, could be seen and photographed by tourists everywhere in Tiwanaku.

Then they arrived at Tejada's husband's collection: everything the man had acquired.

The Horn of Nandi was situated in the Oriental corner, together with various other works of art. Malleus circled the display case, calling up the images Lagrande had sent him on his PDA, and as he did so, he noticed he had several new messages, including a couple from his secretary.

Later.

His PDA analysed the horn in the display case, compared it to the stored images and circled the points where they diverted from each other, either because they were unclear or because there were actual differences.

There are rather a lot. Malleus puffed on his Culebra. 'This is the original?' he asked Soto.

'Of course, Mr Bourreau. I had it checked after receiving the collection.'

'Is it not possible that the thieves left behind a copy for you?' he said without looking at the director, while his PDA zoomed in, finding more and more deviations as it did so. 'Would they not have noticed that during the restoration?'

'That . . . that would be . . .' Soto was clearly fumbling for words. He took out his phone and entered a code, and the glass of the case dropped down on one side.

With great concern on his face, the director pulled out a handkerchief, nervously extracted the horn and examined it.

Malleus, meanwhile, concerned himself with the thought that had just come to him. *What was stolen from Hannes Hein's cubbyhole? The original, or the forgery?*

Had the unknown Collector had it exchanged with a skilful trick?

Or had the exchange only taken place *after* the robbery, in the workshop where they did the restoration?

'How many people could exchange the exhibits in the cases?' Malleus asked, observing the director. The horror on his face was completely genuine.

'Apart from me, only the curator. The alarm system can only be turned off by the fire brigade or the police,' replied Soto absentmindedly, feeling the horn as if his fingertips could tell him more than his eyes could. 'I'm not sure.'

'*Sure*, Sir?'

'About what I'm holding. I'm not sure if it's the real horn or not.' Soto looked at Malleus. 'In any case, thank you for putting me on the right track. The thieves were clearly smarter than we gave them credit for.'

'Not necessarily, but possibly,' remarked Malleus, taking longer puffs as he started to feel dizzy. 'Were there any traces or clues left behind by the perpetrators?'

'No. The investigators found nothing – no fingerprints or anything like that. But because the robbery had failed, they didn't bother looking that hard.' Soto held the horn in his right hand. 'I've got to get this checked out,' he murmured. 'It's unthinkable if . . .' Malleus thought there was one other possibility as to who was behind the allegedly unsuccessful robbery. 'Did you have any enquiries from India relating to a return? It's still a high-value artefact with a direct link to Shiva. I don't think anyone would have been deceived by a simple name change. The exhibit has too many striking characteristics for that.'

'No.'

So it was highly probable they'd know in India that this was a copy and that the original was lost. In Hein's cubbyhole. Malleus felt a sense of uncertainty rise in him. There were too many variables; logic didn't work with such an incomplete formula.

So he'd have to rely on intuition instead.

'Please would you let me know as soon as you know more about the Horn of Nandi, Sir?' asked Malleus. 'I'd like to speak to Miss Tejada and report to her the true nature of the matter.'

'Of course. Of course I'll do that,' replied Soto, making a move to accompany him out, despite still holding the artefact in his hand.

'I'll find my way out. Good day.' Malleus retraced his steps and a few minutes later was standing in the sunshine in front of the museum.

It's still completely opaque. He put on his hat and sunglasses, continued smoking his crooked cigar and scrolled threw the messages on his PDA. *Let's find out what the world wants of me.*

Lagrande was reporting she had had a breakthrough, namely the decryption of the ninth and last artefact. She was also on the trail of what it was that linked them all, which was still perplexing her. She'd explain more when he returned but it appeared there was a sort of mark found on each of the objects. If the other artefacts also had these, it would prove that someone had put the mark on there.

Or had just produced all the artefacts themselves?

Tejada had written to let him know she had found a picture of the Collector. It was at a garden party. Even if she doesn't know his name, this would give Malleus a little more information about his opponent.

A picture! Perfect! As long as it's of the right person. After the episode in the jet, Malleus had a few clues about the man that he could compare with the photograph.

Sirens wailed in the distance: the emergency services appeared to be on their way to the scene of an incident.

Malleus looked up and saw a column of smoke rising in thick black plumes over Tiwanaku. The noise of drums and whistles intermingled with the sirens, revealing the protestors' continuing displeasure.

Malleus, trusting to his sense of direction, worked out that the fire was coming from the same direction as Tejada's house.

Damn it! He ran along the street in the direction of his parked i8, which he had summoned at the push of a button to save valuable time.

It looked as if his opponent wanted to use this fire to wipe every trace of him off the face of the earth.

Celtica, Paris-Lutetia, November 2019

Where are the guards? What do they get paid for if not to come running as soon as there's been a break in? Did the Eighties woman not say anything out there?

That's . . . fuck, the first lot have started shooting at me. Sure, take me for Ingo Rittmann, the friendly watchman, why don't you.

Take cover, get down from the container. My P7 won't be any good, not at this distance. And this lot aren't bad. Two of them are forcing me to stay under cover with machine gun fire.

I can't see what the others are doing.

Down from the container. Jump, land, roll – just in front of one of these idiots' feet.

Raise my P7, shoot, gone. Head-shots are the best.

What gun's this one got? Oh, a Steyr AUG A3. Good, that's better. It rattles and jitters a bit, but it packs a punch, as all good assault weapons should. Now it's mine.

Getting shot at from all sides; these pricks aren't missing by much. Good job this is a massive building – steel and concrete make for the best cover.

Continue stalking, keep my head down.

I can feel myself losing control. My vocabulary leaves something to be desired. Luckily my thoughts are . . .

There's another one! He unleashes a volley and disappears.

Throw myself flat behind the container. A bullet catches the sole of my right foot, but I don't feel a thing. Seems as if luck's on my side.

I swing the Steyr blindly around the corner, unleashing the entire magazine in short bursts; the bullets fly around aimlessly.

Then I step around the corner, raise my P7 and wait for one of them to leave cover. And here he is, today's winner – two shots. Chest, head, dead.

Just two to go.

Change magazine, packing again and ready to rumble. Back to the container with the artefacts.

Where are these masked idiots?

Gently now. Approach carefully . . . hang on, what's that on the door?

Wires!

For fuck's sake! Wires coming from a package of explosives!

Are they fucking stupid? Surely they can't . . .?

Buliwya (Quechua) / Wuliwya (Aymara) / Bolivia (English), Departamento La Paz, Tiwanaku, November 2019

The police had blocked the roads leading to Puma Punku. Malleus had to park the i8 himself, which was no easy task given the number of people and vehicles milling around. Thousands of angry and euphoric locals were congregating along the banks and barriers, holding up placards and maintaining a constant, rhythmic drumming that sounded like they were starting an invocation ritual. He heard cries of 'Inti!' – the Incan Sun God.

I've got to get to Tejada. He pushed through the frenetic crowd and found a gap, taking advantage of their distraction to smuggle his way past the security forces and run into the district, which was ablaze.

Nearly all the houses had turned into torches; flames licked against windows and roofs. Malleus looked over at the fire brigade, who appeared to be content with extinguishing the fires on the houses that weren't part of Puma Punku. *They're doing nothing!* The rift between the Aymara and the Incas had reached the next level, all triggered by his client and her actions.

Malleus opted for a route that kept him as far from the heat as possible as he passed by the flaming buildings. In doing so, he noticed a large amount of blood-spatter on the floor and walls, where it had begun to form pools; drag marks could be seen as well, as if someone had clubbed a seal to death and dragged its body across the blazing corridors in these burning houses.

He couldn't see any police presence, or ambulances. No one was attending to the inferno that was advancing from street to street.

He passed Indios carrying suitcases containing their dearest worldly possessions, their eyes blazing with naked terror and helpless rage, not understanding what was happening. Some had been injured, with cuts on their arms and face.

New era, old hatred. Malleus arrived at the street where Tejada lived.

The fire continued unabated, the dry ground acting as the perfect conductor, spreading the inferno.

People were helping each other; cars were being loaded up until their suspension threatened to break. Children were crying, women were wailing and men cursing as the wall of heat coasted inexorably towards them, picking up more and more speed.

No one was paying any attention to Malleus, the foreigner, running towards Tejada's house.

Then the pounding rhythm started up again.

Nearly a hundred masked people came around the corner, beating their drums in time and shouting threateningly at the Aymara. The sounds of machetes and daggers being unsheathed rang out; bludgeons and clubs were swung wildly around. The masked assailants had no intention of letting those running for their lives from the flames reach safety.

Chaos erupted among the fugitives. Some men stayed and

fought, while others leapt into cars in their attempt to bring their families to safety.

Where are the entities when you actually need them? Malleus took out one of his Apache Derringers in case he needed it to defend himself; the blood smears on the walls and asphalt made him think he might. He didn't dare come to anyone's assistance, no matter how much it pained him to leave them. The mob was incensed and whipped up into a frenzy, and didn't look to be in the mood for the subtleties of argument, especially not from the mouth of a European: *a former conqueror and oppressor.*

He had seen these sorts of scenarios play out during the Great Change; they were now being repeated in Bolivia with other triggers. Only entities or the police or army, with heavy weaponry to gain respect, could be of any help here, but because these institutions consisted primarily of Incan descendants, that would take some time.

If they decide to intervene at all.

Malleus reached his client's house and threw his shoulder against the door.

The marauders are already inside!

'Miss Tejada?' he shouted, listening for a response, his Derringer drawn.

A scraping noise rang out from the living room, which preceded a rattling and a woman screeching. Malleus ran forward, making sure to clear the rooms, checking corners and cubbyholes, and arrived at the entrance of the room.

The three masked men had torn through in a rage: everything had been knocked over and they had covered the walls with slogans Malleus couldn't read. Tejada lay on the carpet, unable to resist the woman strangling her with her bare hands. Tejada's arms and legs were hanging slack and her face had turned a dangerous shade of purple, thanks to lack of oxygen and congealing blood.

A man leapt out, wielding a machete to strike the final blow.

Malleus shot him in the head without warning. These people wouldn't pay any attention to him. *Why should I waste my breath?*

His companion, wearing a headset, shouted from the across the room and withdrew a revolver from his waistband, though not before receiving an Apache bullet through the chest.

The masked strangler pulled back from Tejada and took cover behind a chair. There was a loud clicking noise: she too was obviously carrying a firearm, and it sounded as if it were in her bag.

What is she doing? Malleus went to take cover behind the door.

There was a strong smell of petrol and a familiar cracking sound erupted from the first floor. Another fire was spreading, and no one would be able to put this one out. Tejada wasn't moving; her eyes were open and her tongue was lolling out of her mouth. He could clearly see a distinct distortion on her throat, caused by the pressure applied by her attacker. Tejeda was finished; a chain was lying broken next to the Indio.

There was a dull thud as the masked woman shot at Malleus through the chair.

The bullets punctured the furniture but whizzed past him harmlessly, burying themselves in the wall and punching holes in the slogans, images of gods and hanging tapestries.

The rattle of a lighter sounded. A second later, a Molotov cocktail flew out from behind the couch.

That's just not on. In a flash of inspiration, Malleus caught the bottle and turned his Apache to where the woman was taking cover; with a jubilant laugh, she appeared momentarily from behind the chair to observe the success of her attack—

—and before she could react, he shot her in the torso, although she was able to get a shot away with her Makarov semi-automatic pistol as she was falling to the ground.

The bullet missed Malleus, instead smashing into the fragile vessel in his hand. The mixture of petrol and diesel spread out immediately over his sleeve.

Shit! He whisked his arm away to the side to stop the burning fuse from catching him. It fell to the floor and set fire to the little pool on the carpet.

A second crack behind him sent shockwaves through his ears and back as a bullet knocked the air from his lungs. Tears were streaming from his eyes. Without the new fabric Karak had used for his clothes, he would have died there and then, caught on the back foot: an undistinguished demise.

All this, and not a deity in sight. Malleus fell to the floor and played dead to earn himself a bit of time; as he fell, he turned and saw through narrowed eyes the policeman who had grudgingly come to his aid in the side street.

He was holding a black Colt M1911 semi-automatic with one hand and pointing towards him as he approached with caution. 'How many dead foreigners do we need?' he said in English over a radio. 'I've already got one.'

'Good. Then we'd have four tourists,' came a soft reply. 'Can you bring him with you, or shall we just leave him here?'

'No, there's no point. Leave him here to burn. They've already started the fire.' His face was still turned towards Malleus. 'He's a cop. That'll give the media a field-day.'

'A cop? How on earth do you know that?'

'I've already met him once today.' The policeman laughed. 'Something French. Bourreau, I think.'

What's all this about? Malleus could feel the fire starting to lick at his leg. He'd have to deal with that soon.

'Did you just say *Bourreau*?' his companion asked, alarmed.

'Yes. Wait a minute, I can check. He's got his Interpol pass on him – waving it around and trying to look important.'

The other man cursed loudly. 'Shit, shit, *shit!*'

'What?'

'He's a friend of Exitus'!'

A jolt ran through Malleus. *They know Ove?*

'How was I supposed to know that?' replied the policeman, his mirrored visor preventing his face from being seen. 'He didn't have a shield or letter of recommendation or anything on him.' He looked down at Malleus, cursing. 'What are we going to do now?'

'Leave him. He's supposed to burn, at least according to our new instructions. Let's just hope Exitus doesn't come, otherwise we're both fucked.'

They're from GodsEnd!

'He's still being detained by the cops in hospital.' The policeman put the muzzle of his Colt against Malleus' head.

'Yeah, and who knows how long that'll be for?' The other man took a deep breath. 'It's shit, but there's nothing we can do about it. Then come back and look for another tourist.'

'Okay.'

'The riot is going well, I trust?'

'It is indeed. It was a brilliant idea, getting those flyers out in circulation. The old woman hadn't got the faintest idea about what she ordered and what she didn't.' The policeman stood up. 'I'm getting out of here.'

'Good. Just make sure he can't be identified by anyone, understood? No dental remains, no fingerprints, nothing.'

'Understood.' He ended the conversation and put his gun away, muttering away in his own language and turning towards the hall to get to the kitchen, where he'd certainly be looking for poultry shears and a meat cleaver: utensils for mutilating a body.

Malleus followed him silently and grabbed the man around his legs. He smacked his head on the wall and sagged to the ground, but his helmet kept him conscious and he reached for his semi-automatic straight away.

That won't make any difference. Malleus shot him through the hand with his Derringer; the bullet passed through, ripping blood and tissue. The policeman's fingers spread apart unintentionally – his tendons had been damaged and were now completely useless. 'Don't move,' he ordered him, standing up. 'Pull up your visor.'

The man gave a loud groan of anguish, but did as he was instructed. A clean-shaven Indio face, clearly in a lot of pain, appeared.

'What are *GodsEnd* trying to achieve here? A public uprising? To prove what exactly?' Malleus asked, uncertain. 'You're pitting the Aymara and Incas against each other!'

'The more people die and the more catastrophes there are, the more people start to question the gods,' replied the policeman, panting. 'Why don't they take any action if they really exist? This will wake people up to reality, if not here, then in Europe and the rest of the world. And if not by fire and the massacre of the Aymara, then let it be from our next act. We'll never stop. *Never!*'

Malleus felt an urge to hit the man. *What scum, Vile to his very core.*

He couldn't imagine that Ove felt the same way, that killing hundreds of people was the only way to show everyone that the gods were nothing more than con-artists.

It's not even proof. These are just terrorist acts that they've legitimised by telling themselves it'll make people change their way of thinking.

Malleus stared furiously at the policeman. 'You're under arrest,' he declared. 'I'll have you up before a judge.'

'But we're on the same side, you and I,' responded the man with a groan, getting up as blood gushed from his hand. 'You don't believe in the gods, and neither do we.'

'That's precisely the reason why I *don't* commit abhorrent acts that turn different types of people against each other! Religion has that stuff covered,' he told him, reaching for the man's belt to take his handcuffs. 'Put your hands behind your head.'

After he had safely secured him, he wanted to look for the picture and find Tejada's tablet to take with him.

He hoped he'd be able to find a picture of the Collector. His investigations into the Horn of Nandi had taken a back seat, especially as he was convinced from the analysis done by his PDA that the artefact in the museum was just a copy. *What a job.*

The policeman tried to head-butt him with his helmeted head.

Malleus dodged the attack and punched him in the abdomen, making him fall over once again. He walked around him and smoothly handcuffed him. They snapped shut with a click. He kicked him behind the knee for good measure and tied his shoelaces together.

'Wait here.' Malleus went back into the living room and made his way over to the prone Tejada and her three assailants as the flames and smoke continued to rise steadily.

As he was searching, he forced himself to stay calm, securing the tablet and at the same time discovering an old photograph under the side table that depicted a party scene. *That's got to be it!* Malleus stashed it away and headed back into the corridor.

The policeman's discarded shoes were lying on the floor; the man had scarpered. With him had gone his only witness, and any proof that the riot had been instigated by *GodsEnd*.

Maybe he's still outside. Malleus groped his way into the corridor and headed downstairs to avoid being engulfed in smoke. Through the open front door he could see the inferno spreading, raging through the Puma Punku district and destroying all before it. It was clear that no descendant of the Aymara would ever settle in Tiwanaku again, not after this appalling incident.

Only time would tell whether this would boost support for *GodsEnd*, but Malleus doubted it. People always found excuses to apologise for the failures of their gods, no matter how paradoxical it sounded. They had become accustomed to the fact that there was no such thing as an omnipotent and omnipresent deity.

Malleus was expecting the attack that came from the kitchen. He stepped smartly to one side and the onrushing policeman hurtled past him.

Malleus struck him on the knee with his Derringer's knuckleduster, producing a loud crack. 'Afraid you won't be going anywhere without me, Sunshine!'

As he fell, his opponent threw himself backwards against Malleus, hoping one of the two long carving knives he was clutching in his hand would catch his adversary.

Damn it! Malleus felt one of the blades sliding over his stomach, but his new clothing stopped the knife in its tracks. He was able to fend off a second attack with the titanium rings. The top of the kitchen knife arced upwards as the two men fell to the ground.

The policeman let out another shout before his body went slack.

I need him as a witness! Malleus rolled him over. *He can't . . .*

The long blade had been driven into the man's spine as he fell.

For fuck's sake! The only proof he had that *GodsEnd* were behind all this turmoil had just died on him.

Malleus' next task was to keep himself alive in this overwhelmingly hot oven of a district. He hurried out of the house, crouching to offer as small a surface as possible, and avoid the heat roaring through the streets. Bathed in sweat, gasping for breath and with stars in his eyes, he reached the gates to the enclosure, away from danger, and pushed himself through. Dizzy and exhausted, he sank into his i8 a few minutes later and drank down a mug of water.

The only good thing this case had brought him was the picture of the Collector.

Is this him? Malleus took it out and looked at it: there were roughly forty people there, some large, some small. At first glance he couldn't see anyone that could possibly resemble his dangerous adversary.

A sour taste of defeat and disappointment filled his mouth that not even the dark purple Culebra could remove.

And all the while, Puma Punku was burning to the ground.

Celtica, Paris-Lutetia, November 2019

Marianne Lagrande had imagined her dinner with Malleus Bourreau would be a little more romantic than this. But that's often the way life works: your dreams never quite come true, with or without gods. *Thanks a bunch, Belenos.*

They were sitting in a beautiful little brasserie just off Montmartre with a spectacular view, spoiled somewhat by the case documents scattered around the table, plus a tablet containing the latest data they had compiled.

She was wearing a tight red dress with a short leather jacket and black shoes with metal spike heels. Her backcombed blonde hair was tied back with a slender band.

They had just had soup to start and Lagrande feared that there was nothing else to come. In any respect. *Annoying*. She hadn't sacrificed to Belenos for *this*.

However, she was still captivated by the events of the case, and the latest developments sounded spectacular indeed.

Bourreau looked over her research on the bronze dagger supposedly wielded by the Celtic god Goibniu himself. The fact that this didn't tally with the age of the weapon was less of a consideration in the mythology. Things like this were always being declared as divine after the fact.

Lagrande took the tablet and brought up the photographs of the horn he'd taken in Tiwanaku. She looked at the various details. 'This is a fake.'

Bourreau looked back at her. The gaze from his blue contact lenses pierced her, giving her goosebumps; his smile in turn warmed her, though she showed neither of these feelings on the outside. 'You haven't even analysed its age yet. How do you know?'

She held out the display. 'The photos you've taken are good. You can see all the details, and your PDA has found several discrepancies. The one thing I can't see at all is the symbol that can be found on the rest of our artefacts.'

Bourreau stroked the ends of his Fu Manchu with his thumb and forefinger. 'Then it would appear our Collector doesn't just use force, but he's also got a bit of cunning about him, as we saw from the break-in in your office and in Bolivia,' he summarised. 'But he still hasn't quite found the right balance as to what is the more appropriate course of action.'

Lagrande immediately thought about the airport and the incident at *Tresoriale*.

Their adversary's commandoes had used force and brutality to gain access to the vault, stolen the artefacts and vanished. They'd left two of their men dead and one guard seriously injured; he'd been hospitalised from his injuries from the blast.

Lagrande wondered where the overzealous man had come from who'd got into a fight with the troops; he'd not been part of their arrangements. *Perhaps a have-a-go hero?*

Bourreau seemed to be able to read her thoughts. 'You were beyond brave, Madame. A meal is wholly insufficient as recompense.'

She smiled. 'It was fun, having something to do other than boring secretarial work. And I can look after myself, Inspector, as well you know.' She still had her Beretta U22 Neos in her jacket pocket. For security.

He nodded and waved the waiter over. 'Order whatever you want.'

Lagrande chose an expensive bottle of wine and a seafood pancake that particularly took her fancy. 'Obviously they'd be better if we were by the sea,' she added.

'Quite right. The ones in Brittany are the best. Have you ever been there?'

'No, I haven't been able to get out much since I started taking on your research.'

'We ought to make up for that. Maybe one of our cases will take us there.'

So he wants to keep me on. Lagrande nodded and suppressed her next burgeoning romantic idea, given the disappointing relationship between her previous one and reality. 'Have you already had a response?'

'The artefacts are on the move, but it appears they haven't yet reached their destination.' Bourreau ordered the lamb with couscous and a light red wine. 'All three bugs are rigged to set off a small, passive ping to the next radio tower, meaning we'll be able to know where they are at any given time without the thieves being able to detect any sort of transmission impulse.' He placed his hand on hers. 'Very good work, Madame Lagrande.'

'All I did was follow your friend's advice.' She beamed internally at his intimate gesture. 'Using such small devices was easy – they didn't seem to be more than tiny scraps of transparent paper.'

'So far this is the best trick up our sleeve against the Collector. He'll be thinking he's won a decisive victory, but in fact, we've turned the tables on him.' Malleus squeezed her hand once again in gratitude and drew his fingers away from her, to her great disappointment.

She knew that everything had been agreed with Lautrec. The guards at *Tresoriale* had been given instructions to only offer light resistance and then withdraw. Jean-Luc and Jonathan had also been ordered not to try to prevent the robbery. And the second unit remained at a distance to remain safe. This was the crucial difference from the previous attack: controlled conditions.

This had led to a brief exchange of shots in front of the entrance, which produced no other casualties than the two dead soldiers.

That is until our hero appeared. I hope he pulls through.

Lagrande pointed at the PDA. 'Where are they now?'

Bourreau looked at the display. 'The last signal came from Calais. Our robbers appear to be set on making their way over the Channel to England. And I know why, as well: that's where they do the fewest customs checks. They haven't got to subject the artefacts to standard airport handling, where they'd just have to hope that they'd be approved for transit.' He took out the picture from his pocket and passed it over to her.

'A garden party,' said Lagrande. 'They scrub up all right.'

'I've got to give it to Crick to have it digitalised at the highest resolution possible. I've been told the Collector is in here somewhere.' Bourreau suddenly looked deadly serious.

'I'll scan it and send it to him.' Lagrande could see their food approaching and bundled up the photographs of the artefacts. She had identified all nine stolen objects, from the fan to the brick, from the harpoon tip to the dagger. 'A wide range of cultures and eras, but *one* symbol,' she murmured.

'That's something I think about all the time,' he agreed, tasting the red wine and nodding at the waiter. 'The fact that these objects have value per se was obvious to Hannes Hein, but I don't think he knew about the symbols that linked them.' He stroked his Fu Manchu moustache again. 'So what does the Collector want with them? Where does their *true* value lie?'

Lagrande started eating. 'We'll find out soon enough.'

Bourreau smiled at her. 'I can't wait for the next revelation. And now, *bon appétit.*' He raised his glass. 'You've more than earned it.'

They began to eat, the light chinking of crockery adding to the ambience of the brasserie.

A message popped up on his PDA, which Lagrande could see. *Belenos, if you ever want another sacrifice from me again, then* ... Malleus opened the message and his face darkened. Then he rose and bowed apologetically without having even tasted his lamb.

'I'm sorry, but I've got an urgent matter to attend to,' he said, his voice filled with agitation. 'I'll see you in your office tomorrow. Gods willing, that is.'

'But . . .' Lagrande suddenly thought the world a very unfair place. The first slight hint of closeness – which her boss hadn't even registered – had been cruelly snatched away from her.

'I have no choice, Madame.' Bourreau pointed at the bottle of wine. 'Enjoy it in peace. Everything's been paid for. Please forgive me for my hasty departure.' He laid a hand warmly on her shoulder and hurried to the exit. 'See you tomorrow.'

The i8 pulled up outside, summoned with the autopilot, then he ran past the brasserie's window, waved at her one last time and got in. The BMW roared away.

'Yes, see you tomorrow,' answered Lagrande in a small voice. *Merde*. She drank her glass of wine in a single gulp and poured herself another. *Enjoy it. You bet I will. Far too quickly to appreciate it properly.* Frustration spread throughout her body. *Belenos, you unreliable, evil god. Evil, evil god.*

Now in a foul mood, she flicked through her phone to see if there was anything on the news that warranted Malleus' hasty retreat. She continued looking until she came across an emergency report of a spectacular escape: the alleged *GodsEnd* terrorist Ove Schwan had broken out, leaving several policemen injured in the process.

Of course. She sighed and let the effect of the alcohol wash over her. But Malleus didn't say what he was going to do. *Is there another reason?*

Instead of an answer, she received a message from Lautrec, saying that the guard who had been injured in the incident at *Tresoriale* and taken to hospital had turned out to be a *fake* guard. His relatives had come to visit him and were baffled to find an unknown man lying in the bed. But when the security team at the hospital arrived to find out what was going on, he had fled, despite having sustained serious injuries. They still didn't know where the *real* security guard was.

It was clear to Lagrande who had slipped into the shoes of the guard. *It had to be my shadow.* He had clearly tailed her in an attempt to reach the inspector. But in this case he had chosen his disguise poorly. *Escaped again – but there's surely got to be a photo of him now. A proper one.*

She considered contacting the hospital immediately, but stopped herself: Bourreau had told her to sit here and enjoy herself. And research would take time.

'Good evening, Madame Lagrande,' a female voice said unexpectedly from behind her, and an unknown woman took the seat where Bourreau had been sitting only minutes before. She was wearing a simple but elegant turquoise dress and had long black hair; she was clearly younger than Lagrande. There was a slightly mad, unsteady look flickering in her green eyes.

'May I join you?' She promptly picked up the cutlery and began to eat the lamb the inspector had ordered. She gave a contented sigh and closed her eyes. 'That is truly delicious.'

Lagrande was not sure what the etiquette was for these sorts of situations, although the wine helped. 'Actually I was planning to eat alone,' she replied coolly, resisting the urge to reach for her Beretta. *Who is she?*

'Yes, I know, because Malleus had to leave a little earlier than he intended.' The mysterious woman smiled and tasted the wine. 'I wanted to take this opportunity, Madame, to warn you to keep your grubby little fingers off him. Otherwise you'll be making an enemy you could do without.' The sharp knife passed through the flesh of the lamb and cut off a small piece. Red juice seeped out, forming a pool on the plate.

He's already spoken for – that's clear now! Lagrande felt as if she had been hit in the stomach with a hot poker. *What a shitty evening.* 'Oh . . . I'm very sorry. I thought . . . You're his . . .?'

The black-haired woman shook her head and gave her a wink. 'Not yet. But soon. And I really don't need any interference from you.'

Lagrande felt as if she were being interrogated. She had a rival who was trying her hardest to intimidate her.

She didn't let it show. She laughed, undeterred. 'And you would be?'

'Marina. And I've already been rather close to him. Several times, in fact.' She licked the knife with her tongue, right along the edge – but didn't appear to hurt her. 'Don't lie to me.' She pointed to the left-hand side of her body. 'Your pistol won't do you any good either.'

She swept the final piece of lamb into her mouth, drained the last of the wine and stood up to take her leave.

Did that really just happen? Marianne Lagrande dared not move.

It wasn't just that Belenos had disappointed her and her romantic dreams had gone up in smoke, but that she had also managed to incur the wrath of a madwoman.

A woman whose sharp tongue could defy a blade.

BOOK 9

Episode 9: After the Storm

‘For they have sown the wind, and they shall reap the whirlwind.’

Hosea 8:7, Bible,
King James Version

‘Storm!
Over the sea
Spray of white gout
Rolls the clouds
Black sea.
Free
From the depths of the grave
Rise my comrades,
Wailing’

Ferdinand Avenarius, ‘Sturm am Meer’,
Wandern und Werden, 1881

‘A storm can only extinguish a weak flame.
If it has already started to spread, it will only make it stronger.’

Sophie Mereau, *Observations*

Celtica, Paris-Lutetia, November 2019

Malleus Bourreau was annoyed.

Sitting at Interpol headquarters, he listened half-heartedly as his boss, Ilja Lautrec, proceeded to talk at him in his office. His thoughts were far more occupied with the movements of the bugged artefacts from which nothing had been heard for quite some time after the signal had dropped off in the middle of the English Channel. Television and internet news provided a solution to this apparent mystery: a ferry had sunk and the robbers had almost certainly gone down with it.

Rescue forces searched the site for shipwrecked survivors, who would have been able to survive for only a few minutes in the icy Atlantic waters without a lifeboat.

The fact that none of the three bugs were giving out any sort of signal could mean that they had been in contact with water and high pressure for a long time, and in that case they'd be together with their unwitting courier or couriers in the sea somewhere between Britannia and Celtica. *A calculated move*. Malleus felt a deep sympathy for the passengers, though his anger about the lost artefacts overrode this in a matter of seconds. *All three of them at the bottom of the sea in one fell swoop.*

So both the Collector *and* Malleus would be deprived of their triumph, given how difficult it would be for Malleus to capture his adversary and hold him to account for all the terrible deeds he had initiated.

There's still so much that needs to be explained. Frustrated, Malleus puffed on his sepia-banded Culebra. The smoke sank like a heavy fog from his lips before coming to rest at his feet like a tamed animal waiting for a command from its master.

But he wasn't sitting at Lautrec's desk because he had taken such a heavy risk with their most valuable evidence and lost it, but rather, to receive instructions about his next case – something Malleus was not at all interested in at this very moment.

He still held out a faint hope that Marcus Roy Crick would,

with the aid of the photograph Malleus had found in Bolivia, manage to find someone who could plausibly be the unknown Collector. Then Malleus would be able to come up with a new plan of action for how he could catch up with him.

His adversary was rich and unscrupulous and cared not one jot for laws or rules. This gave him plenty of options for avoiding justice, such as hiring the best lawyers and bribing witnesses. It would have been far more straightforward and unequivocal if the artefacts were still around.

'You should get going in the next hour or so, Bourreau. You've got rather a long journey ahead. You can read up about everything you've missed while you're on your way. That'll be all.'

Damn it. Didn't catch any of that. Malleus cleared his throat and moved his feet, breaking up the smoke and causing it to dissipate into the carpet. 'Sir, I'm afraid I've rather lost my way,' he apologised. 'Sorry.'

'Because you're still annoyed about your lost bait,' observed Lautrec, who was far more convinced of the tastefulness of his dress sense than reality indicated he should be. He combined this so effortlessly with his almost perpetual bad mood that it could almost be considered a style in its own right – despite the somewhat painful effect it had on one's eyes. Today, his yellow shirt and green jumper were set off by a patterned red tie lying askew. 'But if you had been listening to me, you'd know that there might well be a connection.'

'Between?'

'Between the ferry accident and your new case.'

Malleus' irritation grew. 'I have to admit, I—'

Lautrec made a weak movement with his finger, as if failing to summon up the energy to flick a fly away from him; his black curls bounced up and down. His bearded face reflected nothing but displeasure. 'I'll send it to you.' He looked at his watch. 'Frankly, I've neither the time nor the inclination to explain it all to you again.' He got up. 'And don't forget about Lagrande. She's waiting for you downstairs, ready to go.'

'Why Lagrande?'

Lautrec looked at him with narrowed eyes – one of his favourite faces. 'You really weren't listening to a word I said, were you?'

'No.'

'Then she can tell you everything while you're on the road. I'm off home.' He threw on his ugly brown jacket, which would have turned even the most stylish outfit into a fashion disaster. Lautrec was utterly undeterred by this, however. 'I am most curious to hear how your investigations proceed, Inspector.' He turned to Malleus with a look that left him under no illusions that he was to get up and leave immediately. 'Make sure you report back as you go along. Even if you think this could have some connection to the ferry.'

The glass door shut behind Malleus, barely avoiding the glowing tip of his Culebra, and the roller blind on the other side was pulled down.

'What a charmer,' Malleus murmured to himself, turning around and passing through the criminal investigation department, which dealt with all manner of cases, from murder to every other capital crime.

With his specialism in divine incidents, Malleus was a striking exception to this rule; his colleagues' reactions to him ranged from polite acknowledgement to admiration to outright resentment.

So I'm driving, am I? Where? And why is Lagrande coming with me?

He had nothing against her – on the contrary. She was of enormous help to him: a woman who knew how to defend herself and was highly ambitious, who made herself up like an older woman to avoid unwanted attention from younger men. She was fundamentally the perfect partner in crime – but he preferred being a lone wolf. He was more than happy with her title of research assistant.

But for some reason or another he was supposed to bring her along.

Malleus went downstairs and met Lagrande in the foyer.

She had a small travel suitcase next to her and was wearing disconcertingly normal clothes that bore no resemblance to her normal eighties look. She wore high black boots over ripped jeans, and a dark green waxed jacket with a hood. Her long dyed-blonde hair was concealed beneath a large green hat, while a thin black scarf was wrapped gracefully around her neck.

'Inspector,' she called out in high spirits, 'ready for our little trip?' Lagrande could see he hadn't packed anything. 'Oh. You didn't read my message, did you?'

He took another puff, his irritation growing further. It wasn't showing any signs of improving. 'No, I didn't. Where are we going?'

'First we're going back to your flat to pick up a few things. And then we're off to the English seaside. Cornwall, to be precise.'

'Aha.'

She grinned. 'You didn't listen to anything Lautrec was saying, did you?'

'Not one word.'

Lagrande picked up the suitcase just as he bent down to do the same. 'Just to be clear, I'm a big girl – I think I can just about manage.'

Malleus could see the bulge underneath her jacket, betraying the presence of her Beretta U22 Neos. She wouldn't leave home without a gun, even though the danger posed by the Collector could be considered negligible given the disappearance of the artefacts. But his shadow was still out there, and he had recently shown up around her once again. *The Glyph Killer.*

'It's not a matter of *size*,' he replied, taking the luggage out of her hands. His BMW i8 coasted up to them, guided by its autopilot. 'So now would you care to tell me why we're going to Cornwall?'

They walked out together and climbed into the bastion of comfort that was his sleek electric car.

'Maybe we should fly instead?'

'By the time we've found a flight and hired a car at Heathrow, we'll already be over there,' he replied curtly. 'The traffic in the Channel Tunnel will be completely clear at this time. Piece of cake.'

'Think of my poor back though,' she complained as she got in.

'Don't worry, Madame, you can adjust the seat. You'll be far more comfortable here than if you were sitting in the office,' he promised her, loading her luggage into the car before swinging himself back into the driver's seat and taking back control of the vehicle. Their first destination was his little flat at the Place du Tertre. 'Now, please tell me what we're supposed to be doing in this beautiful corner of England? And, what's more, why I've got to bring you with me?'

Lagrande laughed back at him. 'Oh what a charmer you are, Monsieur l'Inspecteur.'

'You know what I mean, Madame.'

'Yes, you've made that abundantly clear.'

Malleus stroked his Fu Manchu moustache, then flicked the remains of his cigar stub out of the open window. 'Do forgive my terrible mood. It's got nothing to do with you.'

'Ah, I bet it has just a little bit. You hate the idea of having your partner with you on a case.'

Malleus secretly agreed. 'It's because of the artefacts,' he replied half truthfully, 'and how we managed to lose them after all the effort to acquire them.'

'I know. That's why I can tolerate your foul mood. For now, at least.' She switched on the BMW's on-board computer and its window projection function, prompting the facts about their current case to be displayed in luminous green writing on the windscreen. 'You're off the hook for now. Anyway, people keep disappearing around the Lizard Peninsula in Cornwall – on walks, boat trips, that sort of thing. Sometimes locals; sometimes tourists.'

That still wasn't the sort of thing you'd call in an investigator like him for. 'Before the return of the gods as well?'

'There are records dating back to 1732. The first incident was a fishing vessel going missing under clear skies; later they found its washed-up wreckage, but no one could explain how it happened. There were large parts that had holes in them in the shape of claws, and it is claimed that they also found a tooth the size of a finger. So began the legend of a sea monster.'

A seafarer's yarn. Malleus nodded. 'Carry on, Madame.'

'Now, for the last eight weeks, after every storm, body parts are being washed up on the shore – and it looks like they belong to people who have been reported missing. The local police have been using DNA analysis to work out who these people are; their relatives have been asked to give hair samples.'

'Could this not just be the work of some psychopathic serial killer?' Malleus had heard about Cornwall, how peaceful and beautiful it was meant to be, but frustration was stopping him from fully engaging with the story. He was far more interested in the mysterious Collector and the fact that the only lead they had for him was an old photograph and Crick's network.

'The wounds they found on the remains of their bodies didn't match any known weapon or animal,' continued Lagrande, 'and *that* is why the King of Britannia asked for you specifically, Monsieur l'Inspecteur: as a specialist, knowing you wouldn't need too much discussion.'

'The king, eh?' *Perhaps this might be interesting after all.* In Malleus' mind, the information he'd just heard combined to form yet more questions: What dwelled on the Cornish coast and what had it done with these people? What entity could have been responsible for this? *Or is there a far more earthly, prosaic explanation for the whole thing?* 'Right, very well then. Let's see what this is all about.'

Lagrande grinned. 'As if you have a choice in the matter.'

'We're lucky this isn't the tourist season. Otherwise the number of missing people would no doubt be considerably higher.' Malleus brought up the images of the body parts that had been found on the display as the i8 slowed to a halt at the traffic lights.

There were several half-hands, a right lower leg with no foot, two thighs and the torso of a woman with her breasts torn off. From their extended submersion in water, they appeared puffy and waxy and the limbs gave the impression of having been half cut off and half torn off.

Malleus increased the luminosity of the display so as to be able to see the details more clearly, enlarging the display as well. *I don't recognise these wounds at all.*

In the absence of any other explanation, the autopsies described a finely serrated, heated knife or very sharp, hot teeth. In two cases cuts had reportedly been made by a sharp blade, and with a large amount of force. The flesh wasn't bleeding, as if the cuts had been sealed up afterwards with invisible glue.

'Maybe we ought to do without the pictures while we're driving through town,' observed Lagrande.

'Why?' Malleus looked at her in surprise. 'The sooner I can—'

She pointed towards the pavement.

Several pedestrians were standing stock-still, staring in horror at the BMW. The green man at the pedestrian crossing had disappeared again; two passers-by raised their phones and took a photograph. One woman was throwing up into a drain, while a child cried hysterically into his father's rain-soaked coat.

Then the i8 continued on its way.

'You're right.' Malleus switched off the projection and turned his mind to what he'd pack for the trip. He didn't need very much. 'So why am I bringing you with me again, Madame Lagrande?'

'You just can't let it go, can you?'

'I'm just asking! It's an entirely harmless question!'

'Lautrec said I should go and see Crick and give him a grilling,' she replied, grinning. She was having a wonderful time making him feel uncomfortable. 'Monsieur le Chef has received a few tips from some of our colleagues in artwork recovery that Mr Crick has developed a tendency to turn to illegal means to achieve his ends.'

'Did he not say that it was his son who had a tendency to use the dark arts?'

Lagrande nodded. 'But that doesn't appear to be the whole truth of the matter. No complaints have ever been raised about him directly – only his middlemen.' She put her hat down, her long hair falling onto her jacket with a gentle sound, releasing the aroma of her perfume. 'I don't trust him. He could very well be double-crossing us.'

'To get his hands on the artefacts himself.' Only yesterday Malleus had written to Crick to tell him not to do anything, even if he had any suspicions about who was responsible for his son's death. 'And why has Lautrec given you this task?'

'Don't you think I'm up to it?' She started to twist her hair into a plait.

'Well, *actually*, it is *my* case.'

'*Actually*, I was the one who worked out what the artefacts were,' she said pointedly. 'And *actually*, I was the one who made sure they were secure, who got shot at by soldiers and—'

'Yes, yes, fine, Madame,' conceded Malleus. *Not such a bad partner after all.* 'But I'll be accompanying you.'

Lagrande picked up her Thermos and poured coffee, bubbling gently, into two paper cups. 'I suspected as much, Monsieur l'Inspecteur.'

Sounds more like that was what she was hoping for.

His thoughts wandered of their own accord to Oona Milord, to her kiss – the one he suddenly realised, to his surprise, needed to be repeated. But his past was still far too ingrained in his very bones, in the very depths of his soul. When he had comforted little Bala, he had felt the pain and mourning for his own daughter coursing through him as if he had lost her only the day before. *His child, his wife.*

He never again wanted to suffer such a punishing blow. *Not with Milord, nor Lagrande. I won't allow my heart to be broken like that again.*

The car stopped in front of the block of flats where his little apartment was.

Malleus got out of the vehicle with great haste.

Celtica, north of Paris, November 2019

I look like fucking Frankenstein's monster – starting to feel a bit like him as well, given how rapidly my self-control is dissolving away. The same old pattern. My therapist warned me about this. Having any sort of say about my thoughts and words is a thing of the past.

But is that really a surprise, after those pricks blew up the vault all around me? They made the organ dealers look like absolute pussycats.

It was a good job they thought I was the guard, albeit briefly. That was just enough to keep me alive. They must have laid a trap at Tresoriale *to get their hands on those objects. A little obvious for my tastes, but it still worked.*

But what those arseholes didn't realise is that I managed to stick a bug to one of the robbers before they made their escape. My prey will be following him as well, so if I stay on his tail I'll be able to get back to him. There's no way he'll let those artefacts go.

It's as simple as that: my beautiful little chain; a secret polonaise.

The signal's stable – somewhere around Calais, staying more or less where it is and never leaving the city.

Pity they weren't on that ferry that sank – that would have been hilarious. Actually no, it would have been a disaster. The artefacts would have been lost for ever.

Ah, it's back again. I sound like I come from Vulgaristan. I'm starting to get a handle on things a little better now. Much better. I can't lose control or else my chance to be close to him once again will slip by . . .

I'm feeling about as well as I did in Calais; the painkillers have pretty much taken away all sensation. It's not the healthiest way of going about things but I've got to intersect with him, no matter what.

And I've managed to get my hands on an APB! Faster than I had imagined, actually. I still need to carve the ammunition, otherwise how else will everyone know I'm back in business after that prick Schwan shot at me? I've already got a Dremel in case I'm unable to find anything better, like a hunting shop with its own workshop. I'd much rather that, obviously.

It's a decent piece of kit, this APB, even though it hasn't quite got the same feel as my old one. I need to give it a proper runout first.

Schwan. Stupid little arse-licker. I'll see to him as well.

But first Calais.

Stay on the lookout.

Work on getting my control back.

Just be. Wait and look forward to my reunion with him, even though the joy will be unrequited.

He owes me a great deal.

Britannia, Kernow (Cornwall), near the Lizard Peninsula,
November 2019

In his mind, Malleus had always linked Cornwall to trashy stories about the trials and tribulations of love, without really knowing much at all about this county that had decided to remain in England during the Great Change.

But it was and would always be Celtic, its strong roots enabling it to retain a special status over the centuries. Even the old Cornish language, which had once been close to extinction, was undergoing a dramatic recovery.

After a speedy journey of just a few hours, the i8 entered the region and Malleus and Lagrande immediately saw the beauty of the area; you could forgive a bit of kitsch when surrounded by scenery like this.

Farmhouses and cottages of stone and thatch gave way to verdant gardens spilling over into those of their neighbours, even as the harshness of winter was approaching. Gentle hills gave way to vertiginous cliffs, while the sea and sand stretched out as far as the eye could see.

'By Belenos, it's stunning here,' exclaimed Lagrande for the tenth time. She knocked back the last of her coffee, despite it being all the worse for the journey. It kept her awake though. 'I need to go on holiday here, urgently.'

'Let's just wait and see how this case pans out,' warned Malleus, enjoying the interplay of colours rippling over the land and sea. Sunbeams broke through the clouds, their fingers of light pointing down as if to cast particular significance or illumination on certain areas. *She'd have loved this.*

Lagrande brought up more information about Cornwall on the display. 'I've prepared something for us, Inspector. There's a veritable treasure trove of burial mounds, stone circles and dolmens here. The Celtic gods defied all change, whether Roman or Anglo-Saxon.'

'Cornwall for ever,' muttered Malleus. 'So do they pray to the usual gods?'

'Yes. Dechristianisation also ended the dispute about who their national hero should be.' Lagrande swiped the information away, causing new material to appear on the inside of the windscreen. 'The first thing I thought was that Lizard Point was a reference to the monster.'

'Which is clearly not the case, judging by your tone of voice.'

'No indeed. It comes from the Cornish, *Lys Ardh*, roughly translated as High Court. The English, in their ignorance, turned it into Lizard.'

'Thus came a lizard from a High Court.' Malleus stroked his black beard in amusement.

'Yes, well, anyway, we can't expect the solution to be quite that simple.'

'Sometimes it is, Madame.' Malleus leaned back. In a few minutes they'd be arriving at the village where their English colleagues were waiting for them. The hotel had been booked; the guests were mainly composed of a specialist police force, including search and rescue teams, two forensic experts and a coroner. 'Are there any other myths about a monster apart from the one you've already mentioned?'

'No. The next closest creature would be the Welsh dragon, but I hardly think—'

'He came here on holiday?' Malleus laughed. 'My dear Madame Lagrande, one thing is for certain. *Everything* has to be factored in, even the most simple and obvious things. Holmes and Houdini would say the same.' He brought up some details about the Welsh dragon on his PDA. 'He fought against a white dragon, so the legend goes. But it doesn't say what happened to the white one.'

'Well, he was obviously killed.'

'Either that or he survived and starting swimming around Cornwall looking for a feed.' Malleus looked at the new message that appeared on his screen. 'But that sounds a little too far-fetched as well.'

'And as we well know, gods aren't born from legends,' interjected Lagrande.

'There are no gods.'

Malleus didn't believe that they were the same creatures of legend. Just because the gods had returned, that didn't mean the world was suddenly some fantasy amusement park, a playground for everything that had ever been mentioned in legends and fairy tales. *If that were the case I'd have shot myself a long time ago.*

The email was from Germania. At his request, the Germanian authorities had offered to put a Russian APB Stechkin up for sale as a decoy, advertising it aggressively until they came across an arms dealer.

The dealer was in turn overseeing a small criminal investigation team to see whether there were any customers interested in this weapon. A few had been sniffing around, but no sale had actually been made – until, not long before the team had been about to withdraw their surveillance unit, the dealer sold the APB in a very hasty transaction indeed. The black marketeer hadn't seen the dealer before making the transaction and had no idea that the picture they had put up on the advertisement was a phantom image. Malleus was in no doubt whatsoever that this particular customer was his shadow.

Granted, the buyer escaped without being recognised, but Malleus' Germanian colleagues had taken precautions by inserting a tracking device into the handle of the fully automatic pistol, which would silently report where the weapon and its owner were.

Calais. Malleus shook his long black hair and brushed it back over the shaved part at the back of his neck, which felt short and bristly. *What on earth is he doing in Calais?*

He had counted on the coordinates being Dover or London or maybe somewhere just a few miles behind them. *Is the buyer not our Glyph Killer?*

'Something about our case, Inspector?'

Malleus shook his head. 'No, just a message about something else.' He didn't want to overburden Lagrande. Once the APB's coordinates were within a mile of them, there'd be time enough to give her some warning.

The i8 turned in to the village; just like everything else around them, it looked like the set from a trashy romcom. But you couldn't blame Cornwall for this – it was just so beautiful, even without gruff Sir Jack and Wilbur the roguish stable boy, who would secretly be the son of a minor aristocrat, without strict Lady Charlotte and her tearaway, secretly adopted young daughter, and without all the Johns and Emilys and whatever they're all called in those hyper-romantic films.

Up ahead, Malleus could see the picturesque hotel in the small village of Lizard. *Yet another idyllic place.* He had the impression that Cornwall was surrounded by the sea on all sides, but in fact they were on the southern tip of a peninsula.

Malleus cast his mind back to the aquatic curse put upon him by the goddess Brigantia: he would never be safe – and might even drown – whenever he was around her element, or something like that.

Malleus was delighted to discover that, especially given the proximity of the waves all around him, he didn't care one jot.

'Why do you keep going on about Houdini, Inspector?'

Malleus looked at Lagrande, who was putting on her make-up next to him. 'Houdini wasn't just an escapologist; he made it his life's work to expose charlatans in the world of psychic mediums and séance organisers,' he explained. 'He didn't believe in the supernatural. He knew all the tricks of the trade far too well.'

The i8 stopped in front of the hotel, around which a large number of police cars had parked. Lizard was one of the safest places in the world, thanks to its extremely high level of security.

After they had found a gap between the cars and swung the BMW into it, they unloaded their luggage and headed inside the small hotel, which reminded Malleus of his case in Brittany. Luckily, the Cornish-Celtic décor and the hotel's furnishings meant there wasn't too much of an overlap.

Several moustachioed policemen were standing at reception,

engaged in deep discussion over a cup of tea, their hats clamped under one arm. The British accents were impossible to ignore.

Lagrande just about manage to conceal her laughter at this sight with a cough, though she did draw attention to herself in doing so. 'The only thing missing here is a game of bridge,' she muttered to Bourreau.

'Good afternoon, gentlemen,' said Malleus in English, removing his hat. 'My name is Bourreau. I am an inspector at Interpol, and this is' – *I can't say she's my secretary* – 'my assistant investigator, Marianne Lagrande.' He could feel her astonished gaze falling upon him. 'Would one of my colleagues be so kind as to take me to the leader of the task-force?'

The bobbies looked at him in silence. One of them took a loud sip of tea, another stroked the tips of his moustache demonstratively, while a third scratched his sideburns. Nobody said a word.

This wall of passive-aggressive tea drinking and silence made it obvious to Malleus that they thought he was just in the wrong place. The whole thing appeared to be a highly English (or indeed, Cornish) affair, where no one wanted to offer any assistance.

Hurried steps could be heard approaching from outside. Lagrande took a step forward, away from the entrance.

A few seconds later the door burst open and a bearded policeman stormed in, holding his hat in his hand out in front of him in a vain attempt to protect himself from the gale blowing outside. 'Everyone to Lizard Point right away. Tommy's gone missing!' he shouted breathlessly.

The men calmly placed their cups down on the counter, put on their hats and hurried past Lagrande and Malleus into the open, before getting into the police cars and racing off into the distance. 'I think we'd better follow these friendly gentlemen,' said Malleus, putting his hat back on.

'Tally-ho, yippety-dip and zing zang spillip,' added Lagrande, holding back laughter once again. 'I actually thought one of them looked rather like General Melchett.'

'Who?'

'*Blackadder.* A television programme. Never mind. That's why I had to . . . Oh forget it.' Lagrande walked towards the BMW. 'May I drive? As your *assistant investigator*?'

Malleus sighed. 'They drive on the left over here, Madame. Don't forget.'

Celtica, Calais, November 2019

Calais.

Can't stand the place. Too many lorries and far, far too many cops who think they've got to go around controlling everything and everyone.

The signal's coming from . . . the hotel.

Very well. I'll go and knock on some doors and see if anyone opens up.

Time for me to show off my mad acting skills again. I think I'll be a secret agent today, meaning I'll just casually wander through reception, keeping my face hidden and carrying on as if I'm reading, climbing the stairs and following the signs.

First floor, second floor, third floor . . .

So far, so good. But my pulse is racing, my heart's beating faster and faster and my head is pounding. The painkillers are wearing off. Fuck, it's really starting to hurt now. They extracted three fragments of metal from my body, stuck me back together and stitched me up again.

Those pricks are due their comeuppance for that. I take it rather personally when people try to blow me up.

Stay calm now; think about your choice of words.

Here we are, room 333.

Knock, wait. 'Housekeeping, sir,' *I call out.*

Someone's shuffling around in there.

I don't need to wait long to give him my wake-up call, right in the face!

Through the door with my silenced APB in my right hand.

A guy in a dressing gown is lying on the carpet in front of me, trying to drag himself up the wall. He slumps down again, failing like the fat, stupid slug that he is. It smells of bathwater. Someone's really let himself go here.

I grab him by the hair, drag him over to the bed and start kicking him in the ribs until they crack and break under the force of my attack.

He curls himself into a ball on the sheets, howling and spitting, staring back at me and taking short, shallow breaths. Looks as if I kicked his ribs right into his guts. That should make it clear enough that I'm not here for a friendly chat.

I look at my display once again. Good, my signal's definitely coming from here.

'Where are the artefacts?'

'Go fuck yourself,' *he hisses.* 'Lay another hand on me and they'll . . .'

He provoked me, honestly. The heavy silencer smashes into his mouth; his lips burst open. He lets out another cry, then falls silent.

'Where's your little friend?'

'What friend?' *he mumbles, blood oozing everywhere, basting his chin in crimson jus.*

'The one I haven't killed yet.' *The APB is pointing straight at his head.* 'I'm the guard you attacked, and now I want my stuff back. No one steals from me and gets away with it!'

Sounds a bit like Psycho. *I really ought to be an actor.* 'Where are they?' *I move the barrel of the pistol to point at his crotch.*

'They're dead! Dead!' *he cries out in panic, spreading his legs apart as if he could possibly evade any bullets if I were to decide to shoot him. Moron.*

'And your friend?'

'He drowned with the rest of them.'

'And what are you doing in Calais?'

'Waiting for the team to arrive.'

I think I've broken him. But if I shoot him now, the room will end up looking like an abattoir – and I could actually put it to good use first.

'A team that's on its way to pick up the artefacts?' *I ask him.*

'I don't know. Maybe.'

'And who's your client? Have you even got one?'

He wipes the coagulating blood from his chin. 'No idea,' *he mumbles again.*

'How can you have no idea?' *I pull a face of disbelief.* 'Colleague, trust me, I want to—'

A cracking sound can be heard from the entrance and the door swings open. A man enters, clutching a brown package in his right hand.

'I've been shopping,' *he says without looking.* 'It's chaos out there. Full of reporters and cops. I had a hell of a time getting through it all. Have you heard from Triton yet?'

I smile at my new friend in the dressing gown and put a bullet through his head, with one in the chest for good measure afterwards.

A medley of red splashes up the bed and walls, the blood running into the thick fabric, which absorbs it like a dye. Good quality robe, that.

The APB swings back under my control and points calmly at the newcomer.

'I've got a few questions for you,' *I say, admiring the smoke curling up from his mouth like a sexy zephyr. The scent smells better than any Asian or Indian incense; I start to feel relaxed. I should bottle it, turn it in to a perfume. Men would definitely buy it.*

'Questions or bullets. Which would you prefer?'

Britannia, Kernow, Lizard, November 2019

Malleus sat in the passenger seat of the BMW with no small degree of surprise. When Lagrande set off with a juddering start, he surmised that this could well be a rather memorable journey.

Lagrande was in pursuit of the last police car, cutting corners and testing the BMW's roadworthiness and cornering ability. 'I've been wanting to do this for a long time,' she confessed, her eyes shining as they flickered up and down between road and dashboard. 'You need to put this sort of car through its paces every now and again.'

'Well you're certainly putting my stomach through its paces.' Malleus looked at the display, which showed that they were now only about a mile away from the last police car. They'd surely be able to catch up to them without him having to endure a serious bout of nausea. The roads were bumpy tracks passing through an area of outstanding natural beauty.

Their journey ended suddenly at an old car park.

The policemen rushed out of their vehicles and ran down the steps leading to the beach.

Lagrande switched on the i8's automatic parking function and gave Malleus a cheeky grin before patting the steering wheel and leaving the car.

He followed her, relieved that the journey hadn't been too long. *But she certainly knows how to drive.*

Lizard Point was the southernmost point of the peninsula, where the Celtic Sea met the English Channel. The two octagonal, eighteenth-century lighthouses served as a grim reminder of how dangerous this area had once been for seafarers; according to what Malleus had read on the way over, the waters all around them were a real nautical graveyard.

One of them was still performing its honourable duty as dusk approached, casting its light deep into the suffocating darkness, with no ability to recall it.

More lances of light flickered around on the beach below, as if they were the children of the giant spotlight above them. Dark figures with neon high-vis jackets were walking slowly in a line, one alongside the other, searching carefully.

Malleus stood at the edge of the cliff, put his hands in his pockets and gazed out at the beauty of the calm evening sea. *Too beautiful to be without danger.*

'I bet,' he said to Lagrande, drawing the hood of his waxed jacket over his hat, 'that this Tommy is our next victim.' He took out a Culebra – one with a green band – from its case and lit it with the chip. The smoke presciently took on the form of a sailing boat before gently vanishing.

How often did I take them to the sea?Far too seldom. Malleus turned his gaze towards the cliff wall to help distract him from the painful memories that had come flooding back. He couldn't help but notice how it appeared to be made of black and white stripes, as if painted by an artist.

What is that?

He directed the lens of his PDA to face it, which soon told him that the rock was serpentinite. *Snakestone. Quite the coincidence, if one were predisposed to believing in water serpents and mystical dragons and so forth.*

One of the policemen came running past an abandoned building and up the stairs.

'Another General Melchett,' whispered Lagrande. 'It's uncanny. They all look identical.'

'Are you the inspector from Interpol, sir?' came the man's voice from halfway up.

'Yes, sir.'

'Then come down. I've got something for you.' The uniformed policeman in the high-vis jacket turned around and headed back to the beach.

Malleus and Lagrande followed him down the steep wooden steps and crossed the pebbled beach to the small building. It looked to Malleus like an abandoned outpost whose garrison had vacated it to rescue a shipwrecked crew after a disaster.

On the beach were several large dinghies that the officials had used to search around the shoreline. They looked like swollen black puddings, bent and welded into shape; being on board one of those when the waves were choppy would not have been a pleasant experience.

The policeman in the black uniform and with an implausibly British demeanour was waiting for them underneath a small canopy from which a battery-operated torch hung. The bright light illuminated a severed arm lying on a tarpaulin.

'Our catch of the day, sir,' announced the policeman, reaching out to shake Malleus and Lagrande by the hand. An enormous moustache protruded from beneath his nose. 'Charles Thomas Blackadder, head of the investigation team. I'm rather glad His Majesty sent for you, in fact. We could learn a thing or two from you.'

An indefinable noise briefly erupted from Lagrande.

The policeman laughed, his ruddy complexion resembling that of a man who'd happily follow half a dozen beers with a few whisky chasers. 'Yes, I'm familiar with the programme, Miss. And believe you me, I've thought about changing my name more often than you've had hot dinners.'

Malleus paid no attention to either of them. *Now that's odd.* He knelt beside the sinewy arm which, unlike the other corpses, had not swollen up at all. Instead, it looked almost mummified: its flesh and skin appeared somewhat wrinkled and dry, where contact with the water should have made it plumper and softer.

'Have you got any disposable gloves, sir?'

Lagrande wordlessly handed him a pair.

Malleus put them on and examined the arm, which had been severed rather sharply just below the shoulder. 'Looks like a blade. No frayed tissue.' He looked at the cut a little more closely. 'No, it's completely smooth.'

'Guillotine,' interjected Lagrande.

Malleus stored her suggestion away, though he had been thinking more along the lines of a cigar cutter. The surface of the wound looked as if it had sealed off by clingfilm or something. *Just like the pieces as well.*

He carefully ran his fingers over the lines on the wrinkled, heavily tanned skin, then cautiously opened up its clenched fingers to see whether there was any sort of clue to be found in its hand.

But there was nothing inside apart from thick calluses and scars. *These hands have seen better days.* He filmed the limbs, paying particular attention to the gnarled fingers. You'd have to have spent years pulling on rough ropes to acquire those scars and deformations. Not even Roy Crick's hands looked like that, and he was an avid sailor.

This led Malleus to a rather unusual, albeit obvious, idea. 'Sir, please could you ask the coroner to examine the cells and bone structure with regard to their age?'

'He doesn't have to, sir. The arm belongs to—'

'Sir, I do not mean the age he appears to be,' interrupted Malleus politely as he rose. 'His *actual* age.'

Blackadder looked nonplussed. 'I'm afraid I don't understand.'

'Before its ... *removal* ... this hand had been subjected to a large amount of hard work. So hard, in fact, that any company doctor would have his work cut out for him if his firm treated its employees like this,' Malleus said, voicing his suspicion.

'The arm is more than one hundred years old,' continued Lagrande. 'That's why it's mummified.'

Malleus spotted something further up that he had missed the first time, due to his preoccupation with the fingers.

He bent down quickly and shone the torch of his PDA onto it. 'You can just about make out a faded tattoo there,' he noted. The old ink didn't appear to have been able to withstand the rapid shift between dryness, cold and seawater.

'*Vinner*,' he read out in a dramatic voice, looking at the policeman. 'Does that mean anything to you, sir?'

'No. But it could also be *Vinnen*,' Blackadder mused, flattening his walrus-esque moustache. 'That's the name of a German ship – *Adolf Vinnen*, the last serious casualty of Lizard Point. At the beginning of the 1920s, if I recall correctly. Since then there have been only minor incidents. In 2004 the Point accounted for a French fishing vessel.'

Malleus nodded and looked over at Lagrande, who was already tapping away on her phone to confirm Blackadder's supposition, which she did with a brief gesture. 'So then the question becomes, where did the arm come from? Where had it been before? And why has it only just washed up now?'

'And how did it get into this condition?' continued Lagrande, all the while taking notes. 'Mummification requires a great deal of heat and dryness.' She looked around demonstratively. 'It's mild here, yes. But hot and dry, no.'

Blackadder's radio crackled. 'Sir, we've just found Constable Iron,' came the report.

'What's his condition?'

'Dead, sir.'

'Then try to resuscitate him.'

'Sir, that ... that wouldn't have much of an effect.' The policeman retched audibly.

'Shine a light where you are and we'll come and find you.' Blackadder hurried off, with Malleus and Lagrande following him along the beach to where beams of light were projected in the air as torches flashed all around.

Soon afterwards they discovered the remains of the unfortunate constable.

Resuscitation would indeed have been somewhat problematical, with his limbs lying discarded beneath the overhanging cliff whose black and white serpentinite had recently been stained with blood spatter. His torso and head were nowhere to be found; there were no tracks on the beach.

Malleus looked at the pallid faces of the policemen, who were visibly angry and disgusted. *No clues among the pebbles here.* He looked out at the sea. *Either tentacles* – he raised his eyes to the sky – *or claws.* To his mind there could be no other possibilities. *But what does the assailant want with the rest of him?*

Malleus puffed away and looked over at Lagrande, her eyebrows raised as she stared at the cleanly severed arms and legs, more with curiosity than horror.

The perfect investigator.

Celtica, Calais, November 2019

'I'll answer anything you want,' *he replies stiffly.*

'Very wise.' *I gesture to him with my other hand to come closer. I take extra care to be very precise with my choice of words. Really.* 'I'm the watchman you set a trap for,' *I say by way of introduction.*

'At *Tresoriale?*'

'Precisely.'

'Oh. Mm.' *He puts down the bag slowly.* 'Sorry.'

'Wow, really? Sorry? One whole sorry?' *I purse my lips.* 'Fuck it, that's one more than I had expected.' *Place the APB carefully on the armrest, so it's always in his field of vision.* 'I want the artefacts back.'

'They were on that ship, the one that sank.'

'I've heard that one before. But he' – *I point to the corpse* – 'said there's a dive team on its way.' *It's really rather rude to shoot someone before you've even asked them their name. Should I get used to it? Maybe as a new quirk of mine?*

'It's possible.'

'You chose to answer my questions, but are now right on the brink of facing the alternative,' *I say, reminding him of the bullets that await him.*

'I don't think it would be a good idea for me to say too much.' *What do these fuckwits think I'm packing here? Marshmallows? Do they just think they'll get diabetes if I decide to shoot them?*

'This is the last chance for . . .' *His name. Suppose I'd better ask, at least this time.* 'What's your name?'

'Killian.'

'So, Killian: this is your last chance. When is the team coming, what do they plan to do and who's responsible for this massive clusterfuck that's resulted in innocent people like me almost losing their lives?' *I've sworn now, fuck!*

He tilts his head slightly. 'There's no way on earth you're a watchman.'

'That's none of your business. I'm the one with the gun here. Look.' *I shoot him through his right forearm and he cries out. Another fountain of red, but after I've . . . dealt with this, they'll need to renovate the place anyway.* 'Well? Do you want another one, or would you rather answer my questions?'

He stares at the wound, groaning and raging, and kicks the bag in agony.

Mm. Well I did warn him.

Pull the trigger twice. Heart and head – finito. Here lies Killian.

I start to rummage through their stuff. I'm sure I'll be able to find something of use.

There's always something.

Britannia, Kernow, Lizard, November 2019

Lagrande and Malleus were working their way through the autopsy results over a coffee at the hotel before turning their focus to local legends that might provide clues about the potential monster, not to mention the list of shipwrecks off the Cornish coast since records began.

As they were doing so, the attentive landlady brought over salmon sandwiches and scones with jam and clotted cream; the hint of brine in the salmon provided the perfect contrast to the scones' subtle sweetness.

'I really ought to have brought coffee beans with me,' said Lagrande, adding more milk to her drink with a theatrical sigh.

He nodded absentmindedly and reached over for the Culebra, which was lying extinguished in the ashtray. He inhaled it deeply in spite of the fact that it was out, enjoying its comparably weak taste as he mulled over the most recent reports about the missing persons.

'There's nothing here that links them,' he muttered to himself, stroking his beard.

'What about that smell?' retorted Lagrande, sniffing distrustfully at her cup.

Malleus looked at her. 'Now *that* is a truly excellent deduction, Madame.'

'You're more than welcome,' she said, smiling mischievously. 'It's obvious really, because *everyone* would smell.'

'Or not at all.' Malleus looked at the names. 'They all disappeared at Lizard Point, at different times of the day. Now, if we are to assume that this has got something to do with the smell, then the time at which it happened is of no significance,' he mused to himself. 'But why are the body parts appearing now? And why can't they be linked to any weapon?'

'And why did it only take the constable's head and torso?' chimed in Lagrande. 'Was there something specific it was after?'

'Why do you keep saying *it*?'

'What do you suggest I say, then?'

Malleus sighed with exasperation. 'We still don't even know whether this is the work of an entity, a person or an animal.'

'Inspector, I know you don't want to hear this, but we can rule out this being a person immediately,' ventured Lagrande. 'The king wouldn't have asked for our help otherwise.'

The king hasn't got a clue. 'But it could equally be the case that that's what we're *supposed* to believe, and that this is in fact the doing of some highly sophisticated mass murderer wreaking havoc in and around Lizard.'

Lagrande appeared unconvinced. 'Then let's split up our brain power,' she suggested. '*You* can take care of everything earthly, while *I'll* deal with the rest.'

Malleus liked her suggestion, despite his having no intention of turning a blind eye to the potential involvement of entities. But it would be a good way of seeing what his new assistant was capable of. 'Agreed. But if you start to freeze up in terror when faced with what you might find, I'll have to put you back in the office.'

'By Belenos, do you really think I'd do that?'

Malleus lit his Culebra and took a few quick puffs, completely enshrouding Lagrande in smoke. 'Your mind is like this: engulfed by a strange haze, blowing in all directions around you, yet you never ask where this is coming from and why they're doing it.'

'I believe in the gods, Inspector, and not all of them are bad,' she replied, waving the smoke away with a sheaf of papers. 'You can't take that away from me. But I'll always remain critical, and I will never let them get away with it.'

'You don't understand the concept of the gods, Madame: you *have* to let them get away with it. Otherwise you'd be a goddess yourself.' Malleus drank his coffee. 'That's what the smoke was all about. You're still playing their game.'

'And you're not, Inspector?'

'Someone's got to keep his head among all this madness and try to bring light back into the darkness the gods have created,' he responded. 'If that means adapting to the situation, then so be it. But I am not giving in to them.'

Lagrande looked at him thoughtfully. 'Understood loud and clear, Monsieur.' She suppressed a cough. 'What do all these bands on your cigars mean?'

Malleus' smile grew warmer. 'They stand for various aromas and tobacco strengths. The other effects are my little secret.' He thought about Oona Milord, who had tried one without asking and had been astonished by the force of its effect. *Not for beginners.*

His mind sought to linger further on the brunette agent, but he forbade himself from doing so. His priority had to be the case. *No women, no loss, no pain.*

'Since, according to our little agreement, I'm responsible for everything earthly' – he looked at the map on the tablet in front of them – 'I'm inclined to consider another possibility.'

'I'm listening, Inspector.'

Malleus re-read the last confirmed locations of the latest victims around Lizard Point and the surrounding area before drawing a circle around each one and marking a spot on the sea with a straight line leading to each circle. 'Does anything come to mind, Madame?'

'You can see the sea from all the places where they were last seen. And this point . . .'

'Think more dangerous.'

'You can' – she considered briefly – 'see all the spots from this point in this sea. And shoot.' Lagrande blinked with surprise. 'You think this was a gun? Someone's been *shooting* from the sea?'

'Since we can't find any traces of it on land, the attack must have been carried out from the air,' replied Malleus. 'That could easily have been done with some sort of new weapon. Rays that vaporise or destroy tissue and seal up the cuts. It doesn't have to be a monster or some ill-tempered local marine entity.'

'You'd need a lot of energy for that.'

Malleus rubbed his Fu Manchu moustache. 'I've had a closer look at the accident with the French vessel in 2004. There was some speculation at the time that a submarine might have been involved.'

'A killer who just happens to be wandering around the Cornish coast with a mini-submarine, popping up every now and again to randomly vaporise people and tear them limb from limb?' concluded Lagrande. 'That's way beyond presumptuous, Inspector. There's no way I could stand before the king and tell him that.'

Malleus leaned back, the smoke from his Culebra following him like a clingy toddler. He drew the outline of a submarine with its glowing tip, the red lines holding together. 'Why not? A modern-day Captain Nemo, only this time coming up against . . . people. Or something even more cunning than that – making it *look* as if it's an entity, using the missing people to exert authority over the inhabitants, promising to bring them back if everyone behaves themselves and is willing to be subservient?' It made sense to him.

He could see it made no sense whatsoever to Lagrande.

'Or someone has found an artefact in one of the old sites, maybe under a dolmen or on some barrow, and is using it to kill people? Or in discovering it has invoked the wrath of some entity, who's now wreaking revenge,' she retorted. 'Or it's none of those things and it's actually just some beast that's been ravaging around for centuries.'

Malleus laughed. 'Something like our frustrated white dragon?'

'Are you taking the piss?'

'Not at all. I'm just presenting you with a few more options.'

'Oh yes, as if a made-up magical submarine with a super-weapon is any better, Inspector.' She grinned disdainfully and ran her fingers through her long hair. 'Anyway, for now it's immaterial. Neither of us has any evidence.'

Malleus raised his Culebra in agreement, painting something new in the air with its smoke. 'So here we are. And we have no explanation as to where the seafarer's old arm comes from, despite it apparently having belonged to a German sailor.'

Lagrande stood up, put on her hat and drew her hood over it. 'Let's see if anything rears its head.'

'What are you doing, Madame?'

'Going for a walk and thinking. The moon's looking beautiful tonight.'

'You most certainly are not.' Malleus knew Lagrande's provenance as a banlieue girl made her less susceptible to fear than most, but what she was planning definitely fell under the category of gross negligence, especially given that they had no idea about what was lurking in the darkness.

'The incidents didn't just occur at night,' she replied curtly. 'It won't make the blindest bit of difference if I'm out and about in daylight or at night.' She tapped lightly on her jacket, which concealed her Beretta. You can listen out for my screams, or use your PDA to do so. Either way I'll let you know if I notice anything.'

She stalked towards the exit and disappeared out into the night.

Soon afterwards, Malleus could see her silhouette heading directly towards the headland barely a mile away.

She's starting to become a bit reckless. Malleus got up to go back to his room, find his Cobray Derringer and lend some assistance with some slightly heavier artillery. A walk couldn't hurt.

He entered his room – and smelled perfume.

He could make out Marina in the moonlight, her black hair spreading out across the pillow like a halo, lying completely naked in a seductive pose on his bed. Her green eyes shimmered in the dim light, while the suggestive expression on her face reflected raw desire; her smile was reminiscent of a beast of prey.

'We didn't get to say a proper goodbye in Gomorrah,' she said by way of greeting.

'I think it's a bit late to make amends for that now,' he replied, his voice still friendly. There was no doubting how attractive she was; her aura was bursting out at him, practically enveloping him, as if she intended to overpower him and drag him onto the bed. *Into* bed.

'Then you'd better say hello properly.'

Malleus noticed how her voice switched from playful to serious in the same sentence, making her appear almost schizophrenic. He looked not at her breasts, nor at her slender waist, her thighs or her femininity, as any other man would have done, but instead fixed on her eyes. 'I told you at the Vatican: now is not the time. And there'll never be a good time for it.'

'There's no such thing as a good or a bad time. Just the moment we're in,' she replied, sitting up as hair fell around her. She slid over to the end of the bed and opened her legs slowly. 'Just *one* moment, Malleus. You'll never get it back.'

He smiled weakly, thinking about her kiss, then about Oona Milord's kiss and how different the two felt. One was beautiful but empty;the other unanticipated, leaving him with a tingling sensation that still stayed with him.

Malleus opened his mouth to reply.

But as Marina raised her head slightly as if to embrace him passionately, her features became sovereign, imperious. 'I mean it, Malleus. If you reject me a second time, there will be unimaginable consequences.'

'I've never liked being threatened.'

'It's a statement of fact. A promise,' she corrected him. 'Then I'll do *everything* to achieve my goal, the one I was first sent to you for.'

Malleus' ears pricked up. 'What—?'

Marina stood up slowly, like a queen rising from her throne to inflict justice on all those who dared to contradict her. 'This *one* moment, Malleus Bourreau, will decide your future. Either we spend the night together and I will give myself entirely to you and promise you the best night of your life, in which case nothing will happen to you, or you refuse – and you'll be destroyed.'

Malleus was used to hearing those sorts of threats, but her voice carried a level of conviction and certainty that he had rarely experienced before. This lovesick woman who wanted to sleep with him clearly posed no threat. *But who is she?* Their lips met again.

He didn't return her probing kiss, which she accompanied with an impassioned sigh. Malleus simply stood there with his hands in his pockets, letting it all pass over him. Gentle, grateful rejection.

Then Marina took a step backwards.

'I see you've made your decision,' whispered the beautiful young woman regretfully, a tear rolling down her cheek; the droplet flamed as it drifted downward, leaving behind a burning trace on her face, though she didn't look injured. 'It is decided.'

Her words had sparked urgent questions which Malleus could feel bubbling up within him.

But a loud scream from outside pushed aside all those thoughts.

Lagrande! Malleus grabbed his Cobray from the open suitcase and stormed out of the room.

Celtica, Calais, November 2019

Looks as though I was successful.

Nice little message here from a certain Triton, saying the dive team will be arriving in the next eight hours.

So someone clearly wants the artefacts back.

Sitting here between killed Killian and terminated Trevor. It says Trevor on his ID card. Trevor Leftfield. That won't be of much use to him now either.

Of course I replied as if I were Killian.

It would be spectacularly funny if I were to retrieve the artefacts for my prey. I could give them to him as a present, or even make him run some errands for me before I let him have them. An errand for an artefact. A hero of my own.

I've got one minor complaint about my latest acquisition, though: my APB has warped slightly. It could well be that it's a bit dirtier than I had thought.

The only thing that'll help it is dismantling it into all its component parts and cleaning it carefully with gun oil. My babies love that.

You've also got to blow into the silencer. Killian the killed's got a cleaning kit on him. That'll do just nicely.

There's a bit of play in the right-hand grip. I can't stand that because it pinches the skin and hurts like fuck when I take a shot.

Fuck.

What the fuck? . . . A bug!

That's just . . . They've gone and put a tracker on me. Great, now I've lost control again! HE must be behind this. Without a doubt. The little shit knew I'd buy an APB and he set me up. The clever bastard!

But why haven't they pounced yet? Because they didn't expect me to be in Calais?Because they're in danger?

I've got to get rid of this bug straight away. Send it off in the post somewhere. I can just change the delivery address online, meaning they won't have the faintest idea about what's going on.

Need to take another look at my APB in case there are any more surprises. I'll make the bullets myself; I found a weapons shop online earlier, one specialising in hunting. They must have a workshop.

And then I'll send another reply as curtailed Killian.

* Α Ω *

Oh no, what now?

They want to meet in Dover and dive from there. Less going on there, according to Triton.

For me as well. Then straight on to Britannia.

Britannia, Kernow, Lizard, November 2019

Malleus ran out of the hotel and looked out at where he had last seen Lagrande's silhouette. *Where is she hiding?*

His radio earpiece crackled to life: there was an incoming call. 'Yes?'

'Lagrande here,' came her reply, breathlessly. He could hear the crunch of gravel under her feet – she was running. 'I'm close to the edge, a few yards away from the hut on the beach. I think I might have a suspect.'

Malleus ran off, thrashing his way cross-country through the nature reserve. The i8 was wedged between the police cars. 'Was it you who cried out?'

'No, Inspector. That came from above the escarpment. Another victim.' Lagrande cursed; the crunching noise stopped. 'Call your colleagues from the coastguard. They need to send out a search vessel. He's trying to get out to sea by boat.' Her steps started up once again. 'I'm taking one of the more powerful outboards down here; it's the only way I'll have a chance of catching up with him.'

'Will you be able to?' Malleus panted as he spoke, running over Cornish heath, the local variant of heather, dodging obstacles as he approached the beach. He never had to worry about his fitness doing this job.

'What?' said Lagrande.

Malleus could see the steps appearing before him, but instead jumped down the slope, sending sand and gravel everywhere, before landing next to the hut. 'Can you drive an outboard?'

'Surely it can't be that difficult?' Lagrande's breathing became louder and she looked back over her shoulder at the noises she could hear behind her. 'There you are!'

'I couldn't just let you go wandering off on your own, could I, Madame?'

Malleus helped her push the heavy rubber boat into the sea. As he was doing so, he could see the second boat was already a fair way ahead and getting further and further away from the coast. The sound of its engine roared across the water as a figure in a hooded anorak looked back at them.

Malleus and Lagrande jumped into the boat; she started the propeller with the press of a button and let out the throttle. 'Just like a motorbike,' she shouted over the cacophony.

He adjusted his balance forwards, took the rope from the bow and lifted the prow slightly to reduce resistance against the waves. *Reinforcements.* With one hand he wrote a message to Blackadder to keep the police abreast of what was going on. Then he stood up, keeping one leg slightly in front of the other on the narrow foredeck as his coat was buffeted by the wind.

The black waves with their argentine crowns of foam reminded him of the curse that had been put on him by Brigantia, the goddess who had vowed to ensure his demise should he ever venture into her realm again. Hopefully the Celtic mori weren't considered part of that.

He had a clear aim in mind: capture the man or woman responsible and interrogate them. He wouldn't let anything sway him. *Not even the thought of my own end.*

Lagrande proved to be more than competent, steering the boat expertly across the water, all the while catching up to their prey. No matter how hard he tried to pull away, he couldn't widen the gap any further.

Malleus saw the suspect switching off the engine and heading to the edge of the boat; he dropped one hand into the water, as if to test the temperature. *Or perhaps he's giving some sort of underwater signal.*

'Watch out,' Malleus called to Lagrande. 'We could well be attacked at any minute.' He looked on as a cable rose out of the water towards the man's other hand. It blinked abruptly as it reached his middle finger.

'Turn right!' he shouted. '*Right!*'

Lagrande's reactions were exemplary; the boat lurched suddenly to the right as Malleus did everything he could to not topple overboard.

A bleak, milky beam of light shot out above them; Malleus looked over his shoulder just as it struck the abandoned beach hut. On impact it spread out, cutting deep holes into the old wood, while other pieces were immediately disintegrated.

So now we know what sort of weapon we're dealing with here. Malleus suspected it was some sort of divine artefact.

Their boat was now running a zigzag course in an attempt to avoid the next attack. They were barely a hundred yards away from their unknown assailant, which gave him ample opportunity to fire off another shot and send them under.

An illuminated ship suddenly appeared around the tip of the peninsula; the water displaced by the propellers looked like it was bubbling uncontrollably. Two powerful searchlights flashed across the surface and pointed directly at the suspect's boat.

Malleus couldn't understand what was being said through the loudspeaker. The sound was muffled. Small fountains of water erupted around the suspect's boat. *Warning shots.*

Another light appeared in the sky, accompanying the two frantically blinking stars that were poised above them. Blackadder had called upon the full resources available to the coastguard, including a helicopter that had begun to climb.

Good work. Malleus gestured to Lagrande to throttle the outboard. *He's got nowhere to go.* He looked pleased as he glanced over at his assistant investigator. 'I look forward to hearing what he's got to say for himself.'

Then the milky ray shot out again from the object on the suspect's finger, striking the steel hull of the coastguard vessel.

A hole the size of a door immediately opened up and the sea began to rush in, gradually dragging the ship underwater.

But the soldier on board the sinking ship wasn't deterred by this sudden assault and returned fire, overwhelming the suspect's boat with a volley of bullets that tore through the wooden panels, the small structure and the figure himself.

With a sharp cry the suspect fell back – yet somehow managed to raise his hand and fire off an attack at the helicopter.

The turgid grey energy from his weapon annihilated the rotor and the upper part of the turbine and the helicopter dropped like a stone, smouldering and then bursting into flames before crashing down into the dark sea in a thousand pieces.

The heavy machine-gun continued to fire, but the angle became impossible as the ship sank further before disappearing beneath the waves.

Malleus could see sailors jumping overboard; there wasn't enough time to launch any lifeboats. He hoped beyond hope that Blackadder and the rest of his unit would be able to rescue them before they froze to death.

However, he still had an important task to complete.

'Let's go – head straight for the boat,' Malleus ordered Lagrande, who turned around and took them over to the collapsing vessel in a matter of seconds; the full-metal-jacket rounds had done their job and it was starting to sink.

Malleus leapt over to his fatally wounded opponent, pointed the Derringer straight at him and pulled the hood away from his face.

It was a middle-aged woman; the blood splattered all over her face had begun to smudge.

'He warned me,' she said in a soft voice. 'He said you'd come and try to take it from me. But it belongs to me. Only to me. *To me!*'

Malleus looked at her hand. A cable ran from a ring on her middle finger to an enclosed device of some sort lying harmlessly on the narrow deck. A small compartment gave off a cool blue light; two diodes glowed red like the eyes of Amarud's pet. There were no runes or inlays, nothing that might give any indication of its origin. At first glance he couldn't see how it worked. 'Who gave you that?'

'He said I could take it and use it however I wanted. And I' – she coughed up blood – 'I had a great deal of fun with it! Until you came and ruined everything. He did warn me.' Her gaze faltered. 'We'd have loved to, back there,' she breathed, her head drooping. 'It was so beautiful. What he showed me was just so beautiful. And I . . .' The light left her eyes once and for all, before she could even finish her sentence. His unknown adversary was dead.

Quick, before the boat sinks. Malleus grabbed the ring from her hand and picked up the device before hoisting her corpse over his shoulder and jumping back onto his own boat.

'We've got our murderer,' he said to Lagrande. *Though we still haven't got the faintest idea why she did this, or what else was going on.*

Lagrande nodded. 'Shall we start helping our colleagues out of the water?'

Malleus looked back at the beach, where he could see a large number of boats rushing to where the coastguard and helicopter crews had fallen in. That improved their chances of saving as many people as possible. 'Yes. Take it slow though.'

The boat chugged into life.

Malleus took out the torch from the small chest on the bow,

then produced the flare gun and shot it directly above him into the night sky. As the stranger's boat sank with a gentle bubbling into the sea behind them, they started their journey towards the wreckage.

Malleus helped one sailor after another into the boat until it became dangerously full, then they turned around and proceeded carefully back to shore.

He was still thinking about the device he had confiscated, which was now in his jacket pocket. He didn't think it was a divine artefact – he considered it more likely that it was a technical item of some description that had no right to be on this earth.

It was this idea that gave him an official reason to contact Oona Milord again. Of course he had no ulterior motive whatsoever.

Britannia, Dover, November 2019

'Unspectacular.' Oona Milord observed the device Malleus had placed on the desk in front of her. 'Compared to its effect, its appearance is beyond underwhelming.'

She was sitting in a quiet corner of the hotel, drinking mineral water and an espresso.

Malleus had checked it several times over to make sure the object wasn't concealing any hidden dangers, but the little lights all remained extinguished. There was no noise or heat coming from it – nothing that gave any indication of activity.

Milord picked it up, turned it over and twisted it this way and that, running her fingers over its blue surface, checking the wire connection between the ring and the device, as well as the diodes and the little viewing window. The only thing that aroused any attention was a small row of ventilation holes.

Malleus watched her inconspicuously, basking in her presence.

She wore a black business dress with a short grey jacket over the top and white gloves; her high-heeled shoes had narrow platforms. He could smell the same perfume he remembered from last time; it reminded him of the sea, fresh grass and sweet flowers.

Milord put it back on the table. 'Please would you tell me what you and Lagrande found out after saving the others?' With a graceful movement of her head she tossed her long brown hair back over shoulder; the reddish strands on the left-hand side of her forehead glimmered in the soft light.

'Of course.' Malleus attempted to hide his happiness. 'The woman shot by the coastguard was identified as Caswyna Silversmith, forty-nine years old, widowed, recently divorced from her second marriage. She lived in Helston and was, by all accounts, nothing more than a friendly devotee spending her life in service to the god Lir, giving Celtic invocations every day. By day she worked on the till at a bakery. The police and I searched her home and found drawings of dozens of places where the god had wanted her to go.' He made an apologetic gesture with his hand. 'My first thought was that this could be some foreign entity. That's why I called you.'

'You were right to be cautious. But what do you know about her journeys to these other places?'

'She had marked the date on each one. I'll send the files to you.' Malleus felt himself sinking into her deep brown eyes. He didn't want to fall in love. Not now. Not with her. *Not with anyone.* 'She acquired the artefact four years ago, she very proudly noted down in her diary.'

'And since then the area around Lizard and the surrounding villages has been subject to an increasing number of disappearances,' continued Milord.

Malleus nodded. 'There are several entries in her diary about how much she hated people who didn't give everything to their gods or do their every bidding. There are all sorts of murderous fantasies in there, some of which are a few years old, for which she found a new outlet once the gods reappeared.' He considered allowing himself a Culebra, one of the new ones that tasted so strongly of the Orient, but decided to wait a little longer. That could lead to quite an emotional rollercoaster. 'She started to increase the gaps between murders she committed at sea, sometimes from the boat and other times with diving equipment.'

'I understand. But how do you explain this whole matter of the arm belonging to someone from the nineteen twenties?'

'Miss Silversmith found the mummified body in a cave when she was on one of her dives. She was experimenting with energy and managed to put him in this state purely by accident. She wrote all this down as well. 'Malleus finished his espresso and waved over to order another one.'

'Case closed. Congratulations.'

'Thank you. I've heard the king is pleased with me as well.'

'*This*' – Milord laid her index finger on the object – 'is something I've seen before, though not intact.' She ran her fingernail over the slit; it rattled lightly. 'The device was designed to be used underwater. It sucks in seawater and converts it – somehow or other – into energy. It can be a tool, but it can also be used as a weapon.'

'As we saw with Silversmith.' Malleus listened with interest. 'And where does it come from?'

'Funnily enough, we found it on the corpse of one of Loki's followers. He appeared to have got himself embroiled in a dispute over this present. It looks like the gods enjoy bringing their followers along for the journey as well.'

Malleus could see why this present had been so well suited

to Loki: it was nothing more than a tool, but the person could decide what he did with it, whether it was for good or for evil.

Milord lifted up a small metal suitcase, opened it and placed the device inside. 'We'll keep this for now and ask Loki about it as soon as we get the chance. The priests should finally take action against him, seeing how he's obsessed with objects that bring nothing but death and destruction.'

As if an entity would take the blindest bit of notice. Malleus nodded nonetheless; he didn't want to be a killjoy. 'It's better off with you. Otherwise it could easily fall into the wrong hands again.'

'Thank you again for thinking of me.' Milord gave him a smile that stopped his heart. She was playing with her white-gold pendant: Aeracura and Dis Pater, the goddess of death and the Lord of the Underworld. 'You've been around a lot lately, Mr Bourreau.'

'That's often how it is.'

'One of these days I'd like you to have more pleasant things to do than just investigating crimes.' She got up and extended her hand to him. 'Should you ever find yourself in Stockholm, drop me a message. I'd be happy to show you around the city.' The look she gave him was a clear invitation than he should get in touch *soon.* 'If you want, of course.'

Malleus jumped up. 'I'll be sure to keep that in mind.' He grasped her hand.

She leaned forward and kissed him three times on the cheeks. He could feel her warmth, smell her perfume again clearly and feel her hair tickle his skin. 'See you soon, Inspector.' Oona Milord smiled at him once more and left through reception.

Malleus sat back down slowly in the armchair and watched her leave. 'Stockholm,' he repeated.

Does she live there? Is that where DEM have their headquarters?

A young man appeared across the hotel's reception area; he had noticed him before, because he looked and acted so different to everyone else in Britannia – and this was a country that was as ethnically diverse as ever.

The man made no secret of his origins. His impeccable tailored suit of ochre-coloured fabric and black leather contained neatly embroidered animalistic images which, together with his facial features, led Malleus to conclude that this was a representative of the First Nations.

He wore bracelets of embossed black leather on his wrists and his fingers were adorned with bejewelled silver rings. A series of faintly visible tattoos of stylised crows ran all the way up his neck. He headed towards Malleus. 'Mr Bourreau,' he said, his voice friendly, when he was about a yard or so away, before bowing deeply. His black hair was clipped at the back of his head by a clasp made of bone. 'My name is Keish, and my father has sent me to talk to you.' His eyes were the unusual colour of rock crystal which, on first impression, made the young man appear blind. His actions and the expressiveness contained within his black pupils told another story, however.

Malleus gestured to the chair where Oona Milord had been sitting. 'You're one of the Tlingit people, presumably here about the drum and mask,' he said in anticipation of the reason behind this surprise encounter.

'Thank you.' Keish, who must have been in his mid-twenties, sat down. 'You are correct, Mr Bourreau. My father is the chieftain of Hoonah, the largest settlement of my tribe. He had never given up researching the disappearance of our artefact, and I was entrusted to help him.'

'Then you came upon on the case of Hannes Hein.'

'We knew the route the drum and mask had taken, but we

arrived too late to save them.' Keish ordered a mineral water from the waiter who was clearing away Milord's cup and glass. 'I have since learned that you are the one conducting the investigation.' He looked at Malleus expectantly, but his expression was irritating.

'You want to know how far along we are with the investigation.'

'I'm here to offer you help. You need it desperately.'

The impetuousness of youth. 'With all due respect, sir, I hardly think . . . My team and I are taking care of this. But I'll keep you and your father abreast of everything that's going on.'

The waiter returned; Keish took the water and drank a sip. 'It's not a question of finding them, sir. I've done some research about you, and it appears you are an exceptional investigator.' He narrowed his bright eyes. 'The sole purpose of my help is to prevent a catastrophe.'

'In what way?'

'If the drum and the mask are used together by someone who is *not* a Tlingit, the reaction is far from desirable,' he explained carefully. 'Should this occur, I can hold back the catastrophe – as long as I'm close enough.'

'Are you talking about something like an explosion?'

'Think of it more like in *Indiana Jones*, when the Ark of the Covenant is opened by the wrong people: it will open a gateway for all manner of ancestral spirits, who will examine everyone they pass and kill all those whom they do not recognise as being Tlingit.'

There's nothing about that in Hein's description. Malleus took out his case. *The mask and drum are far away from their home.* Keish must be one of the only First Nation Tlingits in the whole of Europe.

That in turn meant there would be much for these spirits to destroy.

Far too much. Malleus took a deep breath and cleared his throat as he exhaled. It was time for a Culebra.

I know just the one.

Marianne Lagrande sat on the edge of the smoking area outside the hotel, underneath an umbrella and next to a couple of patio heaters. Several hotel guests had decided to take their pints of Guinness or glasses of wine out with them. The refreshing wind, which was due to turn into a storm later on, played with her clothes.

A few people had tried to chat her up, but she merely smiled back and replied in her most guttural banlieue French. None of the men could understand her, so she was left in peace. Lagrande looked at her tablet, on which a rather unwelcome message from Crick had just arrived. He was refusing to meet her and Bourreau because he was on a business trip.

That would have been too easy. She took the Culebra stub, which she had stolen in secret, from her anorak pocket. If the inspector didn't want to reveal what made his cigars so special, she'd have to test it out for herself. Out of curiosity.

She had cut off a chunk of the cut end, which had also removed about a third of the band, but it was enough to use as a sample and start solving the mystery. *Just curiosity.*

She lit the remaining stub on the heater and took several puffs.

First it just tasted of smoke, slightly spicy, reminding her of a cigarillo. After another few breaths she could start to taste menthol in her mouth; the minty flavour rose through her throat and nose and directly into her brain, jerking it awake.

Lagrande looked at the stub, suppressing a cough. *Pas mal.*

Her mouth filled with saliva and she mimed at the waiter through the window to order another beer before setting about replying to Crick's message while Bourreau was inside talking to Oona Milord.

To her annoyance, the agent wasn't pug-ugly.

None of the women who swarm around him are hideous, she thought with resignation, remembering her disaster at Montmartre.

She chose to focus her concentration, which now surged through her like electricity thanks to the Culebra, on Crick's email.

With every breath she took it was becoming apparent that she could smell more around her than she had ever noticed before. And sounds were clearer; there were nuances in everything.

She could make out details from the corner of her eye: a quick glance or a small noise was enough. Even the otherwise smooth display on her tablet now displayed a little unevenness.

No wonder Bourreau's so good, she thought with amusement, and took another puff. *This is the stuff of miracles.*

Crick had written to say he had looked at the group photo Bourreau had taken with him from Bolivia and used it to identify two men who matched Bourreau's vague descriptions from the virtual meeting in the jet. Both had the eye and pyramid elements on their crests, and you could roughly make out their stature.

One was Gaff Olmos, an American-Mexican multi-millionaire with properties all over the world, containing *objets d'art* that were the envy of many museums. His links to Nazi art theft dealers were often subject to investigations by the tabloid press.

The other was called James Wu Chew, a Chinese man who had made vast sums of money in Shanghai and Hong Kong, which he immediately invested in art as he didn't trust any paper currency in the current climate.

Lagrande looked closely at the photographs of the men; they looked to be over seventy. *I hadn't counted on that.*

The smells and sounds around her were starting to gradually annoy her. Everything was too intense, too obtrusive, as if she were on an out-of-control Ferris wheel. She discarded the stub, throwing it as far as possible to prevent Bourreau from finding it.

But its effect on her nerves didn't subside.

Lagrande focused on the second email that had come through from Interpol. It was about the phantom image of the shadow. The inspector had drawn it up based on Ove Schwan's statement and it had been run against the information in their database. After several checks, the program concluded that the man had not been active in any Interpol-affiliated states. In addition, dossiers had been compiled containing information about men who possessed a certain degree of similarity to this unknown stalker, and Lagrande now counted almost fifty criminals, from notorious thieves and fraudsters to killers and brutal bank robbers.

He's got to look through this himself. Her beer was brought over to her and she gulped it down. If she had known before that it would be like this, that stump of cigar would never have passed her lips.

The Ferris-wheel feeling continued and she suddenly wanted a pair of sunglasses to protect her from the harsh light of her surroundings. She cursed the droning of every car that drove past, with their obnoxiously bright headlights and unbearable squeaking of tyres. Her eardrums could hardly stand it.

I'll never touch one of his Culebras ever again! she swore to herself, noticing her dizziness increasing. Her legs were becoming as weak as overcooked spaghetti, boneless and powerless. Even if a hundred wild bulls were to charge down the road at her, she'd have no option but to remain sitting and become a victim of the stampede. She doubted she'd even be able to run away from a snail.

Lagrande finished the last of her beer hastily, hoping the alcohol would provide some sort of buffer against the tobacco. This was *completely* unlike cannabis or any other drugs she had tried.

Amid the throng on the pavement she could make out the raven-haired madwoman she had last encountered in the brasserie in Montmartre – the one with the indestructible tongue. She headed slowly towards Marianne, her green eyes shining uncomfortably brightly.

Wonderful. Now I'm hallucinating things, thought Lagrande, and closed her eyes. *I need another beer.*

* Α Ω *

Britannia, Dover, November 2019

Just as shit as Calais. Must be because there are ferries here, plus a few lorries and cops. Nothing to make you feel at home

The dive team has checked into a hotel at the ferry point. The weather's horrific, alternating between drizzling and pissing it down. They've written to say the services of my friend Killian are no longer required. No shit.

You were planning to sell the poor guy out.

I had a bit of a whinge, made a few threats and wrote them a letter from his mother. And one from me.

If they thought they could get rid of me, they've got another think coming.

I'm looking carefully at everyone passing through the port, because they sent me – or rather, Jeremy from the dive team sent me – a photo of Triton, his profile picture. Idiot.

That's how I'll get to them, then I'll have my hands on the artefacts again.

I've already been through two hotels, and now . . . oh! I can't believe it. There's that mad nun!

But . . . that must mean . . . he's here as well!

My prey!

What was her name again? That's it – Marina. The same as that old song. A pretty fucking terrible one at that, though once it was in your head you couldn't get it out.

She's coming this way, across the road towards the hotel, turning into the smoking area and . . . there's the Eighties woman!

Is she drunk? Sitting there with her eyes closed, looking like an absolute space cadet.

Anyway, I've got them all back – they're all here! How wonderful.

I start to approach, bit by bit, heading towards the smoking area with my back to both of them and my ears firmly open. I can see what's going on over the reflection of the patio heaters.

'. . . told you to keep your hands off him.'

Oh, quite the little cat fight we've got going on here. Or is the mad-woman intent on bringing everything to a close?

'Piss off,' *says Blondie angrily and, ha ha, her eyes are still shut.* 'You're just a figment of my imagination.'

It's absolutely teeming down. The smokers are heading inside in a hurry. A storm is on its way; the rain starts to pelt down around the canopy.

'No, I'm not.' *The mad nun grabs her thigh and produces the dagger I saw on her last time. That decorated old thing she had strapped to her at the Vatican.* 'But stay calm anyway and keep your eyes closed. That way it won't hurt as much.'

Now she opens her eyes sleepily. 'A dagger?' *She reaches into her jacket, trying to pull out a gun.* 'I've got something far better than that.'

Damn this wind, rattling against the screen. Where's it coming from?

The mad nun laughs. 'This is the dagger that my mother will one day wield. But Bourreau has stopped her from returning three times now. So she has sent me to wreak revenge.' *She raises the dagger.* 'And since he has refused to love me back, I can see no reason to spare him any longer. Neither him nor anyone else around him.'

Blondie needs to do something now.

Right now.

Immediately.

Ah fuck, she's too groggy to even lift her arse up off the chair!

And fuck all this verbal derailment!

I told the mad woman last time that I'd stop her. And I keep my promises. All of them.

The wind is scattering umbrellas everywhere, creating a nice little forest of baffles for me. Better be off!

The mad woman, graceful, and apparently unaffected by the rain teeming down all around her, goes to strike a horizontal blow to slit the Eighties woman's throat with her blade.

I get my APB out, silencer on, and turn around, grab the blonde woman and let her fall so that I'm lying beneath her.

The dagger flies just above us. I've always had a good eye. That's something you can't teach. My right hand reaches under the Eighties woman's anorak and pulls out her Beretta. Elegant yet heavy. Remove the safety and wait.

My left hand turns the silencer to face the mad woman, who's staring at me as if I were the mad one. 'You dare? I'm the daughter of Kostianaia Noga, a demigoddess who—'

Like I give a shit.

Switch over to automatic.

The catch chatters metallically back and forth, carried by the noise of the storm roaring all around us. I leave my finger on the trigger and the APB rides the recoil, etching the fake nun with a line from her navel all the way up to her throat; then I shoot her again with the Beretta, empty the entire magazine. I don't want to make it too easy for them to trace. Christ, that's loud. Kicks like a mule, but it's accurate.

And . . . off with her head. Shame, as she's not half bad to look at. But it's better this way – don't want her coming back any time soon. I could really do without that.

Right, put the U22 back in the Eighties woman's hand and make myself scarce. The chairs and greenery have provided ample cover. No one's spotted me.

And Blondie's quite the heroine.

That's just the way it is sometimes.

* A Ω *

Britannia, Dover, November 2019

Malleus helped Lagrande out of the ambulance where she'd been examined. The official diagnosis was that she was suffering from mild shock, though he was sceptical of this. Lagrande had been through far worse than this in her own flat or in Treva and come up smiling at the other end.

I know precisely what happened. Malleus could see in her eyes, with their slightly altered pupils, something only the most experienced doctors would have been able to spot if they had been looking for it. It was different from any known signs of drug-taking, and could pass any screening. *She smoked one of my Culebras.*

But none of his crooked cigars were missing in his case, so she must have got her hands on the tobacco some other way. *Perhaps a stub?*

The area at the front of the hotel was completely locked down. The British forensics team tromped through the hastily erected pavilion in their white protective gear, past Marina's body, taking photographs and marking out the spot where the corpse lay, along with the dagger and the casings.

Lagrande had had to hand over her Beretta, which had evidently been used to shoot the woman. The British investigators had announced that they wanted to take her in for questioning.

Malleus knew she'd need a fair while before the effects of the cigar would completely wear off. Until then he'd have to keep the detectives off her back.

But *his* curiosity still demanded some answers.

They headed back into the hotel. Before they sat down once again in the dark corner by reception, he took a moment to tell Keish, who was still standing at the bar, that he'd return to him shortly to continue discussing their collaboration. He asked the waiter to bring him some water.

Lagrande slumped down into the chair. Malleus handed her the glass.

'I've seen her before,' she said as she brought the glass to her pale lips. This was the first time he had seen her looking fragile rather than a fearless woman who could steer a dinghy across the sea as if it were something she did every day, or thrash an i8 through a nature reserve.

'Did she threaten you?' The Culebra with the dark purple band was lying in the ashtray, half-smoked. He picked it up, knocked off the ash and put it back in his case.

'Yes. In the restaurant in Montmartre, after you had left.' She drank deeply, her hands trembling.

Malleus looked dismayed. 'Why didn't you say anything?'

Lagrande grimace and leaned back into the cushion. 'I thought I could handle it myself.'

'What did she want?' Malleus thought he knew the answer already.

'Something personal.' The clear undertone to her voice made it obvious it was really some *person.*

Was it about . . . me? He didn't know what to say.

'She introduced herself as the daughter of Kostianaia Noga. It must have had something to do with the case in Riga,' she said, her voice trailing off. She sounded exhausted. 'She had been given the task of getting revenge because of what you did, Inspector, and I was to be her starting point. Oh, and because you weren't in love with the mad bitch either. Otherwise everything would have been dandy.' Lagrande finished her water and banged the glass down too quickly, making a loud clanging sound. 'Forgive me. I think I had one beer too many, and the wind was buffeting those umbrellas around; the breeze tore through me and the mad woman was just . . . there. Then I guess I must have taken out my Beretta and . . .'

Malleus listened closely, contemplating all she had said.

At least that went some way to explaining what Marina had been talking about in the Vatican Park, with everything she was taking on: the daughter of Kostianaia Noga, falling in love with a mortal and deciding to go against her orders and protect him.

But when he'd rejected her in his hotel room, her manic love turned into something else – hatred.

Tragic. He rubbed his Fu Manchu moustache and looked at the tormented figure in front of him. He had seen the drinks bill, which had come up on his Interpol hotel account. Two beers. Two beers couldn't put a woman like her into this state.

He refrained from making any accusations about the Culebra. This wasn't the time for it. *And how could she have possibly known?*

Malleus smiled soothingly at her. 'Go back to your room, Madame, and sleep off the *beer.* I'll keep our English colleagues away from you for the time being.'

'Thank you.' Lagrande stood up shakily, dragged herself to the lifts and disappeared.

Malleus had requested the dagger from his colleagues as soon as it was released. It appeared to be a very special item, underlining the fact that Marina wasn't merely some deranged stalker.

A dead daughter. Now he had another entity who hated him. Him or Lagrande. Self-defence wasn't an argument that would fly with Kostianaia Noga.

He was just about to wave Keish over when he received a new message on his PDA: an incoming video call, with the name *EXITUS* displayed on the other side of the screen.

Malleus bade himself be calm and dragged his chair over so that the wall was directly behind him, preventing anyone from looking over his shoulder. Then he started up the program.

Ove Schwan's face appeared on the small display in front of a white background. He wore an olive-coloured shirt, his striking face was flecked with stubble and his light blond hair was wet, as if he had just come out of the shower.

'Hello, Koios. I just wanted to let you know I won't be around to stand guard over our little friend. Circumstances have driven me underground.'

'Of course. I understand. And thanks for taking on the job in the first place.' He didn't ask how and when *GodsEnd* had organised his escape from hospital. His friend wouldn't tell him anyway.

'If you've got anything a bit bigger for me, perhaps something that needs a bit of extra firepower, just give me shout. That's something I'll always be able to provide.'

Malleus nodded. *Hardly a surprise.* 'Please tell me you had nothing to do with *GodsEnd*'s little stunt in Tiwanaku,' he said in a low voice.

Ove Schwan's face slipped. 'Where—?'

'I was there, in the middle of the riot your people incited. And your name cropped up.'

'Who?'

'I overheard a radio conversation; they thought they had shot me. As a tourist. Trying to drag Europe into the fray, apparently,' explained Malleus with contempt. 'Ove, what *GodsEnd* are doing here is horrific! You're turning people against one another to prove the gods aren't real – what on earth is the point of that?'

'You—'

'I survived, as you can see,' interrupted Malleus curtly. 'I always had a lot of sympathy for *GodsEnd*, but the things I went through over there mean I can't possibly support them any more. Ever.' He leaned forwards, staring intensely into the lens. 'They were going to let innocent people be slaughtered like animals. Women, children.'

Schwan squirmed. 'I know,' he admitted, 'but I swear I'm doing everything I can to stop that sort of thing from happening again. But I haven't got enough influence. I'm still pretty low down in the hierarchy and . . .'

'And all the while can you not see the chaos and destruction they're causing?'

Ove clenched his jaw, flexing the muscles in his cheek. 'If it weren't for them I'd be in gaol.'

'If it weren't for them, gaol wouldn't even have been on the cards,' retorted Malleus. 'Get out, Ove. Whatever *GodsEnd* are planning, the only thing it will achieve is to plunge the world further into darkness. Do you really want to take responsibility for everything that's happened up to now?'

Ove snorted. 'At least we're doing something against the entities. Unlike you, Malleus,' he counter-attacked. 'You're falling back into your old ways of trying to explain everything, abandoning the world to its simple-minded credulity and going your own way. But you're useless. Great, you've solved all these cases, but nothing has *changed*. People are still worshipping the gods as much as ever.' He leaned forward, his arm outstretched. '*We* are taking care of things, Malleus. *We* are *GodsEnd*.' Then the connection broke off.

Malleus lowered his PDA. He suspected that would be the last time he and Ove would speak. *GodsEnd* was utterly without scruples, rendered blind by the self-righteousness of its ultimate objective. Collateral damage could never be justified.

Who knows what they'll think up next to prove the gods aren't real. Malleus was still smarting from what his friend had called him. *Useless.*

There was a small kernel of truth concealed in his words.

His cases would have to be made more public; he would have to publish them online, wake the people up and go to great pains to point out every minor inconsistency in detail about the Return of the Gods.

But do people really want that? Or will they be comfortable with the deception as long as they are content? Malleus ruminated over this, suddenly feeling a need for one of his cigars and immediately taking one out of its case. Green band. *Good for thinking.* He lit the Culebra and painted wispy smoke images in the reception area. Malleus let himself become immersed in the haze, then thought to check the status of the bug he had planted in the APB.

The weapon was on its way to Celtica, according to the tracker. His unknown shadow appeared to be on the lookout in Lutetia in an attempt to catch up with him, which in and of itself was no bad idea.

Time to get rid of him. Malleus was now in the right frame of mind to deal with this ever-elusive phantom. Nothing was going well at the moment, which bothered him greatly. To be on the safe side, he checked the most recent report about the ferry accident, but there was nothing of interest.

According to the official report, a defective flap lock had caused the ship to fill up with water and sink. Half the passengers were saved; the rest had gone under with the ferry, three hundred feet or so down. They'd drowned or frozen to death in the icy waves.

'Forgive me, Mr Bourreau.'

Drawing a deep puff on his cigar, Malleus turned away unhappily from his PDA and looked up at Keish, whom he had completely forgotten about. 'Oh, I should be the one to apologise,' he said with embarrassment.

The man smiled sympathetically. 'No need. After an incident like that my thoughts would certainly be elsewhere, and you've still got your actual work at Interpol to do as well.' Keish sat down; his corvine tattoos on his neck appeared to move. 'I'm only bothering you because of the urgency of the matter. You said you'd be willing to consider collaborating?'

Malleus was finding it difficult to concentrate on the Tlingit and the matter of the drum and mask. There was Marina, Lagrande, who had barely escaped death, his argument with Ove, the loss of the artefacts – all his endeavours were coming to a sudden halt on too many fronts.

He could see on his PDA that Lagrande had forwarded him the latest intelligence from Crick.

Two suspects, one of whom could perhaps be the Collector. He looked at the photographs of Gaff Olmos and James Wu Chew. *Super rich. Enough money to open as many doors as they desire.*

But if Crick was wrong, Malleus would have nothing to go on.

Not even the faintest scent of a trail. He sucked at his Culebra as if trying to elicit new insight or solutions from it.

'May I tell you more about the artefacts?' offered Keish, jolting him back into the present. He ordered a tomato juice from the passing waiter. 'Even though it feels a little odd speaking to an atheist about matters that are in no way rational.'

Malleus gave a forced smile. 'For me it's even stranger, living in a world in which there appear to be gods. I'd almost be more willing to believe in the spirits you're talking about than that, Mr Keish.'

'Not *Mr.* Keish is fine.' Malleus admired his ability to sit upright on the soft upholstery of the armchair: he wouldn't stand a chance at doing that. 'They were the ancestors of the Tlingit, some animalistic spirits that could be invoked unknowingly.'

'In this instance it's just like with the gods: I can reject them, but cannot escape the effects of their actions,' admitted Malleus. 'This effect where the angry spirits appear and overrun non-Tlingits is all because . . .?'

'They don't want to do evil – it's more just preventing it from being abused,' explained Keish. 'Or they think they're in the middle of a war and have to defend their tribe.'

'I understand: it's just because they want to avoid any more damage. How large' – Malleus made a circle with his Culebra; a fiery ring appeared which grew larger and larger – 'is the radius?'

Keish's face grew worried. 'The last time our shamans knowingly invoked this power, it was about ten.'

'Yards?' asked Malleus; the glowing circle started to retract.

'Miles. Radius.'

The wheel of fire expanded rapidly as if it were an explosion; it shot through the entire reception, followed by the light wind and smoke from the Culebra.

Malleus stroked his Fu Manchu moustache repeatedly. That would be truly catastrophic, particularly if the thief were to use the artefacts in a major conurbation. Millions of lives were in danger.

GodsEnd *would have a field day.* This gave the case a degree of immediacy that would allow him to pull out all the stops with Interpol.

But how could you evacuate an entire city in a matter of minutes?

You can't. We've got to nip the whole thing in the bud.

Malleus looked at Keish. 'I presume you're a shaman?'

He nodded. 'I've got everything I need with me to appease these ancestral spirits, should we manage to get close enough in time.' He swilled the juice around in his glass. 'What do your investigations say to that, Mr Bourreau?'

Not a lot. Malleus puffed away as if he had just started, coming to the sobering realisation that his only clues were moderate at best. Then a notification appeared on his PDA.

TRACKER 1:	Operational . . .
SIGNAL:	Clear . . .
LOCATION:	Calais . . .
DIRECTION:	Northwest . . .
SPEED:	Approx. 150 mph . . .
DEPTH:	Approx. 9000 feet

Malleus raised his PDA and laughed with relief.

However the unknown Collector had managed to organise the recovery of his loot from the wreck, he had just retrieved it. *With a helicopter*, Malleus guessed, given the information at hand. He stood up. 'Let's go, Keish. The hunt is on.'

BOOK 10

Episode 10: Gnosis

Gnosis
Greek γνῶσις, gnōsis: Knowledge

Agnosticism
Ancient Greek ἀγνοεῖν, a-gnoein: Lack of knowledge

Atheism
Ancient Greek ἄθεος, átheos: Lack of belief in a god or gods

'A nation that still believes in itself holds fast to its own god. In him it does honour to the conditions which enable it to survive, to its virtues – it projects its joy in itself, its feeling of power, into a being to whom one may offer thanks. He who is rich will give of his riches; a proud people need a god to whom they can make *sacrifices* . . . Religion, within these limits, is a form of gratitude. A man is grateful for his own existence: to that end he needs a god.'

Friedrich Nietzsche, *The Antichrist*, 1888

'I know of nothing poorer under the sun than You gods!
Indigently You feed Your majesty on proffered sacrifice
And breathfuls of prayer.

You would starve to naught if children and beggars
Were not optimistic fools.
[. . .]
Who came to my aid against the Titans and their insolent rage?
Who delivered me from death, from slavery?
Was it not you, sacred heart ablaze, who achieved it all?
[. . .]
I should honour You?
For what?
Did You ever gentle the ache of my burden?
Did You ever dry the tears of tribulation?
Was I not forged to manhood by Time Almighty
And Eternal Destiny, my masters and Yours?
[. . .]
Behold, here I sit, fashioning men in my own image,
A race after my likeness,
A race that will suffer and weep,
And rejoice and delight with heads held high
And heed Your will no more
Than I!'

Attributed to Johann Wolfgang von Goethe, c. 1771
(unconfirmed)
Extract from an early fragment of the poem *Prometheus*

European airspace, November 2019

Dear Mr Malleus Bourreau, held in the highest esteem by my brothers and me,

We would like to take this opportunity to invite you to collect your latest weapon from our London branch: a whip from a bad *tentacle.*

Congratulations! To my knowledge this is the only example of its kind.

You will have little choice but to spend several hours practising with it, Mr Bourreau, if you wish to master it in the same way as you would a gun.

We therefore recommend that you NOT extend the barbs while training with it, lest a serious injury befall you in the event of any failed attempt at such.

On the handle of the whip you will find a secure slider, with which the barbs may be extended or retracted; they are sitting in the front third of the weapon and are controlled by a tendon in the tentacle itself.

The taxidermist we consulted did make a few cuts while he was handling the piece. He told us that this is the most challenging task he has ever undertaken.

He has provided the following instructions:

a) The load should not exceed half a ton; the treatment method used has made the bad *limb even more resistant.*

b) Make sure to keep the whip away from blades. Just as you were able to cut it off yourself, my dear Mr Bourreau, so the same thing could happen again.

c) Its resistance to cutting should be roughly the same as that of a good nylon mountain-climbing rope. The taxidermist has informed us that any damage to the inner tendon would be irreparable.

Please make sure to keep all that in the back of your mind!

My brother and I sincerely hope that you enjoy your new accessory; it is, after all, an incredibly rare and special phenomenon on this planet.

We remain ever your loyal servants,

Miles Karak et Frères

Men's Clothing

Leipzig/Paris/London/Milan

or anywhere in the world on request

Malleus Bourreau sat smoking at the back of a private jet; his previous flight on such an aeroplane was not one he cared to remember.

He had put the small case containing the rolled-up black whip in front of him on the table and had read the accompanying note from his tailor. The delivery had arrived at the very moment he and Keish had left the hotel. This was the first opportunity Malleus had had to examine this mysterious new weapon properly.

He and the Tlingit were alone on the flight, as Marianne Lagrande had been forced to stay in Dover. Their British colleagues wanted to talk to her about the incident outside the hotel and had refused point-blank to let her go, so now it was just Malleus and the Tlingit in pursuit of the tracker signal which was still functioning on one of the artefacts: the statuette of Oddua.

Is it still there? Malleus was checking the signal about every minute, but it remained consistent. Thanks to their jet travelling faster than the helicopter transporting the loot, they had managed to catch up with the robbers who'd stolen it on the orders of the unknown Collector. They were currently flying over The Netherlands, travelling at around 250 miles per hour in a northeasterly direction, without any prospect of landing soon.

Malleus looked over at his companion. Keish was sitting at the front of the aircraft and had opened a small box of objects involved in shamanistic rituals. He was arranging various small bags and pouches, muttering to himself under his breath all the while. The carved bone clasp on his head appeared to have some hidden meaning; his hair and raven-feather jewellery complemented one another perfectly.

They're all getting ready. Malleus took out the whip and clutched it by its grip; it resembled a coiled snake, ready to spring to life at any moment.

With a slight flick of the wrist he unravelled it, estimating its length to be at least six feet. The weight was not too heavy and not too light: the Goldilocks zone for weaponry heft. The hooks would cause a large amount of damage, able to dig through thin sheets of metal and stick in walls.

And into bad.

Keish, noticing what he was doing, left his seat and strolled towards him cautiously. He smelled of autumn and aromatic smoke, as well as the faint scent of leather from his hide bracelets. 'I've never seen leather like that before,' he remarked.

Malleus hadn't expected the Tlingit with the piercing eyes to say anything different, but he had no intention of telling him precisely what it was. 'It's a special delivery.'

'You want to use a whip? That's a rather ... unfashionable choice of weapon. If nothing else, at least you'll have the element of surprise in your favour against heavily armed opponents.' He tilted his head to one side, which caused the crow tattoos to move around on his neck.

'I've always dreamed of chastising entities – the only thing missing was the right implement with which to do so,' replied Malleus dryly, taking a slow puff on his Culebra.

Keish laughed darkly. 'Interesting idea.'

Malleus rewrapped the whip and returned it to the holster Karak had made so that it could be attached to a belt or coat with a carabiner. 'I'm rather looking forward to performing a pain test on a god.'

Keish looked at the PDA. His clear eyes, Malleus thought, would easily terrify those of a less robust disposition. 'They're flying over open water,' the Tlingit announced.

Malleus followed his gaze. 'I haven't the faintest idea where this artefact will lead us.' He was desperately hoping that the other two objects were on board as well and it was just that the transmitters had been broken by prolonged exposure underwater. 'But we won't run out of fuel.'

'Good to know.' Keish sat down opposite him, his jacket making a slight crunching noise and the animistic pattern on it changing as he did so. 'May I ask you a question, Mr Bourreau?'

Go ahead, Malleus gestured with his Culebra; the embers hung in the air.

'You call yourself an atheist who rejects any notion of divinity.' Keish pointed to the box containing his utensils and the fan-like feathers on the back of his head rustled slightly. 'And that is in every form and any aspect of the supernatural. But imagine . . .'

Malleus interrupted him with a friendly smile. 'I am a denialist with my own explanatory model for the way the world is. I confront the entities because there's no one else who dares to do so.'

'But you play by *their* rules.'

Malleus sighed, breathing smoke towards the Tlingit, which spread out and appeared to form a wall. 'I've had this conversation many, many times, Keish. They won't do either of us any good. There's no such thing as gods, and the powers of these so-called entities are by no means divine.' His explanations – variously involving robots, aliens, government projects and the possibility of his having slipped into a coma – were on the tip of his tongue, but he didn't have the requisite patience to take him through it all. 'Someone's got to do it,' he concluded, looking back at the display. *Still travelling, and at the same speed.*

'You see, there's proof that entities aren't omnipotent. If that were the case, I'd have had a ten-ton weight dropped on me. Or a piano. Or they'd blow me up into a million pieces.' Malleus continued to smoke his Culebra. His uneasiness was rising, which put him in a somewhat ironic mood that could quickly descend into sarcasm.

The riddle of the nine artefacts would hopefully soon be solved and the person responsible for such a great deal of death and violence would be made to face up to their actions.

Lautrec knew he would alert the authorities in whatever country the helicopter landed and make them take emergency measures. Then he'd hopefully have a task force at his disposal if he needed any support on the ground.

Our best-case scenario is if the Collector doesn't touch either the mask or the drum. Malleus watched the luminous dot as it moved further over the map.

The Tlingit laughed again. 'Sarcasm and irony. Your weapons.'

'You'd be surprised – I've found you can injure an entity with those alone,' replied Malleus with a weak smile. 'I'm what you'd call a walking irony for the gods.'

He took out his Apache and Cobray Derringer and laid them one alongside the other on the table, checking the chambers, mechanisms and functional integrity. As he was doing so, he took the occasional puff to prevent the cigar from extinguishing; he carefully tapped the ash into the ashtray alongside him.

Keish watched him silently for a while. 'Have you never considered that you yourself might be a god?' He adjusted his bejewelled rings.

'I think I'd implode under the weight of my own irony if that were the case.'

'I'm not speaking hypothetically, Mr Bourreau.' The Tlingit pressed his hands together. 'What I meant was that you actually *are* one of them.'

Malleus finished his final check and returned the Cobray. 'I'm still considering whether or not to be insulted by that.' He inhaled deeply. 'As an atheist, I ought to be.' Keish's conclusion irritated him, so he ignored it. 'There's nothing supernatural about me whatsoever.'

'The fact you're still alive goes some way to suggesting otherwise, Mr Bourreau, does it not?' He stood up and turned back to his box. 'I am truly honoured to fight alongside you. Let's just hope that the Great Spirit is with us.'

Malleus thought this unbidden assumption rather impertinent, not to mention arrogant, abstruse and devoid of any logic or reason.

Yet his thoughts were unable to detach themselves from the idea. No one knew better than he just how mortal he was; he thought of the life he had previously led and how often he had escaped death during the war.

And that Namtarú had to spare me.

The reason behind that hadn't been explained in Gomorrah either . . . Could there be a kernel of truth in Keish's idiotic theory?

Idiocy. He looked quickly at his PDA. Nothing had ever given him the impression that there was anything divine in him at all. *Pure idiocy.*

The Oddua signal began to descend into Danish airspace without decelerating: the movements of a helicopter intending to land in a few seconds. Undertaking such an unscheduled landing in their jet without disturbing normal working activity would be a challenge for the pilot and the air-traffic controllers alike.

The tracker steadily descended, crossed over the islands – and then stood still. The height shown on the display was identical to the altitude of the location itself. The helicopter had landed.

There is something lazy in the state of Denmark.

Malleus read where at least one of the artefacts now was and hastily informed the pilots, 'We're going to Copenhagen.'

Britannia, Dover, November 2019

The doctors had had to inject Marianne Lagrande with a substance that removed the fog from her brain, and at the same time reduced her hypersensitivity to sensory input.

Now she was sitting, relaxed, opposite the two plain-clothes detectives from the British CID who had deferred her questioning as a matter of courtesy, just as they had promised her at the hotel. It was a small courtesy, nothing more. As a colleague of and assistant investigator to Malleus Bourreau, the case was clear. They were wearing the type of clothing you'd expect to see on a teacher at a college: tasteful, inconspicuous, yet with a touch of panache.

Lagrande smelled the coffee and groaned – not a sound of joy: no amount of sugar and milk would make this drinkable.

'Let's go through the sequence of events one last time, shall we?' asked Inspector Green, who was just as pleasant as his colleague Miller. If they decided to pack in this whole detective lark one day, they could easily find jobs as history teachers. 'Once we're done, you'll be able to leave Britannia.'

History and literature. Lagrande nodded. 'I was sitting outside, going through our case notes and drinking a beer.'

Thanks to the medicine they had given her, she was able to stay calm, even though she knew Bourreau was on the trail of the artefacts while she was stuck here in Dover. Lautrec had told her they'd send for her if Bourreau thought her presence would be necessary. *At the finishing line.*

'Then the woman crossed the street towards me; I recognised her – I had been introduced to her before as both Marina and Marinuschka. She pulled out a dagger and immediately came at me with it.'

Green and Miller cross-checked this, her third retelling of the events, with her previous accounts.

'As she did so, she said she was going to kill my superior and everyone who was close to him,' Lagrande added. 'I fell to the ground, took out my Beretta and took care of her.'

She had decided against telling them the exact details of their conversation. That was neither here nor there. She had already told her boss everything he needed to know; he could fill in the rest himself.

Lagrande was also withholding the fact that she could barely remember the events of that day at all.

She had slipped off the chair and was suddenly lying on the ground; a few quick movements later and she could hear the crack of her U22 Neos.

That fucking Culebra! The fog that had come over her was like nothing she had ever experienced before, neither from smoking weed nor enjoying a few too many schnapps. She was certain that her memory was clinging to the important details but leaving out gaps. There were so many small things missing.

She had no idea when she had actually drawn her Beretta. It must have been at some point between falling and shooting. Or why she had thought the floor had felt soft. Lagrande was amazed at how accurately she had taken the shot in her condition. *Not to mention whether any innocent . . .*

That was something she *definitely* couldn't mention to Green and Miller. *Not on my life!*

'Good, Miss Lagrande,' said Green, interrupting her unpleasant thoughts. 'As far as we're concerned, we're done.' He stopped the recorder and started to gather his things.

But Miller switched the device back on nonchalantly. 'Almost. Let's say I've still got my own curiosity to satisfy.'

Lagrande had never thought there was any real benefit to playing good cop, bad cop. *She's like the sports teacher everyone hates.* Her heart began to beat faster. 'Yes?'

'We asked you to hand in your weapon so that ballistics could have a look at it.'

'And I did so: a Beretta U22 Neos.'

'Correct. There'll be a post-mortem done on the body of Marina or Marinuschka or whatever she's called tomorrow, but forensics found quite a few shells that don't belong to a U22 Neos.' Miller looked at her. 'As an investigator myself, I know you'd ideally like to have a second weapon on you as well, just in case you find yourself under threat. But why didn't you tell us about it?'

Lagrande blinked, then smiled apologetically. 'I don't know what you mean.' She wasn't feigning ignorance here either – her response was entirely honest.

'Oh, just leave it,' muttered Green, reaching for the button.

But Miller batted his hand away. She was insistent that this be on the record. She carefully reached into her jacket pocket and pulled out an empty cartridge case, placing it on the table so that it was illuminated by the desk light.

Lagrande could tell that this was nine millimetres, whereas her U22 Neos shot 22-calibre ammunition. She couldn't use that excuse. To make matters worse, she recognised the engraving on the outside of the cartridge case, which looked like made-up symbols.

The Glyph Killer! He's back! 'I'm afraid I still have no idea what you're talking about.' *Didn't Bourreau say that arsehole was in Lutetia?*

'Do you mean you don't *know*, or you don't *want* to tell us?'

'I don't know.' Lagrande decided to play the honesty card before this annoying detective could conceive of the absurd notion that she might be a serial killer's accomplice.

Miller pulled a face that strongly suggested she smelled a rat. 'Miss Lagrande, we are at the very start of this investigation. But the position of the body, the number and angle of bullet holes and your description of events lead us to the conclusion that the second weapon was fired from the same position as your Beretta.' She folded her arms. 'Lying down.'

Lagrande's own version of events suddenly appeared in her head.

The Glyph Killer had – *just as before* – followed her, spotted Marina, torn over to Lagrande and intercepted her fall with his own body, before using his APB and her Beretta and then fleeing the scene. *The umbrellas. They'd have made the whole area all but invisible.*

But Lagrande couldn't understand why he had protected her. *Being helpful?* Because he still had plans for her?

'What do the symbols on the cases mean?' asked Miller. 'You worship Belenos, yet these aren't Celtic symbols.'

'For fuck's sake, I don't know!' Lagrande was starting to sound like the banlieue girl she was. 'The beer had had too much of an effect on me, and everything happened so quickly.'

'Then *you* didn't use the gun at all?' Miller continued.

'Theresa, just leave it, okay?' Green once more sounded reassuring as he switched off the recorder. 'She's just shot a madwoman who attacked her out of the blue. You've read Bourreau's statement as well. This is not a murder.'

'Yes, yes, I know it's self-defence. But I still need to get to the bottom of precisely *what* happened here.' The detective took a deep breath and leaned forward. 'Well?'

'I don't know.' Everything irritated Lagrande; her scalp was itching and tingling all over. 'I blacked out.' She wanted to be with Bourreau, to help him solve the case on which she'd dedicated so much time and effort – and for which she'd more than once risked her life. And this know-it-all Sherlock Holmes wannabe just wanted to put more and more obstacles in her path.

'You blacked out?'

Lagrande stood up. 'I'll call you if anything comes back to me.'

Green stood up and reached out to shake her hand, but Miller remained sitting, giving her a penetrating stare.

'Inspector Bourreau is expecting me for an important Interpol case.'

Without so much as glancing at Miller, she headed to the lift to collect her suitcase.

It was only after the doors had closed and the detectives had disappeared from sight that she allowed her façade to break; she leaned back against the wall, gasping for air. She had escaped death because a madman had saved her from a madwoman. He had fired both guns and made it look as if she had done the whole thing herself.

He wanted us to know he was back. She put her head in her hands. *What's he going to do next?*

When the lift stopped at her floor, Lagrande peered out into the corridor before getting out.

She didn't even have a gun now.

* Α Ω *

I'm sitting just two tables away, eavesdropping on the conversation between the Eighties woman and the cops with my trusty listening device.

It's lucky for them that they let her go. Otherwise I'd have unfortunately had to show them where the nine-millimetre cartridges came from.

She'll now make her way to my prey, and because I've bugged her she won't have a chance of escaping me.

HE won't have a chance of escaping me.

I put this bad boy on her while we were having our highly unromantic tussle on the ground.

I suppose he's gone with this Indian to hunt the artefacts. I can sense it.

And the Eighties woman, who owes me her life, will lead me to him. Then it'll be time for his long-overdue punishment.

As if I could ever forget his ingratitude! Yet I'm still toying with the idea of bestowing my grace upon him. It all depends on my mood, really. And my mental state.

But it's fine. It's never boring. Better than sitting around in my shitty little hideaway in Rome, drinking and channel-hopping. Only killing can really get my juices flowing nowadays.

I've lost a bit of weight as well. Not that much – I'm never exactly going to be svelte – but my trousers are sitting slightly more loosely now.

And I'm utterly in love with my new APB; it's just as good as the other one.

Although it does mean I can't travel by aeroplane any more. I need to get to the railway station instead to buy a ticket.

Ah, she's coming back with her suitcase and checking out.

On the phone.

'You still don't know *precisely* where you're going? Okay, good, then I'll head to the airport. Lautrec's arranged a helicopter for me so I can just follow you. Very well, Inspector. See you soon.'

She hangs up and makes her way to the exit.

Mm.

She's got her own helicopter. There's no way a train will be able to keep up with that.

. . .

Right, change of plan. Blondie's not just my little bug any more – she's also my ticket out of Britain! I'll be able to get my gun through all the security checks as well, and completely legitimately, at that.

Good job it's not another jet.

Denmark, Copenhagen, November 2019

Malleus and Keish drove through Copenhagen in their rented – and far too small – i3, following the signal Oddua was still transmitting.

The two men were tense, staring at the PDA display as if it was a game they were deeply emotionally invested in. Malleus kept stroking the end of his moustache out of nervousness.

To their relief, the jet had landed very quickly, but Malleus was still worried that the artefact would arrive at its intended destination before they got close enough. If the transmitter were to be discovered before then, their entire enterprise would fail. There was no way they could search the whole city.

'Are they going to Central Station?' asked Keish. 'So they'll be continuing by train?'

Malleus believed otherwise. 'They'd be able to reach their final destination far more quickly by helicopter – it must be somewhere in the city centre.'

The dot changed direction and stopped.

Malleus zoomed in. 'That's the entrance to Tivoli.'

Information immediately appeared on his PDA: Tivoli was the largest and oldest amusement park in Denmark, with new attractions constantly being added and an enormous number of visitors all year around.

Keish and Malleus watched as the red dot turned away from the street and entered the park.

'They'll do the handover there.' Malleus ordered the i3 to stop outside the other entrance in front of the railway station. Even though it took them only a few minutes to get there, time was passing agonisingly slowly for him.

The men produced their tickets and entered Tivoli. Despite the bad weather, the place was still full of visitors.

Fine snowflakes fell from the grey sky, turning the park into a bright, glistening winter wonderland. Aromas of sausages and burnt almonds drifted through the air all around them, together with the occasional scream of delight from exhilarated punters on the rides.

Malleus' PDA displayed a map of the area, and precisely where the red spot was located.

'Over there.'

It led them through the throng of people holding paper cups filled with mulled wine or steaming hot tea. A group of elves occupied the large stage to his right, mocking a tied-up Father Christmas and a baby Jesus wrapped in swaddling clothes. The whole scene vaguely resembled Tim Burton's *The Nightmare Before Christmas.*

Keish and Malleus swung off to the left, heading down a gentle slope towards a pond. On one bank bobbed a large pirate ship. Opposite this was a restaurant in the shape of watermill, advertising home-brewed beer.

The red dot – and Oddua – was here.

There was a high degree of probability that Malleus would recognise someone from the nameless Collector's team. *But Keish won't know any of them.*

He looked at the Tlingit, who had his rucksack containing all his items on his back, and explained his plan. 'Please would you go over and use your phone to stream what you're doing, so that I can see what's going on in the restaurant in real time. I'll stay under cover.'

'And?'

'You don't need to do anything. Just have a drink, look around and observe the people there.'

'Do you think the Collector himself will appear?'

Malleus shrugged, snowflakes dropping from his coat. 'I'd like to see the face of the person carrying the artefacts so we can identify him.' He zoomed in even further. The tracker showed him exactly where the artefact was. 'Here it is. Can you see it?'

Keish looked at the display and headed in. 'I'll make sure you're connected.'

Malleus went on board the pirate ship, which was also a restaurant, and removed his hat and coat.

He had a good view from his table through the small window. He ordered a drink and a small portion of twice-cooked chips, which came after a few minutes. They were impeccably crispy.

The pond between the mill and the ship hadn't frozen over yet; a few hardy ducks and other waterfowl were swimming around in circles as visitors bought feed from the dispensers nearby and lured them over with it.

Keish entered the windmill and was led by a waitress to a free table. His phone was stashed in a small pocket of his overcoat; a narrow wire led to an earpiece and Malleus could see on his PDA the curiosity with which everyone was looking at the Tlingit. With his striking outfit and appearance, he looked as if he could be one of the park's attractions.

The only person who paid no attention to the First Nation member was a bearded, brown-haired man of around forty. He was wearing grey cargo trousers, a dark blue shirt and an all-purpose jacket. He was drinking a beer and chewing on fish fingers with such brutality that it looked like he wasn't sure if the fish in them were dead or not.

How unusual.

'Head left, to the other table,' Malleus instructed him.

A woman in her mid-twenties was also going about her business with an apparent lack of interest on the edge of the verandah. She glanced up at Keish as he was navigating his way between the tables, then returned her focus to her tea and let her gaze wander furtively.

They're the ones who'll be doing the handover.

The waitress briefly tried to deter him from his choice of seat, but his rock-crystal eyes convinced her otherwise. The Tlingit sat down.

Through the camera Malleus could see the outdoor area, which was well equipped with a glass roof and heat lamps to stave off the worst of the Danish winter.

None of the people sitting there looked anything like Gaff Olmos or James Wu Chew. Although there were quite a few tourists in Tivoli of various ages and races, no one of Asian or Mexican descent appeared in the image from the phone camera.

The bearded man ate his fish fingers, never taking his eyes off his phone as he did so. Then he suddenly downed the last of his beer and summoned the waitress over with the bill. At the same time, just as a whole group of pensioners were also standing up, the young woman placed a banknote on the table and left the mill.

'Okay, Keish, get ready.' Malleus paid for his chips and finished them off. He hadn't noticed how hungry he was. 'The game's afoot.'

The Tlingit put his money down on the table and started to move, concealing his own flurry of activity by the departure of the pensioners. 'I'm on it,' he said unnecessarily.

Malleus could see from the blurry image coming from his pocket that Keish was following the couple from a long way away; they were now moving around the pond, picking up waffles along the way and eating them as if they had all the time in the world.

The tracker was working perfectly: the man had the statuette of Oddua on him. Of course, this didn't mean that he *was* in possession of all three stolen objects, but he did have enough space for them in the black laptop bag hanging from one shoulder.

Maybe they've divided them out. Malleus left the pirate ship, not sure how to avoid them. If they were to stay on the same path, they might bump into one another. *Is that what I want? No.*

He made his way to the next café along and stood at the entrance, from where he had a good view of the path. The signal was getting closer and closer, while the lens from Keish's phone gave him the occasional glimpse of their backs.

Then Malleus spotted something.

'Stop! Turn right, please.'

The Tlingit followed his instructions, and as he did so, an elderly white-haired man with a thick, dark grey beard appeared, flanked by three companions whose muscular stature suggested they were no strangers to heavy lifting. They moved forwards purposefully, with the apparent intention of blocking the couple's path.

That's Crick! Malleus cursed. This was anything but a business trip for the antiques dealer. *He must have been withholding information from me.* The pair passed just below him, heading straight for the stage. Keish was still on their tail.

Or . . . Crick has arranged to meet them here. Lagrande had suspected he wouldn't play fair, and once again she appeared to be right.

He was here to take the artefacts for himself. *Or to wreak revenge.*

Malleus left the restaurant and fell into a jog to catch up with Keish. 'Things could get dangerous pretty quickly.'

Crick and his henchmen appeared to their left, but took no notice of the couple.

Instead, they went straight to the palatial building in front of them, which was oriental in appearance and had hundreds of colourful lamps burning on its façade. With the snow falling all around, it looked like a scene straight out of a fairy tale.

'Wait,' said Malleus, surprised, and stopped.

The letters *NIMB* loomed over the entrance. According to his PDA, this was a very plush hotel that had recently changed ownership. The name of the new owner was *Gaff Olmos!*

Malleus looked from the display to the hotel, where he could see Crick and his muscle-bound flunkies advancing through the entrance.

The photo from Bolivia had led the Englishman to correctly figure out who the unknown Collector was; now Crick wanted to handle this himself, seeking retribution for the death of his son.

But this is a hotel. Chew could be here as well. Malleus looked at the pair standing in front of the stage and listening intently. Then the bearded man looked at his watch and, together with his companion, also made his way to the hotel entrance.

Or someone we hadn't even considered.

Keish adjusted the rucksack on his back. 'Shouldn't we do something, Mr Bourreau?'

'That's precisely what we're doing,' Malleus responded cautiously.

But he still hadn't the faintest idea what his plan was going to be.

Britannia, Dover, November 2019

'Marianne Lagrande, Interpol,' she said to the guard at the entrance to the private runway reserved for airport authorities and official delegates. She showed him her pass, concealing her job title as always, since she was officially only a secretary. 'I've been summoned here by your supervisor – an urgent investigation. There's a helicopter waiting for me.'

She pointed to the corpulent man alongside her, his face obscured by a pair of aviators and a baseball cap casting a shadow over his features. He was dressed in French desert camouflage and had a long-barrelled weapon hanging from the holster on his hip and a duffel bag slung over his right shoulder. 'This is my colleague, Capitaine François Chateau, from the Celtica Military Police.'

Chateau's service ID badge bounced up and down on his chest as his gloved fingers snapped into a brisk salute. 'I'm officially not here, comrade.'

The guard looked them both up and down. 'All in order, Miss Lagrande.' He glanced briefly at his tablet. 'But your military colleague isn't on here.'

'This case has brought about military involvement. Well, it doesn't matter, we'll just climb aboard and be on our way.' Lagrande gave him an unnervingly friendly smile.

But the guard still appeared disinclined to move out of their way.

'If you prefer, I could always just take out my gun and shoot you, comrade,' offered Chateau, resting his thumbs on his belt. 'That would certainly speed things up, and then I could simply invoke the mutual assistance pact, the joint commitment between the armed forces of Britain and Celtica, which . . .'

The guard stepped to one side, allowing them onto the runway. 'Oh, on you go then.'

'I was never here, comrade,' added Chateau as he passed by, offering another salute.

Lagrande pulled her little suitcase behind her. Chateau was carrying his duffel bag over his shoulder without any signs of exertion. The helicopter was already waiting for them with its rotors whirring away; the machine belonged to the Royal Marines, from whom Lautrec had requested assistance. In contrast to the soldier next to her, these forces were actually on their own territory.

'Well done,' said Chateau. 'Just hold your nerve now.'

Lagrande didn't reply. An explosive charge the size of a matchbox had been stuck to her spine; he could detonate it remotely if she refused to cooperate or tried to draw attention to herself in any way.

He had intercepted her just outside the airport, stuck his gun in her back and given her a perfectly straightforward task: take him to Bourreau. In the meantime, it had become clear where their journey would take them: Malleus' latest message was from Copenhagen.

But she had no idea what this unknown man wanted.

Lagrande greeted the uniformed troops in front of the helicopter, showed them her pass and introduced Chateau, who saluted and went on board. The military always asked fewer questions once they saw badges of rank on your shoulders.

She and her unknown companion took their seats in the Spartan cabin and fastened their seatbelts, and the helicopter took off immediately, heading in a northeasterly direction. They could communicate through the radios on their helmets; otherwise the noise of the engines would have drowned everything out.

'What do you want with the inspector?' asked Lagrande.

'I like watching over him,' replied the man, his face now covered by the helmet and sun visor.

Lagrande waited in vain for him to clarify before deciding to pursue another avenue of enquiry. 'Thank you for saving my life.'

'Don't mention it. You've paid me back by getting me out of Britain. But don't forget I can undo the favour at any moment.' He fell silent again.

'How long are you planning to play this little stalking game of yours?'

'Not much longer now.'

'How come?'

He released the button for his gun holster. 'He has become all too aware that I'm here. And as soon as he's solved his case, he'll try to get back at me. I'm not stupid.' Chateau laughed darkly. 'He's a bit like a pet you get used to over time, which starts to get on your nerves until you have to have him put down before he starts to bite you.'

Lagrande had no way of knowing how serious the man was being. He must have been at least fifty years old and weighed more than sixteen stone – an imposing mixture of muscle and fat, though with a far less impressive girth. His hair was black, though it could easily have been a wig. His round face was utterly inconspicuous; he could disappear into a crowd immediately. *Perfect for a murderer.*

'Would you have shot him?'

'Who?'

'The guard. At the airport.'

Chateau gave her the thumbs-up. 'It's just a means to an end.'

'How can you live with yourself as a serial killer?' Lagrande blurted out, before considering that it probably wasn't the best idea to provoke a psychopath who'd fastened an explosive device to her back and was carrying a pistol. *I should just leave it.*

But he took it in good humour. 'Perhaps they all deserve it?'

'How could that be?'

'Oh, I'm sure you could think of some reason or another. You just need to do enough research. Or maybe' – his visor turned to face her – 'I'm a god? A god of revenge? With blessed bullets, that sort of thing.'

Lagrande gave a snort of derision. 'You're just how I'd always imagined a god of revenge would be, now you mention it.'

'Is that an allusion to my stature, banlieue girl? I'll have you know this was the frame that stopped your bony arse from being scattered into a million pieces all over the hotel crockery. And if I had bleached blonde hair and loped around everywhere dressed like I was in some eighties tribute act, I'd keep my mouth shut.' He bared his teeth in what could have been considered a smile, if you used enough imagination. 'On that note: you enjoy a spot of research, don't you? What have you managed to find out about my glyphs?'

Lagrande recalled her failure in that matter, even though it hadn't been her job. But she was still annoyed about it now. 'Could you hand me one of your cartridges?'

'We'll see about that. And then you'll see that I truly am a god: one of the better-insulated bacchanal gods.' He patted his belly and his biceps rippled noticeably. 'Is there anything to drink here, or are we flying economy?'

Lagrande noticed an incoming message on her phone.

Chateau's instructions had been for her to only respond exactly as he dictated. *If I don't react at all, maybe Bourreau will realise something's wrong.* She left the device untouched in her jacket, just as she left Chateau's question unanswered, and gazed out of the window.

They were flying over water, across the North Sea to Copenhagen.

Denmark had profited greatly, being one of the states that had accepted the Northern Germanic entities as their gods. The Great Change hadn't hurt the country; the people and infrastructure and economy hadn't been affected at all. The Scandinavians had been far cleverer than many others.

'What's going to happen once we've landed in Copenhagen?' she asked.

'You'll find out where Bourreau is; we'll go there and I'll become invisible again. And if you know what's good for you, you'll keep very quiet indeed about our travel arrangements.' He circled his gloved finger in her direction. 'I've still got you bugged, remember, and my little explosive device isn't going anywhere either. One word out of turn from you, one gesture, anything that annoys me, and *BOOM!*' He folded his arms. 'Just to let you know, it's got steel fragments in it as well. Really awful for the environment. As the saying goes, keep your *composure*.'

Lagrande nodded, imagining the pleasure she'd derive from throwing Chateau out of the helicopter. Regardless of whether you want to call it vigilante justice or ingratitude, this psychopath clearly knew nothing of empathy or compassion. He lived solely to serve his own needs, which he combined with sadism and total indifference.

I hope Bourreau or I will have the chance to arrest you. The explosive charge just above her coccyx was unsettling, occasionally sending her into a panic that the transmitter could potentially be triggered by an external radio signal.

Boom. Lagrande looked back at the mystery man who had followed her and her boss, who had almost killed Ove Schwan and who had gone down in Italian police history as the *assassin di glifo.*

She wished the *boom* on him instead.

With all the force she could muster.

But unfortunately his head refused to explode in response to her thoughts alone.

Denmark, Copenhagen, November 2019

Malleus had no intention of letting the couple complete the handover. He fired off a quick message to Lautrec to tell him where he was and that they were approaching the endgame. Support from their Danish colleagues would therefore be most welcome.

Crick's unexpected intervention had added a new element to the whole affair, meaning another one had to be eradicated quickly. 'You get the woman; I'll handle the man.'

Keish quickened his pace and took out his phone as if to take a video recording of the stage, where the bizarre pseudo-Christmassy lampoon was still in full swing.

'Who owns the Winter Solstice?' shouted the MC into the crowd.

'We do!' replied the children in unison, far louder than the adults around them.

'And who else?'

'Baldur, Baldur, Baldur!' they responded, whereupon an actor entered the stage, bathed in divine light, and started reading from the Edda. Homage would soon be paid to the sun god, as the Solstice was on 21 December.

Keish waited attentively.

Malleus emerged by the side of the bearded man, announcing his presence by doffing the brim of his hat, then briefly showing a glimpse of his Apache Derringer. 'My name is Bourreau, Interpol.'

At the same time, the Tlingit grabbed hold of the woman, who remained calm after giving her companion a placatory look. 'You are in possession of stolen goods, which I must confiscate from you. Please do not resist, sir. We've got units standing by in the park who won't hesitate to strike you down if you offer any resistance.'

They dragged the astonished couple out towards the edge of the crowd and stopped by a snow-covered bench.

Malleus showed them his ID card. 'The artefacts, please.' He raised his PDA to confirm the provenance of the signal.

The bearded man realised the futility of lying, slowly reached into his computer bag and took out a small package. 'We haven't done anything illegal, sir.'

'Your ID, please. And how did you obtain these objects?'

'From a dive. It's our job,' added the woman nervously. 'Inspector, we had no idea that this was illegal – a customer asked us to check the shipwreck of the ferry with our diving robots and get their property back for them before someone came along to steal them.'

Malleus smiled. 'And I'm sure you made them show you their purchase agreement, didn't you?'

The woman lowered her eyes guiltily.

Malleus scanned their ID cards with his PDA, compared the data with Interpol records and received confirmation that the couple were Jeremy James White and Janet Lee White, married, unremarkable, except for twice being cautioned for illegal wrecking. The charges had been dropped on both occasions. *Professionals in their field.* 'How was the handover at the hotel going to happen?'

'In' – White looked up at the clock – 'five minutes we're supposed to go to suite 7 and wait there.' He produced a key from his pocket.

'Good.' Malleus took it from him. That meant they wouldn't have time to wait for reinforcements from the Danish police. 'We've got your information, Mr and Mrs White. Please stay here until the detectives have had a chance to talk to you. If you try to escape, things will be far more difficult for you.'

He gestured to Keish to follow him and walked over to the entrance.

'Do you think they're staying here, Mr Bourreau?' muttered the Tlingit.

'I'm certain of it. And our Danish colleagues will be here in a minute. They won't get away, and they know it.' Malleus considered whether or not to go into the suite himself, given the Collector's prior knowledge of him.

Then he decided it didn't matter any more. He'd go ahead and hide, meaning the Collector – whom he assumed was Gaff Olmos – would first have to talk to Keish, an unknown quantity. 'I'll secrete myself in the bathroom while you do the handover.'

'Understood. We can't have you being recognised *too soon*,' the Tlingit agreed. He looked as calm as Malleus from the outside, though his eyes betrayed his heightening tension.

He and Keish walked through the small reception area and up the stairs towards the suite.

'Do you get the impression that the drum and mask have already been used?' asked Malleus.

'No. We'd know about it if that were the case. The spirits of our ancestors don't hang around if they think their tribe is in danger.'

Malleus wanted to be sure they were preventing the worst from happening. They were in the middle of Copenhagen, a city where hundreds of thousands of people lived, with locals and tourists unwittingly going about their business or wandering through the Tivoli without a care in the world.

The ten-mile radius – or whatever measure these ancestral spirits used – was still lodged firmly in the back of his mind. It could be considerably smaller – or considerably *larger*.

If he weren't an atheist he'd be asking for divine assistance, but on this occasion he only had logic, improvisation and a pinch of luck at his disposal.

Malleus entered the suite, which was still empty.

The room was impeccable. The wooden floor made it look spacious and stylish. The large bed had a raised wooden frame that turned it into a four-poster. There was an espresso machine and actual crockery, oil paintings on the wall, fresh orchids on the coffee table, an antique bureau and wardrobe, not to mention a perfect view out over the lively, brightly lit Tivoli.

Malleus looked at his PDA. 'Two minutes,' he said to Keish and went into the bathroom, closing the sliding doors behind him. His Derringer drawn, he peered through the crack in the middle.

An unwelcome thought popped into his head. *Hopefully there aren't any cameras in the suite*. If there were, there'd be no hand-over – or significantly more violence than planned.

Time passed.

One minute.

Two minutes.

Three minutes.

Four minutes . . .

There came a knock at the door, followed by the announcement, 'Room service!' before a click could be heard and the door swung open.

A brown-haired maid entered, dressed in black trousers and a turquoise polo shirt with the hotel logo emblazoned on it.

Malleus guessed she was about eighteen – she looked as if she were there on work experience. She was carrying a crate full of coffee pods, milk and sugar, and had a tablet clutched in her other hand.

'Oh, excuse me.' She eyed the Tlingit curiously. 'You . . . you are not Mr White. And . . .' She looked at him hesitantly. Her demeanour switched suddenly back into employee mode. 'I think you might be in the wrong room, sir. Can I be of any assistance?'

'I think you'll find Mr White is surplus to requirements,' replied Keish with a smile, taking the package from the bed. 'He was supposed to give this to you.'

The maid appeared indecisive, then looked down at her tablet. 'I . . .'

Malleus suddenly realised what was going on here. *She's the one picking up the package. The Collector is watching through the tablet. Just like in the jet.*

'Turn the camera around,' came the voice of the Collector, and the maid did as she was ordered. 'I want my artefacts!'

Malleus left the lavatory and blocked the woman's path to the door, producing his police ID as he did so. 'Bourreau. I'm a detective with Interpol.'

He took the tablet from her and looked at the display, where he could just about make out the Collector's face.

He had the presence of mind to take a screenshot just before the line was disconnected from the other end. *But I've got you!* His first feeling of elation in such a long time started to spread through him.

The maid was shaking with shock and dropped the box containing the hotel accessories. 'I couldn't help it!' she cried plaintively. 'I didn't have anything to do with it. I was forced to do it, and . . .'

'We're not going to hurt you,' he said in an attempt to calm the young woman down. 'I—'

A loud hue and cry from several male voices suddenly erupted from next door.

That's Crick!

'Keish, come with me,' Malleus ordered, and ran down the short corridor, listening for further signs of disturbance. He hurried into a large room with its double doors hanging open: the hotel bar, in all its opulence.

The stocky, silver-haired Briton was standing over the older Gaff Olmos; Malleus recognised his features immediately. *It was him!* He brought up the photograph to be absolutely certain. *Yes, I'm sure of it.*

Crick had already landed a few blows on Olmos; blood was running down the gash on his face, one of his eyes was heavily swollen and his glasses were hanging from one ear. Five hotel employees in suits were lying on the floor; Crick's accomplices had clearly decided to pave the way for their employer to have some alone time with Olmos.

Two of them turned to face Malleus and Keish, drawing themselves to their full height, threatening expressions etched across their faces. Their extendable batons, complete with inbuilt tasers, were drawn.

'Just give me one more minute, Mr Bourreau, and I'll beat a confession out of him. For the death of my son and the theft of all those artefacts,' Crick called out to him, his knuckles and rings coated in blood.

Malleus could see at a glance that the frail Olmos wouldn't be able to withstand another assault. 'Mr Crick, I must ask you not to—'

'I haven't done anything!' shouted the man, blood running

down over his lips and dripping onto his suit and tie. 'Are you with the police? Save me from this madman! He just burst in while I was in the middle of a meeting and—'

Crick hit him again, this time in the stomach, and Olmos groaned, choking on his own blood. 'Look at what's on the counter, Mr Bourreau, and tell me I shouldn't believe this arsehole has nothing to do with the murders?'

Malleus looked over at the bar and recognised the artefacts, arranged neatly in a row, all the way along to the objects Keish held in his hand.

'I haven't the faintest idea who put them there,' said Olmos, trying in vain to put his glasses back on; the frames had completely buckled. 'I didn't even know there was anything there until this—'

'Idiot! He and his cronies were preparing for a ritual,' Crick chimed in, grabbing the Collector by the throat and lifting him up in the air. 'You had my son killed for all this shit!'

Malleus's view of the confrontation was obscured somewhat, not least because the muscle-bound bodyguards were making no effort to step aside. The fact that he was an inspector was apparently of no interest to them at all. It was clear they were making a fortune off Crick.

He'll kill Olmos unless I step in. He put the tablet slowly in his pocket to free his hands.

He could see Keish trying to get his attention, asking, with subtle movements of his eerie eyes, if they should intervene or not.

'Mr Crick, the police are on their way,' admitted Malleus. 'You'll be liable for prosecution under both criminal and civil law if you—'

'Let him finish him off, Inspector,' a quivering female voice came from behind. 'He's earned his death a *hundred* times over. My father is an *animal!*'

Malleus turned his head towards the entrance. In the doorway stood the maid.

* Α Ω *

There she sits, the Eighties woman, hating me.

And so she should.

We've landed and are now driving to the hotel in her rented car, for which she of course paid. I bet there'll be no shortage of drama going on at the hotel.

I'm actually rather excited to find out who's behind all this, and to see how it's going to end.

Just a short journey from the airport to the city centre.

I'd always thought Copenhagen had more charm than this. How disappointing. Not at all like the fairy-tale world that Andersen painted.

It's all pretty boring, nothing interesting to distract you like in London or Rome or Treva or . . . no, not Lutetia. Lutetia's overrated. Just like Berlin. Whatever.

If this whole thing goes to shit, it's not as if anything in Copenhagen will be missed all that much. Maybe the odd building here and there, though I guess it's more a question of taste than anything. I don't really like that many cities anyway.

Apart from Rome. But that's just because I know it so well.

Ah, the entrance to Tivoli.

Out we get, Blondie paying for us again – how very gentlemanly of her – and straight into the crowd.

No chance of her doing a runner, thanks to the charge and bug I've got on her. What a brave girl she is. Right, in goes my earpiece; I can use this to guide her around. It's nice having my own little plaything, my avatar.

Let her hate me.

Ah, looks like we're going through the back entrance of the hotel.

There's a brasserie through there. Perfect! I can grab a bite to eat while watching the whole spectacle unfold before me. Better than the cinema, this. Beats 3D hands down.

Aha, there's the first lot of cops just pulling up now.

'Let's go, go, go,' *I tell her.* 'Belenos will be with you, I'm sure.'

She gives me the finger. The classic banlieue farewell, I bet.

Let the games begin!

Oh good, it's steak night. That'll do just fine . . .

* Α Ω *

Malleus looked at the maid striding angrily into the bar; she had an undeniable resemblance to Gaff Olmos. Her hands were clenched into fists as she trembled with rage and shot hate-filled glances at him.

'Miss, you are . . .?'

'Maria Magdalena Olmos, the youngest daughter of Gaff Olmos, one of the most heinous men you're ever likely to meet,' she replied proudly, her voice quivering. 'He forced me to be part of his plan; he used me as his servant.'

'What are you talking about?' stammered Olmos. His legs had buckled like a boxer who'd just been through twelve rounds. 'Maria, you—'

Her eyes began to well up. 'He forced me to go along with his plan. Those fucking artefacts!' She pointed at the bar, then to Keish. 'He was obsessed! As soon as he heard about them, he wanted them for himself – no matter what the price!'

Crick let out a dull cry and slammed Olmos against the counter; he bounced off it with a loud crack and fell to the floor. But the Englishman wasn't prepared to offer him any respite; he grabbed his prone adversary by his hair and flung him around like a yo-yo, then grabbed him by the throat and pinned him against the edge of the counter.

Malleus could see Olmos' Adam's apple working vigorously in an attempt to swallow or speak, but Crick's vice-like grip made it impossible. 'Mr Crick! The only authority Olmos has to answer to is the law,' he called out authoritatively. 'Not you. As much as I sympathise with your plight, your actions are criminal and I have no choice but to intervene.'

'For the last year he's thought about nothing else,' said Maria contemptuously. 'The artefacts and what he called "the signs" contained in them. Nothing else was good enough for him: nothing and no one. And I had to help him, otherwise . . .' She started sobbing, 'He doesn't care about human life any more. Nobody matters, not even me. He threw everything into possessing those nine artefacts.'

'The signs, miss?' asked Malleus gently. 'What were they all about? Do you know?' He was feverishly considering how best to stop Crick without it turning into a bloodbath. 'Why all this?'

'He let them kill anyone who got in his way,' muttered Maria faintly. She swayed for a moment, then sank to the floor, crying, 'He killed them and disposed of their bodies. Just like your son, Mr Crick. He said he was scum.'

Olmos began to wheeze; his face was steadily turning blue.

Malleus had to do something – he was with Interpol after all – but he was still trying to fully understand everything that was happening, trying to piece together the whole affair. There was a long way to go, given how many gaps and missing pieces there were.

But saving lives took priority.

He drew his Apache Derringer and raised the revolver in the

air. 'Step aside, gentlemen. And you, Mr Crick, let go of the suspect at once. Otherwise I'll have to arrest you as well.'

Crick's guards looked at the small revolver speculatively; even a nine-millimetre would still be fatal at this distance. They slowly inched to one side, but kept their batons out.

Keish ran past them and attempted to wrestle Crick away, but the Englishman was a powerful man, thanks to years of sailing and other sporting activities, and he pushed the Tlingit back with one hand and followed it with a quick jab to his jaw, sending the man to the ground.

'I'm only interested in justice, Mr Bourreau,' hissed Crick, and looked Olmos straight in the eye. 'The law is your concern, not mine. The deed kills the man.'

Olmos was still gasping for breath, losing consciousness as he hung there, held by the throat in the unflinching grasp of his adversary.

'I warned you.' Malleus knew that any more verbal confrontation would be fruitless, so he aimed his gun at the Englishman's shoulder and fired.

The bullet hit its target and Crick cried out – but instead of releasing his grip, the antiques dealer grabbed the bronze dagger lying on the counter next to the other artefacts.

'No!' Malleus fired again, this time at his leg, and ran towards him, jumping over Keish and the other unconscious bodies, desperate to stop Crick from committing murder.

But the ancient blade was thrust through Olmos' chest and into his heart; the pain brought the helpless man to consciousness with a jolt before he cried out in agony and fell back dead, his eyelids still open.

'That's how it feels when you find out your child has been murdered!' shouted Crick as Malleus hauled him to the floor.

Keish got to his feet and looked at the stricken body pinned to the bar by the blade, unable to sink to the ground. 'There's nothing more we can do, Mr Bourreau,' he announced. 'The knife has gone right through.'

'As it should be!' He was so full of adrenalin that he hadn't noticed the blood pouring out from his own gunshot wounds and pooling on the ground. 'I have avenged my son.'

His acts have condemned him. If Malleus recalled correctly, this was a sentence from Germanian common law that was gleefully followed by the adherents of the Nordic gods. Crick was a known devotee of Odin; to him, it was obvious how he should bring about the demise of his son's murderer.

Malleus' eyes wandered around the bar.

Unconscious staff; armed bodyguards; a wounded Crick; Olmos' daughter, still reeling from shock following her confession that contradicted her father's denials. She would be the most important witness in the coming investigations.

But . . . He took the tablet out of his jacket pocket and brought up the photograph he'd taken during the handover. The image was slightly fuzzy but there was no doubt it was Gaff Olmos, despite the amount of time that had passed in between.

But he must have either been there during the conversation, or already in Crick's clutches. Malleus looked at Maria as she rose unsteadily to her feet, wiping tears away from her eyes with her thumb.

Loud voices and metallic clanking could be heard through the door from the reception on the floor below. The Danish police force had arrived at the scene of the crime.

'Keish,' he called out to the Tlingit, 'go over to Miss Olmos and stay by her side.'

He nodded, giving Malleus a look that said, *I understand. Something's not quite right here.*

Malleus looked at the display for an internet connection, but couldn't find one. Instead he noticed an open video program, and when he opened it, he could see a number of small video sequences with Gaff Olmos; each could be called up individually.

He clicked on the first file.

'Turn the pad around,' came the voice of the Collector from the built-in speaker. 'I want my artefacts!'

Malleus looked at Maria; her shock appeared to have completely worn off.

She held a remote control in her hand and pressed a button. The doors to the bar closed as if guided by an invisible hand and locked with an audible click.

'You and Crick haven't quite ruined my plan, Bourreau, but you've forced me to improvise.' She pointed at her dead father. 'It's all come together beautifully. I'm free from the beast and I've got all the artefacts together.'

Crick stared at her. 'It was *you*?'

Malleus pointed at the pad. 'Animated films and a computer program that switched between them in an attempt to deceive me in the jet. Just like everyone else.'

'My father would never have got away with it; I prepared all the evidence in advance in case the police got too close while they followed the trail of the missing objects. And together with the testimony of an inspector, no one would have been interested in me, the poor daughter who was forced against her will to be an accessory.' Maria gestured to Keish to stay where he was. 'But let's get on with it anyway. You can't stop me.'

'What exactly are you planning to do?' Malleus raised his Derringer.

'You'll see soon enough, Inspector.' She produced a hand-held gas mask and with her other hand pressed another button on the remote. 'As an atheist, I suppose this must be rather a paradoxical pleasure for you, witnessing a mortal turn into a goddess: a goddess who will rule over all the other gods!'

Malleus wanted to shoot her, to injure the young woman so badly that she had to stop, preventing the catastrophe the Tlingit had warned of. *All the entities will come and try to stop her.* Copenhagen would be destroyed in the process. *That cannot be allowed to happen!*

The very thought left him paralysed.

Marianne Lagrande arrived at reception at the same time as the Danish police force and immediately held her ID in the air so as not to be mistaken for a tourist.

'Lagrande, Interpol,' she called out cautiously. 'I'm Inspector Bourreau's assistant investigator.'

'We've been told about you.' One of the helmeted men nodded and gestured her towards him. 'I'm Commander Christiansen. Are you wearing a vest?

'No.'

He made another gesture and the other policeman alongside them handed her a piece of Kevlar armour, which she pulled on over her jumper, hoping she wouldn't set off the explosive as she did so.

At least this way she wouldn't be a danger to her surroundings any more.

'Do you know where Bourreau is?'

Lagrande looked at her phone, where suite 7 could be seen on the screen. 'Upstairs.'

Three armoured officers equipped with MP5Ks walked ahead of her up the stairs. At that moment the doors to the bar slid shut with a slight rumble; a loud clanking could be heard as bolts were pushed into place and locked.

Closing time. The bolts sounded far too secure for Lagrande's liking.

Christiansen had two men check the suite, but they returned immediately. Nothing of note had been found.

'They're in the bar.' Lagrande was worried about the inspector. *He's stopped writing.*

No sound could be heard through the doors. They gave them a cautious tap; clearly the metal was incredibly thick.

Christiansen spoke into his radio. 'I need a hotel manager, someone with a key to open the door for me.'

Lagrande was suddenly overcome with the same sort of dizziness as when she had smoked the Culebra. Two of the policemen slumped to the ground beside her.

'Get out,' said Chateau in her earpiece. 'Someone's let some sort of gas off.'

Lagrande staggered backwards; her weakening legs managed to get her to the staircase and she slid down using the handrail before crawling out into the open on all fours and rolling onto her back in the icy snow.

Some of the policemen had also managed to get out in time and were sitting down or leaning against the façade.

'Breathe, banlieue girl. Deep breaths, in and out,' instructed her invisible companion. 'They must have piped it through the heating system. Everyone in the brasserie has got their face in their plates. Hilarious. But I can forget my steak.'

'What . . . should I . . . do now?' she asked, panting. The winter cold was making her shiver, while her blonde hair was soaked through from the ice and mud, in spite of her hat.

'You're asking me?'

'You ... you've got a better overview of the situation.' If Chateau could bug her and turn her into his puppet, he could damn well tell her what to do now as well.

'I suggest you try to climb onto the roof. There's a light-shaft up there.'

Roof. Climbing. Merde. Lagrande stood up shakily, but at least she was no longer dizzy. Her legs were starting to obey her again, while the cold cleared her head. Passers-by had stopped to help and emergency personnel rushed from waiting ambulances to attend to the dazed police officers.

'It'll take a while for the cops to work out what to do next,' came the voice of her unseen companion, 'and by that time anything could have happened to Bourreau.'

'And what about you?'

'Already on my way to the roof, banlieue girl. I'll meet you up there. Whoever gets there first will have to grant a wish to the other.

Like fuck I will. Lagrande grabbed an MP5K from a semi-conscious policeman, as well as a couple of spare magazines; no one would notice amid all this chaos. The fact that she was already wearing a vest with *Politi* clearly emblazoned across it made it look entirely legitimate for her to be scaling a wall while clutching a fully automatic machine-gun.

She circled the hotel and climbed up the snow-covered Oriental façade, swinging from windowsill to ledge, past a series of dazzling lights. She couldn't avoid being seen by tourists, but that was irrelevant at this stage. There were most important things at stake than inconspicuousness.

Meanwhile, the park staff had begun evacuating the area. All manner of announcements could be heard, imploring visitors to leave at once as they were closing earlier than intended due to a technical error on a central monitoring platform.

Lagrande finally reached the roof, which was covered by a fine layer of powdery snow, but was rather boring in comparison to the spectacular front of the hotel.

There was a large set of footprints, belonging to the man styling himself 'Chateau'. He was already kneeling alongside one of the small windows; he had changed his clothes and was now wearing a snow-camouflage uniform which rendered him almost invisible. He had already lifted up the steel screen on the window.

Lagrande loaded her MP and released the safety catch. *It would be so easy . . .*

'Yo, banlieue girl! You're too late!' he called out good-naturedly. 'The fat old man got up here before you.' He pointed at the sheet; a chink of light from below appeared through a small gap between the metal and glass. 'Frozen over. We can't get in, but at least we'll be able to see what's going on.'

Lagrande looked contemplatively at the gap, which was about a hand's-width wide. The barrel of her MP5K would fit through, though the angle allowed her only to shoot into the corner of the large room containing the bar, several armchairs and a fireplace.

Several people had been stacked one on top of another like sacks to stop them from getting in the way. A moat of blood oozed all around them. Lagrande recognised Gaff Olmos and Marcus Crick, who had had his throat slit in addition to the gunshot wounds on his leg and shoulder. There was nothing she could do to save them.

To Lagrande's great relief, however, Bourreau and Keish were seated on armchairs, with cable ties securing them so tightly to the furniture that they had no chance of escaping. Their eyes were closed; the gas was clearly still having an effect.

'We could always use the explosive on my back to blow the sheet off,' she suggested.

Chateau laughed at her. 'Oh, absolutely – and then you can just shoot me with that fancy little machine gun of yours.' He took out his APB. 'We'll be fine to shoot from here. I'll be happy as long as we save Bourreau's arse.'

He removed his chewing gum from his mouth and stuck it to the steel screen. Holding it with one hand, he placed a pin-like object on the glass and drew a circle around the gum. After tapping on it softly he removed the cut-out piece; warm air escaped up from the bar.

He's come well prepared. Lagrande urged herself not to underestimate this man, despite his brash manner.

Chateau pushed his silencer through the opening and held it in position.

'Don't shoot until I tell you to,' he warned her softly.

'Okay.' *But who will be my target?*

Malleus spared himself the trouble of trying to get to grips with his surroundings after he woke up. Every second in the locked bar counted. He opened his eyes and immediately spotted Maria, who had placed the stolen artefacts from Hannes Hein's cubbyhole in a circle in the middle of the room: the Fan of Susanoo, the Horn of Nandi, the Brick of Chogha Zanbil, the Statuette of Oddua with the diamond alongside it, the Iron Crown of Lombardy, the Harpoon Tip, the Gold Wings, the Dagger.

'Welcome back, Mr Bourreau.' She had arranged the eight objects in unusual positions, in such a way that he guessed the unknown symbols Lagrande had spotted were facing one another. She was holding the Tlingit drum in one hand, the mask in the other.

Malleus' wrists and ankles were bound to the chair by cable ties, making it impossible for him to move his arms and legs. Keish, who was also just waking up, was in an identical position.

He did a quick scan of the room and spotted the others. None of them were still alive: not Crick, nor his bodyguards, nor those attending the meeting, and of course not Gaff Olmos either.

'Miss Olmos, please, stop what you're doing,' he implored, keeping his voice friendly. 'You have no idea what you'll trigger if you use these objects!'

She gave him a look of pity. 'Do you really think I haven't fully explored the history of the artefacts?'

Keish broke in, 'Then you know that our ancestors—'

'Let them! Let them come and annihilate Copenhagen and destroy the city,' she interrupted, her voice euphoric, her indifference to humanity clear. 'By then I'll have become the Queen of the Gods and will have them do my bidding.'

'And just how is that going to happen?' Malleus noticed a movement above him by the light-shaft. The steel sheet hadn't completely closed and a piece of glass had been cut out, through which he could see the barrel of a gun protruding.

My unknown stalker. He made an exception this time and welcomed the stubbornness of the man who had yet again hurried to Copenhagen to save his life. Or so he hoped. It didn't matter how he had found him. *He needs an opportunity.*

The angle made it impossible for him to shoot Maria, so Malleus had to bring her further forward, to get her into his sights.

Maria waved the mask in a circle. 'I call upon Him: I call upon the one whom all shall obey and who created everything.'

Malleus didn't understand. 'Him?'

'The ONE god.'

'If you want to force an atheist to participate in your little project, I'd really like to know what you intend to do,' asked Malleus. He wanted to provoke her, to draw her closer to him, into the line of fire. 'If you can convince me, I'll worship you on the spot, Miss Olmos. For what it's worth, I assume you've already picked out a name to go on all your temples? It needs to be something snappy, something that rolls off the tongue. Original as well: Maria's a bit too . . . well, Christian, don't you think?'

Maria laughed contemptuously. 'It's obvious that a man like you has nothing but scorn and mockery at his disposal. But that won't do anything to change my ascent to power. By destroying my predecessor, I shall become the Supreme Being.' She banged on the drum once with the mask, producing a deep, rich tone. 'As I'm sure you discovered during your research, this symbol can be found in different places on every continent, on all these highly significant religious artefacts and objects.'

'That we did.'

'I discovered the first sign by accident, in my father's collection. From that point on I knew that humanity was only led by ONE god,' continued Maria. She banged the skin of the drum once more, and it emitted a roar that reverberated all around the room, right up to its high ceilings. 'He left his symbol as a demonstration of his omnipresence in time and space. I found the clues he left behind and have gathered together all the evidence, to make sure I don't succumb to any deception.' She turned to face the remaining artefacts. 'But the people still remain blind to all this.' She pointed at the brick. 'That's the wording of the invocation, written down with absolute humility. The mask and drum will force him to come to me, and I shall kill him with the dagger forged by his own hand. Then I shall take his power for myself.' She looked at Malleus with elation. 'Are you convinced?'

'So you're asserting that this *one* god has taken innumerable forms in order to present himself as hundreds of different entities?'

'Yes.'

'To what end?'

'Because all people and every culture need their own deities to look up to. Cohesion. Unity.'

'And what about the Christians, the Muslims and the Jews?' Malleus remarked.

'A failed experiment. The ONE god tried to appear as ONE god, but faith in him was torn into three pieces,' stated Maria with conviction, 'hence returning to his former concept in 2012 with the Great Change.'

Malleus laughed scornfully. 'That's just as feeble-minded and overwrought as every other explanation I've heard from people who believe in an entity or some sort of higher power.' He looked at the Tlingit. 'No offence.'

'None taken,' replied Keish quietly. He appeared to have either accepted his fate or to be deep in concentration in an attempt to stop the spirits of his ancestors.

'You'll soon see, Bourreau, that your time as an atheist has come to an end,' replied Maria with certainty. 'I'll take you at your word and will have you kneel before me.' She struck the drum skin once more with the mask; the tone now caused the bottles on the shelves to shake. Even their clothes were vibrating.

'That'll prove hard while I'm shackled to this chair. Did you plan this whole day down to the last detail?'

'Of course. The handover of the missing items was always to take place today. These idiots just thought the artefacts in the bar were some new chic decorations that I had brought along with me this morning; and I put the gas in place to eradicate the guests, my father and any other problems that might arise.

That way I could begin my invocation without being disturbed. It was also pretty useful against the police.'

A helicopter could be heard overhead, hovering just above the roof of the hotel.

'Gaze upon me now,' said Maria, slipping on the mask. 'Before your eyes shall be born a GODDESS from the ashes of the ONE true god.'

She started to bang the drum with her free hand; her voice through the mask could barely be heard against the sound of the rhythmic beat. She called out to her god in an unknown language, standing dead upright and stock-still with her hand thumping down on the drum skin again and again.

The pounding filled the bar, shattering the glasses and bottles on the counter and making the artefacts vibrate and dance across the room in time with the resonance. The first pieces of plaster began to break loose from the ceiling; cracks snaked their way along the walls like streaks of black lightning desperately seeking a way out.

'They are coming, Mr Bourreau,' whispered Keish, his eyes glimmering with a weak light. 'Whether you believe in them or not, the Ancestors are coming.'

'The stupid bitch isn't moving,' muttered Chateau, sounding irritated. 'Come on, just two or three steps.' Even when he was agitated, his enormous body remained completely still.

He must have been a sniper, Lagrande thought, *or maybe he's simply learned his craft from other occasions like this.*

He and Lagrande were following the conversation in the bar between Bourreau and Maria Olmos. The Tlingit was, rather sensibly, keeping a low profile; or maybe just preparing himself for the worst-case scenario.

The noise of a helicopter thundered overhead; it didn't belong to the police but instead looked suspiciously like a chartered press helicopter. A spotlight flashed over them as snow fluttered down.

'Get rid of them, banlieue girl,' growled Chateau, 'otherwise that bitch down there is going to think the cops are coming in through the roof and shit's going to start going down very quickly.'

That's going to happen whatever we do. Lagrande stood up, pointed at the word *Politi* on her vest and made shooing gestures with her gun.

The helicopter moved away slightly, but remained nearby.

She hastily looked down into the bar through the slit.

The droning had increased; the invocation was gathering momentum. Shockwaves were running through the entire roof, shaking her and Chateau around as if they were sitting on the back of an animal that was trying to throw them off. The cold white wall moved and was thrown up into the air; a low crack could be heard all around them.

'Ha! The Indian's eyes are glowing,' he said thoughtfully. 'It's definitely the Ancestors. That'll make him happy.'

Lagrande let out a loud curse and turned her gaze towards the inspector. He looked to be almost within arm's reach, yet there was nothing she could do to help him. *I could . . .*

A loud crack erupted from next to her and she shrank back.

A smoking brass case flew past her face.

There came a second crack and another one sailed in front of her face.

Who's he shooting at? She looked down into the bar through the glass as Chateau let off a third and then a fourth shot.

The Glyph Killer's precise shots hadn't been intended for Maria

Olmos but were instead aimed at the cable ties on Bourreau's hands and feet. From her vantage point it didn't look as if he had injured the inspector at all.

'Four out of four,' remarked Chateau with a laugh. 'Now for the Indian.' He switched hands. 'It's not such a big deal if I hit him anyway.'

Lagrande thought about the charge in her back and thought it best to keep quiet.

Malleus felt and heard the impact of the bullet with shock; it had released the lock on his right-hand cable tie without so much as brushing his wrist. The projectile passed through the seat and embedded itself in the floor, making splinters fly everywhere.

He quickly turned his other hand and his feet around to make things easier for the shooter. Seconds later he was free; after the next lot of bullets had hit their mark, Keish was also released from his shackles. His psychopathic guardian angel was once again proving to be a dab hand with an APB. *Both in Dover and in Copenhagen.*

Maria was filling the high-ceilinged room with droning. The destruction continued to spread further and further out, tearing plaster from the walls. The masonry beneath began to crumble, breaking off in large chunks that fell to the ground and crashed into the bar.

It wasn't just Keish's eyes that were glowing; the mask and drum were also glimmering with a red light that was increasing in intensity. Out of the glowing light emerged shining figures. They began to surround the young woman, whose invocation showed no sign of stopping.

'What are we going to do?' shouted Malleus over the cacophony, finding the second Derringer in his bag. Maria hadn't taken the trouble to disarm him – as a goddess she wasn't expecting to fear any earthly projectiles. *Or even as a mortal.*

But Keish sat stock-still on the chair; a clearly audible song could be heard emanating from his lips and merging melodically with the drumming. The red glow disappeared.

Malleus realised that the Tlingit was trying to act as a counterweight, attempting to appease the Ancestors by making them aware that one of their own was close by.

But they still had to inflict punishment for the theft of the artefacts, although they appeared unable to break through completely – either that, or the Elamite language was keeping them in check.

This ends here. Malleus slipped on his knuckleduster and broke free from the chair. He ran towards Maria – his plan was simple: destroy the ring of artefacts, force the young woman to the ground and pull the mask off her face. *That should do it.*

A glistening white beam of light broke through the ceiling with a loud humming noise and illuminated Maria as if she were standing in the middle of an anti-aircraft searchlight. Debris fell in rings all around her, deflected away by the energy so that she couldn't be hit. Malleus and Keish avoided the hail by a hair's breadth.

At the same time, the ghostly Tlingit began to pour out of the glowing light, as if they had been waiting for a gap to open up for them and their wrath.

Maria was thrown to the ground by the force of the beam, but she knelt down and continued to strike the drum, still invoking the name of the ONE god.

The . . .

Malleus noticed the beam had brought something else along with it.

Out of the ruins emerged a procession of large beings with ashen skin and tentacled arms; their enormous glowing eyes were staring directly at him. Their elephantine feet with razor-sharp nails crushed the circle of artefacts, bent the Crown of Lombardy, destroyed the filigree harpoon tip and stamped on the Statuette of Oddua. They were unstoppable, advancing alongside one another with their claws fanning out.

The servants of Namtarú! Malleus lowered his Apache Derringer and stared at his four entirely unanticipated new opponents, who appeared to have fallen through the ceiling from the sky. *What do they want here? To stop the ONE god from appearing?*

Maria finally noticed that events had taken an sudden unexpected turn. Still chanting, she looked hurriedly from left to right and saw the *bad*. Her beating hand and the drum started to tremble.

She's afraid of them.

More and more spirits emerged from underneath the mask and drum-skin, flooding out towards the roof.

Keish remained motionless, singing in the chair – and Malleus understood. *He can only stop them from attacking me, but not from breaking away from her.*

One of the *bad* turned its head to face Maria, who broke into a stammer as it roared at her. Its glowing white eyes flickered down at her. Its right arm, a mass of black tentacles, struck out and destroyed the drum, while the second blow threw the mask into the woman's head, bursting both into pieces. He finished her off by stamping on her with his gargantuan foot, pressing her into the ground. She was just a crushed corpse who bore hardly any resemblance to a woman.

Malleus could see the three remaining beings approaching him and he stepped back. *The whip.* It was still in its holder in his jacket pocket.

His adversaries stopped at the same time, their tentacles writhing like serpents. One of the beasts opened its hellish mouth, revealing shimmering rows of deadly teeth. 'Now is the time for you to take your punishment for your intervention in Gomorrah, Malleus Bourreau,' came the voice of Namtarú through his servant. 'Coincidence smiles upon me.'

'Are you the ONE god?'

'Of course I'm a god. Are you wondering how I managed to find you?'

He doesn't understand my question – then he can't be the ONE. 'It was the invocation!'

'Yes: an old incantation for a dead god, irrelevant for centuries now. Someone had to answer the unexpected invitation in his stead,' replied Namtarú spitefully. 'Mortals can be so useful sometimes.'

'Why do you want me dead? For saving a child?'

'Not just any child: *Baal's* child! She should never have been in Sodom or Gomorrah, just like her father. You stopped my servants and prevented me from achieving a great triumph over my adversary.'

'So that time in our trench, there was another small child, one you had to get your *bad* to murder?'

A patronising laugh issued from the throat of the beast. 'You know nothing about what happened back then. It is truly magnificent to see how much it bothers you to this day, and how little you understand. Let it gnaw away at you until your death, Malleus Bourreau. After all, you're just a few heartbeats away from staring into its eyes. Perhaps then you'll realise the truth.' The creature shut its mouth and the remaining beasts broke free from their torpor.

Malleus retreated further, took the whip from out of its container and unwound it. It was his only hope of surviving the fight against the four *bad*, even though he had practised just once. The treacherous weapon could as easily destroy him if he tried to wield it.

His gaze fell on the ruined artefacts and the remains of the mask and drum. *What now?* The Ancestors were flying around Copenhagen and Keish wouldn't be able to banish them back to whence they came.

The *bad* came ever closer, their nails gouging deep grooves into the parquet flooring; entire pieces broke off under their weight, revealing sharp edges that protruded into the air.

One after the other. Malleus raised his arm and let the whip gather momentum. If he failed to subdue these four monsters, he and the Tlingit would surely die – in the process destroying everything in a ten-mile radius.

The bright white eyes of the beasts began to flicker, slowly at first, then increasing in speed and intensity.

Malleus released the hooks from his weapon with a flick of his thumb. *I've got to get a move on.*

* Α Ω *

Fuck me blind—!

A beam of light is pouring out of the night sky like a white rainbow and tearing the roof of the bar clean off. Not a pot of gold in sight, though – not a pot of anything. But good, I suppose: I've now finally got a clear field of vision.

What are—? What sort of creatures are those? Shit, is it the Day of Tentacles in Denmark today or something? They certainly don't look as if they come from around here, but nor do they look like they belong to the ONE god.

Red ghosts are swarming out into the open, circling us once before disappearing further and further away.

What are *they doing?*

'*Bad*,' *says Blondie.*

'Yeah, I'd say it's pretty bad.'

'No, not "bad" as in "evil" – *bad* as in: demons from Gomorrah.'

Ah, so now I'm the idiot! The sign of Namtarú: I can see it now, glowing on their foreheads. Like the one on the neck of that little girl in New Carthage.

'Should I shoot?' *I ask banlieue girl.* 'Are he and those white critters friend or foe?'

She's already taking aim. That's an answer in and of itself. 'Don't shoot until I've started,' *she tells me.*

For all I care.

Mm. Where could such a thing—? . . . Whoa! Has he just crushed Olmos?

Ha ha ha – yes! He crushed her like a beetle. And the drum and mask for good measure. That's it for the Invocation for the ONE god, then.

Ha ha ha! I'm practically pissing myself up here.

All that work that stupid bitch put in; all that money and all those murders – all for nothing. And she's no more either. As flat as a pancake. Blood and intestines clinging to his enormous foot as if he's just stood in something disgusting.

There, screaming.

Lots *of screaming.*

Coming from the city and the park. What's going on down there?

'I'll be right back. Start shooting if anything happens.' *I run over to the edge of the roof. Whoa – the Ancestors are tearing shit up!*

Dead bodies everywhere. Cars driven into one another, smashed-up vehicles, bodies, yet more bodies – some liquefying, others torn to shreds. These Ancestors really aren't much craic, are they?

Why did they ignore us? Almost certainly because of that Indian singing in the chair. His little intercession saved us, I bet.

Okay, I suppose I'll let him live, in that case.

Back to the hole in the roof – what's going on down there is more important. 'Have I missed anything?'

'No.'

But I can hear in her voice that I have.

Bourreau's swinging the whip; the white creatures are moving forward and the redskin's still chanting away. Good. You go, Pocahontas!

All this adrenalin coursing through me is making it fucking difficult not to go completely off the rails.

I've got to stay calm . . .

Banlieue girl suddenly starts shooting; the MP5K spits out short bursts and kicks back a bit. She's clearly not done this much before.

'Hold on tighter. Grip at the front.'

I lie flat on the cold roof – nice little surprise for my balls there. They'll definitely start to swell up, and not in the way I'd like. I raise my APB, already loaded.

Let's get this party started. It's not one to miss.

Hold my breath, fire, breathe out. Headshot.

No reaction . . . oh yes, but . . . ah. *It's regenerating.*

Bit rude.

'Aim for their joints,' *I say to banlieue girl, and I see her nodding out of the corner of my eye.*

Good, then the legs. Until these fuckers haven't got any knees left.

Hold my breath, fire . . .

* Α Ω *

Malleus had no idea how to handle a whip so he had to rely on intuition and his own ability to adapt in order to ensure he didn't accidentally attack himself.

The end with the extended razor-sharp barbs struck the first *bad* and tore its face off. It crashed to the floor, liquid pouring out of it and causing the air to change colour.

He could hear the rattle of a machine-gun erupting through the hole above him and saw the flashes of fire appearing from the barrel. The bullets struck the *bad*, punching holes in them that took barely a second to heal over again.

Malleus was all too familiar with *that*.

The gleaming eyes increased their flickering and Malleus could feel himself approaching the point at which he would lose all control. He avoided the approaching beasts and the rapid arcs of their tentacles, which were ramming welts into the parquet floor, goring deep slits into the wall and hacking the furniture to pieces.

Keish sat among the chaos, looking as calm as ever, murmuring inaudibly. Dirt and dust was stuck to his skin and clothes, as well as to his black raven feathers. He was either completely unaware that death was raging all around him, or this was the only way for him to prevent the far greater catastrophe from happening outside.

Malleus swung the whip and struck an advancing *bad*.

The whirling leather whip cut through its knee joint; the creature fell to the ground, howling in agony with one leg missing, flailing around before being hit by another blow to the head.

That's two down! Lagrande was swapping magazines, but Malleus could still clearly see another beast being shot at the same time. His mystery protector and assistant investigator appeared to have formed an alliance in order to assist him.

The APB bullets were causing substantial damage to their joints.

The creature at the back jerked several times. It looked like it couldn't heal itself any more. It turned around, screeching, and launched its black tentacles up to the roof.

That gave Malleus the opportunity to concentrate on the penultimate *bad*.

The enraged beast attacked with great force, leaping towards him and opening its mouth, trying to grab him with its tentacles and drag him between its murderous jaws.

'Get back!' Malleus twirled the whip above his head like a lion-tamer to keep the *bad* at a safe distance, cutting several tentacles off the beast as he did so.

It let out a roar of anger and pain.

Lagrande and the unknown man were firing upon the second beast as it continued to lash up towards them, gradually increasing the size of the hole in the roof in an attempt to drive them back or drag them down with the rubble.

Malleus could see a gap opening up for him, a clearing within the forest of tentacles. *There!* He reached outside the circle, casting the whip in a wide arc – but it struck an obstacle on the way, tearing parts of the chandelier away and sending it spiralling to the floor.

The enormous light hurtled downwards, missing Keish by a matter of inches before shattering in a shower of crystal splinters that lodged in the back of his chair.

The Tlingit stiffened abruptly; his singing became slower and less powerful.

Shit! Malleus evaded the *bad*, which kept pursuing him. Its tentacles formed a circle around him and it was by only jumping onto the counter and into the remains of the bar itself that he managed to avoid a deadly blow. Everything inside the bar was drenched in alcohol; it smelled strongly of spirits.

A thick black tentacle appeared, as strong and supple as a cable.

Big mistake. Malleus grabbed one of the smashed bottles and plunged it into the exposed flesh; the roar from the other side was music to his ears.

He straightened up immediately and grabbed the whip, striking the *bad* on the chest and cutting deeply into it, revealing a collection of brittle bones that were beginning to leak some sort of liquid.

The beast stamped around in agony, the floor shuddering under the weight of its flailing legs and stomping feet. It hurled the bar top to one side and raised its tentacles to attack.

Malleus had just enough time to duck under the advance.

What do you say to that? Malleus pulled out his lighter and set the contents of the broken bottles of spirits on fire.

A wall of flame sprang up and began to eat away at the *bad*; it disappeared into the blaze, emitting a horrifying scream as it was swallowed up by the inferno. The monster appeared to be completely blinded; its burning tentacles were casting fiery streaks at the floor and walls. Grey skin turned to green and a stench reminiscent of boiling liquorice emanated from its pores.

Malleus thrust the whip into the flames and cracked it once more.

The screeching ended abruptly, then the lacerated body of the *bad* fell out of the fire and lay still. The flames hissed and began to subside under the countless gallons of spilt liquid.

Just one left. He looked around and spotted the last beast, still going hammer and tongs at the ceiling. Lagrande was firing brief salvos down from above, but they were having little effect on her adversary.

Malleus approached the *bad*, but despite the incredible success he had had so far, he couldn't allow himself to feel euphoric. There was still the matter of the Ancestors to contend with. With only Keish to stop them, they were without doubt causing havoc throughout Copenhagen.

He quickly looked over at the Tlingit, who was breathing in fits and starts and willed him to hold on.

'Watch out!' shouted Lagrande from above him, and Malleus instinctively took a step back.

The black tentacles sank into the floor just in front of his feet and tore it apart.

Sharp pieces of rubble struck Malleus' face; he staggered to one side and fell down. The whip slipped out of his fingers.

Putrid smoke from the remains of the fire rolled inexorably forwards, enveloping him.

Everything went dark.

Lagrande loaded the last magazine into her gun. *It'll all be over soon.* She cast her eyes downwards and shouted a warning to the inspector, who had let his guard slip, just for a moment, as he was looking for Keish.

It was only because of her last-ditch attempt to attract his attention that he was able to evade the attack, but he fell – and lost the whip.

Lagrande could see that he had sustained several small wounds to the face; he looked disorientated. Before he could grab hold of the whip, it disappeared into a cloud of steam.

The *bad* approached his opponent menacingly, preparing to eradicate this man who had killed three of its companions – certainly not an everyday occurrence.

She looked around for Chateau, but he had disappeared.

Merde. She was on her own.

Belenos watch over me! Without hesitation she ran alongside the hole in the roof, parallel to the *bad*, and leaped; as she did so, she drew her MP5K and fired at the head, shoulders and tentacles of the beast, which turned around with a bellow to face his newest assailant.

Lagrande took a blow to her knee on the creature's surprisingly hard body and slid down its grey skin. It made a rustling noise as she did so, the sound of a wasps' nest being crushed.

She landed awkwardly, slipped – and fell forward into a roll. She didn't get to do those sorts of stunts all that often in everyday life.

The web of whirring tentacles grabbed her and hurled her into the pile of seats below, which cushioned her fall somewhat. A cut on her arm suddenly appeared; it must have been caused by a tentacle. The pain started to spread the moment she noticed the injury, and it quickly started getting unbearable.

The *bad* stomped around, hurling broken pieces of furniture to one side and lunging forward to strike her down; its black tentacles were coiled in anticipation. Piercing eyes flickered rapidly like a strobe light, making every movement appear utterly surreal.

Take that, you piece of shit! She lifted the MP5K with a groan and fired.

A single shot rang out and the bullet lodged in the beast's chest – but the hole started closing almost immediately afterwards.

The magazine was empty.

The monster moved its arms towards her, tentacles twitching menacingly like a rattlesnake.

Belenos, I am in your hands. She was hoping that being cut to ribbons, which appeared to be an imminent prospect, wouldn't hurt too much when, without warning, the *bad* was struck hard from behind.

It screamed and turned its attention away from Lagrande.

Bourreau's whip had swung entirely around the creature's body. There was a quick jolt and the end containing the hooks was pulled tightly around the beast; the line suddenly went taut and the *bad* was torn in two.

It fell to the ground, flooding the remains of the wooden floor with yet more innards and fluids.

The inspector said breathlessly to Lagrande, 'Hold on, Madame. It's nearly over.' He grabbed the Tlingit's rucksack and ran over to him.

Nearly over. Lagrande breathed deeply and clenched her jaw, letting her empty gun fall to the ground. She groaned, rising from the sofa to help Bourreau in any way she could.

Malleus knelt in front of Keish and opened the rucksack containing the little bags the shaman had been using for his incantation to the ancestral spirits. 'You've got to banish them.'

The Tlingit's crystal eyes gleamed weakly; his gargantuan effort and the injuries he'd sustained had really taken their toll.

Lagrande approached him, a wound on her arm bleeding profusely. Her Kevlar vest was in tatters; you could hardly make out the word *Politi* on it at all – but the *bad* would have torn her to pieces had it not been for that vest.

With a great effort Keish took out several bags and carefully opened the coloured leather straps, all the while continuing his song. From the gestures he was making it appeared he needed a fire: a large one.

'Just a sec.' Malleus hurriedly bundled together some wood from the remains of the furniture and ripped-up parquet flooring, then ran over to the bar to look for bottles that still had some alcohol in them.

He found a couple, knocked back a shot himself for good measure and returned to his makeshift pyre. The flame from his lighter started a blaze that completely consumed the wood. *Hopefully that'll be enough.*

His hands trembling, Keish added more items to the bag, one after the other. To European ears his song already sounded unusual, but now it changed once more, becoming eerier and more haunting.

The smoke began to rise in thick plumes, billowing upwards into the open air as if calling out to the Ancestors and absorbing their very essence, ensuring no more harm could be done.

Malleus followed the movements, spellbound. The flames changed colour, then began to make a different sound as the burning continued. *Will it be enough?*

Drifting figures appeared in the room through the glowing column of smoke, circling the three humans beneath them and one after the other dropping into the fire, where they dissolved with a crackle and a medley of bright sparks.

Blood poured from Keish's lips, but he refused to stop until the final bag was empty. Only then, as the last of the light departed from them, did he close his eyes. His body went limp and he slumped forward in his chair.

Malleus caught him – and saw a sharp piece of wood sticking out of the back of the chair was covered in the Tlingit's blood. But the man who had saved Copenhagen from unknowable destruction was still alive.

'We've got to get out of here,' said Malleus, standing up. 'The remote control to unlock these doors will be somewhere in the middle of all this rubble. Stay with Keish, Madame.' He hurried over to where the remains of Maria Olmos lay, though he doubted very much that he'd find the device intact among the noxious mixture of clothes, bones, skin, organs and blood. *Hopefully the police will manage to break their way in soon.*

'Looking for this?'

At the back of the room Malleus could make out a corpulent figure dressed in winter camouflage, a baseball cap and a pair of sunglasses. He held the remote control in his right hand and clutched his APB in the other. *Ah. My Number One fan. Pity he's fucking mental.* 'Would you please unlock the doors so that the emergency services can attend to Madame Lagrande and Mr Keish?'

'You never write. You never call. Not even a "thanks for saving my life".' The man pulled a face of faux-disappointment, barely recognisable through the darkness.

'Maybe later, sir.' Malleus pointed to his injured friends. 'This is urgent.'

'And then I suppose you're going to arrest me.'

'I'm afraid so, yes. And I'll be glad to do so. You're a murderer, sir. A mass murderer.'

The man laughed. 'I merely dealt with people who deserved to be dealt with. Ask Madame Lagrande. We had a bit of natter, we did. And if you try to arrest me, Malleus Bourreau, I'll blow Moneypenny sky-high. I've stuck a detonator to her back, with a remote fuse.'

'He's right,' she said, her voice downcast.

'That's hardly going to make me more sympathetic to your cause.' Malleus took out his PDA and started to film him. 'Would you be so kind as to tell me your name? Just so I know who I'll be hunting.' Malleus looked at the name badge on his uniform. 'It's certainly not *Chateau.*'

'Ah, unfortunately not. Let's keep it a secret for now. I do love a good mystery.' The man chuckled, his entire face wobbling as he did so. 'Right, the time for talking is over. I just wanted to introduce myself really, to let you know I'm a big, big fan of yours and I fully intend to be kicking around nearby for the foreseeable. If you try to cut me off again, I'll make sure to punish you by hurting the ones you hold most dear. Do we understand each other?'

Malleus nodded.

'And *because* you've already tried to get away from me once, that warrants a punishment. I'm a man of my word, after all.'

Malleus drew his Apache Derringer and pointed it at the unknown man. 'Do not lay a finger on Madame Lagrande.'

'I can blow her up if you prefer.'

'You won't be able to.' Malleus lifted up his PDA. 'Jamming device.'

The man's faced dropped. 'Well, that's just cheating!'

'You are under arrest,' he told him, 'for a number of murders. At this stage it is my duty to inform you that—'

The arm holding the APB jerked upwards.

Malleus pulled the trigger.

Chateau was hit once, twice, three times, four times by the combination of shot and full-metal-jacket all piercing his body, most through and through. Blood began to seep out from his chest. The bullets destroyed his glasses and knocked the hat and wig from his bald head.

The man gave a laugh of disbelief and sank to the ground in silence.

'I *did* warn him.' Malleus went over to the dead body, removed the control from his grasp and searched him, though he couldn't find a remote trigger anywhere. *Nothing*? He hurried over to

Lagrande, who showed him where exactly the charge on her back was situated.

'We're finally rid of him,' she said, the relief in her voice tangible. 'What I would have given to be the one to do it though, Inspector – on the roof, when his back was turned.'

'In my case it was self-defence, but I'm afraid for you that would have been considered murder.' The smell of the substance betrayed what it really was. *That's no explosive.* Malleus pulled it off her back. *It's a lump of dough – with a diode stuck in it.* 'Crisis averted, Madame.' He switched off the unnecessary jamming device and released the lock on the doors.

Malleus rang police headquarters and promptly found himself in the middle of a battle over jurisdiction, so he wrote a message on his PDA to the effect that the matter was under control and requested urgent medical assistance.

Barely ten seconds had passed since his despatch when the paramedics rushed in, accompanied by a pack of policemen under Christiansen's command.

Now it's really over. Malleus watched them attending to Keish and Lagrande. He smiled at her. 'From now on you're officially my partner.'

'I'd have shot you, Monsieur l'Inspecteur, if you had denied me that,' she replied, brushing strands of dirty hair away from her face. She smiled back, despite everything she had been through.

Malleus left the bar with her in tow. The clean-up operations, in the hotel and Copenhagen itself, were beginning. *And all because a mortal flew too close to the sun.* He would give himself a day off before compiling everything he knew about the matter in an attempt to come up with some sort of explanation for everything.

'But at least the case is closed,' he muttered to himself.

The death of Crick and Amarud would attest to the fact that a large amount of justice had been meted out.

* A Ω *

He's just left me here.

Shoots me and leaves to die here like a dog in the street!

Well, I can see where he's coming from. I'd have done the same thing in his position. I might have added a kick in the balls for good measure, just to add to the humiliation.

Can't move – must have done something to my spine. But I can still think. I'll keep my composure right up to my dying breath.

Not long now. Close to the end. Something's leaking inside me – everywhere is warm. Stomach acid, perhaps. Or piss.

I won't survive this.

But I've got to say the last few weeks have been fun.

An absolute blast.

This is a far better way to die than my heart giving out halfway through having a wank in that fucking hovel in Rome.

Cops, yes, and paramedics as well. They're all here. But they're ignoring me. And I didn't even get to tell my prey that I was up on the roof, looking over him.

I'm dying . . .

. . . it's taking a while . . .

Ah, two people have just arrived and are shining a light in my face to check my pupil reflex.

What are you gawping at? Surprised to find this fat old man is still alive?

'What have we here, Professor Loki?'

'I'd say it's a mortal who's just about to live up to that designation, Professor Susanoo.'

They both laugh.

Are they fucking with me? Have these two idiots just taken a bunch of pills or something? I can't see a thing – get that fucking light out of my face, you prick!

'Shall we leave him to die, Professor Loki?'

'I don't know. He's rather entertaining. He's been responsible for a great deal of chaos, Professor Susanoo.'

Oh good, I can see them now. One of them's a Nip, the other . . . Fuck! That's . . . he looks just like Loki, the host of the game show Loki's Lost*!*

'Just like your idea to put those meaningless signs all over the artefacts. To piss off the other gods.'

'Oh I thank you for your help, Professor Susanoo. You placed the symbols with utmost cunning and secrecy. But none of us could have predicted that it would have turned out *quite* this way. Is there anything that little woman didn't interpret as being behind the symbols? And then the invocation completely messed up and Namtarú got scared off. But he should have been pleased, shouldn't he?'

THEY did all this? To annoy *the others? Shit. The gods and their little games.*

Wasn't Susanoo the Japanese god who got himself thrown out of the heavens because of all the pranks he played? Because he took it too far?

And the TWO of them have become friends? Ho ho ho! The Earth had better brace itself.

'Yes indeed. Striking out against our own has caused quite a stir among the humans. But that's what we're here for, isn't it?'

'Quite. We should do this again sometime. Maybe with a new sign?'

'Good idea, Professor Loki. We could even involve a few selected colleagues whom we could send after the mortals. A cheeky *scalp* hunt? Who can collect the most hearts, or something like that? Think of the carnage we could cause.'

Oh great. The gods at war? That's just what we need! As long as they're having fun. How many worlds have they already ruined, I wonder? Give me my APB and I'll put them right! Hmm, no, that won't work. Fuck.

'I've noticed we appear to always be thinking along the same lines. Long live the rogue!'

'Definitely. The Winter Solstice would be the perfect time for it. A mystical date, the longest night and so forth. Baldur's always terribly excitable around that time. Even worse than Odin, Wotan and Freya put together.'

They burst out laughing again.

Winter Solstice? That's not far off. Good job I'll be worm food by then. Won't have to deal with this shit any more.

'So, back to our original question. What are we going to do with the mortal, Professor Loki? He was highly entertaining.'

'Mm.'

'We can play Rock, Paper, Scissors to decide.'

'And then, Professor Susanoo? Shouldn't *he* have the right to play as well? It's his life at stake, after all.'

'Yes of course, how stupid of me. Fine, he can play as well.'

There's a tingling inside me. I can feel my right arm.

'Hey there, mortal. Wiggle your fingers a bit for me,' *says Loki.* 'Just give it a try. Be brave.'

I give him the middle finger.

'Very good. Very bold. I like that. You can play against Loki for your life,' *says the god.* 'Rock, Paper, Scissors. Are you familiar with it?'

I give him the thumbs-up.

'Wonderful. I'll count to three, then you'll each make one of the signs. If you both pick the same one, we'll try again. If the mortal wins, we'll save him. And if Loki wins, then—?'

Do I play along?

Or just sack it all off?

But if I win, I can follow him. Again. Ha ha ha, bet he won't have counted on that!

'. . . I'm sure I can think of something, Professor Susanoo.'

Concentrate. Statistically speaking, the one with the best chance of winning is . . .

'Good. Right, let's get going.'

. . . scissors? No . . .

'One . . .'

Rock, Paper, Scissors . . . and what about Lizard and Spock? Shit, I . . . I should . . . Scissors? Blades are always *an option . . .*

'Two . . .'

No, no, he'll know that as well. Can he actually read minds? Best not to think of anything and just do it spontaneously. Okay, I'll try that.

Right, get on with it, old Slitty Eyes.

'THREE—!'

Denmark, Copenhagen, December 2019

Malleus sat in his hotel room and sent off his closing report to Lautrec. He had named the case 'Gnosis', because it had ended with new knowledge.

He had worked on the case with his Danish colleagues for three days, compiling all the details and even reconstructing what had happened with the aid of Maria Olmos' recordings.

All in all, human hubris had led to catastrophe. *As is so often the case.* Olmos had been utterly convinced by her theory and had sacrificed everything to achieve her goal of becoming a goddess. *The ONE goddess.*

It ultimately proved to be entirely fruitless.

Malleus placed all the blame on the dead, even the *bad*, whose appearance Olmos had made possible.

He was a little annoyed with himself for not having paid enough attention to the text on the Elamite brick during his search for the artefacts. The temple from which the stone had been taken was in honour of Inšušinak. The entity had survived and opposed many other gods and goddesses throughout the ages – and Inšušinak was considered a god of the Underworld and of the dead.

Apparently another guise of Namtarú, who had immediately accepted his invitation to Copenhagen.

The Danes came to the same conclusion; they had consulted their rune oracles just to be on the safe side, as well as making sacrifices to their entities. Odin had apparently also been summoned to be part of the discussion, so that he could explain and clarify the sequence of events.

The artefacts had been destroyed during the battle, lost for ever and no longer possible to abuse. Whatever the symbols on them had meant would never again see the light of day and couldn't form part of Gnosis. Keish, who was still in hospital, wouldn't be happy to hear about the loss of the Tlingit drum and mask.

Better than a second catastrophe the next time they're stolen. Malleus would, when he had the opportunity, do some more research about the meaning of the symbols on the artefacts, but he believed they were no longer of importance now the artefacts were destroyed. No unknown entity had appeared to assist Olmos – a joke among the gods? Or just an inexplicable coincidence? The answer no longer mattered to him.

Without a doubt, Keish's intervention had saved Copenhagen from utter destruction. More than ten thousand people had fallen victim to the wrath of the Ancestors; buildings had gone up in flames or collapsed.

But it could have been far worse.

Malleus had managed to convince the Danish government to shift the blame for this whole mess onto Maria Olmos as well. It would serve no purpose whatsoever to drag the First Nations into all this, given that they had nothing to do with it. People had also told him that the Nordic pantheon had been seen. All was calm, even in the realm of the entities. And his insane stalker was gone. Knowing that he had got rid of that man was enough for him. The Danish authorities would in due course discover who Chateau really was and would report back to their Italian colleague. It didn't matter either way to Malleus.

Gnosis. Malleus stroked his Fu Manchu moustache and stood up. He closed his laptop and crossed over to the small wardrobe, slipped on his shoes, put on his military coat and reached inside the wardrobe for his hat.

As he did so, he caught a reflection of his eyes in the small mirror, their true form concealed behind his blue contact lenses.

Let it gnaw away at you until your death, Malleus Bourreau. After all, you're just a few heartbeats away from staring into its eyes. Perhaps then you'll realise the truth.

There was nothing he could do to escape those words.

Malleus didn't want to know the truth, though. The last few weeks had been utterly exhausting.

I need a bit of peace and quiet.

He turned away and placed the hat on his black hair, took a Culebra with a dark purple band out of its case and opened the door. He should be allowed to celebrate a little.

Before him stood Marianne Lagrande, right on time, wearing a sleek white dress and with her blonde hair pinned up; her black eyeliner brought out her blue-grey eyes. She looked more elegant than in her normal eighties attire. 'My stomach's rumbling, Monsieur l'Inspecteur. Could you hear it?'

'Our table's booked. Good to know that we won't have our supper interrupted this time.' Malleus smiled, shifted forwards and gave her a gentle kiss on the lips. Not so strong as to contain a hint of romance, but not so brief as to appear fleeting and trivial. 'Thank you for saving my life, partner.'

He moved the Culebra from his hand to the corner of his mouth and lit it. The clouds of smoke began to form indefinable patterns, as if confused.

Lagrande grinned. 'Any time.'

Malleus assumed it could easily happen again. As they walked side by side down the corridor towards the lift he allowed himself to enjoy the effect of the cigar with its striking purple band. Karak had sourced a truly wonderful leaf.

His PDA buzzed with an incoming message.

Malleus hesitated at first, but he had no choice but to give Lagrande an apologetic look and check the message.

It was a circular from Interpol headquarters with the latest list of wanted individuals, sent out routinely to all investigators so that they could keep their eyes and ears open while on duty.

What? Malleus' eyebrows rose imperceptibly; he stopped puffing and the smoke plummeted downwards from the tip as if the effect of gravity had somehow dramatically increased.

The first name on the list was unmistakeable: Oona Milord.

THE END